Something moved.

A shadow, soft and darting over the mashed remains some twenty feet in front of her, and at the same time, Claire heard a strange rasping sound, breathing—

—and she looked up, still not sure what she was seeing or hearing—that ragged breathing and the *tick* of talons on wood, the talons themselves, thick and curved, the claws of a creature that couldn't exist. Big, the size of a full-grown man, but the resemblance ended there—and it was so impossible that she could only see it in pieces, her mind struggling to put them together. The inflamed, purplish flesh of the naked, long-limbed creature that clung to the ceiling. The puffed gray-white tissue of the partially exposed brain. The scar-rimmed holes where the eyes should have been.

—*not seeing this*—

The creature's rounded head dropped back, the wide jaw opening, a ropy stream of dark drool pouring out and splattering over what was left of the cop. It extended its tongue, eely and pink, the rough surface shimmering wetly as it slithered out. And out. And out, the snaking tongue uncoiling and whipping from side to side, so long that it actually trailed through the ripped flesh of the corpse.

The creature opened its mouth again and screamed—

Also by S.D. Perry

RESIDENT EVIL: THE UMBRELLA CONSPIRACY
RESIDENT EVIL: CALIBAN COVE
RESIDENT EVIL: CITY OF THE DEAD
RESIDENT EVIL: UNDERWORLD
RESIDENT EVIL: NEMESIS
RESIDENT EVIL: CODE:VERONICA

Published by POCKET BOOKS

RESIDENT EVIL

CITY OF THE DEAD

S.D. PERRY

POCKET BOOKS
New York   London   Toronto   Sydney

For information regarding special discounts for bulk purchases,
please contact Simon & Schuster Special Sales at
1-800-456-6798 or business@simonandschuster.com

This book is a work of fiction. Names, characters, places and
incidents are products of the author's imagination or are used
fictitiously. Any resemblance to actual events or locales or persons,
living or dead, is entirely coincidental.

An *Original* Publication of POCKET BOOKS

POCKET BOOKS, a division of Simon & Schuster, Inc.
1230 Avenue of the Americas, New York, NY 10020

ISBN 13: 978-0-671-02441-3
ISBN 10:   0-671-02441-8

First Pocket Books printing May 1999

20 19 18 17 16 15

POCKET and colophon are registered trademarks of
Simon & Schuster, Inc.

Cover art by Gerber Studio

Printed in the U.S.A.

For Juli, who just keeps growing.

Evil unchecked grows, evil tolerated poisons the whole system.

—Jawaharlal Nehru

CITY OF THE DEAD

PROLOGUE

Raccoon Times, August 26, 1998

MAYOR ANNOUNCES 'KEEP CITY SAFE' PLAN

RACCOON CITY—On the front steps of City Hall, Mayor Harris announced in a press conference yesterday afternoon that the City Council will be hiring at least ten new police officers to join the Raccoon police, in response to the continued suspension of the Special Tactics and Rescue Squad (S.T.A.R.S.), in effect since the brutal murders that plagued Raccoon earlier this summer. Joined by Police Chief Brian Irons and all of Raccoon's Council members, Harris assured the gathered citizens and reporters that Raccoon City will once again be a safe community in which to live and work, and that the investigation into the eleven "cannibal" murders and three fatal wild-animal attacks is far from closed.

"Just because no one else has been attacked in the last month doesn't mean that the elected officials of this city can relax,"

Harris stated. "The good people of Raccoon deserve to have confidence in their police force and to be secure in the knowledge that their political representatives are doing everything possible to ensure each citizen's safety. As many of you know, the S.T.A.R.S.'s suspension is likely to become permanent. That unit's gross mishandling of the murder investigations and its subsequent disappearance from Raccoon City suggests that they don't care about this community—but I want to assure you that *we* care, that myself, Chief Irons, and the men and women you see here today want nothing more than to make Raccoon a place in which our children can grow up without fear."

Harris went on to detail a three-point plan designed to bolster public confidence and keep Raccoon citizens from falling victim to violence. Besides hiring between ten and twelve new police officers, the citywide curfew will remain in place through at least September, and Chief Irons will personally head a task force of several officers and detectives to continue searching for the killers who took the lives of eleven people between May and July of this year. . . .

Cityside, September 4, 1998

RENOVATION OF UMBRELLA COMPLEX PLANNED

RACCOON CITY—The Umbrella chemical plant just south of downtown Raccoon is due for major construction efforts, slated to begin next Monday. This will be the third such structural renovation in the last year for the thriving pharmaceutical company. According to Umbrella spokesperson Amanda Whitney, two of the laboratories inside the main plant will be fitted with several million dollars' worth of new equipment designed for vaccine synthesis, and the building itself will receive a state-of-the-art security system. In addition, all of the connected office buildings will be upgrading computers over the next several weeks. But will this be a problem for downtown traffic? Said Whitney, "With the Raccoon police building just finishing up yet another one of *their* renovations, we know that local commuters are getting pretty tired of blocked streets. We're going to do our best not to get in the way of downtown traffic; most of the construction is internal, and the rest we'll be doing after business hours." The courtyard in front of the RPD building, our readers may remember, was recently repaved and landscaped after several mysterious cracks appeared in the cement and topsoil; traffic had to be diverted around two blocks of Oak Street for six days.

When asked why so many "overhauls" as of late, Whitney replied, "Umbrella has stayed ahead of the competition for as long as it has by keeping up with current technology. It's going to be a busy couple of months, but I think it will be well worth the effort when we're finally through. . . ."

Raccoon Weekly Editorial, September 17, 1998

IRONS TO RUN?

RACCOON CITY—Mayor Harris may be in for a rough race next spring. Weekly sources inside the RPD are saying that Brian Irons, chief of police for the last four-and-a-half years, may be running for the city's top office in the next election, facing off against the popular and as yet unopposed Devlin Harris, already in office for three consecutive terms. Although Irons would not confirm his possible entry into the political arena, the onetime S.T.A.R.S. member also refused to deny the rumor.

With his approval rating at an all-time high ever since the cessation of this summer's savage murders (as yet unsolved) and the planned expansion of the RPD, Chief Irons may indeed be the man to knock Harris out of City Hall; the question is, will voters be able to forget Irons's alleged involvement in the 1994 Cider District land scam? Or his rather expensive tastes in art and interior design, which have turned parts of the RPD building into something more like a museum than a working office? Assuming he means to throw his hat into the ring, this reporter—for one— will be looking forward to examining Irons's financial records. . . .

Raccoon Times, September 22, 1998

TEENAGER ATTACKED IN CITY PARK

RACCOON CITY—At approximately 6:30 P.M. last night, fourteen-year-old Shanna Williamson was accosted by a mysterious stranger in downtown's Birch Street Park on the way home from softball practice. The man came out from behind a row of hedges at the south end of the park and knocked Ms. Williamson off of her bicycle before attempting to grab her. The teen managed to get away with only a few scratches, running to the nearby residence of Tom and Clara Atkins; Mrs. Atkins alerted the authorities, who conducted a thorough search of the park but found no sign of the attacker. According to the girl (through a police statement issued earlier this morning), the man appeared to be a transient; his clothes and hair were dirty, and she described a bad odor coming from him, a "smell like rotten fruit." She also said that he seemed drunk, staggering and falling after her as she ran.

With the plague of cannibalistic murders from May to July still unsolved, the RPD is taking Ms. Williamson's encounter very seriously; the assailant bears a striking resemblance to eyewitness reports of the "gang" members spotted in Victory Park last June. Mayor Harris has called a press conference for later today, and Police Chief Brian Irons has stated already that with the first of the newly hired police officers expected next week, regular patrols will extend their routes to include the downtown park blocks. . . .

Oпe

WITH THE GUYS WAITING OUTSIDE IN BAR-
ry's truck, Jill did her best to hurry. It wasn't easy; the
house had been tossed since the last time she'd been
there, the floors were strewn with books and papers,
and it was too dark to navigate around the debris
easily. That her small home had been violated was
upsetting, though not much of a surprise. She figured
she should just be thankful that she wasn't really the
sentimental type—and that the intruders hadn't
managed to find her passport.

She grabbed random handfuls of clean socks and
underwear in the cramped darkness of the bedroom
and stuffed them deep into her weathered backpack,
wishing she could turn on the lights. Packing a bag in
the dark was harder than it sounded, would be even if
one's house hadn't been trashed; but she knew they
couldn't afford to take any chances. It was unlikely

that Umbrella still had all of their houses staked out, but if there was anyone watching, a light in the window could draw fire.

At least you're getting out. No more hiding.

There *was* that much. They were headed for foreign soil, to storm enemy headquarters and very likely get killed in the process, but at least she wouldn't have to hang out in Raccoon anymore. And from what she'd read in the papers lately, maybe that was for the best. Two attacks in the last week . . . Chris and Barry were skeptical about the danger, even knowing what the T-Virus did to people—Barry thought it was some kind of a PR stunt, that Umbrella would "rescue" Raccoon before anyone got hurt. Chris agreed, insisting that Umbrella wouldn't crap in their own back yard, so to speak, what with the Spencer estate disaster so recent. But Jill wasn't prepared to assume anything; Umbrella had already proven that they couldn't contain their research. And with what Rebecca and David Trapp's team had faced in Maine . . .

Now wasn't the time to think about that—they had a plane to catch. Jill scooped the flashlight off the dresser and was about to head for the living room when she remembered that she only had one bra with her. Scowling, she turned back to the open drawers and started to dig. She had enough clothing already, chosen from what Brad had left behind when he'd fled Raccoon; she and the guys had been holed up in his vacant house for several weeks, ever since Umbrella had hit Barry's house, and although none of Brad's stuff fit Chris's tall frame or Barry's massive one, she'd been able to make do. Lingerie, however, wasn't something the S.T.A.R.S. pilot had stocked up on. She didn't particularly want to hop off the plane in Austria and have to go bra shopping.

"Vanity, thy name is underwire," she muttered softly, pawing through the rumpled heap. She found the elusive article only after she'd gone through the drawer twice, and crammed it into the bag as she jogged toward the small front room of the rented house. It was only the second time she'd been there since they'd gone into hiding; she had the feeling she might not be coming back for a while. There was a picture of her father on one of the bookshelves that she wanted to take.

Stepping nimbly through the dark clutter, she hooded the flashlight with one hand and trained the narrow beam at the corner where the shelf had been. The Umbrella team had knocked the whole thing over but apparently hadn't bothered to go through the books themselves. God only knew what they'd been looking for in the first place. Clues as to where the renegade S.T.A.R.S. were hiding, probably; after the attack at Barry's house and the disastrous mission at Caliban Cove, she no longer had any illusions about Umbrella simply ignoring them.

Jill spotted the book she wanted, a rather lurid-looking paperback entitled *Prison Life;* her father would have laughed. She picked it up and rifled through the pages, stopping when the light fell across Dick Valentine's crooked grin. He'd sent the picture along with one of his more recent letters, and she'd tucked it into the book so that she wouldn't lose it. Hiding important things was a habit she'd gotten into young, one that had just paid off yet again.

She let the book drop, the need to hurry suddenly forgotten as she gazed down at the photo. A faint smile played across her lips. He was probably the only man she knew of who looked good in the bright orange jumpsuit of a maximum security pen. For just a moment, she wondered what he'd think of her current predicament; in a roundabout way, he was responsible, at least for her getting involved with the S.T.A.R.S. in the first place. After he'd been sent up, he'd urged her to get out of the business, even saying that he'd been wrong to train her as a thief . . .

. . . *so I take a legit job, actually working for society instead of against it—and people in Raccoon start dying. The S.T.A.R.S. uncover a conspiracy to create bioweapons with a virus that turns living things into monsters. Obviously nobody believes us, the S.T.A.R.S. that can't be bought by Umbrella are either discredited or eliminated. So we go underground, try to dig up proof and come up empty-handed as Umbrella continues to screw around with their dangerous research and more good people are killed. Now we're off on what will probably be a suicide mission to Europe to see if we can infiltrate the headquarters of a multibillion-dollar corporation and stop them from destroying the goddamn planet. What would you think, I wonder? Assuming you'd even believe such a fantastic tale, what would you think?*

"You'd be proud of me, Dick," she whispered, scarcely aware that she'd spoken aloud—and not at all sure if it was the truth. Her father wanted to see her in a *less* perilous line of work, and compared to what she and the other ex-S.T.A.R.S. were currently up against, burglary was about as dangerous as accounting.

After a long moment, she carefully placed the photo into a pocket of the backpack and looked around at the broken remnants of her small home, still thinking about her father and what he'd say about the strange path her life had taken; if things went well, maybe she'd be able to ask him in person. Rebecca Chambers and the other survivors of the Maine mission were still in hiding, quietly networking through the S.T.A.R.S. organization for support and waiting to hear what she and Chris and Barry could tell them about Umbrella's headquarters. The official HQ was in Austria, although they all suspected that the minds behind the T-Virus had their own secret complex elsewhere—

—which you won't find out if you don't get your ass in gear; the guys are gonna think you stopped to take a nap.

Jill shouldered the bag and took a final look around the room before moving toward the back door, through the kitchen. There was a lingering scent of rotten fruit in the dark air, coming from a bowl of apples and pears on top of the refrigerator that had long since disintegrated into mush. Even though she knew better, the smell caused a chill to run up her spine; she hurried for the closed door, trying to block out the sudden vivid flashes of memory of what they'd found at the Spencer estate . . .

. . . rotting as they walked, reaching out with wet and withered fingers, faces melting with pus and decay—

"Jill?"

She barely contained a cry of surprise at the sound of Chris's soft voice just outside. The door opened, Chris silhouetted against the darkness by a distant streetlight.

"Yeah, right here," she said, stepping forward. "Sorry it took me so long. Umbrella's been through here with a bulldozer."

Even in the bare light she could see the half grin on his boyish face. "We were starting to think the zombies got ya," he said, and although his tone was light, she could hear real concern beneath it.

Jill knew that he was trying to ease the tension but couldn't find it in herself to smile back. Too many people had died because of what Umbrella had unleashed in the woods outside of town; if the spill had happened closer to Raccoon . . .

"Not funny," she said softly.

Chris's grin faded. "I know. You ready?"

Jill nodded, although she didn't feel particularly ready for what lay ahead. Then again, she hadn't felt ready for what they were leaving behind, either. In a matter of weeks, her concept of reality had undergone a massive shift, turning nightmares into the commonplace.

Evil corporations, mad scientists, killer viruses. And the walking dead . . .

"Yeah," she said finally. "I'm ready."

Together, they stepped outside. As Jill closed the

door behind them, she was suddenly struck by a strange and ominous certainty—that she would never set foot in the house again, that the three of them wouldn't be coming back to Raccoon City at all . . .

. . . but not because anything happens to us. Something will *happen, but not to us.*

Frowning, hand on the doorknob, she hesitated for a moment and tried to make sense of the bizarre thought. If they survived the recon, if they were successful in their fight against Umbrella, why wouldn't they come back to their homes? She didn't know, but the feeling was uncomfortably strong. Something bad was going to happen, something—

"Hey, you okay?"

Jill looked up at Chris, saw the same concern on his youthful face that she'd noticed earlier. They'd gotten pretty close in the last few weeks, although she suspected that Chris might like to get a bit closer.

Oh, and you don't?

The sense of impending unpleasantness was already fading, other confusions and uncertainties stepping in to take its place. Jill shook herself mentally and nodded at Chris, letting the feelings go. The flight to New York wasn't going to wait for her to indulge in self-analysis—or to worry about things that she couldn't control, imagined or otherwise.

Still, that feeling . . .

"Let's get the hell out of here," she said, and meant it.

They moved out into the night, leaving the house dark behind them, as lonely and silent as a tomb.

†wo

TWILIGHT HAD SETTLED ACROSS THE MOUN-tains, painting the jagged horizon in shades of purple dusk. The winding blacktop snaked through the gathering darkness, surrounded by shadowed hills that towered into the cloudless sky, stretching toward the first faint glimmerings of starlight.

Leon might have appreciated the majestic view a bit more if he wasn't so goddamn *late*. He'd make it to his shift on time, sure, but he'd been hoping to get settled into the new apartment first, take a shower, get something to eat; as it was, he *might* have time to hit a drive-through on his way to the station. Changing into his uniform back at the last rest stop had saved him a couple of minutes, but basically he was screwed.

Way to go, Officer Kennedy. First day on the job and you'll be picking cheeseburger out of your teeth during roll call. Very professional.

His shift started at nine and it was already just after eight; Leon let his boot ride a little heavier on the gas, even as his Jeep whipped past a sign that told him he was half an hour away from Raccoon City. At least the road was clear; except for a couple of semis, he hadn't seen anyone for what felt like hours. A nice change, considering the traffic tie-up just outside of New York that had cost him most of the afternoon. He'd actually tried to call the night before to leave a message with the desk sergeant that he might be late, but there'd been something wrong with the connection. Nothing but a busy signal.

What little furniture he had was already moved into a studio apartment in the working-class but basically decent Trask district of Raccoon City; there was a nice park not two blocks away, and it was only a five-minute drive to the station. No more gridlock, no more overcrowded slums or random acts of brutality. Assuming he could survive the embarrassment of showing up to his first shift as a full-blown officer of the law without having unpacked his bags, he was looking forward to living in the peaceful community.

Raccoon is about as far removed from the Big Apple as you can get, thank you very much—well, except for the last few months. Those murders . . .

In spite of himself, he felt a tiny thrill at the thought. What had happened in Raccoon was horrible, of course, sickening—but the perps had never been caught and the investigation was really just getting started. And if Irons liked him, liked him as much as the heads of the academy had liked him, maybe Leon would get a chance to work on the case.

Word had it that Chief Irons was kind of a prick, but Leon knew his training had been top-notch—even a prick would have to be a *little* impressed. He'd graduated in the top tenth, after all. And it wasn't like he was a stranger to Raccoon City, since he'd spent most of his summers there as a kid, when his grandparents were still alive. Back then, the RPD building had been a library and Umbrella was still several years away from turning the town into an actual city, but in most ways it was still the same quiet place he remembered from his childhood. Once the cannibal killers were finally put away, Raccoon would be ideal again—beautiful, clean, a white-collar community nestled in the mountains like a secret paradise.

So I get settled in and a week or two passes, and Irons notices how well written my reports are, or sees how good I am on the target range. He asks me to take a look at the case files, just to familiarize myself with the details so I can do some footwork—and I see something that no one else has seen. A pattern, maybe, or a motive on more than one of the victims . . . maybe I run across a witness report that reads wrong. No one else has caught it because they've lived with it for too long, and this rookie cop just comes along and cracks the case, not a month out of the academy and I—

Something ran in front of the Jeep.

"Jesus!"

Leon hit the brake and swerved, shocked out of his daydream as he struggled for control of the vehicle. The brakes locked and there was a screech of rubber that sounded like a scream. The Jeep half-turned to face the darkening trees that lined the road—and came to a stop on the shoulder, dying after a final lurching jolt.

Heart pounding and stomach in knots, Leon opened the window and craned his neck, scanning the shadows for the animal that had darted across the highway. He hadn't hit it, but it had been close. Some kind of a dog, he didn't get a clear look—a big one, anyway, a shepherd or maybe an oversized Doberman, but it had looked *wrong* somehow. He'd only seen it for a split-second, a flash of glowing red eyes and lean, wolfish body. And there was something else, it had seemed kind of . . .

. . . slimy? No, trick of the light, or you were just so shit-scared that you saw it wrong. You're okay and you didn't hit it, that's the important thing.

"Jesus," he said again, softer this time, feeling both relieved and suddenly quite angry as the adrenaline leaked out of his system. People who let their dogs run loose were idiots—claiming they wanted their pets to be free and then acting surprised when Fido got squashed by a car.

The Jeep had come to a stop just a few feet away from a road sign that read RACCOON CITY 10; he could just make out the lettering in the growing shadows. Leon glanced at his watch; he still had almost half an hour to get to the station, plenty of time—but for some reason, he simply sat for a moment, closing his eyes and breathing deeply. Cool pine-scented air breezed across his face; the deserted stretch of road seeming almost unnaturally quiet—as if the landscape was holding its breath, waiting. Now that his heart had resumed a more normal pace, he was surprised to find that he still felt unsettled, even anxious.

The murders in Raccoon. Weren't a few of those people killed by animal attack? Wild dogs, or something? Maybe that wasn't someone's pet dog at all.

A disturbing thought—and even more disturbing was the sudden feeling he had that the dog was still close by, maybe watching him from the darkness in the trees.

Welcome to Raccoon City, Officer Kennedy. Watch out for things that may be watching you. . . .

"Don't be an asshole," Leon mumbled to himself, and felt a little better at the sound of his no-nonsense adult tone of voice. He often wondered if he would ever outgrow his imagination.

Daydreaming like a kid about catching bad guys, then inventing killer dog-monsters lurking in the woods—let's try to act our age, eh, Leon? You're a cop, for God's sake, a grownup. . . .

He started the engine and backed onto the road, ignoring the strange sense of unease that had somehow managed to take hold of him in spite of his mind's chiding voice. He had a new job and a nice apartment in a nice little up-and-coming city; he was competent, bright, and decent-looking; as long as he kept his creativity glands in check, everything would be fine.

"And I'm on my way," he said to himself, forcing a grin that felt out of place but suddenly necessary to his peace of mind. He was on his way to Raccoon City, to a promising new life—there was nothing to be uneasy about, nothing at all. . . .

Claire was exhausted, both physically and emotionally, and the fact that her butt had been aching for the last couple of hours wasn't helping matters much. The thrum of the Harley's engine seemed to have settled deep into her bones, a physical counterpoint to the butterflies in her stomach—and of course, the worst of it seemed to emanate from her extremely sore and overheated ass. Plus, it was getting dark and like an idiot she wasn't wearing her leathers; Chris would be totally pissed.

He's going to yell his head off, and I won't even care. God, Chris, please be there to scream at me for being such an idiot. . . .

The Harley buzzed along the dark road, the sound of the engine echoing back at her from the sloping hills and shadow-laden trees. She took the corners carefully, very aware of how deserted the winding highway was; if she took a spill, it could be a long time before anyone happened by.

Like it would matter. Take a spill without your gear on, they'll be scraping pieces of you off the asphalt with a squeegee.

It was stupid, she knew it was stupid to have left in such a godawful hurry that she couldn't be bothered to suit up—but something had happened to Chris. Hell, something may have happened to the entire *city*. Over the past couple of weeks, the growing suspicion that her brother was in trouble had become a certainty—and the calls she'd made that morning had cinched it for her.

Nobody home. Nobody home anywhere. *Like Raccoon moved and forgot to leave a forwarding address.*

It was definitely creepy, although she could give a shit about Raccoon. What mattered was that Chris was there, and if something bad had happened to him—

She couldn't, *wouldn't* think that way. Chris was all she had left. Their father had been killed on his construction job when they were both still kids, and when their mother had died in a car crash three years ago, Chris had done his best to take on a parental role. Even though he was only a few years older, he'd helped her pick a college, find a decent therapist—he even sent her a little money each month beyond what the insurance policies paid out, what he called "walking around cash." And on top of all that, he called her every couple of weeks like clockwork.

Except he hadn't called at all in the last month and a half, and hadn't returned any of her calls. She'd tried to convince herself that she was silly to worry—maybe he'd finally met a girl, or something had turned up on the S.T.A.R.S. suspension thing, whatever *that* was all about. But after three unanswered letters and days of waiting for the phone to ring, she'd finally put in a call to the RPD that very afternoon, hoping against hope that someone there might know what was going on. She'd gotten a busy signal.

Sitting in her dorm room, listening to that soulless

mechanical bleat, she'd started to worry for real. Even a small city like Raccoon had a voice-mail answering system set up to field calls. The rational part of her mind told her not to panic, that a downed line was nothing to get freaky about—but already, her emotional self was screaming foul. She'd gone through her address book with trembling hands, dialing the few numbers she had for friends of his, people or places he'd told her to call if there was ever an emergency and he wasn't at home—Barry Burton, Emmy's Diner, some cop she'd never met named David Ford. She even tried Billy Rabbitson's number, although Chris had told her that he'd disappeared a few months earlier. And with the exception of an overloaded answering machine at David Ford's house, she'd gotten nothing but busy signals.

By the time she'd hung up, the worry had transformed into something close to panic. The trip to Raccoon City was only about six-and-a-half hours from the university. Claire's roommate had borrowed her riding gear to go out with her new biker boyfriend, but Claire had an extra helmet—and with that feeling that was not quite panic spinning through her frightened thoughts, she had simply grabbed the helmet and gone.

Stupid, maybe. Impulsive, definitely. And if Chris is okay, we can laugh about how ridiculously paranoid I am 'til the cows come home. But until I find out what's going on, I won't know a moment's peace.

The last of the day's light was draining from the strip of cloudless sky above, although a waxing, nearly full moon and the Softail's headlight gave her enough light to see by—more than enough to see the small sign ahead on her left: RACCOON CITY 10.

Telling herself that Chris was fine, that if anything weird had happened in Raccoon, *somebody* would have checked it out by now, Claire forced her concentration back to handling the heavy bike. It would be full dark soon, but she'd be in Raccoon before it was too dark to ride safely.

Whether or not Raccoon City would be safe, she'd find out soon enough.

†HREE

LEON REACHED THE OUTSKIRTS OF TOWN
with twenty minutes to spare, but decided that a hot
dinner was going to have to wait. From his previous
visits to the station, he knew that there were a couple
of vending machines he could hit up for something to
tide him over. The thought of stale candy and peanuts
didn't sit well on his growling stomach, but it was his
own damned fault for not taking New York traffic into
account.

The drive into the city proper did a lot to soothe his
still rattled nerves; he passed the few small farms that
lay east of town, the fairgrounds and storage sheds,
and finally the truck stop that marked the separation
of rural Raccoon from urban. Something about knowing that he was going to be patrolling those back roads
before long, keeping them safe, gave him a surprising
sense of well-being and not a little pride. The early

autumn air from the open window was pleasantly brisk, and the rising moon bathed everything he saw in a silvery glow. He wasn't going to be late after all; within the hour, he'd officially become one of Raccoon's finest.

As Leon turned the Jeep down Bybee, heading for one of the main north-south streets that would take him to the RPD building, he got his first hint that something was very wrong. In the first few blocks, he was mildly surprised; by the fifth, he found himself slipping toward a state of shock. It wasn't just strange, it was . . . well, it was *impossible.*

Bybee was the first real city street, coming from the east, where buildings outnumbered empty lots. There were several espresso bars and cheap diners, as well as a bargain movie theater that never seemed to run anything but horror movies and sexy comedies—and was therefore the most popular hangout for the youth of Raccoon. There were even a few generically hip taverns that served microbrew and hot rum drinks for the winter college-student ski crowd. At quarter to nine on a Saturday night, Bybee should have been teeming with life.

But of the mostly single or two-story brick shops and restaurants that lined the street, Leon saw that almost all were dark—and in the few that still boasted some light, it didn't look like there was anyone inside. There were plenty of cars parked along the narrow street, and yet not one person that he could see; Bybee, the hangout for cruising teens and college students, was totally deserted.

Where the hell is everybody?

His mind grasped for answers as he crept down the silent street, searching desperately for a reason—and for some way to alleviate the sweaty anxiety that had once again settled over him. Maybe there was some kind of an event going on, a church function, like a spaghetti feed. Or perhaps Raccoon had decided to take up Oktoberfest and tonight was the big kickoff.

Yeah, but everybody *at the same time? It'd have to be one hell of a party.*

It was then that Leon realized he also hadn't seen a single car on the road since he'd had the scare with the dog ten miles out of town. Not one. And with that thoroughly unsettling realization came the next—less dramatic, but distinctly more immediate.

Something smelled bad. In fact, something smelled like shit.

Jeez, dead skunk. And apparently it threw up on itself before dying.

He'd already slowed the Jeep to a crawl and had planned to take a left on Powell, just a block ahead—but that horrible smell and the total absence of life were giving him a serious case of the creeps. Maybe he should stop and check things out, look around for some sign of—

"Oh, hey. . . ."

Leon grinned, relief flooding through his confusion. There were a couple of people standing at the corner, practically right in front of him; the streetlight was out on their side, but he could see them in silhouette clear enough—a couple, a woman in a skirt and a big man wearing work boots. As he got closer he could see by the way they moved, heading south on Powell, that

25

they had to be monumentally drunk. Both of them staggered into the shadows cast by an office supply store and out of sight; but he was going in that direction anyway—no harm in stopping to ask what was going on, was there?

Must've come out of O'Kelly's. A pint or two too many, but as long as they're not driving anywhere, fine by me. Am I going to feel stupid when they tell me that tonight's the big free concert or the all-you-can-eat town barbecue. . . .

Almost giddy with relief, Leon turned the corner and squinted into the heavy shadows, looking for the pair. He didn't see them, but there was an alley tucked between the supply store and a jewelry shop. Maybe his two drunk friends had ducked in for a bathroom break or something even less legal—

"Shit!"

Leon slammed on the brake as a half-dozen dark shapes fluttered up from the street, caught in the Jeep's headlights like giant whirling leaves. Startled, it took him a second to realize he was seeing birds; they didn't cry out, although he was close enough to hear the brushing of dry wings as they took to the air. Crows, enjoying a late night feast of roadkill, what looked like—

Oh, my God.

There was a human body in the middle of the road, twenty feet in front of the Jeep. Face down, but it looked like a woman—and judging from the liquid red stains that covered most of the once-white blouse, it wasn't some beer-happy college student who'd decided to take a nap in the wrong place.

Hit-and-run. Some bastard hit her and then drove away, Jesus what a mess—

Leon killed the engine and was half out the door before his racing thoughts caught him up. He hesitated, one foot on the asphalt, the stench of death heavy in the cool still air. His mind had latched on to an idea that he didn't want to consider, but knew he had better; this wasn't some training exercise, this was his *life.*

What if it's not a hit-and-run? What if there's no one around because some psycho gunman decided on a little target practice? Everyone could be inside, laying low—maybe the RPD's on the way, and maybe those drunks weren't drunk, they could've been shot and were trying to get help. . . .

He leaned back into the Jeep and fumbled under the passenger seat for his graduation gift, a Desert Eagle .50AE Magnum with a custom ten-inch barrel, Israeli export. His father and uncle—both cops—had gone in together on it. Not standard issue for the RPD, in fact much more powerful; as Leon grabbed a clip from the glovebox and slapped it in, feeling the solid weight of the weapon in his slightly unsteady hands, he decided it was the best present he'd ever received. He stuffed two more clips into a belt pouch on general principle; each only held six rounds.

Pointing the loaded Magnum at the ground, he stepped out of the Jeep and took a quick look at his surroundings. He wasn't all that familiar with Raccoon at night, but he knew that it shouldn't be as dark as it was. Several of the streetlights farther along Powell were either shot out or simply not on, and the shadows past the blood-soaked body were thick; if not for the Jeep's headlights, he wouldn't have even been able to see that.

He edged forward, feeling horribly exposed as he left the relative cover of the Jeep, but aware that she could still be alive; it didn't seem likely, but he had to at least check.

A few steps closer, and he could see that it was definitely a young woman. Lank red hair obscured the face, but the clothes were right, denim pedal-pushers and flats. The wounds were mostly hidden by the bloody shirt, but there seemed to be dozens—ragged holes in the wet cloth exposed torn, glistening flesh and the crimson of muscle beneath.

Swallowing heavily, Leon quickly switched the gun to his left hand and crouched down next to her. The cool, clammy skin yielded easily beneath his fingertips as he touched her throat, pressing his first two fingers against the carotid. A few seconds passed, seconds that made him feel horribly young and afraid as he tried to remember the procedure for CPR and prayed, at the same time, that he would feel a pulse.

Five compressions, two short breaths, keep my elbows locked and come on please don't be dead—

He couldn't find it, and didn't want to wait one more second. He tucked the Magnum into his belt and grabbed her shoulders to turn her over, to check for breathing—but as he started to lift, he saw something that made him lay her down again, his heart a twisting knot in his chest.

The victim's shirt had pulled out of her pants enough for him to see that her spine and part of her ribcage were exposed, the still-fleshy knobs of vertebrae shining and red, the narrow, curving ribs disappearing into masses of shredded tissue. It was like she'd been knocked down and . . . *chewed* on. Information that Leon had disregarded as unimportant suddenly registered, and even as the few facts he had clicked into place, he felt the first inky tendrils of real fear slither into his mind.

The crows couldn't have done this, would've taken them hours, and who the hell ever heard of crows flocking after dark to eat? And that shit-smell, it's not coming from her, she died recently, and—

Cannibal. Murders.

No. No *way*. For that to happen, for a person to have been killed and then partially—*devoured* on a city street with no one to stop it—

—and with enough time to pass for scavengers to come—for that to happen, the killers would have had to slaughter most if not all of the population. Doesn't seem likely? Fine. Then what's that smell? And where is everyone?

Behind Leon, there was a low, soft groan. A shuffling footstep, and another sound. A *wet* sound.

It took him barely a second to stand and turn, hand instinctively snatching for the Magnum. It was the couple, the drunks, staggering toward him, and they'd been joined by a third, a beefy-looking guy with—

—with blood all over his shirt. And his hands. And dripping out of his mouth, a rubbery red mouth set into his pasty, rotting face like an open sore. The other man, the big man with the work boots and suspenders, looked much the same—and the vee of the blond woman's pink blouse revealed cleavage that was spotted with darkness, with what appeared to be mold.

The trio stumbled toward him, past his Jeep, raising pale hands as they emitted moaning, hungry wails. Some dark fluid gurgled out of the beefy man's nose and ran across his moving lips, and Leon was overwhelmed by the understanding that the terrible, shitty smell was decayed flesh, and it was coming from *them*—

—and there was another one, stepping out from a door stoop across the street, a young woman in a stained T-shirt, hair tied back from a slack and mindless face.

A groan from behind him. Leon shot a look over his shoulder and saw a youth with dark hair and rotting arms shamble out from the sidewalk darkness of an awning's shadow.

Leon raised the Magnum and aimed at the closest, the man with suspenders, while his instincts screamed at him to run. He was terrified, but his trained logic continued to insist that there was an explanation for what he was seeing, that he was *not* looking at the walking dead.

Control, procedure, you're a cop—

"All right! That's far enough! Don't move!"

His voice was strong, commanding and authoritative, and he was wearing his uniform, and God, *why wouldn't they stop?* The man in suspenders moaned again, blind to the weapon pointed at his chest and still flanked by the others, now less than ten feet away.

"Don't move!" Leon said again, and the sound of his own panic made him back up a step, darting his gaze left and right, seeing that there were still more of the wailing, lurching people coming out of the shadows.

Something grabbed his ankle.

"No!" he shouted, whipped the gun around—

—and saw that the corpse of the hit-and-run victim was scrabbling at his boot with one blood-crusted hand, working to drag her crippled body closer. Her gasping cry of frantic hunger rose to join those of the others as she tried to bite into his foot, bloody smears of saliva drooling off her abraded chin, dripping onto the leather.

Leon fired into her upper back, the sharp, explosive *crack* of the massive weapon loosening her grip—and at such close range, probably obliterating her heart. Spasming, she dropped back to the pavement—

—and he turned and saw that the others were less than five feet away, and he fired twice more, the rounds splattering red flowers into the chest of the closest. The entry wounds spouted scarlet.

The man in suspenders was hardly fazed by the twin gaping holes in his torso, his stagger faltering for only a second. He opened his bloody mouth and gasped out a hissing mewl of hunger, hands raised again as if to direct him to the source of relief.

Must be on something, firepower like that could drop an elephant—

Backing away, Leon fired again. And again. And *again.* And then the empty clattered to the pavement, another was slammed in, more rounds fired. And still they kept coming, oblivious to the shots that ripped at their stinking flesh. It was a bad dream, a bad movie, it wasn't real—and Leon knew that if he didn't start believing, he was going to die. Eaten alive by these—

Go ahead, Kennedy, say it. These zombies.

Blocked from his Jeep, Leon stumbled away, still firing.

FOUR

SO MUCH FOR THE NIGHTLIFE; THIS PLACE IS deadsville.

Claire had seen a couple of people wandering around as she'd pulled into Raccoon, though not nearly as many as there should have been. In fact, the place seemed spectacularly deserted; the helmet blocked out a lot of visual evidence, but there was definitely a lack of business going on at the east end of town. A lack of traffic, as well. It struck her as weird, but considering the disasters she'd been imagining all afternoon, not all that ominous. Raccoon still *existed*, at least, and as she headed for the twenty-four-hour diner off Powell, she saw a fairly large group of partyers walking down the middle of a side street. Drunken frat boys, if she remembered her last visit clearly. Obnoxious, but hardly the horsemen of the apocalypse.

No bombed-out ruins, no dying fires, no air-raid sirens; so far, so good.

She'd planned to head straight for Chris's apartment before she realized that she'd be passing Emmy's on the way. Chris couldn't cook worth a damn; consequently, he lived on cereal, cold sandwiches, and dinner at Emmy's about six nights a week; even if he wasn't there, it might be worth it to stop in and ask one of the waitresses if they'd seen him lately.

As Claire pulled the Softail to a gentle stop in front of Emmy's, she noticed a couple of rats scurrying for cover from atop a garbage can on the sidewalk. She put down the stand and unstraddled the bike, taking off her helmet and setting it on the warm seat. Shaking out her ponytail, she wrinkled her nose in disgust; from the smell of things, the trash had been sitting out for quite a while. Whatever they were throwing away gave off a seriously toxic stink.

Before going in, she chafed her bare legs and arms lightly, as much to warm them as to wipe off the top layer of road grime. Shorts and a vest were no match for the October night, and it reminded her once again of how dumb she'd been to ride bare. Chris would give her one hell of a lecture . . .

. . . but not here.

The building's glass front gave her a clear look at the well-lit, homey restaurant, from the bolted red stools at the lunch counter to the padded booths lining the walls—and there wasn't a soul in sight. Claire frowned, her initial disappointment giving way to confusion. Having visited Chris pretty regularly over the last few years, she'd been to the diner at all hours of the day and night; they were both night owls, often deciding to go out for cheeseburgers at three in the morning—which meant Emmy's every time. And there was *always* someone at Emmy's, chatting with one of the pink polyester–clad waitresses or hunched over a cup of coffee with a newspaper, no matter what time it was.

So where are they? It's not even nine o'clock. . . .

The sign said Open, and she wasn't going to find out standing in the street. With a last glance at her bike, she opened the door and stepped inside. Taking a deep breath, she called out hopefully.

"Hello? Anyone here?"

Her voice seemed somehow flat in the muted silence of the empty restaurant; except for the soft hum of the ceiling fans overhead, there wasn't a sound. There was the familiar smell of stale grease in the air, but something else, too—a scent that was bitter and yet soft, like rotting flowers.

The restaurant was L-shaped, booths stretching off in front of her and to the left. Walking slowly, Claire headed straight; at the end of the lunch counter was the wait station, and past that the kitchen; if Emmy's *was* open, the staff would probably be hanging out there, maybe as surprised as she was that there were no customers—

—except that wouldn't explain the mess, would it?

It wasn't a mess, exactly; the disorder was subtle enough that she hadn't even noticed it from outside. A few menus on the floor, an overturned water glass on the counter, and a couple of randomly strewn pieces of silverware were the only signs of something amiss—but they were enough.

To hell with checking out the kitchen, this is too weird, something is *seriously fucked up in this city—or maybe they got robbed, or maybe they're setting up for a surprise party. Who cares? Time for* you *to be elsewhere.*

From the hidden space at the end of the counter, she heard a gentle sound of movement, a sliding whisper of cloth followed by a muffled grunt. Somebody was there, ducked down.

Heart thumping loudly, Claire called out again. "Hello?"

For a beat, there was nothing—and then another grunt, a muted moan that raised the hair on the back of her neck.

In spite of her misgivings, Claire hurried toward the back, suddenly feeling childish for her desire to leave; maybe there *had* been a robbery, maybe the customers had been tied up and gagged—or even worse, so badly injured that they couldn't cry out. Like it or not, she was involved.

Claire reached the end of the counter, pivoted left—

—and froze, eyes wide, feeling as though she'd been physically slapped. Next to a cart loaded with trays was a balding man dressed in cook's whites, his back to her. He was crouched over the body of a waitress; but there was something very *wrong* about her, so wrong that Claire's mind couldn't quite accept it at first. Her shocked gaze took in the pink uniform, the walking shoes, even the plastic name tag still pinned to the woman's chest, what looked like "Julie" or "Julia." . . .

. . . her head. Her head is missing.

Once Claire realized what was wrong, she couldn't force herself to un-realize it, as much as she wanted to. There was only a pool of drying blood where the waitress's head should have been, a sticky puddle surrounded by fragments of skull and dark mashed hair and chunks of miscellaneous gore. The cook had his hands over his face, and as Claire stared in horror at the headless corpse, he let out a low, pitiful wail.

Claire opened her mouth, not sure what would come out. To scream, to ask him why, how, to offer to call for help—she honestly didn't know, and as the man turned to look up at her, hands dropping away, she was stunned to hear that nothing came out at all.

He was *eating* the waitress. His thick fingers were clotted with dark bits of tissue; the strange and alien face he raised into view was smeared with blood.

Zombie.

A child of late-night creature features and campfire stories, her mind accepted it in the split-second it took for her to think it; she wasn't an idiot. He was deathly pale and ripe with that sickly-sweet scent of decay she'd noticed earlier, his eyes cataracted and gleaming white.

Zombies, in Raccoon. I never expected that.

With that calm, logical realization came a sudden rush of absolute terror. Claire stumbled backwards, feverish panic turning her guts into liquid as the cook continued to turn, rising from his crouch. He was *huge,* easily a foot over her 5′3″, and broad as a barn—

—and dead! He's dead and he was EATING her, don't let him get any closer!

The cook took a step toward her, his stained hands clenching into fists. Claire backed up faster, almost slipping on a menu. A fork clattered away from beneath one boot.

GET OUT NOW.

"I'll be on my way now," she babbled. "Really, don't bother to show me out—"

The cook staggered forward, his blind eyes glowing with dumb hunger. Another step back and Claire reached behind her, felt air, felt nothing—

—and then the cool metal of the door's handle. A shot of adrenaline triumph bolted through her as she spun, snatched at the handle—

—and screamed, a short, sharp cry of horror. There were two, three more of them outside, their disintegrating flesh pressed to the glass front of the diner. One of them had only one eye, a suppurating hole where the other should have been; another had no upper lip, a ragged, permanent grin scrawled across its lower jaw. They clawed mindlessly at the windows, their ashy, ravaged faces awash with blood—and from the shadows across the street, dark shapes shambled out into the open.

Can't get out, trapped—

—Jesus, the back door!

From the edge of her vision, the glowing green exit sign shone like a beacon. Claire spun again and barely saw the cook reaching out to her from a few feet away, her full attention fixating on the only hope of escape.

She ran, the booths whipping by in a flash of unseen color, her arms pumping for speed. The door opened out into the alley, she was going to hit it running and if it was locked, she was screwed.

Claire slammed into the door and it flew open, crashing into the brick wall of the alley—

—and there was a gun pointed at her face, the only thing that could possibly have stopped her at that second, a man with a gun—

She froze, raising her arms instinctively as if to ward off a blow.

"Wait! Don't shoot!"

The gunman didn't move, the deadly-looking weapon still aimed at her head—

—*gonna kill me*—

"Get down!" the gunman shouted, and Claire dropped, her knees buckling as much from the command as from the cold fingertips suddenly groping at her shoulder—

Boom! Boom!

The gunman fired and Claire snapped her head around, saw the dead cook falling backwards from directly behind her, at least one massive hole now in its forehead. Sluggish spurts of blood jetted from the wound, the white eyes filming over with red. The fallen corpse twitched, once, twice—and stopped moving.

Claire turned back to the man who'd saved her life, and his uniform registered for the first time. *Cop.* He was young, tall—and almost as terrified-looking as she felt, his upper lip beaded with sweat, his blue eyes wide and unblinking. His voice, at least, was strong and sure as he reached down to help her up.

"We can't stay out here. Come with me, we'll be a lot safer at the police station."

As he spoke, she could hear a closing chorus of gasping moans from the street, the wails of hunger growing louder. Claire let herself be pulled up, gripping his hand tightly, taking small comfort in the fact that his fingers were as feverish and shaky as hers.

They ran, dodging dumpsters and heaps of flattened boxes, chased by echoing, haunted cries as the zombies found the dark alley and started after them.

FIVE

LEON RAN ALONGSIDE THE GIRL, DESPER-
ately racking his memory for the city's downtown
layout. The alley should let out on Ash, not far from
Oak, the RPD's street—but the station was at least
another fifteen blocks west; unless they could find
transportation, they weren't going to make it. He was
on his last clip, four rounds left, and from the sounds
reverberating through the alley, there were dozens,
maybe *hundreds* of the creatures at either end.

As they reached the mouth of the alley, Leon held
up his hand and slowed to a jog, scanning the dimly lit
street. He couldn't see much, but from where they
stood to the next streetlight, there were eleven or
twelve of the creatures to the right, staggering and
reeling their way through the stinking darkness. There
were only three of them to the left, not far from—

—*hallelujah!*

"There!"

Leon pointed at the squad car parked across the street, feeling a flush of wild hope. There were no officers in sight, that was too much to ask for—but the front doors were standing open, and the three moaning *things* that roamed nearby wouldn't reach it before he and the girl could. Even if there were no keys, there was a radio and the windshield was bulletproof. They could probably hold out against the walking corpses until help came—

—*and it's the only chance you've got. Go!*

He hesitated just long enough to see the girl nod, her brown ponytail bobbing, and then they were sprinting for the black-and-white, the pavement a blur beneath their feet. Leon kept the handgun half-pointed toward the creatures closest to them, fifty feet away; he wanted to shoot, to keep them from getting one step closer, but he couldn't afford to waste the ammo.

God, let there be keys—

They reached the car at the same time and split, the girl running around to the passenger's side, and Leon realized with a new kind of horror that she probably thought the car was his. He waited for her to slam the door before jumping behind the wheel, a small, deeply frightened part of him screaming that this was his first *day* as he yanked his own door shut.

A prayer answered; the keys were in the ignition. Leon dropped the Magnum into his lap and grabbed them, feeling that wild hope once again, like there were options besides dying.

"Buckle up," he said, barely hearing her assent as he turned the keys and the flashers came on. Ash Street and the creatures that stalked it were bathed in blue and red swirls of pallid color, shadows changing form and thickness. It was a vision of hell and he hit the gas, desperate to get away from it as fast as he could.

The car spun away from the curb with a squeal. Leon pulled the wheel right and then left, narrowly missing a lurching woman whose scalp had been torn half off. Even through the closed windows, he could hear her frustrated howl as they sped away, joined by the cries of many more.

Backup, call for backup—

Leon fumbled for the radio, not taking his gaze off of the road. The creatures were scattered but persistent, dark and shambling monsters that staggered out into the street as if drawn to the sound of the speeding car. As the black-and-white rocketed across Powell and continued on, he had to dodge several more of them.

The girl was talking, staring out at the desolate landscape as Leon hit the com button on the radio, his sense of helplessness rising. No static, no *nothing.* "What the hell's going *on,* I arrive in Raccoon and the whole place is insane—"

"Great, the radio's out," Leon interrupted, dropping the radio and focusing on the road. The entire city seemed like an alien world, the streets strangely shadowed. There was a dreamlike quality to it, but the smell kept him from believing that he was asleep. The stench of diseased flesh had permeated even the interior of the squad car, making it hard to concentrate on driving. At least there was no traffic and no people. No *real* people . . .

. . . except me and the girl. I've got to do my job here, keep her from getting hurt. Poor kid, she can't be older than nineteen or twenty, she's probably terrified; I've got to keep it together and shield her from further danger here, get to the station and—

"You're a cop, right?"

The girl's lilting but somehow sarcastic tone snapped him out of his panicked musings. He shot a look in her direction, noting that while she looked pale, she didn't seem to be quivering on the edge of a breakdown. There was even a trace of humor in her clear gray eyes, and Leon got a sudden strong impression that she wasn't the breakdown type. A very good thing, considering the circumstances.

"Yeah. First day on the job; great, huh? I'm Leon Kennedy."

"Claire," she said. "Claire Redfield. I came to find my brother, Chris. . . ."

She trailed off, staring back out at the passing street. Two of the creatures were staggering into the path of the car from either side, but Leon hit the gas and managed to drive between them. The steel mesh screen separating the back compartment was down, giving him a clear look from the rearview mirror; the two shuffling ghouls were now plodding mindlessly after them.

Hungry. Just like in the movies.

For a moment, neither spoke, the obvious question remaining unspoken. Whatever *had* happened to turn Raccoon into a horror show didn't matter as much as how they were going to survive it. They'd be at the station in a couple of minutes, assuming the roads stayed clear. There was an underground parking lot, he'd try that first—but if the gates were closed, they'd have to cover a short distance on foot. There was a small courtyard in front of the building, a park area—

Four rounds left—and maybe a city full of those things. We need another weapon. . . .

"Hey, open the glovebox," he said. If it was locked, there was a key on the ring that should open it.

Claire tapped the button and reached inside, revealing the back of her pink sleeveless vest; the legend "Made in Heaven" was appliquéd above a voluptuous posing angel holding a bomb. The outfit suited her.

"There's a gun inside," she said, and pulled out a sleek semiautomatic. She raised it carefully and checked to see if it was loaded before digging out a couple of clips. It was one of the RPD's old issues, a nine-millimeter Browning HP. Since the slew of recent murders, the Raccoon force had been carrying H & K VP70s, another nine-millimeter—the difference was that the Browning could only hold thirteen, while the newer issues held eighteen rounds, nineteen if you kept one chambered. From the way she handled it, Leon could tell that she knew what she was doing.

"Better take it with you," he said. The RPD kept a decent arsenal; assuming that there were still cops around, he could pick up his assigned weapon and—

—and why are you assuming anything?

As Leon took the corner of Ash and Third a little too quickly, the realization finally hit him that the station itself might be crawling with corpses. Everything was happening so fast, he just hadn't considered the possibility. He straightened out the car and let up on the gas, trying to come up with an alternate plan as calmly and rationally as he could. Maybe there *was* an organized defense at the station—but it wasn't easy to feel hopeful with the stink of decay so heavy in the air.

We have three-quarters of a tank, more than enough to make it over the mountains; we could be in Latham in less than an hour.

They could drive by the station and if it looked—unfriendly, just get the hell out of town; sounded good to him. He started to tell Claire, see what she thought—

—when the horrible smell of slaughter washed over him and something lunged out of the back seat.

Claire screamed and the monster that had been in the squad car all along grasped Leon's shoulder with icy hands, its flyblown breath gusting into his face. It snatched at his right arm, pulling it toward its drool-slick teeth with inhuman strength.

"No!" Leon shouted as the car veered wildly to the right, jumping the curb and sliding toward a brick building. The creature was unbalanced, losing some of its grip; Leon jerked the wheel but too late to avoid the wall completely. Metal shrieked and a brilliant flash of sparks illuminated the groping hands and leering, ghoulish grin of their passenger as the speeding car shot back out into the street.

The dead thing swung its eager arms at Claire, and without thinking, Leon slammed on the gas and pulled a hard right. The car fishtailed, the back end crunching against a parked pickup truck in another burst of fiery sparks. The drooling corpse fell back into the padded seat but immediately pulled itself forward again, gnashing its teeth and clawing for the girl.

The squad car sped down Third, Leon trying to control the wheel as he grabbed his weapon and half-turned, holding the Magnum by the barrel. He didn't think to take his foot off the gas, couldn't think of anything except that the zombie was about to sink its teeth into Claire's struggling shoulder.

He brought the heavy weapon down and across its face, the butt sliding across flesh that peeled away in a thick flap. Blood gushed from the wound as the grips crushed into its nose, cartilage separating from bone with a wet *crunch*. Gurgling, the creature clutched at its bleeding head and Leon just had time to feel a second's triumph—

—when Claire screamed, *"Look out!"*

—and Leon looked up to see that they were about to crash.

Leon hit the zombie with his gun and Claire instinctively flinched from the splatter of blood, her horrified gaze finding that the street they were on was about to end.

"Look out!"

She caught just a glimpse of his white knuckles on the wheel, his clenched jaw—

—and the car was spinning, screeching, buildings and streetlights flashing by so fast that all she saw was a blur, and then—

BAM!

There was an explosion of sound, of glass shattering and metal compressing as the cop car slammed into something solid, throwing Claire against her safety belt. The impact hurled the zombie forward at the same time, and Claire reflexively threw her arms up as the dead thing crashed through the windshield—

—and then everything was still. There was only the ticking of hot metal and the sound of her own heart thundering in her ears. Claire brought her arms down and saw that Leon had already recovered, was already staring at the bloody, broken mess sprawled across the hood, its head hanging mercifully out of sight. It wasn't moving.

"You okay?"

Claire turned and looked at Leon, suddenly having to fight off a semi-hysterical laughing fit. Raccoon had been taken over by the living dead and they'd just been in a serious car wreck because a corpse had been trying to *eat* them. All things considered, "okay" was not the first word to come to mind.

At the sight of Leon's sincere and stricken expression, the urge to freak out passed. He looked on the edge of a fit himself; allowing her devastated nerves free reign wouldn't help anything.

"Still in one piece," she managed, and the young cop nodded, seeming relieved.

Claire took a deep breath, feeling like it was the first she'd taken in hours, and looked around at where they'd ended up. Leon had managed a complete 180 at the very end of the street where it T-ed, the obviously totaled squad car facing back the way they'd come. There were no zombies in the immediate vicinity, but Claire had the feeling that they wouldn't have long to find cover; from what she'd seen so far, most if not all of Raccoon had been affected by—by whatever it was that had happened. She held the handgun tightly, trying to get her tangled emotions under control.

"We—" Leon started to say something and then stopped, his eyes widening as he stared at the rearview mirror. Claire looked behind her—and for a second, could only think that at some point since she'd left the university, she'd been cursed.

Cursed. Somebody wants me dead, that's all there is to it.

A semi was barreling down the street, still several blocks away but close enough for them to see that it was out of control. The truck veered back and forth, smashing against a blue pickup parked on one side of the street and then plowing under a mailbox on the other. Claire realized with numb horror that it was a tanker—and from the way the haul was sliding dangerously at each frantic swerve, the driver had a full load. In the split-second that it took to digest that information, to pray that it wasn't gas or oil, the tanker had halved the distance between them. She could actually *see* the flames painted across the dark green cab, but even then it wasn't real until Leon broke their stunned silence.

"—maniac's gonna ram us," he breathed, and then they were both stabbing at the seat-belt releases, Claire praying that the crash hadn't locked them somehow—

The sound of the belts letting go were inaudible beneath the rising monolithic growl of the oncoming tanker and the echoing *crunch* of cars being side-swiped left and right. It would be on them in a heartbeat.

"Run!" Leon shouted, and then she was pushing her way out of the squad car, cool air against her sweaty skin and the scream of the truck's engine blocking out everything else.

She took three giant running leaps and then felt as much as heard the impact, the asphalt shaking beneath her feet even as the crash of rending metal thundered behind her.

One more flying step, and—

KABOOM!

—she was being pushed, shoved roughly off her feet by an incredible pressure wave of heat and sound. She managed to kick off against the ground as the tanker's explosion turned night to day in one brilliant instant. An awkward shoulder roll, grit biting into her heat-blasted skin, and she landed behind a parked car in a gasping heap.

There was a brief, clattering rain of smoking debris, and Claire was on her feet, stumbling back into the street to search the towering flames for some sign of Leon. Her heart sank. The tanker, squad car, and what had once been a hardware store were all enveloped in an inferno of chemical fire, the street completely blocked by the mass of twisted, burning destruction.

"Claire—"

Leon's voice, muffled but audible through the wall of curling flame.

"Leon?"

"I'm okay!" he shouted. "Head to the station, I'll meet you there!"

Claire hesitated for a second, staring down at the handgun she still held tightly in one shaky hand. She was afraid, scared of being alone in a city that had turned into a living graveyard—but it wasn't like there was much of a choice. Wishing that circumstances were different was a waste of time.

"Okay!"

She turned, trying to get her bearings by the smoking, flickering light of the wreck. The station was close, a couple of blocks away—

—and there were creatures lurching out of the shadows, from behind cars and inside darkened buildings. With single-minded purpose, they shambled into the strange light of the blazing accident, making small sounds of hunger as they came—two, three, four of them. She saw tattered skin and rotting limbs, gaping blackness where eyes should be—and still they came, moving slowly toward her as if homing in on living flesh.

Beyond the fiery wreck, she heard gunfire—two

shots from perhaps a block away, then nothing—nothing but the crackle of consuming flame and the soft, helpless cries of the shuffling dead.

Leon's on his own now MOVE!

Claire took a deep breath, spotted an opening within the lethal crowd closing in on her, and ran.

Six

ADA WONG FIT THE SHIMMERING DISC OF
metal into the slot on the statue, patting it into the
opening until it was flush with the marble. As soon as
it was in place, she heard the shift of hidden levers
and stepped back to see what would happen. Her
footfalls echoed through the massive lobby of the
RPD building, the sounds reverberating back to her
from three stories of open room.

*Another key? One of the subbasement medals? Or
perhaps the sample itself, hidden in plain sight . . .
wouldn't* that *be a happy surprise.*

If wishes were horses. The water-bearing nymph
made of stone slid forward at a slight angle, the
pitcher at her shoulder dropping a slender piece of
metal atop the lip of the defunct fountain. The spade
key.

She sighed, picking it up. She already had the keys;

in fact, she had everything she needed to search the station, and most of what she needed to get into the lab. If it wasn't for someone at Umbrella dropping the bomb, the job would have been a walk. Easy money.

Instead, I get a three-day vacation sans comfort, I get night of the living standoff, I get to play Put the Bullet in the Brain and Let's Find the Reporter at the same time. The samples could be anywhere by now, depending on who survived. Assuming I make it out of here with the goods, I'm asking for a big goddamn bonus; no one should have to work in these conditions.

Ada slipped the key into her hip pack, then gazed unseeing at the upper balustrade of the impressive hall, mentally checking off the rooms she'd been through and the ones she'd searched more thoroughly. Bertolucci didn't seem to be anywhere on the east side of the building, upstairs or down; she'd spent what felt like hours staring into dead faces, searching the reeking piles of corpses for his square jaw and anachronistic ponytail. Of course, he could be moving—but from the information she had on him, it was improbable; the reporter was very much a rabbit, a hider in the face of danger.

Speaking of danger . . .

Ada shook herself and got moving, heading back to the door that led into the lower east wing. The lobby was safe enough from the virus carriers, they didn't seem to understand the concept of doorknobs—but there were threats besides the infected. God only knew what Umbrella might send in to clean up . . . or what had been freed from the laboratory when the leak occurred. Less frightening but just as bothersome were the live cops that might still be trooping around, looking for someone to save. She'd heard gunfire, some distant, some not, every hour or three since she'd gone to ground; there were still at least a few uninfected left in the expansive old building. Trying to convince a panicky he-man with a gun that she was alive and didn't want an escort made facing the undead seem almost appealing.

Walking on the balls of her feet to avoid additional noise, Ada slipped through the door and then leaned against it at the end of a long hall, safe to decide on her next move; although she hadn't checked out the basement yet and there were still several carriers wandering around in the detectives' room, the hall's doors were all closed; if someone or something wanted to get at her, she'd be able to see it coming and get out in time.

Ah, the exciting life of the freelance agent. Travel the world! Earn money by stealing important things! Fight off the living dead when you haven't showered or eaten a decent meal in three days—impress your friends!

She reminded herself again to insist on that bonus. When she'd arrived in Raccoon less than a week before, she thought she'd been prepared; the maps had been studied, the reporter's files memorized, her cover story set—a young woman looking for her boyfriend, an Umbrella scientist. That part was almost true; in fact, it had been her brief relationship with John Howe ten months before that had landed her the job. More of a one-night stand, actually, and not a very good one at that—but John had thought otherwise, and his connection to Umbrella, though it had probably killed him, had turned out to be a lucky break for her.

So, she'd been ready. But within twenty-four hours of her self-assured check-in at Raccoon City's nicest hotel, her luck had changed; while eating dinner in the vinyl-encased and mostly empty lounge of the Arklay Inn, she'd heard the first screams outside. The first, but by no means the last.

In some ways, the disaster was an asset; there'd be no guards posted around the lab, no endless covert trial runs. The prep work she'd done on the T-Virus had assured her that the airborne was short-lived and dissipated quickly; the only chance of catching it at this point would be through contact with a carrier, so that wasn't a problem—and once she and a couple dozen others had made it to the police station, she'd seen that Bertolucci was among them. Even with the undead factor, it initially looked like things were going in her favor.

Mission objectives: question the hack, find out how much he knows and kill him or ignore him, depending; retrieve a sample of the new virus, Dr. Birkin's latest wonder. No problem, right?

Three days before, with the knowledge of how the Umbrella lab connected into the sewer system and Bertolucci standing right in front of her, the job had looked pretty wrapped. And of course, that's when things had started to go wrong.

The rearranged station, with the rooms shifted around after the S.T.A.R.S. fiasco, making half my preparations obsolete. People disappearing. The barricades that kept coming down. Police Chief Irons, throwing off commands like some cut-rate dictator, still trying to impress Mayor Harris and his whiny daughter even as the dead piled up. . . .

She'd watched Bertolucci closely enough to see that he was going to duck and run, but had missed the exit; she hadn't even had time to make contact before he had disappeared somewhere into the maze of the station, losing himself in the commotion of the first wave of attacks. Ada had decided to fly solo herself when three-fourths of the civilians were wiped out in a single mass assault not an hour later, all because no one had bothered to lower the garage gates. She wasn't willing to die to keep up her cover as a frightened tourist looking for her boyfriend.

And so came the wait. Almost fifty hours of waiting for things to settle, tucked in the clock tower on the third floor, slipping downstairs to find food or to use a bathroom in the lengthening stretches of time between gunplay. Between the echoing clatter of shots and the screams . . .

Terrific. So now you're out and what do you do? Stand around and reflect. Get on with it; the sooner you finish, the sooner you can collect your wages and retire to some nice island somewhere.

Still, for a moment Ada didn't move, tapping the muzzle of her Beretta absently against one long, stockinged leg. There were three bodies sprawled in the hallway; she couldn't stop staring at one of them, crumpled beneath a window counter halfway down the corridor. A woman in cutoff shorts and a halter, her legs crudely splayed, one arm cocked above her blood-soaked head. The other two were cops, no one she recognized—but the woman had been one of the people she'd talked to when she'd first made it to the station. Her name had been Stacy something-or-other, a nervous but strong-willed girl just out of her teens.

Stacy Kelso, that was it. She'd run into town to pick up some ice cream and had ended up caught in the takeover—yet in spite of her own predicament, she was more concerned about her parents and little brother, still at home. A conscientious girl. A good girl.

Why was she thinking about it? Stacy was dead, a ragged hole at her left temple, and Ada hadn't capped her; it wasn't like she had anything to feel personally responsible about. She'd come in on a job, and it wasn't her fault that Raccoon had gone nova. . . .

Maybe it's not guilt, some part of her whispered. *Maybe you're just sorry she didn't make it. She was a person, after all, and now she's as dead as her parents and kid brother probably are. . . .*

"Snap out of it," she said, softly but with an edge of irritation. She tore her gaze from the woman's pathetic form, fixing it instead on a broken ashtray at the end of the hall. Feeling bad about things she couldn't control wasn't her style, it wasn't how she'd gotten to the top of her trade—and considering how much Mr. Trent was putting up to retain her services, now wasn't the best time to be analyzing her empathy skills. People died, it was the way of the world, and if she'd learned anything in the course of her life it was that agonizing over *that* particular truth was pointless.

Mission objectives: talk to Bertolucci and get the G-Virus sample. That was all she needed to worry about.

There was a mechanism that Ada still had to check a few twisted passages away from where she stood, in the press conference room. Trent's notes on the architect's latest additions to the station had been sketchy, but she knew it had to do with the ornate, sculpted gas lamps and an oil painting. Whoever had commissioned all of the work had one serious secret life going on; there were actual hidden passages upstairs, behind the wall of what had once been a storage room. She hadn't gone through them yet, although a quick glance had told her that the room itself had been remodeled as an office. Judging from the overstuffed and neurotically macho decor, it was probably Irons's. Even from the short time she'd been in his company, she'd ascertained that he wasn't the most stable man who had ever walked; there was no question that he was on Umbrella's payroll, but there was also something about him that just screamed dysfunctional.

Ada started down the hall, her dress flats clicking loudly on the scuffed blue tiles; she was already dreading yet another time-consuming mechanical puzzle. Not that there was any help for it; she had assumed from the beginning that the virus was still in the lab, but she couldn't afford to take any chances on passing up an earlier retrieval. The files indicated that there were between eight and twelve one-ounce vials of the stuff, information from a two-week-old video feed—and Birkin's lab was far from impenetrable. With the underground lab connected to the station through the sewer mains, she had to entertain the possibility that the samples had been moved. Besides, Bertolucci could be tucked away in the research library or in the S.T.A.R.S. office on the west side, maybe the darkroom; dead or not, he had to be found. And it would also give her a chance to collect a few more nine-millimeter clips from the fallen RPD.

She followed the passage as it led her past a small waiting area, complete with vending machines that had already been pried open and ransacked. As with the rest of the station, the corridor was cold and badly in need of air freshener; she'd grown used to the smell, but the chill was murder. For the hundredth time since abandoning her table at the Arklay, Ada wished that she'd dressed more casually for dinner. The sleeveless tight red tunic dress and clattery shoes were fine for cover; as mission gear, however, the outfit was somewhat less than practical.

She reached the end of the hall and carefully opened the door to her left, weapon half-raised. As before, the corridor was clear, yet another testament to the faded elegance of the building—dusky sand-colored walls and symmetrically patterned tiles in this one. The station must have been magnificent once, but years of serving as an institutional facility had leeched away its grandeur; the tattered grand movie-house look and the cold, hopeless atmosphere created a distinctly sinister feel—as if at any moment a cold hand could fall across your shoulder, a soft gust of diseased breath whisper across the back of your neck. . . .

Ada frowned again; after this job, she was going to

take a very long vacation. Either that, or it was time to find a new career. Her concentration—her ability to focus—wasn't what it used to be. And in her business a slip at the wrong time could literally mean death.

Big bonus. Trent smells like money. I'll ask seven digits, high six minimum.

In her attempts to let her thoughts go, to let animal awareness take over, she found that she couldn't keep out the persistent image that crept into her mind. A memory of young Stacy Kelso, anxiously pushing her hair behind her ears as she talked about her baby brother. . . .

After what felt like a very long time, Ada shook the troublesome vision and continued down the hall, promising herself that there would be no more lapses of concentration—and wondering why she couldn't make herself believe it.

SEVEΠ

LEON'S BOOTS SCUFFED SHARDS OF BROKEN glass across the floor of the Kendo gun shop as he snapped open drawers, ash-stained sweat trickling down his face. If he couldn't find .50s pretty quick, he was screwed; the few weapons still remaining in the ravaged shop were inaccessible, strung with steel cable, and the front picture window was completely smashed. It wouldn't take long for the creatures to find him, he was down to his last round, and he still had a couple of blocks to go.

Come on, fifty cal action express, somebody in Raccoon must've ordered 'em—

"Yes!"

Fourth drawer, under the deer-rifle case; a half-dozen empty clips and as many boxes of ammo. Leon grabbed a box and turned, slapping it on the counter as he glanced hurriedly at the front of the small shop.

Still clear, if you didn't include the dead guy on the floor. He wasn't moving, but from the freshness of the wounds that oozed from his considerable gut, staining his strappy white T, Leon wouldn't have long to linger; he didn't know how long it took for the freshly dead to stand up—and didn't really want to find out.

Gotta do it fast anyway, it's like I'm a beacon for those things and this place is easy access. . . .

Gaze darting between the crashed front wall and his skittering hands, Leon started to load up.

He'd lucked across the gun dealer's, having forgotten entirely about it in the dizzying, nightmarish run from the wreck. When the fastest route to the station had turned out to be blocked by a pile-up, the best detour was through Kendo's. It was a coincidence that had undoubtedly saved his life. Even killing two of the ex-living on his way, he'd nearly been overwhelmed by the sheer number of them.

"Uuunh. . . ."

A ghastly, skeletal form staggered out of the street's shadows, drunkenly aimed at the front of the shop.

"Hell," Leon muttered, his fingers somehow managing to go faster. One clip down, one more and he could take the rest. If he bolted now, he'd be dead before he could make it to the station.

Another leprous figure was suddenly standing at the mostly empty frame of the shop's glass entrance, the decay so bad on its legs that Leon could see maggots squirming through the fibrous muscle.

—four . . . five . . . done!

He snatched up the Magnum and ejected the clip, reloading even as the mostly-empty hit the floor. The maggoty creature was shouldering its way through the jagged corners of glass still attached to the frame, something liquid in its throat gurgling softly.

Bag, he needed a bag. Leon's fevered gaze swept the space behind the counter, stopping on a grease-stained gym bag propped against a stool in the back corner. Two running steps and he had it, dumping the contents as he ran back to the pile of clips and loose bullets on the counter. Cleaning equipment rattled across the linoleum as Leon swept the clips into the bag, ignoring the scattered rounds in favor of the ammo drawer.

The decayed monster was shuffling toward him, stumbling on the body of the pot-bellied dead man, and Leon could smell how rotten it was. He jerked the Magnum up and leveled it at the creature's face.

The head, just like the two outside—

With a tremendous, thundering kick, the gurgling, pulpy skull blew apart, thick fluids splattering the shop's walls and display cases in a wet slap. Before the decapitated mess could crumple, Leon spun and dropped into a crouch by the ammo drawer. He shoveled the heavy boxes into the nylon sack, his stomach knotted and shaking from the fear that, even now, the back alley could be filling up with more of them, cutting him off from where he needed to go.

Five clips per box, five boxes, get out already—

Pushing off from his crouch, Leon shouldered the bag and ran for the back door. From the corner of his vision, he saw that another creature had made it inside Kendo's; from the *crunch* of powdering glass, there were more of them filing in just behind it.

He opened the exit door and slid through, glancing left and right as the door settled closed, the automatic lock catching with a soft metallic *snick*. Nothing but garbage cans and recycling bins, overflowing with mildewed waste. From where he stood, the alley stretched off to his left and then hooked left again; if his internal compass was still working, the narrow, cluttered passage would take him straight to Oak, letting out less than a block away from the station.

So far, he'd been lucky; all he could do was hope that his fortune would hold out, would let him get to the RPD building alive and in one piece—and, God willing, find a heavily armed contingent of people who knew what the hell was going on.

And Claire. Be safe, Claire Redfield, and if you get there before me, don't lock the door.

Leon repositioned the leaden weight of the ammo across his back and started down the dimly lit alley, ready to blow apart anything that got in his way.

Claire almost made it without having to shoot; the zombies that trickled out into the streets of Raccoon were relentless but slow, and the adrenaline pumping through her system made it easy enough to dodge them. She figured that they were drawn out by the sound of the wreck, then just followed their noses, or what was left of them; of the ten or so that had made it close enough for her to get a good look, at least half were in an advanced stage of decay, flesh falling from the bone.

She was so busy watching the street and trying to sort through all that had happened, she almost ran right past the police station. She'd been to the RPD building twice before to visit Chris, but had never entered from the back—or in the cold and stinking dark, pursued by malignant cannibals. A crashed cop car and a handful of zombified officers had clued her in, sending her through a small parking lot and some kind of an equipment shed that opened into a tiny paved courtyard—a courtyard where she and Chris had eaten lunch once, sitting on the steps that led up to the station's second-floor helipad. As simply as that, she'd made it.

Weaving past the two stumbling, uniformed corpses that wandered aimlessly across the L-shaped yard was easy, and it was such a relief to be somewhere she recognized, to know she was about to be safe, that she didn't see the woman until it was almost too late. A wailing dead woman with one limply hanging arm and a gore-streaked, shredded tank top, who reached out from the shadows at the base of the stairs and brushed at Claire's arm with cold and scabby fingers.

Claire let out a strangled yelp of surprise, stumbling back from the creature's outstretched hand—and nearly fell into the arms of another one, a tall, broad-shouldered rotting man who had emerged from beneath the metal stairs, graceless yet silent.

She dodged sideways and pointed the nine-millimeter at the man, backed up a step—

—and felt her calf hit the unyielding railing of the back steps to the roof. The woman was five feet to her right, the torn, bloody shirt exposing one gouged breast, the hand of her working arm grasping toward

Claire. The man was one step from reaching distance, and she couldn't back up any further.

Claire pulled the trigger and there was a mammoth *boom*, the gun jerking almost out of her hand. The right half of the tall man's slack and withered face disappeared in a burst of dark, liquid streams gushing from his shattered skull.

She whipped the gun around, tightening her grip as she aimed for the woman's pallid, moaning face. Another blast of deafening sound and the rising moan was cut off, the waxen forehead imploding in a spray of blood and bone chips. The woman went over backwards, crashing to the pavement like—

—*like a corpse, which she already was. They won't be walking away from this one.*

It was as if everything finally caught up to her at once, the reality of her situation driven home when she'd pulled the trigger. For a moment, Claire couldn't move. She stared down at the two crumpled sacks of ruined flesh, at the two *people* she'd just shot, and felt like she was only an inch or two from losing it. She'd grown up around guns, been to shooting ranges dozens of times—but with a .22 target pistol, firing at pieces of paper. Targets that didn't bleed, or spew brain matter like the two human beings she'd just—

No, a cool voice inside of her interrupted. *Not human, not anymore. Don't kid yourself and don't waste time on remorse. Leon could be inside by now, looking for you. And if the S.T.A.R.S. got called in, Chris could be here, too.*

If that weren't motivation enough, the two zombie cops that Claire had passed when she first hit the courtyard were on their way, boots shuffling and dragging across the flagstones. It was time to go.

She jogged up the stairs, barely able to hear the *clang* of her steps over the high-pitched ringing in her ears. The nine-millimeter blasts had done a temporary number on her hearing—which explained why she didn't know about the helicopter until she was almost to the roof.

Claire hit the second-to-top riser and stopped dead, a whipping wind pounding rhythmically at her bare shoulders as the giant black vehicle hovered into view, half lost in shadow. It was near the ancient water tower that bordered the helipad at the southwest corner, though she couldn't tell if it had just taken off or was coming in to land.

Couldn't tell and didn't care. *"Hey!"* she shouted, raising her left hand into the air. *"Hey, over here!"*

Her words were lost in the blowing dust that swirled across the rooftop, drowned out by the steady chop of the 'copter's blades. Claire waved wildly, feeling like she'd just hit the lottery.

Somebody came! Thank God, thank you!

A blaring searchlight snapped on from the midsection of the hovering bird, scrawled across the roof—and was going in the wrong direction, away from her. Claire waved more frantically, drawing in breath to call out again—

—and saw what the spotlight saw, even as she heard the desperate, mostly unintelligible shout beneath the 'copter's roar. A man, a cop, standing at the helipad's corner opposite the stairs, backed against an elevated section of the roof. He held what looked like a machine gun and appeared to be very much alive.

"—get over here—"

The officer shouted at the helicopter, his voice tinged with panic; Claire saw why and felt her relief evaporate. There were two zombies lurching through the darkness of the helipad, headed for the well-lit target that was the shouting cop. She raised the nine-millimeter and then lowered it helplessly, afraid of hitting the cornered man.

The spotlight didn't waver, illuminating the horror with brilliant clarity. The cop didn't seem to realize how close the zombies were until they were grabbing for him, their stringy arms extending into the beam of fixed white light.

"Stay back! Don't come any closer!" he cried, and with the pure terror in his voice, Claire heard him perfectly. Just like she heard his howling scream as the two decaying figures obscured her view, reaching him at the same time.

The sound of his automatic weapon ripped across the helipad, and even over the helicopter's clamor Claire could hear the whining *ting* of bullets flying wild. She dropped, knees cracking against the top step as the weapon's clattering fire went on and on—

—and there was a change in the sound of the 'copter, a strange hum that rose quickly into a mechanical scream. Claire looked up and saw the giant craft dip down, the back end swinging around in an erratic, jerking arc.

Jesus, he hit them!

The 'copter's spotlight was going all directions at once, flashing across metal pipes and concrete and the dying struggles of the cop, somehow still firing as the two monsters tore at him—

—and then the helicopter was coming down, teetering sideways, its blades slamming into the brick of the elevated roof with a tremendous crash. Before Claire could blink, the nose of the craft hit—plowing across the helipad in a curtain of screeching sparks and flying glass.

The explosion happened just as the mammoth machine slid to a stop against the southwest corner—directly on top of the fallen cop and his killers. The rattle of the machine gun was finally cut off in the *whoosh* of flame that sprang up after the initial sputtering boom, lighting the rooftop in a burning red glow. At the same instant, something in the roof gave with a rending *crunch,* as the nose of the 'copter plunged through a brick wall and out of sight.

Claire stood up on legs she barely felt, staring in disbelief at the leaping fire that dominated almost half of the helipad. It had all happened too fast for her to feel like it had happened at all, and the smoking, burning evidence in front of her only made the sense of unreality greater. An acrid, sickly-sweet odor of burning meat wafted over her on a wave of heated air, and in the sudden silence, she could hear the soft groans of the zombies down in the courtyard.

She shot a look down the stairs and saw that both of the dead cops were at the foot, blindly and uselessly falling against the bottom step. At least they couldn't climb . . .

. . . can't. Climb. Stairs.

Claire turned her frightened glance toward the door that led into the RPD building, maybe thirty feet from the curling, popping flames that were slowly eating the body of the 'copter. Except for the stairs, it was the only way onto the roof. And if zombies couldn't climb—

—then I'm in some deep shit. The station isn't safe.

She stared thoughtfully at the burning wreck, weighing her options. The nine-millimeter held a lot of ammo and she still had two full clips; she could head back into the street, look for a car with keys in it and go for help.

Except what about Leon? And that cop was still alive—what if there are more people inside, planning an escape?

She thought she'd held up pretty well on her own so far, but she also knew she'd feel safer if somebody else were in charge—a riot squad would be okay, though she'd settle for some battle-scarred veteran cop with a shitload of guns. Or Chris; Claire didn't know if she'd find him at the station, but she firmly believed that he was still alive. If anyone was equipped to handle himself in a crisis like this one, it was her brother.

Whether or not she found anybody, she shouldn't take off without telling Leon; if she didn't, blowing town instead, and he got killed looking for her. . . .

Decision made. Claire walked for the entrance, carefully skirting the blaze and scanning the flickering shadows for movement. When she reached the door, she closed her eyes for a second, one sweating hand on the latch.

"I can do this," she said quietly, and although she didn't sound as confident as she would've liked, at least her voice didn't tremble or break. She opened her eyes, then the door; when nothing jumped out at her from the softly lit hall, she slipped inside.

Eight

CHIEF OF POLICE BRIAN IRONS WAS STAND-
ing in one of his private corridors, trying to catch his
breath, when he felt the shuddering impact rumble
through the building. He heard it, too—heard *something*. A distant splintering sound, heavy and abrupt.

The roof, he thought distantly, *something on the
roof . . .*

He didn't bother following the thought to any kind
of conclusion. Whatever had happened, it couldn't
make things any worse.

Irons pushed away from the stone wall with one
well-padded hip, hefting Beverly as gently as he could.
They'd be at the elevator in a moment, then there was
just the short walk to his office; he could rest there,
and then—

"And then," he mumbled, "that's the question,
isn't it? And then what?"

Beverly didn't answer. Her perfect features remained still and silent, her eyes closed—but she seemed to nestle closer to him, her long, slender body curling against his chest. It was his imagination, surely.

Beverly Harris, the mayor's daughter. Youthful, stunning Beverly, who had so often haunted his guilty dreams with her blond beauty. Irons hugged her closer and continued toward the elevator, trying not to let his exhaustion show in case she woke up.

By the time he reached the lift, his back and arms were aching. He probably should have left her in his private hobby room, the room he'd always thought of as the Sanctuary—it was quiet there, and probably one of the safest areas in the station. But when he'd decided to go to the office, to collect his journal and a few personal items, he found that he simply couldn't stand to leave her behind. She'd looked so vulnerable, so innocent; he'd promised Harris that he would watch out for her, and what if she was attacked in his absence? What if he came back from the office and she was just—gone? Gone like everything else . . .

A decade of work. Networking, making the connections, careful positioning . . . all of it, just like that.

Irons lowered her to the cold floor and opened the elevator gate, trying desperately not to think about all that he'd lost. Beverly was the important thing now.

"Going to keep you safe," he murmured, and did one corner of that perfect mouth rise slightly? Did she know she was safe, that Uncle Brian was taking care of her? When she was a child, when he used to frequent the Harrises' for dinner, she'd called him that. "Uncle Brian."

She knows. Of course she knows.

He half-dragged her into the lift and leaned her in the corner, gazing tenderly at her angelic face. He was suddenly overwhelmed by a rush of almost paternal love for her, and wasn't surprised to feel tears well up in his eyes, tears of pride and affection. For days now he'd been subject to such emotional outbursts—rage, terror, even joy. He'd never been a particularly emotional man, but had grown to accept the powerful feelings, even to enjoy them after a fashion; at least they weren't confusing. He'd also had moments when he'd been overcome by a kind of strange, creeping haze, a formless anxiety that left him feeling deeply unsettled . . . and as bewildered as a lost child.

No more of those. There's nothing else that can go wrong now; Beverly's with me, and once I collect my things, we can hide away in the Sanctuary and get some rest. She'll need time to recover, and I can, can sort things through. Yes, that's it; things need to be sorted through.

He blinked the already forgotten tears away as the metal cage started to rise, unholstering his sidearm and ejecting the clip to count how many rounds were left. His private rooms were safe, but the office was another story; he wanted to be prepared.

The elevator came to a stop and Irons propped open the gate with one leg before lifting the girl, grunting with the exertion. He carried her as he would have carried a sleeping child, her cool, smooth body limp in his arms, her head rolled back and wobbling as he walked. He'd picked her up awkwardly, and her white gown had hiked up, exposing the tight, creamy skin of her thighs; Irons forced his gaze away, concentrating on the panel controls that opened the wall into his office. Whatever harmless fantasies he'd had before, she was his responsibility now; he was her protector, her white knight . . .

He was able to hit the protruding button with one knee. The wall slid open, revealing his plushly decorated and thankfully empty office; only the blank, glassy stares of his animal trophies greeted them.

The massive walnut desk that he'd had imported from Italy was right in front of him and his stamina was going fast; Beverly was a petite woman, but he wasn't in shape the way he used to be. He quickly laid her on the desk, pushing a cup of pencils to the floor with his elbow.

"There!" he exhaled deeply, smiling down at her. She didn't smile back, but he sensed that she would be awake soon, like before. He reached under the desk and tapped the wall controls; the panel slid closed behind them.

He'd been concerned when he'd first found her, asleep next to Officer Scott in the back hall; George Scott was dead, covered with wounds, and when Irons had seen the red splash on Beverly's stomach, he'd been afraid that she was dead, too. But when he'd taken her to the Sanctuary, to his safe place, she'd whispered to him—that she didn't feel well, that she was hurt, that she wanted to go home . . .

. . . *did she? Did she really?*

Irons frowned, snapped out of the uncertain memory by something, something he'd felt when he'd laid her on his hobby table and straightened her blood-stained gown, something he couldn't quite recall. It hadn't seemed important at the time, but now, away from the hidden comforts of the Sanctuary, it was nagging at him. Reminding him that he had suffered one of those confused moments when he'd, when he'd—

—*felt the cold, rubbery jelly of intestine beneath my fingers*—

—touched her.

"Beverly?" he whispered, sitting down behind his desk when his legs went suddenly weak. Beverly kept her silence—and a turbulent flood of emotions hit Irons like a tidal wave, crashing over him, crowding his mind with images and memories and truths that he didn't want to accept. Cutting the outside lines after the first attacks. Umbrella and Birkin and the walking dead. The slaughter in the garage, when the bright coppery scent of blood had filled the air and Mayor Harris had been eaten alive, screaming until the very end. The dwindling numbers of the living through the first long and terrible night—and the cold, brutal realization that had hit him again and again, that the city—*his* city—was no more.

After that, the confusion. The strange and hysterical joy that had come when he'd understood that there would be no consequences for his actions. Irons remembered the game he'd played on the second night, after some of Birkin's pets had found their way to the station and taken out all but a few of the remaining cops. He'd found Neil Carson cowering in the library and had . . . *tracked* him, hunting the sergeant down like an animal.

What did it matter? What matters, now that my life in Raccoon is over?

All that was left, the only thing that he had to hold on to, was the Sanctuary—and the part of him that had created it, the dark and glorious heart inside of his own that he'd always had to keep hidden away. That part was free now. . . .

Irons looked at the corpse of Beverly Harris, laid out across his desk like some delicate and fragile dream, and felt that he might be torn apart by the feelings of fear and doubt that warred inside of him. Had he killed her? He couldn't remember.

Uncle Brian. Ten years ago, I was her Uncle Brian. What have I become?

It was too much. Without taking his gaze from her lifeless face, he pulled the loaded VP70 from its holster and began to rub the barrel with numb fingers, gentle strokes that reassured him somehow as the weapon turned toward him. When the bore was pressed firmly against his soft belly, he felt that some kind of peace might be within reach. His finger settled across the trigger, and it was then that Beverly whispered to him again, her lips still, her sweet, musical voice coming from nowhere and everywhere at once.

. . . don't leave me, Uncle Brian. You said you'd keep me safe, that you'd take care of me. Think of what you could do now that everyone is gone and there's nothing to stop you. . . .

"You're dead," he whispered, but she kept talking, soft and insistent.

... *nothing to stop you from being fulfilled, truly fulfilled for the first time in your life* ...

Tortured and aching, Irons slowly, slowly pulled the nine-millimeter away from his stomach. After a moment, he rested his forehead against Beverly's shoulder and closed his tired eyes.

She was right, he couldn't leave her. He'd promised—and there was something to what she'd said, about all of the things he could do. His hobby table was big enough to accommodate all kinds of animals ...

Irons sighed, not sure what to do next—and wondering why he was in such a hurry to decide, anyway. They would rest for a while, perhaps even take a nap together. And when they awoke, things would be clear again.

Yes, that was it. They would rest, and then he could sort things through, take care of business; he was the chief of police, after all.

Feeling in control of himself again, Brian Irons slipped into a light and uneasy doze, Beverly's cool flesh like a balm against his feverish brow.

Nine

THANKS TO A VAN PARKED IN THE ALLEY behind Kendo's, Leon's straight shot to the station had taken a few detours—through an infested basketball court, another alley, and a parked bus that had reeked from the sprawled corpses inside. It was a nightmare, punctuated with whispering howls, the stink of decay, and once, a distant explosion that made his limbs feel weak. And though he had to shoot three more of the walking dead and was wired to the teeth with adrenaline and horror, he somehow managed to hold on to his hope that the RPD building would be a safe haven, that there would be some kind of crisis center set up, manned by police and paramedics—people in authority making decisions and marshaling forces. It wasn't just a hope, it was a *need;* the possibility that there might be no one left in Raccoon to take charge was unthinkable.

When he finally stumbled out into the street in front of the station and saw the burning squad cars, he felt like he'd been hit in the gut. But it was the sight of the decaying, moaning police officers staggering around the dancing flames that truly wiped out his hope. There were only about fifty or sixty cops on the RPD force, and a full third of them were lurching through the wreckage or dead and bloody on the pavement not a hundred feet from the front door of the station.

Leon forced the despair away, fixing his sight on the gate that led to the RPD building's courtyard. Whether or not anyone had survived, he had to stick with his plan, put out a call for help—and there was Claire to think about. Concentrating on his fears would only make it harder to do whatever needed to be done.

He ran for the gate, nimbly dodging a horribly burned uniformed cop with blackened bones for fingers. As he clutched the cold metal handle and pushed, he realized that some part of him was growing numb to the tragedy, to the understanding that these things had once been the citizens of Raccoon. The creatures that roamed the streets were no less horrible, but the shock of it all just couldn't be sustained; there were too many of them.

Not too many here, thank God . . .

Leon slammed the gate shut behind him and pushed his sweaty hair off his brow, taking a deep breath of the almost fresh air as he scanned the courtyard. The small, grassy park to his right was well lit enough for him to see there were only a few of the once human creatures, and none close enough to be a threat. He could see the two flags that adorned the front of the station house, hanging limp in the still shadows, and the sight resparked the hope that he thought he'd lost; whatever else happened, he'd at least made it to someplace he knew. And it had to be safer than the streets.

He hurried past a blindly reeling trio of the dead, easily avoiding them—two men and a woman; all three could have passed for normal if not for their mournful, hungry cries and uncoordinated staggers. They must have died recently—

—but they're not dead, dead people don't gush blood when you shoot them. Not to mention the walking-around-and-trying-to-eat-people thing. . . .

Dead people didn't walk . . . and living people tended to fall down after they'd been shot a few times with .50 caliber slugs, and didn't put up with their flesh rotting on their bones. Questions he hadn't yet had time to ask himself flooded through his mind as he jogged up the front steps to the station, questions he didn't have the answers for—but he would soon, he was sure of it.

The door wasn't locked, but Leon didn't allow himself to feel surprise; with all he'd been through since he hit town, he figured that it would be best to keep his expectations to a minimum. He pushed it open and stepped inside, Magnum raised and his finger on the trigger.

Empty. There was no sign of life in the grand old lobby of the RPD building—and no sign of the disaster that had overtaken Raccoon. Leon gave up on not feeling surprised, closing the door behind him and stepping down into the sunken lobby.

"Hello?" Leon kept his voice low, but it carried, echoing back to him in a whisper. Everything looked just as he remembered it; three floors of classically styled architecture in oak and marble. There was a stone statue of a woman carrying a water pitcher in the lower part of the large room, a ramp on either side leading up to the receptionist's station. The RPD seal set into the floor in front of the statue gleamed softly in the diffuse light from the wall lamps, as if it had just been polished.

No bodies, no blood . . . not even a shell casing. If there was an attack here, where the hell's the evidence?

Uneasy at the profound silence of the huge chamber, Leon walked up the ramp to his left, stopping at the counter of the reception desk and leaning over it; except for the fact that it was unmanned, nothing seemed to be out of place. There was a phone on the desk below the counter. Leon picked up the receiver and cradled it between his head and shoulder, tapping at the buttons with fingers that felt cold and distant. Not even a dial tone; all he heard was the sound of his own heavily thumping heart.

He put the phone down and turned to face the empty room, trying to decide on where to go first. As much as he wanted to find Claire, he also desperately wanted to hook up with some other cops. He'd received a copy of an RPD memo just a couple of weeks before, stating that several of the departments were going to be relocated, but that didn't really matter; if there were cops hiding in the building, they probably weren't concerned with sticking close to their desks.

There were three doors leading away from the lobby to different parts of the sprawling station, two on the west side and the other on the east. Of the two on the west, one led through a series of halls toward the back of the building, past a couple of filing offices and a briefing room; the second opened into the uniformed-officer squad room and lockers, which then connected into one of the corridors near the stairs to the second floor. The east door, in fact the whole east side of the first floor, was primarily for the detectives—offices, interrogation, and a press room; there was also access to the basement and another set of stairs on the outside of the building.

Claire probably came in through the garage . . . or through the back lot to the roof . . .

Or, she could've circled around and come through the same door he had—assuming she even made it to the station; she could be anywhere. And considering that the building took up almost an entire city block, that was a lot of ground to cover.

Finally deciding that he had to start somewhere, he walked toward the squad room for the beat cops, where his own locker would be. A random choice, but he'd spent more time there than anywhere else in the station, interviewing and working through scheduling. Besides, it was closest, and the tomb-like silence of the oversized lobby was giving him the creeps.

The door wasn't locked, and Leon pushed it open slowly, holding his breath and hoping that the room would be as undisturbed and orderly as the lobby. What he saw instead was the confirmation of his earlier fears: the creatures had been there—with a vengeance.

The long room had been trashed, tables and chairs splintered and overturned everywhere he looked. Smears of dried blood decorated the walls, splashes of it in tacky, trailing puddles on the floor, leading toward—

"Oh, man—"

The cop was sitting against the lockers to his left, his legs splayed, half-hidden by a smashed table. At the sound of Leon's voice, he weakly raised one shaking arm, pointed a weapon vaguely in Leon's direction—then lowered it again, seemingly exhausted by the effort. His midsection was awash with oozing blood, his dark features contorted with pain.

Leon was crouching at his side in two steps, gently touching his shoulder. He couldn't see the wound, but there was so much blood that he knew it was bad—

"Who are you?" the cop whispered.

The soft, almost dreamy tone of his voice scared Leon as much as the still oozing wound and the glassy look in his dark eyes; the man was slipping, fast. They'd never formally met, but Leon had seen him before. The young African-American beat cop had been pointed out to him as sharp, on the fast track to detective, *Marvin, Marvin Branagh*. . . .

"I'm Kennedy. What happened here?" Leon asked, his hand still on Branagh's shoulder. A sickly heat radiated through the officer's ragged shirt.

"About two months ago," Branagh rasped, "the cannibal murders . . . the S.T.A.R.S. found zombies out at this mansion in the woods. . . ."

He coughed weakly, and Leon saw a small bubble of blood form at the corner of his mouth. Leon started to tell him to be still, to rest, but Branagh's faraway gaze had fixed on his own; the cop seemed determined to tell the story, whatever it was costing him.

"Chris and the others discovered that Umbrella was behind the whole thing . . . risked their lives, and no one believed them . . . then this."

Chris . . . Chris Redfield, Claire's brother.

Leon hadn't made the connection before, although he'd known something about the trouble with the S.T.A.R.S. He'd only heard bits and pieces of the story—the suspension of the Special Tactics and Rescue Squad after their alleged mishandling of the murder cases had been the reason the RPD'd been hiring new cops. He'd even read the names of the infamous S.T.A.R.S. members in some local paper, listed along with some fairly impressive career records—

—and Umbrella runs this town. Some kind of a chemical leak, something that they tried to cover up by getting rid of the S.T.A.R.S.—

All of this went through his mind in a split-second; then Branagh coughed again, the sound even weaker than before.

"Hang in there," Leon said, and quickly looked around them for something to use to stop the bleeding, inwardly kicking himself for not having done it already. A locker next to Branagh was partly open; a crumpled T-shirt lay at the bottom. Leon scooped it up and folded it haphazardly, pressing it against Branagh's stomach. The cop placed his own bloody hand over the makeshift bandage, closing his eyes as he spoke again in a wheezing gasp.

"Don't . . . worry about me. There are . . . you have to try and rescue the survivors. . . ."

The resignation in Branagh's voice was horribly plain. Leon shook his head, wanting to deny the truth, wanting to do something to ease Branagh's pain—but the wounded cop was dying, and there was no one to call for help.

Not fair, it's not fair—

"Go," Branagh breathed, his eyes still closed.

Branagh was right, there was nothing else Leon could do—but he didn't, *couldn't* move for a moment—until Branagh raised his weapon again, pointing it at him with a sudden burst of energy that strengthened his voice to a rough shout.

"Just *go!*" Branagh commanded, and Leon stood up, wondering if he would be as selfless in the same situation, working to convince himself that Branagh would make it somehow.

"I'll be back," Leon said firmly, but Branagh's arm was already drooping, his head settling against his heaving chest.

Rescue the survivors.

Leon backed toward the door, swallowing heavily and struggling to accept the change in plan that could very well kill him—but that he couldn't walk away from. Official or no, he was a cop. If there were other survivors, it was his moral and civic duty to try and help them.

There was a weapons store in the basement, near the parking garage. Leon opened the door and stepped back into the lobby, praying that the lockers would be well stocked—and that there would be somebody left for him to help.

†ЕП

FROM THE BURNING ROOFTOP, CLAIRE
moved through a snaking hallway littered with broken glass—and past a very dead cop, a bloody
testament to her fears about the station's safety. She
quickly stepped over the body and moved on, her
nervous tension growing. A cool breeze ruffled
through the shattered windows that lined the hall,
making the darkness alive; there were shiny black
feathers stuck in the streaks of blood that painted the
floorboards, and their soft, wavering dance had her
jerking the semiautomatic toward every shadow.

She passed a door that she thought led back outside
to a set of external stairs, but she kept going, taking a
right toward the center of the building. The way the
helicopter had buried itself in the rooftop was gnawing at her, inspiring visions of the old station going up
in flames.

From the look of things, maybe that's not such a bad idea. . . .

Dead bodies and bloody handprints on the walls; Claire wasn't happy about the idea of touring the station. Still, death by fire didn't carry much appeal either; she needed to see how bad it was before she went looking for Leon.

The corridor dead-ended at a door that felt cool to the touch. Mentally crossing her fingers, Claire opened it—and stumbled back as a wave of acrid smoke washed over her, the smell of burnt metal and wood thick in the heated air. She dropped to a crouch and edged forward again, peering down the hall that stretched off to her right. The hall turned right again maybe thirty feet down, and although she couldn't see the fire proper, bright, fiery light was reflected off the gray paneled walls at the corner. The popping crackle of the unseen flames was magnified in the tight corridor, the sound as mindlessly hungry as the moans of the zombies down in the courtyard.

Well, shit. *What now?*

There was another door diagonally across from where she crouched, only a few steps away; Claire took a deep breath and moved, walking low to stay beneath the thickening blanket of smoke, hoping she could find a fire extinguisher—and that a fire extinguisher would be enough to put out whatever blaze the crashed 'copter had created.

The door opened into an empty waiting room—a couple of green vinyl couches and a rounded counter-desk, with another door across from the one she'd entered by. The small room seemed untouched, as sterile and quietly unassuming as she might have expected—and unlike just about everywhere else she'd been tonight, there was no lurking disaster in the mild shadows thrown by the overhead fluorescents, no stench of rot or shuffling zombie.

And no fire extinguisher. . . .

Not in plain sight, anyway. She closed the door on the smoky corridor and stepped toward the desk, lifting the entrance flap with the barrel of the gun. There was an old manual typewriter on the counter—and next to that, a telephone. Claire grabbed for it, hoping against hope, but heard only dead air through the receiver. Sighing, she dropped it and ducked down to check out the shelves beneath the counter. A phone book, a few stacks of papers—and then, half-hidden by a woman's purse on the bottom shelf, was the familiar red shape she'd been hoping to find, coated with a thin layer of dust.

"There you are," she murmured, and paused just long enough to stick the nine-millimeter into her vest before hefting the heavy cylinder. She'd never used one before, but it looked simple enough—a metal handle with a locking pin, a black rubber nozzle hooked to the side. It was only a couple of feet long, but it weighed a good forty or fifty pounds; she figured that meant it was full.

Armed with the extinguisher, Claire stepped back to the door and started to take short, sharp breaths, filling her lungs. It made her feel light-headed, but the hyperventilation would allow her to hold her breath longer. She didn't want to keel over from smoke inhalation before she'd had a chance to put it out.

A final deep breath and she opened the door, crouching her way back into the now noticeably hotter corridor. The haze of smoke had gotten thicker too, extending down from the ceiling in a dark and choking fog at least four feet deep.

Keep low, breathe shallow and watch your step—

She turned the corner and felt a bizarre mix of relief and sorrow at the sight of the burning wreckage right in front of her. She bobbed her head and took a small breath through the fabric of her vest, feeling her skin flush and tighten from the heat. The fire wasn't as bad as she'd feared, more smoke than substance and not much taller or bigger than she was; the flames that licked up the wall in orange-yellow fingers seemed to be having trouble catching, stopped by the heavy wood of a half-smashed door. It was the nose of the helicopter that drew her attention, the blackened shell of the smoldering cockpit—and the blackened husk of the pilot still strapped to the seat, the melted mouth frozen in a yawning, silent scream. There was no way to tell if it had been a man or a woman; the features had been obliterated, running together like dark tallow.

Claire jerked the metal pin loose from the handle and aimed the hose at the burning floorboards, where the flame danced in white and blue. She squeezed the lever down and a hissing plume of snowy spray *whooshed* out, blasting over the debris in a powdery cloud. Barely able to see through the billowing whiteness, she directed the hose over everything, dousing the wreckage liberally with the oxygen killer. Within a minute, the fire appeared to be out, but she kept up with the extinguisher until it ran dry.

At the last spluttering cough of spray, Claire let go of the handle and took a few more shallow breaths, inspecting the smoking wreck for any spots she'd missed. Not a flicker, but the wooden door alongside the helicopter's flocked cockpit was still leaking tendrils of black smoke. She leaned closer and saw a tinge of glowing orange under the charred surface. The area surrounding the burning wood had already been torched, but she didn't want to take any chances; she stepped back and gave the door a solid kick, aiming for the glowing embers.

Her boot connected squarely with the hot spot, and the door flew open with a splintering *crack,* the scorched wood giving way in a sparking shower of cinders. A few landed on her bare calf, but she drew her weapon before stopping to brush them off, more afraid of what might be waiting behind the ruined door than a few blisters.

A short, empty hallway, littered with jagged pieces of splintered wood and hazy with smoke, then a door at the end on the left; Claire moved toward it, as much to get to some fresh air as to see where it led. With the immediate threat of the fire over with, she had to start looking for Leon—and thinking about what they'd need to survive. If she could check out a few of the rooms along the way, maybe she'd be able to find stuff they could use.

A phone that works, car keys . . . hell, a couple of machine guns or a flame-thrower would be nice, but I'll take what I can get.

The plain door at the end of the hall was unlocked. Claire pushed it open, ready to fire at anything that moved—

—and stopped, feeling mildly shocked by the bizarre atmosphere of the lavish room. It was like some parody of a men's club from the fifties, a large office decorated with an extravagance that bordered on the ridiculous. The walls were lined with heavy mahogany bookshelves and matching tables, surrounding a kind of sitting area made up of padded leather chairs and a low marble table, all set atop an obviously expensive oriental rug. An elaborate chandelier hung from the ceiling, casting a rich, mellow light over it all. Framed pictures and delicate vases were situated throughout—but their classic designs were overwhelmed by the stuffed animal heads and poised, lifeless birds that dominated the room, most gathered around a massive desk at the far side—

—*oh, Jesus*—

Laid out across the desk, like some character from a gothic horror story, was a beautiful young woman in a flowing white gown, her guts ripped to bloody shreds. The corpse was like a centerpiece; the dried and dusty animals stared down at her with dead glass eyes— there was a falcon and what looked like an eagle, their ratty wings spread in simulated flight, as well as a couple of mounted deer heads and that of a nappy furred moose. The effect was so creepy and surreal that for a moment, Claire couldn't breathe—

—and when the high-backed chair behind the desk swiveled around suddenly, she barely held back a shriek of superstitious terror, half expecting to see some vision of dark and grinning death. It was only a man—but a man with a gun, pointed at her.

Twice in one night, what are the odds—

For a second, neither of them moved—and then the man lowered his weapon, a sickly half-smile playing across his pudgy face.

"I'm terribly sorry," he said, his voice as oily and false as a bad politician's. "I thought you were another one of those zombies."

He smoothed his bristly mustache with one thick finger as he spoke, and although Claire had never met him before, she suddenly knew who he was; Chris had bitched about him often enough.

Fat, mustachioed, and as slick as a snake-oil salesman—it's the police chief. Irons.

He didn't look good, his cheeks flushed with high color and his porcine eyes rimmed with puffed white flesh. The way his gaze darted around the room was unsettling, as if he was in the grip of some kind of heavy paranoia. In fact, he looked *unbalanced,* like he wasn't all that connected to reality.

"Are you Chief Irons?" she asked, trying to sound pleasantly respectful as she stepped closer to the desk.

"Yes, that's me," he said smoothly, "and just who are you?"

Before she could speak, Irons went on, confirming Claire's suspicions with what he said next—and with the bitter, petulant tone in which he said it. "No, don't bother telling me. It makes no difference. You'll end up like all the others. . . ."

He trailed off, staring down at the dead woman in front of him with some emotion that Claire couldn't place. She felt bad for him, in spite of all that Chris had told her about his rotten personality and professional incompetence; God only knew what horrors he'd witnessed, or what he'd had to do to survive.

Is it any wonder that he's having trouble with reality? Leon and I wandered into this horror show in the last reel; Irons was here for the previews, which probably included watching his friends die.

She looked down at the young woman on the desk and Irons spoke again, his voice somehow sad and pompous at the same time.

"That's the mayor's daughter. I was supposed to look out for her, but I failed miserably. . . ."

Claire searched for some words of comfort, wanting to tell him that he was lucky to have lived, that it wasn't his fault—but as he continued his lament, the words died in her throat, along with her pity.

"Just look at her. She was a true beauty, her skin nothing short of perfection. But it will soon putrefy . . . and within the hour, she'll become one of those *things.* Just like all the others."

Claire didn't want to jump to any conclusions, but the wistful longing in his tone and in his shining, hungry stare made her skin crawl. The way he was looking at the dead girl—

—you're imagining things. He's the chief of police, not some perverted lunatic. And he's the first person you've met who might be able to give you some kind of information. Don't waste the opportunity.

"There must be some way to stop it. . . ." Claire said gently.

"In a manner of speaking. A bullet in the brain—or decapitation."

He finally looked away from the body, but not at Claire. He turned to gaze at the stuffed creatures perched on the edge of his desk, his voice taking on a resigned but somehow mirthful quality.

"And to think—taxidermy used to be my hobby. No longer. . . ."

Claire's internal alarms were doing some serious jangling. Taxidermy? What the *hell* did that have to do with the dead human being on his desk?

Irons was finally looking at her, and Claire didn't like it one bit. His dark and beady gaze was directed at her face, but he didn't seem to actually *see* her at all. For the first time, it occurred to her that he hadn't asked her one question about how she'd come to be there or commented on the smoke that had leaked into his office. And the way he'd talked about the mayor's daughter . . . no real sorrow at her passing, only self-pity and some kind of twisted admiration.

Oh, boy. Oh boy oh boy, he's not just out of touch here, he's on a different goddamn planet—

"Please," Irons said softly. "I'd like to be alone now."

He sagged down into his chair, closing his eyes, his head falling back against the padded back as if in exhaustion. As simply as that, she'd been dismissed. And although she had a million questions—many of which she thought he could provide answers for—she did think that maybe it was for the best if she just got the hell away from him, at least for now—

A soft creaking sound, behind her and to the left, so quiet that she wasn't even sure she'd heard it at all. Claire turned, frowning, and saw that there was a second door to the office. She hadn't noticed it before—and that soft, stealthy sound had come from behind it.

Another zombie? Or maybe somebody hiding . . . ?

She looked back at Irons, and saw that he hadn't moved. Apparently he hadn't heard anything, and she'd ceased to exist for him, at least for the moment. He'd gone back to whatever private world he'd been in before she stumbled into his office.

So—back the way I came, or do I see what's behind door number two?

Leon—she needed to find Leon, and she had a pretty strong feeling that Irons was a creep, whether he was crazy or not; no great loss that he wasn't up for joining forces. But if there were other people hiding in the building, people that she and Leon could help or who might be able to help them. . . .

It would only take a moment to check. With a last glance at Irons, sagging next to the corpse of the mayor's daughter and surrounded by his lifeless animals, Claire walked to the second door, hoping she wasn't making a mistake.

ELEVEN

SHERRY HAD BEEN HIDING FOR A LONG TIME in the police station, for what must have been three or four days, and hadn't seen her mother yet. Not once, not even when there had still been a lot of people left. She'd found Mrs. Addison right after she'd gotten there—one of the teachers from school—but Mrs. Addison had died. A zombie had eaten her. And not long after that, Sherry had found a ventilation shaft that ran over most of the whole building, and had decided that hiding was safer than staying with the grownups—because the adults kept dying, and because there was a monster in the station even worse than the zombies or the inside-out men, and she was pretty sure that the monster was looking for *her*. That was probably stupid, she didn't think that monsters picked out just one person to go for—but then again, she'd never thought that monsters were real, either.

So Sherry had stayed hidden, mostly in the knight room; there weren't any dead people there, and the only way to get in—besides the ventilation shaft behind the suits of armor—was to go down a long hall guarded by a giant tiger. The tiger was stuffed, but it was still scary—and Sherry thought that maybe the tiger would scare away the monster. Part of her *knew* that that was dumb, but it made her feel better anyway.

Since the zombies had taken over everything in the police station, she'd spent a lot of time sleeping. When she was asleep, she didn't have to think about what might have happened to her parents or worry about what was going to happen to her. The air shaft was pretty warm, and she had plenty to eat from the candy machine downstairs—but she was scared, and even worse than being scared was being lonely, so mostly she'd just slept.

She'd been asleep, warm and curled up behind the knights, when she'd been awakened by a tremendous crash somewhere outside. She was sure it was the monster; she'd only caught a glimpse of it once before, of the giant's broad and terrible back, through a steel grate—but she'd heard it screaming and howling through the building many times since then. She knew that it was terrible, terrible and violent and hungry. Sometimes it disappeared for hours at a time, letting her hope that it had given up—but it always came back, and no matter where Sherry was, it always seemed to appear somewhere close by.

The loud noise that had ripped her from her

dreamless sleep was like the sound a monster would make tearing the walls down, and she'd huddled in her hiding place, ready to dart back into the shaft if the sound came any closer. It didn't. For a long time she didn't move, waiting with her eyes squeezed shut, holding on to her good luck charm—a beautiful gold pendant that her mother had given her only last week, so big that it filled up her whole hand. As it had before, the charm worked; the loud, terrible noise hadn't been repeated. Or maybe the big tiger had kept the monster from finding her. Either way, when she'd heard gentle thumping sounds in the office, she'd felt safe enough to creep out of the case and go out into the hall to listen. The zombies and inside-out men couldn't use doors, and if it *was* the monster, it would have come for her already, clawing down doors and screaming for blood.

It has to be a person. Maybe Mom . . .

Halfway down the hall, where it turned right, she'd heard people talking in the office and felt a burst of hope and loneliness mixed together. She couldn't tell what they were saying, but it was the first time she'd heard *anybody* who wasn't yelling for maybe two days. And if there were people talking, maybe it was because help had finally come to Raccoon.

The army or the government or the Marines, maybe all of them . . .

Excited, she hurried down the hall and was next to the big snarling tiger, right by the door, when her excitement faltered. The voices had stopped. Sherry stood very still, suddenly anxious. If people *had* come to Raccoon to help, wouldn't she have heard the planes and trucks? Wouldn't there be shooting and bombs and men with loudspeakers telling everybody to come out?

Maybe those voices aren't army people at all; maybe those voices are Bad People. Crazy, like that one man . . .

Not long after Sherry had gone into hiding, she'd seen a terrible thing through a grating that led into a locker room. A tall man with red hair had been in the room, talking to himself and rocking back and forth in a chair. At first, Sherry had thought about asking him for help, to find her parents—but something about the way he was talking and giggling and gently swaying back and forth made her wary, so she'd watched him for a while from the safe darkness of the air shaft. He'd been holding a big knife. And after a long time, still laughing and mumbling and rocking, he'd stabbed himself in the stomach. Sherry had been more scared by that man than by the zombies, because it didn't make sense. He'd been crazy, and he'd killed himself and she'd crawled away, crying because it just didn't make any *sense*.

She didn't want to meet anyone else like that. And even if the people in the office were okay, they might take her away from her safe place and try to protect her—and that would mean her death, because the monster surely wasn't afraid of adults.

It felt awful to turn away, but there was no other choice. Sherry started back for the armor room—

Creak!

—and froze as the floor shifted underfoot. The sound of the creaking board seemed incredibly loud and she held her breath, clutching her pendant and praying that the door wouldn't come flying open behind her, that some crazy wouldn't charge in and—and *get* her.

She didn't hear anything, but felt sure that the pounding of her heart would give her away, it was so loud. After a full ten seconds, she carefully started back down the hall, stepping as lightly as she could, feeling like she was creeping out of a cave filled with sleeping snakes. The hall back to the armor room seemed like it was a mile long, and she had to use all of her willpower not to run once she reached the turn—but if there was one thing she'd learned from the movies and TV, it was that running from danger always meant a horrible death.

When she finally reached the entrance back to the armor room, she felt like she might just collapse from relief. She was safe again, she could snuggle back into the old blanket that Mrs. Addison had found for her and just—

The door from the office opened, opened and closed. And a second later, there were footsteps. Coming for her.

Sherry flew into the armor room, no longer thinking about anything at all in the bright and trembling crush of panic that swept through her. She sprinted past the three knights, forgetting her safe place because all she knew was that she had to get away, get as far away as possible. There was a dark, tiny chamber past the glass case in the middle of the room and darkness was what she needed, a shadow to disappear into—

—and she could hear the running footsteps somewhere behind her, pounding over wood as she hurtled into the dark room and into the farthest corner. Sherry crouched down between the dusty brick of the room's fireplace and the padded chair beside it and tried to make herself as small as possible, hugging her knees and hiding her face.

Please please please don't come in, don't see me, I'm not here—

The running footsteps had come into the armor room and were slow now, hesitant, moving around the big glass case in the middle. Sherry thought of her safe place, the mouth of the ventilation shaft that could have taken her away, and struggled to hold back hot tears of self-condemnation. The fireplace room had no escape; she was trapped.

Each hollow, thumping step brought the stranger closer to the dark room in which Sherry hid. She scrunched herself tighter, making promises that she would do anything, anything at all if only the stranger would go away—

Thump. Thump. Thump.

Suddenly, the room flashed into blinding brightness, the soft click of the light switch lost beneath Sherry's terrified cry. She pushed away from her corner and ran, screaming and unseeing, hoping to get past the stranger and back to the air shaft—

—and a warm hand grabbed her arm, tight, keeping her from going one more step. She screamed again, jerking as hard as she could, but the stranger was strong—

"Wait!" It was a lady, the voice almost as frantic as Sherry's hammering heart.

"Let me *go*," Sherry wailed, but the lady was still holding on, even pulling her closer.

"Easy, easy—I'm not a zombie, take it easy, it's okay—"

The woman's voice had turned soothing, the words crooned gently, the hand on Sherry's wrist warm and strong. The sweet, musical voice repeated the gentle words again and again.

"—easy, it's okay, I'm not going to hurt you, you're safe now."

Sherry finally looked at the lady, and saw how pretty she was, how her eyes were soft with concern and sympathy. And just like that, Sherry stopped trying to get away and felt the hot tears trickle down her face, tears that she'd been holding back ever since she'd seen the red-haired man commit suicide. She instinctively hugged the young, pretty stranger—and the lady hugged her back, her slender arms tight across Sherry's trembling shoulders.

Sherry cried for a couple of minutes, letting the woman stroke her hair and whisper soothing words to her—and at last, she felt like the worst was over. As much as she wanted to crawl into the lady's arms and forget all of her fears, to believe that she *was* safe, she knew better. And besides, she wasn't a baby anymore; she'd turned twelve last month.

With an effort, Sherry stepped away from the woman and wiped her eyes, looking up into her pretty face. The woman wasn't that old, maybe only twenty or so, and was dressed really cool—boots and cutoff pink denim shorts and a matching vest with no sleeves. She wore her shiny brown hair in a ponytail, and when she smiled, she looked like a movie star.

The woman crouched down right in front of her, still smiling gently. "My name's Claire. What's yours?"

Sherry felt shy suddenly, embarrassed for running and then trying to get away from such a nice lady. Her parents had often told her that she acted like an emotional baby, that she was "too imaginative" for her own good, and here was proof; Claire wasn't going to hurt her, she could tell.

"Sherry Birkin," she said, and smiled at Claire, hoping that Claire wasn't mad at her; she didn't *look* mad. In fact, she looked pleased with Sherry's answer.

"Do you know where your parents are?" Claire asked, in the same sweet tone.

"They work at the Umbrella chemical plant, just outside of town," Sherry said.

"Chemical plant . . . then what are you doing here?"

"My mom called, and told me to go to the police station. She said it was too dangerous to stay at home."

Claire nodded. "From the look of things, she was probably right. But it's dangerous here, as well. . . ."

Claire frowned thoughtfully, then smiled again. "You'd better come with me."

Sherry felt a cold knot tighten in her stomach, and shook her head, wondering how to explain to Claire that it wasn't a good idea, that it was a very *bad* idea. She wanted more than anything not to be alone anymore, but it just wasn't safe.

If I go with her and the monster finds us. . . .

Claire would be killed. And although Claire was thin, Sherry was pretty sure that she wouldn't be able to fit in the ventilation shaft.

"There's something out there," she said finally. "I saw it, it's bigger than the zombies. And it's coming after *me.*"

Claire shook her head, opening her mouth to say something, probably to try and talk her into changing her mind, when a terrible, furious sound filled the room, echoing in violent waves from somewhere in the building. Somewhere close.

"Rrraaahh—"

Sherry felt her blood turn to ice. Claire's eyes went wide, her skin paling.

"What was that?"

Sherry backed away, breathless, in her mind already running for the safe place behind the three suits of armor.

"That's what I was telling you," she gasped out, and before Claire could stop her, she turned and ran.

"Sherry!"

Sherry ignored the shouted plea, sprinting past the glass exhibit case for the safety of the air shaft. She leapt nimbly over the knight's pedestal and dropped to her hands and knees, ducking her head and scrambling into the ancient stone hole set into the base of the wall.

Her only chance, *Claire's* only chance, was for

Sherry to get as far away from her as possible. Maybe they would find each other again when the monster had gone.

As Sherry crawled quickly through the tight and winding darkness, she hoped it wasn't already too late.

†WELVE

ADA SAT ON THE EDGE OF THE CLUTTERED desk in the office of the Chief of Detectives, resting her aching feet and staring blankly at the empty steel safe in the corner. Her patience was wearing thin. Not only was the G-Virus sample nowhere to be found, she was starting to think that Bertolucci had flown the coop. She'd gone through the break room, the S.T.A.R.S. office, the library—in fact, she was pretty sure she'd covered just about everywhere the reporter would have had easy access to, and had used two full clips to do it. It wasn't that she was low on ammo, it was the waste of time that the bullets represented— twenty-six rounds and no results, except that there were a dozen more virus-riddled corpses lying around. And two of Umbrella's freak hybrids. . . .

Ada shuddered, remembering the warped red flesh and trumpeting shrieks of the bizarre creatures that she'd capped in the press room. She'd never been particularly bothered by greed, corporate or otherwise, but Umbrella had been up to some seriously immoral experimentation. Trent had warned her about the Tyrant retrievers—which, thankfully, hadn't put in an appearance yet—but the long-tongued, clawed, bloody humanoids were an affront to even her sensibilities. Not to mention a lot harder to kill than the virus carriers. If they were T-Virus products, she'd have to keep her fingers crossed that Birkin hadn't done anything with his newest creation. According to Trent, the G series hadn't been put to use yet, but it was supposed to be twice as potent. . . .

Ada let her gaze wander, taking in the plain, functional office. It wasn't the most inspiring environment to take a break in, but at least it was reasonably gore-free; with the door closed, she could hardly smell the officers in the main part of the room. They'd been pretty far gone when she'd put them down, that bonelessly wet stage that apparently preceded total collapse.

Not that it matters if I *can smell* them, *my hair and clothes have absorbed the goddamn smell; when they start to go bad, it seems to happen with a bang . . .*

She wished she'd bothered to learn more on the science end; she knew what the T-Virus was used for, but hadn't thought it necessary to research the physio-chemical effects. Why bother, when she had no reason to think that Umbrella had been planning to spill a shitload of it in their hometown? She was getting plenty of firsthand information about how well it worked, but it would have been nice to know exactly what happened in the infected party's body and mind, what turned them from a person into a mindless flesh-eater. Instead, she could only file away her observations and make guesses at the truth.

From what she'd seen, it took less than an hour for someone infected to turn zombie. Sometimes the victim went into a kind of fever-coma first, which presumably burnt out parts of the brain—and only added to the impression that they were waking from the dead when they stood up and started looking for fresh meat. The symptoms of the virus were the same for everyone, but not the progression rate; she'd seen at least three cases where the victim had turned bloodthirsty within a couple of moments of being infected, the stage she'd started to think of as "going cataract." One of the few constants was that their eyes clouded with a thin film of eggy white mucous when they turned—and although the physical deterioration always started immediately, some fell to pieces much faster than others . . .

. . . and why are you thinking about it? Your job doesn't include finding a cure, does it?

She sighed, bending over to rub her toes. True enough. Still, it was something to think about. Focusing on staying alive was tiring and all-encompassing work; she didn't have a chance to consider the subtleties of the circumstances while clearing out corridors. She was on break, and she needed to let her brain run around a bit, ponder a few of the job's more puzzling aspects.

And there are about a thousand to mull over . . . Trent, what Bertolucci should or shouldn't know . . .

*and the S.T.A.R.S.—what the hell had happened to
that merry crew?*

From the articles that Trent had included in the
info packet, she knew about the S.T.A.R.S.'s suspension—and considering what they'd been investigating, it didn't take a genius to figure out that they'd
been railroaded by Umbrella for uncovering part if
not all of the bioweapon operations. Umbrella had
probably offed them by now, if they hadn't gone into
hiding—and she had to wonder if Trent had played
any part in the S.T.A.R.S.'s little misadventure, or if
he'd tried to contact them before or after.

Not that he would've told her; Trent was an enigma,
to be sure. She'd only had one actual meeting with
him, although he'd contacted her several times prior
to her leaving for Raccoon, mostly by phone—and
although she'd always prided herself on her ability to
read people, she knew absolutely nothing about where
his interests lay, why he wanted the G-Virus or what
his gripe with Umbrella was about. It was obvious
that he had some inside connection, he knew too
much about the company's workings—but if that was
the case, why not just pick up his own goddamn
sample and then quit? Hiring an outside agent was the
act of someone trying to avoid implication—but
implication of what?

Ours is not to question why. . . .

A good principle to live by; she also wasn't getting
paid to figure out Trent. She doubted she'd be able to
even if she *was* getting paid for it; she'd never met
such a supremely self-controlled man as Mr. Trent. In
every interaction they'd had, she'd gotten the feeling

that he had been smiling inside, as if he knew some intensely pleasurable secret that no one else was privy to—and yet somehow, he hadn't come across as arrogant or overblown. He was a cool one, his geniality so natural that she'd been vaguely intimidated; she might not have been able to pick up on his motives, but she'd seen that calm humor before—it was the real face of true power, of a man with a plan and the means to implement it.

So has the spill upset his plans, whatever they are? Or was he prepared for this contingency . . . ? He may not have planned it, but I can't imagine that "caught unawares" is anywhere in Trent's vocabulary. . . .

Ada leaned back, rolling her head tiredly before pushing herself off the desk and stepping back into her uncomfortable shoes. Enough down time, she couldn't spare her aches and pains more than a few minutes and didn't expect to figure out much of anything until she was well away from Raccoon. She still had a couple of areas to check for Bertolucci before heading into the sewers, and she'd noticed that some of the first-floor window barricades weren't as solid as she might have hoped; she didn't want to end up blocked out of a path by a new group of carriers from outside.

There were the "secret" passages on the east side, and the holding cells downstairs past the parking garage. If she couldn't find him in either of those places, she'd have to assume he'd left the station and concentrate her efforts on obtaining the sample.

She decided to try the basement first; it seemed unlikely that he'd stumbled across the hidden corridors. From what she'd read of his work, he wasn't a good enough reporter to find his own ass. And if he was hiding in or near the holding cells, she wouldn't have to spend any more time roaming the station, facing the inevitable invasion; the entrance into the subbasement was downstairs, so barring any complications, she could head straight for the lab.

Ada walked out of the office, wrinkling her nose at the fresh burst of rotting smell pushed at her by the lazily spinning ceiling fans. There had to be seven or eight bodies in the desk-filled room, all of them cops, and at least the three that she'd shot had been fairly rank . . .

. . . and didn't I leave five carriers still walking around in here when I came through before?

Ada paused just outside the large and open room, looking back in from the narrow connecting corridor that led to the back stairs. Had there been five? She knew she'd capped a couple on her first visit; the rest had been too slow to hassle with, and she *thought* there'd been five of them. And yet she'd only had to knock off three when she had returned for her impromptu break.

There were five. I may not be at peak, but I can still count.

She wasn't in the habit of doubting her ability to keep track of such things, and the fact that she'd only just noticed was a sign of how tired she was; two days ago, she would have made the observation immediately. There was no way to tell if the additional corpses had been shot or had simply disintegrated on their own without exposing herself to contact—they were too messed up; but it would be wisest to assume that there were still a few survivors wandering around.

Not for long, one way or another. . . .

Whether or not the zombies managed to break through, Umbrella would act soon, if they hadn't already. What had happened in Raccoon was a shareholder's worst nightmare, and Umbrella certainly wasn't going to ignore the problem; they'd probably already worked up a fail-safe disaster and prepared their own spin to feed to the press. And it was a foregone conclusion that they'd try to salvage Birkin's synthesis before putting their fail-safe into effect, which meant that she'd have to be very careful. Birkin had apparently been somewhat secretive about his work, and Trent had relayed that Umbrella would eventually send in a retrieval team . . . with Raccoon in ashes, that eventuality had probably been moved forward a few notches.

A team of human beings, hopefully. I can handle that. A Tyrant, though . . . I don't need that kind of pain.

Ada turned away from the room, walking toward the closed door that would lead her to the basement steps. Tyrant was the code name for a particular series in Umbrella's organic weapons research, a series that embodied the most destructive applications of the T-Virus. According to Trent, the White Umbrella scientists—the ones working in the secret labs—had just started tests on a kind of humanoid bloodhound, designed to hunt down any assigned scent or substance it had been encoded for with relentless and inhuman capabilities. A Tyrant retriever, a nearly indestructible construct of infected flesh and surgically implanted wiring—just the kind of thing that they might send in to find, say, a sample of the G-Virus. . . .

Once she collected Trent's sample, she was history, paid and drinking margaritas on a beach somewhere. And anything she might or might not *feel* about it, about how many innocents had died or what Trent wanted the G-Virus for—it was just one more thing to put on her list of things the job didn't call for.

Her defenses safely in place, Ada started for the basement to see if she could find the troublesome reporter.

Leon stood in the ransacked basement weapons locker, adjusting the holster straps and thinking about where Claire might be. From what little he'd seen so far, the station wasn't too bad. Cold and dim and stinking of the bodies heaped in the hallways, but not as actively dangerous as the streets. It wasn't much to be grateful for, but he'd take what he could get.

He'd killed two of his fellow officers and a woman in the tatters of a traffic patrol uniform on his way to the basement—the cops upstairs and the woman just outside the morgue, a few yards from the small room that housed the RPD armament. Only three zombies since he'd reached the station, not including the few he'd been able to avoid in the detectives' room—but he'd passed over a dozen corpses on the short journey and had been able to make out the bullet holes on about half of them, through the eyes or directly to the temple. Between the cleanly "dispatched" creatures and the number of weapons missing from the lockers, he dared to hope that Branagh had been right about there being survivors.

Marvin Branagh . . . probably dead by now. Does that mean he'll turn into a zombie? If Umbrella's really behind all this, it has to be some kind of a plague or disease, they're a pharmaceutical company—so how do you catch it? Is it a contact thing, or can you get it from taking a deep breath—

Leon dropped that train of thought, fast; as cool and humid as the basement was, the thought that he could be infected by the zombie sickness made him break out in a sudden feverish sweat. What if all of Raccoon was still hot, and he'd caught it just driving into town? The cluttered shelves of the storage room seemed to close in just a bit, in an anxiety flash of epic proportions.

But before real panic set in, he heard his mind's voice remind him of the reality—and the acceptance of the reality came with it, allowing him to let go of the fear.

If you're sick, you're sick. You can eat a bullet before it gets bad. If you're not sick, maybe you can survive to tell your grandkids about all this. Either way, there's probably nothing you can do about it now—except try to be a cop.

Leon nodded to himself, sighing. A better plan than worrying about it, and he now had the equipment to boost his chances. The electronic lock for the weapons store had been shot through, saving him from having to go searching for a key card or shooting it himself;

the door had obviously been pried open, the external locks and handle practically shredded. On his first dig through the room, he'd been disappointed, and not a little freaked. There had been no handguns at all and very little ammo left in the dented green lockers—but he *had* found a box of shotgun shells, and after a second, more desperately thorough search, he'd uncovered a twelve-gauge hidden behind a high stack of boxes. There were a couple of shoulder harnesses for the Remington model still hanging on a wall hook, as well as a bigger utility belt than the one he already wore; it even had a sidepack deep enough to hold all of the loaded Magnum clips.

With a final cinch on the harness, he decided that it would be best to start searching the most obvious places first, every connecting corridor from every possible entrance. He'd head back to the lobby first, find something to leave a note on—

Bam! Bam! Bam!

Shots fired, close, and the echoing tone said it was the garage just down the hall. Leon yanked the Magnum out and ran for the door, precious seconds wasted as he fumbled at the mangled handle.

The hall was clear, except for the dead traffic cop on the floor to his right. Straight ahead was the entrance to the parking garage, and Leon hurried toward it, reminding himself that he wanted to go in easy, that he didn't want to get shot by a panicked gunman.

Take it slow, get a good look before you move, identify yourself clearly—

The door, set into the wall to his right, was standing open—and as Leon darted a look into wide and open space, his body shielded by the concrete-block wall, he saw something that startled him into forgetting about the shooter.

The dog. It's the same goddamn dog.

Impossible—but the sprawled, lifeless animal in the middle of the car-lined chamber looked the same. Even with the barest glimpse he'd had before, the slimy wet demon in canine form that had nearly scared him into a crash ten miles outside the city could have come from the same litter. Beneath the sputtering fluorescent strips that lit the cold, oil-stained garage, Leon could see how truly abnormal it was.

There didn't seem to be anything moving, and no sound except for the buzz of lights. Still holding the Magnum ready, Leon stepped into the garage, determined to get a closer look at the creature—and saw a second one next to a parked squad car, apparently just as dead as the first. Both lay in sticky red pools of their own blood, their long, skinned-looking limbs splayed brokenly.

Umbrella. The wild animal attacks, the disease—how long has this shit been going on? And how did they manage to keep it quiet after all those murders?

What was even more confusing was why Raccoon wasn't crawling with support services already; Umbrella may have been able to keep their involvement with the "cannibal" murders silent, but how could they keep Raccoon's citizens from calling for help from outside the city?

And these dogs, like carbon copies . . . something else that Umbrella made up in their labs?

He took another step toward the fallen dog-things, frowning, not liking the dark conspiracy theories that were forming in his thoughts but unable to ignore them. What he liked even less was the look of the oil stains on the concrete floor; they were rust-colored—and there were too many of the dried splotches for him to count. He bent down to get a closer look, so intent on putting to rest a sudden terrible suspicion that he didn't register the shot until he heard the high, singing whine when it blew past his head.

Bam!

Leon spun left, bringing the Magnum up and shouting at the same time—

"Hold your fire!"

—and saw the shooter lowering her weapon, a woman in a short red dress and black leggings standing by a van against the far wall. She started walking toward him, her slender hips rolling smoothly, her head high and shoulders back. As if they were at a cocktail party.

Leon felt a rush of anger, that she could seem so calm after very nearly killing him—but as she got closer, he found himself wanting to forgive her. She was beautiful, and wore an expression of genuine pleasure at seeing him; a welcome sight after so much death.

"Sorry about that," she said. "When I saw the uniform, I thought you were another zombie."

She was Asian-American, fine-boned but tall, her short hair a thick and glossy black. Her deep, satiny voice was almost a purr, a strange contrast to the way she looked at him. The slight smile she wore didn't seem to touch her almond-shaped eyes, which were scrutinizing him carefully.

"Who are you?" Leon asked.

"Ada Wong." That throaty purr again. She tilted her head, still smiling.

"I'm Leon Kennedy," he said reflexively, not sure what to ask or where to start. "I—what are you doing down here?"

Ada nodded toward the van behind her, an RPD transport wagon that was blocking the holding cell area. "I came to Raccoon looking for a man, a reporter named Bertolucci; I have reason to think that he's in one of the cells, and I think he might be able to help me find my boyfriend. . . ."

Her smile faded, her sharp, almost electric gaze meeting his. . . . "And I think he knows all about what happened here. Would you help me move the van?"

If there was a reporter locked up on the other side of the garage wall who could tell them anything at all, Leon was eager to meet him. He wasn't sure what to make of Ada's story, but couldn't imagine why she would lie about anything. The station wasn't safe, and she was looking for survivors, just as he was.

"Yeah, okay," he said, feeling caught off guard by her smoothly direct manner. It felt like she had taken control of their meeting, some subtle but deliberate manipulation that had put her in charge—and from the casual way she turned and walked back to the van, as if there was no question that he would follow, he thought she knew it.

Don't be paranoid; strong women do *exist. And the*

more people we can find, the more help I can get to look
for Claire.

Maybe it was time to stop making plans, and just
try to keep up. Leon holstered the Magnum and went
after her, hoping that the reporter was where Ada
thought he was—and that things would start making
sense, sooner rather than later.

Thirteen

SHERRY BIRKIN WAS GONE, AND CLAIRE couldn't fit herself into the ventilation duct to go after her. Whatever or whoever had screamed and scared the little girl so badly hadn't put in an appearance, but Sherry was history, maybe still crawling frantically through some dark and dusty tunnel. She had apparently been hiding by the duct for a while; there were empty candy-bar wrappers and a musty old blanket stuffed in the opening, the pathetic little hideaway tucked behind three standing suits of armor.

Once she'd realized that Sherry wasn't coming back, Claire had hurried back to Irons's office, hoping that he might be able to tell her where the duct let out, but Irons was gone—along with the body of the mayor's daughter.

Claire stood in the office, watched over by the

dumb glass eyes of the morbid decor, and felt really uncertain for the first time since she'd hit town. She'd started out to find Chris, a goal that had expanded to include worries about zombie dodging, hooking up with Leon, and avoiding creepy Chief Irons, pretty much in that order. But in the few moments between meeting the little girl and that strange, howling scream, her priorities had shifted dramatically. A child was caught up in this nightmare, a sweet, little kid who believed that there was a monster stalking her.

Maybe there is. If I can accept that Raccoon's got zombies, why not monsters? Hell, why not vampires or killer robots?

She wanted to find Sherry, and she didn't know how to start. She wanted her big brother, but was just as clueless as to where *he* might be—and she had begun to wonder if he knew anything about what had happened to Raccoon.

The last time she'd talked to him, he'd avoided her questions about why the S.T.A.R.S. had been suspended, insisting that it wasn't anything to worry about—that he and the team had run into some political trouble at the office and it was all going to be sorted out. She was used to his protectiveness, but thinking back, hadn't he seemed overly evasive? And the S.T.A.R.S. had been investigating the cannibal murders, it wasn't much of a stretch to connect the past flesh-eating activity with the current . . .

. . . which means what? That Chris uncovered some evil plot and was hiding it?

She didn't know. All that she knew was that she

didn't believe he was dead, and that for now finding Chris or Leon would have to take a back seat to finding Sherry. As bad as things were, Claire had defenses—she had a gun, she had at least a little emotional maturity, and after nearly two years of daily five-mile runs, she was in excellent shape. But Sherry Birkin couldn't be older than eleven or twelve, and seemed frail in every sense of the word, from the dirt in her pixie blond hair to the desperate anxiety in her wide blue eyes—she had inspired all of Claire's protective instincts—

Thump!

A heavy, hollow vibration rattled through the ceiling, making the intricate chandelier in Irons's office tremble. Claire reflexively looked up, gripping her handgun. There was nothing to see but wood and plaster, and the sound didn't repeat itself.

Something on the roof . . . but what could have made a noise like that? An elephant being air-dropped?

Maybe it was Sherry's monster. The vicious scream they'd heard back in the private exhibit room had come through a duct or the fireplace, the origin of the cry impossible to pin down—but it *could* have been the roof. Claire wasn't particularly keen on meeting up with whatever had screamed, but Sherry had seemed certain that the creature was following her . . .

. . . so find the screamer, find the girl? Not my idea of the perfect plan, but I don't have much else to go on at this point; it might be the only way to find her.

Or maybe it was Irons up there—and although her meeting with him had left a slimy taste in her mouth, she regretted not having tried to get more information out of him. Crazy or not, he hadn't struck her as stupid; it might not be a bad idea to find him again, at least to ask some questions about the ventilation system.

She wouldn't know anything until she checked it out. Claire turned and went to the office door that opened into the outer corridor, where she'd put out the helicopter fire. The smoke had thinned in the adjoining hall, and although the air was still warm, it wasn't the heat of a fresh blaze. In that, at least, she'd been successful. . . .

Claire stepped back into the main hall, averting her eyes from what was left of the pilot—

—and *craa-ack!*

—She froze, and heard a massive splintering of wood followed by the thick, ponderous steps of someone who must be *huge* moving through the corridor past the turn, the sounds deliberate and thundering.

Guy must weigh a ton, and oh Jesus *tell me that wasn't a door being torn apart—*

Claire shot a look back down the small hallway to Irons's office, her instincts telling her to run, her brain reminding her that it was a dead end, her body paralyzed between the two—

—and the biggest man she'd ever seen stepped into view, shadowed by the thin haze of smoke drifting through the hall. He was dressed in a long army-green overcoat that only accented his size, and was as tall as an NBA star—taller, but with proportionate bulk. A thick utility belt was wrapped around his waist, and though she didn't see any weapons, she could *feel* the violence radiating off him in invisible waves. She could just make out his sickly white blur of a face, the hairless, sloping skull—and quite suddenly, Claire was certain that he *was* a monster, a killer with black gloved fists, each as big as a human head—

Shoot! Shoot it!

Claire aimed but hesitated, terrified of making a horrible mistake—until it took one massive step toward her on tree-trunk legs, and she heard the crunch of denting wood beneath its booted Frankenstein feet, and saw the black eyes, black and rimmed with red. Like lava-filled pits in a misshapen white boulder, blank but not at all blind, his gaze found hers—and he raised one meaty clenched fist, the threat unmistakable.

—shootshootshoot—

She squeezed the trigger, one, two times, and saw the impact—a flap of its lapel blew into shreds just below his collarbone, the second shot slicing cleanly through one side of the neck—

—and he took another step, not a flicker of expression passing over his rough-hewn features, the fist still raised, seeking a target, seeking to crush—

The black, smoking hole in its throat wasn't bleeding.

Oh SHIT!

In a rush of adrenaline-boosted dread, Claire pointed the handgun at the creature's heart and pulled the trigger repeatedly, the giant taking another step, striding into the stream of explosive fire without flinching—

—and she lost track of the shots, unable to believe

that it could still be coming, less than ten feet away as the rounds hammered its mammoth chest—

—and the gun clicked empty, even as the monster stopped in its thundering tracks, swaying from side to side like a tall building in a high wind. Without taking her shocked gaze from the reeling giant, Claire grabbed another clip from her vest and fumbled through reloading, her brain crazily trying to name this walking abortion.

Terminator, Frankenstein's monster, Dr. Evil, Mr. X—

Whatever it was supposed to be, the seven-plus semi-jacketed rounds to the chest had finally taken effect. Silently, the towering creature slumped to his right, falling heavily against one smoke-blackened wall and sagging there—not crumpling, but not moving, either.

Weird angle, that's all, he's dead, just propped up by his own weight—

Claire didn't move any closer, keeping the handgun leveled at the motionless giant. Was this the screamer? For as powerful and inhuman as it looked, she didn't think so; this was no primal, furious demon, howling for blood. Mr. X was more like some soulless machine, bloodless flesh that could ignore pain . . . or embrace it.

"Dead now, doesn't matter," Claire whispered, as much to reassure herself as to cut off the relentless stream of useless thought. She had to think, to figure out what this meant—this wasn't some freak zombie mutation, so what the hell *was* it? Why didn't it fall down? She'd emptied a mostly full clip—would somebody hear the shots, would Sherry or Irons or Leon or whoever else might be lurking around the station come find her? Should she stay where she was?

The creature that she'd already started to think of as Mr. X wasn't breathing, its muscular body perfectly still, its face as closed as death. Claire bit her lower lip, staring at the still impossibly standing, leaning creature, trying to think through her confused fear—

—and saw his eyes open, his shiny black and red eyes. Without so much as a wince of pain or effort, Mr. X swayed back to a stand, blocking the hall, his giant hands raising again—

—and with a mighty swing, he crashed his fists through the air, his long arms whipping just in front of her as she stumbled back. The momentum was enough for both of his huge hands to plunge *into* the wall across from where he'd leaned. The impact buried his fists, his arms stuck in the wood and plaster halfway to his elbows.

Me, could've been ME—

Back through Irons's office and she'd be trapped. Without giving the matter any further thought, Claire moved, sprinting toward Mr. X. She flew past him, her right arm actually brushing against his heavy coat, her heart skipping a beat as the material wisped across her skin.

She ran, hung a left and dashed down the hazy hall, trying to remember what was past the waiting room, trying not to hear the unmistakable sounds of movement behind her as Mr. X jerked his hands free.

Jesus, what is that THING—

Back through the waiting room, slamming the door behind her as she ran, Claire decided that she would decide later. She ran, not letting herself think anything at all but how to run faster.

Ben Bertolucci was in the last cell in the room farthest from the garage, crashed out on a metal cot and snoring lightly. Keeping her expression carefully neutral, Ada decided to let Leon wake him up. She didn't want to seem overly eager, and if there was one thing she knew about men, it was that they were easier to handle when they thought they were in control. Ada looked up at Leon with a patience she didn't feel and waited.

They'd checked out an empty kennel and a winding concrete hall before finding him, and though the cold, dank air reeked of blood and virus decay, they hadn't come across any bodies—which was strange, considering the slaughter that Ada knew had occurred in the dank garage. She thought about asking Leon if he knew what had happened, but decided that the less they spoke, the better; there was no point in letting him get used to having her around. She'd seen the manhole in the kennel, rusting and set into a dark corner, and been gratified to see a crowbar on an open shelf nearby. With Bertolucci snoozing in front of them, Ada felt like things were finally starting to pick up—

"Let me guess," Leon said loudly, and reached out to thump on the metal bars with the butt of his gun. "You must be Bertolucci, right? Get up, *now.*"

Bertolucci groaned and sat up slowly, rubbing at his

stubbled jaw. Ada wanted to smile, watching him frown wearily in their direction; he looked like shit— his clothes rumpled, his lank ponytail frazzled.

Still wearing his tie, though. The poor slob probably thinks it makes him look more like a real reporter. . . .

"What do you want? I'm trying to sleep here." He sounded grouchy, and again Ada had to suppress a smile. It served him right for being so difficult to find.

Leon glanced at Ada, looking a trifle uncertain. "Is this the guy?"

She nodded, realizing that Leon probably thought Bertolucci was a prisoner. Their conversation would dispel that particular notion pretty fast, but she didn't want Leon to know more than he had to; she'd have to choose her words carefully.

"Ben," she said, letting her voice carry a hint of desperation. "You told the city officials that you knew something about what's been going on, didn't you? What did you tell them?"

Bertolucci stood up and glared at her, his lips curling. "And who the hell are you?"

Pretending that she hadn't heard, Ada upped the desperation, but just a hair; she didn't want to over- play the helpless female bit, it kind of clashed with the fact that she'd survived this long.

"I'm trying to find a—friend of mine, John Howe. He was working for a branch office of Umbrella based in Chicago, but he disappeared several months ago— and I heard a rumor that he's here, in this city . . ."

She trailed off, watching Bertolucci's expression. He knew something, no question—but she didn't think he was going to give it up.

"I don't know anything," he said gruffly. "And even if I did, why would I want to tell you?"

Original. If the cop wasn't here, I'd probably just shoot him. Actually, she probably wouldn't; Ada wasn't into killing for the fun of it, and thought that she could probably get it out of him using one of her more persuasive methods—if her feminine charms didn't work, there was always a shot to the kneecap. Unfortunately, she couldn't do anything with Officer Leon hanging around. She hadn't planned on their encounter, but for the moment, she was stuck with him.

The cop obviously wasn't happy with the reporter's responses. "Okay, I say we leave him in there," he growled, talking to Ada but staring at Bertolucci with undisguised irritation.

Bertolucci half-smiled, reaching into one pocket and pulling out a set of silver cell keys on a thick ring. Ada wasn't surprised, but Leon looked even more pissed off.

"Fine by me," Bertolucci said smugly. "I'm not about to leave this cell, anyway. It's the safest place in the building. There are more than just zombies running around here, believe you me."

From the way he said it, Ada thought she'd probably have to kill him after all. Trent's instructions had been clear—if Bertolucci knew anything about Birkin's work on the G-Virus, he was to be disposed of; why, exactly, she wasn't sure, but that was the job. If she could just get a few moments alone with him, she'd be able to ascertain how much he actually knew.

The question was, how? She didn't want to shoot

Leon; as a rule, she didn't kill innocents—and besides, she liked cops. Not necessarily the brightest lot, but anyone who took a job that required putting his or her life on the line had her respect. And he had great taste in weaponry—the Desert Eagle was top of the line . . .

. . . so why rationalize? I ditch him first and then circle back, doesn't mean I'm going soft—

"*Ggrraaaa!*"

A violent, inhuman shriek pierced the tense silence. Ada snapped her Beretta around, aiming at the open gate that led back through the empty cell-block area. Whatever it was, it was somewhere in the basement—

"What was that?" Leon breathed from behind her, and Ada wished she knew the answer. The still resonating echo of that furious scream was like nothing she'd heard before—and nothing she expected to hear, even knowing about Umbrella's research.

"Like I said, I'm not leaving this cell," Bertolucci said, his voice breaking slightly. "Now get out of here before you lead it right to me!"

Sniveling coward—

"Look, I may be the only cop left alive in this building," Leon said, and something about the combination of fear and strength in his tone made Ada shoot a look back at him. The officer's gaze was fixed on Bertolucci, his blue eyes sharp and unyielding.

". . . so if you want to live, you're gonna have to come with us."

"Forget it," Bertolucci snapped. "I'm staying here 'til the cavalry shows up—and if you're smart, you'll do the same thing."

Leon shook his head. "It could be days before anyone comes, our best chance is to find a way out of Raccoon—and you heard that scream. Do you really want to get a visit from whatever made it?"

She was impressed; some Umbrella freak could be lurching its way toward them even now, and Leon was actually trying to save the reporter's worthless hide.

"I'll take the risk," said Bertolucci. "And good luck getting out, you're gonna need it. . . ."

The rumpled reporter stepped up to the bars, looking back and forth between them, running a hand over his greasy hair.

"Look," he said, his voice softening. "There's a kennel in the back of the building, with a manhole in it. You can get to the sewers from there, it's probably the fastest way out of the city."

Ada sighed inwardly. Terrific; so much for her hidden route to the lab. If she dumped Leon now, it would take him about five minutes to find her.

You can always kill him, if it comes to that. Or . . . you can get him lost in the sewers and come back for Bertolucci while he's clearing the path for *you.*

Unlike Bertolucci, she didn't want to run into whatever had screamed—and now that she knew he was staying put, luring the cop away was the next logical step.

The things I do to avoid unnecessary bloodshed . . .

"Alright, I'm going to check it out," she said, and without waiting for Leon's response, she turned and sprinted for the gate.

"Ada! Ada, wait!"

She ignored him, hurrying past the empty cells and back into the chilled hall, relieved that the passage was still clear—and feeling a little unnerved by her sudden reluctance to simplify the situation. Things would be a lot easier if she just got rid of them both, a decision she wouldn't have hesitated to make under different circumstances. But she was sick of death, sick and tired and disgusted with Umbrella for what they'd done; she wasn't going to take the cop out unless she had to.

And if she *did* have to, if it came down to some innocent's life or completing the job?

That she could ask herself that question at all told her more about her state of mind than she wanted to admit. She'd reached the door to the kennel; Ada took a deep breath, forcing every twinge of nagging emotion from her thoughts, and stepped inside to wait for Leon Kennedy.

Fourteen

SO BEAUTIFUL . . . EVEN IN DEATH, BEVERLY Harris was radiant, but Irons couldn't risk having her wake up while he wasn't watching; he carefully folded her into the stone cabinet beneath the sink and latched it, promising himself that he would take her out when he had more time. She would become the most exquisite animal he'd ever transformed, posed and forever perfect once he'd prepared her the proper way . . . a dream come true.

If I have time. If there's any time left.

He knew he was feeling sorry for himself again, but there was no one else to commiserate with, no one to marvel at the sheer magnitude of all that he'd suffered. He felt terrible—sad and angry and alone—but he also felt that things had finally become clear. He knew now, knew why he was being persecuted, and that awareness had given him a focus—as depressing as the truth was, at least he was no longer lost.

Umbrella. An Umbrella conspiracy to destroy me, all along . . .

Irons sat on the scarred, stained table in the Sanctuary, his special, private place, and wondered how long it would be before the young woman came for him. The one with the athletic body, the one who'd refused to tell him her name. In a way, she was responsible for his newfound clarity, an irony that he couldn't help but appreciate; it had been her sudden appearance that had provided him with the truth.

She would find him, of course; she was an Umbrella spy, and Umbrella had obviously been watching him for quite some time. They probably had lists of everything he owned, volumes of psychological profiling reports, even copies of his financial records. It all made sense, now that he'd had some time to think; he was the most powerful man in Raccoon, and Umbrella had designed his downfall, tailored each vicious backstab to cause him the most acute agony possible.

Irons stared at his treasures, the tools and trophies that sat on the shelves in front of him, but felt none of the pride they usually inspired. The polished bones were simply something to look at as his mind worked, absorbed with Umbrella's treachery.

Years before, when he'd started taking money to turn a blind eye to the company's doings, things had been different; then it had been a matter of politics, of finding himself a niche in the power structure that really controlled Raccoon. And things had worked smoothly for a long time—his career had progressed on schedule, he'd earned the respect of officials and citizens alike, and for the most part, his investments had paid off. Life had been good.

And then there was Birkin. William Birkin and his neurotic wife and their brat daughter.

After the Spencer estate spill, he'd almost convinced himself that the S.T.A.R.S. and goddamn Captain Wesker had been responsible for all the trouble, but he could see now that it was the arrival of Birkin and his family, nearly a year before, that had started the ball rolling; the destruction of the Spencer lab had only hurried things along. Umbrella had probably started monitoring him the day he'd had the misfortune to meet Birkin—at first, just watching, planting bugs, and installing cameras. The spies would have come later . . .

The Birkins had come to Raccoon so that William could concentrate on developing a superior synthesis of the T-Virus, based on the research being done at the Spencer lab. As quirky and unpleasant as William could sometimes be, Irons had liked him, right from the start. The male Birkin had been Umbrella's boy genius, but like Irons, he wasn't the type to brag about his position; William was a humble man, only interested in fulfilling his own potential. They'd both been too busy to have much of a friendship, but there had been a mutual respect between them; Irons had often felt that William looked up to him . . .

. . . and my mistake was to allow it. To allow my regard for him to cloud my instincts, to keep me from noticing that I was being watched, all along.

The loss of the Spencer lab sent some big ripples through Umbrella's hierarchy, and only days after the explosion, Irons had been approached by Annette Birkin with a message from her husband—a message and a request for a favor. Birkin had been worried that Umbrella was going to demand the new synthesis, the G-Virus, before it was ready; apparently, he'd been most dissatisfied with the application of his previous work, something about how Umbrella hadn't let him perfect the replication process, Irons couldn't remember exactly—and with Umbrella looking to recover from the financial blow of the Spencer loss, Birkin had been concerned that they might compromise the integrity of the untested virus. Through Annette, Birkin had asked for assistance— and offered him a little extra incentive to keep things fair. For a hundred grand, all Irons had to do was help keep the G-Virus under wraps—in short, watch out for Umbrella spies and keep an eye on the surviving S.T.A.R.S., making sure they didn't do any more "discovering" of Umbrella's research.

That was it. A hundred thousand dollars, and I was already watching my city, and *keeping tabs on that rebellious little pack of troublemakers. Easy, easy money, and more to be made if everything went as planned. Except it was a trap, an Umbrella trap. . . .*

Irons had walked right into it, and that was when Umbrella had started plotting against him, using the information they'd gathered to seal his fate. How else could things have gone wrong so quickly? The S.T.A.R.S. had disappeared, then Birkin—and before he'd even had a chance to assess the situation, the attacks had started up again. He'd barely had time to seal Raccoon off before everything had fallen to shit.

And all because I was helping a friend—for the greater good of the company, no less. Tragic.

Irons stood up and walked slowly around the cutting table, idly tracing the dents and scars in the wood with his fingertips. Behind every mark was a story, a memory of accomplishment—but again, he could take no comfort. The cool, quiet atmosphere of the Sanctuary had always soothed him before, it was where he practiced his hobbies, where he was truly able to be himself—but it wasn't his anymore. Nothing was. Umbrella had taken it from him, just as they'd taken his city. Was it so far-fetched to deduce that they'd unleashed their virus to get at him, to rob him of his power—and then sent that scantily clad brown-haired girl to rub his nose in it? Why else was she so attractive? They knew his weaknesses and were exploiting them, trying to keep him from retaining even a shred of dignity . . .

. . . and soon she'll come for me, maybe still playing dumb, still trying to seduce me with her helplessness. An Umbrella assassin, a spy and an exploiter, that's all she is, probably laughing at me behind that pretty face. . . .

Maybe the spill *had* been an accident; the last time they'd met, William Birkin had seemed unsteady, paranoid, and exhausted, and accidents happened even under the best of circumstances. But the rest was fact, there was no other explanation for how completely Irons had been ruined. That girl *was* coming to get him, she was from Umbrella and she'd been sent to murder him. And she wouldn't stop there, oh, no; she'd find Beverly and . . . and *defile* her somehow, just to make certain that nothing he cared about was left.

Irons looked around the small, softly lit room that had once been his, gazing wistfully at the well-used tools and furniture, the sweet, familiar smells of disinfectant and formaldehyde emanating from the rugged stone walls.

My Sanctuary. Mine.

He picked up the handgun that lay on his special cutting table, the VP70 that was still his, and felt a bitter smile curl his lips. His life was over, he knew that now. This whole affair had started with Birkin, and would end here, by his own hand. But not yet.

The girl would come for him, and he would kill her before he said his final good-byes to Beverly, before he admitted his defeat by taking a bullet. But he would see to it that she understood his suffering first. For every torture he'd endured, the girl would pay, the bill settled through flesh and bone and as much pain as he could inflict.

He was going to die, but not alone. And not without hearing the girl scream in agony, creating a voice for the death of his dreams—a voice so clear and true that the echoes would reach even the black hearts of the company executives who had betrayed him.

The S.T.A.R.S. office was empty, cluttered and cold and layered with dust, but Claire was reluctant to leave. After her stumbling, frightened flight through the body-strewn halls of the second floor, finding the place where her brother had spent his working days had left her feeling weak with relief. Mr. X hadn't followed her, and although she was still anxious to help Sherry and find Leon, she found herself lingering, afraid to step back into the lifeless halls—and hesitant to leave the one place that felt like Chris.

Where are you, big brother? And what am I going to do? Zombies, fire, death, your weird Chief Irons and that lost little girl—and just when I thought things couldn't get any more insane, I get to face off with The Thing That Would Not Die, the freak to end all freaks. How am I going to get through this?

She sat at Chris's desk, gazing at the small strip of black-and-white pictures that she'd found tucked in the bottom drawer; the four shots were of the two of them, grinning and making faces, a photo-booth memento of the week they'd spent in New York last Christmas. Finding the strip had made her want to cry at first, all of the fear and confusion she'd been holding back finally surging to the front at the sight of his well-loved smile—but the longer she'd looked at him, at the two of them laughing and having a good time, the better she'd started to feel. Not happy or even okay, and no less afraid of what was to come—just better. Calmer. Stronger. She loved him, and knew that wherever he was he loved her back—and that if the two of them had been able to survive the loss of both of their parents, to build lives for themselves and share a silly Christmas vacation in spite of having no real home to go to, then they could cope with anything. *She* could cope.

Can and will. I'm going to find Sherry and Leon and, God willing, my brother—and we're going to make it out of Raccoon.

The truth was, she didn't really have any choice—but she needed to go through the process of accepting her lack of options before she could act. She'd heard before that real bravery wasn't an absence of fear, it was accepting the fear and doing what was necessary anyway—and once she'd sat for a moment, thinking about Chris, she thought that she could do just that.

Claire took a deep breath, slipped the photos into her vest, and pushed away from the desk. She didn't know where Mr. X had been headed, but he hadn't seemed like the waiting-around type; she would head back to Irons's office and see if Sherry had come back—or Irons, for that matter. If X was still there, she could always run.

Besides, I should have searched his office, tried to find something about the S.T.A.R.S. There's nothing here that can tell me anything. . . .

Standing, she took a last look around, wishing that the S.T.A.R.S. office had offered a little more in the way of supplies or information. All she'd found of any use was a discarded fanny pack in the desk behind Chris's; according to the expired library card in one of the pouches, it had belonged to Jill Valentine. Claire had never met her, but Chris had mentioned her a couple of times, said she was good with a gun. . . .

Too bad she didn't leave one behind.

The team had obviously cleared out all of the important stuff after their suspension, although there were still a surprising number of personal items left around, framed pictures and coffee mugs and the like; she'd spotted Barry's desk right away from the partly finished plastic gun model on top. Barry Burton was one of Chris's closest friends, a huge, friendly bear of a man and a serious gun nut. Claire hoped that wherever Chris was, Barry was with him, watching his back. With a rocket launcher.

And speaking of . . .

On top of everything else, she needed to find another weapon, or more ammo for the nine-millimeter; she had thirteen bullets left, one full clip, and when those were gone, she was SOL. Maybe she should stop and check some of the corpses on the way back to the east wing; even in her panicked run, she'd noticed that some of them were cops, and the hand-gun *was* an RPD issue. Claire didn't like the idea of touching any of the dead bodies, but running out of firepower was distinctly less desirable—particularly with Mr. X running around.

Claire walked toward the door and pushed it open, trying to get her thoughts organized as she stepped back into the dim hall. Leaving the office put a damper on her resolve; she had to suppress a shudder at the still vivid image of Mr. X as she closed the door behind her, suddenly feeling vulnerable again. She turned right and started back toward the library, deciding that she wouldn't think about the giant unless she had to, wouldn't dwell on the memory of those blank, inhuman eyes or the way he'd raised his terrible fist, as if driven to destroy anything in his way . . .

. . . so knock it off already. Think about Sherry, think about getting some goddamn ammo or how to handle Irons, if you can find him. Think about trying to stay alive.

Just ahead, the dark wooden hall turned right again and Claire tried to steel herself against the task ahead; if memory served, there was a dead cop around the corner—

—like I can't tell by the smell—

—and she'd have to search him. He hadn't been too disgusting, at least, not that she'd noticed—

Claire turned the corner and froze, staring. Her stomach knotted, telling her she was in danger before her senses could. The body that she'd jumped over on the way to the S.T.A.R.S. office was now only a bloody, tangled mass, flesh and broken limbs and shredded uniform. The head was gone, although there was no way to tell if it had been taken away or just smashed into an unrecognizable pulp. It looked like someone had taken a sledgehammer or an axe to the corpse in the few moments since she'd passed it, beating it into a clotted smear.

But when, how, I didn't hear anything—

Something moved. A shadow, soft and darting over the mashed remains some twenty feet in front of her, and at the same time, Claire heard a strange rasping sound, breathing—

—and she looked up, still not sure what she was seeing or hearing—that ragged breathing and the *tick* of talons on wood, the talons themselves, thick and curved, the claws of a creature that couldn't exist. Big, the size of a full-grown man, but the resemblance ended there—and it was so impossible that she could only see it in pieces, her mind struggling to put them together. The inflamed, purplish flesh of the naked, long-limbed creature that clung to the ceiling. The puffed gray-white tissue of the partially exposed brain. The scar-rimmed holes where the eyes should have been.

—*not seeing this*—

The creature's rounded head dropped back, the wide jaw opening, a ropy stream of dark drool pouring out and splattering over what was left of the cop. It extended its tongue, eely and pink, the rough surface shimmering wetly as it slithered out. And out. And out, the snaking tongue uncoiling and whipping from side to side, so long that it actually trailed through the ripped flesh of the corpse.

Still frozen, Claire watched in horrified disbelief as the incredible tongue snapped back up, flicking droplets of blood through the shadowy air. The entire process had taken only a second, but time had slowed to a crawl, Claire's heart beating so fast that everything else was in slow motion—even the creature's drop to the wooden floor, its body flipping in midair so that it landed in a crouch atop the mutilated cop.

The creature opened its mouth again and screamed—

—and Claire was finally able to move as the bizarre, hollow shriek erupted from the monster, able to point her weapon and fire. The thunder of nine-millimeter rounds drowned out the howl that echoed through the tight hallway, *bam-bam-bam*—

—and still screaming that chilling, trumpeting cry, the creature was thrown back, its claw-tipped arms flailing. Its spasming legs kicked up bloody chunks of the eviscerated body; Claire saw a ragged flap of scalp, one ear still attached, fly across the hall and smack into the wall with a wet slapping sound, sliding down—

—and the creature got its legs beneath it somehow and flopped forward in a boneless lunge. It spidered toward her, lightning fast, gripping the wood floor with its terrible claws and howling.

Claire fired again, unaware that she was also screaming as three more rounds hit the scuttling thing, ripping through the gray matter that protruded from its open skull. She was going to die, it would be on her in less than a second and its massive talons were only inches from her legs—

—and as suddenly as the attack had come, it was over. Every part of the sinewy body quivered and shook as liquid gray dribbled from its burbling head, the thick claws tapping wildly against the wood floor in a frantic tattoo. With a final whispering whine, the creature died. There was no mistaking it this time. She'd blasted through its brain, it wasn't going to get up again.

She stared down at the monster, her shocked mind digging for something to relate it to, some animal or even a rumor of an animal that came close—but she gave it up after a few seconds, recognizing it as a lost cause. This was no natural creature, and as close as it was, she could finally smell it—the odor was not as pungent as the zombies', it was a bitter, oily smell, somehow more chemical than animal . . .

. . . and it could smell like chocolate-chip cookies, who gives a shit? Raccoon City's got monsters, it's time to stop being so goddamn surprised when you see one of them.

The chiding tone of her mind's voice wasn't particularly convincing. As much as she wanted to feel brave and determined, to step over the monstrous creature and get on with things, she just stood for a moment—and for that moment, she thought very seriously about going back to the S.T.A.R.S. office, going inside, and locking the door behind her. She could hide, hide and wait for help, she could be safe—

Decide, then. Do something, one way or another, stop this wavering and whining, because it's not just you anymore. Will Sherry be safe? Do you want to survive at the cost of her life?

The moment passed. Claire took a careful step over the raw red flesh of the creature and crouched down next to the cop's remains, using the muzzle of the handgun to push a torn piece of bloody uniform aside. She swallowed down bile as she poked through the rotten flesh and bone, working not to think about who the cop had been or how he had died.

Nothing, and she now had only seven bullets left— but she refused to panic, letting the disappointment fuel her determination instead. If she could search one bloody mess, she could search another.

With a last look at the dead animal-thing, Claire stood and walked quickly toward the end of the corridor, her decision made: no hiding and no more running from the fear. At the very least, she could take a few of the monsters with her, raising Sherry's chances of escape.

It would be better to die trying than not to try at all. She wouldn't waver again.

Fifteen

LEON FOUND ADA IN THE KENNEL, STRAIN-
ing to lever up the rusted manhole cover that the
reporter had told them about. She'd turned up a
crowbar from somewhere and had it wedged beneath
the thick iron plate, her well-defined biceps lightly
sheened with sweat as she worked the bar. She'd
managed to raise the cover about an inch, but let it
drop back into place as he walked in, the metallic
clang loud in the cold, empty room.

Before he could say anything, she lay the crowbar
on the cement floor and looked up at him with a
strained half-smile, brushing at her rust-dirty hands.

"I'm glad you're here. I don't think I'm strong
enough to do this by myself. . . ."

He hadn't been sure before, but the helpless look
she gave him cinched it; she was playing him, or
trying to. He'd known Ada for all of twenty minutes,

but he doubted seriously that she'd ever been helpless about anything.

"Looks like you're doing just fine," he said, holstering the Magnum but not making any move toward the manhole. He crossed his arms, frowning slightly. He wasn't angry, just curious.

"Besides, what's the hurry? I thought you wanted to talk to the reporter. About John, your Umbrella friend. . . ."

The woman-in-distress look melted away and her delicate features turned cool and hard, but not in a bad way; it was as though she was letting her real self show, the strong and self-assured Ada he'd first met. Leon could tell that he'd surprised her by not rushing to her aid and was glad to see it; he had enough to worry about without being manipulated by a mysterious stranger. She'd been very careful to avoid his questions, but it was time for Ms. Wong to explain a few things.

Ada stood up, meeting his gaze evenly. "You heard him—he wasn't going to tell us anything. And with this place as dangerous as it is, I don't really want to stand around waiting for him to develop a conscience . . ."

She dropped her gaze, her voice softening. ". . . and I don't even know if John's in Raccoon. But I *do* know that he's not here—and I want to leave before the station's completely overrun."

It sounded good, but for some reason, he had the feeling that she was holding something back. For a few seconds, he struggled to think of a polite way to get her to open up—then decided to hell with it; under the circumstances, social graces would have to be suspended.

"What's going on, Ada? Do you know something that you're not telling me?"

She looked at him again, and again, he had the feeling that he'd surprised her—but her cool, dark gaze was as unreadable as ever.

"I just want to get out of here," she said, and the sincerity of her tone was impossible to deny. If he didn't believe anything else she'd said, he had to believe that much.

And I wish it was that easy—but there's Claire, and even Ben, our asshole friend, and God knows how many others. . . .

Leon shook his head. "I can't leave. Like I said, I may be the only cop left around here. If there are still people in the building, I have to at least try to help them. And I think it'd be best if you came with me."

Ada gave him another one of her half-smiles. "I appreciate your concern, Leon, but I can take care of myself."

He didn't doubt it—but he also didn't want to see her abilities tested. Granted, he was pretty untested himself, but he'd been trained to deal with crisis situations, it was his job.

And be honest with yourself—you lost Claire, you couldn't help Branagh, and Ben Bertolucci could give a rat's ass for your protection skills; you don't want to fail with Ada on top of all that. And you don't want to be alone.

Ada seemed to know what he was thinking. Before he could come up with a convincing argument, she stepped forward and put one slender hand on his arm, the humor fading from her bright eyes.

"I know you want to do your job here, but you said it yourself—we have to find a way out of Raccoon, try and get outside help. And the sewers are probably the best chance we've got. . . ."

The light, gentle touch surprised him—and sent an electric flutter through his belly, an unexpected flush of warmth that left him feeling confused and uncertain. He managed to keep his reaction from showing, but just barely.

Ada continued, frowning thoughtfully. "How about this—help me with the manhole cover, and let's see what's down there. If it looks dangerous, I'll come with you . . . but if it's not bad—well, we can talk about what to do next."

He wanted to protest, but the truth was, he couldn't make her do anything she didn't want to do—and he wanted very much for her to know that he wasn't some overbearing macho type, that he was receptive to compromise . . .

. . . and does the name "John" ring a bell? This isn't a date for Chrissake, stop thinking with your hormones.

Feeling awkward even thinking about it with her hand still on his arm, Leon stepped away, nodding briskly. Together, they crouched down next to the manhole. Leon picked up the crowbar and jammed one end beneath the lid; as he pulled back, Ada pushed on the bar, and with a heavy grating sound the thick metal plate came up. Leon put his back into it and heaved the lid to one side, clearing the opening—

—and both of them recoiled back from the smell that bellowed out of the dark hole, a choking, dark stench of blood and piss and vomit.

"Gah, what *is* that?" Leon coughed.

Ada sat back on her heels, one hand pressed to her mouth. "The bodies from the garage, they must have dumped them down here—"

Before he could ask what she was talking about, a scream of pure terror echoed through the basement halls, filtering through the closed door. The cry went on and on, a man's voice, the panicked scream suddenly changing to a gurgling shriek of pain.

The reporter.

Leon locked gazes with Ada, saw the same startled realization flash across her face—and then they were both up and running, pulling out their weapons and sprinting through the door before the echoes died.

I left him, I shouldn't have left him—

They ran down the corridor for the cell block, guilt driving Leon to run faster than he thought he could. Someone or something had gotten to Bertolucci—and had passed right behind his back to do it.

Sherry stood in Mr. Irons's office, rubbing at her good luck pendant and wishing that Claire would come back. She had crawled through a dozen dusty tunnels to get away from the monster and to lead it away from Claire, and was pretty sure it had worked—she hadn't heard it again, and had come back to find that Claire had left; if the monster *had* found her, she would have been dead and ripped apart.

But she's not here. Nobody is. . . .

Sherry sat on the edge of a low table in the middle of the room, wondering what she should do. She'd gotten used to being alone, and hadn't even realized how lonely she'd been—but meeting Claire had changed that. Sherry wanted to see her again, she wanted to be with other people, she wanted her parents so bad that it made her ache. Even Mr. Irons would be okay, although Sherry didn't like him; she'd only met him a couple of times but he was weird, showy and fake—and his office was creepy besides. Still, she'd gladly put up with him if it meant she didn't have to be alone anymore. . . .

Footsteps. In the hall outside of the office.

Sherry stood up and ran to the open door that led back to the armor room, hoping it was Claire and ready to sprint for cover if it wasn't. She ducked around the door frame and held her breath, staring at the stuffed tiger in the hall and silently praying.

The outer door opened and closed. Muffled steps on the carpet, moving slowly, and she tensed to run, at the same time trying to muster up enough courage to sneak a look—

"Sherry?"

Claire!

"I'm here!"

She ran back into the office and there was Claire,

hole face lit up with a beaming smile. Sherry to her open arms, so happy to see her that she to cry.

was looking for you," Claire said, holding her tight. "Don't run off like that again, okay?"

knelt in front of her, still smiling—but could see the worry behind the smile and in her gray eyes.

"I'm sorry," Sherry said. "I had to, or the monster would have come."

"What does it look like?" Claire asked, her smile fading. "Does it look—kind of red, with claws?"

Sherry swallowed heavily. "The inside-out men! You saw one, didn't you?"

Incredibly, Claire grinned, shaking her head. "Yeah, that's exactly what I saw, an inside-out man . . . good description."

She looked at Sherry more seriously, frowning. "'Men'? There are more of them?"

Sherry nodded. "Yes, but they aren't anything like the monster. I only saw him once, from behind, but he's a man, a giant man—"

Claire seemed excited. "Bald? Wearing a long coat?"

"No, he had hair, brown hair. And one of his arms was all screwed up, a lot longer than the other one."

Claire sighed. "Terrific. Raccoon's got something for everyone, sounds like . . ."

She reached out and took Sherry's hand, squeezing it. ". . . and that's all the more reason that you should stay with me. You've done a really good job of taking care of yourself, and you've been very brave—but until we find your parents, I feel like it's my job for now, to watch out for you. And if the monster comes, I'll—I'll kick its ass, okay?"

Sherry laughed, surprised into it. She liked that Claire didn't talk down to her. She nodded, and Claire squeezed her hand again.

"Good. So we've got zombies, inside-out men, and a monster. And a big bald guy . . . Sherry, do you know what happened to Raccoon? How this all got started? Anything you can tell me, anything at all—it could be important."

Sherry frowned, thinking. "Well, there were a bunch of murders last May, or June I think—like ten people got killed. And then they stopped, but then maybe a week ago, somebody got attacked."

Claire nodded encouragingly. "Okay. Did more people start getting attacked, or . . . what did the police do?"

Sherry shook her head, wishing she could be more helpful. "I don't know. Right before that girl got attacked, my mother called from work really upset, and told me that I couldn't leave the house. Mrs. Willis—that's our next-door neighbor—she came over and cooked dinner for me, and that's how I heard about that girl. Mom called again the next day, and told me that she and Dad were stuck at the plant and wouldn't be home for a while—and then like three days ago, she called again and told me to come here. I went to see if Mrs. Willis would come with me, but her house was dark and empty. I guess things had already gotten pretty bad by then."

aire was staring at her intently. "You were alone at time? Even before you got to the station?"

erry nodded. "Well yeah, but I stay alone a lot. arents are both scientists; their work is important, nd sometimes they can't stop in the middle of hey're doing. And my mother always says that I'm very self-sufficient, when I want to be."

"you know what kind of work your parents do? At Umbrella?" Claire was still watching her closely.

"They develop cures for things, for diseases," Sherry said proudly. "And make medicines, like serums that hospitals use. . . ."

She trailed off, noticing that Claire seemed distracted suddenly, her gaze far away. It was a look she had seen plenty of times before, on both of her parents' faces—and it meant that they weren't really listening anymore. But as soon as she stopped talking, Claire refocused on her, reaching out to pat her on the shoulder—and for some stupid reason, that made Sherry want to cry again.

Because she's listening to me. Because she wants to watch out for me now.

"Your mother's right," Claire said gently, "you're very self-sufficient, and that you've made it this far means that you're also very strong. That's good, because we're both going to have to be strong, to make it out of here."

Sherry felt her eyes go wide. "What do you mean? Leave the station? But there are zombies all over the place, and I don 't know where my parents are, what if they need help or they're looking for me—"

"Sweetie, I'm sure your folks are just fine," Claire

said quickly. "They're probably still at the plant, hiding and safe, just like you were—waiting for people to come from outside of the city, to, to make everything better—"

"You mean kill everything," Sherry said. "I'm twelve, you know, I'm not a baby."

Claire smiled. "Sorry. Yeah, to kill everything. But until the good guys come, we're on our own. And the best thing we can do, the smartest thing, is to get out of their way—to get as far out of their way as possible. You're right, the streets *aren't* safe, but maybe we can get a car. . . ."

It was Claire's turn to trail off. She stood up and walked toward the big desk at the far end of the office, looking around as she went.

"Maybe Chief Irons left his car keys here, or another weapon, something we can use—"

Claire saw something on the floor behind the desk. She crouched down and Sherry hurried after her, as much to stay close as to see what she'd found. She already knew that she didn't want to lose her again, no matter what else happened.

"There's blood here," Claire said softly, so softly that Sherry thought she hadn't meant to say it out loud.

"So?"

Claire looked up at the plain tan wall, frowning, then back down at the big drying splotch of red on the floor. "It's still wet, for one thing. And see the way it's just kind of cut off? There should be some on the wall here. . . ."

She rapped on the dark wood trim that lined the

wall, then on the wall itself. There was an obvious difference; a dull *thump* from the trim, but the wall sounded hollow.

"Is there a room back there?" Sherry asked.

"I don't know, it sounds like it. And it would explain where he took . . . where he took off to earlier. Chief Irons."

She glanced up at Sherry as she started to feel along the baseboards, running her hands up the wall and pushing at it. "Sherry, look around the desk, see if you can find like a switch or a lever. My guess is it would be hidden somewhere, maybe in one of the drawers. . . ."

Sherry started to move behind the desk—and tripped, her foot sliding on a handful of pencils that she hadn't seen. She grabbed at the desktop, trying to catch her balance, but still came down pretty hard on her bare knees.

"Ow!"

Claire was next to her right away, putting an arm around her shoulders. "Are you okay?"

"Yeah. I just—hey! Look!"

Her bruised knees forgotten, Sherry pointed at the switch under the top drawer of the desk, set into a small metal plate. It looked like a light switch, but it had to be for the secret door, she just knew it.

I found it!

Claire reached out and flipped the switch—and behind them, a section of the wall a few feet across slid smoothly upwards, disappearing into the ceiling and exposing a dimly lit room lined with oversized bricks. Cool, damp air breezed into the office; it was a secret passage, just like in the movies.

Together, they stood and stepped toward the opening, Claire holding Sherry back with one arm until she'd looked first. The small room was totally empty—three brick walls and a stained wood floor, and only about half the size of the office. The fourth wall was dominated by a big old-fashioned elevator gate, the kind that pushed to one side.

"Are we going to take it?" Sherry asked. She was excited but nervous, too.

Claire had taken her gun out. She crouched down next to Sherry and smiled—but it wasn't a happy smile, and Sherry knew what was coming before Claire said a word.

"Sweetie, I think it would be safest if I went and looked around first, and you stayed here—"

"But you said we should stay together! You said we could find a car and leave! What if the monster comes back and you're not here, or you get killed?"

Claire hugged her, but Sherry felt almost sick with helpless anger. She was going to tell her not to worry, that the monster wouldn't come, that nothing bad would happen—and then she was going to leave anyway.

Stupid grownup lies—

Claire leaned back, smoothing Sherry's hair away from her face. "I don't blame you for being scared. I'm scared, too. This is a bad situation—and honestly, I don't know what's going to happen. But I want to do the right thing by you, and that means that I'm not going to take you into a situation where you could get hurt, not if I can help it."

Sherry swallowed back tears, trying again. "But I want to come with you . . . what if you don't come back?"

"I'm going to come back," Claire said firmly, "I promise. And if—if I don't, I want you to hide again, like before. Somebody will come, help is going to come soon, and they'll find you."

At least she was being honest; Sherry didn't like it, not at all, but at least there was that—and from the look on her face, Sherry could see that there was nothing she could say to change her mind. She could be a baby about it, or she could accept it.

"Be careful," she whispered, and Claire hugged her again before standing and moving toward the elevator. She pushed a button next to the gate and there was a low, soft hum; after a few seconds an elevator car rose into view, coming to a gentle stop. Claire pulled the gate open and stepped inside, turning for a last look at Sherry.

"Stay here, sweetie," she said. "I'll be back in a few minutes."

Sherry forced herself to nod—and Claire let the gate close. She touched something inside the elevator and the car went down, her smiling, strong face descending out of sight, leaving Sherry by herself in the cold, dark passage.

Sherry sat down on the dusty floor and hugged her knees close to her body, rocking herself slowly. Claire was brave and smart, she'd be back soon, she *had* to come back soon. . . .

"I want my mommy," Sherry whispered, but there was nobody to hear. She was alone again, the thing she wanted least of all.

But I'm strong. I'm strong, and I can wait.

She rested her chin on one knee, touching the necklace her mother had given her for good luck, and started to wait for Claire to come back.

Sixteen

ANNETTE BIRKIN SAT IN THE LABORATORY monitor room, exhausted, staring up at the wall of video screens centered over the surveillance console. She'd been there for what felt like years, waiting for William to appear, and was starting to think that he never would. She'd give it a little longer—but if she didn't see him soon, she'd have to do another search.

Goddamn technology . . .

It was a brand-new system, less than a month old— twenty-five screens with a channel control that should have allowed her to see any and every part of the facility. A brilliant security advance—except only eleven of the screens still worked at all, and over half of those would only show static, an endless dance of electric snow. Of the five she could still get a clear picture from, all she could see—all there *was* to see—

were dead, rotting bodies and the occasional Re3, either feasting or sleeping. . . .

"Lickers. You called them lickers, because of their tongues. . . ."

She thought she'd been past the worst of the pain, but the lonely sound of her own voice in the cold, cavernous chamber and the realization that there would be no answer—that there would never be an answer again—brought on a fresh, knifing wave of grief. William was gone, he was gone and she was talking to no one at all.

Annette lowered her head to the console, closing her weary eyes. At least there were no more tears; she'd wept an ocean of them in the days since Umbrella had come for the G-Virus, but was simply too spent to cry anymore. Now there was only pain, interspersed with fits of violent, helpless fury over what Umbrella had done.

Another month, maybe two, and we would have given it to them. We would have turned it over without a fight, and William would have made the executive board and we would have been happy. Everyone would have been happy—

There was a faint squealing from one of the muted security screens. Annette looked up, hoping and dreading at once—but it was just a licker, one floor up in the surgical bay. It had dropped from its ceiling roost to snack on one of the techs, howling stupidly to itself as it ripped into the corpse's guts. The dead man looked like Don Weller, one of the chemical plant go-betweens, but she couldn't tell for certain; he was almost as mutilated and inhuman looking as the Re3 that was eating him.

She watched the licker feed, watched the small screen but didn't really see; her mind wandered, running over what was left for her to do. She'd already wiped all of the computers and locked in the countdown codes; the lab was ready, and her escape route was secured. But she couldn't finish things until she saw him again, saw that he was back in the Umbrella facility. Destroying the lab wouldn't solve anything if he wasn't in the blast zone; they would find him, and extract the virus from his blood . . .

. . . and Umbrella won't have it. I'll die before I let them have it, so help me God.

Her only consolation in all of this mad, horrible affair was that Umbrella hadn't managed to get their greedy hands on William's synthesis. They hadn't and they never would. Everything that had gone into the creation of the G-Virus would be buried under a thousand burning tons of stone and wood, along with William and all of the monsters they had created for the company. She would go into hiding for a while, take some time to heal, to consider her options—and then she would sell the G-Virus to the competition. Umbrella was the biggest, but they weren't the only conglomerate working on bioweapons research—and when she was through with them, they wouldn't be the biggest anymore. It wasn't much of a revenge, but it was all she had left.

"Except for Sherry," Annette whispered, and the thought of their young daughter made her heart ache, a different pain but pain nonetheless. Since the day

Sherry had been born, Annette had meant to spend more time with her, to focus on the child instead of on her part in William's brilliant work. And yet somehow the years had slipped by, William's promotions had kept coming up, the work had grown ever more interesting and valuable—and although both she and William had made promises to themselves and each other that they would make more of an effort to develop their family life, they had continued to put it off.

And now it's too late. We'll never be a family, we'll never be parents together. All that time wasted, slaving for a company that sold us out in the end. . . .

It *was* too late; there was no point in mourning what could have been. All she could do now was make sure that Umbrella wouldn't get anything else from the Birkin family. William was gone, but there was still Sherry; that part of him would go on, and Annette meant to finally become the mother she should have been all along. Of course she'd have to wait until things cooled down before she could collect Sherry, at least a few months, but the girl would be safe; the cops would send her to live with William's sister, it was in both of their wills . . .

. . . unless Irons is still alive. That fat, greedy bastard could find a way to screw even that up if given half a chance.

She hoped he was dead; even if he wasn't directly responsible for Umbrella's awareness of the G-Virus, Brian Irons was a disgusting, arrogant man with the morals of a sea slug. After years of loyalty to the company, he'd been bought out for a measly hundred thousand dollars. Even William had been surprised, and he'd had an even lower opinion of the police chief than she had. . . .

On the screen, the Re3 had finished its meal. All that was left of the dead man was an empty shell, arched, bloody ribs, and a faceless cup of skull, the surely vibrant colors lost to the video's flat shades of gray. The licker scrabbled out of view, trailing sticky fluids in its wake. Thanks to the T-Virus, all of the reptile series were efficient killers, although the 3s had design flaws—the protruding cerebrum was the most obvious, but they also had a ridiculously high metabolic rate; keeping them fed had been a constant hassle.

Not a problem anymore. Plenty of carrion to go around—and lucky them, they'll get a chance for a hot dinner soon enough. . . .

Annette felt drained of energy, and didn't want to go back out into the facility—but she couldn't just keep hoping that William would happen by one of the working cameras. She'd heard him up on level three, perhaps two days before, but hadn't seen him in almost twice as long; she couldn't keep waiting. Umbrella's people were probably already working on a way in—even with the mainframe wiped, there were other ways to get past the doors—

—and William may have found a way out. I can't keep denying it, no matter how much I want to.

There was an abandoned factory west of the lab, a shipping company that had been bought up by Umbrella to ensure that the underground levels would stay secret; it was how Umbrella had managed to build the complex in the first place without arousing suspicion, hiding equipment and materials in the factory's warehouses and using the heavy machinery lift to transport them. Although the entrances from the factory had still been sealed off the last time she'd checked, there was a slim chance that William had gotten through—and if he could get to the factory, he could get into the sewers.

Annette forced herself to stand up, ignoring the cramps in her legs and back as she picked up the handgun on the console. She didn't know much about guns, although she'd figured out how to use one quickly enough, after—

—after they came for the G-Virus, the men in the gas masks, shooting and running—and William, poor William dying in a puddle of blood and I didn't see the syringe until it was too late—

She took a deep, shuddering breath, trying to push that terrible memory aside, trying to forget about the incident that had taken William from her and turned Raccoon into a city of the dead. It didn't matter anymore. The journey ahead wouldn't be a pleasant one, and she had to concentrate. Escaped Re3s, first- and second-stage infected humans, the botany experiments, the arachnid series—she could run into any of the T-Virus carriers, not to mention whomever Umbrella had managed to send.

And William. My husband, my beloved—the first human G-Virus carrier, who isn't really human anymore.

She'd been wrong to think that she had no more tears inside. Annette stood in the middle of the vast, sterile room five floors beneath the surface of Raccoon and wept lost, racking sobs that didn't even begin to touch the pain of her loneliness.

Umbrella would be sorry. Once she could be sure that William was beyond their reach, she was going to destroy their precious facility, she was going to take the G-Virus and run, she was going to make sure that they understood how badly they'd screwed up—and God help anyone who tried to stop her.

SEVENTEEN

ADA RAN INTO THE CELL BLOCK ONLY A STEP
behind Leon, just in time to see the reporter stumble
out of his cage and fall to the floor. "Help him!" Leon
shouted, and ran past Bertolucci to check out the cell.
Ada stopped in front of the gasping reporter but
ignored the command, waiting to see if whatever had
gotten to him was going to spring out of the open
cell—

—he was behind bars, how did this happen—

She waited, weapon pointed after Leon as he leapt
in front of the open cell, her heart pounding—and
saw the bewilderment on his youthful face, the open
surprise. The way his gaze searched the cell told her
that it was empty. Unless the attacker was invisible . . .

*Not a chance. Don't even start thinking like that,
don't let it get to you.*

Ada knelt next to the reporter, taking in immediately that he was in a bad way—dying bad. He'd crumpled into a half-sitting position, his head against the bars of the cell adjacent to his. He was still breathing, but it wouldn't be long before he stopped. Ada had seen the look before, the far-seeing gaze and the trembling, the pallor—but what she didn't see was *how,* and that scared her. There were no wounds. It had to be a heart attack, maybe a stroke—

—but that scream.

"Ben? Ben, what happened?"

His flickering gaze fixed on her face, and she saw that the corners of his mouth were cracked and bleeding. He opened his mouth to speak, but all that came out was a rasping, unintelligible croak.

Leon crouched down next to them, looking as confused as she felt. He shook his head at her, an unspoken answer to her unasked question; there was apparently no sign of what had happened.

Ada looked down at Bertolucci and tried again. "What was it, Ben? Can you tell us what happened?"

The reporter's shaking hands crawled up his body, resting across his chest. With a visible effort, he managed to whisper a single word.

". . . window. . . ."

Ada wasn't reassured. The cell's "window" was hardly a foot across, maybe six inches wide, and set eight feet off the floor—nothing more than a ventilation hole that opened into the parking garage. Nothing could have gotten through—at least nothing that she'd heard of or read about, and that meant that there were dangers she wasn't prepared against.

Bertolucci was still trying to speak. Both Ada and Leon leaned closer, straining to catch his painful whispers.

". . . chest. Burns, it . . . burns. . . ."

Ada relaxed just a bit. He'd seen or heard something outside of the cell, something that had kicked off a massive coronary; that, she could accept. A pisser for the journalist, but it *would* save her the trouble of killing him herself. . . .

He reached out suddenly and grasped her forearm, staring up at her with an intensity that surprised her. His grip was weak, but there was desperation in his wet eyes—desperation and some frustrated sorrow that inspired not a little guilt for what she'd been thinking.

"I never told . . . about Irons," he breathed, obviously struggling to hang on to life, to get it all out. "He's—working for Umbrella . . . all this time. The zombies—are Umbrella, research . . . and he covered up the murders but I couldn't—prove it all, yet . . . was going to be my—exclusive."

Bertolucci closed his bruised-looking eyelids, breathing shallowly as his fingers fell away from her arm, and she felt a surge of pity for him in spite of herself. The poor dumb jerk; his big secret was that Umbrella was into bioweapons and that Irons was on the take. It would have been a big scoop, too, but apparently he hadn't even been able to get any hard evidence.

He doesn't know dick about the G-Virus, he never did—and he's going to die regardless. Talk about a shit deal.

"Jesus," Leon said softly. "Chief Irons. . . ."

Ada had all but forgotten how clueless the young cop was. He was obviously new, but a couple of times he'd seemed so perceptive that she'd been taken aback; the kid wasn't just a testosterone case, there was definitely something going on upstairs—

—knock it off already, he's not much younger than you. The reporter's about to kick and you need to be on your way, not worrying about Officer Friendly—

Bertolucci spasmed suddenly, his hands clutching at his chest as he moaned, a sharp, tortured cry of agony. His back arched, his fingers hooked into claws—

—and the moan went liquid as blood started to stream from his mouth in a burbling gout. Choking and shaking, Bertolucci's limbs convulsed violently, droplets of crimson spraying out with each racking cough—

—and Ada saw red blossom across his rumpled white shirt beneath his scrabbling hands and heard the thick, wet *crack* of breaking bone. She leapt back as Leon grabbed for the reporter's hands, not sure what was happening but absolutely positive that it was *not* a heart attack—

—holy Christ what IS this?

All at once, Bertolucci went limp, his eyes rolled back and fixed, sightless. Blood still oozed from his cracked lips and there was a sound, a horrible sound of meat being torn, and under the stained fabric of his shirt, something moved.

"Get back!" Ada shouted, pointing her Beretta at the dead reporter, and in the split-second it took her to aim, a *thing* erupted from Bertolucci's bloody chest. A thing the size of a big man's fist, a gore-drenched thing that opened a tiny black hole of a mouth and squealed shrilly, revealing nubs of sharp red teeth. It wriggled out of the corpse with a whipping manta's tail, splashing the cold cement with shreds of wet tissue and gut.

Lashing against the cooling flesh of the reporter, it poured from the body in a gush of blood and onto the floor—and took off like a shot for the open gate back into the hall, propelling itself with its snaking tail and legs that Ada couldn't see, smearing a red path behind it.

It was out the door before she even remembered that she was holding a gun; for the first time since she'd come to Raccoon, since *ever,* she had been so completely shocked that she hadn't thought to react. A chest-bursting parasitic creature, straight out of a sci-fi movie. . . .

"Was that—did you see—" Leon fumbled breathlessly.

"I saw it," Ada said softly, cutting him off. She turned and looked down at Bertolucci, at his face, frozen in a bloody contortion of anguish, and at the gaping wet cavity just below his sternum.

His mouth, cracked at the corners. . . .

He'd been implanted with the creature—by what, she didn't know, and she didn't *want* to know. What she wanted was to get the mission wrapped, as quickly as possible, and then get as far away from Raccoon City as she could. In fact, she thought that she'd never wanted anything quite so badly. When she'd first realized that there had been a T-Virus incident, she'd expected to have to deal with some unpleasant organisms. But the thought of having one of them forced or forcing its way down her throat, nestling inside of her body like some slick, aberrant fetus before eating its way out . . . if that wasn't the most horrible thing she could think of, it ran a close second.

She looked at Leon, giving up any pretense of trying to be reasonable. She was going to the lab, and it wasn't open to discussion.

"I'm getting out of here," she said, and without waiting for a response, she turned and walked briskly toward the gate, careful not to step on the glistening trail of blood that the tiny monster had created.

"Wait! Look, I think—Ada? Hey. . . ."

She stepped into the corridor, weapon raised, but the creature was gone. The blood trail petered out less than halfway down the hall—but she saw that they'd left the door to the kennel open—

—and the manhole cover's off. Terrific.

Leon caught up to her before she'd gone more than a few steps. He stood in front of her, blocking her path, and for just a moment, Ada thought he was going to try to physically stop her.

Don't do it. I don't want to hurt you, but I will if I have to.

"Ada, please don't go," Leon said, not a command but a plea. "I—when I got to Raccoon, I met this girl, and I think she's in the station somewhere. If you could help me find her, the three of us could leave together. We'd stand a much better chance—"

"Sorry, Leon, but it's a free goddamn country. You do what you have to, and good luck—but I'm not staying. I've had enough. If—*when* I get out, I'll send help."

She started to push past him, hoping it wouldn't come to violence and wishing that she could tell him not to get in her way—how dangerous it would be for him to try—when Leon surprised her yet again.

"Then I'm coming with you," he said. He met her gaze evenly, his own unflinching and resolute—and scared. "I'm not going to let you do it alone. I don't want anyone else—I don't want you to get hurt."

Ada stared at him, not sure what to say. Now that Bertolucci was dead, she didn't want to have to ditch Leon in the sewers; it wouldn't be hard, considering how extensive the system was . . . but he was just so goddamn *nice*, so determined to be helpful, that she was starting to—to not want to have to do anything bad to him. Things would be a lot easier if he was just some asshole on a machismo kick. . . .

Okay, so blow your cover. Tell him you're a private agent working to steal the G-Virus, and you don't want company; tell him about the relief you felt when you realized the reporter was about to die, or how you don't have a problem with killing, if it's for a good cause— like getting paid. See how nice and helpful he is after that.

Not an option; neither was trying to talk him out of coming along, it wouldn't make sense. And there was some part of her, some part that she didn't want to admit to, that wanted very much not to be alone. Seeing that thing that had popped out of Bertolucci had shaken her, it had left her feeling that she wasn't as invulnerable as she liked to think.

So let him come, get to the lab and find a safe place to leave him there. No harm, no foul.

Leon was watching her closely, studying her—waiting for her approval.

"Let's go," she said, and the grin he gave her, though winning, made her feel even more uncomfortable.

Without another word, they walked toward the kennel, Ada wondering what the hell she was doing—and whether or not she was still capable of doing whatever it took to get the job done.

Claire stood in front of a medieval door at the very end of the dark, dungeon-like hallway that the elevator had taken her to. The station had been chilly, but the icy damp of this stone hall made the station seem like summer; it was like she'd descended into some ancient, haunted castle straight out of the Middle Ages.

She took a deep breath, trying to decide how to go in; she was pretty sure that Irons wouldn't appreciate a surprise visit, but the idea of knocking seemed ludicrous—not to mention dangerous. There were torches burning in sconces on either side of the heavy wood door, the door itself belted with strips of rusting metal—and if she'd had any doubt before that Irons was crazy, the sight of the twin sputtering torches and the feel of cold, quiet dread that suffused the corridor itself had wiped her uncertainty out.

A secret tunnel, a hidden room complete with moodlighting . . . what sane person would want to hang out down here? It wasn't the disaster that did it—Irons must have been nuts way before the Umbrella accident . . .

Another certainty, although she didn't have any proof—but when Sherry had told her about what her parents did for a living, and what had happened just prior to her coming to the station, something had clicked. Umbrella worked with diseases, and the population of Raccoon had definitely come down with a bad case of *something*. There must have been some kind of an accident, a spill that had released the strange zombie plague. . . .

Quit stalling.

Claire bit at her lip, not sure what she should do. She didn't doubt that Irons was down here somewhere, and she did *not* want to run into him again; maybe she should go back up, get Sherry, and try to find another way out. Just because the area was secret didn't mean that it was some kind of an escape route.

Still stalling, and Sherry is up there by herself. And you've got a gun, remember?

A gun with very little ammo. If this was Irons's hidden lair, maybe he kept weapons inside . . . or maybe it was just another corridor, one that led even deeper into the bowels of the station. Either way, wondering about it was telling her exactly jack shit.

Claire put her hand on the latch, took another deep breath, and pushed it open, the heavy door swinging in slowly on well-oiled hinges. She stepped back, pointing the handgun—

Jesus.

An empty room, as dank and unwelcoming as the corridor—but with furnishings and a decor that made her skin crawl. A single naked bulb hung down from the ceiling, illuminating the creepiest chamber she'd ever seen. There was a table in the middle of the room, stained and battered, a hacksaw and other cutting utensils scattered on top; a dented metal bucket and a mop, slopped against one water-stained wall, next to a portable basin with dried red patches inside; shelves, laden with dusty bottles—and what looked like human bones, polished and pale, set out like macabre trophies. That, and the smell—a thick chemical reek, sharp and acidic, that only just covered a darker smell. A smell like insanity.

Even looking into the room made her want to be sick; "nuts" was maybe the understatement of the year for the police chief—but there was nobody home, and that meant that there could be another secret passage somewhere inside. At the very least, she had to check for weapons.

Swallowing, Claire stepped into the room, glad that she hadn't brought Sherry with her; looking at the private little torture chamber was going to give *her* nightmares, it was nothing to expose a child to—

"Freeze, little girl, or I'll shoot you where you stand."

Claire froze. Every muscle in her body froze as Irons started to laugh from behind her, from behind the door where she hadn't thought to look.

Oh my God, oh, God, oh, Sherry I'm so sorry—

Irons's deep chuckle rose into the hearty, gleeful laughter of a madman, and Claire understood that she was going to die.

Eighteen

TRYING NOT TO BREATHE TOO DEEPLY, LEON reached the bottom of the metal ladder and turned around quickly, aiming the Magnum into the thick gloom. Murky water sloshed over his boots, and as his eyes adjusted to the low light, he saw the source of the terrible smell.

Parts of it, anyway. . . .

The subbasement tunnel stretching out in front of him was littered with body parts, human corpses that had been torn into pieces. Limbs and heads and torsos were strewn randomly through the stone passage, lapped at gently by the few inches of dark water that covered the floor.

"Leon? How is it?" Ada's voice floated down from the circle of light above the ladder, echoing hollowly around him. Leon didn't answer, his shocked gaze fixed on the terrible scene, his brain trying to add up the shredded parts and come up with a number.

How many? How many people?

Too many to count. He saw a faceless head, the long hair streaming around it in a cloud. A heavy woman's decapitated trunk, one breast bobbing above the rippling darkness. An arm encased in the tatters of a cop's dress shirt. A bare leg, still wearing a sneaker. A curled hand, the fingers slick and white.

A dozen? Twenty?

"Leon?" Ada's tone had sharpened.

"It's—it looks okay," he called, struggling to keep his voice from cracking. "Nothing moving."

"I'm coming down."

He stepped away from the ladder to give her room, remembering something she'd said before, something about bodies being dumped. . . .

Ada stepped off the bottom rung, splashing into the dark tunnel. His eyes had adjusted well enough to see a look of disgust cross her delicate features—disgust and something like sadness.

"There was an attack in the garage," she said softly. "Fourteen or fifteen people died. . . ."

She trailed off, frowning, and took a step past him to get a closer look at the severed and mutilated remains. When she spoke again, she sounded worried.

"I didn't see the attack, but I don't think they were torn up like this."

She looked up, scanning the roof of the tunnel, gripping her nine-millimeter tightly. Leon followed her gaze, but only saw algae-thick stone. Ada shook her head, looking back down at the gently rippling sea of broken flesh.

"The—zombies didn't do this. Something got to these people after they were killed."

Leon felt a chill go up his spine. That was about the last thing he wanted to hear, standing in the humid, stinking dark and surrounded by savaged bodies.

"So it's not safe down here. We should head back up and—"

Ada started forward, stepping through the tangled limbs, the sound of her careful, sloshing movements seeming very loud in the otherwise silent tunnel.

Damn, does she ignore everybody, or is it just me?

Watching his step, Leon followed, reaching out with his free hand to touch her shoulder. "At least let me go first, okay?"

"Fine," she said, sounding almost but not quite exasperated. "Lead the way."

He stepped in front of her, and they started forward again, Leon trying to divide his attention between the darkness ahead and the sodden pieces of flesh and bone underfoot. Just ahead, the tunnel turned to the right, and there was some light reflected off the oily surface of the water; the passage was clearer, too, with not as many bodies.

Leon paused just long enough to unshoulder the Remington, checking to make sure he'd chambered a round. Whatever had gotten to the corpses didn't seem to be around, but he didn't want to be unprepared if it came back.

Ada waited without speaking, though he could feel

her impatience—not for the first time, he wondered if there was more to her story than she'd told him. He was scared, and he was also cold and tired and afraid for Claire, who might still be wandering the station— he didn't even know if Claire was still alive; but he hadn't felt right about letting Ada walk into a bad situation on her own.

Ada, on the other hand . . . she was as calm and controlled as a veteran soldier, expressing nothing but a kind of irritable eagerness to get on with things— and if she appreciated his presence at all, she was taking great pains not to show it. It wasn't that he needed or wanted her gratitude—

—*but wouldn't most people be* happy *to have a cop along? Even a rookie?*

Maybe not, and it wasn't the time or place to start asking questions. Leon shut down his thinking and started moving again, stepping gingerly over a chewed-up chunk of flesh that he couldn't identify.

"Stop," Ada whispered sharply. "Listen."

Leon tensed, Remington in one hand, Magnum in the other. He tilted his head, straining to hear, but there was only a distant, hollow drip of water—

—and a soft thumping. A rapid but random sound, like padded hammers on a padded surface. Whatever it was, it was getting closer, coming toward them from where the tunnel turned up ahead.

Why isn't it splashing, why don't we hear water—?

Leon backed up a step, raising both weapons slightly, remembering how Ada had looked at the ceiling before—

—and saw it, saw it and felt his heart stop in

midbeat. A spider the size of a big dog, skittering over the wet stones halfway up the inner wall, its bristling, hairy legs tapping—

—*not possible*—

—and then there was a series of deafening explosions next to his right ear, *bam-bam-bam-bam,* the muzzle flash from Ada's Beretta strobing the hellish tunnel as she fired. The booming echoes pounded through the dark as the giant, impossible arachnid dropped from the wall, splashing into the inky water.

It crawled toward them, wounded, dragging two of its multiple legs through the murk behind it, dark fluids spilling out from its grotesquely rounded body. It humped itself over a human head, the mutilated skull rolling out from beneath its swollen, pulsing abdomen, and Leon could see its shining black eyes, each the size of a ping-pong ball—

—and he squeezed the trigger on the Remington, not even feeling the kick of the thundering blast, his entire focus on the inconceivable arachnid. The round hit it squarely, blowing its alien face into a thousand wet pieces. The spider flipped over backwards with a skidding splash, its thick legs quivering, curling in over its furred body.

His ears ringing, his heart pounding, Leon chambered another round, his mind telling him that he had *not* just blown away a spider that big, the physics was wrong, it couldn't happen because it would collapse under its own weight—

—Ada pushed past him, running ahead, shouting back to him.

"Come *on,* there could be more coming!"

Leon took off after her, forced by Ada's reckless behavior to put his shock on hold. He sprinted through the dark, jumping over the disturbed and gently rocking hunks of flesh, past the closed dead spider that would never have existed in the reality he'd known before Raccoon.

"Drop your weapon," Irons commanded, and the girl did so, hesitating for only a second. The Browning clattered to the floor, and Irons had to resist the urge to laugh again, scarcely able to credit how stupidly she'd acted. The Umbrella assassin had obviously grown arrogant, walking into his Sanctuary as if she owned the place—and her smug, inflated conceit had cost her the game.

"Turn around, slow—and keep your hands where I can see them," he said, still grinning. Oh, what a gloriously easy conquest! Umbrella had underestimated him for the last time.

Again, the girl did as he asked, pivoting slowly, her hands empty and open. The look on her face was priceless, her aquiline features fixed in a mask of fear and shock; she hadn't expected *this,* she thought it would be a simple task to take out Brian Irons. After all, he was a broken man, a shadow of his former self, his city, his *life* taken away—

"Mistaken, weren't you?" he said, feeling the humor leak out of the situation, feeling the anger stir again. He kept the VP70 trained on her ridiculously young face; insulting, that they'd sent a child in to do their dirty work. Even such a pretty one. . . .

"Calm down, Chief Irons," she said, and even

angry, he was pleased to hear the strain in her sultry voice, the edge of fear beneath her useless plea. He was going to enjoy this, even more than he'd imagined . . .

. . . but first, some answers.

"Who sent you? Was it Coleman, from headquarters? Or did your orders come from higher up . . . someone on the board, perhaps? There's no point in lying, not anymore."

The girl stared at him, her eyes wide with feigned confusion. "I—I don't know what you're talking about. Please, there's been some kind of a mistake—"

"Oh, there's been a mistake, all right," Irons spat, "and you made it. How long has Umbrella been watching me? What were your orders, exactly—were you supposed to kill me outright, or did Umbrella want to see me suffer a little more first?"

The girl didn't answer for a moment, obviously trying to decide how much to tell him. She was good, her expression still carefully arranged to show only a bewildered fear, but he saw right through it.

She's been caught, she must know that I won't let her live and she's going to try and conceal the truth, even now. Young, but well-trained.

"I came to Raccoon looking for my brother," she said slowly, her wide gray eyes fixed on the gun. "He was with the S.T.A.R.S., and I just—"

"S.T.A.R.S.? Is that the best you can do?" Irons laughed bitterly, shaking his head. The Raccoon S.T.A.R.S. had fled well before things had fallen to shit—and last he'd heard, Umbrella had already "converted" the organization to their purposes, and was working to eliminate those who wouldn't cross over. As a cover story, it didn't play.

But there is *something. . . .*

He narrowed his eyes, studying her pale, anxious face. "And just who is your brother?"

"Chris Redfield, you know him—I'm Claire, his sister, and I don't know anything about whatever Umbrella did, and I wasn't sent here to kill you." She spoke quickly, all but stumbling over herself to get her story out.

She *did* look like Redfield, through the eyes at least . . . although why she thought that connection would help her somehow was beyond him. Chris Redfield was a pompous, disrespectful upstart who had openly defied him many times; in fact—

"Redfield was working for Umbrella, wasn't he?" Even saying it aloud, Irons could see that it was the truth—and his anger swelled up like a red tide, an acid heat that flushed through his veins and made him feel sick.

Even my employees, all along. Treasonous Umbrella puppets.

"The Spencer estate, the accusations against Umbrella . . . it was all a setup, they had him stirring up trouble to—to *distract* me so they could steal Birkin's new virus. . . ."

Irons took a step toward the girl, barely able to keep himself from pulling the trigger in spite of his plans. The girl, *Claire,* took a step back, holding up her hands, palms out, as if to ward off his righteous fury.

"That's how the S.T.A.R.S. knew to get out of

town," he snarled, "they were *warned* to get out of town before the T-Virus leak!"

He took another step forward, but Claire had stopped, her eyes going even wider. "You mean Chris isn't here?"

Her small, hopeful whisper only fed the red, burning heat that pounded through him—and the feelings were so powerful that they transcended rage, focusing his intentions into something brutal and precise. It wasn't enough that he'd been betrayed by Umbrella and the S.T.A.R.S., it wasn't enough that he'd been manipulated, tormented, *hunted*—

No. No, I have to be lied to by this little girl, a spy and an assassin from a family of traitors. A lifetime devoted to service, a lifetime of hard-won experience and self-sacrifice, and this is my reward.

"A slap in the face," he said, his voice as cold as this new savagery that filled him up, transforming him into the hunter. "Treating me like an idiot. You don't even have enough respect to lie well."

He extended the nine-millimeter and walked toward her, each step measured and deliberate—and her fear *was* real this time, he could see it in the way she stumbled back, her lips trembling, her young chest heaving in a most delicious way. She was terrified, trying to look for a weapon and watch him and get away all at the same time, succeeding at none of them as he marched forward.

"*I* have the power," he said, "this is *my* Sanctuary, this is my domain. You are the intruder. You are the liar, *you* are the evil—and I'm going to skin you alive. I'm going to make you *scream*, you bitch, I'm going to make you wish you were never born. Whatever they paid you, it wasn't enough."

She backed against one of the shelves, tripping over the leg of the worktable, almost falling on top of the covered trap door in the corner. Irons followed, feeling that beautiful, exciting power course through him, feeling excited by her helplessness.

"Please, you don't want to do this, I'm not who you think I am!"

Her pathetic entreaties made him stop and laugh, wanting to add to her terror, wanting for her to know that his control was absolute. She was wedged between a trophy shelf and the covered pit, and Irons stayed a safe distance away, enjoying the look in her glistening, overbright eyes—the panic of a trapped animal, a soft, warm, powerless animal of tender, pliable flesh. . . .

Irons licked his lips, his hungry gaze traveling over her limber, smooth, cowering form. Another trophy, another body to transform . . . and it was time to get down to business, to—

"Graaagh!"

What the—

The board that covered the subbasement entrance flew into the air, splitting with a tremendous *crack,* one jagged piece hitting Irons's hip. He staggered, not understanding—he was *in control* and yet something had gone horribly, horribly wrong—

Something wrapped around his ankle, something that squeezed so tight he heard the bone being crushed, felt incredible, spiking pain travel up his leg—

—and he locked gazes with the girl, her eyes bright with a new terror, and in that instant of contact, of clarity, he wanted to tell her so much, wanted to tell her that he was a good man, a man who'd never deserved any of what had happened to him—

—and the vise-like grip *jerked*, and Irons was falling, dropping the gun, pulled into the pit by the screaming and the pain and the beast that waited for him below.

ΠΙΠΕΤΕΕΠ

ONE MINUTE, IRONS WAS STANDING IN FRONT of her, staring into her eyes with a terrible, wrenching sorrow—

—and in the next, he was gone. Yanked into a hole in the floor by an arm that she only caught a glimpse of, a muscular, dripping arm with foot-long claws. It whipped out of sight, taking Irons with it into the darkness below.

There was another scream from the creature, a powerful, lusty howl that was matched and then surpassed by the intensity of Irons's terrified shriek. Frozen by the piercing screams, Claire could only listen, shock and relief and fear for herself battling through her as the horrible cries swept up through the open hole, pounding her ears in the cold, dismal dungeon that Irons had created—

—until his cries burbled to a stop, only a second or two later—and the slurping, meaty, wet noises began.

Claire moved. She scooped up the handgun that Irons had dropped and ran around the table in the middle of the room, not wanting to be grabbed and pulled under like he had.

It killed him, it killed him and he was going to kill me—

The reality of what had just happened, what *would* have happened, hit her all at once, turning her limbs into rubber. Claire forced herself a few more steps away from the open pit and collapsed against one sweating stone wall, taking in great, whooping breaths of the bitterly scented air.

He had been planning to kill her, but not right away. She'd seen the way his mad gaze had crawled over her body, heard the eager anticipation in his crazy laugh—

There was a low, grunting sound from the corner, a bestial sound, the growl of a well-fed lion. Claire turned, raising the heavy gun, astounded that she could feel any more horror—

—and something burst up from the hole, something with flailing arms, and Claire fired, the shot going wide. A glass bottle on a shelf exploded as the thing hit the floor—

—and it was Irons, but only half of him. He had been neatly bisected, cut in two by the thing that had snatched him; everything below the fleshy waist was gone, trails of torn skin and muscle hanging down over the oozing pool of blood that had replaced his legs.

Claire backed toward the door, the weapon still trained on the opening—and heard the creature, the *monster* scream again, an echoing howl that faded away, falling away into some distance that she couldn't imagine. A second later, she couldn't hear it at all; it was gone.

Sherry's monster. That was Sherry's monster.

She edged slowly toward the mangled corpse of Chief Irons, toward the empty, yawning blackness of the hole—but it wasn't all blackness. She could see light filtering up from somewhere, enough to see that there was another floor below, what looked like the metal grid pattern of a catwalk—and a ladder leading to it.

A subbasement . . . a way out?

She stepped back from the opening, her thoughts racing and disorganized, trying to absorb the information along with what Irons had told her. Chris wasn't in Raccoon, the S.T.A.R.S. were gone—a wonderful, terrible relief, because it meant he was safe, but also that he wasn't about to come running in to save the day. There *had* been a spill at Umbrella, which explained the zombies, at least—but what he'd said about Birkin, about Birkin's virus . . . was that Sherry's father?

And—maybe the zombies are the result of some laboratory accident, but what about all the other things, Mr. X and the inside-out men?

The way Irons had ranted about Umbrella suggested that while the accident was unexpected, the pharmaceutical company wasn't some innocent victim. What had he called it?

"T-Virus," she said softly, and shivered. "There was Birkin's new virus, and there was the T-Virus. . . ."

The zombie disease had a name. And you didn't name something unless you knew something about it, which meant—

—which meant she didn't *know* what it meant. All she knew was that she and Sherry needed to get out of Raccoon, and the subbasement might be a way. It wasn't a dead end, the monster that had killed Irons had gone *somewhere* . . .

. . . and do you really want to follow it, with Sherry? It could come back—and if it actually is *looking for her . . .*

Not a happy thought—but then, neither was hitting the streets, and the station was already crawling with God knew what other creatures. Claire checked the clip of the weapon Irons had held on her, counting seventeen bullets. Not enough to face off with the things in the station—but maybe enough to keep a monster at bay. . . .

It was a chance, but she was willing to take it. Claire took a deep breath, blowing it out slowly, collecting herself. She needed to keep it together, for Sherry's sake if not for her own.

She turned, looking down at the mangled remains of the police chief. It was a terrible way to have died, but she couldn't find it in herself to feel sorry. He had been ready to rape and torture her, he had laughed when she'd pleaded for her life, and now he was dead; she wasn't happy about it, but she wasn't going to shed any tears, either. Her only feeling about it was that she should cover him up before she brought Sherry down with her; the girl had seen enough violence for one lifetime.

You and me both, kiddo, Claire thought tiredly, and started to look around for something to drape over the dead Chief Irons.

Leon caught up to her in the cold industrial hallway that led to the sewer entrance, a few steps up from the flooded subbasement. She'd run ahead to plant the keys that would get them into the sewers, not wanting to have to explain how she'd come by them; she'd just managed to toss them into the boiler room before his footsteps sounded on the metal steps behind her.

At least I don't have to fake being out of breath. . . .

Ada could see by the look on his face that she needed to smooth things over; she started talking the second he stepped into the shadowy corridor.

"I'm sorry I ran," she said, offering him a nervous smile. "I hate spiders."

Leon frowned, studying her—and looking into his searching blue gaze, Ada realized she was going to have to do better than that. She took a step closer to him, not close enough to be invasive but enough so that he could feel the heat of her body. Maintaining eye contact, she tilted her head back to emphasize the height difference between them; it was a little thing, but in her experience, men generally responded well to the little things.

"I guess I'm just in a hurry to get out of here," she said quietly, losing the smile. "I hope I didn't worry you."

He dropped his gaze, but not before she saw a flicker of interest—confused and self-conscious, but definitely interest. Which made it all the more surprising when he stepped away.

"Well, you did. Don't do it again, okay? I may not be much of a cop, but I'm trying—and God only knows what we're going to run into down here."

He met her gaze again, speaking softly. "I came with you because I want to help, I want to do my job—and I can't do that if you go charging ahead. Besides," he added, smiling a little, "if you run off, who's going to help *me?*"

It was Ada's turn to look away. Leon was playing it straight with her, openly admitting to his fears—and his response to her not-so-subtle flirtation had been to step back and tell her that he wanted to be a good cop.

Interested, but not a fool for his tool . . . and man enough to tell me that he's unsure of his abilities.

She was forced to smile back, but it was a shaky affair. "I'll do my best," she said.

Leon nodded and turned to inspect the hallway, letting the conversation drop—much to Ada's relief. She wasn't sure what she thought of him, but was uncomfortably aware that her respect for him was growing; not a good thing, considering the circumstances.

There wasn't much to see in the damp, poorly lit hall; two doorways and a dead end. The boiler room, where she'd tossed the keys—or plugs, rather—was directly in front of them, the sewer disposal entrance in a back corner; according to the sign on the wall, the other door opened into a storage closet.

Ada followed as Leon walked to the closest of the two doors, the storage room, hanging back as he pushed it open with his Magnum and stepped inside. Boxes, a table, a trunk; nothing important, but at least no creepy-crawlies. After a quick search, he stepped back into the hall and they moved toward the boiler room.

"How'd you learn to shoot like that, anyway?" Leon asked as they stopped in front of the door. His tone was casual, but she thought she detected more than casual curiosity. "You're pretty good. Were you in the military or something . . . ?"

Nice try, Officer.

Ada smiled, falling into her carefully rehearsed character. "Paintball, believe it or not. I mean, I went target-shooting some when I was a teenager, with my uncle, but never got into it much. And then a few years ago, a friend at work—we're both buyers at an art gallery in New York—dragged me to one of those weekend survival retreats, and we had a blast. You know, hiking, rock-climbing, stuff like that—and paintball. It's great, we go up every couple of months . . . although I never thought I'd have to use it for real."

She could actually see him buy it, see that he *wanted* to buy it. It probably answered a few questions that he'd been hesitant to ask.

"Well, you're better than a lot of the guys I graduated the academy with. Really. So, you ready to get on with this?"

Ada nodded. Leon pushed the door to the boiler room open, scanning the ancient, rusting machinery in the wide empty space before ushering her inside. She made a point of not looking down, wanting Leon to find the small wrapped package that she'd tossed in a few moments earlier.

She hadn't gotten a good look before. The room, shaped like a sideways "H," was fitted with corroded railings and two massive old boilers, one on either side. Fluorescent lights sputtered overhead, the few that still worked casting strange shadows across the metal pipes that ran down the water-marked walls. The door that led into the sewer system was in the far left corner, a heavy-looking hatch next to an inset panel.

"Hey—" Leon crouched down, picking up the bundle of plugs that would open the hatch. "Looks like somebody dropped something. . . ."

Before Ada could go through the charade of asking him what he'd found, she heard a noise. A soft, slithery noise, coming from the area in the right back corner, neatly blocked from view by one of the boilers.

Leon heard it, too. He stood up quickly, dropping the bundle and raising the shotgun. Ada pointed her Beretta toward the sound, remembering how the door had been slightly ajar when she'd come up from the subbasement.

Oh, hell. The implant.

She knew it even before it crawled into sight—and was shocked anyway. The little bugger had grown, and it had grown *fast,* easily twenty times its former size in half as many minutes—and it was still growing, apparently at an exponential rate. In the few seconds it took for the creature to move into the middle of the room, it went from the size of a small dog to the size—and bulk—of a ten-year-old child.

The shape had changed, was changing, too. It was no longer the alien tadpole that had chewed its way out of Bertolucci. The tail was gone, and the creature that inched its way across the rusting floor had developed limbs, stretching arms folding out of its rubbery flesh. Claws popped out of the tan and swimming skin that swirled over its body, accompanied by a sound like gristle being punctured. Muscular legs unfurled, liquid that snapped into sinewy shape as its stuttering crawl became smoother, almost feline—

The shotgun and Beretta sounded at the same time, a string of massive blasts peppered with the higher whine of the nine-millimeter. The creature was still shifting, standing, mutating into a humanoid shape—and its response to the booming shots that smacked into its twisting flesh was to open its mouth and vomit, a grunting projectile scream of rotten green bile—

—that hit the floor and started moving. The stream that gushed from its wide, flat face was *alive*—and the dozen or so crab-like creatures that tumbled out of the monster's gaping mouth like liquid seemed to know exactly where the threat was to their fetid, mutant womb. The skittering, multi-legged animals swarmed toward Ada and Leon in a silent wave as the implant monster took one massive step forward, pulsing cords standing out on its impossibly long, thick neck.

Leon had the heavier firepower. "Got 'em!" Ada

shouted, already targeting and shooting at the closest of the tiny, bilious green crabs. They were fast, but she was faster; she pointed and squeezed, pointed and squeezed, and the baby monsters exploded into small fountains of dark, ichorous fluid, dying as silently as they'd come.

Leon blasted again and again with the shotgun, but Ada couldn't spare a glance to see how he was faring with the mother beast. Five of the crawling babies left, three more rounds and she'd be dry—

—and she heard the shotgun clatter to the floor, heard the deeper but less powerful fire of the .50 AE rounds resounding through the metal room as she picked off two more of the spidering creatures, and her weapon clicked empty.

Without stopping to think, Ada let go of the Beretta and dropped to the floor. She grabbed the shotgun by the barrel, rolling up into a crouch beneath Leon's line of fire, and swung the weapon down, hard. Two of the mutant animals were smashed into goo by the heavy stock—but the third, the last of them, sprang forward in an unexpected burst of speed—

—and landed on her thigh, catching hold with needle-sharp claws. Ada dropped the shotgun, crying out as the animal scuttled up her leg, the warm, damp weight of it making her frantic with disgust.

Off get it OFF—

She fell backwards, slapping at the creature that had already reached her shoulder and was skittering toward her face, toward her *mouth*—

—and then Leon was grabbing her, roughly pulling her up with one hand as he snatched at the animal with the other. Ada stumbled against him, clutching at his waist to keep from falling. The bug clung tenaciously to the tight fabric of her dress, but Leon had a good grip. He tore it away, shouting as he flung the flailing thing across the room.

"The Magnum!"

The weapon was stuck in Leon's belt. Ada jerked it free, saw the creature land near the giant, motionless heap that had birthed it, blasted to death by Leon—

—and fired, managing to get a clean shot despite how off-balance she was, how deeply unnerved she was by how close she'd come to being implanted. The heavy round *clanged* against the floor, rust chips spattering up—and the creature was blown into an ugly stain against the back wall. Obliterated.

Nothing moved, and the two of them just stood for a moment, leaning against each other like survivors of some sudden, terrible accident—which, in a way, they were. The entire firefight had taken place in less than a minute, and they had come out unscathed— but Ada wasn't going to kid herself about how close it had been, or what they had just managed to destroy.

G-Virus.

She was sure of it; the T-Virus couldn't have created such a complicated creature, not without a team of surgeons—and they'd *seen* it growing; how big, how powerful would the creature have become if they hadn't walked in when they had? The beast might have been some early G-strain experiment, but what if it had been the result of a leak? What if there were more of them?

The sewers, the factory, the underground levels—

dark, shadowy places, secret *places, where anything could be growing. . . .*

Whatever the situation, the trip to the labs wasn't looking like a walk anymore—and Ada was suddenly very glad that Leon had decided to come along. Since he was so goddamn insistent on going first, if something attacked, she'd have a better chance of surviving—

"Are you okay? Did it hurt you?"

Leon, one arm still supporting her, looking into her eyes with a heartfelt concern. Ada realized that she could smell him, a clean, soapy smell, and pushed herself away. She handed the Magnum back to him and straightened her dress, studiously inspecting it for rips to avoid looking at him.

"Thanks, I'm fine. Don't sweat it."

It came out harsher than she meant it to, but she was rattled, and not just by the implant's vicious attack. She glanced at him, and wasn't sure how to feel when she saw that her response had caught him off guard. He blinked slowly, and a kind of coolness settled into his gaze, indicating a strength of character that she hadn't bothered to give him credit for.

"Paintball, huh?" he said mildly, and without another word, he turned to pick up the package she'd planted.

Ada stared after him, telling herself how absolutely ridiculous it was to care what he thought of her. They were about to embark on a journey in which she might have to desert him, or watch him sacrifice his life in order to save her own . . .

. . . *or kill him myself. Let's not forget* that, *friends and neighbors. So who gives a shit if he thinks I'm an ungrateful bitch?*

Straight up. She should thank him, for reminding her.

Ada stooped down to retrieve the shotgun, feeling like she needed to do a better job of keeping her priorities straight—and feeling an emptiness inside that she hadn't noticed in a long, long time.

Twenty

MR. IRONS HAD BEEN A VERY BAD MAN. A *sick* man. Sherry supposed she'd known it all along on some level, but seeing his secret torture chamber, like some mad doctor's workshop, made it a lot more real. The room was just *gross*, bones and bottles and a smell even worse than the zombies. Perhaps that was why seeing the shape on the floor, the incomplete body shape beneath the bloodstained tarp, didn't bother her half as much as Claire seemed to think it would. Sherry stared at it, wondering what had happened exactly.

"Come on, sweetie, let's get going," Claire said, and the forced note of brightness in her voice told Sherry that Mr. Irons had been severely messed up. All Claire had told her was that Mr. Irons had attacked her, and then something had attacked *him*, and that there was a chance they could get somewhere safe if they went

down into the basement. Sherry had been so reliev
to see Claire at all that she hadn't bothered to
questions.

*Not big enough to be a whole person under there
did he get eaten? Or chopped into pieces?*

"Sherry? Let's go, okay?"

Claire laid a hand on her shoulder, gently pull
her away from what was left of the police chief. She
let herself be led toward the dark hole in the corr
deciding that it was best to keep her questions
herself. She thought about saying that she didn't c
that Mr. Irons was dead, but she didn't want
appear rude or disrespectful. Besides which, Cla
was trying to take care of her, and Sherry didn't m
that at all.

Claire went down the ladder first, and afte
second, called up to her that it was safe to come do
Sherry stepped carefully on the metal rungs, feel
really happy for the first time in days. They w
doing something, they were getting out of the R
station and headed for escape; whatever else h
pened, it was a good way to feel.

Claire helped her down the last couple of ru
lifting her and setting her on the metal floor. She
turned and looked around, her eyes widening.

"Wow," she said, and the word whispered a'
into the dim shadows and came whispering ba
reflected off the strange walls.

"Yeah," Claire said. "Come on."

Claire started walking, her boots clanking out
oes, and Sherry followed closely, still looking aro
in amazement. It was like a bad guy's lair in a

movie, some factory passage inside of a mountain or something. They were on a catwalk surrounded by rails, a murky green light coming up through the grate floor from somewhere far below—and although there was rough brick to their right, to the left was an actual cave wall. She could see giant, dripping pillars of stone that stretched off into the dark, natural formations of rock that were stained green by the weak and ghostly light.

Sherry wrinkled her nose. As interesting as it was, it smelled pretty rotten. And she didn't like the way that sound carried in the chill air, making everything seem hollow.

"What do you think this place is?" she asked softly.

Claire shook her head. "I'm not sure. Between the smell and the location, I'd say we're in part of a sewage treatment plant."

Sherry nodded, glad to know—and even more glad to see the way out just ahead of them. The walkway wasn't very long; it turned left, and there was another ladder at the end, one that went up. When they got to it, Claire hesitated, peering up at the opening overhead and then back around at the dark and empty cave.

"I should go up first . . . how 'bout you climb up right behind, but stay on the ladder until I say it's clear?"

Sherry nodded, relieved. For a second, she'd been afraid that Claire was going to tell her to stay down here and wait, like before.

No way. It's dark, stinky, and lonely. If I were a monster, this is where I'd be. . . .

Claire went up, boosting herself easily through the hole, and Sherry clambered up just behind, holding the cool metal of the rungs tightly. After a few seconds, Claire's long, slender arms reached down to help her out.

They were back on solid ground, a short cement hallway that seemed incredibly bright after the cave. Sherry figured they were still in the sewage plant; the smell wasn't as bad, but the hall was bordered on the left by a motionless river of sludge water, maybe a foot deep and five or six feet across; the muddy water ran off in either direction, one end through a low, rounded tunnel, the other stopped by a big metal door. It was all overlooked by a kind of balcony, but Sherry didn't see any stairs.

Which means . . . oh, yuck.

"Do we have to?" she asked.

Claire sighed. "'Fraid so. But look at the bright side—no sane monster would follow us through *that.*"

Sherry smiled. It wasn't particularly funny, but she appreciated what Claire was trying to do—it was the same as covering up Mr. Irons's body, or telling her that her parents were probably safe.

She's trying to shield me from how bad things really are. . . .

Sherry liked that, so much so that she was already dreading the moment when Claire would leave her for good. Eventually, she would; Claire had a whole life somewhere else, her own friends and family, and once they got out of Raccoon, she would go back to wherever she came from and Sherry would be alone again. Even if her parents were okay, she would be alone . . . and though she wanted very much for them to be safe and well, she wasn't looking forward to the end of her time with Claire.

She was only twelve, but she'd known for a couple of years that her family was different from most. The other kids at school had parents who spent time with them, had birthday parties and went on camping trips, and had brothers and sisters and pets. She'd never had any of those things. She knew that her parents meant well, and that they loved her—but sometimes, she felt like no matter how quiet and good and self-sufficient she was, she was still in their way—

"You ready for this?"

Claire's soft, pretty voice brought her back to the situation, reminding her that she needed to be more alert. Sherry nodded, and Claire stepped down into the dark, dirty water, reaching back to help her.

The water was cold and greasy, and came up to Sherry's knees; it was gross, but not puking bad. Claire motioned toward the big metal door to their left with her new gun, looking as disgusted as Sherry felt.

"Looks like we're going to—"

A loud noise from the balcony cut her off, and they both looked up, Sherry instinctively moving closer to Claire as the noise came again. It sounded like footsteps, but too slow and too loud to be normal—

—and Sherry saw a man in a long, dark coat walk into view, and felt her mouth go dry with fear. He was a giant, maybe as tall as ten feet, and his bald skull gleamed as white as a dead fish belly. She couldn't see him clearly because of the angle, but she could see enough—and she could *feel* that he was bad, that there was something very wrong and bad about him. It radiated off of him like sickness.

"Claire?" she squeaked, her voice breaking as the giant man stalked across the balcony, as he started to turn toward them—slowly, so slowly, and Sherry didn't want to see his face, didn't want to see the face of a man that could frighten her so deeply by just walking onto a balcony—

"Run!"

Claire grabbed her hand and the two of them ran, splashing through the thick water toward the sealed door. Sherry concentrated on not falling, on praying that the door would open—

—*don't be locked, don't be locked!*

—and on not looking back, not wanting to see what the giant, bad man was doing. The door was close but it seemed to take forever, each second stretched out as they fought against the weight of the cold and oily water.

They stumbled to the hatch and Claire found its control, slamming at the button in a kind of panic that made Sherry even more afraid. The door split in the middle, one half sliding up into the ceiling and the other slipping beneath the rippling waves.

Sherry didn't look back, but Claire did. Whatever she saw made her leap through the door, pulling Sherry off her feet and hurtling into the long, dark tunnel that lay behind the hatch. As soon as they were through, Claire fumbled at the wall and the door slid closed behind them, sealing them into the dripping darkness.

"Don't move and be quiet," Claire whispered, and in the very dim light that came from somewhere up ahead, Sherry could see that she was holding the gun out in front of her, trying to search the heavy shadows for any new threats. Sherry obeyed, her heart pounding, wondering who, *what* that man had been—it was the man Claire had asked her about before, that much was obvious, but what *was* he? People didn't get that big, and Claire had been scared, too—

Clink.

A metal noise, soft and muffled from the wall behind her—and Sherry felt the water around her feet start to move suddenly, a swift rush of current that pulled on her legs, pulled her off balance—

—and she stumbled, tripped, plunging face-first into the cold and nasty water as the current got stronger, sucking her backwards. Sherry reached out, trying to find something, anything, to hold on to, and felt slimy stone whip beneath her clutching fingers as the waters rushed her away, away from Claire.

—can't breathe—

Sherry kicked wildly, twisting her body, her eyes stinging from the bad water—and managed to take a breath as her head broke the surface, as she realized that she was in a tunnel, a pitch black shaft no bigger than the vents from the station. The swift waters carried her along, Sherry taking deep gasps of the foul air overhead, forcing herself not to struggle against the relentless power of the hissing liquid. The tunnel had to end somewhere—and wherever it came out, she had to be ready to run.

Claire, please find me, please don't give up on me. . . .

She was lost, blind and deaf, sliding down through the dark—and farther and farther away from the only person who could protect her from the nightmare creatures that had taken over Raccoon.

Annette no longer doubted that her husband had escaped the laboratory levels. Not only were half of the facility entrances unsealed, the fences that surrounded the factory had been breached—and the sewer tunnels, the tunnels that should have been mostly empty, were crawling with human carriers that had to have come from outside. Even as advanced as they'd been in terms of cellular deterioration, she'd had to shoot down five of them just to clear a path from the tram to the sewage operations room.

After what seemed an eternity of trudging through the semi-treated, inky waters of the labyrinthian system, she came to the platform she'd been looking for. Annette stepped up into the concrete tunnel, gazing warily at the closed door a few meters in front of her. Closed and undamaged, a good sign—but what if he'd gone through before he'd lost all trace of human intelligence, before he'd grown into an unthinking, violent animal? Even now, he might still retain something resembling memory; the truth was, she didn't know. The G-Virus hadn't been tested on humans yet . . .

. . . and if he did go through? If he made it to the police station?

No. She couldn't, wouldn't entertain the possibility. Considering what she *did* know about the progressive chemophysiologic changes—what he would be capable of doing if the virus worked the way it was supposed to—the thought of him getting to an uninfected population . . . well, it was unthinkable.

The station is safe, she thought firmly. *Irons may be an incompetent ass, but his cops aren't. Wherever William is, he couldn't have gotten past them.*

She couldn't afford to believe anything else; Sherry was there, if she'd done what she was supposed to do—and besides being her own flesh and blood (which, she reminded herself, was reason enough), Sherry played a very important role in her future plans.

Annette leaned against one cold and sweating wall, aware that time was running out but simply unable to go on without resting for a moment. She'd been counting on the encoded territorial instinct to keep him close to the lab, and had been so sure that she would find him, that her live, human scent would lure him to her . . . but she was almost at the end of the contained area, and all she'd found were a dozen ways in which he could have escaped.

And Umbrella will be here soon. I have to get back, I have to activate the fail-safe before they can stop me.

William deserved to be at peace—but beyond that, destroying the creature that had once been her husband would eradicate all of her doubts about the success of her objective. What if she blew the lab and escaped, only to find that Umbrella had captured him? All of her struggles, all of his *work*, for nothing. . . .

Annette closed her eyes, wishing that there was an easy way to make the decision that had to be made. The fact was, William's death simply wasn't as crucial as getting rid of the lab. And there *was* a good chance that they wouldn't find him, that they weren't even aware of his transformation—

—and it's not as though I have a choice. He's not here, he's not anywhere.

She pushed away from the wall, walking slowly toward the door. She would check the last few tunnels, perhaps see if the conference rooms showed any sign of damage—and then she would go back. Go back and finish what Umbrella had started.

Annette pushed the door open—

—and heard footsteps, echoing through the lonely corridor from somewhere up ahead; the hall was shaped like a "T," the sounds melting into themselves, making it impossible to tell from which direction they were coming—but they were the strong, sure steps of an uninfected human, perhaps more than one, and that could only mean one thing.

Umbrella. They've finally come.

Rage boiled up through her, making her hands shake, her lips curl back from gritted teeth. It had to be them, it had to be one of their murdering spies; besides Irons and a few of the city officials, only Umbrella knew that these tunnels were still in use— and that they led to the underground facility. The possibility that it was some innocent survivor of the spill didn't cross her mind, and neither did running; she raised the handgun and waited for the heartless, murdering bastard to appear.

A figure stepped into sight, a woman in red, and Annette fired—

—*bam,* but she was trembling, screaming inside, and the shot went high. It ricocheted off the cement wall with a whining, zipping sound, and the woman was raising a weapon of her own—

—and Annette fired again, *bam-zip,* but suddenly there was another one, a blurred, flying shape that leapt in front of the woman, knocking her out of the way, all of it happening at once—

—and Annette heard the cry of pain, a man's cry, and felt a burst of roaring triumph.

Got him, I got him—

But there could be more, she hadn't hit the woman—and they were trained killers.

Annette turned and ran, her dirty lab coat flying, her wet shoes slapping against the cement. She had to get back to the lab, fast.

Time had run out.

Twenty-One

LEON STOPPED TO ADJUST HIS SHOULDER harness, so Ada walked on ahead, musing over how surprisingly clear the first few tunnels had been. If memory served, this corridor let out right next to sewage treatment ops; past that was the tram to the factory, and then the machine lift to the underground. Conditions would probably get worse the closer they got to the labs, but with the trek as trouble-free as it had been so far, she was feeling optimistic.

Leon had been uncomfortably quiet since they'd opened the path into the sewers, only talking when it was necessary—watch your step, hold up a minute, which way do you think we should go . . . she didn't think he was even aware of the defenses he'd put up, but she was getting better at reading him. Officer Kennedy was brave, he was at least above-average in the brains department, he was a crack shot—and he didn't know dick about women. When she'd blown off his attempt to comfort her, she'd confused and hurt him—and now he didn't know how to interact with her. He'd chosen to withdraw rather than risk another rejection.

Really, it's for the best. No point in leading him on when it's not necessary, and it saves me the trouble of ego-stroking. . . .

She stepped into the intersection of the empty hall, thinking about the easiest place to part company from her escort—

—and saw the woman, just as she fired.

Bam!

Ada felt chips of concrete spray across her bare shoulders as she brought the Beretta up, a blur of emotions and realizations flashing through her in the instant it took to react. She wouldn't be able to return fire in time, the woman's next shot would kill her, anger at herself for being so stupid—and recognition.

Birkin—

She heard the second shot—and then she was hit, shoved out of the way and falling to the cold floor as Leon cried out in pain and surprise, his warm bulk landing on top of her.

Ada took a deep breath, shocked and amazed as she understood what had happened, as Leon rolled off of her and clutched at his arm. She heard running footsteps and Leon's harsh panting, and sat up.

Oh, my God. No shit—

He'd taken a bullet. For her.

Ada stumbled to her feet, bending over him. "Leon!"

He looked up at her, jaw clenched against the pain. Blood seeped through the fingers of his hand, pressed to his left armpit.

"I'm—okay," he gasped, and although his face was pale, his eyes clouded with suffering, she thought he was probably right. It undoubtedly hurt like a son of a bitch, but it wouldn't—*shouldn't*—kill him.

It would have killed me, Leon saved my life—

And on the tail of that thought, —*Annette Birkin. Still alive.*

"That woman," she blurted, the guilt hitting her even as she turned to run. "I have to talk to her."

Ada took off, sprinting around the corner and down the hall, the door at the end standing open. Leon would live, he would be fine, and if she could catch up to Annette, this whole goddamn nightmare would be over. She'd studied the file photos, she *knew* it was Birkin's wife—and if, by chance, the woman wasn't carrying a sample, she'd sure as hell know where one was.

She ran through the door and stopped short of jumping into yet another water-filled tunnel, pausing just long enough to listen, to scan the surface of the rippling murk. No splashing sounds, and there were still lapping waves to the left—

—and a ladder bolted to the wall, leading up to a fan shaft.

—*goes to operations.*

Ada plunged into the water and made for the ladder. There was a hallway farther along, but it was a dead end; Annette would surely have opted for escape.

She quickly scaled the metal rungs, refusing to let herself think about Leon (because he was *fine*) as she peered through the shaft and saw that it was clear. Mrs. Doctor was probably still running, but Ada wasn't going to walk into another bullet.

Through the shaft, a quick peek past the dead, massive blades of the vent fan at the far end, and back down another ladder. The giant two-story chamber that housed the sewage-treatment machines was empty of life, as cold and industrial and strewn with equipment as she'd expected. There was a hydraulic bridge that spanned the room, raised to the level she'd exited on—which meant that Annette must have gone down via the west ladder, the only other way out. Ada flipped through her mental maps as she started across the bridge, remembering that it went down into one of the treatment center's dumping grounds—

"Drop it, you *bitch!*"

Behind her. Ada halted, feeling a pain inside—the pain of a hearty slap to the ego. The second time she'd screwed up, badly, in as many minutes—but there was no way she was going to obey Annette's hysterical command. The woman's aim was for shit and Ada tensed, preparing to drop, to spin and fire—

Bam-ping!

The shot hit the floor next to Ada's right foot, glancing off the rusting bridge. Annette had her.

Ada dropped the Beretta, raising her hands slowly, turning to face the scientist.

Jesus, I deserve to die for this. . . .

Annette Birkin walked toward her, a Browning nine-millimeter trembling wildly in one outstretched hand. Ada winced inwardly at the sight of that shaking gun—but saw a possible opportunity as Annette moved closer, finally coming to a stop less than ten feet in front of her.

Too close. Too close, and she's right on the edge of a total collapse, isn't she?

"Who are you? What's your name?!"

Ada swallowed heavily, putting a stutter into her voice. "Ada, Ada Wong. Please don't shoot, please, I haven't done anything—"

Annette frowned, backing up a step. "Ada . . . Wong. I know that name—Ada, that was John's girlfriend's name. . . ."

Ada's mouth dropped open. "Yes, John Howe! But—how did you know? Do you know where he is?"

The disheveled scientist glared at her. "I know because John worked with my husband, William. You've heard of him, of course—William Birkin, the man responsible for the creation of the T-Virus."

Annette fairly glowed with a mix of pride and despair as she spoke, giving Ada hope; it was a weakness that she could use. Ada had read the files on William Birkin—read about his steady climb through Umbrella's hierarchy, the advances in virology and genetic sequencing . . . and about the scientific ambition that had made him a veritable sociopath. It looked as though his wife was operating on a similar plane—which meant that the Mrs. would have no problem pulling the trigger.

Play it dumb, and don't give her a reason to doubt it.

"T-Virus? What's—" Ada blinked, then widened

her eyes. "Doctor—Birkin? Wait, *the* Doctor Birkin, the biochemist?"

She saw a flash of pleasure cross Annette's face—but then it was gone, and there was only despair. Despair and the flickering of bitter madness, deep in her bloodshot eyes.

"John Howe is dead," she said coldly, "he died three months ago at the Spencer estate. My condolences—but then, you're about to join him, aren't you? You're not going to take the G-Virus away from me, you can't have it!"

Ada started to shake all over. "G-Virus? Please, I don't know what you're talking about!"

"You know," Annette snarled. "Umbrella sent you to steal it, you can't lie to me! William's dead to me now, Umbrella took him from me, they forced him to use it! They forced him. . . ."

She trailed off, her gaze suddenly far away. Ada tensed—but then Annette was back, her eyes welling up with tears, the weapon pointed at Ada's face.

"A week ago, they came," she whispered. "They came to take it, and they shot my William when he wouldn't give them the samples. They took the case, they took all of the finals, both series—except for the one that he managed to keep, the G-Virus . . ."

Annette's voice raised into a shout suddenly, a pathetic and somehow pleading shout. "He was *dying,* don't you see? He didn't have any *choice!*"

Ada understood. She understood all of it. "He injected himself, didn't he?"

The scientist nodded, her limp blond hair falling

across her eyes, her voice a whisper again. "It revitalizes cellular function. It—it changed him. I didn't see—what he did, but I saw the bodies of the men who tried to kill him, afterwards . . . and I heard the screams."

Ada took a step closer, reaching out as if to comfort her, her own features set into a mask of sympathy—but Annette thrust the gun at her again. Even in her sorrow, she wasn't going to let Ada get any closer.

But it's almost close enough. . . .

"I'm so sorry," Ada said, lowering her arms. "So the G-Virus, it leaked, it changed all of Raccoon—"

Annette shook her head. "No. When the Umbrella assassins were—stopped, the case was broken. The T-Virus leaked—the lab workers hit by the airborne were contained, but there were rats, you see. Rats in the sewers. . . ."

She paused, her lips trembling. ". . . unless William, my sweet William has started to reproduce. Implanting embryos, replicating . . . it shouldn't be time for that yet, but I—"

She broke off, her eyes narrowing, the madness sweeping over her again as visibly as a crashing wave. High color flared in her pale cheeks, her red-rimmed eyes glossy with paranoia.

Get ready—

"You can't have it!" Annette screamed, spittle flying from her cracked lips. "He gave his life to keep it from you, you're a spy and you *can't have it—*"

Ada ducked and leapt, pistoning both of her arms beneath Annette's, shoving the gun up and away from both of them. The Browning discharged, sending a round clanging off the ceiling as they fought for control of the weapon. Annette was physically weaker, but she was driven by demons of hatred and loss, the edge of insanity lending her strength—

—*but no sense*—

Ada let go of the gun suddenly and Annette stumbled, not prepared for the unexpected move. She crashed against the railing of the bridge and Ada charged, driving her elbow into Annette's lower belly, hitting her beneath her center of balance—

—and Annette half-turned, her mouth an open darkness of surprise, her arms pinwheeling for balance—and she plummeted over the railing, silently, not a sound until the dull *thump* as her body hit the floor some twenty feet below.

"Shit," Ada hissed, stepping to the rail and looking down. She lay there, facedown and motionless, the gun still clenched in one thin white hand.

That's just great. Walk into an ambush, not once but twice for hell's sake, then kill the one crazy bitch who can tell you where the samples are—

A low moan floated up from Annette Birkin's body—and she moved, hunching her back, trying to roll onto her side.

Shit shit shit!

Ada turned and ran across the bridge, scooping up the Beretta as she hurried for what looked like a control panel next to the fan shaft ladder. She'd have to lower the bridge, get to Annette before she could crawl away—

—except the panel was for the fan, and as another painful moan—a slightly *louder* moan—echoed up through the chamber, Ada knew she didn't have much time.

The dump, I can go through the dump, circle back around through one of the tunnels—

Even as she thought it, she was jogging for the west ladder, hoping that the pitiful scientist was injured enough to stay down for a minute or two. There was a small balcony at the end of the bridge that looked over the dump, and the metal ladder hung down from an opening at the far right. Ada lowered herself down as quickly as she could, dropping the last several feet onto a cement landing.

The dumping area was a large boxy room, the walls heaped with industrial debris—smashed crates, rusting pipes, wire-encrusted panels, and rotting cardboard. She stepped off the landing and into almost three feet of black sludge, the cold, gooey muck rising up to her thighs. She didn't care, she only wanted to get to the lady Birkin, to bring an end to her time in Raccoon—

—except something moved. Beneath the opaque and stinking liquid, something *big* moved. Ada saw what might have been a reptilian spine slice through the murk in front of her, saw and heard a stack of boards topple into the water some ten feet away in the same instant.

You gotta be kidding me. . . .

Whatever it was, it was big enough to change her mind about the hurry she was in to get to Annette. Ada backed to the platform and boosted herself up, never taking her gaze from the indeterminate shape as it curled back through the lapping sludge—

—and rose up in a sudden, violent spray of darkness, coming straight at her. Ada raised the Beretta and started to fire.

There was a tiny elevator platform in one corner of the empty conference room, a square of metal that apparently went down. Claire hurried toward it, fetid water dripping from her clothes, feeling horribly lost and anxious to keep moving, to find Sherry.

Please be alive, baby, please. . . .

She'd found the drainage hole, but no Sherry—and after agonizingly long moments of screaming into the rushing water, of trying to squeeze into the tiny hole, she'd forced herself to abandon the effort. Sherry was gone, maybe drowned, maybe not—but unless the flow of water suddenly decided to reverse itself, she wasn't coming back.

Claire found the controls for the one-man lift and punched a button. A hidden motor whirred and the lift descended, inching down through the floor, probably taking her to some other empty hall, some other blank and unknown room—or worse, directly into the path of yet another unnatural creature.

She clenched her damp hands in frustration as the lift slid slowly down, wishing that it was faster, that there was some way to speed up her search. She felt like she was running blind, taking whatever path was in front of her; from the tunnel where Sherry had been lost, she'd found a dimly lit corridor and then the unadorned and somehow sterile conference room.

It was like an endless funhouse—*sans fun*—and she was feeling pretty shitty for bringing Sherry into it; if the girl *was* dead, it would be her fault—

She shut down the futile thinking before it got any farther, making herself focus. Self-recrimination was a killer, and she couldn't afford it. The elevator was lowering into a hall, and she crouched down, pointing Irons's heavy gun in front of her as her new surroundings rose into view.

The concrete corridor had another lift at the other end, and was intersected by a second hall, maybe forty feet away—and next to the junction there was a body propped against one cement wall, what looked like a cop—

She felt a mix of shock and distress, her eyes widening as she took in the cop's slack features, the hair color, the build . . .

. . . *that's—Leon?*

Before the lift hit the floor, Claire jumped off and ran toward the crumpled figure. It *was* Leon, and he wasn't moving, either unconscious or dead—but no, he was breathing, and as she crouched in front of him, his eyes flickered open. His hand was high on his left arm, his fingers wet with blood.

"Claire?" His blue eyes seemed clear, tired but aware.

"Leon! What happened, are you okay?"

"I got shot, must've blacked out for a minute. . . ."

He carefully took his hand away, exposing a small ragged hole just above his armpit, oozing red. It looked painful, but at least it wasn't gushing.

Wincing, Leon pulled the shredded fabric of his

uniform over the hole and put his hand back over it. "Hurts like all hell, but I think I'll survive—Ada, where's Ada?"

The last was delivered almost frantically, Leon struggling to push himself away from the wall. With a soft groan, he fell back, obviously in no shape to move.

"Lie still, just rest for a minute," Claire said. "Who's Ada?"

"I met her at the station," he said. "I couldn't find you, and we heard that you can get out of Raccoon—through the sewers. The city's not safe, there was some kind of a leak at the Umbrella lab, and Ada wanted to leave right away. Somebody shot at us, and I got hit—Ada went after the shooter, down that hall, she said it was a woman. . . ."

He shook his head as if to clear it, then frowned up at her. "I have to find her. I don't know how long I was out, but not more than a couple of minutes, she can't have gone far—"

He started to sit forward again and Claire stopped him, pushing him back gently. "I'll go. I—I was with this little girl, and she's lost somewhere in the sewers. Maybe I can find both of them."

Leon hesitated—then nodded, resigning himself to his injury. "How's your ammo?"

"Uh—seven in this one—" She patted the weapon that she'd taken from the squad car, tucked in her belt. It suddenly seemed like a million years ago, that wild ride. "—and seventeen in this one."

She held up Irons's gun, and Leon nodded again, his head rolling back tiredly. "Okay, that's good. I should be able to follow in a few minutes . . . be careful, alright? And good luck."

Claire stood up, wishing that they had more time. She wanted to tell him about Chris, about Irons and Mr. X and the T-Virus, she wanted to find out what he knew about Umbrella, or if he knew the way out of the sewers—

—but this Ada might be facing down a sniper right now, and Sherry could be anywhere. Anywhere at all.

Leon had closed his eyes. Claire turned and started down the intersecting hall, wondering if any of them had a chance to make it out of this madness alive.

Twenty-Two

ANNETTE HURT ALL OVER. SHE SAT UP SLOW-
ly, feeling sick from the seeming hundreds of aches
and pains that yammered for her attention. Her neck
and stomach hurt, she'd jammed her right wrist, both
knees felt like they were swelling—but it was the
sharp pain in her right side that was the worst,
because she thought she might have cracked or even
broken a rib.

You horrible, horrible woman—

Annette leaned back, supporting her strained neck
with her uninjured hand, but saw only metal and
shadow; Ada Wong, the bitch from Umbrella, had
apparently run away. She'd pretended not to know
anything, but Annette wasn't stupid; Ada was probably already on her way to the lab—or coming after
her, anxious to finish her off.

Umbrella, Umbrella did this. . . .

Annette crawled to her feet, using the rage to overcome the pain. She had to get out, to get to the laboratory before the spies did—but oh, she hurt so very much! The stabbing sensation in her gut was terrible, a knife sawing at her insides, and the lab seemed a million miles away . . .

. . . can't let them steal his work. . . .

She staggered toward the door to the cavernous room, one arm wrapped around her burning chest— and stopped, tilting her head to one side, listening.

Shots. Echoing through the chill air, coming from the adjacent dumping grounds—and a second later, she heard a thundering hiss, more shots, splashing—

Annette grinned, a tight, humorless grin. Perhaps she'd get to the lab first, after all.

The bridge, lower the bridge, don't let her escape. . . .

Tired and aching, Annette stumbled to the hydraulic's controls and activated the span's descent. The powerful hum of the bridge's motors drowned out the noises of whatever battle was being waged, the platform rotating down and locking into place with a heavy *clang*.

Annette pushed herself away from the wall, falling against the console by the door. She found the switches for the ventilation fan and flicked them up, still smiling grimly as the whining start-up high overhead grew into a dull roar. Ada had run into trouble in the dump, and Annette wasn't going to let her just climb back out of it; with the bridge lowered and the shaft blocked, Ms. Wong would have to fight her way through.

Hope it's a pack of lickers, you bitch, I hope they're tearing you to pieces in there. . . .

Annette turned away from the console—and fell, the pain and dizziness too much, her bruised and swelling knees hitting the floor and sending fresh needles of agony through her legs—

—and the door in front of her opened. Annette raised the gun but wasn't able to aim, expending what was left of her strength just to keep from screaming in suffering and frustration.

William, it hurts so bad, I'm sorry but I can't—

A young woman crouched in front of her, a look of wary concern on her smudged face. She was dressed in cutoffs and a vest, dripping with sewer water—and held a sleek and heavy handgun, not pointing it directly at Annette—but not pointing it away, either.

Another spy.

"Are you Ada?" the girl asked tentatively, reaching out to touch her—and it was more than Annette could stand, to be touched in pity by some heartless, scheming corporate pawn.

"Get away from me," Annette snarled, slapping at the girl's outstretched hand weakly. "I'm not your 'contact,' and I don't have it on me. You can kill me, but you won't find it."

The girl moved back, a look of confusion on her dirty face. "Find *what?* Who are you?"

The questions again, and the fury passed, leaving her numb. Annette was tired of playing games; it hurt too much, and she just wasn't strong enough to fight anymore. "Annette Birkin," she said wearily. "As if you didn't know. . . ."

She'll kill me now. It's over, it's all over.

Annette couldn't help it. Tears trickled down cheeks, tears as futile as her plans. She'd failed William, she'd failed as a wife and a mother and even as a scientist. At least it would end now, at least there would finally be an end to the anguish—

"Are you Sherry's mother?"

The girl's words stunned her, snapping her out of her exhausted collapse as sharply as a slap to the face. *"What?!* Who—how do you know about Sherry?"

"She's lost in the sewers," the girl said, speaking quickly, her voice tinged with desperation as she shoved her handgun into her belt. "Please, you have to help me find her! She was sucked into one of the drainage shafts and I don't know where to look—"

"But I told her to go to the station," Annette wailed, the physical pain all but forgotten, her heart pounding out waves of horrified disbelief. "Why is she here? It's dangerous, she'll be killed! And the G-Virus—Umbrella will find her, they'll take it, why is she *here?"*

The girl reached for her again, helping her up, and Annette didn't fight, too weak and terrified to fight. If Sherry was in the sewers, if Umbrella found her—

The girl stared at her intently, looking somehow guilty and afraid and hopeful all at once. "The station was overrun—where do the drains go? Please, Annette, you have to tell me!"

The truth dawned into her exhaustion and fear like a ray of bitter light.

The drains let out into the filter pool—which happens to be right next to the factory tram.

The fastest route to the labs.

It was a trick. The girl was using Sherry's name to get to the facility, to get information about the G-Virus. Sherry was still at the station, safe and well, and this was all an elaborate ruse—

—but Umbrella knows the way, why would she ask if she knows already? It doesn't make sense!

Annette raised the gun, her aching wrist trembling, and backed away from the girl. Her confusion was too big, the questions too many—and because she couldn't be sure of *anything,* she couldn't pull the trigger.

"Don't you move. Don't you follow me," she snarled, ignoring the pain, reaching back to push the door open. "I'll shoot if you try to follow me."

"Annette—I don't understand, I just want to—"

"Shut up! Shut up and leave me alone, can't you all just leave me alone?!"

She backed through the door, pushing it closed on the surprised and frightened girl, squeezing her arm against her bruised or broken ribs as soon as the hatch was shut.

Sherry. . . .

It was a lie, it had to be a lie—but it didn't change anything, either way. She could still make it, she *had* to make it back to the facility, to finish what she had started.

Turning, limping and gasping, Annette stumbled into the cold darkness of the connecting tunnel, letting each terrible, aching step be a reminder of what Umbrella had done.

* * *

A cold, silent cavern, the walls sheened with ice, and I am lost. I am lost and exhausted, running and afraid for a very long time, so I sit down to rest. So quiet, so cold—but my arm hurts, I'm sitting against a wall that has grown spines, and one of them is digging into my flesh, piercing me. It hurts so badly, and I have to get up, I have to find someone, I have to—

—wake up.

Leon opened his eyes, aware at once that he'd hazed out again. The realization made him catch his breath, the sudden fear jolting him fully awake.

Ada, Claire—Jesus, how long?

He gently pulled his hand away from his arm, the blood gummy and thick between his fingers. It hurt, but not as sharply as before—and the bleeding had stopped, at least at the entrance; the shreds of his torn uniform had clotted to the wound, forming a stiff seal.

He leaned forward, reaching around to touch where the bullet had come out; again, a hardening, tacky patch of fabric beneath the pulsing ache of the wound. He couldn't be positive, but he thought that the bullet had gone straight through the flesh, missing the bone completely—which meant he was extremely goddamn lucky.

Even if it blew my arm off, Ada's still out there—and I sent Claire after her. I have to go after them.

He thought it was the shock of the trauma that had made him black out, rather than the pain or blood loss—and he couldn't afford any more time to recover. Clenching his teeth, Leon pushed himself up with his good arm, his muscles cold and stiff from the damp chill of the concrete.

His left shoulder brushed against the wall, and he gasped as the pain intensified briefly, stabbing and hot—but it ebbed, receding to the duller throbbing sensation after a few seconds. Leon waited it out, breathing deeply, reminding himself that it could have been a hell of a lot worse.

When he was finally on his feet, he decided that he could take it; he wasn't light-headed or dizzy, and although there was blood on the floor and wall, there wasn't nearly as much as he'd thought there would be. Careful not to jostle his wound, Leon turned and walked down the corridor to the closed door at the end, moving as quickly as he could.

Through the door, he was faced with another water-filled tunnel stretching off in either direction; there was a ladder on the wall to his left, but he didn't even want to guess at how to climb it without ripping open the wound—besides which, there was a loudly spinning fan at the top. He struck off to the right, stepping down into the dark water and sloshing forward, hoping that he'd see some sign as to where Ada or Claire had gone.

Chasing after the sniper . . . how could she do that, how could she just leave me there?

After their confrontation with the vomiting monster-thing, he'd sworn to himself that he wouldn't assume anything else about Ada Wong; she was alternately flirtatious and standoffish, and if she'd learned how to shoot by playing paintball, he was a bank executive. But in spite of her confusing behavior and probable duplicity, he liked her; she was smart and confident, she was beautiful—and he *had* assumed there was a good, decent person beneath that contradictory facade . . .

. . . and yet she left you to chase after the shooter, left you rolling on the floor with a bullet in your arm. Yeah, she's great; you should propose.

He'd reached a split in the tunnel, and blocked out his wandering attempts to figure out Ada's actions, reminding himself that he could ask her when he found her—*if* he found her. There was a locked gate to the right, so Leon turned left, peering uneasily into the thickening shadows as he trudged onward. He shouldn't have let Claire go after Ada alone, he should have pulled himself together and gone with her—

He stopped, hearing something. Shots, distant and hollow, coming from somewhere up ahead, distorted by the winding maze of tunnels that made up the sewer system.

Still holding the Magnum tightly, Leon pressed his wrist against the bullet wound and started to run, the pain going sharp again, making him queasy. He couldn't manage much better than a shagging jog, the water slowing him down almost as much as the nasty bite of the wound—but as the last echo of the shots faded away, he somehow found the motivation to go faster.

There was a dimly lit offshoot to the tunnel ahead and to the left, pale yellow light streaming out across the softly slopping water. Even before he reached it, he saw that he would have to make a choice. Straight in front of him was a platform of sorts, a heavy door set into the ragged bricks of the tunnel's end, water dripping down from the ceiling in slender rivulets.

An obvious choice, except—

Leon stopped in the elongated patch of murky light, looking down into the offshoot. Another door, and he didn't have *time* to decide, the shots could have come from anywhere—

Bam-bam!

To the left. Leon jumped up from the tunnel, feeling new pain, feeling hot wetness against his wrist as the wound started to seep. He ignored it, hurrying to the door and pulling it open, hearing more rounds fired as he started down a wide and empty hall.

The corridor he'd entered was as shadowy and cold as the sewage tunnels, but much bigger, wider, presumably some kind of transport hall for heavy equipment. It twisted left and then left again, boxes and a rack of steel canisters against the second corner, just past some kind of a loading door.

. . . acetylene, maybe oxy, good GOD what takes that many bullets and doesn't die?

He heard another string of shots, splashing water— and a different sound, a deep and guttural *hissing* that chilled him to his core. Strangely familiar, but too loud to be possible.

A million snakes, a thousand giant cats, some primordial, terrible dinosaur—

He ran, finally giving up trying to hold the bullet hole closed, needing his arm free to pump for more speed. The end of the tunnel was close, he saw a panel of blinking lights and an opening to the left, another huge loading door—

—and he stopped just short of running into the line

of fire as another rapid succession of shots sounded, as a thundering crash of water sprayed out, water raining down on the floor in a thick sheet.

"Stop, I'm coming in!" He shouted—

—and heard Ada's voice, and felt a sweeping relief in spite of whatever horror was ahead.

"Leon!"

She's alive!

Magnum raised, his wound bleeding freely now, he stepped in front of the open door—and saw Ada across a lake of churning muck, boxes and broken boards swimming through the turbulent liquid. She was standing on a small ledge of concrete beneath a ladder, her Beretta pointed into the thrashing pool.

"Ada, what—"

Splash!

A giant burst out of the lake and slammed him off of his feet, knocking him back into the corridor. It happened so fast that he didn't actually *see* it before he was flying through the air, his mind feeding him the picture as he hit the ground. He fell on his injured arm and cried out, as much from the shock of what he'd seen as from the stinging blast of pain.

—crocodile—

Leon was on his feet and stumbling away before he even knew he could get up—and the giant lizard, the croc that was thirty feet long if it was an inch, stepped into the corridor behind him with a mighty, bellowing roar. The cement trembled as the mammoth reptile crawled up from the waters of its home, gallons of black water streaming from its toothy, grinning jaws.

—jaws as big as me, bigger—

Leon ran, there *was* no pain, his heart hammering in a primal panic. It would eat him, it would shred him into a hundred screaming, bloody chunks—

—and the beast roared again, an impossibly low bellow that rattled his bones, that urged sweat to burst from every quaking pore—

—and Leon shot a look back, and saw that he was much, much faster than the grinning lizard. It was still climbing through the loading door, its tree-trunk legs short and squat, its incredible bulk too huge to maneuver so easily.

Leon swapped weapons in a daze of terror, his wound shrieking as he chambered a round into the Remington. He sidled backwards in an uneven gait, reaching a turn in the hall—

—and unloaded all five shells as quickly as he could pump them, the heavy rounds blasting the monster crocodile's hideous snout.

It roared, swinging its head from side to side, blood erupting from its grinning face in buckets—but still it came, lumbering forward, dragging its armored tail from the pool of slime behind it.

Not enough, not enough power—

Leon turned and ran again, horrified at having to retreat, afraid of what would happen to Ada when he left the crocodile behind, but knowing that it would take another fifty rounds to stop it—that or a nuclear blast, and why was he still *thinking,* he needed to get away and then worry about what to do.

Hang on, Ada—

The booming steps of the giant filled his ears as he ran past the boxes, past the row of steel cylinders—

—and stopped running. His instincts cried out for sanity, but he had an idea—and as the terrible lizard took another twisting, thundering step, Leon turned and went back.

Let this work, it works in the movies, please God be listening—

The row of five gleaming canisters was inset on a thick shelf cut into the wall, held into place by a steel cable. There was a release button for the cable on the side of the shelf. Leon slapped it, and the heavy wire drooped, one looped end falling to the floor.

Dropping the shotgun, he grabbed the closest of the cylinders, his muscles straining, blood pouring from his injured arm. He could feel thin, trickling trails of it sliding down his sweat-slick chest but didn't stop, rocking back on his heels to free the can of compressed gas.

—there!

Leon jumped back as the silver can fell off the shelf, hitting the ground and rolling a few inches. He looked up and saw that the croc had covered another fifty feet—close enough for him to see the dull, dirty pits in its six-inch teeth as it roared again, close enough for him to smell the rotting-meat stench of its hot breath only a second later.

Leon raised one boot to the canister and shoved with all he had, the can lazily rolling back toward the gaining lizard. By some incredible stroke of fortune, the corridor floor had some slant to it; the two-hundred-plus pounds of cylinder seemed to pick up speed, spinning in the croc's direction in a loose semicircle.

Backing away, he yanked the Magnum from his belt and pointed it at the shining can, forcing his fingers not to pull the trigger. The crocodile plodded forward, its tail slapping the walls so hard that stone dust rained down with each violent whip. Leon was in a state of total awe, in the grip of an instinctual terror so deep that it was all he could do not to turn and flee.

Come on, you bastard—

Less than a hundred feet away, the crocodile and the canister met—and Leon pulled the trigger. The first shot *pinged* off the floor in front of the rocking can—and the grinning jaws opened, the massive beast lowering its head to catch at the obstacle, to push it aside.

—steady—

Leon fired again, and—

KA-BOOM!

—was thrown to the ground as the canister exploded. In a blast of curled steel and igniting gases, the creature's head was *obliterated,* disappearing like a popped balloon. Almost simultaneously, a wave of steaming gore hit Leon, bits of tooth and bone and shredded, smoking flesh clapping over him like a thick wet blanket.

Gagging, his ears ringing and arm bleeding, Leon sat up as the headless carcass settled to the floor, the legs crumpling beneath the brainless weight of the reptilian monster. He pressed his blood-covered hand against the wound, exhausted, sick, in pain—and as deeply satisfied as he'd felt in quite some time.

"Gotcha, you dumb shit," he said, and smiled. When Ada came jogging up the corridor a moment later, that's how she found him—staring at his handiwork in dazed and dizzy triumph, bloody and bleeding and grinning like a little kid.

Twenty-Three

LEON WAS WEARING A WHITE UNDERSHIRT beneath his uniform; Ada tore it into strips and bandaged his arm with it, fashioning a kind of sling for him to wear once she'd slipped his ruined shirt back on. He'd lost enough blood to be dazed, almost helpless, and Ada used his mild shock to explain herself as she tended to him, feeling mildly shocked herself by the complex emotions that warred inside of her.

". . . and I thought she looked familiar. I thought I'd met her through John, and I almost caught up to her—but she must have slipped past me. I got lost in the tunnels, trying to find my way back. . . ."

Nothing of truth, but Leon didn't seem to notice— just as he didn't seem to notice the gentle, careful way she touched him, or the very slight tremor in her voice as she apologized for a third time, for leaving him behind.

He saved my life. Again. And all I have to give him in return are lies, calculated deceit in exchange for his selflessness. . . .

Something had changed for her when he'd taken the bullet in her stead, and she didn't know how to change it back. Even worse, she didn't know that she *wanted* to change it back. It was like the birth of a new feeling, some emotion that she couldn't name but that seemed to fill her up; it was unsettling, uncomfortable—and yet somehow, not altogether unpleasant. His clever solution to the problem of the nearly invincible crocodile—the creature that she'd only just been able to hold at bay, in spite of her best efforts—had made the unnamed feeling even stronger. The hole in his arm was only a flesh wound, but from the streaks of fresh blood across his smooth chest and stomach, she knew that it had been hurting bad—draining him, *killing* him as he'd worked to save her ass.

Get rid of him now, her mind hissed, *leave him, don't let this affect the job—the* job, *Ada, the mission. Your* life.

She knew it was what she had to do, that it was the *only* thing to do—but when he was fixed up as best as she could manage, and her pathetic cover story had been told, she conveniently forgot to listen to herself. Ada helped him to his feet and led him away from the gut-splattered scene of the monster reptile's demise, spouting off some nonsense about having found what looked like an exit when she'd been lost.

Annette Birkin was gone; as soon as Leon had led the crocodile out of the dump, she'd scaled the ladder and checked—and seen that Annette had retained enough sense to start up the fans and lower the bridge before running, effectively blowing Ada's other options for escape. The woman was possibly psychotic, but not a moron—and although she'd been wrong about Ada's source of purpose, she'd been dead on as to the purpose itself. To wrap the mission, Ada would have to get to the lab as quickly as she could, before Annette could do anything . . . *final*—and Leon, silent and stumbling Leon, would add to her time by half.

Drop him! Lose the weight, you're not a nursemaid, for Chrissake, this isn't you, *Ada—*

"I'm thirsty," Leon whispered, his breath warm across her neck. She looked up into his gore-stained, blinking face and found that the voice inside was easier to ignore this time. She'd have to leave him, of course, in the end there would have to be a parting of the ways—

—but not yet.

"Then we'll have to find you some water," she said, and steered him gently in the direction she needed to go.

Sherry woke up in the dark, a terrible, bitter taste in her mouth, a river of cold gunk tugging at her clothes. There was a rumbling sound all around her, a sound like the sky was falling, and for a second, she couldn't remember what had happened or where she was—and when she realized that she couldn't move, she panicked. The thundering sound was fading, fading and then gone—but she was stuck in some awful stinking river, pressed against cold, wet *hardness,* and she was alone.

She opened her mouth to scream—and then remembered the screaming monster, the monster and then the giant bald man, and then Claire. Remembering Claire stopped her from screaming; somehow, the image of her was like a soothing touch, easing through the blind terror and allowing her to think.

Got sucked into a drain hole, and now I'm—somewhere else, and screaming won't help.

It was a brave thought, a *strong* thought, and it made her feel better to think it. She pushed herself away from the hardness at her back, treading the dark water, and discovered that she wasn't stuck at all; she had been up against a row of bars or openings in the rock, and the force of the current had held her there—held her, and probably saved her from drowning. The disgusting goop was flowing around her, tinkling and burbling like a regular old stream, not nearly as strong as before—and the bad taste in her mouth meant that she must have swallowed some of it. . . .

Thinking *that* opened up the rest of her memory. She'd been floating along and then had gotten twisted somehow, and had gulped some of the horrible, chemical-tasting liquid and freaked out—*passed* out, she thought.

At least the noise had stopped, whatever that had been, a sound like a moving train, maybe, or a giant truck, roaring away . . . and now that she was more awake, she realized that she could see. Not very much, but enough to know that she was in a big room filled with water, and there was a tiny, feeble shaft of light coming down from high above.

There has to be a way out. Somebody built this place, they had to have a way out. . . .

Sherry swam a little farther into the big room, and kicking, she felt the toes of her shoes glance off against something hard. Something hard and flat. Feeling stupid for not thinking of it already, she took a deep breath, lowered her legs—and stood up. The water was all the way up to her shoulders, but she could stand.

The last traces of panic slipped away as she stood in the middle of the room, turning slowly, her eyes finally getting the most from the weak light—and saw the ladder shape against the far wall. She was still scared, no question, but the sight of the shadowy rungs meant she'd found the way out. Sherry lifted her feet and paddled toward the ladder, proud of how she was handling herself.

No screaming, no crying. Just like Claire said. Strong.

She reached the ladder and pulled her knees up to the bottom rung, a few inches above the surface. She got her feet beneath her and started to climb, grimacing at the thick, slimy feel of the metal bars beneath her pruned fingers. The ladder seemed to go on forever, and when she risked a look down to see how high she'd gone, she could only see a tiny, shimmering patch of the water's lapping top where the light hit it directly. She could see the source of the light, too—a narrow slit in the ceiling, not much higher than where she was.

Almost to the top. And if I fall, I won't get hurt. There's nothing to be scared of.

Sherry swallowed heavily, willing the thought to be true, and looked up again.

A few more rungs, and when she reached up for the next, her hand touched a bumpy metal ceiling. She felt a burst of accomplishment, pushing at it with one hand—

—and it didn't move. Not at *all*.

"Shit," she whispered, but it didn't sound annoyed, the way she'd hoped; the word sounded small and lonely, almost like a plea.

Sherry hooked an elbow through the rung she was holding, touched her pendant for luck, and tried again, really pushing this time. Straining with all of her might, she thought she felt it give, just a little— but not anywhere near enough. She lowered her hand, cursing silently this time; she was trapped.

For several minutes she didn't move, not wanting to go back down into the water, not wanting to believe that she really *was* stuck—but her arms were getting tired, and she didn't want to jump, either. Finally, she started down, much more slowly than she'd come up. Each step lower was like admitting defeat.

She was perhaps a third of the way back to the water when she heard the footsteps overhead—a light thumping at first, more of a vibration than anything, but then quickly redefined into separate steps, getting louder. Then closer—and getting louder still, approaching the top of the pit where she'd awakened.

Sherry gave about a second's thought to ignoring the footsteps and then scrambled up the ladder, deciding that it was worth the risk; it might not be Claire, or even anyone who meant her well—but it could be her only chance at escape.

She started shouting before she got back to the top. "Hello! Help, can you hear me? Hello, hello!"

The footsteps *seemed* to pause, and as she reached the ceiling again, still calling out, she hit the metal several times with her fist.

"Hello, hello, hello!"

Another smack with her decidedly sore hand—and suddenly she was hitting air, and a blinding light was in her face.

"Sherry! Oh, my God, sweetie, I'm so glad you're okay!"

Claire, it *was* Claire, and Sherry couldn't see her but was nearly overwhelmed with delight at the sound of her voice. Strong, warm hands helped her up, warm, damp arms were hugging her tightly. Sherry blinked and squinted, and started to be able to make out the features of a vast room through the brilliant white haze.

"How did you know it was me?" Claire asked, still holding her.

"Didn't. But I couldn't get out by myself, and I heard walking. . . ."

Sherry looked around at the big room that Claire had pulled her into, feeling stunned amazement that

Claire had heard her at all. The room was huge, spanned by a series of thin metal catwalks laid out in diagonals—and the section of floor that she'd come out of was at the farthest corner of the darkest part of the room, the panel that Claire had lifted only a couple of feet across.

Man. If I hadn't knocked, or if she'd been going any faster. . . .

"I'm very glad it's you," Sherry said firmly, and Claire grinned, looking just as happy and amazed as Sherry felt.

Claire knelt in front of her, her smile fading a little. "Sherry—I saw your mom. She's okay, she's alive—"

"Where? Where is she?" Sherry blurted, excited by the news—but feeling a kind of nervous uncertainty tensing her muscles suddenly, making it hard to breathe.

She looked into Claire's worried gray eyes, and saw that she was thinking about lying again—that she was trying to figure out the best way to tell her something unpleasant. Even a few hours ago, Sherry might have let her do it, too—

—but not anymore. Strong and brave we have *to be. . . .*

"Tell me, Claire. Tell me the *truth.*"

Claire sighed, shaking her head. "I don't know where she went. She was—scared of me, Sherry. I think she thought I was someone else, someone bad or crazy. She ran away from me—but I'm pretty sure she came this way, and I was trying to find her again when I heard you calling."

Sherry nodded slowly, struggling to accept the idea

that her mother had been acting weird—weird enough for Claire to try and sugar-coat it.

"And you think she came in here?" Sherry asked finally.

"I can't be positive. I also ran into this cop, Leon, before I saw your mother; I met him when I first got to the city, and he was in one of the tunnels I went through after you disappeared. He was hurt, he couldn't come with me to look for you—so after your mom took off, I went back to get him, but he was gone."

"Dead?"

Claire shook her head. "Nope. Just gone—so I backtracked, and as far as I can tell, this is the only way your mom could have gone. But like I said, I'm not sure. . . ."

She hesitated, frowning, gazing at Sherry thoughtfully. "Did your mom ever tell you about something called the G-Virus?"

"G-Virus? I don't *think* so."

"Did she ever give you anything to hold onto, like a little glass container, something like that?"

Sherry frowned back at her. "No, nothing. Why?"

Claire stood up, putting her hand on Sherry's shoulder and shrugging at the same time. "It's not really important."

Sherry narrowed her eyes, and Claire smiled again. "Really. Come on, let's see if we can figure out where your mom went. I bet she's looking for you."

Sherry let Claire lead the way, wondering why she was suddenly sure—almost certain, in fact—that Claire didn't believe what she was saying . . . and wondering why she couldn't find it in herself to ask any more questions about it.

The factory machine lift, like the tram, was exactly where Annette had left it. The margin had surely tightened, but she was still ahead of the spies, of Ada Wong and her ragged little friend . . .

. . . lies, telling me lies like they all tell lies, as if losing William, suffering such pain and loss isn't enough to shame them. . . .

She fumbled the control key out of her torn lab coat pocket, leaning heavily against the mounted controls as she inserted the key and turned it. Her shaking fingers touched the activation switch and a trail of lights appeared on the console, too bright even in the moon-filled darkness. Cool autumn air brushed over her aching body, a friendly, secret wind that smelled like fire and disease . . .

. . . like Halloween, like bonfires in the dark when they brought out their dead, burning the pestilent flesh of the plague-riddled bodies . . .

Four squealing, blaring honks sounded into the night sky, the massive elevator room telling her that it was time to go. Annette staggered up the gray and yellow steps, unable to remember what she'd been thinking about before. It was time to go, and she was so, so tired. How long had it been since she'd slept? She couldn't remember that, either.

Hit my head, yes? Or just sleepy, mayhaps. . . .

She'd been exhausted before, but the relentless pain of her injuries had sent her to some delirious place that she'd never imagined could exist. Her thoughts came in spiraling, uneasy bursts of feeling that she couldn't seem to sort through, at least not to her satisfaction; she knew what had to be done—the triggering system, the subway gate opening, the hiding in the shadows and waiting to heal—but the rest had become some strange, disjointed grouping of free association, as if she'd taken some drug that had overloaded her senses, and would only let her think a bit at a time.

It was almost over. That was something she could hold on to, one of the only constants in her muddled mind. A positive and somehow magical phrase that she could still see, no matter how blind she became. On her way through the factory, she'd coughed and coughed and then vomited from the pain a thin and acidic string of bile that had made dark bubbles burst in front of her eyes, the darkness staying for so long that she thought she might actually lose her sight—

—*it's almost over.*

Clutching the thought like a lost love, she found the latch to the metal room and went inside. The controls, pushed. The movement and sound of movement engulfing her as she lay across one soft metal bench and closed her eyes. A few moments of rest, and it was almost over. . . .

Annette sank into the dark, the humming motors lulling her into a deep and instant sleep. She was going down, her muscles relaxing, her aches and miseries loosening their hold—and for some endless reach of time, she found a silence—

—until a howling, terrible scream knifed into her darkness, a shriek of such fury and pain that it spoke for her heart, and she jerked back to life, panting and afraid—

—and then realized what had snapped her out of her dreamless sleep, and her thoughts came together, giving her one more clear and constant thing to hold on to.

It was William. William had come home, he had followed her—and Umbrella would have nothing, because the thing that had been her husband had come back into the blast radius.

The scream sounded again, this time echoing away into one of the lab's many secret places as the lift went down and down.

Annette closed her eyes again, the new thought joining her lost love from before, the two of them together making her happy at last.

William has come home. It's almost over.

The third followed naturally, added as she slipped back into the silence, knowing that she had to get up too soon, to begin the final journey. When the lift stopped, she'd wake up and be ready.

Umbrella will suffer for what they've done—and everybody dies at the very end.

She smiled, and fell asleep, dreaming of William.

Twenty-Four

LEON FINALLY STARTED TO FEEL LIKE HIM-
self again, sitting in the control room where Ada had
left him. She'd found a medkit in one of the dust-
covered cabinets, along with a bottle of water; she'd
only been gone for about ten minutes, but the aspirin
was starting to kick in, and the water had worked
wonders.

He sat in front of a switch-covered console, trying
to piece together what had happened after the explosion in the sewers; the last thing he really remembered
clearly was seeing the headless crocodile collapse, and
then being overwhelmed by a light-headed weakness.
Ada had bandaged him up and then led him through
tunnels—

*—and a subway, we were on a subway for a minute
or two—*

—and finally to this room, where she'd told him to

rest while she went to check on something. Leon had protested, reminding her that it wasn't safe, but had still been too fuzzy to do much more than sit where she'd put him. He'd never felt so helpless, or so totally dependent on another person. Once he'd gulped about half of the gallon jug of water, though, he'd started to snap out of it. Apparently, blood loss tended to dehydrate . . .

. . . *so she gave me the water and then went to check on* what, *exactly? And how did she know to come this way?*

He'd barely been able to walk, let alone ask any questions—but even in his delirium, he'd noticed how certain she was, how she'd chosen their path with unwavering precision. How could she know? She was an art buyer from New York, how could she know *anything* about the sewer system of Raccoon City?

And where is she? Why hasn't she come back?

She'd helped him, she'd most probably saved his life—but he just couldn't keep believing that she was who she said she was. He wanted to know what she was doing, and he wanted to know *now,* and not just because she'd been keeping secrets; Claire was still somewhere in the sewers, and if Ada knew the way out of the city, Leon owed it to her to try and find out.

Leon stood up slowly, holding onto the back of the chair, and took a deep breath. Still weak, but no dizziness, and his arm didn't hurt as badly, either— the aspirin, perhaps. He drew his Magnum and walked to the door of the small, dusty room, promising himself that he wasn't going to accept any more vague answers or smiling brush-offs.

He opened the door and stepped out into an open-ended warehouse almost big enough to be an aircraft hangar; it was empty, decrepit, and heavily shadowed, but the brisk night air that breezed through made it almost pleasant—

—and there was Ada, stepping onto a raised platform just outside of the hangar, disappearing behind what looked like a section of a train. It was an industrial transport lift—and from the well-oiled look of the rails that ran through the warehouse, it was one part of the abandoned factory that hadn't been completely abandoned.

"Ada!"

Keeping his wounded arm tightly pressed to his body, Leon ran toward the lift—and felt dull anger as he heard the rising thrum of the transport's engines, the heavy mechanical sound spilling out into the clear night sky. Ada was leaving, she hadn't gone to "check" on anything—

—*but she's not going anywhere until she tells me why.*

Leon ran out into the moonlit open, hearing the door to the transport slam shut as he skirted a control console and stepped up to the vibrating metal platform, nearly tripping on the brightly painted steps. Before he could catch his balance, the transport started its descent; three-foot-high panels of corrugated metal rose all the way around the train, containing the large platform as it slid smoothly down into the ground.

Leon grabbed for the door handle as the darkness swept up around the humming transport, the sky dwindling into a smaller and smaller starry patch overhead. The cool, pale light of the moon and stars was quickly replaced by the electric orange of the transport's mercury lamps.

He stumbled inside, and saw the startled look on Ada's face as she stood up from a bench bolted to one side, as she half-raised her Beretta and then lowered it again—and a flash of guilt, there and gone in the time it took for him to close the door.

For a moment, neither of them spoke, staring at each other as the room continued its smooth descent. Leon could almost *see* her working to come up with an explanation—and as tired as he was, he decided that he just wasn't in the mood.

"Where are we going?" he asked, making no effort to keep the anger out of his voice.

Ada sighed—and sat down again, her shoulders sagging. "I think it's the way out," she said quietly. She looked up at him, her dark gaze searching his. "I'm sorry. I shouldn't have tried to leave without you, but I was afraid. . . ."

He could hear real sorrow in her voice, see it in her eyes, and felt his anger give a little. "Afraid of what?"

"That you wouldn't make it. That *I* wouldn't make it, trying to keep both of us safe."

"Ada, what are you talking about?" Leon moved to the bench, sitting down beside her. She looked down at her hands, speaking softly.

"When I was looking for you, back in the sewers, I found a map," she said. "It showed what looked like some kind of an underground laboratory or factory—

and if the map was right, there's a tunnel that runs from there to somewhere outside of the city."

She met his gaze again, honestly distressed. "Leon, I didn't think you were in any condition to make a trip like that, like *this*—and I was scared that if I brought you with me, if it was a dead end or something attacked us. . . ."

Leon nodded slowly. She'd been trying to protect herself—and him.

"I'm sorry," she repeated. "I should have told you, I shouldn't have just left you there like that. After all you've done for me, I—I at least owed you the truth."

The guilt and shame in her eyes wasn't something that could be faked. Leon reached for her hand, ready to tell her that he understood and that he didn't blame her—

—when there was a resounding *thump* outside. The entire transport shook, just a slight tremble, but enough to make both of them tense.

"Probably a rough spot in the track. . . ." Leon said, and Ada nodded, gazing at him with an intensity that made him pleasantly uncomfortable, a warmth spreading through his entire body—

BAM!

—and Ada flew off the bench, thrown to the floor as a massive, curled *thing* slammed through the wall, crashing through the sheet metal of the vehicle's side as though it were made of paper. It was a fist, a fist with bone claws, each of them nearly a foot long, the claws dripping with—

"Ada!"

The giant hand withdrew, its bloody talons ripping new holes in the metal wall as Leon dropped to the floor, grabbing Ada's limp body, pulling her into the center of the transport. A terrible shriek pealed through the moving darkness outside—and it was the same furious cry that they'd heard in the station but louder, more violent—and even less human than before.

Leon held on to Ada with his one good arm, feeling the warm trickle of blood seeping out from her right side, feeling her dead weight against his heaving chest.

"Ada, wake up! Ada!"

Nothing. He lowered her gently to the floor, then pulled at the bloody hole in her dress, just above her hip. Blood was welling up from two deep punctures; there was no way to tell how bad, and he ripped at the fabric, tearing off the bottom few inches of her short dress and pressing the wadded material against the wound—

—and again the monster screamed, and the rage in its throaty howl was nothing to what Leon was feeling, staring down at Ada's still and closed face. He stretched her tight dress over the makeshift bandage, fixing it in place as best he could, then stood up and unstrapped the Remington.

Ada had taken care of him, had protected him when he couldn't protect himself. Leon loaded the shotgun grimly, feeling no pain at all as he prepared to return the favor.

When they reached what looked like the end of the line, it was Sherry who figured out where her mother must have gone. They'd walked into yet another open, shadowy room, but it only had the one door; there seemed to be no other way out of the cavernous chamber, unless Annette had jumped off the raised floor and trekked off through the unlit emptiness that surrounded them.

They stood at the edge of the darkness, trying to see down into the shadows and having no luck. The room was set up almost like a loading dock: a railed platform ran from the door along the back wall, then ended abruptly, giving way to a seemingly endless void. Either Annette had climbed down and navigated some secret path through the dark, or Claire had been mistaken about which way she'd gone.

So what now? Go back, or try to follow?

She didn't want to do either one—although going back pretty much beat the crap out of the idea of walking into a pitch-black abyss. And Leon was probably still back there somewhere . . .

"Could it be a train? Is this like a train station?" Sherry asked, and as soon as she said "train," Claire gave herself a solid mental kick in the ass.

Platform, railings, about a thousand overhead "pipes.". . .

Claire grinned at Sherry, shaking her head at her own stupidity; she was getting flaky, no doubt about it.

"Yeah, I think it is," she said, "though you guessed it, not me. My brain must be on strike. . . ."

The small computer console on one side of the platform, the one she'd dismissed as unimportant, was probably the control board. Claire headed for it,

Sherry following along and clutching absently at her gold locket as she described the noises she'd heard, down in the drainage well.

". . . and it was moving away, like a train would. It scared me pretty bad, too. It was loud."

Sure enough, just beneath the small monitor screen on the standing console was a recall command code and a ten-key. Claire tapped in the code and hit "enter"—and the chamber was filled with the smooth hum of working machinery: the sound of a train.

"You're one smart cookie, you know that?" Claire said, and Sherry practically beamed, her entire face crinkling with her sweet smile. Claire wrapped an arm around her shoulders and they walked back to the edge of the platform to wait.

The tram's light appeared after a few seconds, the tiny circle of brightness getting bigger as they watched. After the trials they'd been through, Claire decided to be as fantastically optimistic about this new development as she could—primarily to keep from worrying about what horrible thing would probably happen next. The train would lead out of the city, of course, and it would be well-stocked with food and water; it'd have showers and fresh, warm clothes—

—*nah, scratch that. A hot tub, and a couple of those thick terry robes, for after. And slippers.*

Nice, but she'd settle for anything that didn't include monsters or crazy people. She glanced at Sherry, and noticed that she was still rubbing her locket.

"So what's in there?" she asked, wanting to make Sherry smile again. "You got a picture of your boyfriend, or what?"

"Inside? Oh, it's not a locket," Sherry said, and Claire was pleased to see a faint blush rise in her cheeks. "My mom gave it to me, it's a good-luck charm—and I *don't* have a boyfriend. Boys my age are totally immature."

Claire grinned. "Get used to it, sweetie. As far as I can tell, some of them never grow out of it."

The train was close enough now for them to see its shape, a single car about twenty or twenty-five feet long riding smoothly along its overhead track.

"Where do you think it goes?" Sherry asked, and before Claire could answer, the door to the platform exploded.

The hatch blew inward, torn off its hinges in a squeal of metal and *clanging* to the floor—

—and Claire grabbed Sherry, pulling her close as the towering Mr. X stepped into the room, bending low and sideways to squeeze through the opening, his soulless gaze turning toward them at once.

"Get behind me!" Claire shouted, pulling Irons's handgun, risking a glance back at the approaching train. Ten seconds, they needed ten seconds—

—but X took a giant step toward them, and she knew they didn't have them. His bland, terrible face, expressionless, his giant hands already rising, still twenty feet away but only four steps in his massive stride—

"Get on the train when it stops!" Claire screamed, and pulled the trigger.

Four, five, six shots, beating into his chest. The seventh hit one dead-white cheek, but Mr. X didn't blink, didn't bleed—and didn't stop. Another mighty

step, the black, smoking pit in his face a testament to his inhumanity. Claire lowered her aim, *legs, knees—*
Bam-bam-bam!
—and he paused as the rounds smashed into him, at least one a direct hit to his left knee, the black eyes fixed on her, *marking* her—
"—*here, come on!*"
Sherry was pulling at her vest, screaming, and Claire backed away, squeezing the trigger again. Two more rounds hit him in the gut—
—and then she was on the train, and Sherry had found the control for the door. It *whooshed* shut, Mr. X framed in the tiny window, not coming forward anymore but still not falling. Not dying.
"Follow me!" Claire shouted, spotting the board of blinking lights to her right, knowing that the door wouldn't hold for a second if the giant, terrible creature started walking again.
She ran for the control board with Sherry at her side, thanking God that the designer had been user-friendly as the red "go" button snapped down beneath her shaking hand—
—and the train was moving, sliding away from the platform, away from the indestructible un-man and into the black.

Annette sat in the staff bunk room on level four, waiting for the mainframe to respond to the power-up and debating whether or not to initiate the P-Epsilon sequence. Once the fail-safe system was triggered, all of the connecting corridor doors would unlock, and those doors that were electronically powered would open. The creatures that had been trapped these last days would be free to roam, and most of them would be hungry . . .

. . . hungry and hot, bleeding pure virus from their clotted flesh . . .

She didn't want to run into any—unpleasantness upon her departure, but as the first lines of code spilled across the screen, she decided against running the sequence. The P-Epsilon gas was an experiment anyway, something a couple of the microbiologist techs had worked up to appease the Umbrella damage-control staff. If it worked, it would knock out the Re3s and all of the human carriers that had been infected by the initial airborne—the first wave—ensuring her a safer trip to the escape transport tunnel; but the spies were coming, and Annette didn't want to make things easy for them. She'd heard the lift being recalled as she'd stumbled her way to the synthesis lab—which was fine, great, they'd be just in time for the finale, and she wanted them fighting for their lives as she sped away from the facility, away from the brilliant explosion that would consume the multibillion-dollar facility . . .

. . . and it'll burn, it'll all burn and I'll be free of this nightmare. Endgame and I win. Umbrella loses, once and for all, the sneaking, murdering animal bastards—

She felt good, awake and aware and in very little pain; she'd meant to go straight to the nearest computer outlet upon her return to activate the fail-safe even before collecting the sample, but she'd barely been able to see straight as she'd stumbled off the lift;

she'd been afraid of forgetting something—or worse, of falling and being unable to get up again. A trip to the meds locker in the synthesis lab had fixed all that; already, the terrible pain was a distant memory, along with the bizarre, deluded thought processes that had made it so hard to concentrate. When her little cocktail shot wore off, she'd pay for the temporary reprieve, but for the next couple of hours, at least, she was as good—she was *better*—than new.

Epinephrine, endorphin, amphetamine, oh my!

Annette knew she was high, that she shouldn't overestimate her abilities, but why shouldn't she feel happy? She grinned at the small computer in front of her and started to tap in the codes, her fingers flying over the keys, feeling like her teeth would crack as the synthetic adrenaline pounded through her dilated veins. She'd made it back to the lab, William had come back, and the sample, the very last viable G-Virus sample in the facility, was tucked into her pocket. She'd hidden it in one of the fuse cases before she'd gone looking for William, and picked it up on the way to the staff room—

—76E, 43L, 17A, fail-safe time . . . 20, vocal warning/power cut, 10, personal authorization, 0001Birkin—

—and that was it. Annette couldn't stop grinning, didn't want to stop as she lightly stroked the "enter" key, the triumph a hot and liquid joy spinning through her numb and tattered flesh. One touch, and there was nothing on earth that could stop it. In ten minutes, the taped warnings would start to run, and the transport lift would shut down, cutting the facility off from the surface; in fifteen, the audio would begin the countdown—five minutes to reach the minimum safe distance by train, another five and—

Boom. Twenty minutes before the explosion. More than enough time to get to the tunnel and power up the train, no matter what is loosed; enough time to speed away from the ticking clock, beneath the city streets, through the isolated foothills at the outskirts of Raccoon. Enough time to get to the end of the track, walk out into the private plot of land, turn around—and see Umbrella lose it all.

As the clock ticked to zero, the plastique fail-safe charges in the laboratory's central power core would be activated. Even if all but one of the twelve explosive packets failed, that one blast would be enough to set off the secondary charges that were built into the walls themselves; Umbrella's fail-safe system had been designed to take it all down. The lab would become an inferno, blasting up into the dead city, visible for miles—and she'd be there to see it, to know that she'd done what she could to make things right.

This is for you, William. . . .

The thought was bittersweet . . . for some time, they hadn't—*enjoyed* their relationship as husband and wife. William was so brilliant, so devoted to the work, that the pleasures of synthesis and development had taken the place of the perks of married life. She had come to recognize his genius, to learn the joy of supporting him without the nuisance of relationship struggles—but now, her finger resting on the end to it all, she found herself suddenly wishing very much that there had been more between them in the last few years, more than her adoration for his incredible gifts, his appreciation of her assistance. . . .

This is our last kiss, my love. This is my contribution to the work, my final loving act for what we shared.

Yes, that was right, that was the *feeling*. Annette pressed the key, her heart singing, and saw the locked code flash across the monitor in glowing green.

"I respectfully tender my resignation," she said softly, and started to laugh.

†wenty-five

THE DARK SLID PAST THE MOVING PLAT-
form, metal darkness bathed in murky orange light,
and whatever had punched through the wall of the
transport was gone. Leon had edged his way around
the enclosed room twice, and seen nothing at all,
heard nothing but the smooth hum of the working
motors.

When the creature finally howled from the shadows
atop the roof, and Leon snapped the shotgun up, what
he saw actually made him freeze. In the second it took
him to really *see* it, his vengeful fury blew away like so
much dust, replaced by an absolute bone-chilling awe.

Holy shit—

The thing was still shrieking, its head thrown back,
the brutal, gurgling scream like the voice of hell in the
moving dark. It had been a man, once—arms and
legs, shreds of clothing still hanging from its hulking

body—but everything human about it had changed, was still changing as it bellowed its rage into the cold black, and Leon could only stare.

Its body was swollen and rippling with strange muscles, the bare chest puffed and bloated with its endless scream. Its right arm was six inches longer than the left, the stained bone claws jutting from the pulsing hand. And the bulbous moving tumor in its right bicep looked like nothing so much as an eyeball the size of a dinner plate, jerking wetly from side to side as if searching—

—and the scream was changing, too, getting deeper, rougher, the shaggy face falling forward—and *melting* into its chest. Like hot wax, like a movie effect, the creature's head flowed into its upper body, disappearing smoothly into the inflamed and greedy skin—

—and at the same time, another face was forming, growing, rising up from the back of its neck with a horrible *snapping* sound, like fingers being broken. Slitted eyes cracked open, a bony red hole of a mouth forming, taking up the furious cry with a new voice—

—and Leon squeezed the trigger in denial, a denial of the monster's unholy existence.

Boom!

The shot hit its chest, and a thick, purplish blood sprayed out, cutting off the creature's scream—but that was all it did. The monster's new face angled toward Leon, the domed head tilting—

—and it hopped down onto the platform, landing in a half-crouch on legs as big around as Leon's chest.

It took one jumping, crooked step forward and was close enough for Leon to smell the strange, chemical musk that poured from its glistening skin—and see that the wound on its chest had stopped bleeding, that the strange flesh was *eating* the tiny holes.

The creature raised its mighty claw and Leon stumbled backwards, pumping another round and firing as the talons came down—

—*shhink!*

—and sparks flew up from the metal rail as the shot blasted into the creature's stomach, more purplish fluid spattering from its body. The almost point-blank range of the heavy round barely fazed the towering monster. It took another step, and Leon backed away, pumping another round—

—and he tripped on the steps that led up to the transport room, tripped and fell on his ass, the round going high over the creature's bullet-shaped head. One more step and it would be on him—

—*dead I'm*—

—except it didn't take the step. Instead, it turned toward the railing, its bizarre head tilting, the pits of its rudimentary nostrils flaring—

—and silently, almost gracefully, it leapt over the edge of the platform, out into the passing darkness.

For a moment, Leon didn't move. He *couldn't,* he was too busy trying to understand that the monster hadn't killed him. It had smelled or sensed something, it had broken off the attack that it most certainly would have won—and had jumped off the moving transport.

I'm not dead. It's gone, and I'm not dead.

Why, he didn't know, and couldn't begin to guess. Accepting that he was alive was enough—and a short time later, maybe no more than a few seconds, his knotted thoughts and senses told him that the transport was slowing down, that the shaft was getting lighter, the blackness washing to gray.

Leon crawled to his feet and went to check on Ada.

Sherry had heard the monster from far away, from somewhere deep in the giant hole, and felt even more scared than she had when the giant—Mr. X, Claire called him—had come into the train station. Claire had said it probably wasn't even the monster, that it was most likely some machine problem, but Sherry wasn't convinced. The sound was so distant and strange that it *could* have been something else . . .

. . . but what if it isn't? What if Claire's wrong?

They stood outside a warehouse in the chill of the dark, stood over the big hole in the ground and waited for the mechanical noises to stop. The almost-full moon was low in the sky, and Sherry could tell by the deep blue light of the horizon that it was very early in the morning; she didn't feel tired, though. She felt scared and anxious, and even with Claire holding her hand she didn't want to go down into the black hole where the monster could be.

After what seemed like a long time, the humming noise of the machinery stopped, and Claire stepped back from the hole—the transport shaft, she said— and turned back toward the warehouse.

"Let's go see if we can recall the—Sherry?"

Sherry hadn't moved to follow her. She stared down into the hole, holding her charm and wishing that she was brave like Claire—but she wasn't, she knew she wasn't, and she didn't want to go down into the dark.

I can't, I can't go down there, I'm NOT like Claire and I don't care if that's where my mom went, I don't care at all—

Sherry felt warmth across her back and looked up, startled, to see that Claire had taken off her vest and was slipping it over her shoulders.

"I want you to have this," Claire said, and in spite of her fear, Sherry felt a sudden rush of confused happiness.

"But—why? It's yours, and you'll get cold. . . ."

Claire ignored her for a minute, helping her put it on. It was too big for her and it had some dirt on it, but it was the coolest thing Sherry thought she'd ever worn.

For me. She wants me *to have it.*

Claire knelt in front of her, now wearing only a thin black T-shirt and shorts. She looked at her very seriously, pulling the vest closed over Sherry's chest.

"I want you to have it because I can tell that you're scared," she said firmly, "and I've had it for a long time, and when I wear it, I feel like I can kick ass. Like nothing can stop me. My brother has a leather jacket with the same design on the back, and *he* kicks ass— but he got the idea from me."

She smiled suddenly, a tired, warm smile that made Sherry forget about the monster, just for a minute.

"So now it's yours, and every time *you* wear it, I

want you to remember that I think you are the best twelve-year-old who ever walked."

Sherry smiled back, hugging the faded pink denim to her body. "And it's a bribe, huh?"

Claire nodded without hesitation. "Yes. And it's a bribe. So what do you say?"

Sighing, Sherry reached for her hand, and they walked back into the warehouse to find the controls for the elevator.

Ada woke up as Leon set her gently on a creaking cot, woke up with a pounding headache and a pain in her side. Her first thought was that she'd been shot— but as she opened her eyes, and Leon's worried, pale face swam into focus, she remembered.

He was going to kiss me, I think—and then . . .

"What happened?"

Leon reached down and brushed her hair off of her forehead, smiling a little. "A monster happened. The same one that got Bertolucci, I think. It put its hand through the wall of the transport and knocked you over. You hit your head, after it—clawed you."

Virus!

Ada struggled to sit up, to look at the wound, but the headache knocked her back. She reached up and carefully touched the throbbing spot just over her left temple, wincing at the feel of the sticky lump.

"Hey, just stay put," Leon said. "The wound isn't too bad, but you took a pretty serious knock. . . ."

Ada closed her eyes, trying to collect herself. If she'd been infected, there wasn't anything she could do about it now—and really, what an irony that would be—if it *was* Birkin who'd stabbed her and he was still hot, she'd end up collecting a G-Virus sample in an extremely personal way.

Deep breath, keep it together. You're not in the transport anymore, what does that tell you?

"Where are we?" she asked, opening her eyes.

Leon shook his head. "I'm not sure. Like you said, it's an underground lab or factory of some kind. The transport is just outside. I brought you to the closest room."

Ada turned her aching head enough to see the small windows, over a cluttered counter, looking out into the transport bay.

Gotta be fourth level, where the lift stops. . . .

The main synthesis lab was on the fifth level.

Leon was staring down at her so sincerely, his bright blue gaze so achingly tender, that for just a few seconds, Ada thought about aborting the mission. They could go down to the escape tunnel together, they could hop on the train and get out of the city. They could run away, run far, far away—

—and then what? Call Trent and tell him that you'll offer a refund? Sure. Then maybe you can meet Leon's parents, get a ring, buy a little white house with a picket fence, have a couple of kids . . . you could take up crochet, and rub his feet when he comes home from a hard day busting drunks and making traffic stops. Happily ever after. . . .

Ada closed her eyes again, unable to look at him as she spoke.

"My head hurts pretty bad, Leon, and the tunnel I saw, on that map—I don't know where it is, exactly. . . ."

"I'll find it," he said softly. "I'll find it, and then I'll come back for you. Don't worry about anything, okay?"

"Be careful," she whispered, and then felt his soft lips graze her forehead, heard him stand up and move toward the door.

"Just stay here, I'll be back soon," he said, and the door opened and closed, and she was alone.

He'll be okay. He'll get lost trying to find the tunnel, he'll come back, he'll see that I'm gone and take the lift back to the surface . . . I can find the sample and escape, and it will be over.

Ada counted a minute and then sat up slowly, grimacing at the pounding in her skull. A bad knock indeed, but not a debilitating one; she could function.

There was a noise outside, and Ada stood up, walking to one of the small windows. She knew the sound even before she looked, and felt her heart sink a little; the transport was heading up, probably recalled to the factory by an Umbrella team . . .

. . . which means I don't have a lot of time. And if they find him—

No, Leon would be okay. He was a fighter, he had the sense to run from danger, he was strong and decent—and he didn't need to have someone like her in his life. She'd been crazy to consider it, even for a moment. It was time to wrap things up, to do what she'd come to do, to remember who she was—a freelance agent, a woman with no qualms about stealing or killing to complete a job, a cool and efficient thief who could take pride in a career with no misses. Ada Wong *always* walked away with the goods, and it would take more than a few hours with one blue-eyed cop to make her forget it.

Ada pulled the key cards and master from her pouch and opened the door, telling herself that she was doing the right thing—and hopeful that in time she'd come to believe it.

Twenty-Six

ANNETTE HAD RUN INTO SOME TROUBLE.

The trip down to the cargo room hadn't been bad; she'd only run across one carrier, one of the first-stagers, and had blown a hole into its ashy, withered skull with the first shot. She'd passed under a sleeping Re3, but it hadn't stirred from its ceiling bed, and it seemed that the other creatures still lurking in the facility shadows hadn't yet figured out that they were free. Either that, or more of them had disintegrated into mush than she'd imagined . . . in any case, she'd be gone before she had to worry about it either way.

In all, she made it to the cargo room hall in under three minutes, and had punched in the key code with a sense of grand accomplishment; the high from the shot was wearing off, but she was still feeling good—

—until the hatch to the cargo room refused to open. Annette had tapped the simple code in a second time, more carefully—and nothing. It was one of the only doors in all the facility that didn't open automatically on fail-safe triggering, but it shouldn't have been a problem—there was a verification disk in the slot beneath the controls, the disk that was *always* there in spite of Umbrella's insistence that only the section heads were supposed to have access—

—and of course, upon checking, she'd seen that it wasn't there, that it wasn't where it was supposed to be. Someone had taken it.

Annette stood in front of the locked hatch in the empty hall and felt the first bright tendrils of panic reach into her mind, a hysteria that she couldn't allow to take hold.

The lab's going to blow up, and I've wasted four, almost five minutes now and where's the goddamn disk?

"Easy, take it easy, you're okay, it's okay. . . ."

A gentle echo, a whisper of reason in the shining hall. She'd simply have to take the elevator from a different level; she had the master key, she had a weapon, she had time. Not as much, but enough.

Breathing deeply, Annette started back toward the hall that led to the stairs, reminding herself that all was well and that it didn't really matter, that Umbrella was going to pay whether or not she made it out alive. She didn't want to die, she wasn't *going* to die, but the gleaming, blood-splattered corridors and once-sterile labs were going to burn either way, so there was no need to panic—

—and as she turned right and moved quickly down the connecting hall, her footsteps loud and hollow in the silence, a ceiling panel crashed down in front of her—

—and an Re3, a licker, dropped to the floor and screamed for her blood.

No!

Annette fired, but only hit its scrabbling shoulder as it darted forward, reaching out with one deformed claw to swipe at her. She felt a sharp red pain in her forearm, and fired again, shocked and disbelieving—

—and the second one caught it in the throat, and it screamed, blood spraying from its torn neck, its trumpeting shriek a garbled and spitting cry as it lunged at her again.

The third shot blew into the gray jelly of its brain, and it flopped to a spasming stop just inches from her trembling legs.

Gasping as she realized how close she'd been, Annette looked down at her bleeding arm, at the thick scratches that had torn through her lab coat—

—and something gave. Something in her mind.

Her racing mind, her pounding heart, the blood and the licker, William's licker, dead on the floor in front of her—all these things whirled and danced, spinning into a circle that came together and focused into a single, stunningly simple thought. A thought that made sense of it all.

It isn't theirs.

It was so clear, so crystal clear. She couldn't run from pain, because pain would find her wherever she ran; she had proof, dripping down her arm. William had understood, but had lost himself before he could explain, before he could tell her what she really needed to do. She had to *confront* her attackers, and make sure they understood—that the G-Virus wasn't theirs—because it *didn't belong to them.*

But will they understand? Can they?

Maybe, maybe not. But she was so overwhelmed by the profound simplicity of the truth, she knew that she had to try, to make them see. The work was William's. It was his legacy, and now it was hers; she'd known that before, but now she *knew* it, a ray of light in her mind that made everything else trivial.

Not theirs. Mine.

She'd have to find them, tell them, and once they accepted the truth of it, they would have to leave her alone—and then, if there was still time, she could go her own way.

But first, she needed another shot. Smiling, her eyes wide and starry, Annette stepped over the licker and started for the stairs.

Leon thought he heard shots.

He was in some kind of a surgical bay, the first room at the end of the first passage that he'd taken after leaving Ada, and he looked up from the pile of crumpled papers he'd found, listening—but the distant *cracks* didn't repeat, so he went back to his search. He rifled quickly through the pages, desperate to find anything besides the endless lists of numbers and letters beneath the Umbrella letterhead.

Come on, there must be something useful in all this. . . .

He wanted out, he wanted to get Ada and get the hell *out.* The disemboweled corpse slumped in the corner was reason enough, but it was more than that—the very air of the room, of the hall outside the room, and, he was willing to bet, of every room in the facility, was just *wrong*. It stank like death, but worse, there was an atmosphere of something darker, something amoral. Evil.

They performed experiments here, they ran tests and God knows what else here—and they'd created a zombie plague, they'd created the monstrous demon that attacked Ada, they'd murdered an entire city. Whatever they meant to do, they were practicing evil.

—Evil on a grand scale; the transport had taken them into a secret Umbrella facility, and it was a big one. From the numbers on the walls, he knew he was on the fourth floor, whatever that meant—and the catwalk he'd taken to get to the strange operating room, only one of three choices, had stretched over what had to be sixty or seventy feet of open space, the bottom to it lost in shadow. He didn't know how deep he and Ada had come, and he didn't really care; what he wanted was a map like the one she'd found in the sewers, a clear and simple diagram with an arrow pointing to *out*.

And it ain't here. . . .

Frustrated, Leon pushed the useless papers aside—and saw there was a computer disk lying on the steel table that had been hidden beneath the stack of chemical readouts. He picked it up, frowning—"For Cargo Room Verification" was printed on the label in smudged block letters.

Sighing, Leon slipped it into his pocket and rubbed at his aching eyes with his right hand, his left arm basically useless again after carrying Ada from the lift. He didn't want to look for a computer to see what was on the disk, he didn't want to go wandering from room to room looking for the exit, seeing what atrocities Umbrella had played with before they'd shut themselves down. He was tired and in pain and worried about Ada . . . and he decided, as he walked back to the door, that he should go back and talk to her. He'd wanted to ease her mind, saying that he would find the way out, but the place was just too goddamn huge; if she even knew the direction, or could remember the floor number. . . .

Leon opened the door, stepped into the hall—

—and a woman with a gun was standing in front of him, a nine-millimeter pointed at his chest. She was bleeding, thin streams of crimson pouring from one arm and dripping down her dirty white lab coat—and the look on her face, the strange, wide-eyed glassy look that played across her features, told him that making any sudden moves would be a very bad idea.

Oh, Jesus, what is this?

"You murdered my husband," she said, "you and your partner and the girl, too—all of you, you wanted to dance on his grave but *I have news for you!*"

She was high on something, he could hear it in her high, trembling voice and see it by the way her skin twitched and ticked. He kept his hands at his sides, kept his voice low and calm.

"Ma'am, I'm a police officer, and I'm here to help, okay? I don't want to hurt you, I just—"

The woman dipped her bloody hand into her pocket and held up something, a glass tube full of some purple fluid. She grinned wildly, raising it over her head, the gun still trained on his chest.

"Here it is! It's what you want, isn't it? Listen to me, do you *hear* me? *It isn't yours!* Do you understand what I'm saying? *William* made it, and I helped him, and it doesn't belong to you!"

Leon nodded, speaking slowly. "It doesn't belong to me, you're right. It's yours, absolutely—"

The woman wasn't even listening. "You think you can take it, but I'll stop you, I'll keep you from taking it—there's plenty of time, time for me to kill you and Ada and anyone else who tries to take it!"

Ada—

"What do you know about Ada?" Leon barked, taking a half-step toward the madwoman, no longer feeling so calm. "Did you hurt her? Tell me!"

The woman laughed, a humorless, insane cackle. "Umbrella sent her, you stupid shit! Ada Wong, Miss Love-em-and-leave-em herself! She seduced John to get the G-Virus but it's not hers, either! It's *not,* it's NOT YOURS IT'S MINE—"

A massive shock rocked the floor, pitching Leon to the ground, a rumbling vibration that shook the walls—

—and *crash,* pipes and plaster rained from the ceiling, a thick beam striking the woman down with a dull *thump.* Leon covered his head as bits of concrete and white chunks of drywall slapped at him—

—and it was over. Leon sat up, staring at the woman in shock, not sure what had happened. She wasn't moving. The metal beam that had struck her still hanging from the ceiling, one of her arms pinned beneath it—

—and a cool, clear voice suddenly blared from hidden speakers somewhere in the walls—female, calm, and punctuated by the rhythmic bleat of a honking alarm.

"The self-destruct sequence has been activated. This auto-destruct sequence cannot be aborted. All personnel should evacuate immediately. The self-destruct sequence has been activated. This program cannot be aborted. All personnel should evacuate immediately—"

Leon scrambled to his feet, took one running step toward the fallen woman—then reached down and plucked the glass cylinder from her outstretched hand, shoving it into his utility pack. He didn't know who she was, but she was too crazy to be holding *anything* in a test tube.

Ada—he had to get to Ada and they had to get out. The throbbing, screeching alarms blasted through the echoing halls, chasing him through the door to the catwalk along with the indifferent-sounding female's repeating message of imminent destruction.

The recorded voice didn't say how long they had, but Leon felt quite certain he didn't want to be around when the clock ran out.

†wenty-Seven

THE COOL, DARK RIDE DOWN THROUGH THE
elevator shaft ended in a squeal of hydraulic brakes—
and then silence, as the engines shut down and
trapped them somewhere in the seemingly endless
tunnel.

"Claire? What—"

Claire held a finger to her lips, hushing Sherry—
and heard what sounded like an alarm from somewhere outside, a repeating, muffled bleat of honking
noise. There seemed to be talking, too, but Claire
could only make out the faintest mumble.

"Come on, sweetie, I think the ride's over. Let's see
where we ended up, okay? And stay close."

They moved out of the transport room and onto the
platform, the distant sounds not so distant anymore—and there was light, coming from somewhere
behind the lift. Claire took Sherry's hand as they

walked quickly around, not wanting to worry the girl but feeling pretty sure that it *was* an alarm they were hearing. There was definitely someone speaking over the rhythmic squeals, too, and Claire wanted to know what they were saying.

The lift had stopped only a few feet down from some kind of a service tunnel, the light she'd seen coming from a caged bulb that hung down from the tunnel's ceiling. There wasn't a door, but there was a decent-sized crawl space at the end of the short passage; it would have to do.

It's either that or climb back to the surface, probably only a mile or so up. . . .

Not a chance. Claire boosted Sherry up and then climbed after her, moving to the front and then crouch-walking to the dark hole. The bleating sound got louder the closer she got to the crawl space, the mumble transforming into a woman's voice. She strained to hear the words, hoping that she'd catch "elevator malfunction" and "temporary"—but she still couldn't make it out. They'd have to abandon the lift and hope that they were leaving it for something better.

Claire swiveled around, sighing. "Looks like crawl time for me and thee, kiddo. I'll go first, and then—"

SLAM!

Sherry shrieked as something landed on the roof of the transport behind them, crashing through the top in a thundering clap of rending metal. Claire grabbed her, pulling her close, her breath caught in her throat—

—and a hand, two hands appeared through the hole in the roof. Two thick arms, clad in shadow—

—and the gleaming white of Mr. X's enormous skull rose up from the destroyed lift, like a dead moon on a starless night.

Claire turned and pushed Sherry toward the darkness of the crawl space, her heart hammering, her body suddenly slick with sweat.

"Go! Go, I'm right behind you!"

Sherry disappeared into the curving black, darting out of sight like a frightened mouse, and Claire didn't look back, was too scared shitless to look back as she followed Sherry into the hole, their relentless stalker surely climbing through the shattered elevator to continue his determined and unfathomable hunt.

Ada had heard pieces of Annette's screaming rant from the shadows of the catwalk hub, where the three metal spans joined. She'd forced herself not to rush to Leon's aid, promising herself that if she heard shots, she'd reconsider—

—but then the laboratory facility had been violently shaken, and the bland voice of the recording started its loop.

Shit!

Ada staggered to her feet, furious at the woman scientist, a part of her aching for Leon, knowing what this meant. Annette had triggered the fail-safe, which meant they probably had less than ten minutes to get the hell out of Dodge—

—*and Leon doesn't know the way.*

No, not important. If she was going to collect the

sample, which Annette surely had on her, she needed to do it *now*. Leon wasn't her problem, he'd never *been* her problem, and she couldn't quit now, not after the hell she'd been through to get Trent's precious virus.

Ada took a single step away from the main fuse panel that connected the three catwalks—and heard the pounding footsteps coming toward her, footsteps too heavy to be Annette's. She slid back into the shadows and around to the span that led west, pressing herself against the hub's frame.

A second later, Leon went running past, probably back to where he thought she'd be waiting for him. Ada took a deep breath, blowing it out as she swept Leon from her mind, and hurried across the southern bridge to find Annette.

Ada was gone.

"—has been activated. This auto-destruct sequence—"

"Shut up, shut *up*—" Leon hissed, standing helplessly in the middle of the room, his stomach knotted, his hands balled into fists.

When she'd heard the alarm, she must have panicked and run. She was probably stumbling through the giant facility, lost and dazed, maybe looking for him as that infernally calm voice repeated, as the sirens blared and rang.

The transport lift!

Leon turned and ran back through the door—and saw that it was gone, a large empty hole a few feet deep where it had been. He'd been too intent on getting to Ada, he hadn't even noticed that it wasn't there anymore—

—we have to find that tunnel, we have to! Without the lift, we're trapped here!

With a silent howl of frustration, Leon turned and ran back toward the catwalks, praying that he would find her before it was too late.

The crawl space ended abruptly, stopping over at least a seven-foot drop to an empty tunnel. Her ears ringing, her mouth dry as dust, Sherry grabbed the edges of the square hole, closed her eyes, and jumped.

She swung out over the hall and let go as soon as she was straight up and down, landing crooked and falling as her right leg crumpled. It hurt, but she hardly felt it, scrambling on hands and knees to get out of the way, staring up at the hole—

—and there was Claire, her head coming out, her wide, worried eyes taking in that she was okay, that the hall was empty and safe . . . except that there were bells ringing and a woman on an intercom was talking, and Mr. X was coming.

Claire stretched her arm down as far as she could with the gun. "Sherry, I need you to hold this, I can't turn around."

Sherry stood and reached up, grabbing the barrel, amazed at how heavy the gun was as Claire let go.

"Don't point it at anything," Claire breathed, and then she actually *dove* out of the hole, curling her body and landing on her shoulder, her head tucked in tight. She did a half-somersault and then her legs banged into the concrete wall.

Before Sherry could even ask if she was all right, Claire was on her feet, taking the gun and pointing to the door at the end of the hall.

"Run!" she said, and started to run herself, one hand pushing on Sherry's back as they sprinted for the door, as the intercom voice told them to get out, told them that a self-destruct sequence had been activated—

—and behind them, a sound of crashing metal tore through the blaring noise of the sirens, and Sherry ran faster, terrified.

Twenty-Eight

ANNETTE BIRKIN CRAWLED OUT FROM BE-
neath the crushing weight of the cold metal, still
holding the gun, the G-Virus gone. As she opened her
mouth to scream her fury, to rail to the Gods at the
injustice of her terrible plight, blood dribbled out
across her lips in a thick streamer of clotted drool.

—mine mine mine—

Somehow, she made it to her feet.

Ada told herself that she didn't deserve Leon Kennedy's good opinion anyway. She'd never deserved it.

Forgive me . . .

As he ran back across the catwalk from the transport bay area and swung west, running blind with fear
for her, she stepped out of the hub's shadows and
pointed the Beretta at his back.

"Leon!"

He spun around, and Ada felt her throat lock at the relief that spread across his face—and struggled not to feel anything more as the joy turned sour, his grin fading.

Oh, Jesus, forgive me!

"I've been waiting for you," she said, and felt no pride at how smooth and steady her voice sounded. How very cold.

The alarms blared, the mechanical voice almost as icy as hers, telling them that the fail-safe couldn't be shut down. She didn't have time to let him get used to the idea, that she was as much a monster as the Birkin-thing or one of the soulless zombies.

"The G-Virus," she said. "Give it to me."

Leon didn't move. "She was telling the truth," he said, no anger but more pain than Ada wanted to hear. "You work for Umbrella."

Ada shook her head. "No. Who I work for is no concern of yours. I—I—"

For the first time in years, since she'd been a very young girl, Ada felt the sting of tears—and suddenly she hated him for that, for making her hate herself.

"I tried!" she wailed, her composure blown by the fierce torrent of anger that coursed through her. "I tried to leave you, back in the factory! And you had to take it from Birkin, didn't you, you couldn't just leave it alone!"

She saw pity on his face, and felt the fury pass, swept away on a wave of sorrow—for what she'd lost, with him; for the part of herself she'd lost a long, long time ago.

She wanted to tell him about Trent. About the

missions in Europe and Japan, about how she'd become what she was, about every event in her miserable, successful life that had brought her to this place—holding a weapon on a man who'd saved her. A man she might have cared about, in a different time and place.

The clock was ticking.

"Hand it over," she said. "Don't make me kill you."

Leon stared into her eyes, and said, simply, "No."

A second gone, then another.

Ada lowered the Beretta.

Leon steeled himself for the shot, for the bullet from Ada's gun that would kill him—

—and she slowly lowered the weapon, her shoulders sagging, a tear running down one porcelain cheek.

Leon blew out his held breath, feeling too many things, a jumble of sadness and betrayal—and pity, for the tortured struggle in her beautiful dark gaze—

—and a shot rang out from the shadows behind her. Ada's eyes went wide, her mouth falling open as she pitched forward, the gun hitting the floor, her body hitting the rail and flipping over.

"Ada, no!"

He ran and dove, and somehow she caught the rail as he grabbed her wrist, her body dangling over the bottomless dark, blood spouting from her hanging, shattered shoulder.

"Ada, hold on!"

* * *

"Mine," Annette whispered.

She raised the handgun again, intending to shoot the other, to take back what was hers, to make them all pay—

—and the gun was too heavy, it was falling, and she was falling with it. Together, they fell to the dark metal, the dark, the dark spinning up into her mind and finally taking her pain away.

William—

It was her very last thought before she went to sleep.

The door opened into a room filled with screaming machines, the howls and hisses of the humming, rattling giants drowning out the shrill call of the alarm warning.

Claire ran, pulling and pushing Sherry along, looking desperately for a way out, knowing that the monster was close.

What does he want, why us?

There, a platform in the corner some six feet off the floor, a stack of crates pushed to one side just beneath it.

"This way!" Claire screamed, and they ran, past the rows of shuddering metal consoles, heat pouring from the machines as Claire pushed Sherry up and then climbed after her.

Crash!

She turned, saw that the massive creature was ripping through the door across the room, striding into the screaming heat and searching, searching—

At the end of the platform, a double metal hatch. They dashed for it, Claire not thinking of anything but how to get away, how to destroy a thing that had survived all that it had—

—the door was unlocked, and they ran onto another platform; the heat in the shadowy chamber was searing, terrible—

—and a dead end. Claire saw that before they'd taken a half-dozen running strides into the massive room. They were on the overseer's platform in a foundry, the boiling heat rising up from the heavy smelting vats below.

She had twelve bullets, split between two guns.

Claire stumbled to the edge of the platform, Sherry next to her, the electric orange of the molten metal bathing them in its fevered glow. Hot enough to burn anything. . . .

How? How do I make him jump?

"Sherry, go over there!"

She pointed to the farthest corner of the platform, and Sherry shook her head, her small face trembling with fear.

"Do it! Now!" Claire shouted, and with a cry of terror, Sherry ran, her locket banging against the open flaps of the denim vest—

—*not a locket*—

—and Sherry screamed, and Claire turned, and Mr. X was coming.

He walked into the chamber, as stiff and huge and impossible as when she'd first seen him, the eerie orange light turning him into even more of a nightmare. Claire stood her ground, jamming Irons's gun into her shorts, the half-formed plan running through her frightened mind. It probably wouldn't work but she had to try—

—he reaches for me, I jump over the railing, I grab on, he falls—

Mr. X turned his blank gaze toward her as he took his floor-shaking, measured steps, the black bullet holes in his face and throat just pockets of shadow in the smooth, terrible pumpkin light—

—and he turned toward Sherry, and raised his fists, and started for her.

"Hey! Hey, I'm here!" Claire screamed, and he didn't hear her, didn't *see* her, his entire monstrous being focused on the cowering, sobbing girl huddled against the far wall, clutching her locket—

—and Claire knew what he wanted. The half remembered phrases from both Sherry and Annette came together in a flash of awareness, forming the answer.

G-Virus, rip her apart, good luck charm—

Not a locket.

"Sherry, he wants the necklace! Throw it to me!"

If she was wrong, they were both dead. Mr. X closed in on the girl, blocking her from Claire's view—

—and the pendant, the G-Virus pendant that Annette Birkin had inflicted on her young daughter came flying through the heated dark, hitting the floor in front of Claire's feet.

Mr. X reeled around, following the path of the thrown pendant with his black eyes, forgetting Sherry the second the necklace left her grasp. It was true.

Good girl!

S. D. PERRY

Claire scooped it up, waving it at the monster, feeling a rush of incredible anger and malicious glee as the bloated giant started toward her with unwavering intent, fists raising again, his lifeless features fixed on the glittering pendant.

"You want this?" Claire taunted, the words spilling out of the fury, for the wasted bullets, for the fear that she and Sherry had suffered. "Yeah? Then come and get it, you miserable, mindless *freak!*"

The monster was less than five feet away when Claire turned and threw it into the bubbling, burning hot pool, the necklace disappearing into the melted iron—

—and the superman creature that had terrorized them throughout the endless night walked straight into the rail, the metal bars snapping in his all-powerful wake—

—and plunged silently into the giant vat, a great wave of sizzling metal sloshing over the blackened sides, spontaneous eruptions of flame dancing up from the dark shape of his body as he disappeared beneath the surface of the molten lake.

Triumph, sweet and wonderful—and then the cool voice of the recording changed suddenly, wiping away the joy of seeing Mr. X take a lava bath.

Over the shrill blasts of the mechanical sirens—

"There are five minutes to reach minimum safe distance. All remaining personnel should evacuate immediately. Please report to the bottom platform. Repeat, please report to the bottom platform. Repeat. . . ."

Sherry was at her side, and Claire grabbed her hand, and they ran.

The pain was incredible, and Ada closed her eyes, wondering if she would die from it.

"Ada, hang on! Just hang on, I'll pull you up!"

Through the throbbing, pounding sirens that assaulted her ears, Ada heard the countdown for the fail-safe start to run. Five minutes.

He tries to save me, we both die.

Leon's grip was strong, the determination in his panicked, pleading voice almost as strong as her own will. Almost, but not quite.

Ada turned her face up to his, saw that in spite of it all, he still wanted her to survive, he wanted to help her up and carry her away to the safety of escape.

Not this time. Not for me. . . .

Her life had been about selfishness, about ego and greed. She'd seen a lot of good people die, and somewhere along the way, she'd lost the ability to care—telling herself that even the effort was a waste of time and a sign of weakness.

And I was wrong, I was selfish and wrong and now it's too late.

Not too late. Whatever waited beneath her, the decision was made.

"Leon—go down, west, and find the cargo room, past the—row of plastic chairs. You'll need the disk, it's in my—pouch—"

"Ada, I have it! Cargo disk, right, I have it, I found it—don't talk, just hold on, let me help you!" He fumbled at the rail, trying to maintain his grip.

Talking was a horrible effort, but she had to finish, had to tell him before time ran out.

"The code is 345. Get to the elevator, Leon. Take it down. The subway—tunnel leads out. Have to—run full throttle . . . and watch out for Birkin, the G-carrier, he—he's changing by now. Got it?"

Leon nodded, his blazing blue eyes filling her up.

"Live," she said, and it was a good word, a word to go out on. She was tired, and the mission was wrapped, and Leon would live.

She let go of the railing, and Leon screamed her name, and the sound of it followed her down into the dark like a bittersweet good-bye.

Twenty-Nine

SHERRY WAS SCARED, BUT MR. X WAS DEAD
and he must have been the monster all along, not the
one at the station but the *real* monster, the one that
had wanted to rip her apart all along—

—but she didn't have time to think about it as
Claire sprinted, jerking her along back the way they'd
come, through the machine room, through the hall
with the crawl space and around a corner—

—and Sherry screamed as a zombie reeled toward
them, a dead white creature made of dusty bone, and
Claire raised her gun and shot—

—*bang,* and the dry white head caved in, the
moaning dead creature crumpled to the floor, and
then Claire was dragging her over the body and
running for the door at the end of the hall.

It was an elevator, and Sherry collapsed against one
wall after Claire pulled her inside, trying to catch her

breath as Claire punched the controls. After the speed of their run from Mr. X, the elevator's descent was a crawl, a softly humming crawl.

"We're gonna make it," Claire gasped, "just a little longer."

Sherry nodded, her heart pounding even harder as the intercom voice told them that they had four minutes left to be safe.

Leon felt like he didn't know how to stand up and walk away. The image of her composed, beautiful face in the second before she'd let go . . . *she's gone. Ada's dead.*

He reached for the Beretta, fresh grief washing over him as he picked it up, the weapon still warm from her touch—and it was too light, too light by half because it wasn't loaded. There wasn't even a clip. She'd never meant to hurt him; she'd lied, she'd lied all along, but she'd never meant to hurt him at all.

". . . are four minutes to reach minimum safe distance. All remaining personnel should evacuate immediately. Please report to the bottom platform . . ."

Four minutes. He had four minutes to get far enough away to fulfill Ada's last request.

He stood up and turned for the door—and stopped, reaching into his pocket, pulling out the tiny glass tube full of purple fluid. He knew he didn't have time to spare, but it only took a second to pull his arm back and throw the sample as hard as he could, wanting it as far away from him as possible.

If the laboratory responsible for so much death was going to burn, let the G-Virus burn with it.

"Yes!"

The elevator door opened—and there was a train, a secret subway train in shining silver. It was silent and dark, not the powered-up, thrumming machine that Claire had hoped to see, but it was still the most beautiful escape vehicle that she'd ever laid eyes on, hands down.

Sherry holding on to her arm, they ran to the door at the front of the three-car subway, the bleating alarms still sounding, echoing through the concrete tunnel. The woman's bland voice, the voice that Claire had started to hate long moments ago, informed them that they had three minutes to get to the minimum safe distance.

They hurried aboard, Claire noticing and not caring that there weren't any seats, just a wide, empty space for the passengers to stand in. The control booth was to the left.

"Let's get this show on the road," Claire said, and the bright and radiant look of hope on Sherry's dirty, tired face made Claire's heart break, just a little.

Oh, baby . . .

Claire looked quickly away, hopping up the steps to the control room, making a silent promise to herself that if the train didn't work, she'd carry Sherry through the tunnel herself. Whatever it took to see that the fragile hope in her eyes wasn't broken.

* * *

The code and the verification disk he'd found in the operating room opened the door just as Ada had said, the broad hatch opening into a short hall. With three minutes left, Leon dashed down the cold corridor, through another overwide door, a biohazard symbol emblazoned across the front, and found himself in the cargo room.

He didn't have time to stop and get a good look, his focus on getting to the elevator before the recording told him he couldn't possibly get out of the facility alive. Leon ran to the back of the wide, strangely red-tinted room, found the controls for the large warehouse-type elevator, and slapped the button for down, ready to jump in and go—

—and nothing happened, except that a row of tiny lights—perhaps *twenty* tiny lights over the elevator door—started to flash in descending order. Slowly.

Leon reached forward and slapped the button again, feeling something like numb disbelief as the elevator crept down, pausing for what seemed like minutes between floors, as the alarms blared and the countdown to the lab's destruction ticked closer and closer to the end.

"Jesus!" He turned around, feeling like he'd scream if he had to wait much longer—

—and for the first time, got a clear look at the room he was in. The two tall, wide shelves that ran the length of the chamber held a very specific kind of "cargo"—and although the half-dozen giant glass containers that lined each shelf held nothing but clear red fluid, Leon felt a chill just looking at them. Each cylinder was large enough to hold a full-grown man, and it made him wonder what they'd been built for.

Doesn't matter, they're gonna be blown to shit in a matter of minutes, and so am I if this goddamn thing doesn't hurry UP—

He turned back to the elevator, almost glad to be angry, frustrated, to have something to feel besides loss—

—and the ceiling over the elevator started to shake and rattle . . . Leon backed away, pointing his Magnum at the solid metal ceiling panel as it *crashed* down and out—

—and the monster from the transport lift landed in front of him, the same demonic creature that had hurt Ada, that should have killed him—

Birkin—?

—and from the way it threw back its strange head and howled, the vicious, feral sound drowning out the buzz of the alarms, he could tell it had come to finish the job.

The subway was ready, it was powered up and ready to go—except it seemed that the tunnel gate release had malfunctioned; a console full of green lights, and a single red dot that insisted the gate needed to be opened manually.

Two minutes to safe minimum distance.

Won't make it, we'll never make it—

"Stay here," Claire said, and went outside to find the release, praying that it was nothing.

* * *

Leon turned and ran as the monster started walking toward him, each powerful stride thundering through the chamber, the echoes of its terrible shriek still spinning through the room.

Think!

The powerful shotgun hadn't been enough, he had to hit it someplace vulnerable, *the eyes, use the Magnum—*

Leon was back at the door. He spun and fired, aiming the Magnum at the creature's face—

—except that the face was changing again, the jaw dropping, falling away as it screamed. Great jagged spikes of tooth or claw slid out from what was left of the mouth, from out of the top of its pulsating chest—and as another scream burst out of its mutating throat Leon saw two new arms unfurl from its sides. The limbs snapped into place, elbows locking, thick worms of taloned fingers growing from the tips.

Bam-bam-bam!

The shots grouped tight, blowing into the thin-stretched skin over its slitted left eye. The monster roared, this time in pain, and Leon saw shards of bone and pus-purple fluid splatter out, a small stream of dark blood obscuring the yellow ball of its eye.

It shook its head back and forth, flinging more liquid, squatting down on its haunches like a mutant frog—

—and leapt into the air, springing up and right, landing on one of the seven-foot-high shelves with an animal grunt.

Oh shit, how'd it do that—

He couldn't see its eyes, couldn't see anything but its back as it slumped down—but it was changing again, he could hear the wet *snapping* sounds and see the knobs of spine rising up through the purpled flesh of its back.

He didn't want to see what it was becoming, but the elevator hadn't landed yet, and he had two goddamn *minutes.*

Leon grabbed another clip and slapped it home, then fired at what he could see—a shape with six legs, a shape that no longer looked like anything human.

The shot hit one of its muscular shoulders, and the creature jumped. Like some wild, spidering beast it leapt back to the floor, landing a few feet in front of him. Its chest had become a wall of strange teeth, of spikes that opened and closed as it panted—and when it screamed again, the sound was a demon cry, like nothing he'd ever heard, like the dying screams of a thousand damned souls.

Leon got two shots off into the cluster of moving teeth and stumbled away, and beneath the constant blare of the sirens, he heard the bright and cheery *ping* of the elevator's arrival.

Claire ran to the front of the train, looking at the series of levers and switches set into the tunnel wall, frowning, finding the red and white handle in less than ten seconds and slamming it down. She heard the grating of metal somewhere in front of the train and turned to run back to the door—

—when she heard metal again—the ripping, tearing sounds of steel being bent and hammered out of shape, coming from somewhere behind the subway, from somewhere in the back of the tunnel—

No, no way.

She stared toward the back of the train, past the metal bars of a closed gate that led back into shadows—and heard a sound like bone on concrete, a grinding heavy noise that repeated, and again.

Footsteps.

Claire ran for the door, knowing that it couldn't be X, absolutely could *not*—he was melted, gone, and they didn't have the G-Virus anymore—

—and she caught a glimpse of movement past the bars of shadow some thirty feet away. A glimpse of something tall, wisps of smoke curling through the darkness—and the bitter, choking stench of something burned. It stepped out of shadow, stepped toward the back of the train car, raising charred, massive fists—

BAM!

—and the car actually rocked, as Claire realized that it was Mr. X, or what was left of him—and that he was surely a demon straight from hell.

She'd combined the clips on their elevator ride; eleven rounds left; there was no way it would be enough, but it was all they had.

Claire raised Irons's gun, wondering if this was the end.

Leon ran, around the shelf to his right, heading back for the elevator, and there were galloping, thundering footsteps *right behind,* he couldn't stop.

Another turn, back through the middle of the room—

—and he was hit in the back, propelled forward and down as the beast rammed him, hot, rubbery flesh slamming him into the floor.

Leon rolled and it was on top of him, its dripping teeth poised to drive through his skull, its thick legs pinning him down. The tumor like an eye was still there, opening out of the shoulder, *looking* at him—

—and he jammed the barrel of the weapon against its drooling chin and pulled the trigger, screaming, emptying the heavy rounds into its thrashing head.

The beast shrieked, flailing, falling sideways off Leon. In a flash, he was up and running, straight for the open elevator. The enormous, freakish animal was still howling as Leon sprinted into the lift and turned, hitting the control marked down—

—and saw the beast shuddering, changing, screaming, and spitting chunks of bone and flesh and blood as it also turned and started for the elevator. It picked up speed with each staggering step, the door closing slowly, the terrible creature almost flying now—

—and Leon had the shotgun in his hands, pumped a shot and squeezed. The blast hit its barrel chest, knocking it back—

—and the door closed, Leon was going down, and there was only one minute left.

THIRTY

BAM!

Sherry felt the train rock violently all around her.

Claire!

She ran to the door, remembering that Claire said not to leave and not caring; she didn't know what it was or what she could do to help, but she couldn't just *stand* there—

BAM!

—and the car shifted again, another loud, banging crash blasting through the stale air, the floor trembling beneath her feet. Sherry reached the door and hit the open switch, her heart hammering, sweat dribbling through the dirt on her face.

The door slid open—and there was Claire, pointing her gun at something Sherry couldn't see, something at the back of the car.

Claire's gaze flickered to her, and her shouted words quaked with fear and panic.

"Don't come out! Shut the door!"

Sherry reached for the controls and hesitated, terrified for Claire, wanting to see what it was—

—*quick look*—

—and she darted her head out, just for a second, searching for the source of Claire's fear, for whatever was slamming into the train car. A smell like chemicals and burnt meat had filled the dimly lit platform, coming from—

Sherry screamed when she saw it, when she saw the tattered, charred monster that was rocking the subway, just past a wall of metal bars. She saw its giant fist pound the steel wall of the train, but it was the monster's face that she couldn't look away from.

Mr. X.

The skin was burnt away from his face, from his whole body. Smoke drifted up from the blackened, melted lump of his skull, but the eyes were still alive—red and black and steaming with acrid smoke, but still very much alive.

"Sherry! *Do it, now!*" Claire screamed, not taking her gaze from the smoking monster, from its terrible, giant body coated with red, metallic muscle, as red and burnt as its awful eyes.

Sherry hit the controls, the door closing as Claire started to fire.

The elevator *did* go down, though not as Leon had expected, and not nearly as fast as he needed it to go.

The wide platform slipped down an angled tunnel, like a slide, neon gridwork on black walls humming past. Slowly.

". . . now forty seconds to reach minimum safe distance."

"Go go go—" Leon breathed, every ache and pain in his body forgotten in the rising dread that beat at his brain. The voice had stopped telling him to report to the bottom platform, now only making announcements in ten-second increments. As much as he loathed the repeated instructions, it was much worse not hearing them; the silences between the statements were telling him not to bother trying.

To make it this far and then die because of a slow elevator. . . . He couldn't accept that. He'd been through too much. The car crash, Claire, the running and the monsters and Ada and Birkin—he *had* to make it, or it was all for nothing.

There didn't seem to be a real floor beneath the descending platform, or he would've tried it on foot—but the lift seemed to be lowering by grooves cut into either side of the darkness, by some mechanism that he couldn't begin to guess at.

". . . twenty seconds to reach . . ."

Leon started to shake, the tension running through his muscles, tightening them, making it hard to breathe. What was safe distance? When that cool, inhuman voice reached zero, how long before the explosion?

Full throttle, she said full throttle—

The train would have to be fast. And he had ten

seconds left to get to it, as the strange elevator continued its smooth, unhurried trek down into the dark.

The door slid shut and Sherry was safe. For the moment. Claire's thoughts had kicked into overdrive, spinning through her limited options in a flash.

Can't let him knock it off the tracks—

She knew she couldn't hope to injure the creature, but she might be able to distract it long enough for them to get away. She wished she'd bothered to show Sherry the simple controls for the train, wished that the train was already moving, taking Sherry to safety—

—but I didn't and we have to go NOW.

The recorded message was counting down the final ten seconds to reach a safe distance. As the smoking remains of Mr. X dealt another hammering blow to the dented subway wall, Claire aimed for its mutant head and fired.

Five shots, four of them smacking into the bizarre material that made up its flesh, about where a human's ear would be. The fifth went wide, and as the explosive thunder echoed through the shadows of the chill platform, the thing that she'd dubbed Mr. X turned slowly toward her.

Now what?

The recorded female voice distracted her for a split-second, as Mr. X took a single step toward her, a lumbering, monstrous step that pulled it out of the shadows.

". . . three. Two. One. Safe distance minimum now required. Self-destruct will occur in five minutes. There are now five minutes until detonation."

The alarms still blared, but at least the voice had shut up. She wouldn't have noticed in any case, her wide-eyed gaze fixed on the creature. It was hideous, all the more so for its still humanoid shape, like a mockery of reality, of sanity. In spite of the charred, smoking patches that covered most of its body, its unnatural flesh hadn't lost its elasticity; the reddish matter beneath the burns flexed and contracted like real muscle. It looked like a skinned giant that had crawled from beneath a burning building—and if it had suffered from its molten metal bath, she couldn't see it. Another mighty step, and the arms rose, the barred gate was ripped down, the iron bars were crashing to the concrete.

Slow at least, at least there's still that—

It was the only thing she had going for her. Claire sprinted for the subway door, still afraid, but the smoking monster was slow, powerful but unable to really move—

—and suddenly, Mr. X wasn't just walking anymore. The creature bent at the waist, bent its knees—

—and pushed off the ground in a dynamic lunge that tore gouges in the concrete, its deformed feet propelling it toward her at a full run.

Claire didn't think. She dodged right and took off past the hunched, loping monster, running as fast as she could. It almost got her anyway, its reflexes faster than fast—as if losing its facade of skin had freed it somehow, the liquid metal paring it down to its core strength. As she leapt over the broken gate and into the shadows, she heard the screech of not-flesh fingers raking across the cement, saw that Mr. X had brought one mighty arm up, slashing through the air where she'd been only a second before. It meant to *disembowel* her—

—but why, no G-Virus, no reason—

Claire ran deeper into the echoing darkness as the intercom system calmly informed her that they had four minutes left.

"There are now four minutes until detonation. . . ."

Shit shit shit!

Just when he thought he might have a stroke from the frustration, the elevator had finally stopped. Leon jerked at the handle to a thick metal door, tensing himself to run—

—and the door opened into one wall of a passage, a sterile concrete corridor lit by flickering overhead bars. And there were no signs telling him which way to go.

Left or right?

The few seconds that he hesitated could cost him his life—*if* he still had any chance at all.

He'd heard once that when faced with a choice, most people instinctively turned in the direction of their dominant hand. With the crappy luck he'd had throughout his long, long night in Raccoon, he decided to go the other way.

Left. Leon ran, his boots pounding the floor, wondering if he should even bother.

* * *

Not far past the broken gate, Claire saw a walkway that crossed over the train, the stairs hidden by deep shadow—

—and she heard the pounding of Mr. X behind as it started after her, each running step a violent slap of mutant flesh against cement. The terror drove her on, her feet hardly touching the ground, not caring if she ran head-on into a wall in the deepening dark. Maybe that would be best, it was tremendously powerful, it was fast, it was impossible to kill—she didn't stand a chance if it caught her—

—and the steps were getting louder, faster, she heard the ripping scrape of its clawed fingers plowing up concrete. She had maybe a second before that hand tore into her—

—and she dodged right again, throwing herself into a well of darkness just past the stairs. Mr. X flew past, a mammoth, hulking blur, and she actually felt the wind from his moving hand whisper against her leg as she hit the cold floor.

Sharp pain shot up her arm, her elbow cracking hard against the cement. She ignored it, jumping to her feet, searching for the monster in the dark.

Can it see, does it see me?

Her hand found an angled wall to the right, cement against her back and on the left. She was in the space beneath the stairs, and she had no idea where the impossibly silent X was; the shadows wouldn't help her if it could see in the dark.

She ran her hands over the walls, found a switch and punched it. The texture of shadow changed as dim light filtered down from somewhere above—and she saw the monster less than fifty feet away just as it turned, its thick red gaze scanning evenly across the deserted platform—

—and finding her. Marking her. The only sound was a soft crackling coming from its still-smoking flesh—until it took a step for the stairwell, and cement crunched beneath one purpled leg.

Six or seven shots left, get the eyes—

Claire stepped quickly out of the shadows and raised Irons's gun, squeezing the trigger, backing toward the stairs.

Bam-bam-bam—

—and X was positioning itself for another attack, the bullets smashing into its melted face, two of them ricocheting from the matter of its skull as it aligned to her position.

—bam-bam—

She was at the stairs, sidling up a step, the rounds useless, Mr. X starting its lurching run. It would be on her before she could turn, before she could get up the steps.

—I'll die—

—but at least I'll hurt it first—

Mr. X took one—two powerful strides, halving the distance between them as Claire aimed, determined to make the last shots count. She would die, and her only regret was for Sherry, her only wish that she would be able to incapacitate the nightmare X before it killed her.

She fired, and the monster's left eye exploded, a burst of inky fluid splattering its wretched, inhuman face.

Yes!

Mr. X veered to its right, not stopping but not coming straight at her anymore—it would still hit the base of the stairs—too close!—she had to try for the other eye and she had about two seconds left—

Claire aimed, found her mark, and—

—*click!*

—there were no bullets left, and the monster was slamming into the base of the steps, the smell of roasted meat washing over her as it raised its giant hand up, and its giant, terrible body was all she could see.

Claire rolled down the concrete stairs, hunching herself into a ball—

—and screamed as Mr. X's ragged clawed fingers raked across her left thigh, and a distant voice told her that they had three minutes left.

Thirty-One

HE'D GONE THE WRONG WAY. TWISTS AND turns in the cold and empty hall had led him to a storage room—a dead end.

"There are now three minutes until detonation."

Leon turned back the way he'd come, and with what felt like the very last of his strength, forced himself into a stumbling run. He was too exhausted to feel disappointed, to worry about his impending death, to wish that things were different; it took all of his energy just to keep moving.

He'd make it or he wouldn't; either way, he didn't think he'd be surprised.

Claire hit the floor at the base of the stairs and leapt to her feet, blood running down her leg in a hot pulse of stinging pain. She staggered away, nothing broken—

—but she knew her clawed leg was just the beginning of what it would do to her, a prelude to the real pain.

Mr. X was still bent over the railing of the steps, but as she stumbled away, back toward the broken gate of the platform, the monster pushed itself off. It turned its immense body in her direction, the open blackness of its empty eye socket drooling out some dark and ichorous liquid. It would compensate for its altered senses, she was sure—it would compensate, realign, run at her again—and would slaughter her like the merciless machine it was, there was nothing she could do to stop it.

At least I'll die in the explosion—

Claire tripped on the metal bars of the gate, barely catching herself, blood pattering to the ground as she staggered another step, *please let it be quick—*

"Here! Use this!"

Claire spun, saw that Mr. X was positioning itself for its killing strike—and saw the silhouette high above, on the walkway over the train. A woman's voice, a woman's shape, the shadowed figure throwing something—

—who—

—that clattered across the concrete, landing between her and Mr. X. It was metal, it was silver—she'd seen them in movies, it was a *machine* gun—and Claire ran for it. Another final hope, another chance, however slim, that she and Sherry would survive.

She reached the weapon, dropped, saw X pushing

itself toward her, the thunder of its steps shaking the ground—

—and she scooped up the heavy gun, kicking against the floor and rolling onto her back, her shaking hand finding the trigger, her body moving to accommodate the weapon. Stock on the ground, arms twisted around the cold metal, aiming—

—*please please*—

The monster was only a step away when the spray of bullets crashed out of the gun, a clattering, rattling string of tiny explosions that shook Claire's entire body—and whammed into the gut of the beast, the sheer force of so many rounds stopping it in mid-stride—and pushing it back.

—*tattatattatatta*—

She felt the vibrating metal trying to shake itself free of her grip, so she held it tighter, the butt of the weapon tapping against the floor at a manic pace. The bullets were still pounding into the creature's abdomen, so fast and so many that she couldn't hear her own gasping cries of fury and pain and exaltation—

—and Mr. X was trying to move forward, but a strange thing was happening, a strange and beautiful thing. Its gut was being *shredded* by the endless stream of rounds, its midsection gaining depth and texture, black fluids coursing down its lower half from the ragged, growing wound. X's mouth was open, an empty hole like its eye socket—and like the socket, thick liquid was pouring out, obscuring its pitiless face.

—*tattatattatat*—

Claire held on, directing the hail, watching the creature try to stand against the pulsing, crashing spray. Watching it bleed. Watching as it seemed to— *condense*, its massive body crumpling, its torso sinking down.

The bullets still flying, Mr. X raised its arms—

—and split in two.

Claire took her finger off the trigger as X's upper body toppled to the cement, a wet *slap* of heavy meat, and its legs collapsed, falling to one side, more strange blood gushing from both halves. Pools of shiny black grew around the massive pieces of its broken body, forming stinking puddles. The creature was dead— and even if it wasn't, it didn't matter anymore. Unless it could pull itself across the floor as fast as she could run, her battle with the terrible mystery that had been Mr. X was finally through—

—*hell with all that, no time, MOVE!*

Claire was on her feet in a second, ignoring the squelch of blood in her boot and the pain that had caused it, her gaze searching the upper platform for her unknown savior. No one was there, and she didn't know if another minute had ticked by, the warning lost in the gunfire.

"Hey!" Claire shouted, backing toward the subway car. "We have to go, now!"

No answer, no sound but the ringing in her ears and the echo of her trembling words. If she wanted to save Sherry . . .

Claire turned and ran.

* * *

"—two minutes until—"

Leon pushed himself to go faster, the twining tunnel a blur of gray that spun past his aching, breathless perception. He'd lost all track of the turns and twists of the corridor and was rapidly losing hope, a voice in the back of his mind telling him that maybe it would be best to stop, to sit and rest—

—and then he heard it, and that tiny, despairing whisper was obliterated by the sound.

The sound of heavy machinery stirring to life, somewhere up ahead. Not far ahead.

Train!

Faster, legs distant, rubbery, lungs working, heart pounding—one way or another, it was almost over.

Thirty-Two

CLAIRE BURST INTO THE TRAIN, HOLDING A giant rifle and with one leg covered in blood, barely pausing to hit the controls to the door before running for the engineer's booth. Sherry knew that they were in trouble, that it was going to be close, so she didn't waste time asking questions; she followed, relieved beyond measure that Claire was okay but keeping it to herself.

Okay, she's okay and we're going now. . . .

A small, tinny version of the intercom voice and alarms blared out of the tiny room's control board.

"There are two minutes until detonation."

Claire had dropped the oddly shaped rifle and was hitting buttons, throwing switches, her attention fixed on the console. A giant mechanical hum suddenly enveloped them, a growing, whining rumble that made Claire grit her teeth; Sherry couldn't tell if it was a smile, but *she* smiled as she felt the train lurch—

—and start to move, taking them away from the platform.

Claire turned, saw Sherry standing behind her, and tried to smile. Claire rested one hand on Sherry's shoulder, but didn't say anything—so Sherry didn't either, waiting to see what would happen.

The train started to go faster, sliding past dimly lit halls and platforms, the tunnel in front of them dark and empty. Sherry let the warmth of Claire's hand remind her that they were friends, that whatever happened, Claire was her friend—

—and she saw a man, a policeman, stumble into view ahead on the left, and then the train was gliding past him, his eyes wide and searching and desperate in his dirty face.

"Claire!"

"I see him—"

Claire turned and ran out of the booth, her footsteps clattering through the metal train car, sprinting to the door. She hit the control and the door slid open, the booming, grinding sounds of the subway billowing into the closed space.

"Leon!" she screamed. "Hurry!"

She jerked back suddenly, a wall sliding by, and spun around looking as desperate as the man—Leon—had. After another second she turned back and closed the door.

"Did he make it?" Sherry asked, realizing that Claire couldn't possibly know, even as the words came out of her mouth.

Claire came to her and put an arm around her, as the train kept going faster and her face knotted with worry—

—and the voice in the intercom told them they had one minute left—

—and the door in the back of the car opened. In stumbled Leon, his arm wrapped with a shredded, stained bandage, his hair matted with dark, dried goo, his eyes bright and blue in the mask of dirt.

"Full throttle!" he shouted; Claire nodded, and Leon blew out a heavy breath. He staggered toward them, the train shifting back and forth, speeding now, rocketing through the tunnel. He put his arm around Claire, and Claire hugged him tightly.

"Ada?" Claire whispered. "Ann—the scientist?"

Leon shook his head, and Sherry saw that he might cry. "No. I didn't—no."

". . . thirty seconds until detonation. Twenty-nine . . . twenty-eight . . ."

The woman's voice kept counting down, the numbers seeming to come twice as fast as they should, and Sherry buried her face in Claire's warm side, thinking about her mom. Mom and Dad. She hoped that they'd gotten out, that they were safe somewhere—

—*but they're probably not. They're probably dead.*

Sherry could hear Claire's heart pounding, and she hugged her friend tighter, thinking that she would think about it later.

". . . five. Four. Three. Two. One. Sequence complete. Detonation."

For a second, there was no sound at all. The alarms

had finally stopped, and the clattering movement of the racing train was all there was to hear—

—and then there was an explosion, a **muffled** sound, a *shoomp* sound that kept going, growing, becoming huge.

Sherry closed her eyes and the train rocked suddenly, horribly, and they were all thrown to the metal floor as bright, burning light flickered through the window, as the sounds of a car crash blasted all around them, heavy *thumps* raining over the roof—

—and the train kept going. It kept going, and the light went away, and they weren't dead.

The blinding flash dissipated, faded, and Leon felt the tension leaking out of his body. He rolled onto his side, and saw Claire sitting up, reaching for the hand of the young girl next to her.

"Okay?" Claire asked the girl, and the child nodded. Both of them turned to him, their faces expressing what he felt—shock, exhaustion, disbelief, hope.

"Leon Kennedy, this is Sherry Birkin," Claire said, saying the words carefully, the slightest accent on "Birkin." He got the message even without the intensity of her gaze, nodding his understanding before smiling at the girl.

"Sherry, this is Leon," Claire continued. "I met him when I had just gotten to Raccoon."

Sherry returned his smile, a weary, too-adult smile that seemed out of place; she was too young to smile like that.

One more rotten deed to lay at Umbrella's door, innocence stolen from a child. . . .

For a few seconds, they just sat there on the floor, staring at one another, smiles fading all around. Leon hardly dared to hope that it was really over, that they were leaving the terror behind. Again, he saw his feelings mirrored in front of him, in Sherry's worried brow and Claire's tired gray eyes—

—and when they heard the distant squeal of metal coming from somewhere at the back of the train, he didn't see any surprise. A rending, tearing screech—followed by a heavy, somehow stealthy *thump*—and then nothing.

Should've known it isn't over—

"Zombie?" Sherry whispered, the word almost lost in the gently clattering sound of the speeding train.

"I don't know, sweetie," Claire said softly, and for the first time, Leon noticed that her left leg was ripped to shit, blood oozing from several ragged scratches; he'd been too amazed at his, at *their* narrow escape to see it before.

"How about I go take a look?" Leon said, taking his cue from Claire, keeping his voice mild and even; no point in scaring Sherry any worse. He stood up, nodding toward Claire's leg.

"Sherry, why don't you stay here with Claire, keep an eye on that leg? I'll see if I can find some bandages while I'm checking things out; don't let her move, okay?"

Sherry nodded, her small face intent with purpose that again was too old for her years. "Got it."

"I'll be back in a minute," he said, and turned toward the back of the swaying train, praying that it was nothing at all and knowing better, as he reached for the Remington and went to see.

Leon opened the door, the sounds of the rolling train amplified for a second before it closed behind him. Claire couldn't see him enter the next car from her position on the floor, and wished she'd been in shape to go with him; if there *was* something else on the train, Sherry wasn't safe, none of them were—

—*don't think like that, it's nothing. It's over*—

—*like it was over with Mr. X?*

"What should I do?" Sherry asked, pulling Claire away from the disheartening thoughts. "Direct pressure, right?"

Claire nodded. "Yeah, except we're both pretty grimy, and I think it's starting to clot. Let's see if Leon comes back with something clean . . ."

She trailed off, her thoughts going back to Mr. X. There was something nagging at her but she was a little dizzy from the blood she'd lost—

—*G-Virus. It wanted the G-Virus before.*

Why *had* Mr. X come to the subway platform? Why had it been trying to get inside the train, unless—

Claire struggled to get up, fighting her swimming head and the throbbing pain in her leg.

"Hey, don't move," Sherry said, a look of deep distress in her eyes. "Leon said to stay still!"

She might have been able to overcome her physical problems, but seeing Sherry on the edge of panic was too much; if there *was* some G-Virus creature on board, if that was why Mr. X had come, Leon would have to face it alone. She couldn't leave Sherry. If Leon didn't come back, she'd have to figure out how to detach their train car, or stop the train so they could get off before the creature could get to them—

Claire shut the thoughts off, forcing a smile for Sherry. "Yes ma'am. I just wanted to make sure he got through the second car. . . . ."

She could see the relief sweep across Sherry's face. "Oh. Well, forget it, I'm taking care of *you* now, and I say you stay still."

Claire nodded absently, hoping that she was wrong, hoping that Leon would be back any second—

—*Bam! Bam! Bam!*

The thunder of the Remington was loud and clear. Sherry grabbed her hand as two more shots blasted the hope from Claire's fuzzy mind, as the train sped through the dark.

The second car was clear, the same wide-open space that Leon had entered the train by, all dusty steel and not much else. Whoever had designed the escape vehicle had obviously figured the Umbrella employees would have to be packed in like sardines.

Just us three, though—and our stowaway. . . .

There was nothing to see, but Leon moved slowly nonetheless, carefully scanning the shadowy corners and steeling himself for whatever was in the last car. Whatever it was, it couldn't be as bad as the thing that had jumped him in the cargo room, the Birkin-thing, if that was what it was. The thought that the creature had anything at all to do with Claire's young friend was deeply unsettling, even obscene. A monster and a madwoman, both destroyed, both parents of the little girl. . . .

He reached the back of the dim and rocking train car and peered through the door, pushing all other thoughts aside as he tried to make out anything at all in the last car. Darkness, and nothing else.

Hell.

Maybe there wasn't anything to see, but he had to look. He felt his heart start to pound fresh adrenaline through his body, felt his weariness fall away. Nothing, it was surely nothing, but it *felt* bad. Wrong.

Last thing, very last thing. . . .

He took a deep breath and opened the door, stepping into the loud, whipping breeze of the outside, holding on to the rail. The rattle of the train drowned out the thumping of his heart as he moved to the last car, opened the door, and stepped into darkness.

Immediately, he raised the shotgun, all of his senses telling him to run as the door slid shut behind him. He reached back, slapping for a light switch. Darkness, but there was a powerful smell like bleach or chlorine, and there was the soft sound of *wetness,* of movement—

A single bare bulb flickered on in the middle of the car as he found a button, and he thought for just a second that he'd lost his mind.

A thing. A creature that wasn't even vaguely humanoid, except for a strange, pulsing tumor protruding from one side, a slick orb that looked very much like an eye.

Birkin.

The creature was a giant, stretching *blob* of dark,

slimy matter, spanning the width of the car; Leon couldn't tell how tall it was. The Birkin-thing had thick streamers extended out, tentacles of wet and elastic goo attached to every part of the space in front of it—the ceiling, walls, and floor. And as Leon watched, the alien beast pulled itself forward, the dark limbs contracting, bringing the mass of the body a few feet ahead of where it had been.

Not crazy. He was seeing it, seeing the brackish, moving colors of black and green and purple in its tentacles as it stretched out again, the viscous material latching to the metal of the car somehow, dragging the blob a few more feet ahead. The body itself was nothing so much as a gaping maw, a wet cave that still had teeth—

—and that would reach him pretty soon if he didn't snap out of his disgusted stupor.

Leon aimed into the giant hole of its mouth and pulled the trigger, pumping in another round, firing, pumping, firing—

—and then the shotgun was empty, and the giant semi-liquid *thing* was still moving steadily forward.

He didn't know how to kill it, didn't know if the rounds had even damaged it. His mind raced for an answer, for a solution that would end the terrible life of the G-Virus monster. He could detach the last car, fire through the pins and chains that held it together, *if* he could find the locking mechanism—

—*and it would still be alive. Still living and changing in the blackness of the tunnel, becoming something new*—

The stretching elastic of its nebulous form inched

forward, and Leon reached back for the door control. He'd have to try unhooking the cars, there was no other choice—

—*unless*—

He hesitated, then unholstered his Magnum and pointed it at the impossible mass. At the strange tumor that peered out of a slit in its rubber flesh, the eye that had been in every form that Birkin had taken. Careful aim, and—

—*BAM!*

The effect was immediate and total, the heavy round piercing the rheumy sphere—and a hissing, screaming whine or whistle pouring out of the toothed maw, like nothing on Earth, like the howl of something mechanical and insane. The tendrils of unformed matter shrank inward, turning black, shriveling—

—and the thing imploded, pulling in on itself, withering into a steaming black mass less than a quarter its original size. Like a deflated beachball, the gelid blob wrinkled and shrank, collapsing into a flattening thickness, drooling itself into a wide puddle of bubbling slime.

"Suck on *that*," Leon said softly, the last bubbles popping, the pool a dead and inanimate thing. He watched it for a few moments, thinking about nothing at all—and finally turned to join the others, to tell them it was over.

First day on the job, he thought.

"I want a raise," Leon said, to no one at all, and couldn't help the grin that broke across his face, a tired, sunny grin that faded quickly . . . but for the few seconds he wore it, Leon felt better than he had in a very long time.

Leon was back, and had found a jumpsuit that he tore into pieces and used to bind up Claire's leg. All he'd said was that they were safe now, although Sherry had seen him and Claire exchange a look— one of those "we-shouldn't-talk-about-it-right-now" looks. Sherry was too tired to take offense.

She snuggled into Claire's arms, Claire stroking her hair, the three of them not talking. There was nothing to say, or at least not for a little while. They were alive, on a train thundering through the dark—and from somewhere not far ahead, a soft light came filtering in, coming through the window in the control booth, and Sherry thought it looked very much like morning.

EPILOGUE

THEY SAW THE AFTERMATH OF THE EXPLO-
sion from ten miles outside the city, a black and
billowing cloud that rose up into the early morning
light and hung over Raccoon like a terrible storm—

—*or a bad dream,* Rebecca thought, *a recurring
one. Umbrella.*

She didn't say it aloud, because it wasn't necessary.
John and David hadn't gone through the Spencer
estate nightmare, but they'd been at the Cove facility,
witnesses to what Umbrella was capable of; they
knew.

Nobody spoke as David stepped up the speed, his
knuckles white on the wheel. For once, John didn't
crack any jokes about what might have happened.
They all knew that it was bad; before Jill, Chris, and
Barry had left for Europe, Jill had wired them with
her suspicions about another accident, and asked

them to keep tabs. When the phone lines had gone down, they'd loaded up the SUV and left Maine to see what could be done. The only question was how many people had died this time.

Maybe this is the end, finally. A blast like that . . . Umbrella can't cover this up so easily, not if it's as bad as it looks.

John finally broke the silence, his deep, mellow voice uncharacteristically subdued. "Fail-safe?"

David sighed. "Probably. And if there *was* a spill, we're not going in; we'll circle the city and then call for help from Latham. Umbrella is surely sending in its cleanup staff already."

Rebecca nodded along with John. They weren't technically part of the S.T.A.R.S. anymore, but David had been a captain before, and with good reason. They fell back into a tense silence, the dawn-touched trees spinning past the utility vehicle, Rebecca wondering what they would find—

—when she saw the people, staggering up into the road, waving their arms.

"Hey—" she started, but David was already hitting the brakes, slowing down as they neared the threesome of ragged strangers. A cop with a bandaged arm and a young woman in shorts, both of them holding weapons, and a little girl in a pink vest that was much too big for her. They weren't infected, or at least not showing signs that Rebecca could see—but they looked like hell nonetheless. With their ripped clothes and their faces pale and shocked beneath masks of dirt, they certainly could have passed for walking death.

"I'll talk," David said, his crisp British accent mild but firm, and then they were pulling up beside the Raccoon survivors.

David opened his window and killed the engine, the young cop stepping forward as the woman slipped one grimy arm around the little girl's shoulders.

"There's been an accident, in Raccoon," he said, and although they were obviously tired and wounded and badly in need of help, there was a wariness in the cop's tone, a guarded, careful note that suggested just how bad things had been. "A terrible accident. You don't want to go there, it's not safe."

David frowned. "What sort of accident, Officer?"

The young woman spoke up, her mouth a set and bitter line. "An Umbrella accident," she said, and the cop nodded, and the little blond girl buried her face against the woman's hip.

John and Rebecca exchanged a look, and David hit the switch to unlock the doors.

"Really? Those tend to be the worst kind," he said gently. "We'd be happy to help you, if you'd like, or we could call for help. . . ."

It was a question. The cop glanced back at the woman, then met David's gaze for several long beats. He must have seen something in David's face that he felt he could trust; he nodded slowly, then motioned for the woman and girl to come forward.

"Thanks," he said, the exhaustion finally coming through. "If you could give us a ride, that'd be great."

David smiled. "Please, get in. John, Rebecca— would you assist . . . ?"

John grabbed a couple of blankets out of the back as

Rebecca reached for her medical kit, careful not to uncover the rifles tucked next to the wheel well.

An Umbrella accident . . .

Rebecca wondered if they knew how lucky they were to have survived it—but another look into those three exhausted, shell-shocked faces told her that they probably did.

They started talking even before David turned the vehicle around—and in a very short time, they discovered that they had a lot in common, as the child fell asleep and they drove back the way they'd come, leaving the burning city behind.

About the Author

S.D. (Stephani Danelle) Perry writes multimedia novelizations in the fantasy/science-fiction/horror realm for love and money, including several *Aliens* novels, the novelization of *Timecop,* and *Virus.* Under the name Stella Howard, she's written an original novel based upon the television series *Xena, Warrior Princess.* The *Resident Evil* books mark her first foray into writing novels based upon video games. She lives in Portland, Oregon, with her husband and a multitude of pets.

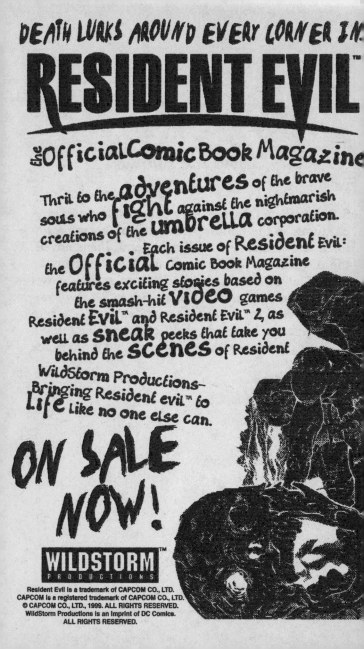

DEATH LURKS AROUND EVERY CORNER IN

RESIDENT EVIL™

the Official Comic Book Magazine

Thrill to the **adventures** of the brave souls who **fight** against the nightmarish creations of the **umbrella** corporation.

Each issue of **Resident Evil: the Official** Comic Book Magazine features exciting stories based on the smash-hit **video** games Resident Evil™ and Resident Evil™ 2, as well as **sneak** peeks that take you behind the **scenes** of Resident

WildStorm Productions— Bringing Resident evil™ to **life** like no one else can.

ON SALE NOW!

WILDSTORM™
PRODUCTIONS

Praise for

FIGURES
IN A
LANDSCAPE

"A portrait of an optimist with curiosity and affection for humanity in all its forms, as well as a ravenous appetite for the literary efforts of others... Theroux's sweet spot happens to be spinning a convincing narrative through wandering conversations with any citizens who cross his path... Emotionally affective." — *New York Times Book Review*

"Novelist and travel writer Theroux is at the top of his game with his third collection of essays, a magisterial grouping of intimate remembrances, globe-trotting adventures, and incisive literary critiques... A highly versatile, appealing writer, Theroux casts a wide net with pleasing and entertaining results." — *Publishers Weekly,* starred review

"[Theroux's] stories are less travelogues than well-curated meditations on some of the places, people, and moments he has experienced in a lifetime of rambles... His spare, unhurried prose style, which is rarely long-winded, betrays a novelist's relish for illuminating details and devastating turns of phrase... A masterfully simple and satisfying collection." — *Kirkus Reviews*

"Those who've missed these thirty pieces where previously published will be impressed by the breadth of his interests, the depth of his research, and the scrupulousness of his prose. A profile of Elizabeth Taylor... works a miracle, allowing us to view the icon with unjaded eyes. A lengthy profile of a dominatrix... offers genuine insight into both spanker and spanked. Appreciations of Conrad, Greene, Maugham, and Simenon show how book introductions ought to be done. And the closing, more personal pieces... add emotional heft and shape to this wide-ranging, thought-provoking, and eminently browsable collection." — *Booklist*

Theroux's observations are so keen and writerly skills so sharp that he
utter-slices narratives with a razor-thin surgeon's scalpel, masterfully
erving up both the world's dark underbelly and its gloriously uplifting
ustenance of love, longing, and *wonder*-lust." — *Forbes*

'In short, there is something for everyone . . . His talky, big-hearted book
will make a heavenly companion at the beach."
— *Honolulu Star-Advertiser*

"His new collection of essays, like its illustrious author, is full of surprises."
— Forbes.com

FIGURES
IN A
LANDSCAPE

BOOKS BY PAUL THEROUX

FICTION

WALDO

FONG AND THE INDIANS

GIRLS AT PLAY

MURDER IN MOUNT HOLLY

JUNGLE LOVERS

SINNING WITH ANNIE

SAINT JACK

THE BLACK HOUSE

THE FAMILY ARSENAL

THE CONSUL'S FILE

A CHRISTMAS CARD

PICTURE PALACE

LONDON SNOW

WORLD'S END

THE MOSQUITO COAST

THE LONDON EMBASSY

HALF MOON STREET

O-ZONE

MY SECRET HISTORY

CHICAGO LOOP

MILLROY THE MAGICIAN

MY OTHER LIFE

KOWLOON TONG

HOTEL HONOLULU

THE STRANGER AT THE
PALAZZO D'ORO

BLINDING LIGHT

THE ELEPHANTA SUITE

A DEAD HAND

THE LOWER RIVER

MR. BONES

MOTHER LAND

CRITICISM

V. S. NAIPAUL

NONFICTION

THE GREAT RAILWAY BAZAAR

THE OLD PATAGONIAN EXPRESS

THE KINGDOM BY THE SEA

SAILING THROUGH CHINA

SUNRISE WITH SEAMONSTERS

THE IMPERIAL WAY

RIDING THE IRON ROOSTER

TO THE ENDS OF THE EARTH

THE HAPPY ISLES OF OCEANIA

THE PILLARS OF HERCULES

SIR VIDIA'S SHADOW

FRESH AIR FIEND

DARK STAR SAFARI

GHOST TRAIN TO THE
EASTERN STAR

THE TAO OF TRAVEL

THE LAST TRAIN TO
ZONA VERDE

DEEP SOUTH

FIGURES IN A LANDSCAPE

PAUL THEROUX

FIGURES
IN A
LANDSCAPE
PEOPLE
AND
PLACES

ESSAYS: 2001–2016

Mariner Books
An Eamon Dolan Book
Houghton Mifflin Harcourt
Boston   New York

First Mariner Books edition 2019

Copyright © 2018 by Paul Theroux

For information about permission to reproduce selections from this book,
write to trade.permissions@hmhco.com or to Permissions, Houghton Mifflin Harcourt
Publishing Company, 3 Park Avenue, 19th Floor, New York, New York 10016.

hmhco.com

Library of Congress Cataloging-in-Publication Data
Names: Theroux, Paul author.
Title: Figures in a landscape : people and places : essays: 2001-2016 /
Paul Theroux.
Description: Boston : Houghton Mifflin Harcourt, 2018. |
"An Eamon Dolan book."
Identifiers: LCCN 2017045486 (print) | LCCN 2017048160 (ebook) |
ISBN 9780544866669 (ebook) | ISBN 9780544870307 (hardback) |
ISBN 9781328592781 (pbk.)
Subjects: LCSH: Theroux, Paul. | Theroux, Paul—Travel. | Authors,
American—20th century—Biography. | BISAC: TRAVEL / Essays & Travelogues.
| BIOGRAPHY & AUTOBIOGRAPHY / Personal Memoirs. |
LITERARY COLLECTIONS / Essays.
Classification: LCC PS3570.H4 (ebook) | LCC PS3570.H4 A6 2018 (print) |
DDC 814/.54 [B] — dc23
LC record available at https://lccn.loc.gov/2017045486

Book design by Jackie Shepherd

Printed in the United States of America
DOC 10 9 8 7 6 5 4 3 2 1

Write the vision
And make it plain on tablets,
That he may run who reads it.

—HABAKKUK 2:2

CONTENTS

INTRODUCTION: STUDY FOR FIGURES IN A LANDSCAPE

I am a novelist and only now and then an essayist or a chronicler of my travels. How I wish it were possible for me to describe the snail trail of my fiction writing — that groping interior journey of false starts and bad days and sudden enchantments — without uttering pompous approximations and absurd sanctimonies. Even that rambling attempt is pretentious and irritating, so you see the problem.

If I can't stand listening to the rabid vanity of other writers talking in abstractions about their work, why should I do it myself? I am happier to see people write fiction well without moaning about how they did it. When writers complain about how tough a job writing is, making a meal of their pain, any fool can see that what they are saying is a crock. Compared with a real job, like coal mining or harvesting pineapples or putting out wildfires or waiting on tables, writing is heaven.

Besides, I am possessed by the great gnawing fear of many writers, that if I anatomize the craft of fiction writing, I might never write another word of fiction again. Better not to vapor on about it. Every writer must find the secret of fiction within. Misery helps, so does muddle and loving books, so does leaving home. I grew up with the notion, well expressed by the traveler Norman Lewis, "The farther I was from home, the better it would be," and it proved to be true.

But if fiction writing is a ritual in the dark, obscure and so ungraspable that you don't understand a word of what you've written until you're done, other sorts of writing involve a plainer and more practical approach.

Writing travel. I can talk about that. I have certain guidelines. The first one is, in travel be as unofficial as possible. Evidence of the dangers of official travel is everywhere. Nothing in the world is more misleading than the sponsored visit, the press junket, the press pool, the pool feed, the fact-finding mission. The subtext of the official visit is always tendentious, and it is laziness, self-importance, and greed that impel the official visitor to accept the auspices and lap up the lies. The whole point of the red carpet is to dazzle the visitor and obscure the truth.

"Uganda's doing great," President Clinton said to me at a gathering when I told him I had been traveling there.

I said, "No, it's not. The government is corrupt. It persecutes the opposition. Life in the bush is much worse than it was in the 1960s, when I was a teacher in Kampala. And, as I said, I was there a month ago."

"Hillary just came back." The president smiled at my ignorance. "It's doing great."

And now it was my turn to smile.

"Who do you think you are, saying those awful things about Iran? You're lying!" Marion (Mrs. Jacob) Javits howled at me backstage in the NBC-TV studio in New York City in August 1975, after I published my first book of travels, *The Great Railway Bazaar*. Iran was a stable, prosperous, and well-governed country, she said. Really? I had traveled overland by train and bus from west to east, ending up in the holy city of Meshed. I heard nothing but stories of torture, repression, and tyranny from very angry Iranians, who spoke of ridding themselves of the shah. It turned out that Mrs. Javits was a paid consultant to the government of Iran, and her husband, Jacob, the U.S. senator, no stranger to Iranian junkets and free caviar, courtesy of the shah, who was overthrown fourteen years later.

"There is no fate so uncertain as the fate of books of travel," Joseph Conrad wrote in his preface to Richard Curle's *Into the East*. "They are the most assailable of all men's literary productions. The man who writes a travel book delivers himself more than any other into the hands of his enemies."

In my 1988 book of China travels, *Riding the Iron Rooster* (name a Chinese train and I took it), I suggested that the Chinese cops, the People's Armed Police and the Chengguan "peace officers," had a taste for beating up students. I had traveled in China for a year; I had seen many demonstrations. The conventional wisdom in the West was that the Chinese government was reform-minded and tolerant. Reviewers spanked my book. But this was a year before the Tiananmen Square massacre.

True travel and the inquiry of the essayist requires the simpler stratagems of being humble, patient, solitary, anonymous, and alert. These are not qualities one normally associates with duck-butted legislators on a fact-finding mission, or agents of virtue looking for someone to encumber with charity and free food, or journalists reporting high-level meetings, all of them in search of a welcome mat.

That I am a well-off, fairly old, semi-well-known writer who can afford to fly first class and rent nice cars and stay in good hotels makes it all the more important that I travel in old clothes, on a small budget, on a bus or train or cattle truck. My natural element (and it has been the stuff of the travel narrative since Herodotus) is the low-level meeting. In Africa in 2001, I received little enlightenment from politicians, but quite a lot from talking to truck drivers, migrants, prostitutes, and farmers. Writers are also a source of inspiration, especially those writers who seem part of a particular landscape. In Buenos Aires I sought out Borges, in Tangier Paul Bowles, in Brazil Jorge Amado, in Turkey Yaşar Kamal and later Orhan Pamuk. Traveling in Africa, I spent time in Egypt with Naguib Mahfouz, and in Johannesburg with Nadine Gordimer. All travel writing and many essays seem to me to be summed up in the title of the enigmatic Francis Bacon painting *Study for Figures in a Landscape.*

I enjoy comfort as much as the next traveler. And no one knows better than a writer how pleasant is the life removed, how dreary it is to haunt assemblies where youth and cost a witless bravery keeps. Sound familiar? This paraphrased admonition is the Duke in Shakespeare's *Measure for Measure,* who is a good model for the traveling writer. In order to find out what is really going on in his dukedom, the Duke says he needs to assume a humble disguise, such as a friar's habit, "to visit both prince and people."

The example of Harun al-Rashid, caliph of Baghdad in the eighth century, is also salutary. The caliph habitually disguised himself as a commoner and went to the marketplace to find out how people lived, what complaints they had, what exercised their minds, what made them proud. The great travelers of the past peregrinated in this same mood of discovery — the medieval friars who visited China, the Japanese mendicants, the wandering diarists quoted extensively by the French historian Fernand Braudel in my favorite of his books, *The Structures of Everyday Life*. Official travel does not tell you what the world is like; unofficial travel, by the eavesdropper and the buttonholer, does.

Making my way from Cairo to Cape Town, peregrinating for my book of Africa travels, *Dark Star Safari*, I found myself in buses, on trucks, on ferries, canoes, and trains. I never had a name; I was never able to pull rank. I was sometimes *effendi* or *faranji*, but throughout Swahili-speaking Africa I was *mzee* — pops, grandpa — which is how I wanted it to be, an anonymous elder. There are risks, of course, in solo travel, but there are also great rewards. One is privileged enough in being an American traveler, but I don't see how it is possible to get at the truth of a country without seeing its underside, its hinterland, its everyday life. Not bureaucrats in offices, but figures in the landscape.

The most revealing part of any country, and especially an African country, is its border. Anyone can land at the airport in the capital and be fooled by modernity, but it takes a certain nerve to ride a bus or a train to the frontier, always the haunt of the rabble, the dispossessed, people struggling to leave, trying to get in, the bane of officialdom. The customs and immigration officials at border crossings are not noted for their graceful manners, yet they are more representative of life in the place than any number of meet-and-greeters in the capital's international airport.

If you are unofficial, traveling by improvisation, what is your support system? Except for your nerve, you have none. You show up and hope for the best. The wisest travel advice I have ever received was from a beachcomber camped in Australia who was planning to sail around the Cape York Peninsula. This would be a hair-raising trip in a large vessel, yet he was planning to do it on a small homemade raft. He had no doubt that he would survive the swift current and strong winds of the Torres Strait and perhaps strike out for Papua New Guinea.

He said, "What I find is that you can do almost anything or go almost anywhere if you're not in a hurry."

It seems all the good advice I have ever received has been from people who have nothing but a desire to move — optimists, all of them. Traveling for my 1992 book *The Happy Isles of Oceania*, sailing on an outrigger canoe with some fishermen in the Trobriand Islands, I was told by the steersman that he went hundreds of miles to sea looking for fish.

"The ocean looks empty, but it is not," he said. "There are rocks and little islands everywhere in it where you can tie your canoe and stay the night."

The greater part of travel is nuisance and delay, and no reader wants to hear about that. I do my best to be prepared. I seldom solicit names of people to look up. Anxiety and improvisation are helpful to the traveler, who is made watchful and resourceful when constantly reminded that he or she is a stranger. Before I set out, I am a scrutinizer of the most detailed maps I can find, a compulsive reader of guides for the budget traveler. It helps to have money, but time is much more valuable. Apart from a small shortwave radio, I carry no high-tech items — these days a phone, never a camera or computer, nothing fragile or irreplaceable. In South Africa my bag was stolen and I was robbed of almost everything I owned: a good lesson. I had my notes. Who steals notebooks?

The writing, then. I carry a pocket-sized notebook and scribble in it all day. In the evening I transcribe these notes into a larger journal, making an orderly narrative of the day. My average daily entry is about a thousand words, sometimes less, often more. En route, whenever I have a chance I photocopy these pages, say forty or fifty at a time, and mail them home. By the end of a trip I will have filled about seven or eight student notebooks, and these are the basis for the book. Interviewing someone for a profile, especially a potentially litigious celebrity, I keep a tape recorder running while I write the person's answers in a notebook, as a guide to the highlights. Afterward, I transcribe the entire interview myself from the tape, skipping the boring parts. I have never employed a secretary, assistant, or researcher. Though I have written many more novels than travel books, I could never be so specific or certain about my fiction writing method, if indeed I have a fiction writing method.

After *Sunrise with Seamonsters* (1984) and *Fresh Air Fiend* (2001), *Figures in a Landscape* is my third volume of essays, a total of 134 essays written over 53 years. And in that time I have published novels, short stories, and travel books. Millions of words! But what may look like graphomania or *furor scribendi* is no more a compulsion than the natural impulse of an average artist who makes many paintings and sketches in a lifetime of creation. Like the painter, immersing myself in writing has been a way of making sense of my life, as well as earning my living. I am in sympathy with Ford Madox Ford, who in his dedication to his exhaustive survey, *The*

March of Literature, described himself as "an old man mad about writing — in the sense that Hokusai called himself an old man mad about painting."

When I quit my job at the University of Singapore in 1971, I vowed never to have a boss again or to have to obey the memo "Department meeting on Thursday. Be there." I had published four novels and was working on a fifth, *Saint Jack*. I thought: I can't be a part-time writer. I have to commit myself entirely to this, even if it means living poor.

"The value of anything equals what you will give up to possess it." This apothegm, in my son Marcel's novel *The Secret Books,* elegantly expresses how I felt forty-six years ago, having chucked job security, a possible pension, a certain amount of prestige, and a monthly salary to live precariously in a small, badly heated stone cottage in a remote part of Dorset, in rural England. The first draft of *Saint Jack* was completed there, happily.

Necessity showed me that I could also pay my bills by taking writing assignments: book reviews, travel pieces, profiles of people both well known and obscure. Anthony Burgess once wrote, "I refuse no reasonable offer of work, and very few unreasonable ones." Burgess, who was a friend and generous to my work, is someone I identify with, along with all the other writers who financed their novel writing by taking assignments. Graham Greene, V. S. Naipaul, V. S. Pritchett, Jonathan Raban, and many other writers I've known started their careers as freelance writers. I like the term "freelance," its suggestion of independence and potential power, the armed horseman roaming at will, not answerable to any knight, but open to negotiation, and with a willingness to do battle. Speaking of his fiction, Henry James wrote, "It is art that makes life, makes interest, makes importance, and I know of no substitute for the force and beauty of its process." Yet this noble sentiment must be set against the fact that James was also someone who wrote travel pieces and book reviews to make a living.

When Jonathan Raban published his first collection of essays in 1987 he titled it pointedly *For Love and Money,* a motto for the escutcheon of the freelance. It is undeniable that a writer takes an assignment in order to pay bills, because, as Dr. Johnson said, "No man but a blockhead ever wrote except for money." But no one ever wrote well without a love of writing.

Though no official patronage has come my way, I do not disparage the Guggenheim fellowships, the Fulbright awards, the MacArthur genius grants, or the posts of writer-in-residence. But they can mislead and bewitch the writer. The glamour, and the social advantages that accompany such awards, may inspire the delusion that it is the patronage, and not the work itself, that confers a distinct elevation. One of the consequences of patronage is complacency, the presumptuousness of celebrity, the inevitable hobnobbing and a certain unreality. I notice, too, an unwillingness of such fortunate writers to launch themselves into the unknown. Worse than any of these is an attitude — a reflex often found in the sponsored, awarded, garlanded author — that dismisses the freelance as a hack resident of Grub Street. So I suppose, having written that, I am, after all, a trifle umbrageous and disparaging when it comes to the matter of patronage.

The freelance is guided by curiosity, and must, in its pursuit, be uncompromising, never betraying his or her gift by writing badly, or in haste, or at the bidding of the magazine editor who insists on a certain style. Being free — to travel or take an assignment at short notice — is essential in living such a life. But seizing even the simplest opportunity can start a chain of events.

For example, eager to paddle my kayak the length of the Zambezi River, I successfully pitched the notion to *National Geographic*. While on the trip, which I wrote as a piece for the magazine, I met a handsome couple who were on a luxury safari on the Zimbabwe side of the river. The woman wore high boots and a tailored safari jacket; the man was bearded and gruff in the Hemingway mode, and he too was kitted out in stylish khaki. They were New Yorkers, I took them to be man and wife, and when we parted the woman said, "Do keep in touch."

Back in the States, I called her to hear her impressions of Africa, and in the course of the conversation I inquired about her occupation. "I'm a dominatrix," she said. "That man I was with is one of my clients. I often spanked him on that safari."

That was how I met "Nurse Wolf," who agreed to talk to me for the piece printed here, which appeared in *The New Yorker*. And the Zambezi trip and the *New Yorker* payday allowed me to embark on a more ambitious African journey, overland from Cairo to Cape Town, which became my travel book *Dark Star Safari*.

At its best, the freelance writer lives a life of happy accidents. A magazine assignment in China in 1980, on a Yangtze River cruise, led to more assignments in China and ultimately the yearlong travel for *Riding the Iron*

Rooster. A story on New Zealand in the late 1980s stimulated my curiosity and, a few years later, my traveling all over the Pacific for *The Happy Isles of Oceania,* and later my becoming a resident of Hawaii.

Now and then my curiosity gets the better of me and I write something off my own bat and hope a magazine will be interested. After reading many of Oliver Sacks's books, I wrote him a letter inviting him for lunch, to discuss his theory of "street neurology" — identifying the conditions of random pedestrians in New York City. We went for walks, Oliver diagnosing strangers' tics and compulsions. We became friends. I kept detailed notes and turned these into a profile of the man, and a magazine published it. My pieces here on Hawaii, on living in London, on autobiography, on raising geese, on taking the psychedelic drug ayahuasca, on a life of reading, and the many op-eds I have written, all were self-assigned. The piece here about my father, "Dear Old Dad," was written on the Trans-Siberian Express in the winter of 2007, when I had nine days of idleness (and 5,772 miles) ahead of me. Beginning in Vladivostok, I set down my memories of my father, writing as the birches and the snowy versts of bleakness flashed past, and finished as the train pulled into Yaroslavsky Station in Moscow. This essay on my father led to a broader meditation on my family, and scrupulous note-taking, that became my novel *Mother Land.*

There is the other sort of piece, one based on a request or a conversation with an editor. Often the suggestion, which comes out of the blue, has the merit of keeping one in touch with books, with the world, with complex figures, with distinctive landscapes. The assigning editor wonders whether one might be interested in writing the profile of a celebrity, or an introduction to a book, or an essay about a writer. If it's an author or book I admire, I say yes. Thus, Henry David Thoreau, Henry Morton Stanley, Joseph Conrad, Somerset Maugham, Graham Greene, Paul Bowles, Muriel Spark, Hunter Thompson. I first read Georges Simenon's *Chez Krull* as a teacher in Africa, and continued to read him, discovering with pleasure that he had himself traveled in Africa in the 1930s (and wrote three novels with an African background); that he had sailed through the Pacific, lived in Arizona and Connecticut, and published hundreds of novels. After fifty years of reading Simenon, I was delighted when an editor asked me to write the introduction to a reissue of his novel *The Widow.*

One of the satisfactions in the randomness of this sort of writing life is that one is making a reasonable living without having to put one's work aside and enter a classroom, or apply for a fellowship, or be some sort of consultant. Another satisfaction is the notion that writing occasional pieces, along with books, produces the encouraging illusion of respectable employment, that one is fully occupied and has work to do. Because the great dread of a writer is that writing goes so slowly it is more like a perverse hobby than a stable occupation, and nothing at all like a real job.

Much of this is old hat, the workings of a world and the elements of a dated literary life that are passing away. I recently sold my papers to an illustrious library; they sent a truck to cart them off. But this, too, is becoming an anachronism, because I write my first drafts in longhand, the only way I know. How much longer will writers possess a paper archive? Even now the truck may be superfluous; many writers are able to put their whole archive on a thumb drive or two.

As I write, magazines are closing, few television programs interview serious writers, and (apart from NPR) radio is mainly music and sports talk. The writing profession that I have always known is changing, old media is ossified, and what I know of new media is that it is casual, opinionated, improvisational, largely unedited, full of whoppers, often plagiarized, and poorly paid. But as I set this down, I feel I am probably wrong, confusing (as my son once wrote of old men) the end of my life with the end of civilization, and that it is fogeyish to disparage innovation, or to suggest in tones of astonishment that the barbarians are at the gate, because they have always been there, giving writers a reason to be vigilant, and unsparing, and fully employed.

FIGURES
IN A
LANDSCAPE

1

MY DRUG TOUR: SEARCHING
FOR AYAHUASCA

When I first read The Yage Letters, *William Burroughs's cackling account of his drug search in Peru and down Colombia's Río Putumayo to find what he referred to in* Junky *as the grail of psychotropics ("Yage may be the final fix")—a trip in which he was rolled, robbed, starved, diverted, and endlessly bullshitted in his quest to find a high that towered way beyond your average stoner's dreams of doobage—I closed the book and thought: I really must repeat his trip sometime.*

This was in the 1960s, when the book first appeared, to cries of execration by the usual hypocrites. The book is an encouragement to any prospective quester, and very funny, too. "In all my experience as a homosexual I have never been the victim of such idiotic pilfering," he writes of a flirtation with a boy in Peru, then quickly adds, "Trouble is I share with the late Father Flanagan—he of Boys Town—the deep conviction that there is no such thing as a bad boy."

Yage is *yajé, Banisteriopsis caapi:* vine of the soul, secret nectar of the Amazon, the shaman's holy drink, the ultimate poison, a miracle cure. More generally known as ayahuasca, a word I found bewitching, it was said to make its users prescient if not telepathic. Rocket fuel is another active ingredient: in an ayahuasca trance, many users have testified, you travel to distant planets, you meet extraterrestrials and moon goddesses. "Yage is space time travel," Burroughs said. A singular proof of this is the collection of trance-state paintings by one of ayahuasca's greatest proponents, the shaman and *vegetalista* Don Pablo Amaringo. *Ayahuasca Visions,* Don Pablo's book (written with Luis Eduardo Luna), is a meticulous pictorial record of his many ayahuasca sessions. But there are risks in the drug, too, not least of which are convulsive fits and ghastly spells of vomiting. Many of Don Pablo's paintings include an image of someone engaged in picturesque puking.

Even my closest friends have seldom succeeded in exerting a malign influence on me: I am by nature pitch-averse, resistant to the selling mechanism. A persuasive sales pitch is no pitch at all, but rather something like a tremor that causes in me a distinct throb of aversion. Praise a product or a person to me, boost something or someone in my estimation, urge me to care deeply about a cause or a campaign, and my shit detector emits a high-pitched negative squeal that blorts in my head and sends me in the opposite direction.

Yet for all my circumspection, I have been seriously led astray by books. Reading about Africa made me want to go there; I spent six years in Malawi and Uganda in the 1960s, enthralled. Under the spell of Conrad I went to Singapore, not for a visit but for three years on that tyrannized and humid island of sullen overachievers — though my lengthy sojourn was relieved by trips to north Borneo, upper Burma, and Indonesia. Books led me to Africa, to India, to Patagonia, to the ends of the earth. I travel to find obstacles, to discover my limits, to ease the passage of time, to reassure myself that innocence and antiquity exist, to search for links to the past, to flee from the nastiness of urban life and the paranoia, if not outright dementia, of the technological world. *The Yage Letters* possessed me. Burroughs had written simply: "I decided to go down to Colombia and score for yage."

Years passed. Then I was in the middle of a novel and stuck for an idea, and in this period of Work in Stoppage I remembered "The Aleph," the great story of visions by Borges, in which a man finds the inch-wide stone, the Aleph, that allows him to see to the heart of himself and the world. I realized the moment had arrived for me to find the insight and telepathy of ayahuasca, which would be my Aleph.

Some friends, former amigos of the old gringo and self-exiled writer Moritz Thomsen, told me they knew of *ayahuasqueros* among the river people in eastern Ecuador. I was given the name of an outfit that shepherded aliens into the tributaries of the upper Amazon where traditional healers abounded. I made arrangements and soon found myself in a cheap hotel in Quito, awaiting the arrival of the other travelers on this drug tour.

"Drug tour" was my name for it. "Ethnobotanical experience" was the prettified official name for it, and some others spoke of it as a quest, a chance to visit a colorful Indian village, a clearing in the *selva tropical* where, just a few decades before, American missionaries sought early martyrdoms among the blowguns and poison-tipped arrows of indignant animists resisting forcible conversion to Christianity.

The people who organized this drug junket characterized it as a high-minded field trip, eight days in the rainforest, for eco-awareness and spiritual solidarity, to learn the names and uses of beneficial plants. One of those plants was ayahuasca. There was no promise of a ritual, yet heavy hints were dropped about a "healing." We would be living in a traditional village of indigenous Secoya people, deep in Ecuador's Oriente region, near the Colombian border, on a narrow branch of Burroughs's Putumayo, where the ayahuasca vine clinging to the trunks of rainforest trees grows as thick as a baby's arm.

But I had a bad feeling from the beginning. I am not used to traveling in groups, and this was a nervous and ill-assorted bunch, eight or ten people, a larger number than I had expected. The great attraction for me — it was the reason I had signed up — was that Don Pablo Amaringo would be our *vegetalista*. But even Don Pablo, in his stirring lecture in Quito before we set out, spoke of the conflicting vibrations he felt among the people in our group.

Don Pablo's gentle manner, shy Amazonian smile, and wide knowledge of jungle plants made him instantly persuasive. He was golden-skinned and slight of build, and his expressions were so animated and responsive it was impossible to tell his age. An experienced taker of ayahuasca, he had as a master painter been able to capture the experience in his pictures. He is a respected shaman, though he seldom used the word. "Shaman" is a term from the Siberian Evenki people that has gained wide acceptance. In Quechua, the word for shaman is *pajé*, "the man who embodies all experience."

Don Pablo was also a teacher; he ran an art school in Pucallpa, Peru. In 1953 Burroughs had found ayahuasca in Pucallpa. I trusted Don Pablo from the moment I met him. He remains one of the most gifted, insightful, and charismatic people I have met in my life. Don Pablo correctly diagnosed that I had unfinished business back home — my wife unwell, my affairs in a muddle; he seemed to know I was stuck in writing my book. His shrewdness reminded me that a substance named telepathine had been isolated from ayahuasca.

"Your mind is partly here and partly at home," he told me.

The others disturbed me. Except for a psychiatrist-poet and a young man who was on the trip to add a chapter to his book about his drug experiences (not long before, he had been roistering at the Burning Man festival), these people were not travelers. Even in Quito they looked out of their depth, and later, as we penetrated the Ecuadorian interior, they seemed to wilt. One woman cried easily, one man proclaimed militant Zionism, another her spirit search; a man confided to me that he was on a quest for spiritual fulfillment, another sobbed, "I need a healing." One lovely girl was beset by a chronic case of the squitters.

They thought of themselves as searchers. They seemed to have a touching faith in the efficacy of this trip, yet they seemed abysmally ill prepared for its rigors. The sobbing woman did not bother me much; I was more concerned by the anxious screeching facetiousness of some of the others. They seemed to me innocents. They were easily spooked, yet looking to repair their lives. Most had never been in a jungle before, or slept rough. They looked confused, giggling desperately in sweaty clothes, as though expecting to be ambushed. The organizers did their best to soothe the nerves of these people, yet I remained querulous and discontented, unused to so much apprehension. One woman was menstruating: the ceremony was forbidden to her.

Finally assembled, we left Quito late; we procrastinated at the Papallacta hot springs. Idling there at the edge of the forest, Don Pablo showed me a blossom, angel's trumpet, of the brugmansia family. There are many varieties, but this one was especially potent. "They call it datura — *toé* in Guarani. It can give you visions. In some ways this is more powerful than ayahuasca."

"In what way?"

"Great visions," he said, rubbing a leaf the way a Chinese connoisseur evaluates a piece of silk, "but it can make you blind."

Night fell as we traveled east, going slowly on bad roads. We arrived in darkness at Lago Agrio, a boomtown that had grown to accommodate the sprawl of American oil companies, which were exploiting the rainforest and displacing the Indians. At the hotel we took pains to hide our bus ("or it will be stolen"). We went to sleep in the stinking town of furtive shadows and sharp clicking heels; we awoke in a hot, bright place, a confusion of traffic and the sour-creamy stink of spilled oil and the toxic saturated earth.

Lago Agrio was a blight in the harsh equatorial sun. Because of a delay in our departure for the river, I lingered over coffee and fell into conversation with Joaquín, a local resident and volunteer guide who claimed to be a *vegetalista*. He was a young man, no more than thirty, with the look of an ascetic — long hair, faded shirt, sandals — that was also the look of a risk taker. He told me that the noises I had heard all night were the scurryings of prostitutes. It was, he said, a town of whores, drugs, gunrunning, rebels, and oil prospectors. You could buy anything here, at any time of day. Even the whorehouses never closed. It was then eight thirty in the morning.

"The *burdeles* are open even now," Joaquín said.

I challenged this, so he took me on a ten-minute taxi ride to a low building on a dirt road. Inside, women old and young, all of them in bathing suits, sat primly on folding chairs in front of little cubicles that surrounded a large dance floor. No one was dancing, though the music was loud. Two men were fighting, knocking over chairs. Eight or ten other men were drinking beer. The morning sun slanted through the building's small windows.

"They work all night in the oil fields and come here in the morning to get drunk and find a woman."

Joaquín led me through the back streets of the ramshackle town, where in little shops merchants whispered and handed me bones. "Endangered species!" The polished skulls of jaguars — called *tigres* — were for sale. There were also hunks of tortoiseshell, stuffed bats, mounted lizards, dead spiders transfixed by needles, and weapons of all sorts — blowguns, poison darts, machetes, wicked-looking shivs, bows and arrows.

"This was once rainforest. Just Indians and animals." Joaquín asked me what I wanted. I could have anything — a monkey skull, a tiger skin, drugs, guns, a fourteen-year-old girl. He could even arrange what he called a Toxic Tour, a survey of the local blight caused by Halliburton and Occidental Petroleum.

I told him I was going down the Río Aguarico with my group of gringos, to a village of the Secoyas. He recognized this as shorthand for a drug tour, and he made an elbow-bending motion and a drinker's gesture.

"Ayahuasca," I said.

"You could drink it near here. I know people," he said. And in one shop he showed me bags of medicinal herbs and plants, and fat dusty lengths of cut-off ayahuasca bulging in gunnysacks.

"No, I want to see the village."

What had started as a fairly straightforward search for the ayahuasca experience was becoming more complex, crowding my head with images — the oil squirting from bandaged pipes running alongside the road, the faces of the prostitutes — young fearful girls, old resentful women, the devilish faces of their customers — the grinning tiger skulls, the spiders as big as my fist, the heat, the dust.

And terrorism. Joaquín had told me that the previous night on the bridge into Colombia, about ten miles away, some guerrilla soldiers of the FARC had stopped twenty cars. At gunpoint they had given the drivers cans of gasoline and said, "Douse your car and burn it, or we'll shoot you."

Twenty flaming cars blocked the San Miguel Bridge to Colombia, at La Punta, the frontier, that day.

"It is to discourage visitors," Joaquín said with Ecuadorian understatement.

Leaving Joaquín, I rejoined the ecotourists. We took a bus to the muddy settlement of Chiritza, on the banks of the Aguarico River. In Lago Agrio, on the roadsides, in Chiritza, and along the riverbanks were mud-spattered signs, all bearing the same message: *Prohibido el Paso.* Keep Out. We then boarded a dugout canoe and crouched inside this enormous hollowed-out tree trunk and set off downstream, powered by a farting outboard motor.

The river narrowed from a hundred yards or more to fifty, then thirty, in less than an hour, the jungle overhanging it like thatch, drooping bamboo and trailing vines and big-leaved trees. The nervous chatter of the passengers in the dugout drowned the cries of flitting birds.

Such a river, deep brown from the silt of runoff from the rains, and such a fragile-seeming boat, in such a distant place, created a sense of uncertainty among the gringos. The anxiety of traveling slowly down the gullet of the jungle suggested that a place so hard to get to would be equally hard to get out of. We were in the hands of the monosyllabic guides and the taciturn boatmen. I did not like the feeling of being in the same boat with these others. I need a degree of control over my coming and going. I am not happy in a herd, especially a herd of debutantes.

Daylight drained from the sky, the jungle darkened, the river gurgled at the hull of the dugout; yet the river, amazingly, was still visible, holding the last of the light, as though the day glowed undissolved in its muddy current.

"*Remolino*," a boatman said. Whirlpool.

Beyond that swirl, and a long reach of the river, was the village: men in orange smocks, one or two wearing coronets of feathers and vines, boys snatching at the bowline and helping the visitors ashore.

We were directed to a communal platform, where we would all sleep on mats or in hammocks. I resisted this, partly because furry knuckle-sized insects were bumping and batting the glaring lanterns, but mainly because I wished to sleep alone. I had brought my small tent — packed, it was the size of a football — and my down-filled sleeping bag, much smaller in its bag than the tent. I set up camp in a clearing at the edge of the village.

For the following two days the creepy feeling I'd had at the outset deepened. I felt an uncertainty awaiting me back home, a sense of misfortune and dread; and also a disarray, a greater uncertainty, here. The awareness of killing time wore on me in the sadness and decrepitude of the Secoya village.

I sat on a fallen log with Don Pablo, making notes while spiders and ants crept across the pages of my notebook and the river sucked at the muddy bank. I told him I was having trouble with my novel. He spoke to me about the Eye of Understanding.

"This eye can see things that can't be seen physically," he said. "Some people have this third eye already developed. And for others the Eye of Understanding can be acquired through ayahuasca or some other jungle plants."

Each morning the group had same question: "Tonight?"

"Not tonight."

Not auspicious, or was it that a certain shaman had not arrived as planned, or that signals had been crossed? A great sleepy uneasiness, dank with the moss and mildew of the forest, settled over us.

If someone seemed at a loss for something to do, he or she was told, "You can weed Juana's garden."

Or we could paint pictures, or help build one of the structures, or consult the healers on botanical strategies. Most of the gringos were happy to pitch in, but impatience was growing, a sense of discomfort, disorganization. The gringos who had seemed so tidy in Quito were looking grubby, sweaty, careworn. The Frenchman among us ridiculed America and the young writer objected to his casual abuse; a woman described her life as a series of sorry episodes and began to cry. A low level of bickering began as a barely audible hum in the jungle clearing.

"Where have you been?" people began asking me.

"Looking around," I said, annoyed that my absence had been noticed. In fact, I was spending time on the riverbank at the edge of the village making notes, or in my tent, away from the spiders, listening to my shortwave radio.

One morning Enrique, an Ecuadorian man, was denounced for his drunkenness the night before. As he was being humiliated and asked to apologize before the gringos, I smiled at his accusers' sanctimony.

When they were done, I pointed out that all this man's persecutors were chain smokers and drug users. What was the problem with alcohol?

"Alcohol has taken a terrible toll on the indigenous people here," one of the American guides said.

And I was also thinking: Where's the ayahuasca? Don Pablo went on explaining it to me. Ayahuasca was like death, he said. "When you drink it, you die. The soul leaves the body. But this soul is an eye to show you the future. You will see your grandchildren. When the trance is over the soul is returned."

One day, bored and restless in the village, I found a Secoya man to take me deeper into the rainforest.

He said, "We can see flowers. Birds. Big trees."

Preceding me, he slashed with a machete; a small Secoya boy followed. This was like Burroughs's trip, just as aimless and improvisational. People went on such drug tours in a mental quandary, it seemed. They were unused to being at close quarters in a simple village, and they were growing impatient waiting, as I was, for the shaman to summon us to the ayahuasca ceremony. I was happy to be away from their agitated laughter.

We walked for three hours in the humid heat on a muddy track under the high rainforest canopy. The flowers I saw growing wild were those I associated with Hawaii: brilliant heliconias, beaky strelitzias, wild-eyed blossoms, pink torches of wild ginger, and the attenuated datura, angel's trumpet, which gave people visions and made them blind. Ayahuasca, too: the vine was unprepossessing and serpentine on the tree trunks.

Only the dimmest daylight penetrated to the forest floor. The greenish air was littered with gnats and filtered sunlight, and here and there a large woolly wheel of a spider's web, the spider crouched at the edge like a small dusty plum with legs.

Just as I was thinking that it was possible to believe that, though humans had passed nearby, none had interfered with it, nor had ever bent a stem, nor plucked a flower, that this was a little Eden of the Secoya people, the small boy called out, "*Escucha,*" tilting his head to listen.

There came a far-off chugging, like a motorboat plowing invisibly through the sky, and when it drew closer it became a more distinct *yak-yak-yak.*

"*Mira! Helicóptero,*" the boy said, his hair in his eyes.

A shadow like a big brown cloud passed overhead, a gigantic Russian helicopter.

The forest dome with its branches and leaves prevented us from seeing the progress of the helicopter, yet we still heard it and were able to follow its percussive sound, the drumbeat of its engine burps in the distance.

We were off the path now and chest-high in ferns and big leaves as we saw ahead a brightness, perhaps a clearing, and then the descending shadow of the chopper settling to earth.

We were stopped by a head-high chainlink fence that ran through the forest, razor wire coiled along the top edge, and skull-and-crossbones signs lettered in red, *Prohibido el Paso,* every twenty feet or so. Sunlight scorched the clearing within the fence — sunlight and steel towers and box-like prefab structures and oil drums, and the huge sputtering helicopter, its twin rotors slowing, as men in yellow hard hats rushed back and forth from its open cargo bay, unloading cardboard boxes.

The encampment was entirely encircled by the fence and the forest. No road led here. And there was no break in the fence — no opening, not even a gate. When the sound of the helicopter died down, we could hear the softer but regular pulsing of an engine and could see a steel cylinder moving up and down in the center of the clearing, pounding the earth with gasping and swallowing noises, and the lurch of unmistakable grunts that sounded like squirts of satisfaction, pumping oil.

Near the entrance to one of the new bright boxy buildings an Ecuadorian all in white — white shirt, white apron, tall white chef's hat — was conferring with another swarthy man in a short black jacket and striped trousers and a bow tie. This second man, obviously a waiter or a wine steward, held a tray on his fingertips, and on the tray was a pair of thin-stemmed wine glasses and a wine bottle in an ice bucket.

Gringos, clearly Americans, were climbing out of the cockpit of the helicopter.

"*Petroleros*," the Secoya man said, and added that we must leave at once.

It was one of the ugliest things I had ever seen in my life.

"This is Secoya land," I said. "How can they be drilling for oil?"

"We own what is on top," he said. "The government owns what is under the ground."

Later, I learned that the local people had been paid a pittance by the American oil company so that the fence could be erected, but no profits would accrue to them, and it was only a matter of time before this part of the rainforest would have the shops and brothels and bars and oil-spattered roads of Lago Agrio.

The vision of this oil well in the virgin forest added to my sense of derangement and demoralized me. I consulted Don Pablo.

"You are not calm," he said, and held my hands.

This was an understatement. I crawled into my tent that night, listening to the chatter of the gringos on the sleeping platform, wondering whether I had the stomach for this. My search for the final fix was turning into a stubborn stall of procrastination. That night I had a nightmare: my wife was very ill and calling out for me. In the morning I put this down to ambiguous guilt, my unconscious mind justifying my confusion and apportioning blame.

Sitting on the riverbank pondering what to do, I saw three gringo women from our group dressed in shirts and shorts begin swimming across the river from the far bank. They were chirpy, gargling water as they clumsily paddled in the swift brown stream. One cried out, "I lost my ring! It just dropped off my finger!"

The two others hesitated, and as they stopped swimming they were pulled downstream. The woman who lost the ring said, "Never mind. It was meant to be," but the river was too much for her, too. I kicked off my sandals and dived in, reached her after a few strokes, and brought her to shore. One of the others was thrashing but didn't need much help, so I went after the third, who was heading toward Brazil in the churning current.

She was blowing and gasping as I got to her. Her clothes were dragging her down, she could barely lift her arms, but her shirt gave me something to hang on to, and so, slowly — cautioning her not to grab me; I feared her panicky grip — I tugged her to shore.

Perhaps she was in shock. She whinnied a bit, mirthless laughter. She didn't thank me. She said, "I think I could have made it on my own."

In that moment of ingratitude, near tragedy, and plain foolishness, I decided to bail out. My bad feeling about this group and this place seemed justified. What was I doing here? I had come for the drug, and I had seen the horror of Lago Agrio — whores and drugs and stories of burned cars and the Toxic Tour. Looking for the purity of the jungle, I had found the violation of the oil people. These reckless women who had almost drowned themselves seemed proof that worse might be in store. And besides, my wife was ill.

I rolled up my sleeping bag, folded my tent, and found a Secoya man who said he had a boat with an outboard motor. I paid him the $100 he asked for — pretty steep, I thought — and he took me upriver to Shushu-findi, where I found my way back to Lago Agrio.

As soon as I was alone I could think straight. Instead of eco-chic, ethno-botany, the rainforest experience, shamanism, or visions, I had encountered child prostitutes, gunrunners, Big Oil, and blighted jungle, the place surrounded by FARC guerrillas. The diminishing number of Secoyas seemed doomed. That village would soon be swallowed by the encroachment of oil people, who were only half a day's march through the forest.

Perhaps this was meant to be my adventure, though I had not known it at the outset. The whole point of adventure is that it is unplanned; a leap in the dark, verging on the unfortunate, offering glimpses of danger; and what separates adventure from disaster is that you live to tell the tale.

Back in Lago Agrio, I found Joaquín. He made the swigging motion with his hand and arm and gave me an inquiring smile.

In Spanish, I said, "No. It's a Chinese story."

Meaning, as the idiom has it, long and preposterous.

"Maybe I can help you," he said.

The others downriver were perhaps preparing for their ceremony. I had come all this way, and yet sitting there in that dreadful town I felt calm, even happy. I was on my own. I called my wife — yes, she had been ill, but with worry because she hadn't heard from me. So I had a reprieve, and now I had no sense of urgency.

My ayahuasca ceremony was private, one-on-one in a large, open-sided shed inside the walled compound — *Prohibido el Paso* — of a large house at the edge of Lago Agrio. Don Pablo had briefed me, so I was prepared, though I would have preferred him to be my shaman. After all I had seen, I feared this ceremony would be an anticlimax. This was not a Secoya village, yet the shaman was real enough, and as for the ayahuasca, my barfing convinced me of its potency, the way poison can be medicinal.

Crouched and retching, I slipped into a time warp, twisting in a hammock to an auditory gust, a cataract of sound, of tinkling song, and matching images — torrents, and a waterfall of snakes, the serpents slithering in lakes of oil, the bleeding trees and spiders, helicopters that could have been spaceships, the scaly greasy river, which bunched and swelled like an anaconda. The rasping hum in my belly might have been the chanting of the shaman. My whole body was vibrant with a syncopation of grunts and murmurs, but the colors I saw were subdued, like enlarged pixels.

The visions, though disturbing — the sticky oil flow, the twisted snakes — did not strike fear into me, but seemed to be part of something whole and coherent, fitting into a harmonious world of creation and destruction. The harmony was both the sound of the chanting and the glitter of the foliage and flitting birds and, as in a poem by Rimbaud, monstrous mouth-like blossoms.

I woke drooling and gasping, somehow on the floor of an open-air pavilion, my face stuck to a raffia mat. I had scored for *yajé*.

Back home, I was reassured that my wife was fine now. For the whole of my time downriver she had felt short of breath, almost asthmatic with the anxiety that I was in danger. Some time later, I talked to a few people from the tour who had joined the ayahuasca ceremony in the Secoya village. On one or two of them the drug had had no effect; others had experienced the moon shot. And there was a visitor — me, in my Panama hat and Hawaiian shirt.

"Two people saw you," one of the *ayahuasqueros* told me. "You were there in our visions, watching us."

That ghostly visitation was like a metaphor for being a novelist. Not long afterward I threw away what I had begun of my novel and started the real thing. Having experienced the blinding light of this drug tour, I felt I understood my subject. My novel went well, and in the several years of my writing it I often thought: Sometimes there's a spider in your cup that you don't see. You drink and move on, never knowing the creature is lurking in the liquid. But I had guzzled the whole cup and had a glimpse of the poisonous insect. I was resolute, with one of my favorite lines from Shakespeare murmuring in my mind: "I have drunk and seen the spider."

Truly, I had not known what I was in for before I went. I now knew where, and what it had done to me. "A place where the unknown past and the emergent future meet in a vibrating soundless hum," Burroughs wrote of his ayahuasca experience in *The Yage Letters*. "Larval entities waiting for a live one."

That was a lyrical way of putting it. And I had been "the live one." Ayahuasca was the formal reason for my journey, but the whole point of a leap in the dark is that you cannot foretell your fate. Many things I had seen on this trip had mattered much more than the ayahuasca. A few gringos dabbling in psychotropic drug potions was just a charade compared to everything else that was going on beyond the village.

In a sense, the effect was like that of datura, the brugmansia drug that made you blind. The systematic oil search and the frantic drilling amounted to a conspiracy by American oil interests as they connived with the Ecuadorian government to take the oil and change the face of the rainforest forever. The result was — what? Enough oil to run Los Angeles for a week or so, vast profits for a few people, and more hookers, gunrunners, guerrillas, and homeless people in a bigger sprawling Lago Agrio. It was a terrible vision to take home, but one I went on living with. As in "The Aleph," I also saw the circulation of my own dark blood. Adventure is the unexpected experience of discovery, of course; but it is also a kind of death, an end of innocence.

2

THOREAU IN THE WILDERNESS

Henry David Thoreau was so emotionally attached to his home in Concord that he found it almost impossible to leave. In fact, after 1837 he did so only for short periods: thirteen days on the Concord and Merrimack Rivers, some visits to Cape Cod, three trips to the Maine woods, brief spells in Staten Island and Minnesota. He was never alone on these excursions, always went with a friend or relative. He was one of the earliest climbers to the heights of Mount Katahdin, but that was a bold exception, and he probably did not achieve the highest peak. The canoe trip of 325 miles he writes about in "The Allegash and East Branch" in The Maine Woods *was his most ambitious trip — and a hard one — but the book shows that for all Thoreau's enthusiasm for the wilderness, he was sometimes lost and confused in the deep woods. The experience convinced him that he would never be able to live there on his own.*

The Maine woods were wilderness, but Thoreau emphasizes their proximity: they are only a matter of hours from easily accessible Bangor. Walden Pond was a pleasant walk to his family home, where he lived for almost his entire life. During his famous experiment in his cabin at Walden, moralizing about his solitude, he did not mention that he brought his mother his dirty laundry and went on enjoying her apple pies. His friend William Ellery Channing wrote that, after his graduation from Harvard, when his mother broached the subject of his leaving home, Thoreau became weepy — and didn't leave.

Though his friend and literary mentor Emerson went to England in search of inspiration, and other contemporaries traveled widely on the globe — Hawthorne to England, Washington Irving to Spain, Melville to the Pacific — Thoreau was not impressed. The reports of such peregrinations roused him to be defiant and sometimes condescending. He was self-consciously a contrarian. He cultivated his eccentricity and talked it up in his writing, but his personality was a great deal stranger than he knew, and perhaps beyond cultivation.

His characteristic response to his world-traveling friends was (as he confided to his journal), "Methinks, I should be content to sit at the backdoor in Concord, under the poplar tree, henceforth forever." Is Thoreau in this saying any more than Dorothy in *The Wizard of Oz* in her final epiphany: "If I ever go looking for my heart's desire again, I'll never look further than my own back yard"? Perhaps not, but Thoreau's deflations are often paradoxes. Anyway, why leave Concord when, as he wrote in a poem,

> Our village shows a rural Venice,
> Its broad lagoons where yonder fen is;
> As lovely as the Bay of Naples
> Yon placid cove amid the maples;
> And in my neighbor's field of corn
> I recognize the Golden Horn.

This is Thoreau's usual attitudinizing, the lovable but maddening stay-at-home stubbornness of an American village explainer who has never seen Venice, Naples, or Turkey, and doesn't intend to. Its special pleading seems suspect, and you have to question his insistence on staying put and the fact that he seldom mentioned foreign parts except to belittle them. The inherent provincialism of the attitude, which so caught Henry James's critical eye, lies at the heart of Thoreau's desire to chronicle the wildness in Maine. He wanted to find it spooky and saturated with the past and wild enough to report that it had never been seen by a white man before — a claim he makes on his first trip, in just those words.

Thoreau was assertively American, in a manner of conspicuous nonconformity inspired by Emerson. Thoreau's passion was for being local, and that included being a traveler in America — to show how to care about the country, what tone to use, what subjects to address. By the way, in adopting and refining these postures, he became our first and subtlest environmentalist. In Maine his subjects were, as he listed them in a letter, "the Moose, the Pine Tree & and the Indian." The last words he spoke on his deathbed were "Moose . . . Indian."

Thoreau's three Maine trips, from 1846 to 1857, overlap the publication of Melville's greatest works. There is no proof that Thoreau read *Moby-Dick*, but there is ample evidence that he read *Typee*, which appeared at the time of his first visit to Maine, and which he discussed in a discarded early version of "Ktaadn." Somewhat combative in comparing wildernesses, Thoreau argued that he experienced deeper wilderness in Maine than Melville had as a castaway in the high volcanic archipelago of the remote Marquesas, among the lovely maiden Fayaway and the anthropophagous islanders. It seems a stretch, but there it is.

Among other things, Thoreau's trips to the Maine woods were a deliberate search, like that of his contemporary George Catlin, to understand the Indian as an American ideal. Thoreau was an early and unbigoted chronicler of Native Americans and as great a portraitist of them in words as Catlin was on canvas. But Catlin was traveling in the Far West, and Thoreau never saw the finery and feathers or the dignity of Catlin's subjects. Speaking of an Indian in one of the more lyrical and mystical passages at the end of "Ktaadn," he concludes, "He glides up the Millinocket and is lost to my sight, as a more distant and misty cloud is seen flitting behind a nearer, and is lost in space. So he goes about his destiny, the red face of man."

Against Thoreau's longest trips away from home, two futile months of illness in Minnesota, six homesick months in Staten Island, we must consider the accomplishments of the heroic travelers of his time: Sir Richard Burton in Arabia and Africa, Sir John Franklin in the Arctic, Sir Joseph Hooker in Tibet, Henry Walter Bates on the Amazon, Darwin in the Galápagos, Alfred Russel Wallace in the Far East. I mention these travelers because Thoreau, who read widely in travel narratives — this literary genre was one of his greatest enthusiasms — read the books of most of these men. He was fascinated by Burton in Arab disguise in the holy cities of Mecca and Medina, and as a writer and thinker was profoundly influenced by Darwin's *Voyage of the Beagle* and *On the Origin of Species*.

Thoreau's denigrating witticism, "It is not worth the while to go around the world to count the cats in Zanzibar," is well known, yet he much preferred books of African travel. Arctic travel books were another passion and taught him how to write about the freezing and thawing of Walden

Pond. He also read Lewis and Clark (the account of their expedition was first published in 1814) and was keenly, almost competitively, aware that in his lifetime America was still being ambitiously explored. At roughly the period Thoreau was hiking and paddling in the Maine woods, John Frémont and Kit Carson were exploring in the Rocky Mountains.

In his reading and in his own travel, Thoreau — obsessed with unspoiled America and in search of primeval forest — was insistent that Maine was wilder than more distant parts of the country. The logging metropolis of Bangor he describes in a lovely image as "like a star at the edge of night, still hewing at the forests of which it is built." And as for wilderness, he says that "some hours of travel" north of Bangor "will carry the curious to the verge of a primitive forest, more interesting, perhaps, on all accounts, than they would reach by going a thousand miles westward." A thousand miles westward would have landed him in Columbus, Ohio.

Thoreau traveled for information and experience, but he also traveled in search of metaphors and, most of all, to carry back with him a narrative structure. He traveled (as *A Week on the Concord and Merrimack Rivers* shows) in order to have the bones of a trip to flesh out with wisdom and insight, aperçus, poems (his own and others'), and asides so extensive they amounted to essays. The conceit of *A Week* was that it was a week of floating down rivers. It is anything but that, and is hardly a travel book in any conventional sense. Each day is a lengthy chapter of philosophy and natural history, with plenty of breezy denunciations of Christianity and mocks against organized religion (this obsessive secularism killed the book's chances with readers at the time). One of his best essays (on friendship) is a later insertion. *A Week* is replete with such insertions, and *Walden* went through seven different handwritten drafts.

With such an appetite for revision, narrative plumping, second thoughts, tidying up, and rewriting, it is little wonder that Thoreau published only two books in his lifetime, though he had plans for a number of others. *The Maine Woods* was to be one of them, *Cape Cod* another, and he spoke of a book about Indians. It is important to point out that, for all its insights, *The Maine Woods*, published posthumously, is a set of three narratives in various states of completion; not a unified book, but rather a three-decker sandwich of woodland excursions. As a record of impressions, a work in progress, it is all the more interesting for that. "Ktaadn" is a polished and youthful piece, "Chesuncook" finished and mature, and "The Allegash and

East Branch" somewhat provisional, though containing a wealth of information.

The whole book is rife with repetitions, contradictions, and loosely organized matter. A trivial example: the name Sunkhaze is used early in "Ktaadn." It is a small stream near Oldtown. "We crossed the Sunkhaze, a summery Indian name." But almost three hundred pages later, Sunkhaze is defined by Joe Polis with his characteristic (and hardly summery) allusiveness, "Suppose you are going down Penobscot, just like we, and you see a canoe come out of bank and go along before you, but you no see 'em stream. That is *Sunkhaze*."

I feel compelled to point out to an unsuspecting first reader of *The Maine Woods* that each narrative begins in the most pedestrian, almost off-putting way, with a date of departure and a recitation of unadorned bits of information, with all the plodding factuality of a traveling salesman's route report. Each section begins in the same way, but soon after, in each case, when he has left the settlements behind and is in the woods, Thoreau hits his stride. He is an inexhaustible observer ("A spy in the camp," he describes himself in his note-taking). Anyone who reads Thoreau must inevitably regret that he did not at some point leave the American continent and travel abroad, for he was in the whole of literature one of the most sensitive and scrupulous noticers of nature and man.

In "Ktaadn" he defines the essence of wilderness. "It is difficult to conceive of a region uninhabited by man," he begins modestly. Then comes his hammer stroke: "Nature was here something savage and awful, though beautiful. I looked with awe at the ground I trod on, to see what the Powers had made there, the form and fashion and material of their work. This was that Earth of which we have heard, made out of Chaos and Old Night. Here was no man's garden, but the unhandselled globe. It was not lawn, nor pasture, nor mead, nor woodland, nor lea, nor arable, nor waste-land. It was the fresh and natural surface of the planet Earth, as it was made forever and ever."

It is a wonderful passage. You may wonder what Thoreau was doing in his cabin at the shore of Walden Pond for two years. One of the things he was doing was writing sentences like those, for he took his first Maine trip when resident at Walden and worked it up into a article there, which he used as a basis for public lectures. He was twenty-seven years old and at his most lyrical, most prone to the dazzling set piece and to the minute observation that he had learned from reading Darwin.

He went to Maine again seven years later. He was still the poet, still lyrical, but with a writing style of satisfying particularity. Consider the passage in "Chesuncook" where his Indian guide Joe Aitteon shoots and wounds a moose. The moose flees and Aitteon follows. Thoreau is closely watching: "He proceeded rapidly up the bank and through the woods, with a peculiar, elastic, noiseless, and stealthy tread, looking to the right and left on the ground, and stepping in the faint tracks of the wounded moose, now and then pointing in silence to a single drop of blood on the handsome shining leaves of the Clintonia Borealis, which on every side covered the ground, or to a dry fern-stem freshly broken, all the while chewing some leaf or else the spruce gum."

In another passage in "Chesuncook," justly famous for its beauty and its accuracy, Thoreau describes a tree falling some distance off in the forest: "Once, when Joe had called again, and we were listening for moose, we heard come faintly echoing, or creeping from far through the moss-clad aisles, a dull, dry, rushing sound with a solid core to it, yet as if half smothered under the grasp of the luxuriant and fungus-like forest, like the shutting of a door in some distant entry of the damp and shaggy wilderness. If we had not been there no mortal had heard it. When we asked Joe in a whisper what it was, he answered, 'Tree fall.'"

Thoreau took his last Maine woods trip in 1857. He was forty then, and you can see by his prose style that he is a different sort of traveler: humbler, affronted by the changes he sees in the eleven years since his first visit, no longer a quoter of Milton, a praiser of lumberjacks, or a hyperbolic observer of the mystical Indian. He is now a denouncer of the logging industry and a clear-sighted diarist. Indians fascinated Thoreau, and this third trip in Maine offered him his best opportunity to study them. Through his guide Joe Polis, Thoreau was able to record firsthand the life and habits of a Penobscot Indian who still retained something of his people's traditions.

He had searched for Indians on his first trip, but did not find any companions. The Indians in "Ktaadn" were living in "shabby, forlorn, and cheerless" houses, and the single woman he saw was "shabby." One man he met was a "stalwart, but dull and greasy-looking fellow." The Indians were "woebegone," they were drunks, and worst of all they were Christians.

Seeing a well-built Catholic church in Oldtown, Thoreau (the young, the quipping, the contrary, the hyperbolic traveler) remarked, "I even thought that a row of wigwams, with a dance of pow-wows, and a prisoner tortured at the stake, would be more respectable than this."

The Indians in "Ktaadn" are glimpsed from a distance and summed up with typical Thoreauvian briskness and presumption. No Indian accompanies him in "Ktaadn." Louis Neptune, a possible guide, lets him down. With Joe Aitteon in "Chesuncook" Thoreau scruples to look deeper and finds someone unexpected. Aitteon is "a son of the Governor" (the tribal governor). He is twenty-four years old, "good looking," "short and stout," with narrow "turned up eyes," and sturdily dressed. After these mundane details Thoreau offers us this: "When afterward he had occasion to take off his shoes and stockings, I was struck by the smallness of his feet." We at once see Joe Aitteon as perhaps delicate and slightly more interesting.

"I narrowly watched his motions, and listened attentively to his observations, for we had employed an Indian mainly that I might have an opportunity to study his ways." What Thoreau sees is that Aitteon has a peculiar gait, that he is a great tracker, that he whistles "O Susanna" and says "Yes, sir-ee" and "By George!" That he is illiterate ("though he was a Governor's son"), that he knew little about the history of his people. Thoreau reveals his own naïveté as a traveler among native peoples in being disconcerted by Joe Aitteon's apparently slender grasp of distances. But in the rough terrain of folk societies, miles are meaningless; actual travel time is what counts. This is the chief distinction between the person with a map (Thoreau) and the person with profound experience of the region (Aitteon), for Aitteon could tell "at what time we should arrive, but not how far it was."

Thoreau notes that Joe Aitteon had difficulty conveying an abstract idea —presumably in the English language—for hearing Aitteon's fluency in his mother tongue of Abenaki one night gave Thoreau the feeling that as an outsider he "stood, or rather lay, as near to the primitive man of America, that night, as any of its discoverers ever did." That Crusoe moment, Thoreau believed, was one of his triumphs as a traveler in the Maine woods.

It is apparent that Joe Aitteon was not the Indian archetype Thoreau was looking for. Aitteon was too familiar with the white world. His "O Susanna" and his catchphrases grated on Thoreau's finely tuned ear. On Thoreau's third visit he found the man he sought. True, Joe Polis was a Christian, and so he refused to work on Sunday; he had a sweet tooth; and he had been to Washington, D.C., and New York City. He had met (and been rebuffed by) no less a personage than Daniel Webster. But he is more knowledgeable than Aitteon, has considerable skills as a woodsman, is a master of wilderness topography, and knows the names of plants, trees, landscape features — and this information he shares with Thoreau. Indian-fashion, he uses his teeth ("often where we should have used a hand"). Joe Polis is wellborn, "one of the aristocracy." He is shrewd, enigmatic, given to gnomic utterances. Asked by Thoreau how he finds his way home through the trackless forest, Polis just laughs. "O, I can't tell you . . . Great differences between me and white man." On a later occasion, discussing the mending of a canoe with pitch, Polis confides "that there were some things which a man did not tell even his own wife."

One of the most heartfelt descriptions of Joe Polis is Thoreau's recording the Indian's memory of almost starving to death on a trip through the woods in winter as a boy of ten. This harrowing story, simply related, occurs toward the end of "The Allegash." The Indian is admirable for his toughness, but what impresses Thoreau most about Joe Polis is his self-possession and the simplicity of his life. In his style of dress and travel he is the Thoreauvian ideal: "He wore a cotton shirt, originally white, a greenish flannel one over it, but no waistcoat, flannel drawers, a strong linen or duck pants, which had also been white, blue woollen stockings, cowhide boots, and a Kossuth hat. He carried no change of clothing, but putting on a stout thick jacket, which he laid aside in the canoe, and seizing a full-sized axe, his gun and ammunition, and a blanket, which would do for a sail or knapsack if wanted, and strapping on his belt, which contained a large sheath-knife, he walked off at once, ready to be gone all summer."

In the portrait of Joe Polis, the man seems as eternal as the trees and the rocks. "I have much to learn of the Indian, nothing of the missionary," Thoreau writes, pondering his guide. Thoreau's method, as he relates it to Joe Polis, is, "I told him that in this voyage I would tell him all I knew, and he should tell me all he knew." Thoreau's experiences in the Maine woods have a humbling effect on him, turning him from an explainer into a student. Earlier, in "Chesuncook," seeing an Indian making canoes, he writes, "I made a faithful study of canoe-building, and I thought that I should like to serve an apprenticeship at that trade for one season, going into the woods for bark with my 'boss,' making the canoe there, and returning in it at last."

Hearing Joe Polis divulge the identification of birdsong, Thoreau wishes again to be tutored. "I observed that I should like to go to school to him to learn his language, living on the Indian island the while." Polis taught Thoreau so many Abenaki words that a glossary ("A List of Indian Words") was included in an appendix to most editions of *The Maine Woods*. After Polis shows him the traditional way of making soup from lily roots, Thoreau tries to cook some himself. And at the end of the trip (rather late in the day for this lesson), Polis teaches Thoreau the Indian method of paddling a canoe.

Throughout *The Maine Woods*, Thoreau disabuses himself of the presumption that the Indians are preservationists. Joe Aitteon readily admits that he cannot survive in the woods as his ancestors ("wild as bears") did. The woods are not a residence for Indians, but rather their hunting ground, he says, yet he blames them for their opportunism. "What a coarse and imperfect use Indians and hunters make of nature! No wonder that their race is soon exterminated!" Although this is unreasonable (he said earlier the Indians had been hunting there for four thousand years), he correctly envisages that indiscriminate logging and hunting will ultimately change the face of the forest forever.

One of the most dramatic episodes in the book is the killing of a moose by Joe Aitteon. Thoreau's descriptions of moose are inspired and fanciful: "They made me think of great frightened rabbits," and "It reminded me at once of the camelopard," and its "branching and leafy horns — a sort of fucus or lichen in bone." In all these descriptions there is affection and awe. The killing of a moose is in Thoreau's view a tragedy ("nature looked sternly upon me on account of the murder of the moose"), but Thoreau grudgingly acknowledges that moose are hunted by Indians out of necessity — for their meat, for their hides, as part of Indian custom and tradition.

In one of the great passages in "Chesuncook" Thoreau writes how the moose and the pine tree are linked in his mind. "A pine cut down, a dead pine, is no more a pine than a dead human carcass is a man." He speaks of the "petty and accidental uses" of whales and elephants, turned into "buttons and flageolets." He continues, "Every creature is better alive than dead, men and moose and pine-trees, and he who understands it aright will rather preserve life than destroy it."

The Indian is no more a friend of the pine than is the lumberjack; indeed, the only friend of the pine — and the moose, and the wilderness — is the poet. Change nothing, kill nothing, neither moose nor pine, he says in rolling hortatory sentences. This wonderfully humane argument ends with Thoreau extolling the pine tree, what he loves most: "the living spirit of the tree." He ends with, "It is as immortal as I am, and perchance will go to as high a heaven, there to tower above me still."

When "Chesuncook" appeared in the *Atlantic Monthly*, the editor of the magazine, James Russell Lowell, cut that last sentence. The circumstances of this, and Thoreau's reaction, are telling. Lowell had recently taken over as editor. He had no great liking for Thoreau as a person: they had attended Harvard at the same time, but Lowell was something of a socialite and a dandy, and Thoreau was Thoreau. Lowell asked for a magazine piece. Thoreau submitted "Chesuncook." The proofs were corrected and sent to Thoreau, who saw the sentence provisionally crossed out. Thoreau wrote "stet" in the margin. When the piece appeared, the sentence was gone. Thoreau suspected, perhaps rightly, that Lowell found it heathenish in its nature worship, excessively hyperbolic, a little too mystical and druidic, unworthy of inclusion in a magazine Lowell intended to be welcome in all households. Whatever, Thoreau said that cutting without his permission was "mean and cowardly."

It is easy to see that the offending sentence sums up Thoreau's view of the world. In omitting it Lowell showed his disapproval of this view and thus rejected one of Thoreau's core beliefs. And Thoreau, who distrusted authority of all sorts, came down hard on him. His letter is a small masterpiece in defense of authorship. Among other things, he wrote to Lowell: "The editor has, in this case, no more right to omit a sentiment than to insert one, or put words into my mouth. I do not ask anyone to adopt my opinions, but I do expect that when they ask for them in print, they will print them, or obtain my consent to their alteration or omission. I should not read many books if I thought that they had been thus expurgated. I feel this treatment to be an insult, though not intended as such, for it is to presume that I can be hired to suppress my opinions."

After insisting that the sentence be printed in the next issue — it never was — Thoreau went on, "I am not willing to be associated in any way, unnecessarily, with parties who will confess themselves so bigoted & timid as this implies. I could excuse a man who was afraid of an uplifted fist, but if one habitually manifests fear at the utterance of a sincere thought, I must think that his life is a kind of nightmare continued into broad daylight."

Thoreau had gone to Maine in search of such epiphanies as he described in the pine tree sentence. He had strongly, even erotically identified with trees, not just in his famous declaration "All nature is my bride," but in an owlish quip he committed to his journal in 1856: "There was a match found for me at last. I fell in love with a shrub oak." In slashing the sentence Lowell was denying Thoreau the central thought of his argument, his love for the forest, and I think we should see in Thoreau's reaction what he values in his book. That is a sentence, and a belief, Thoreau wants us to remember. It is a summing up of the very spirit of the book.

The spirit of *The Maine Woods* is youthful. One of Thoreau's chief characteristics is his boyishness — even his mother love, his playful puns, and his staying close to home are aspects of this. So, I believe, are the many instances of simple happiness in his freedom in the Maine woods. And what are those enthusiastic yearnings to acquire Indian skills — learning how to speak Abenaki, to make a canoe — except wishes to be a young student again? The talk of eating off birch-bark plates with forks whittled from alder twigs, sampling cedar tea, and gloating that his supper is being eaten using a large log for a table all seem to me examples of Thoreau taking such ostentatious pleasure in the primitive that he sounds like a gleeful Boy Scout.

"I began to be exhilarated by the sight of the wild fir and the spruce tops," he writes in "Chesuncook." "It was like the sight and odor of cake to a schoolboy." One of the portages in "The Allegash" becomes a frolic — Polis races him — and it is obvious that Thoreau approves when, at last out of breath, the Indian says, "O, me love to play sometimes." Thoreau went to the Maine woods with serious intentions, and he left us a valuable record of this time and place. But there is also no question but that the woods gave Thoreau the freedom to play and be youthful, for the pine tree and the moose and the Indian loomed over him, as they would a small boy.

His ambivalence is also part of his youthful outlook. When contemplating a solitary hunter, he makes a point of comparing his lot to that of someone living in "the rowdy world in the large cities," where people gather "like vermin." He extols life in the forest, yet he cannot imagine thriving there as the Indians do. The hunter's life is beyond him, and so is the life of "the solitary pioneer or settler . . . drawing his subsistence directly from nature." To the admirer of Thoreau's resourcefulness, one of the revelations of *The Maine Woods*, and it is something of a shock, is Thoreau's honest admission that he cannot live there, that this essentially sociable man needs the society of his own town, that he is happy once again to go home.

But this book is much more than a chance to become better acquainted with the turbulent obscurity of Thoreau's inner conflict. The three trips build in their power to evoke a changing landscape. Because of settlers and missionaries and loggers, he saw that the Indian's way of life was changing beyond recognition, that cities were becoming nastier, and that the forest was doomed unless we set some of it apart to be conserved, and he specified that they be national parks. He was prescient in condemning the damming of rivers and streams; he foresaw the consequences, all the damage of flooding and loss of habitat. He was not alone in denouncing loggers, but his denunciations are memorable: "The wilderness feels . . . ten thousand vermin gnawing at the base of her noblest trees." Vermin again. In the same way, instead of prettifying his nights at Walden, he recorded the harsh sound of the first railway locomotives passing within earshot of his cabin. Writing retrospectively in *Walden*, he said, "But since I left those shores the woodchoppers have still further laid them waste . . . How can you expect the birds to sing when the groves are cut down?"

The Maine Woods is one of the earliest and most detailed accounts of the process of change in the American hinterland. Thoreau showed us how to write about nature, how to know more, how to observe, even how to live. "Our life should be lived as tenderly and daintily as one would pluck a flower." Of course, Thoreau is capable of writing like an angel, but that felicity is not his only or even his greatest value. Because Thoreau was so faithful in recording what he saw and heard, his writing suggested what the future had in store. In this book he illustrates the powerful lesson of the truthfulness of dogged observation: that when the truth is told, the text is prophetic.

3

LIZ IN NEVERLAND

It says something for Elizabeth Taylor's much-criticized voice that I could hear it clearly above the loud hack-hack-hack of the helicopter during our ascent at sunset one day over Michael Jackson's Neverland Ranch. Girlish, imploring, screamy, piercing the titanium rotor blades, as she was clutching her dog, a Maltese named Sugar, and saying, "Paul, tell the pilot to go around in a circle, so we can see the whole ranch!"

Neverland, the toy-town wilderness of carnival rides and dollhouses and zoo animals and pleasure gardens, was dropping beneath us as, characteristically, Elizabeth asked for more.

Even without my relaying the message — even with his ears muffled by headphones — the pilot heard. He lifted us high enough into the peach-colored sunset so that Neverland seemed even more toy-like: lots of twinkling lights looking futile because (apart from the security staff) there were no other humans in sight, only the reptile house with its Frisbee-shaped frogs and fat pythons, where both a cobra and a rattlesnake had smashed their fangs against the glass cage trying to bite me; the ape sanctuary, where AJ, the big bristly shovel-mouthed chimp, had spat in my face and Patrick the orangutan had tried to twist my hand; the skittish giraffes, the expectorating llamas, the aggressive swans in the lake, Gypsy the moody five-ton elephant, which Elizabeth had given to Michael; the empty fairground rides — Sea Dragon, the Neverland Dodg'ems, the Neverland carousel playing Michael's own song, "Childhood" ("Has anyone seen my childhood . . . ?"); the large, brightly lit railway station; the lawns and flower beds where loudspeakers disguised as big gray rocks played show tunes, filling the valley with unstoppable Muzak that drowned out the chirping of wild birds. In the middle of it, a jumbotron the size of a drive-in movie screen showed a cartoon, two crazy-faced creatures quacking miserably at each other. All of this very bright in the cloudless dusk, not a soul watching.

"That's the gazebo, where Larry and I tied the knot," Elizabeth said, moving her head in an ironizing wobble. Sugar blinked through prettily combed white bangs which somewhat resembled Elizabeth's own lovely white hair. "Isn't the railway station darling? Over there is where Michael and I have picnics," and she indicated a clump of woods on a cliff. "Can we go around one more time?"

Elizabeth is at her most Elizabethan asking for more. And once again the long scoop of the Neverland Valley, all three thousand acres of it, revolved slowly beneath us, the shadows lengthening from the pinky-gold glow slipping from the sky.

"The Neverland Movie Theater . . . Flowers . . . Michael loves flowers," Elizabeth said. "Look at the swans on the lake! Whee!"

With swans like that you hardly need Rottweilers, I was thinking. Even though no rain had fallen for months, the acres of lawns watered by underground sprinklers were deep green. Here and there, like toy soldiers, were the uniformed security people, some on foot, others riding golf carts, some standing sentry duty, for Neverland is also a fortress.

"Please can we go around just one more time?" Elizabeth said.

"What's that railway station for?" I asked.

"The sick children."

"And all those rides?"

"The sick children."

"Look at all those tents." It was my first glimpse of the collection of tall tepees, hidden in the woods.

"The Indian village. The sick children love that place."

Even from this height I was reminded that this valley of laboriously recaptured childhood was crammed with statuary. Lining the gravel roads and golf-cart paths were little winsome statues of flute players, rows of grateful grinning kiddies, clusters of hand-holding tots, some with banjos, some with fishing rods. And large bronze statues, too, like the centerpiece of the circular drive in front of Neverland's main house with its dark shingles and mullioned windows, a statue of Mercury (god of merchandise and merchants), rising thirty feet, winged helmet and caduceus and all, balanced on one tippy-toe, the last of the syrupy sunset lingering on his big bronze buttocks, making his bum look like a buttered muffin.

By contrast, the next valley was scattered with cows. We passed over them, and then spun toward the sprawl of Santa Barbara.

"Tell the pilot we want to go low! Lower!"

It was a different voice again, even younger, with the *More, please!* pitched as a small girl's squeak. The pilot had heard. He was jerking his thumbs-up. He brought us past downtown Santa Barbara and over the shoreline, almost at the level of the breaking waves.

Elizabeth began to cry out in a shrill little voice, "Whee! We're skimming! What a rush! Whee!"

Surf was breaking in fat white bolsters, releasing feathers of foam two feet below the helicopter's runners. Not far away at the famous Rincon surf break, lollygagging surfers lined up on boards waved to us. Startled pelicans flew up as we approached, and they seemed as cinematic and outrageous as Neverland and its jumbotron cartoons, its statues and swans, and its interminable contending music.

Our nearness to the ocean amplified the rotor noise, but Elizabeth, undaunted by the racket, was still chatty. She leaned forward and shouted into my ear, "Have you ever done this before?"

"In Vietnam!" I yelled.

"No — here!" She seemed annoyed, as though I had deliberately contradicted her. "Sometimes the water hits us. Sometimes we go so low we get wet. Whee!"

The helicopter corkscrewed past Ventura, where we turned inland over strawberry fields and fruit trees, and then flew east under a dark sky, toward Van Nuys Airport and a waiting limousine.

But Elizabeth was looking back at the western sky and its lingering light.

"It's like a Whistler *Nocturne,*" she said quietly. The girl's voice was gone. This was a different tone, thoughtful, adult, a little sad, with the characteristic Elizabethan semiquaver, from a lifetime of lotus eating. And what struck me was her precise characterization of the sky, perfectly Whistlerish, with blobby light and ambiguous shadows hovering over the place where Neverland lay.

· · ·

"So you're Wendy, and Michael is Peter?" I had asked a month before, at her house in Bel-Air.

"Yeah. Yeah. There's a kind of magic between us."

"Magic" had an odd sound in this setting. Upright, her large impressive head and smooth face on a small, much frailer body, she looked like a fugitive chess piece. She is only a few inches taller than five feet. A bad back, three hip operations, a brain tumor, a broken ankle, "and I fell seventeen times — I was like the Flying Nun!" All of this in just the past few years has given her a struggling sideways gait, that too like a peculiar chess move.

Now sipping water, Elizabeth was propped against cushions to favor her back. Her feet in thin slippers were braced against a coffee table on which there was a mass of shattered meteorites (or were they geodes?), forty or more of them, with purple crystals glittering in their interiors. Behind Elizabeth a wall of masterpieces, cheek by jowl, van Gogh jammed against Monet, Rouault against Mary Cassatt, Matisse on top of Modigliani, and three Utrillos side by side, past the Tiffany lamp and the table of cut glass and crystal, one diamond the size of a coconut. "From Michael," Elizabeth explained later. "He said he wanted to get me the biggest diamond in the world. It's a crystal — isn't it fun? Go on, lift it." It must have weighed twenty pounds, and its sparkle reached the Franz Hals, which was hung over the fireplace, with shelves of bronze horses sculpted by Eliza Todd. The Picasso was over the fish tank. The carpet was white, of the same whiteness as Elizabeth's hair, Sugar's fur, her slippers, most of the furniture. The trophy room was next door, the Michael Jackson portrait in the hall ("To my True Love Elizabeth — I'll love you Forever, Michael"), a Hockney and two Warhols — one a silk-screen icon of Elizabeth — in the library, and four Augustus Johns in, pedantically enough, the john.

It was late afternoon. Elizabeth, a night owl and a notoriously bad sleeper, had risen from her bed not long before, where she had been listening to the Italian singer Andrea Bocelli's album *Romanza*. It would be a normal day: rising in midafternoon or so, lots of music, some TV, a turn around the house, a chat with me. A date was planned for later, but nothing special. Rod Steiger was expected. For the past year and a half he has been picking Elizabeth up in his little Honda and taking her out for burgers or fried chicken.

"I was agoraphobic for almost four years," she said. Medical terms trip off her tongue. "Didn't leave the house, hardly got out of bed. Rod Steiger got me out of here. He said I was depressed. Then we dated."

"Dating" is a maddeningly opaque word. In addition to Rod Steiger, who denies any romance, she is currently also dating another man, Cary Schwartz, a Beverly Hills dentist who is in his midfifties and accompanied her on her birthday at the Bellagio Hotel in Las Vegas (and to hear Andrea Bocelli) with his two grown sons, and José Eber her hairdresser, and Dr. Arnie Klein — Michael Jackson's dermatologist — and Michael Jackson himself. Both Dr. Klein and José had shown me the commemorative birthday snapshot, all of them beaming at a restaurant table, Michael looking distinctly chalky as he presented Elizabeth with a birthday present, an elephant sculpture, football-sized, covered in jewels. It had been inspired by the big, real, trumpeting elephant, Gypsy, she had given him.

Her friendship with Michael Jackson is something she obviously values, but, unlikely as it seems, in the context of her own turbulent life it is almost unremarkable.

"I've had some things happen in my life that people wouldn't *believe*," she said, apropos of telling me that she could not bear looking back on her life and would never contemplate an autobiography. "Because some of it has been so painful, I couldn't relive it. Which is one of the reasons I've avoided psychiatry. I couldn't go back to some of those places and totally relive them. I think I'd go out of my mind."

A writer sits indoors over the years, fantasizing, creating fictional lives, and multiple marriages, and fortunes, and appalling accidents — an exasperating but fairly tidy, risk-free occupation involving paper and pencil. But Elizabeth Taylor — imagination made flesh — has lived out her desires, a series of overlapping lives, with a cast of thousands. But never mind the full life. She has, she claims, even died.

"I went through that tunnel," she told me, speaking of her tracheotomy operation in 1959 during which she had been pronounced dead. "I saw the white light and it said, 'You have to go back.' It actually happened. I didn't talk about it, because I had never heard about it, and I thought, This is Loony Tunes!"

She admits she is the opposite of reflective. Perhaps it is this lack of introspection in her, her unwillingness to look at the past, that accounts for her optimism.

She conceded that, as Mrs. Larry Fortensky, she had had to grit her teeth to go to a marriage counselor. "But I thought, Why not? I'll try anything."

Because Larry was acquainted with the counselor — indeed had seen her before, in the course of one or both of his previous marriages — Elizabeth said, "They had a conversation which had become a sort of code. I felt left out. But we did it. Got into the car. Did it. Then we wouldn't speak until the next appointment."

And she laughed, with a peculiar sort of self-mocking mirth that makes her likable. This fatalistic laugh at her own expense comes after a mention of anything absurdly catastrophic — marital disaster or hospitalization or accident, or the back-from-the-dead story. It puts you at ease. Its subtext is "I must be mad!" It is also a displacement activity, for the prospect of someone's pity or regret, she says, can reduce her to helpless tears.

What began as a friendship with Michael Jackson has developed into a kind of cause in which she has become almost his only defender.

"What about his" — and I fished for a word — "eccentricity? Does that bother you?"

"He is magic. And I think all truly magical people have to have that genuine eccentricity." There is not an atom in her consciousness that allows her the slightest negativity on the subject of Jacko. "He is one of the most loving, sweet, true people I have ever loved. He is part of my heart. And we would do anything for each other."

This Wendy with a vengeance, who was a wealthy and world-famous preadolescent, supporting her parents from the age of nine, says she easily relates to Michael, who was also a child star, and denied a childhood, as well as viciously abused by his father. There is a "Katherine" steam engine and a "Katherine Street" at Neverland; there is no "Joseph Street," nor anything bearing his father's name.

And Michael, who indulges in obsessive iconography, had for years collected images of Elizabeth Taylor, as he had of Diana Ross and Marilyn Monroe and Charlie Chaplin — and for that matter of Mickey Mouse and Peter Pan, all of whom, over the years in what is less a life than a metamorphosis, he has come physically to resemble. It cannot have escaped Michael's notice that Elizabeth, too, in the almost sixty years of her stardom, has similarly altered. The winsome child has relentlessly morphed from Velvet Brown to Mrs. Flintstone, via Cleopatra and the Wife of Bath. Each movie (there are fifty-five, and nine TV films), each marriage (eight), each love affair (about twenty on record), has produced a different face and figure, a new image, while at the same time the woman herself is unchanged: straightforward, funny, truthful, impulsively game ("I'll try anything"), outward-looking, a risk taker, and somehow still hungry for more.

When, out of the blue (they had not yet met), Michael offered her tickets for one of his Thriller Tour concerts at Dodger Stadium, she seized them — indeed, she got fourteen tickets. The day was auspicious, February 27, her birthday and also her son's. But the seats were in a glass-enclosed VIP box, a distance from the stage. "You might as well have been watching it on TV." Promising to get a video of the show, she led her large party home.

"Michael called the next day in tears and said, 'I'm so sorry. I feel so awful.'" He stayed on the line. They talked for two hours. "And then we talked every day." Weeks passed, the calls continued. Months went by. "Really, we got to know each other on the telephone, over three months."

One day Michael suggested that he might drop by. Elizabeth said fine. He said, "May I bring my chimpanzee?" Elizabeth said, "Sure. I love animals." Michael showed up holding hands with the chimp, Bubbles.

"We have been steadfast ever since," Elizabeth said. "I was supposed to go with him on that trip to South Africa."

"To meet President Mandela?"

"I call him Nelson," Elizabeth said. "Because he told me to. Nelson called me and asked me to come with Michael. We chat on the phone. 'Hi, Nelson!' Ha-ha!"

"Do you see much of Michael?"

"More of him than people realize — more than I realize," she said. They go in disguise to movies in Westwood and elsewhere, sitting in the back, holding hands. Before I could frame a more particular question, she said, "Everything about Michael is truthful. And there is something in him that is so dear and childlike — not childish, but childlike — that we both have and identify with."

She said this in the most adoring Wendy-like way, but there is in such an apparently sweet manner something of a child taking charge, something defiant, almost despotic.

"I love him. There's a vulnerability inside him which makes him the more dear," Elizabeth said. "We have such fun together. Just playing."

• • •

"Yeah, we try to escape and fantasize," Michael Jackson told me. "We have great picnics. It's so wonderful to be with her. I can really relax with her, because we've lived the same life and experienced the same thing."

"Which is?"

"The great tragedy of childhood stars. And we like the same things. Circuses. Amusement parks. Animals."

At a prearranged signal he had called me. There was no secretarial intervention of "Mr. Jackson on the line." The week's supermarket tabloids' headlines were JACKO ON SUICIDE WATCH and JACKO IN LOONY BIN and, with a South Africa dateline, WACKO JACKO KING OF POP PARASAILS WITH 13-YEAR-OLD. In fact, he was in New York City, where he was recording a new album.

My phone rang, and I heard, "This is Michael Jackson." The voice was breathy, unbroken, boyish — tentative, yet tremulously eager and helpful. That was its lilting sound, but its substance was denser, like a blind child giving you explicit directions in darkness.

"How would you describe Elizabeth?" I asked.

"She's a warm cuddly blanket that I love to snuggle up to and cover myself with. I can confide in her and trust her. In my business you can't trust anyone."

"Why is that?"

"Because you don't know who's your friend. Because you're so popular, and there's so many people around you. You're isolated, too. Becoming successful means that you become a prisoner. You can't go out and do normal things. People are always looking at what you're doing."

"Have you had that experience?"

"Oh, lots of times. They try to see what you're reading, and all the things you're buying. They want to know everything. There are always paparazzi downstairs. They invade my privacy. They twist reality. They're my nightmare. Elizabeth is someone who loves me — really loves me."

"I suggested to her that she was Wendy and you're Peter."

"But Elizabeth is also like a mother — and more than that. She's a friend. She's Mother Teresa, Princess Diana, the Queen of England, and Wendy."

He returned to the subject of fame and isolation. "It makes people do strange things. A lot of our famous luminaries become intoxicated because of it — they can't handle it. And your adrenaline is at the zenith of the universe after a concert. You can't sleep. It's maybe two in the morning and you're wide awake. After coming offstage you're floating."

"How do you handle that?"

"I watch cartoons. I love cartoons. I play video games. Sometimes I read."

"You mean you read books?"

"Yeah. I love to read short stories and everything."

"Any in particular?"

"Somerset Maugham," he said quickly, and then, pausing at each name, "Whitman. Hemingway. Twain."

"What about those video games?"

"I love X-Men. Pinball. Jurassic Park. The martial arts ones — Mortal Kombat."

"I played some of the video games at Neverland. There was an amazing one called Beast Buster."

"Oh, yeah, that's great. I pick each game. That one's maybe too violent, though. I usually take some with me on tour."

"How do you manage that? The video game machines are pretty big, aren't they?"

"Oh, we travel with two cargo planes."

"I see. Have you written any songs with Elizabeth in mind?"

"'Childhood.'"

"Is that the one with the line 'Has anyone seen my childhood?'"

"Yes. It goes," and he liltingly recited, "'Before you judge me, try to . . .'" He continued with six lines more.

"Didn't I hear that playing on your merry-go-round at Neverland?"

Delightedly, he said, "Yes! Yes!"

We talked about the famous Neverland wedding, about Larry, whom Michael said he liked. About Elizabeth as an inspiration, and about their mutual friend Carole Bayer Sager, who had written some of the songs on the *Off the Wall* album. About childhood, how Elizabeth used to support her family when she was a young girl.

"I did that, too. I was a child supporting my family. My father took the money. Some of the money was put aside for me, but a lot of the money was put back into the entire family. I was just working the whole time."

"So you didn't have a childhood, then — you lost it. If you had it to do again, how would you change things?"

"Even though I missed out on a lot, I wouldn't change anything."

"I can hear your little kids in the background." The gurgling had become insistent, like a plug hole in flood. "If they wanted to be performers and lead the life you led, what would you say?"

"They can do whatever they want to do. If they want to do that, it's okay."

"How will you raise them differently from the way you were raised?"

"With more fun. More love. Not so isolated."

"Elizabeth says she finds it painful to look back on her life. Do you find it hard to do that?"

"No, not when it's pertaining to an overview of your life rather than any particular moment."

This oblique and somewhat bookish form of expression was a surprise to me — another Michael Jackson surprise. He had made me pause with "intoxicated" and "zenith of the universe" and "pertaining," too. I said, "I'm not sure what you mean by 'overview.'"

"Like childhood. I can look at that. The arc of my childhood."

"But there's some moment in childhood when you feel particularly vulnerable. Did you feel that? Elizabeth said that she felt she was owned by the studio."

"Sometimes really late at night we'd have to go out — it might be three in the morning — to do a show. My father made us. He would get us up. I was seven or eight. Some of these were clubs or private parties at people's houses. We'd have to perform." This was in Chicago, New York, Indiana, Philadelphia, he added — all over the country. "I'd be sleeping and I'd hear my father. 'Get up! There's a show!'"

"But when you were onstage, didn't you get a kind of thrill?"

"Yes. I loved being onstage. I loved doing the shows."

"What about the other side of the business. If someone came up after the show, did you feel awkward?"

"I didn't like it. I've never liked people-contact. Even to this day, after a show, I hate it, meeting people. It makes me shy. I don't know what to say."

"But you did that Oprah interview, right?"

"With Oprah it was tough. Because it was on TV — on TV it's out of my realm. I know that everyone is looking and judging. It's so hard."

"Is this a recent feeling, that you're under scrutiny?"

"No," he said firmly, "I have always felt that way."

"Even when you were seven or eight?"

"I'm not happy doing it."

"Which I suppose is why talking to Elizabeth over a period of two or three months on the phone would be the perfect way to get acquainted. Or doing what we're doing right now."

"Yes."

At some point Michael's use of the phrase "lost childhood" prompted me to quote the line from Léon Bloy, "In the lost childhood of Judas, Jesus was betrayed," and I heard "Wow" at the other end of the line. He asked me to explain what that meant, and when I did, he urged me to elaborate. What sort of a childhood did Judas have? What had happened to him? Where had he lived? Whom had he known? Twenty minutes of biblical apocrypha with Michael Jackson ensued, and well over an hour later, we talked about his plan to perform in Honolulu, and the progress of his album. We returned to the subject of Elizabeth. He told me what pleasure it had given him to take her and her entourage to Las Vegas — to give her the jeweled elephant. I said I had seen a snapshot of the birthday party.

"That was great. It's the way we really are. We go out and have fun."

Given Elizabeth's past, her once insisting to Oprah that "Michael is the least weird man I have ever known" is not the hyperbolic statement it sounds. She was put down as credulous at the time, but it is a clever rebuttal, and it is a fact that she has known — been married to, had affairs with, been mixed up with — some of the weirdest, most abusive, addictive, profligate, polymorphously perverse men imaginable — drunks, brutes, even convicted felons, big and small. Henry Wynberg, one of her lovers, was busted for fiddling with the odometers of the secondhand cars he was selling. Elizabeth first got into the perfume business with Wynberg.

She was slapped around by Nicky Hilton, cheated on by Richard Burton, badmouthed by Eddie Fisher. She sold a 69-karat diamond and her purple Rolls to help get John Warner into the Senate. And Larry Fortensky — poor, beer-swilling Larry, who was treated to his first ride in a plane and his first foreign country by Elizabeth — Larry, you gather, might use some of his two-million-dollar settlement to pay for a course in anger management. And then there are the lovers, who reputedly range from Max Lerner to Ryan O'Neal, with Carl Bernstein, Bob Dylan, and the former Iranian ambassador somewhere in there, too.

Next to this bunch, Michael — who doesn't smoke or drink — must truly seem to her like Peter Pan. He is famous for his whisper. *Whee!* is one of his trademark expressions, too. His generosity toward this woman, who adores receiving presents, makes him as much her patron as her playmate, though it is as playmates that she describes the relationship.

But it seemed to me that every relationship of Elizabeth's involved her in a sort of role-playing, as if a marriage was a movie, with a beginning, middle, and end; yet each a different movie with a different leading man, different costumes and locations and story points; each one even had a "look," as though an inventive art director had had a hand in the design. Looking over the decades of photographs, you notice a startling dissimilarity in the Elizabeths: the fresh young all-American Mrs. Hilton, the English Mrs. Wilding, the Jewish Mrs. Todd, the stage wife Mrs. Fisher, the much-louder and somewhat Welsh Mrs. Burton, the podgy political campaigner Mrs. Warner, and finally the svelte Mrs. Fortensky, in a leather jacket and jeans, famous for showing up, looking terrific, at Larry's construction sites. Even for the lovers her look changed: deeply tanned on the arm of George Hamilton, somewhat of a moll next to Wynberg, and with slick Hispanic hair, in a ruffled polka-dot dress, with her Mexican lover, Victor Luna.

Some of the marriages were melodramas, a few tragedies, a farce, a comedy or two. Nicky Hilton — young, rich, drunken, wasteful — was straight out of an F. Scott Fitzgerald script; the Wilding effort — transplanted English actor wilting in Los Angeles — was an Anglo-American culture clash; the short, intense Todd marriage, tragically ending in a plane wreck, had a sequel, with music — the marriage to Todd's friend Eddie Fisher, a farcical and faltering lounge-act movie about failure and pills; the Burton business was a two-parter, with serious drinking and spending, highly emotional, complex, and passionate, proving Freud's dictum that in all love affairs four people are involved. One of her Utrillos depicts a château in Switzerland near where she says she secretly met Burton after the filming of *Cleopatra;* the painting she values less for its being a masterpiece than the scene of what she says is one of the most romantic moments in one of her two (the other was Todd) great loves. The last pair of marriages — to the rising politician John Warner, to truck driver Larry — amounted to comedy, with all the excruciating pain that true comedy requires.

• • •

Wifehood as a role? Marriages as movies? I decided to ask her.

One night, just before going out to meet Elizabeth, I saw John Warner on television, talking about the war in Kosovo. He is the chairman of the Senate Armed Services Committee, but even the most charitable assessment of the senator makes him seem doltish and vain — unpersuasive, self-important, his closely set eyes and narrow skull giving him the ingratiating face of a spaniel.

Speaking about the John Warner marriage, she said, "It seemed to me that if I didn't get out of it soon I'd go crazy — out of that situation where you have no opinion of your own, just the candidate's wife."

"That's like a movie title, *The Candidate's Wife*," I said, and asked her whether her own marriages had seemed that way, so specific and so unreal at the same time.

Elizabeth considered this, then said, "You don't start a movie expecting it to crash. You get married expecting it to be forever. That's why you get married."

But that was not my point; it wasn't a matter of intention, but rather that the result had been so cinematic. It seemed to me that a child star, trained for the changing demands of specific circumstances, was perfectly suited for a life of endless adaptation, of multiple roles. Of course no one entered a marriage expecting it to end, but in fact all of her marriages had ended, all her love affairs had crashed.

Elizabeth was, of course, the wrong person to ask about this, yet everything she told me made it seem as though her marriage, *The Candidate's Wife*, was infinitely more watchable than the movies she made during this period: *A Little Night Music, Winter Kills, The Mirror Crack'd,* and *Return Engagement*.

"I had to go along with the party line," Elizabeth said. "I was told I was not allowed to wear purple. The Republican women's committee said, 'It denotes royalty.'

"I said, '*So?*'

"'And it denotes passion.'

"I said, 'What's the matter with that?'

"They said, 'You're the candidate's wife!'"

Cut.

Elizabeth bought herself a conservative suit — "I hate suits!" — and campaigned for the next two months, five or six places a day, no time to eat, the candidate frenetically stumping for votes, the candidate's wife smiling bravely. One day on their way to a Republican function, they enter the building through a rear entrance, candidate and wife hurrying.

Passing a tray of food, Candidate Warner, whose pet name for his wife was Pooters, said, "There's some fried chicken right there, Pooters. Grab some fried chicken, and get a breast or something down into your stomach. This is the last chance for us to eat for the rest of the day."

"So I grabbed a breast," Elizabeth said, "and all of a sudden — *aargh!* You know these two-and-a-half-inch bones? One of them got stuck in my throat. John Belushi did a whole sketch on it, on *Saturday Night Live*, the bastard! Choking on a chicken bone in Little Gap, Virginia!"

In a bizarre improvisation of first aid, Elizabeth snatched a bread roll, broke it in half, and "swallowed half of it to push [the bone] down further, because evidently I was changing colors."

This did not work. Elizabeth was taken to the hospital, and warming to her theme as she told the story, she described how the doctor took a long rubber hose and stuck it down her throat. "To get the bone into my stomach — with no anesthetic, not so much as an aspirin — and they got it into my stomach. But the jokes! I was teased for a year!"

After Warner was elected, a luncheon was given for Elizabeth by the Republican ladies, to thank her for her contribution to the victory. Little did they know how great the contribution had been: Elizabeth had sold one of Burton's more extravagant gifts, "my great big 69-karat diamond . . . to maintain my half of the marriage."

For the luncheon, "I took my purple Halston pantsuit out of mothballs, had it all spruced up, and wore it in all my glory. I said, 'Judy' — she was the manager of the campaign — 'I'm wearing this in your honor!'"

Were this a film, this scene would have been the high point, toward the middle, with the later action suggested in something Elizabeth said to me: "As the candidate's wife I found it very hard to keep my mouth shut." Warner was now in the Senate. Elizabeth was redundant. "Washington is the cruelest city for a woman in the world." She was idle. He was, she says, obsessed with showing up for roll call votes; he wanted to record his perfect attendance. And he succeeded. "He was one hundred percent on his roll call vote. 'John Warner?' 'Aye!'" From this exertion in the Senate he returned home exhausted.

"And he'd say, 'Why don't you pour yourself a Jack Daniel's, Pooters, and go on upstairs and watch TV.'

"So Pooters would pour herself a large Jack Daniel's and go upstairs and watch TV and wait for another day. And on and on, and I thought, My Jack Daniel's are getting larger and larger, and if I don't get my finger out, I'm going to drink myself either to death or into such a stupor that there is going to be no life for me."

At this low point in Washington, melodramatic and self-mocking in Elizabeth's telling, she thought, "What is the most challenging thing I can think of to do in the world, the most difficult to me physically, mentally, but within the realm of possibility? Ah, do a Broadway play."

Against the advice of nearly everyone she knew, she settled on *The Little Foxes.* "I went to a fat farm, to lose weight and get some energy back — stop drinking, feel good about myself. Took the script with me."

Rehearsals were in Florida, and though Warner didn't show up for opening night, Tennessee Williams did. He had told Elizabeth he had always thought of her as "a Tennessee Williams heroine," and she proved it, playing his heroines in *Cat on a Hot Tin Roof, Suddenly Last Summer,* and *Sweet Bird of Youth.* She says that she felt liberated by *The Little Foxes;* she liked the theater people and the applause and the family atmosphere of a show. This play went on the road, and so did Elizabeth, in every sense. She was soon divorced from Warner but continuing with the London run of the play.

It is the perfect ending to *The Candidate's Wife.* The star who has forsaken acting to assume the real-life role as the wife of a rising politician finds that she is superfluous after he gets elected. Seeing that she is dying as a Washington wife, she chooses freedom by getting herself a part in a play, another role-within-a-role. She can only be herself and "feel freedom and joy" by acting.

And then the actress who is liberated by the play falls for Tony Geary, a soap-opera star, and she makes a number of guest appearances on the TV series *General Hospital.*

Life to life, role to role. Ten years pass, and the next movie is *The Trucker's Wife.* The jewels are gone, Elizabeth is in jeans, the adoring spouse of a monosyllabic blue-collar worker named Larry. He has never been in an airplane, never set foot outside the United States. "I got such a vicarious kick out of taking him to places that I had never gone to, so that I wouldn't have an advantage over him and that we could share the newness together." She takes him for his airplane rides — to Morocco, to Thailand. Because they are the guests of the Thai royal family, they have a motorcycle escort. There are never any other cars in view when they are on the road; the roads are cleared of all traffic for them. Larry, in his innocence, believes all foreign travel is like this, empty roads and saluting policemen. But he hates foreign food. He is bored. "He always wanted to go to McDonald's, wherever we were."

Back home in Bel-Air, "I used to get up at four in the morning and have breakfast with him. After Larry went to work, I went back to bed. Then he would come home and it was wonderful — he was sweaty, he had dirty hands, he was beautiful, and he played with his [homing] pigeons.

"I was so proud of him for working. I was kind of hurt when he stopped."

And when Larry the trucker stopped working, and began drinking, his famous temper sometimes flared. Idle, there was only daytime TV and beer for him. It could only end with the trucker's departure from Bel-Air. End of movie.

Far from my belittling these doomed love affairs by comparing them to movies, I felt Elizabeth warranted praise for putting her heart and soul into them, for throwing herself into the role of spouse with such gusto. By changing roles she has kept her vitality, though her biographer Sheridan Morley observed to me how she was like a certain sort of character in a Henry James novel: "innocent, yet at the center of death and destruction."

With the exception of Eddie Fisher ("Let's say we're not exactly intimate buds"), she remained fairly close to all her ex-husbands. And while she pokes fun at them, she is never unkind; if there is abuse, she lets the facts speak for themselves.

"It's a mixed blessing, discovering boys," she said after a long, pleasurable recollection of her riding horses as a young girl. In the beginning, Elizabeth had two or three strictly chaperoned romances, and then, after a short courtship, she and Nicky Hilton were married. "I was a virgin — I was halfhearted. That was a foolish thing, let me tell you."

Her voice became drier and she quailed slightly, crouching on the sofa, seeming almost physically to contract, as she continued. "He started drinking two weeks after we got married — I thought he was a nice, pure, all-American boy. Two weeks later, *wham! bam!* All the physical abuse started.

I left him after nine months of marriage . . . after" — she paused and looked into the middle distance — "having a baby kicked out of my stomach."

"That's terrible," I said.

"He was drunk. I thought, This is not why I was put on earth. God did not put me here to have a baby kicked out of my stomach. I had terrible pains. I saw the baby in the toilet. I didn't know that I was pregnant, so it wasn't a malicious or on-purpose kind of act. It just happened."

Without another word, she got up, holding herself, and left the room. Some minutes passed before she returned, saying that the memory had given her physical pains in her abdomen. She said, "I have never spoken about this before," and changed the subject, to Montgomery Clift, how she found him his first lover.

How had she known that Monty was gay?

"I don't know how I knew. I loved Monty with all my heart, but I knew there would never be a romance for us. No one had explained it to me, but I knew it. Monty was in the closet, and I think I knew what he was fighting. He was tormented his whole life. I tried to explain to him that it wasn't awful. It was the way that nature had made him."

If there is a constant in her endlessly altering life, it is the friendship of gay men. Husbands and lovers have come and gone, but there has always been a gay man — and usually more than one — acting as an escort, confidant, friend, almost sister. Roddy MacDowell was a friend from 1942, when they appeared in *Lassie Come Home,* until his death in 1998. Montgomery Clift. James Dean. Rock Hudson. Tennessee Williams. Halston. Malcolm Forbes. Andy Warhol. Truman Capote. Actors, directors, dress designers, hairdressers, writers, nearly all of them adoring and, even she admits, among the closest friends she has in her life. Her lovers have been abusive, but there is not a recorded instance of even a spat with one of her gay friends.

When AIDS began to claim the lives of some of them, she reacted. A near martyr to hedonistic self-indulgence seems only at first sight to be a poor candidate for good works; in fact, a life of ramping sexual excess and living large is the usual apprenticeship for the moral crusader, the object of self-denial being, very often, simple atonement. Shocked by these AIDS deaths, Elizabeth distinguished herself by calling attention to the disease and being the first person in Hollywood to raise money for AIDS research, with the American Foundation for AIDS Research (AMFAR) and then also with the Elizabeth Taylor AIDS Foundation.

"If you're famous, there's so many good things you can do," she told me. "If you do something worthwhile, you feel better. I spent my whole last fifty years protecting my privacy. I thought, Wait, you're getting angry — you can turn your fame around and use it for something positive. I resented my fame until I realized I could use it."

In the beginning of the AIDS outbreak people "were getting bent out of shape, getting angry and hateful. They weren't doing anything. I got so upset."

She hosted the first AIDS fundraiser in Hollywood, a landmark event in 1985, much to the horror of people in the industry who had tried to conceal the fact that anyone in Hollywood was gay. That fundraiser was a $1 million success. Many more have followed.

"I am this dreaded famous person. I can get under their skin," Elizabeth says. Always rather liking the idea that she has been rebellious, it was also a way to make rebellion work. Her efforts have earned so much money for AIDS research — some $150 million — that even the most skeptical bystanders admit that the money has made a profound difference in AIDS research by raising the funds to develop the life-extending protease inhibitor.

"That's why I do photo shoots — to keep my fame alive. So people won't say, Who's that broad?"

She laughs about Hollywood fame, how it has changed since she was a child star. "Being under contract was heinous." It was the sort of thing that Michael Jackson easily related to. As Elizabeth describes it, "Being loaned out for $500,000 and getting $5,000 a week — which really pissed me off — excuse me. It just wasn't fair."

But in spite of the independence and the big money, there is something missing in Hollywood today. It is not the star system, though Elizabeth can be said to be the last star. It is not even the decline of the studios and the rise of the independent filmmakers. Not the scandals and the marriages and murders — there are still some of those. What is it?

"There's no tits anymore," Elizabeth said. "And if they are, they're fake balloons. I mean, you can spot them a mile off. It's all become slightly androgynous. That's not very sexy."

"So Hollywood's titless these days — that's the message?" I said. "But I don't want to put words in your mouth."

Laughing, she said, "Didn't I say that?"

That evening, Rod Steiger showed up in his little Honda, wearing sneakers. Shaven head, square shoulders, all in black, he could have been Mussolini on an off-day, paying a call on Clara Petacci. Sunk in depression, Steiger had not been able to work for eight years and was nearly broke when, with medication and doctoring, he began acting again. A year and a half earlier, he visited Elizabeth, whom he hardly knew, to propose that she appear with him in *Somewhere* — a script he cowrote — a sequel, Oz revisited, all the characters grown older. In this version, Elizabeth would play the older Dorothy. But Steiger was shocked at the sight of Elizabeth. He saw her as blue and housebound, if not clinically depressed and agoraphobic, and having been through the same things himself, he decided to make her his mission. He insisted that they go out together, and he kept up the pressure for her to socialize. And so Elizabeth was returned to the world. Steiger wrote a poem about Elizabeth, called "The Price" — the price she has paid for the life she has led. Steiger, who sees her as "an enchantress who has become a victim of her powers to enchant," says, "She'll go anywhere for fresh air."

Michael Jackson is fresh air. Perhaps her ultimate film is the one she is enacting with him now — truer to the spirit of her life than Steiger's *Wizard of Oz* update. There are two books on the coffee table in the library of Michael's house at Neverland, *Peter Pan* and a picture book, Michael's own *HIStory*. The house is full of Peter Pan iconography. Almost consciously, Elizabeth and Michael are role-playing in their sequel to Barrie's book, but *Peter and Wendy* in their version is stranger, more highly colored, more complete, and longer-running than any of the marriage movies that I had alluded to with a reluctant Elizabeth in Bel-Air — *The Crooner's Wife, The Candidate's Wife, The Trucker's Wife,* and the others have much less potential than this one about Wendy grown older and the reclusive, refusing-to-age Peter. There is no conflict, nor any likelihood of it; no sex, no struggle, no deprivation. I had the impression they hug a lot and share confidences. It is all about lost childhood, secret pleasures, picnics, food fights, and instant gratification. If they crave an elephant or a concert or a game or a jet plane to take them away, they have it immediately. For their purposes, the Neverland Ranch is perfect: the girlish mother, the boyishly patron-like son, the frisson of sex existing in the pulses of the air — the touching, holding, teasing, hugging, life as play and plenty of money — even pirates! Already, *Peter and Wendy* has shown that it has legs. This friendship has lasted longer than any of Elizabeth's actual marriages.

Elizabeth had an appetite for life, and appetite was the word that kept occurring to me when I thought of her: it was a zest, and a hunger, that somehow was never satisfied. In this hunger she is at her most Elizabethan. Of course it is a metaphor, but she is not a metaphorical person. Her feet are squarely on the ground, she is literal-minded, and her appetite is literally that, a desire to devour. She has said many times that when she was fat it was not a result of unhappiness; it was that she loved to eat. And she adored the most fattening foods — ice cream, fried chicken. Steiger brings her hot dogs from a joint in Malibu, the dentist takes her out for burgers.

Everyone who has known her (and many who don't) has a theory about the way she has lived her life. Most are stories about her being fabulous, about excess, her nine lives, her accidents, her aliments, many about the oddity of her being at the center of so much catastrophe. Mike Nichols, who directed her in his first film, and one of Elizabeth's best, *Who's Afraid of Virginia Woolf?,* has been the most succinct: "There are three things I never saw her do: tell a lie, be unkind, or arrive on time."

Though Elizabeth says she examines nothing in her life or behavior, her unpunctuality is the richest of the many aspects that repay scrutiny. Her lateness amounts almost to a title, Her Serene Lateness. There is a lateness story associated with everything she has ever done, and this is in itself extraordinary, for she has apparently never done anything on time. Her film career began when she was ten, but that was, metaphorically speaking, the only recorded instance of her ever having been early.

Lateness is a theme in her life, as illness importantly is, and yet they are not related. Illness does not explain her unpunctuality, and even unpunctuality is a lame word for her chronic and incurable condition of reluctance and delay, which verges on the despotic, if not the pathological. We all know, and in our hearts resent, people who are habitually late. Thinking about Elizabeth, I realized what a rich subject this is, one deserving a monograph, a whole textbook, as dense as a book might be on the subject of the manipulative personality or spousal abuse — two areas lateness overlaps with, because it is not a solitary affliction, but rather one that involves at least two people, the latecomer and the waiter. In Elizabeth's case the waiter might be me in her living room, or many hundreds of people in a theater wondering when the curtain is going to rise on *The Little Foxes,* or a thousand people on the set of *Cleopatra* awaiting her arrival, or John Warner, tapping his foot on his wedding day, for she was late to that event, too. In the theater, the curtain has been held. Directors have raged in vain. Heads of state, Queen Elizabeth II, the pope, her closest friends — no one has been privileged to see her on time. She is impartially unpunctual. What about airplanes? I asked a person who sometimes travels with her. Planes have takeoff slots and flight plans and must leave on the minute. But many times commercial flights have been held for her. Was your plane unaccountably late in taking off from LAX? Chances are, Elizabeth had a seat in first and someone made a call.

That lateness is a neurotic sense of entitlement, and a bid for power, is perhaps obvious. It raises the ante in a relationship. It is a consistent feature in courtship and sexuality: the aroused person is made to wait, the act is delayed until the loved one appears, and even then there is delay until the seventh veil is dropped. *Meet me in the dressing room — we'll make love,* ran a stripper's line in a seedy show I saw as a youth in Boston's Scollay Square. *If I'm late, start without me.*

Lateness is a diva's trait, allowing her to make an entrance. It is also classically passive-aggressive. The narcissism in lateness is undeniable, and what makes this egocentric demand absurd is the latecomer's expectation that you will be on time. It is not really a contradiction. A late person places a high value on punctuality; everything must commence the moment the latecomer arrives; the latecomer is never made to wait — this is one of the demands of lateness. When Elizabeth arrives the curtain goes up, the camera rolls, the pictures are snapped, the music plays, the show begins. No one else must be late. I was privy to Elizabeth saying, "If he is not here in fifteen minutes, then fuck him. I'll never see him again."

No one has ever said that of her. She expects to be taken on her own terms, so her lateness functions as a sort of test. If you are not willing to wait for her, she is not interested in you. You must never expect her to wait for you; you must always be on time, despite knowing that she will not be. What right have you to be late? But for her it is a privilege, a flourish that functions as a reminder in everything she has done. To say it is a queenly attribute is probably wrong, since royalty are notorious timekeepers. It is more characteristic of the ball-breaker, the manipulator, the control freak, someone deeply insecure. It is the trait of the bullying man, the coquette, the cockteaser, the person needing reassurance, anyone who wishes to assert control. You must wait for me; I will never wait for you.

What puzzled me was — given the fact that she is not in films anymore, that her workload is light, that she doesn't read, that she has little more to occupy her mind than her dates and her dog — what on earth is she doing when she is not where she is supposed to be? Like a little girl, Elizabeth disingenuously apologized for being late when we met, and I always made a point of asking her what she had been doing. "I was upstairs, singing and dancing," carried away by the music of Andrea Bocelli, she told me once. But she also fusses endlessly, changes her clothes — her whole outfit — adjusts her makeup, kicks off her shoes and tries others, dithers over her jewelry, cuddles Sugar, talks on the phone.

This deeply dislikable quality ends friendships, but of course, since it is designed to test friendships, that is inevitable. In Elizabeth it is an accepted mode of behavior, on a par with a handicap, as though she is a figure worthy of sympathy, like a limper or a twitcher, in her case someone seriously time-challenged. But I saw it as another detail in the ongoing drama of *Peter and Wendy,* for most of all it is a trait of the troubled child, who is often a foot-dragger without really knowing the deeper reason, and in the case of the foot-dragging child there is always a deeper reason.

It is an Elizabethan characteristic, but it does not sum her up. Writing this story, I was able to spend enough time with her to see her at her most Elizabethan, that moment — like the moment in a movie — when so much is revealed by a look or a line.

There was the shocking business about Nicky Hilton — but less the revelation than her getting up just afterward and haltingly leaving the room, her hands against her stomach, undoubtedly in physical pain.

And at Neverland, in Michael's dining room, a much lighter moment, when she was with the chef and debating what to eat. She finally settled on a big cheese omelet with ketchup, and as she was tucking into it, she saw someone else with a plate of french fries — the twiggy frozen Mickey D. kind — and she said with real gusto in a hungry voice, "Hey, where did you get those?" And in minutes, she too had a big plate of fries.

"Please, God, super-size my life" has always been Elizabeth's prayer, as eating has always been an Elizabethan theme. A friend of Elizabeth told me how Elizabeth looked into a refrigerator and began speaking fondly to the food she saw on the shelves: "I'm going to eat you . . . and then I'm going to eat you . . . and then I'm going to eat you . . ."

One day she was telling me, very slowly, with real feeling, about a photo shoot she had done for her line of White Diamonds perfume — an enterprise that assured her a substantial income and eliminated the necessity ever to act again.

"I had on a 101-karat diamond," she said, pausing after each word. She licked her lips and there was a chuckle of pleasure in her throat. "No flaws!" And again pausing between the words, "Talk about a rush!"

She clutched her finger on which the imaginary, emerald-cut diamond ring was fitted, and a shudder of hunger shook her small brittle body as she lifted the finger to her mouth and said, with a shout that barely concealed a shriek, "I wanted to swallow it!"

Another day she was listening to a Bocelli ballad and singing along, then interrupted herself and said, "*Più! Più!* I love *più!* What does *più* mean?"

"It means 'more,'" I said.

"*Più!*"

The essential Elizabeth I was not privileged to observe, but I had it on good authority. After we'd had a particularly fruitful session of talk at her house, we said goodbye. Later, speaking with a mutual friend, Elizabeth said, "Is Paul married?"

4

GREENELAND

1. ONE OF FATE'S FUGITIVES

Graham Greene lived, and thrived, in an age when writers were powerful, priest-like, remote, and elusive. They were risk takers, romantics, lovably disreputable, seldom interviewed but often whispered about. You did not see them at your local bookstore; you did not pluck their sleeve; you had no opportunity to hand them a manuscript or to ask for tips on travel or to observe, "What is your problem?"

It is impossible now for any American under the age of sixty or so to comprehend the literary world that existed in the two decades after World War II, and especially the magic that fiction writers exerted on the public. Henry Miller comes to mind. He was one of many borderline outlaws, but in an age of censorship — the *Chatterley* ban and all that — all writing is a dodgy business. Until the past twenty years or so, writers were not accessible to the reading public. They did not turn up for readings at bookstores; they did not give free talks at the library or sign your book. They were not visible. They were the more powerful for being somewhere else, only whispered about. They are all dead, but some of the writers who enjoyed that sort of fame as conspicuous absentees (Mailer, Bellow, Styron, and other heroic octogenarians) lived on into this age of intrusion, where publishers conspired with bookstores to bully writers into the open and make them part of the selling mechanism. This weird and philistine exhibitionism is now the way of the world. Greene was spared.

The period I am thinking of — which began to decline in the 1960s, perhaps when publishers became corporate, middlebrow monsters — was also an age of censorship. Greene caused a huge fuss by choosing the Olympia Press edition of *Lolita* as his Book of the Year in 1955. His singling out the book got it serious attention and substantial contracts in London and New York, and of course howls of execration. The Vatican took a dim view of Greene's novels, though the adulteries in them kept them on the top shelf. Growing up in an age of literary censorship, I regarded all serious writing as a shady, faintly subversive business, which was another attraction to me.

Graham Greene, born in 1904, was just such a subversive hero, self-consciously seeking out (in Browning's words) "the dangerous edge of things," someone who lived everywhere and nowhere, a man whom few people ever knew. "One of fate's fugitives," in the words of his biographer, Greene published two memoirs, *A Sort of Life* (1977) and *Ways of Escape* (1980), which are notoriously reticent, not to say misleading. Though he was more hospitable to being interviewed than he admitted, he allowed only the highest standard of interviewer. V. S. Pritchett, Anthony Burgess, and V. S. Naipaul all made their way to Antibes to genuflect to the master and subsequently say nice things about him in Sunday newspapers. Greene must have known that such men would not spill the beans about his irregular life or ask awkward questions, though Burgess famously teased him for being a God-botherer and a poseur, and was banished.

Aware that he led a hidden life, Greene developed a habit of evasion, which was an almost pathological inability to come clean. His secretiveness led him at times to keep a parallel diary, in which he might chronicle two versions of his day, one rather sober and preoccupied, the other perhaps detailing a frolic with a prostitute. Betrayal was one of Greene's obsessive subjects. Reluctant, too weary, or too wary to write an exhaustive autobiography, Greene appointed Norman Sherry, an acclaimed biographer and a professor of English, as his official biographer. (It so happened that in 1968 I joined the English department at the University of Singapore and occupied the office chair that Professor Sherry had kept warm for the four previous years.) Greene had read and admired Sherry's books about Joseph Conrad, notably *Conrad's Eastern World,* and had been impressed by Sherry's stamina in following in Conrad's footsteps, to fictional settings and old stomping grounds.

With his customary circumspection, Greene summoned Sherry for drinks and meals in 1974, and after considerable scrutiny offered him unlimited access. Greene said, "No lies please. Follow me to the end of my life." In 1976, after two years of spadework, Sherry started writing his *Life of Graham Greene,* and in 1989 published the first volume, covering the years 1904–1939. Greene lived to read that book, but he had been dead three years by the time the second volume (1939–1955) appeared in 1994. A decade later, with the publication of the long-awaited third volume (1955–1991), Sherry's work, a total of 2,218 closely printed pages, is now complete.

For anyone interested in Greene's life and work, this three-volume biography is incomparable; as an intellectual and political history of the twentieth century it is invaluable; as a literary journey, as well as a journey across the world, it is masterful; as a sourcebook and rogues' gallery it is fascinating. Sherry is not the stylist that Leon Edel was when he wrote his five-volume life of Henry James, but this work can be compared with Edel's achievement. It is as satisfying and as exhaustive, and evokes a much more intimate and physical sense of his subject.

In volume three we encounter Greene the playwright and the traveler to Cuba, which resulted in *Our Man in Havana;* the journey to the Congo, which produced *A Burnt-Out Case;* the Haiti trips and *The Comedians;* the South American trips and *The Honorary Consul,* as well as *Travels with My Aunt* and *The Human Factor.* Even financially destroyed, Greene becomes venerable in his last decades, is awarded prizes, endures a fuss over the Nobel Prize, which seems little more than the Swedish lottery. He turns down a knighthood but receives the bigger gong, Companion of Honour. He becomes involved in a French scandal and writes *J'Accuse.* He teams up with a Spanish priest and writes *Monsignor Quixote.* He is befriended by Omar Torrijos, premier of Panama, and writes *Getting to Know the General.* One great love affair ends, another runs its course, and he finally finds a companion, a devoted (but married) woman in whose arms he dies. His last words as he lies in pain: "Oh why does it take so long to come."

In this period he wrote "May We Borrow Your Husband?" His biographer somewhat undervalues the story, yet it remains one of my favorites. It contains this observation: "At the end of what is called 'the sexual life' the only love which has lasted is the love that has accepted everything, every disappointment, every failure and every betrayal, which has accepted even the sad fact that in the end there is no desire so deep as the simple desire for companionship."

Greene was a restless traveler, a committed writer, a terrible husband, an appalling father, and an admitted manic-depressive. He was relentlessly sexual, ardently priapic. "I think his sexual appetites are voracious, frightening," one of his close male friends remarked, though the man was English, so the word "frightening" must be taken with a grain of salt. But certainly Greene was a tireless sensualist. Like many other sexually obsessed men he tended to be noncommittal, evasive, given to unexplained vanishings and sentimental utterances, but forever feverishly on the prowl. He often complained of writer's block, but where women were concerned he was hypergraphic. He had the lecher's bouts of romanticism and fits of fantasy; these he set down on paper.

Much of volume one was given over to his pursuit of a suitable wife, and when the young Greene had settled on Vivien Dayrell-Browning he wrote her more than two thousand letters before finally convincing her to marry him. But less than two years after his marriage he resumed frequenting prostitutes. His marriage faltered with the arrival of children. He was so lacking in the paternal instinct, he seriously considered putting at least one of them up for adoption. "How I dislike children," he wrote to one of his lovers, and he continued to complain about his offspring — their selfishness, their demands — long after he left home, after twenty years with Vivien, some of which were spent traveling in Liberia and Mexico, writing masterpieces, philandering, or simply avoiding her.

Though he talked of dumping Vivien, he never divorced her. His marriage kept him from ever having to commit himself entirely to his mistresses: Dorothy Glover, whom we meet early in volume two, he was seeing as his marriage ended, and others, notably Catherine Walston, with whom he had a passionate affair (much of volume two) and finally a friendship that lasted until her death. This Walston affair is recounted in thousands more letters. A passionate affair for Greene might inspire a fifteen-page letter but did not imply fidelity. For one thing, many if not most of his affairs were conducted with married women whose cuckolded husbands could do little except sigh or issue meaningless ultimatums. He had his own reasons for choosing married women and for constantly being involved in ménages à trois — or quatre, or cinq for that matter. On her conversion to Catholicism, Catherine Walston developed a thing for priests — and, being madly attractive, she encouraged the priests to become her lovers. By way of response, Catherine's husband, Harry, just shrugged and took up with the cast-off Dorothy Glover, and while Greene objected to the priests, he himself was involved (we are now in volume three) with Anita Björk, a Swedish actress, and then with Yvonne Cloetta, the wife of a diplomat in Cameroon, whose husband did not have a clue. Is it any wonder that Greene's books are full of adulteries? "Greene's truth is in his fiction," Sherry says, and demonstrates this again and again. One might also add that, since childhood looms large in Greene's work, there is something in the very nature of a Greene adultery — and perhaps adultery in general — that can make it seem as thrilling as a child's game: the hiding, the secrets, the lies, the playacting, the giggling satisfaction, the guilt, even the furtive sex itself.

An illustrative moment of Greene's childish perversity occurs in Jamaica in 1959, when on vacation with Catherine he writes to a friend, "In spite of the pleasant life here (& my 500 words a day) my mind strays an awful lot to Douala [Yvonne] — not to speak of Stockholm [Anita]. Perhaps the Dutch widow is the real solution!" Since he is still married to Vivien, he has five women in his life at this point (and is working on *A Burnt-Out Case*). A month later, he is traveling in the Pacific with a male friend, Michael Meyer. Though a previous biographer, Michael Shelden, suggested Greene had spells of homosexual behavior, Sherry disputes the claim. He takes the line that Greene preferred married women because they asked so little of him. "Married women are the easiest," Querry says in *A Burnt-Out Case*. My own feeling is that there is something ambiguously homoerotic in a man's conducting a lengthy affair with a married woman who remains at home and continues to sleep with her husband. This was a habit of Greene's. And there is the twisted logic of Greene's proclaiming his fidelity to his mistress while cheating on his wife and also of course seeing hookers, for whom he had a hopeless penchant.

"I could never understand the attraction of having a prostitute," Michael Meyer said with bemused disapproval, "which seems to me like paying someone to let you beat them at tennis."

This is funny but wide of the mark, for Greene was not a Casanova, not vain in his conquests, not a scorekeeper (though he kept a detailed list of his forty-seven favorite prostitutes, given by Sherry in an appendix). Greene was insecure, needy, insatiable, interested in variation, and always willing to have a go. He preferred his women to be waif-like, boyish, petite — he himself was six foot four. The women in his novels tend to match that description, but of course they are all based on women he had loved.

"He has a definite quirk for brothels," a woman friend remarked. Sherry straps on his brothel creepers and proves this to be so. Way back in volume one, Otto Preminger was quoted as saying, "Though he gives a first impression of being controlled, correct and British, he is actually mad about women. Sex is on his mind all the time."

You might say, So what? But this compulsive sexuality seemed to shape the pattern of his life, his travel, his fictional subjects, and his faith. Obsessive and easily bored, he was incapable of being sexually faithful to any woman. He reveled in being a wanderer, an eavesdropper, a stranger. His sexuality both depressed him and relieved his gloom. It damned him in his own faith, made him a sinner, and filled him with remorse, provoking him to say things such as, "I've been a bloody fool" and "I've betrayed very many people in my life" and "I wish I didn't have so much to be remorseful about."

He converted to Catholicism to win over Vivien, but it seemed as though he remained a Catholic in order to strengthen his control over his sexual appetite. All his faith did was to make him feel guiltier, tying himself in knots to reconcile his belief with his sinning, but at least, as a believer, he could obtain absolution and sanctifying grace. In *The Heart of the Matter, The Power and the Glory, The End of the Affair,* and many other books he struggled to portray sinners as ultimately virtuous. Charles Péguy's observation, "*Le pécheur est au coeur même de chrétienté*" (The sinner is at the heart of Christianity), is part of the epigraph of *The Heart of the Matter*. The conundrum went on tormenting Greene and made him a moralist.

While there is something humdrum about being bad, and an irritating banality in the act of doing wrong, high drama can be achieved with the words "sinning" and "evil." Greene indulged himself by casting his actions in these terms. Right and wrong did not much interest him, but good and evil did. He was a sucker for diablerie. Orwell remarked that Greene seemed to share the idea, "which has been floating around since Baudelaire, that there is something rather *distingué* about being damned."

Greene travels to Haiti in volume three. Haiti summed up just about everything he required in a foreign destination, especially one that he intended as the setting for a novel. It was distressed, tropical, ramshackle, overcrowded, poor, and on the brink of civil war. It was governed by a bogeyman. It was famous for its brothels, its slums, and its weird expressions of religious faith — Catholicism and a mishmash of African ritual. Its women, especially its prostitutes, were celebrated for their beauty. Its ornate hotels were in a state of decay, yet there was enough alcohol available for a guest to tie one on. The only expatriates in the place were shady businessmen and foreign ambassadors, with the requisite number of bored wives. Add to this Voodoo, political tyranny, rum punch, and sunshine, and the result is the colorful horror show we see in *The Comedians*.

The travel, the sex, the writing, the romances, were — so Norman Sherry suggests — all attempts by Greene to relieve his depression. He was an authentic melancholic. He attempted suicide several times and spoke often of ending his life. His untrusting nature kept him from revealing his gloom to anyone, except Catherine Walston, who was capable of lifting his spirits. It was she who said, "Graham's misery is as real as an illness." Another (male) friend spoke of how Greene "was only happy when he was being unhappy." Greene the novelist created central characters who were notoriously gloomy, and Greene the traveler was hardly cheery either. Of Mexico and Mexicans in *The Lawless Roads*, he said, "I hate this country and this people."

Money was often on his mind. The quest for solvency is a subtheme in the three volumes, for he never stopped sending money to his wife and went on supporting his children long after they were adults. Greene was an unusual English writer of his time in having held a number of different full-time jobs: at least four editorial jobs on newspapers and magazines, regular film reviewing (at which he excelled, as evidenced in his collection *The Pleasure Dome*), and two important and active positions in London publishing houses. Volume three describes his work as a playwright, his great success (*The Potting Shed*) and ultimate failure (*Carving a Statue*), as well as his screenwriting, not just *Our Man in Havana* and *The Comedians*, but offers from Hollywood, such as the feeler for him to work on *Ben-Hur* ("I might help if there's a lot of money & if my name was kept out"). In his early sixties he discovered that his accountant was a crook who had cheated him. Faced with financial ruin, Greene moved to France for tax reasons and regained his solvency through scriptwriting. His celebrated trips to Panama, where he became involved in the canal imbroglio, were paid for by General Torrijos, who sent him complimentary air tickets. On his death, all his money (but it was a modest estate) went to his wife, whom he had not lived with for over forty years.

There is in most literary biography a simple detail that speaks volumes about its subject. Thoreau never left home, Henry Miller was henpecked, Borges lived in fear of his mother, James Joyce was afraid of thunderstorms,

Freud was angst-ridden on railway platforms, Wittgenstein was addicted to cowboy movies, Wallace Stevens to candy, Nabokov never once visited Moscow, Jack Kerouac had stacks of the *National Review* by his bed when he died.

Many such equally curious details occur in this Greene biography. Greene's dislike of children seems predictable enough; it is a characteristic of many writers of children's books (Greene wrote three). He also disliked adverbs, though you can find them in his books. It seems he did not ever fire a gun, yet his novels are full of gunplay. Living amid the great cuisine of Provence, he said how he sorely missed English sausages.

He was the least domesticated of men. After he left his marital household in 1939 he did not share a house with any woman — and he died in 1992. His ultimate lover, Yvonne Cloetta, visited him at his Antibes apartment, cooked his evening meal, consoled him, and then went home to her husband. Greene could not cook, was incapable of using a typewriter, did not wield a mop; he was a naturally dependent, if not helpless, man. Add to this the astonishing fact that, though a traveler, a seeker of danger, a deeply curious wanderer who was seldom home, he could not drive a car. I think we can easily understand his need for a lover. But it is bewildering to reflect how he was lost without a driver, a cook, a cleaner, a typist; all his life he needed someone to look after him. Is it any wonder that in all the thousands of (handwritten) letters Sherry includes, so many of them have the tone of a lost boy?

I knew Greene, though not the complex Greene of Sherry's biography. As Sherry says, no one knew this man. He was very generous to me and many other writers. A name not mentioned here is that of Etienne Leroux, the South African writer (he wrote in Afrikaans) whose brilliant novels (*Seven Days at the Silbersteins* and others) Greene championed. And whenever I feel undervalued, unread, or misunderstood, I remember a story (not recounted in the biography) that Greene told me of an evening he spent in Paris with some film people. A famous French director, and an admirer, praised his epic walk through the Liberian bush, described in his travel book *Journey Without Maps* (1936). He said, "This is Graham Greene. He has traveled through West Africa!"

The actress beside him said, "How did you do this?" She stuck out her thumb. "*Autostop?*" (Hitchhiking?)

2. THE TRAVELER

Journey Without Maps is such an assured trip, so portentous in its Conradian shadings, you keep having to remind yourself that the book is a young man's balancing act. Come to think of it, Conrad's own inspirational trip, his piloting the *Roi des Belges* up the Congo River in September 1890, was also a balancing act: Conrad (still Captain Korzeniowski) was thirty-two, needed money, was thinking of ditching the sea forever, and was making tentative progress on his first novel, *Almayer's Folly*. African travel changed both men's careers by offering them epic subjects and jungly ambiguities. Long afterward, Greene called the nervous journey he had taken, at the age of thirty, "life altering." Conrad said something similar about his own hectic river trip.

Greene's book is one of many on the travel shelf that suggest a mythical penetration of Africa to its essence, much like its predecessors, *Heart of Darkness,* Stanley's *Through the Dark Continent* and *In Darkest Africa,* as well as its many successors, among them Laurens van der Post's *Venture to the Interior.* The quest myth elaborated in these books has its parallel in a boy's adventure story: the ordeal that the white traveler must endure and overcome (with all the stereotypical obstacles of primitivism) in order to find life-changing revelation at the remote heart of Africa. This fanciful supposition of the heroic romantic in a pith helmet, that *l'Afrique profonde* contains glittering mysteries, is one of the reasons our view of Africa has been so distorted. In Conrad's case the revelation was "The horror, the horror." In Greene's it was nuisance, homesickness, African porters wailing "Too far!," and psychoanalytic confirmation. But really, there is no mystery, only the obvious truth that difficult journeys, such as overland trips through Africa, tell us many things about ourselves: the limits of our strength, our wits, our spirit, our resourcefulness, even the limits of our love.

Greene's book is an ingeniously worked-up account of only four weeks in the Liberian bush by an absolute beginner in Africa. Greene admits this early on. "I had never been out of Europe before; I was a complete amateur at travel in Africa." Amazingly, he brought his young female cousin Barbara along for company. "You poor innocents!" a stranger cried at them in Freetown. He didn't know the half of it.

Out of his element, Greene is gloomy, fidgety, nervous, and Barbara has no discernible skills. But the pitying man in Freetown can see from their helpless smiles and lack of preparation that theirs is a leap in the dark. *Journey in the Dark* was one of the rejected titles for the book. How innocent was Greene? Here is an example. Just before setting out from Freetown to start his trip, he confides, "I could never properly remember the points of the compass." Can a traveler be more innocent than that?

Greene and his cousin are not deterred by their incompetence. They seek guidance. They hire porters and a cook. They board the train for the Liberian frontier and start walking around the back of the country. They have twenty-six poorly paid African porters carrying their food and equipment. They have a pistol, they have a tent (never to be used), they have a table and a portable bath and a stash of whiskey. They even have trinkets to hand out to natives — but the natives prefer gifts of money or jolts of whiskey to trinkets. The trip is eventful: the travelers suffer fatigue, Greene falls ill with a serious fever, there are misunderstandings and wrong turns. There is a great deal of foot-dragging on the part of the porters. A little over a month after they set off, the Greenes are back on the coast, and in a matter of a week or so (the book skimps on dates) they are on a ship heading back to Britain.

It was 1935. Young, presentable, confident, well-educated, well-shod, and presumptuous Englishmen were showing up in remote corners of the world, boasting of their amateurishness, wearing comic headgear (Greene sported a pith helmet), with the assurance that all would be well. People would respect them for their Englishness and would fall into line and be helpful, and if they didn't fall into line, if the natives were cranky and colorful and mangled their English idioms, the trip would be a hoot. Back home, the book would get written and talked about. That was the case with the travels and writings of Greene's contemporaries — Evelyn Waugh, Robert Byron, Peter Fleming, and others whose works over the past decades have been much praised, even (to my mind) overpraised.

Journey Without Maps is seldom lumped with those books, perhaps because it lacks humor, it is dark, it is broadly political. It is frankly appreciative of half-naked African women, though. The book had an unlucky publishing life. Eighteen months after it first appeared, it was withdrawn because of a threatened libel action. That killed its chances at the beginning. As for his being a tenderfoot, it seems to me that Greene's nervousness and inexperience contributed to his memory of battling with the challenges of the trip, enlarging them perhaps, making more of a drama; and his fears heightened his consciousness of every passing hour, making the trip seem something of a saga. It is Greene's first and best work of travel.

At some point in the early 1930s Greene conceived this idea of walking through the African bush. He was a young man, six years married and with a one-month-old baby girl. He had never written about travel, which is not surprising — he had hardly traveled. He had made jaunts out of England, but in a hilarious, weekending way, and had never ventured beyond Europe. He knew nothing of Africa, had never camped or slept rough or been on a long sea voyage or a long hike of any consequence — certainly not a trek through the bush. Probably influenced by the journeys his friends and contemporaries were taking, he got it into his head to hike with porters and carriers through an unmapped part of the Liberian hinterland. He did not know exactly how many miles he would have to walk, or how long it would take, or what his actual route would be.

Much odder than this vagueness — to me, at any rate; this impulse, not to say batty notion, has never been seriously questioned — was Greene's decision to take his young cousin Barbara with him. She was twenty-seven and had never been anywhere. She'd had a privileged upbringing and was not much of a walker. But Greene was lucky — though Barbara was a socialite, she was also a good sport. She learned how to hike and how to cope, and the trip hardened her to the rigors of travel. Though she was self-effacing in her role as part of the team — she hardly appears in Greene's book — Barbara was his equal on the trail, if not on the page. Her own account of the trip, first published in 1938 as *Land Benighted,* and reprinted (with my introduction) in 1982 as *Too Late to Turn Back,* is a modest but helpful gloss on Greene's allusive and at times ponderous book.

Why Greene took Barbara, why he did not go alone, why he did not choose an experienced man, are questions he does not answer in his book, nor are they seriously addressed in any biographies. In an aside, Greene put the invitation down to his impulsiveness — too much champagne at a party. It is hard to imagine anyone so casual, so reckless, in choosing a partner for such a daunting journey. An inexperienced young traveler, lacking the ability to use a compass, and his younger debby cousin in Africa, with (so she said) a volume of Saki's stories in her luggage, sounds like satire. Or was Greene infatuated? He could be impulsive where women were concerned. Barbara was lovely; Greene had been unfaithful to Vivien within months of his wedding. There have been whispers of his having an affair with Barbara. His largely excluding her from the narrative could be interpreted as a sheepish reflex, adulterer's remorse, a mood that afflicted the womanizing Greene for much of his life.

We don't know, and it probably does not matter, but our being aware that Greene was sharing his hardships with this young woman makes much of the mystique fall away. Imagine Kurtz with his intended by his side at the Inner Station and he at once seems less of a loner, less of a leader, less of a problem solver and mystery man — as Greene does with Barbara. Toward the end of the trip, Greene became feverish and took fewer notes and began to hurry. "I remember nothing of the trek to Zigi's town and very little of the succeeding days. I was so exhausted that I couldn't write more than a few lines in my diary." For details on that last part of the journey the reader has to turn to Barbara's narrative. She was not ill; on the contrary, she claimed in her book that she became stronger on the journey, as Greene grew weaker.

A male companion might have challenged Greene, might have ridiculed his sketchy plans and all his improvisations. At the outset Greene did not have a clear idea of where he was going or how he would get there. He says he had only a hazy notion of his journey. "I intended to walk across the Republic [of Liberia], but I had no idea of what route to follow." Yet Greene saw it through to the end with the help of his cousin. He penetrated the hinterland; he reached the coast. The reason the book is one of his best is perhaps that he was desperate the whole way through, and that in some important aspects the trip was the fulfillment of his childhood fantasies.

In later life, Greene often spoke of how he had been deeply influenced as a child by stories of adventure, of derring-do, of pirates and exiles, the colorful ordeals of travelers, of swordsmen and sinners. Most of us leave these books on the nursery shelf, but Greene never forsook them or their bright colors, their themes, their stark moralities, their preoccupation with heroes and villains, their exotic settings. Before he left for Africa he read a British government report about atrocities in Liberia, which caused him to remark, "The agony was piled on . . . with a real effect of grandeur." He is not shocked — he is excited; and the judgment is not a bad description of, say, *King Solomon's Mines*. In his essay "The Lost Childhood," Greene was to reflect on that book, saying it was his "incurable fascination of [the witch] Gagool with her bare yellow skull, the wrinkled scalp that moved and contracted like the hide of a cobra that led me [to Africa]."

Greene was a dreamy, at times brooding boy. He was feared to be suicidal. He so alarmed his parents with his dark withdrawals that he was psychoanalyzed while still in his teens, an early candidate for the then novel treatment of talk therapy and the interpretation of dreams. *Journey Without Maps* is crammed with evidence that it was written by someone who has spent time on a psychiatrist's couch. Speaking of his fear of rats and mice, moths and other flying creatures ("I shared my mother's terror of birds"), he explains, "But in Africa one couldn't avoid them any more than one could avoid the supernatural. The method of psychoanalysis is to bring the patient back to the idea which he is repressing: a long journey backwards without maps, catching a clue here and a clue there, as I caught the names of villages from this man and that, until one has to face the general idea, the pain or the memory." His African trip, he is saying, is therapeutic, a fresh-air confrontation with his fears.

His boyhood was a humdrum existence (but with a terror of birds and moths) in an unremarkable English market town noted for its boys' school and its furniture-making. Greene was unwillingly conspicuous. A gawky failure-prone student at the school where his father was headmaster, he was too tall and too morose, a natural target of bullying and taunts, not only from other boys but also from his own rivalrous siblings. Greene fantasized escaping into the remoter and more vivid struggles of a hero out of Rider Haggard, Kipling, Captain Marryat, Robert Louis Stevenson, or G. A. Henty. He yearned to be someone else and to be elsewhere — a writer's yearnings; but the fulfillment of them made Greene the writer we know.

He seems to have settled on Liberia because it was the sort of setting he had encountered in his early reading. Or at least that was what he imagined: jungle, mud huts, natives, witch doctors, talk of cannibals. He managed the trip in an old-fashioned way, leading a file of heavily laden porters down a foot-wide path. On his return to England in April 1935, he began writing the book. That same year, he also put his Liberian experience into one of his best short stories, "A Chance for Mr. Lever." In addition, he was working on a thriller, *A Gun for Sale*. He finished both books by the new year and they appeared in 1936.

In spite of mediocre sales and the threat of a libel action, the story of his Liberian trip secured Greene's reputation and became part of his personal myth, setting his life on course, fixing this melancholy and evasive soul in readers' imaginations as a stoical adventurer. People still read the book in order to understand his cast of mind, in which none of those deficits figure. Greene found a setting and a way of writing about travel that was quite different from his literary contemporaries. Greene's book is self-consciously strewn with literary allusions, with many tags and quotations, from Conrad, Burton, A. E. Housman, Henry James, Céline, Baudelaire, Firbank, Santayana, Kafka, Sassoon, Saki, Milton, Thomas Paine, Samuel Butler, Walter Raleigh, and the Bible. On the subject of travel, he compares the relative merits of two of his near contemporaries, Somerset Maugham and Beverley Nichols.

In the book he dismisses Soviet junkets and (an odd assertion for Greene) Soviet-inspired hypocrisy. And he opted for the disorderly West African coast rather than the more orderly farming towns of British East Africa. Though a questionable claim, it seems like praise for him when he writes that in Liberia, "civilization ends fifty miles from the coast." He would have correctly guessed that in East Africa, hundreds of miles from the coast, there were towns with coffee growers, cattle raisers, polo players, tea plantations, and gymkhana clubs. And Liberia had been in the news. Not long before, in 1926, the Firestone rubber company leased — for a pittance — a million acres of the republic for its production of latex. In 1930, the League of Nations investigated Firestone and the Liberian government for unfair labor practices and exploitation, forced labor and slavery — the precise abuses Conrad had witnessed in King Leopold's Congo in 1890. These facts got Greene's attention.

Greene claimed that the maps of Liberia were largely blank, with the tantalizing white spaces that Marlow speaks of early on in *Heart of Darkness*. Writing almost fifty years later, Greene seems to be promoting the notion (as he does throughout the book) that much of Liberia is terra incognita. But Liberia had been an independent republic since 1847. Until 1919, the country was beset by continual border disputes from the neighboring French colonies, French Guinea and the Ivory Coast. Greene's blank-map claim seems extraordinary, since to meet such territorial challenges, accurate mapping would have been essential.

Greene also maintained that the American maps he examined were designated in certain places *Cannibals*. Fanciful claims of this sort do appear on eighteenth-century maps of Africa, but are improbable in the twentieth, for the very good reason that cannibalism was not practiced except in the minds of timid fantasists, whom one does not normally lump together with modern cartographers. Still, you can see what Greene is driving at. The country is blank, the bush is trackless; it is filled with magic and devil dancers and anthropophagous tribes; it is *l'Afrique profonde*. Because he is so scared, he is emphatic about dangers. Even in his own book he alludes now and then to cannibalism. This is a libel on his hosts, of course, but it puts him firmly in the company of Conrad, who made cannibalism one of the insistently whispered motifs in his own richly ambiguous narrative of the Congo.

But even though he later lived for a year — a miserable year, so he said — as a British spy in Freetown, Greene was essentially a visitor to Africa. He dropped in, he did some journalism, he wrote pieces. He romanced Africa and, like many another ardent suitor, was uncritical. Africa rewarded him by showing him its drama, its ambiguities, but seldom its ordinariness or true virtues — flourishing family life and self-sufficiency come to mind. Greene loved Africa in the way only a visitor can — never a long-term expatriate, the long-suffering alien, the belittled missionary, the overworked doctor, the despised schoolteacher.

Greene would have found it hard as a resident writer in the African bush, had he chosen to live there for any length of time. His exasperation with details of bush life shows in his book. Halfway through the trip — that is, a mere fourteen days into it — he is sick and impatient for the thing to end. "Now all I wanted was medicine, a bath, iced drinks, and something other than this bush lavatory of trees and dead leaves." A few days later: "I was happy with the sense that every step was towards home." On the seventeenth day: "I felt irritated with everyone and everything." Soon after that: "I felt crazy to be here in the middle of Liberia . . . It was like a bad dream. I couldn't remember why I had come." In his diary at Bassa Town, he referred to "this silly trip," but this — and his more serious apprehensions — he kept out of his published book. Less than a week later he is at the coast, and the whole thing is a memory.

In retrospect, rationalized on the page, the journey was both breezier and more profound, with suspenseful highlights and shaped to seem as though it was plotted — an unexpected ordeal for this unprepared traveler. Yet his struggle elevated it in Greene's mind. He realized that what he had accomplished was unique and difficult, and of course it was: the amateur had broken through and acquired experience. "I wanted to laugh and shout and cry; it was the end, the end of the worst boredom I had ever experienced, the worst fear and the worst exhaustion." His instinct had been right: this was a trip he needed to take.

Claims are made that Greene was a superior sort of traveler, that his trips were monumental, even groundbreaking. I don't see this at all. He was a fortunate traveler. His life had been sheltered. He was rather fearful and manic-depressive, as he himself confided in his autobiography. He always had a taxi waiting. His achievement was that such a nervy soul was able to succeed in such challenges, for he was essentially an urbane man who boasted of disliking exercise and valuing his privacy and his comforts.

His fears made Africa vivid — for himself, for the reader. The uneasy traveler, the dilettante, which Greene was (always looking up contacts, always dependent on being shown the way), tends to invent the landscape he is traversing. Out of muddle he imagines it as much wilder than it is. There are robust assertions of cannibalism in *Journey Without Maps*. But there are no cannibals in Liberia. He mentions at one point "a tribe, about a week ahead . . . still supposed to practise cannibalism," and traveling "in the land of the Manos, where ritual cannibalism practiced on strangers has never been entirely wiped out," and in Ganta, "Human sacrifice had once been offered at the falls." Equally unlikely, in a country that a few years earlier had made the important deal with Firestone for rubber plantations (and the eagerness of Firestone to possess the country), are "the places where I and my cousin were the first white people to be seen in living memory." These are the endearing self-deceptions of a man inventing a landscape he first imagined as a child in England, scaring himself rigid with images of the witch Gagool.

Greene's Africa is worth studying because so much of it is in his head. He sees the bush as hostile, not neutral. If the ants and rats and cockroaches fail to nibble you to death, then answering a call of nature at the latrine you are likely (so he says) to be bitten by a poisonous snake. Yet the snakes can be decorous: "Once, a beautiful little green snake moved across the path, upright, without hurry, bearing her bust proudly forward into the grasses like a hostess painted by Sargent, poisonous with gentility, a Fabergé jewel."

Greene's Africa is a place for an outsider to go to pieces, a dramatic backdrop, not always as specific as a landscape but often an atmosphere —

heat and dust, insects and birdcalls; it represents romance and the possibility of reinvention. There is no big game in Greene's Africa, but there are predatory people — whites usually — and there is illness, betrayal, adultery, and lost love. Politics hardly figure at all, and except for Deo Gratias in *A Burnt-Out Case* and a couple of the carriers in *Journey Without Maps*, few Africans are delineated or have personal histories.

Returning to Freetown in 1942 to do wartime intelligence work, Greene got better acquainted with Sierra Leone. Even so, he stuck to the city. The novel that came out of his experience, *The Heart of the Matter*, is set in the coastal capital, with excursions to Pende in the bush. Africa is not the subject but the shadowy backdrop for this essentially inward-looking novel that questions the elements of belief and damnation, heaven and hell.

A Burnt-Out Case (1961) was an even more deliberate book, the result of another African trip, which Greene described in the short nonfiction account he titled *In Search of a Character*. Many parts of the novel are direct transcriptions from his notebook and portraits of people he met on his stay at a leprosarium in the Belgian Congo. By the time this novel appeared, Greene was well established as a describer of tropical decay and disorder, of drunken expatriates, whose prose was never lacking in an uneasy awareness of the judgmental presence of the omniscient Christian God, the deity peeping especially into the humid bedrooms of Greene's wayward characters. Africa looms large in these two novels, but Christian faith looms much larger. Africa is the stage on which adulterers wonder if they have spoiled their chances for salvation. Africa suits Greene because it is unformed, suggestive of risk and danger and disease, something like a war zone without the shooting. Such is Africa's power to bewitch the credulous.

When Greene finally found a true rebellion in Africa, reporting the events of the Mau Mau uprising in colonial Kenya in 1953, he was less inclined to sympathize with the rebels than with the British farmers in the so-called White Highlands. He did not stay long enough to understand the exploitation, political unfairness, and fundamental racism of British Kenya, yet by inclination he was fair-minded himself and a well-wisher in the cause of African independence. Greene's Africa, unlike the more particular landscapes of London, Brighton, Saigon, and Port-au-Prince, is a landscape of the mind, a set of vivid, sometimes stereotypical images which, precisely because they match our own stereotypes in their oversimplification, could account for the success of his vision of Africa as seedy.

"The deep appeal of the seedy" is adumbrated in his Liberian journey, but it seems to me that "seedy" describes little more than the down-at-heel coastal communities of expatriates, a far cry from the sense of everlasting-ness of the bush, which is the true heart of Africa.

Greene was an admitted sentimentalist where Africa is concerned. This sentimentality occurs very early in his work; indeed, it first surfaces in *Journey Without Maps*. One of his memories of England is of sitting in a bar where a young woman is crying. Drinking and watching her, "I thought for some reason even then of Africa, not a particular place, but a shape, a strangeness, a wanting to know. The unconscious mind is often sentimental; I have written 'a shape,' and the shape, of course, is roughly that of a human heart."

This thought is unlikely to occur to the long-term expatriate in an African country, who would never think of a map of the whole continent. Such a person, unsentimental for reasons of survival, would think of Africa as the small town or clearing he is working in. Any maps he thinks of would be maps of his district, or at the very most, his province.

Greene's reaction to Africa is literary and somewhat abstract, derived from Conrad, who, though he had strong views on Belgian colonialism, hardly knew Africa at all beyond the banks of the river. Yet, in his typically virile and spontaneous way, and perhaps as a side effect of his anxiety in the bush, Greene is highly responsive to Africa. In this respect he was ahead of his time, unprejudiced, and true to the spirit of his boyhood adventure stories. In a word, for Greene Africa is naked. Some of the women greatly entrance him. The book is a compendium of brown breasts. The unforced, and I should say unconscious, way Greene notices the pretty women is like a grace note in the book. Only Sir Richard Burton, in East Africa, demonstrated an equal connoisseurship of brown breasts.

Though he could be contradictory, for *Journey Without Maps* is a moody book in which he changes his mind about Africa a number of times, in general Greene regards Africa as representing life and hope and vitality. Greene's shipboard observations of the green continent contrast with Marlow's in *Heart of Darkness* as his ship approaches the Congo, for while the vantage point is the same, the conclusions are different. Marlow saw a continent beset, possessed, fired upon, and spooky; Greene sees on the lush coast a happier place, "a sense of warm and sleepy beauty" that reminds him of Baudelaire at his most sensual.

For Greene, Africa also represents visceral excitement, freedom, "the life one was born to live." At this early joyous point in the book he has glimpsed his first African women in a market, with "lovely features ... young and old, lovely less from sexual attractiveness than from a sharp differentiated pictorial quality." In a bright memory farther down the coast he refers to "the neat tarts of Dakar." His gaze lingers in Freetown when a young woman approaches the car he is riding in: "her bare breasts were small and firm and pointed; she had the neat rounded thighs of a cat." A few days later, peering from the train as he travels upcountry, he sees "the women pressed up along the line, their great black nipples like the centre point of a target." Arriving at the border of Liberia and French Guinea, he fastens onto a figure as the very embodiment of the place, "something lovely, happy and unenslaved, something like the girl who came up the hill that morning, a piece of bright cloth twisted above her hips, the sunlight falling between the palms on her dark hanging breasts."

He had gone to some trouble to arrange a meeting with Liberia's president, Edwin Barclay, but on the day Greene is less impressed by this powerful man than by a woman who is present, looking "more Chinese than African ... She was the loveliest thing I saw in Liberia; I couldn't keep my eyes off her." In a bush settlement Greene calls "The Horrible Village" he measures the village by its women and concludes, "Only a few of the women broke the monotonous ugliness of the place ... There was one small girl in a turban with slanting Oriental eyes and small neat breasts who did appeal to European sexual tastes even in her dirt." Detouring through French Guinea, he approves of the women, who "lived up to the standard of a country which provides the handsomest whores and the most elegant brothels" — and he goes on to provide a minutely detailed description of their coiffures and their distinctive makeup.

Greene's response to the nakedness of African women is clearly an aspect of his relief at being liberated as well as tantalized. At these times Africa seems Eden-like. Farther on in the French colony Greene is entertained by a chief whose daughter is present and is slightly drunk. Greene eyes the girl: "her thigh under the tight cloth about her waist was like the soft furry rump of a kitten; she had lovely breasts; she was quite clean, much cleaner than we were. The chief wanted us to stay the night, and I began to wonder how far his hospitality might go." Even at the end of his tether, sick and impatient, staggering near the conclusion of his journey in Bassa Town, noticing hardly anything in his feverishness, he is aware of women watching him. To his now practiced eye, he sees one woman as representing an advanced culture, "a sign that we were meeting the edge of civilisation pushing up from the Coast. A young girl hung around all day posturing with her thighs and hips, suggestively, like a tart. Naked to the waist, she was conscious of her nakedness; she knew her breasts had a significance to the white man they didn't have to the native."

The "tart" is an exception to Greene's equating African nakedness with innocence. As a spectator at a village dance that sounds like a ghastly rigadoon ("emaciated old women slapping their pitted buttocks"), he is happy: "the freedom of Africa began to touch us at last." In the next paragraph he presses this point about the attraction of a country — and he quotes — "that hath yet her maidenhead, never sacked, turned, nor wrought . . . the mines not broken with sledges, nor their images pulled down out of their temples." This quotation is unattributed — I had to ask a scholarly friend to identify it, which he readily did: Sir Walter Raleigh — but the message could not be clearer. It is still early enough in his journey (about ten days) for Greene to be fascinated by the notion of Africa as undefiled. He believes he has gone deep. His notion is that he is in virgin territory, and "There is not so much virginity in the world that one can afford not to love it when one finds it."

This was not a final judgment. Later, dispirited and ill, he confessed that Liberia was hellish and that he could hardly wait for the trip to end. He hated the last two weeks and was glad when it was all over. So the book is contradictory, but the contradictions are truthful reflections of Greene's traveling moods. Greene is scrupulous in dramatizing all the stages of his emotional journey, from anxiety to fear to bewitchment to romance to disillusionment and back again (reflecting in tranquility) to fascination.

Now, seventy years later, Liberia is more dangerous than it was when Greene walked through with his cousin, depending on the kindness of strangers and receiving hospitality. For decades, not much changed in Liberia's political system, characterized by patronage, corruption, and nepotism, Homburg hats and three-piece suits. When President William Tubman, who ruled much in the Barclay mode, with U.S. backing, died of natural causes, William Tolbert succeeded him. After nine years of rule he was overthrown by a young upstart soldier, Samuel Doe, who presided over a reign of terror. In his turn, Doe was overthrown. Captured, his ears were cut off and he was brutally killed. After a few years, his murderer,

Prince Yormie Johnson, who did not replace him as president, was forced to flee to exile in Nigeria.

The country was plagued by armed gangs, child soldiers, and self-appointed leaders. In 2005 Liberia had an interim government, anticipating free elections in 2006, but the country was (as in Greene's time) one of the poorest in Africa. There are roads (though bumpy ones) where in Greene's time there had been bush tracks. You can trace his route on a modern map. Peace Corps volunteers staff the schools in some of the very settlements Greene mentions—for example, Tapeta (Tapee-Ta), where he and his cousin spent "a Victorian Sunday" and met Colonel Elwood Davis ("Dictator of Grand Bassa"). Even in its distress, Liberia remains a stronghold of the Firestone rubber empire and a continuing source of illegal diamonds.

Greene never returned to Liberia. His trip, like many difficult trips, remained glamorous in retrospect. Yet it turned him into a more ambitious traveler. Within a few years he was in Mexico, riding on a mule for *The Lawless Roads* (1938). He began to explore more of Africa, and other equatorial places, in Southeast Asia, the Caribbean, and Latin America. He developed an instinct for troubled countries with dramatic landscapes, where the women (whom he never stopped scrutinizing) were lovely. In his seventies, on an anniversary of the trip, he wrote to Barbara, "To me that trip has been very important—it started a love of Africa which has never quite left me . . . Altogether a trip which altered life."

3. THE COMEDIAN

Graham Greene clucked about the abuses in Haiti and wrote outraged letters to newspapers on Haitian subjects, and even a piece of journalism, but the "nightmare republic," as he called it, was perfect for him. As a traveler, he greatly preferred nightmare republics to healthy democracies, though as a resident he chose more salubrious places: the isle of Capri, a fashionable district of Paris, and Antibes. He moved to the south of France in 1966, as a tax exile, the year *The Comedians* was published.

On the walls of his Antibes apartment he hung valuable paintings by the Haitian artists Salnave Philippe-Auguste and Rigaud Benoit. It so happens that Brown, the narrator of *The Comedians*, also owns paintings by these artists. Brown describes the macabre details of the Philippe-Auguste, then adds, "Wherever that picture hung, I thought, I would feel Haiti close to me." Greene must have felt this nostalgia among the lotus-eaters in Antibes. But he was hardly the first novelist to surround himself with fine art and gourmet restaurants in order to write horror stories. Many of his scribbling neighbors were doing much the same. The tidy Côte d'Azur is just the sort of place to inspire *nostalgie de la boue,* the *boue* in this case being (again Greene's description) a "shabby land of terror."

Greene first traveled to Haiti in 1954. He kept going back until, a dozen years later, *The Comedians* incurred the wrath of Haiti's president, François "Papa Doc" Duvalier. National novelists are routinely banned by repressive regimes, but what other visiting writer has been personally denounced, and his book reviewed, by a head of state for making his country the landscape of a novel? Greene pretended to be annoyed, but his pleasure in Papa Doc's pamphlet, "Graham Greene: Finally Exposed," was unmistakable; it is clear Greene regarded the attack as a badge of honor.

Haiti was also tainted by American meddling. Duvalier's regime existed, in Greene's estimation, because of the patronage of the United States government. This, too, animated Greene, who for much of his writing life teased interviewers with anti-American remarks. (In 1960 a French journalist asked him, "What is it that you dislike in today's civilization?" Greene replied, "America.") The U.S. government reciprocated this contempt. After Greene's death it was revealed that for forty years the FBI had monitored his movements and his provocative statements, recorded in secret reports.

Though he traveled as a foreign correspondent, reporting crises in Vietnam, Malaya, and Africa, Greene was not a natural journalist, which is to say he had no stomach for the grind of journalism, the delays, the daily filing of stories. He often repeated that he disliked journalists. His natural form was the thoughtful essay. He looked for vivid and life-defining experiences, not scoops. In general, his reportage was not distinguished. Yet he wrote about Haiti, not as breaking news or an account of great events, but rather as a summing up of the mood of the place. This portrait of a small miserable country, titled "Nightmare Republic," was published in the London *Sunday Telegraph* in 1963, three years before *The Comedians* appeared. (In the novel he specifically mocks this sort of journalism, and even quotes the title of this piece in a belittling way.) To anyone who wishes to understand Greene's personal attitude toward Haiti — as opposed to his apparent novelistic impartiality — the piece is helpful.

From the first few sentences, in which a Voodoo *houngan* (priest) bites the head off a chicken, through the descriptions of poverty and ruin, violence and terror, it is clear that many details have been chosen for their shock value. "Some strange curse descended on the liberated slaves of Hispaniola," Greene writes, and he goes on, "They live in the world of Hieronymus Bosch." Your first thought on reading such sentences is that it is surprising that Greene claimed to dislike journalism, since these are examples of the most lurid excesses of the tabloid form.

But "Nightmare Republic" has its subtleties, too. Quite early in the piece, Greene writes, "A reign of terror has often about it the atmosphere of farce," and you guess at once that it is farce — the absurdity of evil — that appeals to Greene. He portrays Papa Doc as a tyrant, a torturer, an embezzler, a practitioner of Voodoo, and a part-time goblin. "Baron Samedi, in his top hat and tails, who haunts the cemeteries smoking a cigar and wearing dark glasses, spends his days, so some believe, in the Presidential Palace, and his other name is Dr. Duvalier."

Greene enumerates the farcical aspects — the empty hotels, the extravagant rumors, the bullies manning roadblocks. "Anything may happen, any time, anywhere." Mass is celebrated at the cathedral in Port-au-Prince, but "when the excommunicated President puts in his one appearance at Mass, the Tontons arrive armed with submachine-guns and search, even behind the altar." And "a kind of evil farce enters even into the religious conflict." Intending to suppress Voodoo, a prominent bishop demanded that Voodoo charms be collected, and "he was accused of robbing the country of archaeological treasures."

Trade has failed, agriculture has failed, even rebellion has failed. "Everyone is some sort of prisoner in Port-au-Prince." Hunger is the rule. "It is impossible to exaggerate the poverty of Haiti." And when Greene asks himself whether there is any hope for this "beautiful and bedeviled country," he seems at a loss to find a single example, except that "Haitian pride cannot be exaggerated." After Greene's devastating account of this futile place, one cannot resist wondering: pride in what?

Deforested, slum-ridden, tyrannized, exploited, disgraced, divided and at war with itself, and a horror to the people who live there, Haiti is a gift to Greene. As a regular visitor, he saw it alter through several regimes, and perhaps it was the writing of "Nightmare Republic," in which he depicted it as the apotheosis of failure, that he was convinced that its best expression would be in fiction. *The Comedians* is characterized by many of the points

Greene made in the piece, and the mood of the essay pervades the novel, that dark blend of terror and farce.

Greene conceived and wrote *The Comedians* at a time of crisis in his life. He had been dealt a severe financial setback, through the mismanagement of his accountant. He had decided to move to France, claiming health reasons, but it was in fact tax avoidance. Because of his financial bind he was once again, as in an earlier time in his life, writing for money. He had cut his ties with England, sold his London residence, and had taken stock of his romantic life. He had fallen in love with a married woman who lived in France. Though she remained married, and so did he (but his marriage had effectively ended twenty-five years earlier), she would be accessible to him in the south of France. He was in his early sixties, not as solvent as he had once been, uprooted, and restless.

These circumstances inform the book. Everything about *The Comedians* has the implication of crisis: its setting, which is the rotting Republic of Haiti, and its characters, each of whom is beset with an unsolvable problem. It is a novel of insecurity. Haiti is hopeless, the Haitians are hopeless. There is no food. The government is parasitical and oppressive. Nothing works. What to do? Well, there is sex — that works. There is faith — Voodoo has its excitements, and for the Catholics, God is in His heaven, offering salvation. There is love — not much of that here. There is comedy — quite a lot of that; indeed, it is insisted upon. Tragedy is quite near to farce, Greene once wrote. When all else fails — and this is a novel in which all else fails — there is always laughter.

From the outset, none of the characters are who they really seem. The voyage out on the Haiti-bound cargo ship *Medea* shows the small number of paying passengers to be dissemblers, great and small. "Aspects are within us," says the epigraph. The course of the novel reveals who these people are. In a word, tragic or troubled though they may appear to be, they are nearly all of them comedians.

The first paragraph is one of Greene's best openings, suggesting all the ambiguities of the novel with a kind of mock eloquence, and concentrating on Jones. Jones is obviously a liar, a chancer, a charmer, with a gift for obfuscation. Apparently Greene based Jones somewhat on the accountant who got him into his financial muddle. Greene wrote in his preface to the novel that he based Mr. and Mrs. Smith on a kindly American couple he had met on one of his trips — they were artistic and were going to bring art into Haitian classrooms. This fact is mildly interesting, and art instruction seems rather more useful than the Smiths' obsession with vegetarianism. But if you have vegetarians in your narrative, and the book is a dark comedy, there is room for mentions of prepackaged vegetarian meals with names such as Yeastrel and Barmene, all of which Greene seems to have found hilarious.

The character Petit Pierre was based on an impish journalist and man-about-town in Port-au-Prince named Aubelin Jolicoeur — at least Jolicoeur took credit for it in an interview, and there seem to have been some resemblances. Brown's hotel, the Trianon, was based on an actual hotel called the Oloffson, just as empty and decrepit and ornate. The brothel is Mère Catherine's, and Catherine was the name of the woman whom Greene had loved and lost before moving to France. Greene was in the habit of cracking private jokes in his books. But do any of these correspondences to Greene's life matter? I don't think so.

The voyage on the *Medea* is a wonderfully sustained episode of tantalizing hints and character sketches — Greene seldom writes of shipboard life in his fiction, though there is a Mexican voyage in *The Lawless Roads*. The *Medea*, with its close quarters and hijinks, is a somewhat sunny prologue to the darkness that lies ahead in Haiti. The isolation of an ocean crossing is perfect as both revelation and titillation, for raising doubts and setting up all the action that follows. The central characters are introduced. They are plainly named Smith, Jones, and Brown, and Greene seems to intend their names as a wheeze of sorts, as though in the setup of a laborious joke: "See, there were these three people — Smith, Jones, and Brown . . ."

The novel is not one of Greene's best or his favorite (among his favorites were *The Power and the Glory* and *The Honorary Consul*), but it is one of his most characteristic efforts, showing many of his strengths and his weaknesses. The plot is easily related. Brown is returning to the decrepit hotel he inherited from his blowsy mother. Jones is involved in a private adventure. The Smiths are evangelizing vegetarians and had also been Freedom Riders in the American South, idealists in the civil rights movement of the late 1950s. Mr. Smith had been a presidential candidate in 1952, espousing vegetarianism.

On their arrival in Port-au-Prince, these characters appear to go their separate ways, but — this being a small and inbred country at a time of political crisis — their paths cross. After the body of a Haitian, Dr. Philipot, is found in Brown's empty swimming pool, apparently a suicide, various Haitian characters emerge: the gossiping gadfly figure of Petit Pierre, the sententious Dr. Magiot, Captain Concasseur ("Steamroller"), and the thuggish Tontons Macoute. Though he makes no appearance, the presence of Papa Doc constantly hovers. Brown is cynical throughout; the Smiths' idealism is tested; Jones proves to be the ultimate opportunist, and it is his undoing. The pivotal meeting places are Brown's hotel and Mère Catherine's brothel. It is revealed that Dr. Philipot cut his throat to escape the Tontons Macoute. As initiates in a Voodoo ceremony that Greene lifted whole from his newspaper piece, Philipot's son and Brown's employee are turned into rebels. To entice the posturing Jones away from his mistress, Brown involves him in the guerrilla opposition. The rebellion fails, though in the course of it Jones becomes a hero. Brown's love affair collapses. The Smiths depart, sadder but wiser. Brown at the end becomes a mortician. Haiti is unchanged.

From the voyage onward, the persistently self-referential Brown (we are not told his first name) muses on his rootlessness. He is a man who is truly at sea. The paradox is that the more conscious he is of it, the more he sees his resemblance to Jones. "Perhaps he's like me and he hasn't anywhere else to go," Brown says. "I divide the world into two parts — the toffs and the tarts," Jones asserts, adding that he is a tart. This seems ridiculous until he explains that tarts hustle for a living, stay alert, keep moving, and live by their wits, and his description fits Brown. Although Jones's sense of humor sets him apart from Brown, the men are presented as sharing certain affinities. Jones even ends up as a houseguest of Brown's mistress, Martha, the German wife of a South American ambassador. As a woman who carries on her intrigue while opting to remain married to her complaisant husband, Martha is a stock character in Greene's fictional repertoire. To Brown's annoyance, Martha finds Jones good company and a far more amusing companion than Brown, who is relentlessly gloomy.

Jones is "foreign," and at the very end reveals himself as half Indian, passing himself off as a British war hero. He is a man with a shadowy past that he is anxious to conceal in his dissembling and his tall tales. Brown is just as emphatically a man from nowhere who, when he learns the truth of Jones's ancestry, says, "It was like meeting an unknown brother." Jones was born in Assam, Brown in Monaco: "that is almost the same as being a citizen of nowhere." Elsewhere Brown says, "No region of the earth had taken the place of home."

"I should never have come to this country, I was a stranger," he says at another point. "My mother had taken a black lover, she had been involved, but somewhere years ago I had forgotten how to be involved in anything. Somehow somewhere I had lost the capacity to be concerned."

As for his hotelkeeping in his empty hotel in Haiti, "I felt a greater tie here, in the shabby land of terror, chosen for me by chance." But we never see any expression of Brown's tie to the country. In fact he had left to go to New York in order to sell his hotel, but understandably there were no takers.

A trait that the rootless Brown does not mention is his monumental egotism. Self-protecting, he thinks obsessively of himself. You wonder why Brown is in this desperate dictatorship, of all places, for his self-centeredness prevents him from ever entering into Haiti's drama. He hints at one reason he lives there, for the advantage of being rootless, Brown says, is that "one accepts more easily what comes . . . We have chosen nothing except to go on living, 'rolled round on Earth's diurnal course, with rocks and stones and trees.'" But this Wordsworthian essence leaves him on the sidelines as a dispassionate observer. His concern is little more than perfunctory. Things happen to him; he does not act. Is this existentialism? No, it is egotism.

Brown has no allegiances to disclose; Jones is an egotist of concealment. Yet Jones's boasting so convinces others that he is impelled to act. When Brown calls his bluff, his reversal from impostor to guerrilla leader is the payoff to the great joke of his bluster. Of all the comedians in the novel, Jones is the most comic. It is impossible to miss this theme — that terror inspires farce. "Life was a comedy, not the tragedy for which I had been prepared," Brown reflects on board the *Medea*, speaking of his belief in God, "and it seemed to me that we were all . . . driven by an authoritative practical joker towards the extreme point of comedy."

You need a sense of humor to believe in God, he says, but humor is also useful in Haiti. A sense of humor takes the place of commitment: the Smiths are laughable for their vegetarianism and their ideals, and Jones is a joke for the pickle he gets himself into. But what of the Haitians? They are jolly, but in effect they don't matter much, for this is a novel of Europeans going to pieces in a hopeless tyranny, not a novel about the plight of Haiti.

Haiti is a horrific backdrop to instances of infidelity, self-doubt, domestic tragedy, and the pretensions of foreign opportunists.

Each character is described at one point or another as being a comedian. Brown's extravagant mother, with her debts and deceptions and her lovers, is one. Brown says, "I knew very little of her, but enough to recognize an accomplished comedian." Mr. Smith says, "Perhaps we seem rather comic figures to you, Mr. Brown," and though Brown denies it and says they are heroic, he finds the vegetarianism, presidential candidacy, and freedom-riding rather ludicrous. The Smiths are typical Americans — figures of fun.

"I am no comedian," Martha says, though her husband conjectures, "Perhaps even Papa Doc is a comedian." When Brown first meets Captain Concasseur at Mère Catherine's, Concasseur gives a little speech about humor, saying, "You have a sense of humor. I appreciate humor. I am in favor of jokes. They have political value. Jokes are a release for the cowardly and the impotent."

Jones's comedy is his saving grace. Jones makes Martha laugh; he amuses the prostitute (another annoyance, she is one of Brown's favorites: "In age one prefers old friends, even in a *bordel*") at Mère Catherine's; and as a leader of the rebels he is a success: "The men loved him. He made them laugh." One of the few truly comic episodes in the book occurs when Jones escapes from a ship in disguise, dressed as a woman. He carries it off with a panache that implies he has been in this position before, using shaving powder for makeup and wearing a black skirt and a Spanish blouse.

> "At the foot of the gangway," he told the purser, "you must kiss me. It will help hide my face."
>
> "Why not kiss Mr. Brown?" the purser asked.
>
> "He's taking me home. It wouldn't be natural. You have to imagine that we've passed quite an evening together, all three of us."
>
> "What kind of evening?"
>
> "An evening of riotous abandonment," Jones said.
>
> "Can you manage your skirt?" I asked.

"Of course, old man." He added mysteriously, "This is not the first time. Under very different circumstances, of course."

Later, when we are told several times that Jones's weakness is flat feet, we are inclined to associate his flat feet with a clown's flapping feet. The implication throughout the novel is that comedy is meaningless but is at least a relief from misery or sadness. "We belonged to the world of comedy and not of tragedy," Brown says of himself and Martha. Earlier, Martha denied she was a comedian, but Brown concludes that she was perhaps "the best comedian of us all." For all the talk of comedy (and there is more talk of comedy than fleshed-out instances of it), the love affair between Brown and Martha seems neither comic nor tragic, but instead sullen, passionless, abruptly sexual, and characterized by jealousy, misunderstanding, ambivalence, and resentment. It is the end of an affair, a dying away of desire.

"Semi-attached" is how Brown defines his love affair with Martha, and his characterization of it gives a clue to the Haitian world of the novel. Their life as lovers had been important, he says, because it "seemed to belong now exclusively to Port-au-Prince, to the darkness and the terror of the curfew, to the telephones that didn't work, to the Tontons Macoute in their dark glasses, to violence, injustice and torture."

But by asserting that the failing love affair is suited to the crumbling of Haiti, he is romanticizing their selfishness while at the same time belittling the plight of the millions of Haitians. And he is dramatizing the disorder, without using that ordinary word; the messy love affair matches the chaos and casual violence of Haiti. But so what? Because the love affair is enacted on the fringe of a much greater chaos, we know too much about the former and not enough about the latter. One of the problems of the novel is that Greene — and his mouthpiece Brown — never shows us why we should care about these petty, humorless, selfish, unfaithful, and discontented lovers. It is not enough to say that we are all comedians; the point is not proven, though in a blunter, crueler sense some of the characters behave like fools.

At the very end of the novel Brown confesses that he is spiritually empty. Readers of Greene's novels find this a familiar disclosure. Brown envies anyone with belief — he envies Dr. Magiot for having political beliefs. "I had felt myself not merely incapable of love . . . but even of guilt." Throughout the novel Brown sounds rather sedated, and even in sex he is joyless. Making love to Martha, he says, "I flung myself into pleasure like a suicide on to a pavement." He takes his real problem with Martha to be that he has no sense of humor or, as he puts it, "has not learned the trick of laughter." He ends up admiring Jones for his humor, and for at last becoming a man of action, not only the ultimate comedian but also a hero. The novel begins with a recollection of Jones, and it ends with Brown's dream of him. Jones is clearly the pivotal character; the trouble is that in describing Jones's simplicities, Brown's complexities get in the way.

Greene was candid about his superficial experience of Haiti. In a newspaper interview with a young and obviously dazzled V. S. Naipaul in 1968, Greene said, "The political situation [in *The Comedians*] is accurate. But I feel that my knowledge of Haitian life and manners was surface." (He also pointedly said to Naipaul, "Are you satisfied with what you've written?") It's true, the texture of Haitian life is not represented. And the novel is tepid without a firsthand account of the rebellion. The action, which is the climax of the narrative, sputters unconvincingly somewhere in the background, given in muted second- and thirdhand versions, like Shakespearean stage directions ("Alarum. Flourish of trumpets. The armies clash") and we never see a skirmish. We take it on faith that there is an armed opposition to Papa Doc piling on from somewhere over the border in the Dominican Republic.

The writers who influenced Greene (so he said) were the authors of books of action and adventure — Anthony Hope, the Kipling of *Kim* and "The Man Who Would Be King" — and he never ceased to praise Marjorie Bowen's *The Viper of Milan* (1906). Odd, then, that he seldom attempted to write action himself, usually contenting himself with summaries. *The Comedians*, which takes place during an attempted insurrection, has no gunplay in it and, in effect, no insurrection. In the place of action there is talk of action. The book is constructed of a series of epigrams and almost-epigrams.

"Violent deaths are natural deaths here," the sententious Dr. Magiot says. "He died of his environment." And Magiot again: "A witness here can suffer just as much as the accused." Brown says, "An innocent victim nearly always looks guilty," "Courage even in the brave sleeps before breakfast," and, of Petit Pierre, "He had the courage and humor of the defeated." And, "Violence can be the expression of love; indifference never." And, "Death is a proof of sincerity." From these observations Greene intends to drive his argument, but each of them is debatable. In the novel the republic of rebellion and upheaval is reduced to a republic of talk, and the wordy pretensions give the novel a static quality.

Yet there is an unmistakable stamp of authorship on the book. This could only be a novel by Graham Greene: a doomed love affair in a back-water, the talk of belief, and especially the talk of belief in principles, the rotting hotel, the cheery brothel, the strong drinks — it is all Greene. The mentions of "mistress" strike me as dated, and in a way so do the discussions of a belief in God. A Haiti without AIDS is also old hat. A sea voyage with hijinks thrown in is a thing of the past. The novel was written only a little over forty years ago and already seems old-fashioned.

Greene would probably have disagreed, but the quaintness of these details is part of its appeal, for the world has changed, and the world Greene wrote about is gone. But Greene made Haiti accessible, gave it a visible landscape, and by demonizing Papa Doc, Greene made the shabby dictator seem important, even unearthly ("Baron Samedi walked in all our grave-yards"). After Papa Doc died, his son — nicknamed Baskethead for his fatness and his stupidity — took over, and was deposed in a coup. A few more coups later (Haiti has had thirty-odd of them), a president was chosen in Haiti's first free election.

I am writing this in March 2004, the year of Haiti's bicentennial. In 1791, Haiti went to war with itself in the celebrated slave revolt led by Toussaint Louverture and his comrade Boukman (who was a Voodoo *houngan*). The result was Haiti's independence in 1804. Two hundred years later, Haiti is again in the news as a nightmare republic: riots in the streets of Port-au-Prince, mayhem in the provincial towns, thousands dead, and even — as in *The Comedians* — endangered Haitians seeking refuge in foreign embassies. The elected president, Jean-Bertrand Aristide, protested that he was kidnapped by the U.S. Marines and flown to Africa against his will. An interim president has been chosen. A rebel leader with a proven record of atrocities as a leader of Haitian death squads is presently maneuvering to be the next Haitian head of state.

"Haiti was not an exception in a sane world; it was a small slice of everyday taken at random." So it must have seemed forty years ago. There are other countries that resemble Haiti. Political geographers have put the number at about forty-five, most of them in Africa, though Albania is one, and so is Afghanistan. They are known as failed states. They might have begun as colonies, or kingdoms, or provinces of larger republics, countries that had become prosperous through possessing a mineral or a crop that is no longer in demand. Haiti in 1780 grew 60 percent of the world's coffee.

Now it has relatively few coffee bushes, or any other kinds of bushes: Haiti's need for fuel has resulted in its deforestation. It is the poorest country in the Western Hemisphere.

As a failed state, Haiti has little hope of financial independence or political stability and seems destined to remain one of the world's slums. Greene understood Haiti to be a problem place — he had a nose for such places — and he chose to write about it in the early 1960s when the war in Vietnam was in the news. The great value of *The Comedians* is not its theology (a Jansenist tract, as some critics have called it), nor its philosophizing, nor its plot. It reads like an extended piece of self-criticism, and, written by a man who claimed not to know much about the place, its value most of all is its setting. Greene's obsessive love for the place in all its gruesome comedy rings true even if the drama does not. Haiti had no fiction — and hardly had a face — until Greene wrote this book.

5

HUNTER IN THE KINGDOM OF FEAR

1

The suicide of a satirist such as Hunter S. Thompson is particularly disturbing. You remember the things he wrote, the threats, the promises, or just the extravagance of his titles and subtitles — Kingdom of Fear: Loathsome Secrets of a Star-Crossed Child in the Final Days of the American Century; Better Than Sex: Confessions of a Political Junkie Trapped like a Rat in Mr. Bill's Neighborhood; Death of a Poet; Fear and Loathing in Las Vegas: A Savage Journey to the Heart of the American Dream — *and you think, He wasn't kidding.*

Hunter made something of a fetish for seeming to use words idly, as the bombast of comic effect, particularly his repetition of "fear and loathing." But the fear and loathing were real to him. He tended not to pull his punches or deal in ambiguities. "You are a trigger happy little bastard," he wrote to me affectionately. And also, "The pig has gone into the tunnel. But so what? We are champions." He knew how to buck one up. As for the rest of humanity, politicians in particular, for whom, as a fascinated journalist, he had lots of time but no sympathy, his usual cries were: Swine! Pig! Weasel! Crook! Fascist! Nazi! Diseased cur! He was a living reminder that satire at its best is a savage business. He was unsparing, self-punishing in the way he lived his life. His friends adored him. Such a brooding presence could not be the life of the party, but he was always its soul.

He could also be an oblique and fearful man, less a drug addict than (as he sometimes called himself) a dope fiend. "The brutal reality of politics alone would probably be intolerable without drugs," he said. "Anybody who covers this beat for twenty years — and my beat is 'The Death of the American Dream' — needs every goddamned crutch he can find." He also said, "It may be that every culture needs an Outlaw god of some kind, and maybe this time I'm it."

He was a boisterous recluse who also needed to be seen and heard. He was by nature a prowler, a social animal, inviting disapproval, provoking insults. He seldom dealt with books; he was no reader. Except for snippets from the Book of Revelation, which he knew almost by heart, his literary quotations have the odor of the anthology about them, or the simplicity of having been overheard or borrowed, not quarried from a dense text. You need to be able to sit still to be a reader.

There is a peculiar sort of irritable, sober, and timid Mr. Hyde who is always attempting with the use of drugs to transform himself into a bolder and happier Dr. Jekyll, to transform himself for the purposes of art and science from a cranky destructor into a student of human behavior. It is the Stevenson story turned on its head. I saw this in Hunter. Released from his rages and his babbling, he acquired a much sunnier mood, and after the drugs had taken hold, he was calmer, more rational, with a greater attention span; under the influence, Hunter called himself "Doc."

He was always stuffing something into his mouth, and his chain-smoking wasn't even half of it. I wonder if I ever saw him sober. He wasn't an alcoholic, but he was certainly a drunkard. And though he could be compulsive, I don't think he was a drug addict — not an obsessed and needy user of addictive drugs, at any rate, but what is generally known as a stoner and a sniffer. An addict is helpless, but drug-taking was for him a decision. Not shy but strangely timid (he never traveled alone and was innocent of the practical details of travel), Hunter at his most extroverted could be almost psychotic. He was deaf and distracted in the way serious drug takers become, even when they are sober, either shouting or whispering. I have no idea how he managed to write a word, but he wrote a dozen memorable books. He hardly slept, and he kept the strangest hours. Any friend of Hunter's can recount the phone ringing at 3 a.m. and the low conspiratorial growl, "It's 'Unner!"

He loved Hawaii for its fine weather and its air of tolerance and its remoteness. Here he is in the luxury suite of a beachside hotel, sitting amid a clutter of room-service food, drinking beer and smoking and bantering and watching a basketball game. He was all his life a passionate sports fan. (Until his death he had a weekly column on the ESPN website.) He happened to be in Hawaii to cover the Honolulu Marathon, but at the same time was keeping up with the NFL playoffs and the front-runners in the NBA. He was barking at the TV and picking at his food. Much of the time he could be unintelligible, and there were times when I had no idea what he was talking about. It wasn't just his Kentucky accent (he habitually called himself a hillbilly); it was the hoarse drawls and throat-clearings, all the things in his mouth, for he was now drinking whiskey and the cigarette was gone, replaced by a doobie he was sucking.

"Want to get high?" he called to his fiancée (soon to be his wife, and now his widow), Anita. Hunter took out a vial and tapped powder into his palm. Anita replied that they had a plane to catch around midnight and that she had to pack all their bags. She was not cross. She was being reasonable: it was not possible to take hits of cocaine and also fold shirts and zip up duffels.

Within minutes, Hunter had become serene — tranquilized is the perfect word. He was legless, of course, but more cheerful, more comprehensible, more relaxed and rational, more affectionate, more conscious of the ups and downs of the basketball game, not barking anymore. He was Doc again, talking about the results of the marathon, and urging me to consider joining him as an associate professor in the School of Arts and Sciences at the University of Hawaii.

"We'll offer a course on writing," he said. "And not just writing, but life, travel, philosophy, books, journalism, the whole thing. Do it together, you and me up there in the lecture hall. Every goddamned student will want to take the course. It'll be great. We'll meet girls, we'll make money, check out the surf. I'm sick of the horrible winter and all the snow in Colorado. This is the place, man. We just have to think of a name for the course. Hey, I've already cleared it with the president."

He wasn't joking. The president of the University of Hawaii was an old friend. Hunter knew everyone — writers who saw him for the true satirist he was, actors who wanted to appear in films about him (two feature films had been made of his exploits, Bill Murray playing him in the first, Johnny Depp in the second), journalists looking for a profile (five substantial biographies of Hunter were published in his lifetime), artists who wanted to paint him, photographers who wanted him to pose — and he would sometimes oblige, naked, drinking, shooting a .44 Magnum, sometimes all at once.

After he arrived back in Colorado from that night of transformation in Hawaii, he told me he had made an important travel discovery at the airport.

"If you're really stoned — really mellow, really coked up," he said, "they put you in a wheelchair and you're the first passenger to board! It was a great flight. Went by in a flash."

I have not seen his like in Europe, but he was a familiar American type, not much louder but a lot more imaginative, a country boy ("I was a juvenile delinquent") who had served in the U.S. Air Force for two years, traveled to South America, worked on small-town newspapers in such places as Middletown, New York. He made his name forty years ago by chronicling the Hells Angels and writing an excellent book about the outlaw motorcycle culture. He was always looking for the newest excitement. The dignified and appreciative prose style (even when describing gang rape and mayhem) of his *Hell's Angels* does not much resemble the controlled hysteria and satirical abuse of his later books. He quickly realized that true objectivity was not possible and that he was at least as important as whatever he was writing about. To this personal intrusion, which is the heart of his writing, he gave the name "gonzo journalism."

Already obituarists are speaking of his demons. But his demons are familiar, because they are our demons, most of ours anyway: fatuous politicians who see war as an answer, the junking of toxic waste, an increasingly more poisoned planet, the selling mechanism, weasels in government, posturing celebrities, brainless academics, fat lazy children, liars in power.

President Nixon said that Hunter represented "that dark, venal and incurably violent side of the American character," and Hunter saw that Nixon was, of course, describing himself. He returned the compliment and went on attacking Nixon. On Nixon's death he spat on his grave. It is one of my favorite Thompson pieces (reprinted in his collection *Better Than Sex*). As the funeral orations were being delivered and everyone was praising Nixon, Thompson wrote "He Was a Crook," one of the best, the funniest, the most sustained polemics I have ever read. Midway through it, in a burst of candor, Hunter reflects on his harsh words and says, "But I have written worse things about Nixon many times, and the record will show that I kicked him repeatedly long before he went down. I beat him like a mad dog with mange every time I got a chance, and I am proud of it."

The epigraph to *Fear and Loathing in Las Vegas* is Dr. Johnson's statement, "He who makes a beast of himself gets rid of the pain of being a man." It would not be a bad epitaph. He liked getting liquored up and doing battle — his memos to various magazines reek of alcohol but are readable for their truth and their boozy wit. He called himself "a political junkie." Late in Bill Clinton's first campaign for the presidency, Hunter flew to Little Rock and spent an afternoon with the man and saw into his heart, describing him as humorless, ambitious, and eager to please. The piece ran in *Rolling Stone*, and Clinton must have been stung by it, because he continued, in notes on White House stationery, to patronize Hunter ("Dear Doc"), even when Hunter replied with mocking jibes or po-faced scorn.

America is a country that celebrates fakes and posturers, but Hunter Thompson, who shot himself to death inside his walled compound, Owl Farm, in Colorado, on February 20, 2005, was the real thing. The genuine article, as he would have said; the real McCoy. He lived the life he wanted, as half outlaw, half hero, without any inhibition. He broke the law when he felt it impinged upon him, was beholden to no one, shot holes in any fakery he found — either with a .44 Magnum or a breezy vocabulary — and died the same way, at the moment of his choosing, probably in great pain.

2

Kingdom of Fear combines memoir, polemic, satire, abuse, diablerie, and something new for Hunter Thompson: a nice line in prophecy. It opens with a memory of childhood, but this being Thompson's childhood, the memory is of a nine-year-old's battle with the FBI, "in the case of a Federal Mailbox being turned over in the path of a speeding bus." This was in Louisville, Kentucky, the formative years. New York, San Francisco, Big Sur, and Rio de Janeiro came later. After Rio, "suffering from amoebic dysentery and culture shock," he retired, at the age of twenty-nine, to hunt elk and breed Doberman pinschers in a fortified compound in Woody Creek, Colorado, where much later he beat a rap for sexual assault and also ran for county sheriff — memoir elements of this book. No one can accuse Hunter Thompson of not living his philosophy: "When the going gets weird, the weird turn pro."

Little Hunter and his school friends were guilty of the mailbox crime. As a federal offense, mailbox vandalism carried a five-year sentence. But this was not mindless mayhem; it was purposeful. Even then, it seems, he adhered to the Bob Dylan dictum he loves to quote: "To live outside the law you must be honest." The mailbox was part of an elaborate scheme to get "revenge on a rude and stupid bus driver who got a kick out of closing his doors and pulling away just as we staggered to the top of the hill and begged him to let us on."

The avengers, using ingenuity and speed, ropes and pulleys, created a booby trap of the mailbox. When the bus driver sped away, he became an agent of his own destruction, smashing into the mailbox that was yanked into the path of his bus. Subsequently, refusing to confess or crack under questioning, Hunter ("What witnesses?") is declared innocent, and everything works out fine: a new bus driver is hired, and a lesson is learned: "Never believe the first thing an FBI agent tells you about anything."

This is more of a Huck Finn than a Tom Sawyer story, but the tone is unmistakable, which is to say that when he is in the zone, in full flow, there is no one like him: "I have seen thousands of priests and bishops and even the Pope himself transmogrified in front of our eyes into a worldwide network of thieves and perverts and sodomites who relentlessly penetrate children of all genders and call it holy penance for being born guilty in the eyes of the Church . . . Whoops! I have wandered off on some kind of vengeful tangent here."

Reviewers despairingly compare Thompson's persona to a coked-out prophet in Revelation, a hillbilly bookworm on speed, a psychopath with an arsenal of high-powered weapons, a paranoid gun junkie, a womanizer, a drunk, and worse. While all these characterizations are provable in various degrees, the truth is far weirder: Hunter Thompson is most of the time a strangely modest man, a serious thinker, a great wit, a superb satirist, and a sports fan. He is sixty-something, and he grew up, as I did, at a time when the greatest American writers were remote and powerful figures.

Hunter Thompson is probably the last American writer of that kind. "He is known as an avid reader, a relentless drinker and a fine hand with a .44 Magnum" ran the author's bio in *Hell's Angels*. But a kind of magic still attaches to Thompson.

My own feeling is that the magic arises not from the self-promotion, the publishing hype, or the living-legend stuff. I think Thompson has remained a writer of significance because, essentially a satirist, he has displayed an utter contempt for power — political power, financial power, even show-biz juice.

For his first book-length subject he chose the Hells Angels. He rode with them, chronicled their lives and their customs. They were an outlaw tribe living at the edge of society, and he identified with their need for space, their love of binges, and their hatred of authority.

Fear and Loathing in Las Vegas, probably the best book ever written about that city in the desert, began as an assignment to cover a motorcycle race. The prospect of writing about the Honolulu Marathon induced Thompson to visit Hawaii, and the result was personal history, Hawaiian mythology, and the usual mayhem, in *The Curse of Lono.*

Last year, well before the Iraq War, Thompson wrote, "We have become a Nazi monster in the eyes of the whole world — a nation of bullies and bastards who would rather kill than live peacefully. We are not just Whores for power and oil, but killer whores with hate and fear in our hearts. We are human scum, and that is how history will judge us."

That is included in *Kingdom of Fear,* along with another prescient piece, written on September 12, 2001, in which he predicted "a religious war, a sort of Christian Jihad, fueled by religious hatred and led by merciless fanatics on both sides. It will be guerrilla warfare on a global scale, with no front lines . . . We are going to punish somebody for this attack, but just who or what will be blown to smithereens it is hard to say. Maybe Afghanistan, maybe Pakistan or Iraq, or possibly all three at once."

Kingdom of Fear is angry, prophetic, full of vitality, and enormously funny. In almost forty years of battling the confederacy of dunces, Thompson's energy has not flagged. He is not coy about his choice of poisons, but when asked specifically about them, in a piece here ("Yesterday's Weirdness Is Tomorrow's Reason Why") he makes a nice reply: "I haven't found a drug yet that can get you anywhere near as high as sitting at a desk writing, trying to imagine a story no matter how bizarre it is, as much as going out and getting into the weirdness of reality and doing a little time on The Proud Highway."

6

CONRAD AT SEA

Joseph Conrad was famous for saying that the writing of fiction is not accidental or impulsive, but rather a deliberate act, the writer consciously creating effects to arrive at a particular result. This view seems to have a lot of authority: This is your captain speaking! But in fact the whole matter is debatable, and is probably a delusion. As Conrad's stories show, a writer can say much more than he or she intends, or a lot less.

Yet Conrad, holding to this belief in well-laid plans, was just as deliberate in his life. He chose the life he wanted — two lives, actually, and both involved serious risk. He first chose to be the single, seafaring, Polish- and French-speaking Captain Józef Korzeniowski. Then, after twenty years, when he was in his late thirties, he turned his back on all that and invented a new man, an English-speaking writer, with a wife, a new country, a new language, a new career, and a new name. He went ashore in 1894 and wrote fiction; he never set sail again.

He was not just a young sailor who ended up writing books, but a highly regarded master mariner who became a major writer. Conrad could not have made his decision at a better time. The great age of sail, involving a large, overworked crew, had given way to the motorized vessel, which was — in terms of propulsion, at any rate — a simpler matter. Both are represented in his two long stories "The Nigger of the *Narcissus*" and "Typhoon." The *Narcissus* is a sailing ship; the *Nan-Shan*, in "Typhoon," is steam-driven. One of the dramas in "The Nigger of the *Narcissus*" is concerned with the way seamen cope in adversity. The sailing ship is a perfect setting for such a challenge, a seagoing obstacle course that Conrad represents with the subtlest nautical distinctions, all sorts of weather, which involves all sorts of sails, all sorts of emotions, specialists, and conflict and with a complex command that makes the sailing ship, in Conrad's own words, like "a fragment detached from the earth . . . like a small planet."

For his literary life, Conrad chose the right time, the right country, even the right part of that country, the middle of Kent. At the time that Conrad was writing in Kent, his neighbors were Henry James, Ford Madox Ford, Stephen Crane, H. G. Wells, and Edward Garnett, among others. Recognizing a true exile and a kindred spirit who knew his subjects intimately, these writers became friends and benefactors — Conrad, whose books never sold well, needed such encouragement. Ford, fifteen years younger, became a collaborator on four novels. Henry James, fourteen years older, became a champion of Conrad's writing, and we can take James's criticism seriously, for while he was the sweetest of men socially, he was an unsentimental literary critic. He said, "'The Nigger of the *Narcissus*' is in my opinion the very finest and strongest picture of the sea and sea-life that our language possesses — the masterpiece in a whole great class."

It was Henry James who supplied the epigraph. In the winter of 1897, the two men had lunch, and afterward, flipping through Pepys's diary where the diarist is speaking about Charles II's return from exile in the ship *Naseby*, Conrad happened upon, "My Lord in his discourse discovered a great deal of love to this ship," and wrote it down and took it home to use.

The finely argued, slightly pompous, but persuasive theorizing in Conrad's own preface, one of the most incisive essays ever written on the art of fiction, does not quite prepare us for the rough-and-ready stories that are included in the same volume. In "The Nigger of the *Narcissus*" an ill-assorted crew of men, many of them strangers to each other, serve on a voyage from Bombay to London. One of the men, Donkin, is a foulmouthed, shiftless, and mutinous Cockney; several are gloomy Scandinavians; one is a talkative Ulsterman; and the central figure is a black man from St. Kitts, who does almost nothing except cough, complain, quarrel, and die. An entire chapter, and the center of the story, is a gale. "Typhoon," a shorter but sharper voyage, is almost all storm and conflict. The other stories are distinctly odd, ranging from a village woman's relationship with a castaway to suggestions of cannibalism. All of it a far cry from the pieties expressed in the preface.

For the American publication, so as not to offend American racial sensibilities, "The Nigger of the *Narcissus*" was retitled "Children of the Sea." It is questionable how delicate these sensibilities could have been in a racially segregated country that at the time had just fought the Spanish-American War, annexed the Philippines and Cuba, and overthrown the Hawaiian monarchy. These events inspired Kipling, another of Conrad's neighbors, to write "The White Man's Burden," in which the typical native was characterized as "half-devil and half-child." Conrad's lame-sounding title is appropriate, for Conrad often describes the crew in terms of being childlike.

"They were the everlasting children of the mysterious sea," Conrad writes at one point. He speaks of the contentments and the "simple hearts" of deckhands when they are fully occupied and far at sea, but when they argue, they are "obstinate and childish." Toward the end of the voyage he describes two men as looking like "decrepit children." The crew of the *Narcissus* is a very mixed bunch, and crucially some are new and apparent malingerers. The captain, like many Conradian captains, is a Scotsman, but other hands come from Ireland, "Russian-Finland," Scandinavia, England's West Country, London, and the West Indies. Two newcomers, the destitute Donkin and the sickly James Wait, antagonize the others. Donkin is lazy, quarrelsome, and mutinous, and Wait is dying but so overbearing in his terminal illness that he tests the patience of everyone on board. Conrad bestowed an ambiguous name on this latter man, and gets a great deal of mileage out of it from the moment he arrives on the ship, bewildering everyone with his shout of "Wait!" His sickness forces the crew to wait, and wait on him; as his name suggests, Wait is the personification of delay.

Who better to challenge the crew with his death agony than someone they see as a racial type but are forced to understand as a man? (At about this time, Stephen Crane, whom Conrad admired, posed a similar dilemma in one of his greatest short stories, "The Monster," about a black man who is horribly disfigured by an act of heroism.) Creating a black character was a novelty. The moment Wait steps on board there is a hum: "the suppressed mutter of the word 'Nigger.'" Conrad anatomizes the racial differences, commenting on Wait's height ("Those West India niggers run fine and large"), the whites of his eyes, his gleaming teeth, his whole face ("the repulsive mask of a nigger's soul"), his inscrutability ("a nigger does not show"), the woolly quality of his hair, his lips, even suggestions of womanizing. Conrad makes it clear that Wait is rightly offended by this, and Wait never uses the word "nigger" himself. "Is your cook a coloured gentleman?" is one of his first statements, and later, in distress, he says to the Ulsterman Belfast, "You wouldn't call me nigger if I wasn't half dead, you Irish beggar!" Another memorable riposte is "'Don't be familiar,' said the nigger." After a time, James Wait's blackness is the least remarkable thing about him.

Conrad was to write even more subtly of the delusion of racial superiority in *Heart of Darkness*. One of the achievements of "The Nigger of the *Narcissus*" is that it is about neither race nor bigotry. James Wait is an unexpected and unwished-for victim, a human sacrifice; his dying and death is a distraction, something that must be reckoned with at the most inconvenient time, in the midst of a terrible storm. So everyone's humanity and sense of duty are tested.

The image of the doomed black crewman on an otherwise white ship is brilliant, but there are many other satisfying things in the story: the beautiful description of the *Narcissus* leaving Bombay in the first few pages of chapter 2 and the storm that follows; the strife that amounts almost to a war on board; the lingering death of Wait and the burial at sea.

In this early story there are some peculiar locutions, Conradian near misses as he struggles with the English language, like "the unprosperous breeze," and the sentence "They lay in a solid mass more inabordable than a hedgehog," in which Conrad is slipping into his second language, French, where *inabordable* means "inaccessible." Often in Conrad a sort of comedy is failing to surface, as though one is hearing a joke being told in a heavy accent. Conrad's hyperbole, which he might have learned from reading Melville, is seldom a success; he can only approximate dialect or a foreign accent ("sooperfloos," "seez," "concloode"), and approximation is often worse than no attempt at all.

Conrad regarded this novella-length story as a natural companion to "Typhoon." There is the ambivalence of the seaman, cursing the weather, fearing the storm, pining — sometimes dishonestly and sometimes with sincerity — for the life of a landlubber. There is conflict and fear in both stories, the phrase "white devil" occurs in both, and both stories depict a devastating storm. But "Typhoon" is chiefly about one man, Captain Mac-Whirr, about his rigidity in decision-making, about a certain cast of mind and judgment, all this thrown into stark relief by an inscrutable alien presence. James Wait served that purpose on the *Narcissus*. On the *Nan-Shan* it is the Chinese, who are continually referred to as cargo, not passengers; they constitute a big unwieldy mass not of humanity but of squealing creatures — they might be some sort of temperamental animals. "A cargo of coolies" is how they are described, just a mob with racial traits, easy to panic, money-grubbing. "They are only Chinamen." There are two hundred Chinese on board, and only one Chinese name occurs in the entire story, Bun-Hin. As though to reinforce this notion of cargo, someone says at one point, "But they say a Chinaman has no soul." Never mind a soul, these Chinese are so lacking in personality they are nameless and indistinguishable.

The crisis in "Typhoon" is simple and horrible: in the middle of the worst storm he has known, Captain MacWhirr looks at the barometer, sees that it shows "the lowest reading he had ever seen in his life," and refuses to alter his course. At that point in the story, the storm has already battered the ship, but the captain realizes "the worst was to come." This is the nub of the story. The captain has a choice. He can sail around the storm, as the sailing manual advises, thus losing time but having a greater chance of surviving, or he can sail directly into the storm, risking everything. MacWhirr does not even hesitate. He goes headfirst at the storm like a bull at a gate. He puts his experience as a seaman above the authority of the book, saying, "They may say what they like, but the heaviest seas run with the wind. Facing it — always facing it — that's the way to get through." And to his mate Jukes, who is petrified, he adds, "You are a young sailor. Face it. That's enough for any man. Keep a cool head."

But surely the point is that his mind is mechanically "macwhirring"; he does not really know what he is doing. He has been forewarned by the barometer that the storm in progress is worse than any he has ever known. Still, in this ignorance of the terror of the storm, he heads into the unknown. He nearly loses his ship, the crew, the "cargo" of Chinese. What he does is against the advice in the manual, but this does not seem to matter — indeed, he is emphatic. He says, "You don't find everything in books," and repeats it two more times, significantly at the end.

It is possible that such attitudes drove Conrad from the sea — the inflexibility of such men and the demands of the budget-conscious businessmen who wanted every voyage as short as possible, even if it meant hideous discomfort. MacWhirr's contempt for books seems to go against everything Conrad stands for. Surely Conrad believes that you find much more in books than on the sea? Here is where the story becomes enigmatic, for MacWhirr is not really against books, but against the authority of books.

Conrad, who saw his writing as new and recognized it as strange and original — he often said so — was in his way like MacWhirr, taking the most difficult route against all advice, a Polish sea captain landlocked in Kent, facing the headwind of English literature, which must have seemed like a typhoon that would either destroy him or prove he was right in his instinct.

In contrast with the captain's level-headedness, Jukes's fear is remarkable. Jukes believes he is going to die. That MacWhirr has no patience with this is less a comment on his bravery than his inability to entertain the thought that the ship will be lost. In this sense, Jukes is the more imaginative man, but the more fainthearted for it. Were this merely two men in a storm, we would have a parable about willpower, but the Chinese in the hold throw into relief the actions of the men above deck, for they are the cargo that needs to be saved — they represent profit. We had to see James Wait as human and the equal of his shipmates on the *Narcissus* before the implications of the story became fully clear; we must understand the humanity of the Chinese in order to understand the risk in Captain MacWhirr's rigidity. My difficulty with the story is that Conrad does not show Captain MacWhirr making a decision. He is programmed, without a thought process, to take the shortest route, save money, and face the storm; in fact, he makes no decision.

Put this way, the captain, who is one of those maddening narrow-minded men who always know better, is not such an irritant, but a figure who commands some admiration. The case is not, of course, so neat. Conrad leaves the matter open to debate whether MacWhirr, informed by experience, made a good decision or a bad one. What Conrad seems to stress, though, is that MacWhirr himself is convinced that he did the right thing.

There is an apparent clumsiness in the way these stories are told. And there is a definite lopsidedness in "Amy Foster" and "Falk," which are stories that mean much more as part of this larger sequence than they do on their own. "Amy Foster" is like a crude gloss on Conrad's own life: the weird-seeming Eastern European fetching up in an English village after being washed ashore, befriended and then rejected by Amy. The gibbering foreigner, Yanko Goorall (like James Wait and the Chinese), poses a problem, which is also a challenge, in this case to a tidy village. At first, as with the other aliens, you think, What is he doing there? Yet there can be no story, and we would not understand the English village, without him. But what do we understand? To my mind, both "Amy Foster" and "Falk" are too turgid and obliquely observed to have any force, and the revelation of cannibalism in "Falk," instead of giving the story more force, limits it and makes it seem more like a yarn.

"Typhoon" is the most accomplished in terms of construction, but even so, we have multiple points of view. Though he keeps saying "we," it is not entirely clear whether the narrator of "The Nigger of the *Narcissus*" is one of the crew (numbering thirteen — "twenty-six pairs of eyes"), because he is never shown actually doing anything until the end of the story, onshore, when he becomes "I" and nods at them and describes himself walking away.

A seaman in one of these stories speaks of how he "wished to end his days in a little house, with a plot of ground attached — far in the country — out of sight of the sea." That is a pretty good description of Conrad's house in Kent. It is perhaps an odd wish for a seaman, but in this book of pieces, which Conrad claimed belonged together, for their having "a unity of outlook," he did not idealize the sailor's life. Seamen could be fearful, confused, cowardly, combative; when the worst happened they hankered to be on dry land. In "Falk" he writes, "He who hath known the bitterness of the Ocean shall have its taste for ever in his mouth." The sea might be impartial, or an enemy, but was never a friend. Conrad abandoned the sea in order to spend the next thirty years of his life sitting at a desk, transforming the world he had known into fiction. It is not surprising that these stories contain a great deal of ambivalence toward the sea and her children.

7

SIMENON'S WORLD

Two startlingly similar short novels appeared in France in 1942. At the center of each narrative was a conscienceless and slightly creepy young man, unattached and adrift, the perpetrator of a meaningless murder. One was Camus's L'étranger, the other Simenon's La veuve Couderc. Camus's novel rose to become part of the literary firmament and is still glittering, intensely studied, and praised — to my mind, overpraised. Simenon's novel did not drop, but settled, so to speak, and went the way of the rest of his work — rattled along with decent sales, the occasional reprint, and was even resurrected as a 1950s pulp-fiction paperback, The Widow, with a come-on tag line ("A surging novel of torment and desire") and a lurid cover: busty peasant girl pouting in a barn, her skirt hiked over her knees, while a hunky guy lurks at the door — price, twenty-five cents.

Camus had labored for years on his novel of alienation; his *Carnets* record his frustration and false starts. "The fewer novels or plays you write — because of other parasitic interests — the fewer you will have the ability to write," V. S. Pritchett once wrote, lamenting his own small fictional output. "The law ruling the arts is that they must be pursued to excess." Simenon had published three other novels in 1942, and six the previous year. *La veuve Couderc* (in English, variously, *The Widow* and *Ticket of Leave*) became another title on the extremely long list of Simenon works, none of them regarded as a subject for scholarship.

If reading Camus represents duty, Simenon represents indulgence, a lavishness that seems frivolous, inspiring a greedy satisfaction that shows as self-consciousness in even the most well-intentioned introductions to his work, the critic's awkwardness over a pleasurable text, together with a shiver of snooty superfluity, and the palpable cringe, common to many introducers of a Simenon novel: What am I doing here?

Simenon takes some sorting out, because at first glance he seems easily classified, and on second thought (after you have read fifty or sixty of his books) unclassifiable. The Camus comparison is not gratuitous — Simenon often made it himself, and André Gide brought the same subject up a few years after *L'étranger* appeared, favoring Simenon's work, especially *La veuve Couderc*. And (in a 1947 letter to Albert Guerard) Gide went further, calling Simenon *"notre plus grand romancier aujourd'hui, vrai romancier."*

Born ten years apart, both Camus and Simenon had arrived raw and youthful in metropolitan France from the distant margins of literary Francophonia, Camus a French Algerian and polemical journalist with a philosophical bent, Simenon a self-educated Belgian who began his writing life as a cub reporter with a taste for crime stories; Camus the pedant and Simenon the punk, both with an eye for the ladies. Camus seems to have taken no notice of Simenon (no mention at all in any Camus biography), though we know that Simenon was watchful and somewhat competitive with the decade-younger Camus, whose complete works (he must have noted) can be accommodated between the covers of one modest-sized volume. The indefatigable Simenon, confident of winning the Nobel Prize, predicted in 1937 that he would win it within ten years. The literature prize went to others — Pearl S. Buck, F. E. Sillanpää, Winston S. Churchill. Hearing the news in 1957 that Camus had won it, Simenon (so his wife reported) became enraged. "Can you believe that asshole got it and not me?"

What to make of the gifted and unstoppable writer who has a rarefied existential streak but also a nose for what the public wants? The universities are seldom any help — no one is less welcome in the literature departments than the accomplished filler of multiple shelves of books. Like many self-educated people, Simenon tended to be anti-intellectual in a defiant and mocking way, despising literary critics and giving literature departments a wide berth. The universities returned the compliment, rubbishing him and belittling or ignoring his work. The academy is uncommonly fond of the struggler and the sufferer; scratch even the most severe academic and you find an underdogger. How can (so the argument seems to run) a prolific and popular writer be any good? Usually, like Ford Madox Ford or

Trollope, they are nailed as graphomaniacs and subjected to cruel simplification, represented by one book, not always their best.

Professorial philistinism dogged Simenon; so did snobbery. And it was after all a bitter, provincial university librarian who wrote of

> ... the shit in the shuttered château
> Who does his five hundred words
> Then parts out the rest of the day
> Between bathing and booze and birds

Simenon was the living, intimidating embodiment of Larkin's envious lines, plenty of booze and birds available, though his daily output in the château was more like five thousand words.

Simenon considered himself the equal of Balzac. He regarded his novels as a modern-day *Comédie humaine.* His one foray into literary criticism was a long and insightful essay on Balzac, which took the form of mother-blaming. "A novelist is a man who does not like his mother, or who never received mother-love," words that applied to himself and that also inform one of his memoirs, *Letter to My Mother.* He was the Balzac of blighted lives, writing out of a suffering that was not obvious until the end of his long career. Material success, one of Balzac's major themes, is not a theme that interested Simenon, who dwelled on failure in spite of the fact that he himself was a great success, and made a point of crowing about it.

Incredibly, for such a productive soul, Simenon was at times afflicted with writer's block, and though in Simenon it seemed almost an affectation, it perturbed him to the extent that he used it as an occasion to keep a diary, to recapture his novel-writing mood. In the diary he recounted his obsessional subjects — money, his family, his mother, the household, and other writers. During the writing of this diary, Henry Miller visited him and extravagantly praised him as someone who lived an enviable life. While Simenon humored him, and anatomized his character, he unblocked himself with this unusual and valuable journal, later published under the title *When I Was Old.*

His many straight detective novels based on the character of Chief Inspector Jules Maigret fit a pattern, as compact case studies, problems of lingering guilt and subtle clues, with a shrewd, even lovable detective of settled habits. He came up with the rounded and believable and happily married Maigret in 1930 and did not stop adding to that shelf until 1972, seventy-six volumes later. But what about the rest of the books? The immensity of Simenon's life and letters baffles and defeats the simplifier. How to square the years in Liège, as a reporter and an admitted hack, with his postwar retreat to rural Connecticut? The trip through the Pacific in 1935, with the year he dropped out to travel by barge through France? The Arizona novels? The many châteaux? The classic cars he collected? The gourmandizing, the womanizing? "Most people work every day and enjoy sex periodically. Simenon had sex every day and every few months indulged in a frenzied orgy of work," writes Patrick Marnham, in *The Man Who Wasn't Maigret*. Simenon lived long enough to have made love to Josephine Baker and to stare priapically into the cleavage of Brigitte Bardot. What of his ability to write a chapter a day and finish an excellent novel in ten or eleven days, and write another one a few months later?

Simenon's detractors put him down as a compulsive hack; to his admirers, who included not just the hard-to-impress Henry Miller and the sniffily Olympian Gide, but also the generally aloof Thornton Wilder and the quite remote Jorge Amado, he was the consummate writer. He had no time for his other contemporaries. It wasn't a question of his believing he was better than any of them; he simply took no notice of them. Even at the height of his friendship with Henry Miller he did not read Miller's work; he suggested it was unreadable, but shrewdly analyzed Miller the man in *When I Was Old*. He claimed in the *Paris Review* to have been inspired by Gogol and Dostoyevsky, but he wrote nothing insightful about them.

Like many other writers, he hated anyone probing into his life, and habitually lied, laid false trails, or exaggerated his experiences. In 1932, he traveled through central Africa. Typically, he claimed he had been in Africa a year. The actual time was two months. Never mind, he made the best of it and wrote three novels with African settings. The three novellas in *African Trio* were written in the thirties and forties, at a time when colonials were villains and Africans practically unknown. In these tales, Africans are rather decorative, but little more than shadows. Very few even have names. And yet one gets the message: "Colonialism in Africa has no future" — the motto is repeated throughout Simenon's tumbling narrative.

It is helpful to be reminded of the crimes of colonialism, principally its ignorant racketeering. And it is interesting that an observant man like Simenon can visit Africa and emerge knowing next to nothing about Africans. They drum, they dance, they cook yams; in the last story, depicting a rambling sea voyage from Matadi to Bordeaux, they scarcely appear at all except in several passengers' nightmares. But Simenon visited Africa in another age, when it was still possible to believe that the European was in general an obstacle to progress, and that liberation — and prosperity — would come when he folded his tent and stole away. The idea is so quaint and so profoundly vitalized by Simenon's deadpan description that it imbues *African Trio* with the sad, steamy period detail of that other age. It is a timely reminder that Africa knew another kind of brutality. Simenon did not know that it would be supplanted by an equal viciousness and that the Congo he wrote about would know more pitiless regimes.

These stories are attractive for their single-minded dissection of the threadbare and arrogant colonial world. Simenon deals with Africans by excluding them or attributing to them a watchfulness and silence that imply a stolid heroism. It is perhaps why he remained optimistic, because if he had made the logical — and, one might say, more Simenon-like — deduction and seen that the machinery of government and agricultural enterprise was unworkable and antique, he might have been less cheerful about the chances of the inheritors.

He hid himself, never more than when he was promoting one of his books, as the dapper writer, puffing his pipe, obscuring himself with phenomenal statistics. But the statistics were misleading in the way that record-breaking is misleading: merely the helpless adoration of the exceptional. Simenon trotting out his big numbers sounds to me like a man's mendacious reckoning, no different from the modestly endowed group of islanders in Vanuatu who wear enormous phallocrypts and call themselves Big Nambas.

Yet, though they invite suspicion, the most unlikely figures associated with Simenon are probably true, that the roundabout 400 works of fiction he claimed to have published are verifiable. A hundred and seventeen are serious novels, and the rest are Maigrets and books written under pseudonyms. He dropped out of school at thirteen to become a reporter. The facts associated with him take such an extravagant form that he seems a victim of his own stupendous statistics — the numerous novels, the 500 million copies sold, the 55 changes of address, and his often quoted boast that he bedded 10,000 women. (His second wife put the figure at "no more than 1,200.")

It is perhaps not surprising that such a freakish example of creative energy is not seriously studied (though there exists a Centre d'études Georges Simenon at the University of Liège). Apart from the Nobel omission, Simenon did not feel slighted. He said, "Writing is not a profession but a vocation of unhappiness." But the consequence is that every new reissue of a Simenon merits a reassessment like this, because he seems (like many of his characters) to come from nowhere. Well, he agreed. He said that as a Belgian he was like a man without a country.

Though he claimed that none of his books were autobiographical, his work is a chronicle of his life: his young self is vivid in *Pedigree* and *The Nightclub;* his mother looms in *The Lodger* and *The Cat;* his daughter in *The Disappearance of Odile;* his second marriage in *Three Bedrooms in Manhattan;* his ménage à trois in *In Case of Emergency;* his travels in the novels with foreign settings — *Tropic Moon, Aboard the Aquitaine, Banana Tourist, The Bottom of the Bottle, Red Lights, The Brothers Rico,* and many others; and in all of them the particularities of his fantasies and obsessions. Feeling that he was an outsider, he had a gift for depicting aliens: the nameless African in *The Negro,* the immigrant in *The Little Man from Arkangel,* the Malous (in fact the Malowskis) in *The Fate of the Malous,* and Kachoudas in *The Hatter's Phantoms.* By contrast, in Camus's *The Plague* you'd hardly know you were in a foreign country — all the characters are Frenchmen, and incidentally, *The Plague* is a novel without any women.

"You know you have a beautiful sentence, cut it," Simenon said. "Every time I find such a thing in one of my novels it is to be cut." Simenon is exaggerating; he sometimes lets slip a pretty sentence, but generally his writing is so textureless as to be transparent and never calls attention to itself ("It's written as if by a child"). No love of language is ever obvious, and he remains anti-lapidary. The only new words one is likely to find in Simenon are the occasional technical terms, like the medical jargon in *The Patient, The Premier* with its descriptions of French governance, and some bridge-playing episodes elsewhere; you will never learn a new word in a Simenon. And you will never laugh. Comedy is absent, humor is rare. A bleak vision and relentless seriousness earned his non-Maigrets the appellation *romans durs,* because *dur* is not just "hard" but implies weight, seriousness, not only a stony quality, but density and complexity — a kind of challenge, and even a certain tedium. (A *dur* is a bore in some contexts.) Simenon's characters read newspapers, usually bad news or crimes; they plot, lie, cheat, steal, sweat, have sex; frequently they commit murder, and just as often they commit suicide. They never read books or quote from them. They don't study (as Simenon did, to mug up on detail). They are generally fussing at the margins of the working world, coming apart, hurtling downward, toward oblivion.

For any writer, it is not possible to be productive without being possessed by a strict sense of order, and guided by discipline. One of Simenon's shrewdest French biographers, Pierre Assouline, sees the clock as his dominant metaphor. His novels are full of timepieces and clock watching. Simenon himself timed all his movements, not just his writing, clocking in, clocking out; even meals were timed to the minute. He famously made calendars chronicling his novel writing — usually eight or nine days of furious composition, a chapter a day.

His sexuality, too, involved the stopwatch. Simenon, even at his most ithyphallic, was anything but a sensualist. A sex act in his books usually takes a few lines at most. In *The Bells of Bicetre:* "They stayed a long time almost motionless, like certain insects you see mating." *The Man on the Bench in the Barn:* "I literally dived into her, suddenly, violently, there was fear in her eyes" — and then it's over. *The Nightclub:* "She looked at him in astonishment. It was over already. He couldn't even have said how he set about it."

These hair-trigger instances echo the love life Simenon recorded in his *Intimate Memoirs.* One day, he approaches his wife in her office as she is speaking with her English secretary, Joyce Aitken. His wife asks him what he wants.

"You!"
That afternoon she simply lies down on the rug.
"Hurry up. You don't have to leave, Aitken."

The Widow is exceptional in depicting several seductions that go on for a few pages. A sentence that repeats so often in a Simenon as to be a signature line is "She wore a dress and it was obvious that she had nothing on underneath." *The Widow* also contains a variation of this sentence: "Still wearing her blue smock, with next to nothing underneath it . . ."

Unlike most of his characters, Simenon was someone whose self-esteem was in good repair. His personal world seemed complete. He moved from grand house to grand house — and they were self-contained, holding his family, his lovers, his library, his recreations; his appetites, his pipes, his pencils, his fancy cars. He lived the life of a seigneur, the lord of his own principality, where everything was ordered to his own specifications. The completeness of Simenon's life is impressive: the man who lives with his ex-wife, his present wife, and his loyal servant, all of whom he sleeps with, while still finding time to be unfaithful to all three with prostitutes, and keeps writing. That was what thrilled Henry Miller. Well, what philanderer wouldn't be thrilled? And Miller didn't know the half of it. One day (according to Marnham), seeing a young serving girl on all fours dusting a low table, Simenon on an impulse took her from behind. The girl told Madame Simenon, who laughed it off as being typically Georges. Witnessing this drollery, another serving girl wondered aloud, *"On passe toutes à la casserole?"* (So everyone has a go at this pot?)

In great contrast to the apparent coherence, the fatness, of his own life are the insufficiencies in the lives of his characters, who are usually strong enough to kill but seldom resourceful enough to survive. And it must be said that having spent many decades vigorously writing and living in style, his last years, twenty-three of them — after the suicide of his beloved daughter — were spent in a kind of solitary confinement and protracted depression in a poky house with his housekeeper, sitting in plastic chairs because, among his phobias, he held the belief that wooden furniture harbored insects.

A number of Simenon's novels, among them *The Venice Train, Belle, Sunday,* and *The Negro,* can be grouped around the general theme of *malentendu,* or cross-purposes — the title of a Camus play that is Simenonesque in its cruelty. *The Widow* is firmly in this category, though its descriptions of violence and sexuality are unusually graphic for Simenon; and it is one of the few Simenons with a strong woman character in it. The woman in *Betty* and the woman narrator of *November* are similarly strong. But his women tend to be one-dimensional, guileful, opportunistic, coldly practical, unsentimental, or easy prey. Tati the widow is a peasant who knows her own mind and possesses an ability to size up strangers.

The action of *The Widow* takes place in the Bourbonnais, the dead center of France, in a hamlet by the canal that joins St. Amande with Montluçon. Apart from omitting the "e" from Amande, Simenon is very specific in his provincial geography.

An odd solecism occurs in the first paragraph of the novel. A man is walking down a road that is "cut slantwise every ten yards by the shadow of a tree trunk" — Simenon at his most economical in precise description. It is noontime, at the end of May. The man strides across these shadows. Then his own shadow is described: "a short, ridiculously squat shadow — his own — slid in front of him." The sun seems to be shining from different angles in the space of two sentences, creating two sorts of shadow. It is perhaps not a riddle. Simenon hated to rewrite.

The young man boards the bus outside St. Amande, bound for Montluçon. He has nothing on him, no impedimenta, no obvious identity. "No luggage, no packages, no walking stick, not even a switch cut from the hedge. His arms swung freely." Among the women returning from the market he is a stranger, though for the reader of Simenon he is so familiar as to be an old friend: the naked man, someone at a crossroads, a bit lost, a bit guilty, on the verge of making a fatal decision.

The widow Couderc sizes him up, seeing something in him no one else sees. Later, we understand why: he somewhat resembles her son, a waster and ex-con who is in the Foreign Legion. She sees that this bus passenger is going nowhere, that he has nothing. She understands him and she wants him.

In this beautifully constructed first chapter, with a subtle building of effects, the young man notices the woman, too, and in the midst of the nosy chattering market women, the two "recognized each other." He also needs her.

The woman, Tati, gets off the bus, and soon afterward the young man, Jean, does the same. Jean asks if he can give her a hand with her bundles, a gesture she had been expecting ever since their eyes met. He moves in with her. A few days later, on a Sunday, after she returns from church — a nice touch — she pours him a few drinks and they end up in bed.

She is not beautiful, but she is tough, even fearless, the sort of indestructible peasant who would feel at home at the table in van Gogh's *The Potato Eaters.* Unloved and frumpy, slatternly in an old ragged coat, her slip showing, and with a hairy mole on her cheek, she is at forty-five more than twenty years older than Jean. She gives Jean to understand that he can expect occasional sex but that she must also sleep with her abusive father-in-law from time to time, because she is living in his farmhouse.

Belying Tati's rumpled clothes and precarious existence among her quarrelsome in-laws is her animal alertness, a peasant shrewdness, especially as regards her niece. The teenage mother Félicie lives nearby; the effect of this pretty young woman on Jean disturbs Tati. Her suspicions of Jean's past are quickly borne out after a visit by the gendarmes: Jean has recently been released from five years in prison (thus the *Ticket of Leave* alternate title), and his precariousness resembles hers. She had taken him for a foreigner — he seems foreign throughout, a true outsider — but in fact he is from a distinguished family in Montluçon, son of a wealthy woman-izing distiller. Estranged from his family, he is "free as air . . . a man utterly without ties." And "he was free . . . like a child . . .

"He did not walk like other people. He seemed to be going nowhere." But Jean has walked into a trap. He does not know it yet, though for him, as for Meursault in *L'étranger,* there is no future. He lives in a "magnificent present humming with sunshine."

He has murdered a man, he tells Tati, almost casually and partly by accident. A woman was involved, though he didn't love her. Far from being seriously affected by the crime, the trial, and the years in prison, Jean "scarcely realized that it was himself it was happening to." He has been cast adrift by the crime, and after prison, nothing mattered: "he was committed to nothing, nothing he did possessed either weight or importance."

In his lack of remorse or pity, he resembles the coldhearted killer Frank Friedmaier in *Dirty Snow,* and Popinga in *The Man Who Watched the Trains Go By.* And, of course, he prefigures Camus's Meursault, even to the solar imagery, for at a crucial point in the novel, recognizing his desire for Félicie, "at one stroke the sun had taken possession of him. Another world was swallowing them up."

He succeeds with Félicie as he succeeded with her aunt, but wordlessly, rutting among the farm buildings. He continues to make love to Tati, and is always abrupt, if not brutal: "He undressed her as one skins a rabbit." And in this ménage, another familiar Simenon situation ensues, that of lovers separated by a physical barrier, the passions of propinquity, jealousy always figuring in the plot. In *The Widow* the lovers in nearby cottages are separated by the canal, in *The Door* a communicating door, in *The Iron*

Staircase an iron staircase, and a similar shuttling back and forth in *Act of Passion*. All these novels end in murder.

In this springtime pastoral — conflict in the countryside: fertile farmland, browsing animals, quarreling peasants — Jean slowly goes to pieces, consumed by self-disgust and fatalism. Typically for Simenon, by the subtle building of effects, Jean's condition is suggested rather than analyzed. Feeling possessed by the desperate older woman who won't let him go and by the younger woman who is indifferent to him, Jean realizes that he is at a dead end, that a crime is inevitable, and "he waited for what could not fail to happen."

The novel becomes implicitly existential, though Simenon would scoff at such a word: there is no philosophical meditation in the narrative. Jean has been put on a road to ruin by Simenon — been set up, indeed. Many if not all Simenon novels describing the occurrence of *malentendu* imply that there is no exit — and the maddening thing is that even though the doomed character does not see a way out, the reader does. It does not occur to Jean that he can just walk away or get back on the bus. He protests that he is indifferent to his crime, but he is damaged, guilt-ridden, possessed, and when she begs him to stay and love her, he is helpless to do anything but smash Tati's skull. "It had been foreordained!"

In describing this lost soul and his desperate act, Simenon was reflecting the fatalism of his time. He wrote the book in a dark period, on the French coast — Nieul-sur-Mer is given at the end as its place of composition, a town near La Rochelle. France was at war, German occupation not far off, and doomsday seemed imminent. In this uncertain war, only violence or an act of passion gave meaning to the passage of time. Like Meursault, Jean is headed to certain execution — the notion of it occurs to him throughout the last third of the novel — and he is the author of his fate. He had stumbled into an idyllic setting without at first realizing that it was not idyllic at all, but an Eden that has become a snake pit of corruption matching his own loss of innocence.

Rereading the novel, one realizes that, as with most Simenons, Jean had been doomed from the first paragraph, when he walked through the shadows. And we can easily see why he was so angry that Camus won the Swedish lottery, because in novel after novel, Simenon dramatized the same sort of dilemma, the life with narrowing options (but always with subtle differences of plot, tone, location, and effects), the risk-taking of the man with nothing to lose, his vanity, his presumption, his willful self-destruction, the *acte gratuit*. Earlier, Jean yearns for commitment and for fate to intervene, but when he meditates on it (and ultimately gets his wish) — "He wanted something definite and final, something that offered no prospect of retreat" — Simenon seems to be talking to himself, sending another of his characters to his death in a world without happy endings.

8

DR. SACKS, THE HEALER

Oliver Sacks was sipping tea, juggling a cookie, his knees together, his fumbling hands making him seem unsure and a bit hunted, like Edward Lear — the same Socratic beard, the same gaze, twinkling with myopia — and stammering his gratitude to the hostess, who was a stranger to him. Oliver also looked lost, like a big befuddled and bearded boy.

Famously absent-minded, the next minute Oliver was preoccupied with some papers he thought he had mislaid. He slapped his pockets. "Bugger," he muttered. I was thinking, Where has his cookie gone to? Oliver said, "And where are my car keys? What have I done with my keys?" The hostess was active, talking most of the time about something else, with wearying intensity, while Oliver fussed, rummaging for his lost papers, his lost keys. "No, that's not it — that's my biscuit," Oliver said, pulling cookie crumbs from his pocket. He was the picture of confusion. His shirt had become untucked because of his muscular shoulders, and yet he looked schoolboyish, desperate as he floundered. Even his dimples had been sucked flat in an expression of pure panic. Then, sighing with relief, he put his hands on the papers, and the keys, too.

A few minutes later we were in the street.

"What did you make of her?" I asked, referring to the hostess.

A calm descended on Oliver. He had tucked in his shirt. He weighed his car keys in his hand. He said in a diagnostic tone, "Frail, yet explosive. Definitely compulsive. Possibly — though this might be a bit strong, this word might need refining — psychotic. I wouldn't like to be around her when she goes off. But I'd like to see her again."

In the crispest way, he had precisely described the woman we had casually met. Even slapping cookie crumbs in his pocket and fearing the worst for his keys, he is the most perceptive of men. There is something of Sherlock Holmes in his shrewd summing up of scattered neurological clues, and it is probably appropriate, since Arthur Conan Doyle based Holmes's deductive ability on one of his medical school teachers, a hawk-eyed diagnostician. Oliver has that concentration, and his "street neurology" was something I had longed to see ever since I read about it in "The Possessed," a chapter of *The Man Who Mistook His Wife for a Hat*. The phrase "street neurology" refers to the assessment of a person's condition after observing their behavior in a casual setting — the street, a bus, a movie line, a room full of strangers.

Among the many antecedents of "street neurology," Oliver said, was James Parkinson, who "delineated the disease that bears his name, not in his office, but in the teeming streets of London." And for the illness to be understood, it had to be seen in the world. This was perhaps truer of Tourette's syndrome. The preface to the seminal book *Tics and Their Treatment* (1901), by Meige and Feindel, described a *ticqueur* in the streets of Paris. "The clinic, the laboratory, the ward are all designed to restrain and focus behavior." A clinic could be scientific and helpful, but Oliver advocated a more open, "naturalistic neurology."

One day after seeing "Witty Ticcy Ray," Oliver's first Touretter, Oliver saw three Touretters on the streets of New York. A woman of about sixty, the most "florid" of the three, seemed to be convulsing or having a fit. In fact, her mode of Tourette's was the compulsive caricaturing in an accelerated and parodic way of everyone who passed by her. She was possessed by each person for an instant. "In the course of a short city-block this frantic old woman frenetically caricatured the features of forty or fifty passers-by." The whole sequence of possessions took little more than two minutes.

Seen in the street, the particularities of the woman's condition were more obvious than they would have been in a clinic. For variety and context, Oliver said, there was really no place better for observing people "than a street in New York — an anonymous public street in a vast city — where the subject of extravagant, impulsive disorders can enjoy and exhibit to the full the monstrous liberty, or slavery, of their condition."

I asked Oliver about this the first time I met him, in 1997. He said to me, "I had a Tourette's patient in my office. I talked with him and saw quite a lot of him. But I thought, What is this man's life like? So we went outside. I saw him in the street, in the world. Then I understood him much better."

A writer's life is almost unapproachable except through the writing, which is inevitably full of ambiguities. You spend time with a writer and you get — what? — wool-gathering, silences, rants, evasions, the contents of a cracker barrel; anyway, most such visits are just excursions into tendentiousness. But if the writer also happens to be a doctor, there is a visible and unambiguous human dimension that can be seized: Voltaire squeezing leeches onto a patient's skin, Chekhov poking someone's tonsils, Freud closely questioning the hysterical Anna M., William Carlos Williams delivering a baby. Oliver Sacks happens to be a marvelous writer, with a range of expression that is both exact and poetic, his neurological writings praised by no less a stylist than W. H. Auden. Even Oliver's footnotes fascinate. The footnotes to his *Island of the Colorblind* are wonderfully informative and original, with a casual brilliance. For example, in his essay on the scientist Sir Humphry Davy, his point of departure is the little-known fact that the poet Coleridge attended Davy's lectures; Oliver speaks in his footnote of how other poets have been lovers of scientific language:

> Coleridge was not the only poet to renew his stock of metaphors with images from chemistry. The chemical phrase "elective affinities" was given an erotic connotation by Goethe; "energy" became for Blake, "eternal delight"; Keats, trained in medicine, reveled in chemical metaphors. Eliot, in "Tradition and the Individual Talent," employs chemical metaphors from beginning to end, culminating in a grand, Davyan metaphor for the poet's mind: "The analogy is that of the catalyst . . . The mind of the poet is the shred of platinum." One wonders whether Eliot knew that his central metaphor, catalysis, was discovered by Humphry Davy in 1816. A wonderful metaphoric use of chemistry is Primo Levi's *The Periodic Table*. Levi was himself both a chemist and a writer.

I mentioned to Oliver that the composer Borodin had been trained as a chemist. But of course he knew that. "Borodin was a friend of Mendeleev," he said. Literary references in his piece about a chemist are not gratuitous. The pathology of literature is one of Oliver's favorite subjects, and he published a paper in the *British Medical Journal* titled "Tourette's Syndrome and Creativity." He has brought his neurological experience to bear on such figures as Dostoyevsky, Bartók, Kierkegaard, Mozart, Nabokov, Klee, and de Chirico. "Samuel Johnson was probably Tourettic," he has said. "Sherlock Holmes possibly autistic."

The visionary mystic Hildegard of Bingen Oliver diagnoses as "migrainous" in his book *Migraine*. One of her visions, "The Fall of the Angels," is a shower of stars, which she describes with lyrical rapture. Dr. Sacks notes that Hildegard experienced a severe migraine and "a shower of phosphenes in transit across her visual field, their passage being succeeded by a negative scotoma." He is profoundly sympathetic, even admiring of the episode, and he adds in brilliant interpretation, "Invested with this sense of ecstasy, burning with profound theophorous and philosophical significance, Hildegard's visions were instrumental in directing her towards a life of holiness and mysticism. They provide a unique example of the manner in which a physiological event, banal, hateful, or meaningless to the vast majority of people, can become in a privileged consciousness, the substrate of a supreme ecstatic inspiration."

One of the many satisfactions in spending time with Oliver Sacks is hearing such an astonishing range of references, each one a little glimpse into his erudition and his life. "Something that repels me about damascene blades is that after heating the steel they used to quench it by shoving them into the bodies of slaves." Or, "Mendeleev had a dream in which he saw the arrangement of the periodic table. In the morning he wrote it down . . . I had an intense boyhood interest in metals . . . I dreamed of manganese one night . . . They use beryllium for the nose cones of rockets." Or, "Nabokov has a lovely description about trees in winter looking like the nervous systems of giants."

I also liked the references that were flashes of other Olivers: Oliver the word lover ("festination," "volant," "apodictic"); Oliver the confidant of Thom Gunn, A. R. Luria, and W. H. Auden; Oliver the weightlifter (he once held a California weightlifting record, doing a full squat with six hundred pounds); Oliver the motorcyclist, with an extensive knowledge of classic English machines, like the Norton he used to own, as well as esoteric motorcycle writings (T. E. Lawrence's *The Mint*, for example); Oliver as Wolf Sacks, using his middle name for its lycanthropic associations, consultant physician to a California chapter of the Hells Angels; Oliver the former dabbler in hallucinogenic drugs and morning glories.

But his "druggy excitements" ended on the last day of 1965, when he looked into a mirror, saw his skeletal self, and said, "'Unless you stop you will not see another New Year.' And I stopped."

One day we were talking about autism. Oliver said, "When I was at a summer camp in Canada for autistic and Tourettic children, one of them saw a goat and asked, 'Is it a diagram?' Imagine the degree of alienation! I wonder whether, with the largest dose of LSD possible, one would ever see a goat as a diagram."

"Probably very easily," I said. "But I don't know. I have never taken LSD."

"Oh, I have. It wouldn't produce that hallucination," he said. "One time at my house in Topanga Canyon after a huge overdose of morning glories I thought the cacti were gigantic insects — gigantic motionless insects. Still, an insect is a living thing, whereas a diagram is an abstraction."

Or this sort of conversation, discussing the brain: "Those so-called Aztec birdmen that were exhibited in circuses? They were microcephalic. The face was normal size, but the head went back like this" — he squinched his face in imitation. "They were exhibited with macrocephalics." These strange skulls were also exhibited in the Royal College of Surgeons Museum, where Oliver's mother used to take him, to show him other oddities, such as the Irish Giant and the twenty-inch-tall Sicilian woman who weighed seventeen pounds. Oliver can still recall their names: Patrick Cotter and Caroline Crachami.

"Does a microcephalic person have language?" I asked.

"Oh, yes, the brain may be smaller than a cat's, but they have language. Brain sizes are interesting. Turgenev's endocranial cast is 2,100 cc, versus Anatole France, who had barely 1,000 cc of brain."

"So brain size doesn't matter?"

"I am not saying that. I am saying that in the severest human idiocy there is always some language. Especially language. The microcephalic person may be a lot less intelligent than the average chimp, yet they are human. They will have some language."

Chimp language is another of his scientific interests. In *Seeing Voices*, Oliver discusses the question of whether chimps have language. "It seems they don't," and though they can make certain guttural signifying sounds, their method of communication is a "gestural code."

There seemed nothing he did not know, or had not seen or experienced.

. . .

But Oliver the doctor was the person I wanted to know better: Oliver in a ward; Oliver making a house call; Oliver on the street, on the move, in the world, observing; especially Oliver in New York, treating patients. It is obvious from his writing — and he has said this explicitly — that "patients" is a misleading word for the people he writes about. They are his friends, some as dear to him as family members, and he has gained understanding by having developed relationships with these people over many years.

Oliver's bumbling is neither an act nor a deliberate diversion. He really is nearsighted and cack-handed. He constantly loses things. He is hesitant and forgetful. In his dreamiest and perhaps most intellectual productive moods he stumbles and trips. He has fallen on his face and sustained many injuries. He wrote a whole book, *A Leg to Stand On,* about one bad stumble, which resulted in a severe leg injury. Looking at waves on a Hawaiian beach, he shook his head and said to me, "I can't swim there. If I got into those waves I'd end up a quadriplegic."

Once in the water, he never falters. Distance swimming, snorkeling, and diving, he is a porpoise. I have swum with him in the dankest waters of Lewis Bay in Hyannis and Waimea Bay in Hawaii. He is a strong swimmer and stays in the water for a long time. "It takes forty minutes in the water just to warm up, and then the real swimming starts."

He says he is happier among invertebrates, among cephalopods, among plants — ferns and cycads. One of his dreams is to swim in Jellyfish Lake, on one of the Rock Islands of Palau, in the western Pacific. I described to Oliver how I had swum there myself. The water was thick and yellowish, a stew of jellyfish, some like parasols and some like nightcaps. They had no sting, but they bulged with gelatinous ectoplasm and filled the small volcanic pool. My whole body was pressed at each stroke by the strongest wobble of slime, my fingers tangling in their greenish masses of tentacles. I did it on a dare and was glad finally to pull myself out of the water. Oliver said there was nothing he relished more than the thought of spending a whole day swimming among the millions of jellyfish.

On dry land he is less certain. He is a careful if overcautious driver. His bumper sticker reads *American Fern Society.* The decal on his window says *British Pteridological Society.* Fluctuating temperatures make him irritable. He complains if the temperature inside or out does not hover around 65 degrees, and has been known to carry a foot-long thermometer into restaurants, especially in the summer, to establish at the outset whether the dining experience will be a comfortable one.

He cannot cook. But he is not fussy about food; indeed, he dislikes culinary variety. One of his unshakable habits is to eat the same meal every day. A large pot of stew (say) is prepared for him on the weekend, and he warms up portions of it through the week. He is not odd in this, and as Oliver would be the first to point out, most of the world's people eat the same meals every day. When I visited him at his City Island bungalow I saw a selection of ferns on the kitchen table and stacks of books on his stovetop: the thick, exhaustive *Dictionary of Applied Chemistry* and some others on the front burner, and a tome simply titled *Manganese* on the back burner.

Until he moved to the West Village, he spent part of the week at that house, which he bought in the 1980s for its nearness to swimming and his hospitals. Apart from books, Oliver says, "I own nothing of value." His New York apartment is Sacks Central, both a comfortable home and an efficient office. Oliver types swiftly — as fast as his secretary — with two fingers on a old manual typewriter, but in his office he has access to every modern innovation, not just machines and computers and databases and a secretary, but Kate Edgar — assistant, minder, amanuensis, friend, and midwife to his last five books. Like many people with active minds, he is a bad enough sleeper to rank as an insomniac. He is tall and powerfully built from his daily swimming; he is physically strong, but he also carries on his body the bumps and scars and stitch marks of his mishaps.

Oliver is at ease working in the hospital, but says he is sometimes wary even there. He says that he fears he might become very flustered one day at a hospital and, because of his stammering and shyness, will be confused with a patient and locked up.

"Without my badge and my white coat I am indistinguishable from many patients here," he said to me. "In Bronx State, a state mental hospital I used to work at, I always used to carry my white coat and my identity pass, because I was never sure that if I lost it I would be able to prove my sanity. 'Oh, yes, yes,'" he says, mimicking a sarcastic doctor. "'Delusion of being Oliver Sacks.'"

It is the nightmare of Chekhov's "Ward No. 6," a story Oliver often refers to — in which the doctor, Andrei Yefimich Ragin, mistaken for a mental patient, is unable to talk his way out of the ward, and he is left there, and beaten by a brutal watchman, while the other doctors smile at the poor doctor's protestations. One of the characteristics of a strong protest is that it sounds delusional and paranoid. "I must go out!" he cries. He is told to shut up. He is beaten repeatedly, and at last the doctor dies in his own hospital.

A cruel variation on this is the story Oliver tells about the former medical director of Beth Abraham Hospital in the Bronx, who had retired. Three years later the doctor was admitted to the same hospital with symptoms of an advancing dementia. One day, returning to his old habits, this man slipped into his white coat, went to his old office, and began scrutinizing the patients' charts. Over one complex chart he muttered, "Poor bugger," then closed it up, and when he did, he saw his own name on the file. He exclaimed, "My God!" and turned ashen. He started shaking and crying in horror, seeing that he was the patient with irreversible dementia and not the director. In that terrible lucid moment he saw it all.

"It was one of the most awful things I have ever seen. One out of a nightmare. He was devastated. Ultimately he became profoundly demented," Oliver said, finishing his story with a grim sense that one of the paradoxes of neurology is that there is not always a clear distinction between sanity and madness — one often resembles the other, and transformation is constant. Many people in the hospital could function on the street, and many people on the street are demented.

Oliver's parents, Samuel and Elise Sacks, were physicians, and just as important, they were "medical storytellers," who saw their patients as long-standing friends with complex histories. Elise's father had had eighteen children, and there were nearly a hundred first cousins. On his father's side, Abba Eban, the Israeli politician and diplomat, was Oliver's cousin, and so was the cartoonist Al Capp.

Oliver, the youngest of four boys, was a lonely member of this vast extended family. At the onset of the Blitz, in 1939, he was sent out of London for safety's sake. Oliver was just six. It was to be a four-year ordeal of separation. He was exiled and isolated; he experienced physical cruelty, discomfort, the wintry mendacity of authority figures. He was first placed in a boardinghouse in Bournemouth, and then — a further disruption — was moved to Brayfield, near Northampton. This painful period in Oliver's life could have destroyed him. It certainly marked him, as the blacking factory marked Dickens and the House of Desolation (fictionalized in "Baa Baa, Black Sheep") marked Kipling. It also sharply resembles the rustication that Orwell recounted in "Such, Such, Were the Joys." It was a form of child abuse verging on soul murder, in the phrase of Dr. Leonard Shengold (a close friend of Oliver's), who discusses such traumas in his book *Soul Murder*.

"I became obsessed with numbers, as the only things I could trust," Oliver says. He was reassured by the periodic table, seeing "order and harmony in the family of elements."

By wounding him, the experience made him the sort of scientist who is brother to the poet.

In his childhood attachment to the periodic table, to colors, to metals, to science and solitude, he related to Humphry Davy, a kindred soul. As a university undergraduate in the late 1950s Oliver experienced England's first postwar sparkle, an intellectual rekindling that included writers dubbed "the Angry Young Men"; *The Goon Show,* a radio series featuring Peter Sellers; and the comedy revue *Beyond the Fringe*—Jonathan Miller, one of its writers and performers, an embodiment of that period's humor, intelligence, and glamour, is one of Oliver's closest friends and a fellow doctor. Oliver came to America just as it was being energized. He was twenty-seven in San Francisco in the early 1960s, where everything was happening. He lived for five years in California—years of medical residence and reading, years of experimentation, motorcycle years. Nineteen sixty-five was devoted to the study of earthworms at New York's Albert Einstein College of Medicine: he gathered worms by the thousands to extract myelia from their nerve cords, an episode that was inflated in the movie *Awakenings*.

In October 1966, he arrived at Beth Abraham Hospital, and there he has remained, working for thirty-two years, earning the New York rate of $12 for each patient he sees. This hospital, the "Mount Carmel" of *Awakenings*, is in that hinterland of the Bronx, an hour or so from midtown Manhattan by subway. Its nearest stop is Allerton Avenue. Beth Abraham was once a charity hospital. The patients here, and at the hospital of the Little Sisters of the Poor not far away, where Oliver has been working since 1972, are generally older men and women.

Over the decades that Oliver has spent caring for these people, he has seen them age, sometimes showing improvements, sometimes degenerating or regressing. Many are in a kind of suspension. One brain-damaged man said to Oliver, "I've recovered enough to know that I'll never recover enough." Another man is immobilized in a chair. He was mugged in Manhattan in 1986, when he was twenty-two, and received severe head injuries that put him in a coma. After being treated in acute-care hospitals, he improved a little. But now he is just sitting, a wounded man, but conscious of his condition.

I asked, "Does he know where he is?"

"He is aware enough to be enraged," Oliver said.

"Agnes is our senior centenarian," Oliver says, smiling at a bright-eyed woman in a wheelchair. "Twenty years ago she chased me up four flights of stairs, vociferating. She was Parkinsonian. Violently, writhingly choreic." Oliver has a habit, when using an expression such as "writhingly choreic," of giving a deadly accurate imitation of the affliction. "And, um, yes, I was frightened."

One of the days I was at Beth Abraham, Oliver showed me a patient's thick record. This was Grace, also Parkinsonian; written in her file: "An enigma since 1929." Hers was a static neurological condition — writhing movements, tics, oscillation of the eyes. She was on no medication because one of Oliver's reiterated dictums is "Ask not what disease the person has, but rather what person the disease has."

Oliver observed that Grace felt an energy with her condition. "With medication, she would have devitalized."

Her husband had been very important to her. Grace had said, "I have the drive, he has the patience. We make a good pair."

A note Oliver had made in Grace's record said, "I cannot avoid the feeling that she is preparing for her death."

Grace died two months later.

Without the dullness induced by medication, a Parkinsonian patient had the possibility of the freedom to live, the energy to react, to "borrow" postures or gestures from other people. ("Repetition can be an absorption of posture," Oliver says.) Sometimes people are rigid until they see a friend or an animal or a pattern, until they hear music or are asked to go out for bagels.

Such patients, seemingly comatose or indifferent, react when they see Oliver. They smile, widen their eyes. In many cases the first reaction of a patient is to reach out and touch him, and he returns the touch, which is almost a caress. Many are rigid until they see Oliver, and they become animated as he speaks to them, or hums a tune, or touches them. He embraces them; they hug him in return.

"Here is our senior resident," Oliver says. "Hello, Horace" — and he clutches the man, who smiles shyly and says, "Dr. Sacks." Oliver holds his hand and speaks to him directly, softly, inquiring how he is. His arms and legs are stick-like, his fingers are twisted. He has a wan smile of innocence and sadness.

Horace has never walked. He has had cerebral palsy since birth. He was admitted in 1948, when he was twenty-three and the full name of the hospital was the Beth Abraham Home for Incurables. At the time, he was selling newspapers in Times Square. He functioned fairly well and was a familiar sight on the corner of 42nd Street. American cities then were full of such newspaper vendors. He could sell papers, he could move his arms, he could speak and give change. Like many patients, he had been looked after on the outside, but when he ceased to get help he was sent to Beth Abraham. He has been there now for fifty years, staring out the window. I remarked on the sadness in Harry's expression.

"He is rather sad now," Oliver said. "Horace was very attached to another patient, Ruth." They sat side by side in their wheelchairs, holding hands. They ate together. "Since Ruth died he has deteriorated. He has lost his goals."

Outside the hospital, Oliver can become tongue-tied attempting to buy a ballpoint pen in a corner store, or appear helpless fiddling at the cash register in a coffee shop, his thick fingers futile and unresponsive in his coin purse. But he is alert and focused when he is seeing a patient — like the Tourettic surgeon and pilot he wrote about who never has tics when he is operating or flying a plane. In the hospital Oliver is efficient, as completely at home as the patients, unshockable in a place that occasionally requires real nerve.

One day at Beth Abraham Oliver and I were getting into the elevator with one of his colleagues when a woman in a wheelchair propelled herself toward the door, her left leg sticking straight out like the sort of weapon police reports ominously describe as "a shod foot." Her hair was tangled; she was old and energetic and angry.

"You fucking bastards!" she screamed at us. "You bastards! Let me on the elevator! I want to get on! Let me fucking on! Fuck you!"

The door shut on the woman's howling. Everyone in the elevator was rattled except Oliver, who said softly, with serene puzzlement, "I think I recognize her. I am sure I know her. Didn't she used to be on the second floor? Ethel-something?"

A person's anger does not make Oliver angry; it appears to calm him and make him more watchful, for rage is a symptom, like a tic or a gesture.

At the Little Sisters of the Poor, I was with him when he saw Janet, a paranoid woman who had been violent. Before Janet entered, the nurse gave Oliver the woman's records.

"She thinks there are men attacking her," the nurse said. "Men trying to rape her. She reported the priest and a workman — and I can tell you there was absolutely nothing in it. She's yelling and screaming."

"Was the attacker on her right or her left?" Oliver asked.

The nurse was not sure. I asked Oliver why he wondered this.

"She has a blind side, apparently," he said, turning pages. "Do you know the term 'blind sight'? The sight that reaches consciousness. There are blind rats which don't fall off the edge of a table."

Janet was about seventy, with bulging thyroidal eyes and yellowy-white hair in a small girl's pageboy cut, neatly dressed in slacks. Her puffy, almost coquettish face looked like Bette Davis's playing Baby Jane. She was eager to see Oliver, and had been waiting several days for his visit.

"Janet, isn't it? How are you doing, Janet?" Oliver asked.

"There are a couple of men here who are bothering me," Janet said, smiling at me. "One of them is frightening me to death. Following me!"

"Yes?" Oliver said. "On the left side or the right side?"

"On all sides! He ran out and tried to get me. He was being a smart aleck."

Oliver said, "What did he say?"

But the woman began to protest. "I am a decent woman. I was raised in Greenwich Village by a good Irish family." She said loudly, "It wasn't as though I was wearing a bikini!"

"You said there were two men," Oliver said.

"There's a Catholic brother — his shirt sticks out like it's a penis," Janet said. "He's staring and looking at me. This is a Catholic holy place! I dress modestly. I got into my room about ten at night. I was sleeping alone — I have to mention that. I have never married. All of a sudden I hear a fist banging on my room! I was afraid. After a while I looked out. No one there, but I saw Julia across the hall. Julia said, 'It was the brother.' The loud sound of fists on my door!"

She said this looking at Oliver and me with popping eyes, smiling, smoothing the thighs of her slacks. She made Oliver promise to return soon, winked at me, and left.

"Notice the erotic content in what she said," Oliver said. "'I sleep alone.' The mention of the bikini. The priest's shirt like a penis."

Afterward, the nurse said, "I forgot to tell you that when she is in her room, she goes about stark naked. She answers the door without a stitch on. Just stands there in the doorway, naked."

"Paranoia and eroticism often go together," Oliver said, making a note in Janet's file. Each file is a detailed narration of a person's condition — a story, in many cases a long, episodic story.

He sees to the heart of the person. The first thing I learned at the hospital is that his patients are his friends. These are close relationships, developed over years. There is intense understanding and compassion. Perhaps no treatment is ever possible unless a human relationship is given a chance to develop.

"This woman can't speak, but she can sing," Oliver said as a smiling woman propelled her wheelchair toward him. He introduced me to the woman, Jane, and to the music therapist, Connie Tomaino.

Jane smiled and, as patients seem to do, clutched his hand, hugged his arm, but she said nothing. Oliver, who cannot sing, compensates for this by becoming a conductor. This does not always work. I could not accommodate him when, introducing me to a song-responsive patient, he said, "Sing something by the Grateful Dead."

Connie began to sing "What a Friend We Have in Jesus."

Jane found her voice and joined the hymn, and the singing of it, regarding Oliver as she sang, was like a greeting. She became livelier, her facial expressions became friendly, and for the duration of the hymn she was totally animated. When it ended, she entered a sort of blankness.

Jane was aphasic. She could utter one word, "fine," in conversation, but the rest was what a neurologist would describe as memory deficits. She could sing fluently.

Connie has found, in her work over the past twenty years, that memories aren't really lost, at least with apparent aphasia or dementia. What is lost or damaged is the patient's ability to access these memories. "What music can do, or at least music that is familiar, is tap into those memories or unleash them. Sometimes the music is enough to cue those lost memories and bring them back to immediacy."

Oliver read his notes from Jane's file: "She is vehemently expressive despite her aphasia. She continues to be able to sing, to recite, she is an excellent musician and has an uproarious sense of humor. With the Lord's Prayer, the cadences continued, and the inner meaning, while the words degenerated into cadenced garble . . ."

I looked over his shoulder. In Jane's file, another doctor had written "this demented woman," and beside it Oliver had written, almost scoldingly, "Not demented!"

Oliver stood aside and let his protégé speak. What looks like modesty or deference is a technique for creating a moment. Oliver's standing aside was part of his method for obliquely watching a patient react to strangers. Oliver encouraged me to talk, to interact. He seemed to like the thought that the patient and I were strangers; he let the patient speak. Oliver, the author of *Musicophilia* (music helped him walk again when his leg was injured), said nothing, just smiled, watched all this, and then urged Connie to say something.

"First there is an initial recognition," Connie said. The effect of music on a person with aphasia is strange at first for the patient. "There is a possibility of connection, and an uncanny feeling of restlessness and uneasiness," she said. "It is like their being in a strange place. After that, there are connections."

One woman who was not verbal at all, who could not utter her own name, began talking about her son after hearing a certain piece of music. After eight weeks of treatment, which was music therapy, she became verbal. The music that unlocked her memory was "Does Your Mother Come from Ireland?" Other Irish songs contributed to her fluency. She was in her mideighties, born in Ireland.

"I played recordings, of songs that would have been popular in the thirties," Connie said. "The first three sessions were only facial reactions, smiles and crying. I played 'It's a Long Way to Tipperary' and she burst into tears."

As Irish songs worked with this woman, Chinese songs worked with a Chinese man, and songs in Spanish with a Puerto Rican. Patients who were described as demented or aphasic remembered events and people and acquired a sort of comprehension of their personal history.

Oliver gestured toward an old woman slumped in a wheelchair. "She may speak to you. Her voice is a little slurred and ataxic."

"How long have you known her?"

"I have been seeing her since '66."

Thirty-two years: one of the thousands of patients Oliver has seen and described minutely in their hospital records, but who have not become subjects for his neurohistories.

Oliver looked wistful. "It's sort of sad in a way that we've never been able to make a radical change in her condition."

Stefan, whom Oliver has known for twenty-six years, came in 1972. Stefan, in a warm-up suit, sat aggressively in a wheelchair, leaning on his forearms, his face forward.

"I always think of Stefan as a young man with a lot of hair. And how does he see me?"

Stefan shook his head negatively when Oliver approached him.

Oliver said, "I don't think he has ever forgiven me for bringing him here. But I wonder. Was his so-called schizophrenia itself an expression of his disease?"

Mild dementia, a stroke, and a fall had incapacitated Gladys, a seventy-year-old black woman. But it had been discovered that Gladys had played the piano in clubs in her time. A piano was found. Gladys recaptured an entire repertoire of songs, and while we stood there she played "Moon River," "The Birth of the Blues," "All the Things You Are," and "Take the A Train," moving her fingers skillfully, playing from memory.

The other patients stopped gabbling and sat up. They turned away from the television set. They listened, and when it was over, they applauded.

"While the music was playing it wasn't a hospital," Oliver said.

As Gladys had so vastly improved, I wondered whether the same happened to other patients.

"Sometimes," Oliver said. "I saw a chap this morning who is going to leave the hospital. I don't know whether he has improved so vastly. He was involved in a motor vehicle accident. He was brain-injured, but his wife has got a large settlement, so they will be able to manage. But it was for this reason that the post-encephalitics used to be so envied. People used to come up and say, 'I wish I were post-encephalitic' — instead of having multiple sclerosis or cerebral palsy or something — 'because you could *do* something for me. I'd have a chance.'"

I asked, "Does music treatment have any effect on Parkinson's patients?"

"Yes," Connie said. "In the case of Parkinson's it works as 'rhythmic cueing' — people get out of their chair and just start dancing. What is the mechanism?"

Oliver said, "People have trouble generating their own rhythm. People with Parkinson's, their sense of timing is off. You have to give them timing. Tempo. And it's an almost incorruptible tempo. Music imposes a tempo and prevents acceleration."

"Or people can internalize a musical phrase and thereby know when they need to breathe," Connie said. "I did this with a small grant with people who had dysarthria and other kinds of muscular damage. When they started, they could only do three syllables. 'How–are–you?' was the best they could do. By the time we finished, and this was after only two months, they were up to nineteen syllables."

"Did they also take medication?"

"No," Connie said. "It was learning a technique and listening, feeling it, breathing. But there was such an improvement, people were asking, 'Did they have new medication?'"

Oliver said, "People with Alzheimer's are able to play music very well. Why is one ability preserved and another lost? There are people who are too drunk to stand who dance well, and when the music stops they fall down."

When we left the ward, Oliver was smiling — he had loved the way the atmosphere there had been transformed by the music. Three years before, introducing me to a hospital, Oliver had said to me, "However sad or frightening, there is something positive here."

Pursuing the idea of "street neurology," I suggested walking around New York, just looking at the people on the sidewalks — limping, twitching, "vocalizing." To an outsider, the city appears to be overrun by people on the verge of a nervous breakdown, and a New York nutter can seem world class. Was this something to do with the way the city, so cellular, so like an asylum, an island of vertical compartments, isolates people and intensifies psychosis? Dr. Sacks might have the answer.

To me, New Yorkers generally look like creatures who have adapted to their environment, like the blind fish and glowing eels that live in deep water. New Yorkers often say they could not live anywhere else. But I wondered what Oliver would say about the chattering Afghan taxi driver, or the hurrying wild-eyed Lubavitcher snatching at his side curls, or the slumped-over man selling gum in the rain. There were always people talking seriously and loudly to themselves, muttering menacingly. There were always people taking refuge in doorways or doubled up with laughter — what's so funny? Or hunkered down in front of shops babbling "Blee-blee." There were ranters, people looking for trouble, people with tics and palsy, people who had been discharged years ago from hospitals and were "decompensating." Decompensating might mean howling in the street or taking a swing at passersby, cackling in a subway car or masturbating at moving traffic. There was nearly always someone looking desperate, lying in the doorway of the Harry Winston jewelry store on Fifth Avenue or squatting in the alcove of Sotheby's auction house on Madison.

Oliver liked the idea of doing street neurology, but it would have to be limited — his foot was bothering him.

He said, "I'd like to show you two people, one with Parkinson's and one with Tourette's. They are both artists."

Oliver, very shy, is the man who has proven in his work that a person's so-called handicap often causes the development of new skills or the discovery of assets. He is far less emphatic about "deficits." He says there are sometimes greater compensations for the person who has an affliction like the Andean villagers in the H. G. Wells story "The Country of the Blind," who understand everything and miss nothing, precisely because they are blind. In that story, it is the sighted man who is at a disadvantage.

He has known Ed Weinberger, a furniture designer, for fifteen years. He has never written about him. As with many people in Oliver's life, there is no clear distinction between friendship and treatment. The people are part of his life — perhaps the largest part of his life. Ed's story has taken many turns, but it is still unfolding. Ed lives on the eighth floor of a building on the Upper West Side. When he answered the door he was canted over — he has Parkinson's. Oliver stepped aside and said almost nothing. It was what I had noticed at the hospital, a sort of group dynamic in which no one is a patient, no one is in charge.

Oliver does not speak of cures. His genius lies in his understanding of patients, which draws on friendship and love and the long-term relationship.

Faced with a patient who has a severe neurological problem, Oliver is open to anything: aromatherapy, music therapy, group therapy, acupuncture, hugging, hand-holding, fresh air, outings in the countryside — and of course medications, though as Oliver says, drugs often obscure the real cause of a problem and create misleading symptoms of their own. He wants to go beneath the symptoms to find the problem and treat it. Because this takes so much time, Oliver offers more hours to his patients than any other doctor I know, which perhaps explains why his medical earnings last year were $7,000 — a figure that was reduced to zero after he paid his malpractice insurance.

He is a listener of seismographic sensitivity, a clear-sighted and inspired observer, attentive, with an eloquence that allows him to describe a person's condition with nuance and subtlety. Oliver has said that his shyness — possibly caused by the wartime separation from his family — is a sort of disease, and should be considered one. Shyness plays a part in his observation, giving him a vantage point, for shy people can be intensely watchful. It makes him patient. His patience and the tenacity of his observation make him the most compassionate and tolerant of men, with a capacity for seeing abilities where another doctor would see only deficits.

For the first half hour or so at Ed's, Oliver hardly spoke. He did not want to intrude; he wanted me to form my own impressions. I soon saw that Ed's leaning was echoed in the furniture. In every table or chair, in desks and shelves, angles had been cut out of their surfaces, the corners were bisected, the legs seemed to lean, and everything stood solid — the more solid for the way the angles supported them.

"Look at this." It was a photograph of Ed, crouched on a legless corner of a table that seemed to defy gravity.

Ed was a collector of well-made objects: old cameras and spyglasses and telescopes, Chinese jades and bronzes. He also had a vintage car, a 1948 Bristol, made in England.

"That's a lovely desk," I said.

"I call it my bridge desk."

Arched like an eyebrow, the desk was unusual, built of mellow, pale orange pear wood, sanded by hand, the details of grain matching the joinery carefully chosen, giving the illusion of lightness. The legs were splayed, somewhat like Ed's own.

The cantilevered legs, he said, were based on a bridge designed by Robert Maillart. Maillart was a Swiss engineer who revolutionized the design of bridges, making them stronger and more slender, combining the whole — arch, girder, and road — into one piece.

"And those angles I saw on the eye features of a Kwakiutl Indian ceremonial mask," Ed said. "The structural features of the mask interested me, especially the tension between the solidity and the surface."

Many objects and pieces of furniture in the room looked as though they were about to topple over. Canted over himself, Ed said it was all a trick of the eye. He showed me a red desk with jutting planes and said that he had derived some of its features, too, from the Indian mask. "I wanted to give it the illusion of an extruded form."

It was more solid and foursquare than anything upright. He showed me the angle of the desk and said, "Would you imagine this to be a ninety-degree angle?"

It seemed to me much smaller, but by placing a square piece of cardboard in the angle, he showed me that it was absolutely square. It was important to him, he said, that the angles in his furniture reflected the angles in his body and life. Needing his life to be angular, he redesigned the furniture in his house and, in so doing, contrived to invent a totally new sort of furniture, a Parkinsonian style, which was a way of standing and living. What another person might take to be an obstacle had given him a new conception of the objects around him.

Oliver then spoke for the first time. He said, "It so reminds me of the person in *Awakenings* who says, 'If only the world were composed of stairs, then I would be happy.'"

"Before my operation a year ago, I began to think about buying a car and driving it," Ed said.

His choice of car was interesting, Oliver said. The vintage Bristol had an angular body. It was a substitute body. Ed would open the angular doors — with angles as interesting as the ones he designed for his furniture, angles as radical as his own posture — and he inhabited that body.

"I drive around Central Park on Sundays, when there is no traffic," Ed said.

"Ed's passionate about cars," Oliver said. "My version of that, I suppose, is the motorbikes I used to ride — Nortons."

When Oliver was a medical resident at UCLA, there was a quadriplegic woman who said she wanted to go for a ride with him. Oliver knew that the woman did not have long to live. "I thought I would grant her this wish, and so my friends helped me get her on the back of the bike. They wrapped her up, tied her firmly on the seat, and off we went. She loved it. We all rode together, about six or eight motorbikes, the quadriplegic woman on the back of mine."

He smiled, remembering the incident, and he fidgeted as though he had dislodged conflicting memories. "We returned to face an aghast and curious crowd," he said, and seemed to see the crowd of astonished faces, the untying of the quadriplegic woman from the pillion seat. "My whole residency was characterized by episodes like this. As far as the department was concerned, I was somewhere between an embarrassment and an ornament."

The quadriplegic woman had loved being sprung from the hospital and delighted in the sensation of racing down the road on the back of the roaring Norton.

Already I was glad we were away from the hospital and just having lunch in a New York apartment. I would never have known this fact about Oliver's motorcycling if Ed had not prompted it. As for the puzzled response of Oliver's department, that was to be repeated later, when in 1991 Oliver was let go after twenty-four years working at Bronx State–Bronx Psychiatric Center, whose unimpressed executive director was quoted in the *New York Times:* "Dr. Sacks was not considered particularly unique here. I am not sure he complied with state regulations."

At the mention of hospitals, Ed described various horrific experiences he had had in hospitals about four years before, when, heavily sedated with Elavil, Halcion, and codeine, he had had a severe nervous reaction and hallucinations. From being a patient with Parkinson's, he was then diagnosed as psychotic.

"I thought I was being attacked by terrorists. I thought I was being set up. There were many episodes. I had the fantasy that I was being persecuted."

He had to be restrained by male nurses. He was treated as someone who was out of his mind. The doctors who were supposed to be taking care of him were merely sedating him, but the effect was alarming. "I was really crazy. The food was a problem, too. If you have Parkinson's, you have throat problems — it's hard to swallow. They gave me rough food, not soft food. That could have choked me. I said, 'You should give me soft food,' but they paid no attention. I spat it out. They thought that was very amusing."

One day he overheard them saying that, although his condition was pretty bad, they wanted to go on giving him a certain experimental medication in order to finish their trial. This enraged Ed. He told them they were irresponsible. This had little effect.

"Then I called my own neurologist and told him to get me out of there or I would sue. That's what did it. The next day I was out of the hospital."

"One shudders to think how much this may go on," Oliver said. "There was a woman who ran from Brookhaven, who then began to live among the fields and hedgerows of Long Island. They said, 'She has discharged herself against medical advice.' You can't spend years — or even days — in a mental hospital being treated as mad without it doing something terrible to you."

Ed at home was easier to diagnose than Ed in a hospital. I said, "So hospitals can be dangerous?"

"I come across many people who have been in hospitals for twenty or thirty years because of being misdiagnosed," Oliver said. It was the old horror from "Ward No. 6." "These so-called designer drugs — designer heroin. There are forms of it that render people profoundly Parkinsonian. Deaf people are mistakenly diagnosed as retarded. Post-encephalitics are sometimes locked up in mental hospitals as schizophrenics."

Ed said, "The doctor who was in charge of me was only interested in his work. To him I was just a body. It was like a prison camp. It was all ruthless indifference. Sometimes, in order to be treated properly in a hospital you have to act crazy."

An operation called a pallidotomy had saved him. He had opted for the procedure because of his terror of hospitalization and his severe Parkinson's, which at times had given him episodes — some as long as six hours — of utter immobility, one rigid posture in which he had been unable to move. But the surgery had been risky: it involved targeting a very precise area in the brain and destroying it. There are risks of intellectual and speech impairment due to the location of the target area. The procedure worked

— Ed was liberated. Before the operation he had been immobile: could not walk, could not talk, could not get up from his chair.

"I have been reborn," Ed said. "I have a new life."

It seemed to me that Oliver's friendship and insight was as essential to Ed's understanding as the surgeon's knife. Ed's ambition was to fly to England, pick up a new Bristol — the angular car for the angular man — and drive to Switzerland, to look at the gravity-defying angles of Maillart's bridges.

Street neurology, Oliver said, allowed "the spur and play of every impulse." The true test of this was perhaps accompanying a very ticcy Touretter (Oliver prefers this word to Tourettic) through New York. Shane F., who is mentioned in passing (another splendid footnote) in *An Anthropologist on Mars*, happened to be visiting New York from Toronto, so Oliver suggested that the three of us go to the Museum of Natural History. In Shane, Oliver said, I would see "Tourette's as a disease. As a mode of being. As a mode of inquiry."

When we met Shane in front of his hotel, he rushed to Oliver, hugged him, touched his face, and became excited, vocalizing an urgent and eloquent grunt — "Euh! Euh!" — as he described an auto accident he had just witnessed.

"But some people came up to help!" he said in his hurried, stuttery way, like a child trying to discharge a whole thought and stumped by syntax in the excitement.

He went on describing it, and from that first moment he dominated us. Also from that moment Oliver seemed to withdraw. He was a presence, no more than that, sometimes a shadow, sometimes a voice, always a friend, and often his figure — protective, supportive, yet entirely unintrusive — was that of an ideal parent.

Shane was thirty-four, but seemed younger because of his explosive gestures and great energy and eagerness. He had black hair and bright eyes; he was handsome and vital, humorous and talkative, too impatient in asking, chattering, to wait for an answer.

He did an imitation of President Clinton, then one of Oliver. He said, "I can't drive, but I was driving Oliver's car! Euh! Euh! Oliver was saying, 'Do pull over, Shane. Just pull over.' And I was driving. Not too fast, but fast! 'Do pull over.'"

He caught the Englishness and the slight stammer in Oliver's voice. This was the first indication I had that when Shane was mimicking someone's voice or accent, he was so concentrated he ceased to be Tourettic.

We got into Oliver's Lexus (the air conditioner preset at 65 degrees) and headed off to look for a parking space. Oliver had two large plastic cuttlefish on his dashboard. One fell off, and in righting it, Oliver swerved and Shane cackled. Oliver was disoriented, he took several wrong turns, and none of us had any idea where we might park. And so for fifteen or twenty minutes, while Oliver murmured, narrating his mistakes in driving, Shane was gesticulating, ignoring the search for a parking spot, and talking excitedly.

"Oliver's writing about Pingelap and Pohnpei — did he tell you, or is he too shy? He was writing about the achromatopes. Euh! Euh! He went there — Euh! — twice. Toronto's my town, but you know the people are more aggressive in my city than they are here. Euh! I find people a lot friendlier here. I prefer New York. I like the frenetic strange — euh! Oliver is Mister Mushroom Maniac."

"Not really, but I love lichens," Oliver said, and then, "Just put it in this lot," still narrating his movements at the wheel, and he parked the car.

Leaping out, Shane ran around to Oliver again and hugged him, touched his face, grunted, stamped the heels of his boots. Oliver just smiled — it was like father and son — and said, "Yes, yes, well . . ."

As soon as we crossed the street, Shane took off without even grunting in farewell. He shot down the sidewalk, sprinting toward the museum like a hunter-gatherer through tall grass, very fast, his arms pumping.

"Imagine Shane in space," Oliver said, watching him with pride. "One violent movement and he would push the shuttle off course." Oliver smiled at the thought of a space capsule jerked out of orbit by the Tourettic astronaut inside. Several times Oliver mentioned with genuine amusement the possibility of highly sophisticated technology upset or destroyed by such tics or flailings.

West 78th Street seemed the perfect place for a Touretter. Shane smelled a light pole, then gripped it and swung around it. He moved on, touching posts, stooping to touch the curbstone, the sidewalk, the parking meters.

Then he sniffed the parking meters. He rushed back. He touched both my elbows, then Oliver's, dashed on ahead again, found some more parking meters to sniff, and ran on. Now I knew why the heels of his boots were so worn.

"Why does he touch those posts?"

Oliver was implacable. "Ask him," he said.

Shane smiled to my question. He said, "You're looking for a rational reason. Euh! Euh! But if I told you, would you believe me? Would you think I was telling you the truth? I touch them because they're down there, this one and then that one." He twisted his head and grunted again. "Is the reason I gave you the right reason?"

Soon he was moving too fast for me to keep up with him and persist in my questions. Oliver just smiled.

On this June afternoon, a cool day after days of heat, people were strolling but few of them noticed Shane. This was New York City. Shane did not seem unusual; he did not stand out in the crowd. He waited for the Walk sign. He jeered at the bad drivers, the honkers, the speeders, and when the light changed and we walked across Columbus Avenue, Shane was running, stopping to touch the low stone walls of the museum, or the gateposts, or the trees. Now and then he hugged a tree and sniffed it, pressing his face against it.

"He remembers everything," Oliver says. "Everything he touches. Everything he smells."

Shane seemed like someone making a new map of the city, his very own map, on which every object had a unique shape, temperature, smell, and texture. In his Manhattan, every parking meter was different. There was no such thing as "a parking meter." There was only, say, "the sixth parking meter on the north side of West 78th Street, east of Columbus Avenue," like Funes in the Borges story "Funes the Memorious," who can't understand why the word "dog" stands for so many shapes and forms of the animal, and more than that, "it bothered him that the dog at three fourteen (seen from the side) should have the same name as the dog at three fifteen (seen from the front)."

Shane ran on, calling out, "Hup! Hup! Hup!" A white dog on a leash sensed Shane's hurrying, became agitated, and leaped into its mistress's lap. This interested me, because no one else paid much attention, but the dog reacted to him as if to another creature — not as a threat but as something large and alive with whom it would have to share its space. The dog began barking — not at Shane, but in a generally upset and distracted way, alarmed and excited. Shane laughed and replied with his own "Euh! Euh!" because he had sensed the dog, too.

Apart from that, Shane was lost in the crowd. Odd and ticcy as his behavior was, it was not more extraordinary than that of the gigglers and shouters, the rollerskaters, the youths with hats on backward and carrying boom boxes, the woman pushing a supermarket trolley crammed with plastic bags, the two haggard men sharing a bottle wrapped in brown paper, the screeching girls, the murmuring old men, the snuffling man raggedly dressed as a cowboy. Now and then someone smiled at Shane — no more than that, a smile as a shy query. Only the little white dog was truly alarmed, and the woman who owned the mutt was more alarmed than the dog, as the dog skittered on the woman's skinny thighs.

So far, in terms of street neurology, it seemed that a world-class Tourettic was just about invisible on a New York sidewalk except to a small dog.

"Sometimes Shane creates misunderstandings," Oliver said. "And occasionally they are serious misunderstandings. But usually it is no worse than this."

We entered the museum. I bought the tickets, Shane barked and coughed and chattered, and he smelled the turnstile as he went through it.

Running ahead, Shane loudly read the signs — all the signs: "It says you can't cross this . . . 'Danger, Man-Eating Plants' . . . You know this type of tree . . . Look, there's a little chipmunk in this . . . I didn't know they go underground . . . 'Winter is a period of inactivity' . . . Euh! Euh! Babies over here . . . You see what's buried under there? It's a food cache . . . Nuts. Nuts."

He touched and pinched Oliver, touched walls and doorways, ran his fingers over plaques, moved rapidly from one exhibit to the other. He drew a long breath and seemed to inhale everything he saw. Then he said, "Let's sit down and take a good look," as though willing himself to be still.

We sat in front of a diorama of rural winter, a cross-section of the countryside. Dead leaves on the ground, mulch below that, rodent tunnels and rotting vegetation.

"Tree roots remind me of the brain for some reason," Shane said.

"Yes, dendrites," Oliver said. "So they can make maximum contact."

"Look at that decay," Shane said. "It looks like what goes on inside my refrigerator."

The sight of decay launched Shane into a frenzied description of the movie — his favorite, he said — *Soylent Green,* its prophetic visions of a dying planet: ozone depletion and dead oceans and overpopulation. This explanation calmed him a little, and he finished by saying that he wanted to see the tigers. We found three stuffed tigers in a glass-fronted exhibit.

Knowing that Shane is an artist, and judging from some of the paintings Oliver had shown me, a very good artist, I said, "What do you see?"

"This is meant to inspire nobody. It doesn't inspire fear or awe. This is a base comparison to the real thing. Euh! Euh! This is a mausoleum-like glass enclosure, sort of pathetic. It's like a memory, the ghost of a ghost. There is no reality to this. It doesn't make sense. Why don't they stuff humans and put them in here? You know, the tiger in life can stand very still. A tiger can stand breathless and frozen. As Oliver would say," and here he slipped into Oliver's donnish accent again, "'It's Parkinsonian . . . It's . . . it's lithic.' But these tigers have only the shape and the memory but not the lithe movements. In other words, a sculpture could better this. They're not infused with life."

"What do you think of the tigers in the zoo?" Oliver asked. I wondered whether he asked it because of Shane's love of tigers and his own tigerish movements, his leaping and pouncing.

"They're in cramped quarters, and they're depressed and even regressed. One we saw had a pacing behavior. But you know the two-edged sword is that the zoo is meant to protect them."

"But do you have any sense of Blakean wonder at the zoo?" Oliver asked.

"Yeah, I did. Euh! Euh! Because it was a living tiger. But I don't know — it's a captive. A captive in your imagination. You can never really capture a tiger. I'd like to have an exhibition of my tiger paintings."

Shane hurried on to the room signposted INVERTEBRATES, and Oliver paused, smiling gently, making a note on a small pad. We moved on to GIANT INVERTEBRATES.

"I love the gelatinous," Oliver said. "I love the cephalopods."

A giant squid, fifty feet long, dangled from the ceiling. Oliver smiled at it. Shane was walking quickly in circles among the exhibits of squid, touching benches, smelling signs. He moved purposefully, his head up, his hair damp with perspiration.

"I met someone the other day who had been bitten by an octopus," Oliver said. "The octopus is very intelligent. One was being examined in a tank. In another tank an octopus was watching." He glanced at Shane, who was sniffing and touching, and said, "It makes you wonder whether parts of the brain die because they aren't fed and stimulated."

"Brains, brains, euh! Aarrgh!" Shane was hugging Oliver again.

"We used to eat brains all the time," Oliver said as Shane poked at him. "I remember my mother serving it — sheep brains — and cutting the cerebellum. 'There's the dentic nucleus, Oliver. Eat it.'" He smiled.

"What about your family, Shane?"

"My father's Jewish. My mother's crazy." He tapped my notepad. "Put down Canadian." He began pacing again.

A thin, leathery-faced Indian man approached Oliver. He woggled his head and said, "I heard you speak in Rotterdam."

"Yes?" Oliver said.

The Indian said, "Do you remember my question?"

Oliver stepped backward to get a better look at the man.

The Indian said, "About Tourette's. Can it manifest itself at an elderly age?"

"Oh, yes," Oliver said. "But I can't remember what I told you. Not long ago I met a woman whose Tourette's manifested when she was fifty-two. So it is possible."

"Oliver, Oliver, Oliver, Oliver," Shane was chanting, and he was grunting, too. He called Oliver's attention to a pair of dinosaur skeletons, an allosaurus attacking a long-necked diplodocus. Shane then began to imitate the movements of each creature, the leaping allosaurus, the roaring diplodocus.

Nearby, a man was making a charcoal sketch of the allosaurus on a large drawing pad. Some people were sitting on benches, lovers were holding hands, kids were squalling. Shane paced up and down, making dinosaur faces, dinosaur gestures. He approached the man sketching and began commenting on his picture. The man listened. Shane asked for a piece of paper. Without a murmur, the man tore off a large piece for Shane.

"Newsprint," Shane said, and twitched violently. "It's not good quality."

With a mixture of charm and chutzpah, and uttering sudden sounds, he put his hand out. I thought the man was going to hit him, but he gave him a piece of charcoal. Shane threw the piece of paper onto the floor and crouched on it, poised like the attacking allosaurus, and started sketching rapidly.

Oliver had been pacing, not impatiently but merely, it seemed, to get some sort of perspective. I approached him. He said, "I have never seen him do this before."

Oliver slipped away. I drifted over to Shane as, I suppose, Oliver thought I might. The next time I looked up, I saw that Oliver was studying Shane and me. In pursuit of street neurology, I had believed that I would be observing Oliver, and of course I had, to an extent. But Oliver was elusive: he evaded my glance, stepped out of sight, or stayed firmly in the background. He listened and let others talk, and only when they were done did he put his oar in.

Some people gathered to watch Shane swiping at his sketch, ignoring the man who was slowly scraping away on his pad. In minutes, Shane was done.

"The gesture, the gesture, see? Hup! Hup!" Shane said. "The whole movement, euh!"

Shane dropped the picture and began pacing rapidly again, vocalizing, for he had been still throughout the making of his sketch. I picked up the drawing and brought it over to Oliver.

Oliver said, "One wonders to what extent these gifted people's imaginations may be flavored by the gesture, the movement. It immediately seizes and is seized. Some of Shane's pictures are of animals in motion. But there are also some highly symbolic ones, about starvation, exile, torture."

Shane's picture was amazing for its speed of execution and its accuracy. It was the allosaurus in motion, and even the other artist approved, and so did passersby. Shane was skipping around the room, touching the walls, smelling the pillars, tapping the benches. From time to time he would return to Oliver as if to a reference point, touching his arms and shoulders, and hugging him. Oliver simply smiled.

As we left the museum, Shane sprinted— "Hup! Hup! Hup!"—and vaulted a planter by a doorway. He called to Oliver, "You do it!"

Oliver said in a self-mocking, Edward Lear–like way, "I am an elderly gentleman and can't be expected to do that."

Shane was not listening. He was headed down the sidewalk, his arms pumping. "Hup! Hup! Hup!" He touched the posts of an awning. He drummed his fingers on a curbstone. He saw a bench — he sat on it quickly and just as quickly leaped up, saying, "Euh! Euh!"

Seeing him, a woman ran to her baby carriage, and with a quick step that spoke of alarm, she rushed away, thrusting the carriage in front of her, away from Shane.

I said, "Why did that woman leave in such a hurry?"

"She was frightened," Shane said.

"Why do you suppose she was frightened by you?"

"I'm a man."

"So she's afraid of men?"

"She saw a man moving. That maybe bothers her. She's nervous. She's got a little kid with her."

"Why should she be worried about you?"

"This is New York."

We went to a café. Oliver seemed baffled by the menu. He stammered and then decided on tea. Shane ordered tea, too, but talked so energetically he did not drink it. He talked about Robin Williams, Lenny Bruce, ecology, deforestation, floods, dumping raw waste ("Bizarre plumbing practices"), tourists, AIDS in Thailand, the Galápagos, Victorian science, and coprolalia.

"Sometimes in Tourette's there's coprolalia—compulsive swearing. I don't have coprolalia, except sometimes when I'm alone," Shane said. "When I'm painting, then sometimes I swear. All the words, ahem! Euh! Lenny Bruce's performances were attacked and he was prosecuted for his obscene language. He was told to modify it or fuck off. There are so many ironies—the police themselves use that language in the police station."

Oliver said, "You swear less than most policemen."

"I swear when I have touching tics. I touch my bed. My comments usually involve my family."

"In the eight years I've known you, I really haven't heard this," Oliver said. "Only ten or fifteen percent of Tourette's patients have it. Some people have severe motor tics but no coprolalia. The only identical behavior I've found has been Tourettic twins in Atlanta. They both have elaborate erotic phantasmagoric behavior, such as calling out the window, 'My father's raping me!' Or there was a time at the beach when they shouted, 'Shark! Clear the beach!'"

"I did that!" Shane said. He was rising. He was fidgeting again.

Out of the café, he sprinted ahead and began talking loudly, chattering to people on the sidewalk. I tried to catch up with him, but I was weary —nothing was more fatiguing than an outing with a Tourettic. But he was still bright. A young woman smiled at him. She was about twenty-five, in cutoff jeans and a blue-patterned bandanna.

"Hi, hi, hi," Shane said.

"I know you," the woman said. "You're famous, aren't you?"

Shane was vocalizing—barking and coughing. He touched her elbow very gently. She took his hand and they started down the sidewalk together, holding hands. Shane then sprinted with her, hurrying her forward. As though energized by him, the woman laughed excitedly.

Behind me, Oliver said, "The car's up here," and pointed in the opposite direction.

Seeing Oliver standing so calmly, I saw again, as I had in the museum, that he was helping me get to know the process of approaching neurohistory by setting up such a meeting. But the encounter served him, too, by offering him contrasts and different points of view. To Oliver, human behavior was prismatic, multilayered, and his life and his work proved that revelations came over time. In this natural neurology, treatments in the fourth dimension, personality was not painted in primary colors but shown in a million subtler hues, delicately shaded, and even, as Oliver had written in another context, "a polyphony of brightnesses." A solitary person was monochromatic. When others were present, the personality was suffused with color. I remembered something Oliver had said about a man at Beth Abraham whom a hasty doctor might term a vegetable. Oliver had spent decades treating the man. True, the man was confined to a wheelchair, but —the phrase stayed with me—"he is emotionally complete."

Oliver was looking past me, in the direction Shane had taken.

"I'll get him," I said. But I could not see Shane.

Shane and the young woman had gone two blocks before I reached them. It was only because of their being blocked by traffic that I caught up with them at all. Shane could easily have hurried the woman away. She looked as if she wanted to be hurried away.

To this young, fresh-faced New Yorker, Shane was not a Tourette's sufferer, nor ticcy, nor gesticulating wildly, nor hurrying up and down in an inexplicable manner. He was another New Yorker, an energetic young man, talking fast and stammering and grunting. He wore a black jacket and cowboy boots. Had the young woman looked, she would have seen that in an afternoon of sprinting through streets and museum corridors the heels of the boots had been worn flat. One person had been frightened by Shane — the woman with the baby. A few people had smiled at him. Most had not noticed him. Only the dog had been spooked.

This young woman was madly attracted, but she scowled at me when I approached and spoke to Shane.

"We have to go," I said. "Oliver's way down there, waiting for us."

"Shane, who's this guy?"

After a two-block sprint she was already on a first-name basis with him.

"I have to go," Shane said. "Dr. Oliver Sacks. Down there! Euh! Euh! Give me your number. I'll give you a call."

"If you blow in my ear," she said, and screeched with pleasure.

Shane blew lightly into her ear as she wrote her name and telephone number on Shane's museum brochure.

"Do it more! Oh, that's nice!" Then she hugged him. "Call me Baby Doll."

"Euh! Euh! Baby Doll."

"I love you!" she said, and kissed him.

Shane smiled at her. He had made a friend — he could easily have spent the night with her. I stood watching with my arms hanging down. Then Shane was off, sprinting again. I started after him, but he surged ahead, dodging people on the sidewalk, and leaped across the street, ahead of the traffic. He got to Oliver before the light changed, the nimblest pedestrian in New York, leaving me on the wrong side of the street, but both of them watching me.

I understood then that at the hospitals, with his friends, in the street, and now at the end of the day, it had always been part of Oliver's intention to observe me, and more, to see the interplay between the patient and me — the aphasic, the choreic, the paranoid, the Parkinsonian, the Touretter, even the colleague and the close friend. I was not an observer, and this was not an interview, but part of his life and the psychodrama of a New York outing, street neurology in the widest sense.

9

NURSE WOLF, THE HURTER

The man she called "the bug cruncher" used to show up at her studio fur-
tively carrying old, cloudy Tupperware containers labeled with strips of
masking tape scrawled Lasagna April 97 or Spaghetti Sauce. Never mind
the labels; the Tupperware contained insects the man had carefully caught
on Long Island, where he was a construction worker. He started with bee-
tles, and then he brought roaches and slugs. As time passed the creatures
got bigger. One day he brought a live mouse.

Nurse Wolf said to him, "I draw the line there. I never said I'd do a mouse."

"Do the mouse," the man pleaded. "It's half dead anyway." It had been in
the Tupperware container with no breathing holes.

"I'm like, 'No way!'" Nurse Wolf told me. But she agreed to do the others. "I had to wear shoes. He was very specific. Open-toed mules with these
high heels."

The man lay on his side, on the floor — "the bug's-eye view," in Nurse
Wolf's phrase — tumescent, touching himself.

"Stab it with your heel, slowly." He wanted Nurse Wolf to tease and torment the creatures. Then he would say suddenly, "Crush it!" and clutch
himself.

The bug cruncher's fetish was unusual even in Nurse Wolf's wide experience. And it was difficult for her to squash insects by aiming a stiletto
heel at them — they often kept slipping, and the slugs were just impossible.

"I liked the freaky side of it," she said, yet she was soft-hearted toward all
creatures. She collected stuffed animals, she loved having pets, she owned a
large collection of animal skulls. She had an oryx skull, a giraffe skull, and a

stuffed beaver she called Hoover in her studio, which she sometimes called her dungeon.

Her psychotherapist remained thoughtful when Nurse Wolf told her how, as a dominatrix, she sometimes imagined herself a furry creature with sharp little teeth. When Nurse Wolf added, "And with a long tail. I have a major tail fetish. I wish I had a tail. I used to wear a tail," the therapist said, "That could be penis envy."

"I *have* a penis!" Nurse Wolf shouted at her, and began laughing. "I have lots of them! I have a long purple one with glitter on it. I have big ones and small ones. Some are electric. Why should I be envious?"

Some time later, Nurse Wolf said to me, "I love women with tails."

She also told me, "I love little fat Hispanic boys with breasts. I have an ass-fetish. I can't describe the perfect one, but I know it when I see it. I love old men. I love big fat soft men. A few of the fattest and oldest men are my babies. I put diapers on them. I like the ones that just lie there and love the smell of talc. I love the rotten ones, too, the ones that are naughty and have to be spanked very hard. Other babies need treatment. I say, 'Mommy wants to take your temperature. This is good for you. This is part of your treatment. I'll make this as comfortable for you as possible.' I use a dildo, or I might use my finger. If it's my finger, I wear gloves, two gloves, one over the other. For fisting I use long-sleeved autopsy gloves that a doctor friend gave me. They're totally great gloves."

In the world turned upside down, people in search of pain are nearly as common as people seeking relief from it. This is the other side of treatments. Nurse Wolf was my name for this queen of algolagnia — pleasure from pain. She gave pleasure by inflicting it, she got pleasure from causing it. "Nurse Wolf" because in our talks she described one of her most frequent roles as a nurse in a medical scenario, and it suited her perfectly. I could see the white shoes, the white nurse's outfit, the brisk gestures, the busy hands. In her early thirties, attractive, the picture of health, still looking more like a Texas cheerleader than an art student — she had been both — it was easy to see her as the efficient and unflappable nurse.

She often referred to skills and actual medical knowledge. In her studio she had a medical room and a lot of implements: tongs and scalpels and electrical devices. I remarked several times on her expertise, the specific operations she mentioned, for it cannot be easy to sew buttons on a man's skin, or stitch his penis to his thigh, or put in sutures (even given a dominatrix's skill in tying knots), or use the sharpest scalpels in the manner that people in her line of work call "blood play." But she rejected my compliments and dismissed such procedures as fairly simple — her modest dismissal was very nurse-like — shaking her head and saying, "It's only home surgery.

"Typically, I'm an evil nurse," she explained.

The ritual and theatrical aspects of sexuality were subjects I often pursued with Oliver Sacks. He told me how sadistic attacks on plants were for some men a sexual ritual. He also said, "The universals of costume and uniform become heightened and ritualized in fetishism. Posture is very important. One shows one's posture in one's dress."

In her wardrobe, which included a French maid's outfit and black leather items of her biker-babe role — and much else — Nurse Wolf also had the white dress, the hat, the shoes. And then she enlarged on the eroticism in finding dramatic uses in her nurse scenario for rectal thermometers, high colonics, and the simple exposures and insertions in the more provocative aspects of prostate-poking — sex as proctology.

"'This is for your own good,' I might say. Or it's an examination. 'You have to bend over and we have to see if you're worthy to be my slave.' With the cross-dressers it's, 'Are you a virgin?' It can be a slave-auction scenario or sheer humiliation. There's something incredibly humiliating and exciting about someone they're overpowered by, and being penetrated by."

"So you're a wicked nurse?" I asked.

"There's always that wicked side, but the question is, how pronounced is it? 'Mommy wants to take your temperature.' Nurse does that, too. It's the same kind of line. 'This is part of your treatment.' I am more or less in control that way."

Her authority and assertiveness in the role-playing derived from the discussion beforehand in which all the options were considered. "I say, 'Paint me an image if you don't know the words for it,' and they go, 'I used to watch this show, and this woman used to wear . . .' and they describe it. A lot of people love catsuits. They love Catwoman in *Batman*. And they love that woman Emma Peel from *The Avengers*."

If the role-play was nurse-patient, she urged the client to recount his history — had he had an experience of nurses or hospitals, or physical examinations, and what about a childhood illness?

The promise of "authentic medical exam room" is often made in the advertisements for mistresses in the S & M press. Nurse Wolf's medical room was well fitted out and, with the possible exception of the handcuffs and whips, would not have disgraced a professional gynecologist's examining room, which it greatly resembled. And there was much more equipment elsewhere in the place. "Dungeon" seemed an apt name for two of the rooms, given the furnishings: a black coffin, a steel cage, flogging posts and flogging stools, a rubber body bag that was winched up so that a man could hang like a bat. I had never seen so many clothes or such equipment.

"You wouldn't believe my overhead," Nurse Wolf said.

After many lengthy conversations I seriously wondered whether there was anyone whom Nurse Wolf did not welcome to her place.

Her answer surprised me.

"If someone calls on the phone and says, 'I'm very attractive. I work out all the time and make a lot of money,' I have no interest," Nurse Wolf said. "And younger men are no good. They think they're so handsome. They don't show up on time. They're not respectful — I don't like the young guys at all. Those you're-going-to-tie-me-up-and-keep-me-forever guys. What I want to hear is: 'I haven't had an extensive amount of real experience, but I want to grow in this area, and I fantasize about X, Y, and Z.' Maybe they don't know what it means in their life — that it has a place. I have a lot of great clients."

"What makes a great client?"

"They have a good sense of humor. They respect your time. They like the same things I do. They trust me and appreciate it. I like grateful and really respectful people. The only downside is that after you beat the hell out of them, they call you twenty times afterward to thank you."

As with any other treatment center, a person is not accepted as a client without first being screened and interviewed, and there is always the question of money. Nurse Wolf charges $200 an hour for clients of long standing, $250 for newer clients, sometimes more for lengthy sessions. "I love the crazies and the psycho people, but they are so unstable."

"I imagine flogging someone is pretty exhausting, isn't it? How many would you do in a day?"

"Not many. But I might do longer sessions."

"What's a long session?"

"The longest I like to do is ten hours."

Which is $2,000, but as Nurse Wolf quickly points out, it requires considerable preparation and a lot of cleaning up afterward. "This business can be profitable. Some people make it very profitable. But I travel so much. Also, I am selective. I don't see it as a business as much as I should. Another mistress would have other people working for her. Or would not have so much equipment. They would try to keep their overhead lower. I don't want to do that. I know people who have 900 lines and websites. They offer videos and phone sessions."

Screening is essential. Walk-ins are out of the question: no drop-ins, no strangers. Even men Nurse Wolf thought she knew well have become stalkers, and there are nonstop phone freaks. She knows that when she is alone with her clients anything can happen. Last summer, a dominatrix on the Upper West Side was found bludgeoned to death in her dungeon.

"I am worried about that," Nurse Wolf said. "The clients know where you are, and they think they have something over your head."

One of Nurse Wolf's objections to working in a house — as she did early in her career — was that the clients were not properly screened. Some men wanted sessions with her but considered her unclean, wanted her to cover herself completely in Saran Wrap, and others implored her to strip, "which was out of the question." And others did not want to be dominated at all. "One guy stuck my head in a toilet. I had no idea that I was expected to be a slave at times. I had limits. And of course, in a house they want you to do volume."

So, as Nurse Wolf, and sometimes as Mistress Wolf, or Mommy, she screens everyone beforehand. "I have them write letters. There are a number of things they have to do for me. They have to draw a portrait of themselves on the outside of the envelope, and the envelope also has to contain a picture of their pet, or someone else's pet. Choosing a pet picture tells me a lot about a person. What they're like, their sense of humor. A lot."

After that she talks to the prospective clients on the phone. And when they arrive for their session there is more preparation — discussion, perhaps an hour or more of it, before the session starts.

I asked, "If I said, 'Would you see my friend?', would you?"

"I would want to know a lot — whether it was personal or professional.

I'd ask what sort of experience he's had. 'Who have you really enjoyed seeing?' If someone says, 'No one' — a first-timer — I'm not going to see them, because I'm not sure what I am going to find."

She is one of the busiest and most successful mistresses in Manhattan. As for the preferences, there are all sorts, but a certain random synchronicity develops day by day.

"It goes in waves. I don't know how it happens — it's like being in the subway and everyone's chosen to wear green. One day will be all sissy-maid-cross-dressers-slut day. And the next day very heavy leather."

We met, she and I, as travelers, by chance, both of us being cagey about what we really did for a living, like a bishop and an actress thrown together on the Zambezi. She said she was a photographer; I mumbled something about journalism. In fact, I was working on a novel and she was traveling with one of her slaves, whom she buggered every morning and beat every night, though I was never privileged to observe this unusual spectacle (unusual, at least, in the mellow monotony of a jungle setting). She said she traveled extensively, and it had to be true, for she was knowledgeable and confident. But it was only long after, when we came clean about how we were both self-employed ("I have a dungeon," "I'm a novelist") that she told me how she travels with some clients, prosperous businessmen, heads of companies, tying them up and whipping them back at the hotel after all the day's meetings are over. She especially favored traveling in Germany, Holland, and England. She liked all her clients, but she had a special fondness for the English ones.

"They have a cutely developed sense of kink. They love games. They're also very polite — respectful and formal. And they can be real sluts," she said, smiling with genuine approval. Her descriptive language interested me, because it did not come out of books — she had read almost nothing, yet she sometimes used the neurological or psychological phrases that Oliver Sacks used. For example, speaking of the English, she said, "What matters more is that it's all about some structure and ritual."

I took to her and she to me. "We both have people skills," I said. She laughed at that. She laughed a lot — I liked her cheery mood. "Hey, I'm busy, I've things to do and people to beat," she said sometimes. Or, "Come on over and let's see what we can whip up."

Such lines were the well-honed ripostes of a professional pleaser, but most revealed the good humor a person derives from sheer fulfillment. I saw my fictional doctor, Lauren Slaughter, resident of Half-Moon Street —daytime postgraduate student and nighttime escort—as the embodiment of much of the ambition and self-delusion of the eighties. Nurse Wolf I saw as a Dr. Slaughter for the nineties, not just servicing flagellomaniacs but also having a cultural perspective: she really was a photographer, a record-cover designer, and a maker of videos; she liked the movie *Crumb* and all sorts of performance art. She had an enthusiastic appreciation of modern art. Talking about Francis Bacon one day, I mentioned that he was a masochist who was whipped every evening by his Cockney lover. ("Ready for yer frashing now, Frawncis?") She gushed, "I *love* his paintings. I would *love* to have whipped Francis Bacon." Pop music, even if it wasn't mainstream, was a passion. She knew everything about rock groups like Nashville Pussy or acts such as the Pain-Proof Rubber Girls. There were two Rubber Girls, who contorted together in erotic postures on a bed of nails. They also put cigarettes out on their tongues.

After telling me how people did something shocking like that, Nurse Wolf would say, "Maybe they don't do it in your world, but they do in mine." I liked that very much, her referring to my world and her world.

Her world I knew from advertisements in magazines. It has never been hard to figure out the personal ads; indeed, they have become less entertaining as they have grown more specific. "Cute Jewish male, 55, very fit, own business, seeks full-figured Jewish female, 22–35, for travel southern CA coast" is not necessarily about marriage, whereas "Marriage-minded Catholic female, 34, seeks smart, fun, white successful professional NYC male who has never been married" certainly is. The more upbeat such ads sound, the more desperate they seem, but the subtext of loneliness and frustration is obviously part of the attraction.

Alongside such ads is another sort of classification that, until recently, I had found pretty hard to decode. For decades, "massage" and "relaxation therapy" have been euphemisms for masturbation, but the category of "Role-Play" in mainstream weekly magazines I found distinctly peculiar. The wording of a typical ad, "Sultry Diva—Let me train you . . . Now!— Fetish Exploration/Behavior Modification/Nurse Therapy," just baffled me.

Role-playing was one of Nurse Wolf's specialties. And in a profession where talk costs money and the meter is always running, Nurse Wolf was easygoing and talkative. Her garrulity appealed to me because she was so candid. And her work was not just a job. She was clearly sexually obsessed. Her role-playing was less a living than a way of life that she had been refining since puberty. She had grown up in a suburb, a middle-class home with a swimming pool, in an indulgent family, and was still in regular touch with her folks. She was educated in private schools; she had gone to a great art college. Almost more than anything, I was fascinated by her prosperous upbringing, her prep school, and her cheerleading. What struck me in her reminiscences were her distinct and detailed memories of her girlhood, her close touch with her sexual memory.

"I have a suspicion that obsessive sexuality goes with a clear, continuous, and conscious memory of childhood sexual desire, fantasies, and even activity, without the latent period that other people have," Oliver Sacks once said to me.

To a novelist, latency is a nuisance, and access to the past is a kind of magic — all the better when what is revealed is something forbidden or strange. What I regarded as unspeakable rituals she would term "play." Again, a psychologist's term. And I was fascinated by how immediate her history was to her. Perhaps, as Oliver said, it was part of her obsessive sexuality.

And then there was the question of her world, which was an actual world, one that more and more was referred to in my world with the algolagnic imagery in fashion ads — the long metal heel of a Gucci shoe (called "the Stiletto") pressed onto a man's hairy chest. Gucci offers a stylish nipple ring in silver for $895. In an ad for Bass Ale a man is shown licking a woman's latex boot ("In a world of strange tastes, there's always Bass Ale"). "Tongue for Rent" is the heading in an ad for a New York wine merchant, and there is predictably pervy imagery in an ad for Fetish perfume. Add to these the allegations of the sexual amusements of a well-known sportscaster waiting in fishnet stockings and a garter belt for his date; and a political adviser in a Washington hotel room with a call girl enjoyed (according to the call girl) being naked on all fours, wearing a dog collar, and barking, "Woof-woof!"

The Robert Mapplethorpe photographic exhibition that traveled across America from 1988 to 1990 was a significant event in publicizing the varieties of sexual experience: black leather bullies, men in chains and wearing muzzles and leashes, urolagnia, genital mutilation, fisting, clamping, and piercing were all lovingly adumbrated, along with the photographer's self-portrait in which a bullwhip was rammed up his bum. Mapplethorpe regarded his show as news, and he was satisfied when he achieved his goal of shocking the straight world. Was this inspirational? Perhaps so. It gave at least one Versace fashion show a style: bondage clothes. The work of another photographer, Eric Kroll, is just as bizarre yet in a sense more appealing than Mapplethorpe's — no blood, for one thing. Kroll's photographs of women in bondage, *Beauty Parade* and *Fetish Girls,* have an allegorical quality, though many are also straightforward pornography. Books that would have been available only from specialty bookstores are now mass-market items.

One night after looking over my Nurse Wolf notes I saw a TV comedy, *Just Shoot Me!,* in which one of the characters, Dennis Finch (played by David Spade), becomes madly attracted to a fashion model and ends up suspended in her bedroom in a cage — an actual cage, a classic piece of S & M apparatus, with the laugh line about the willowy fashion model being a closet dominatrix. This gimmick went through various permutations, but the plot point was insistent in implying that Dennis rather liked the experience and happily went back for more punishment. That was shown on NBC, in prime time, on a weeknight a few days before Christmas.

Nurse Wolf has just such a cage in her dungeon, which is in an older red-brick building in a busy neighborhood in Manhattan. It is no more than a numbered door in the middle of a block, the sort of place that is easy to slip into and out of unnoticed.

Go up one steep flight to a small landing, through a door, to a narrow corridor and small rooms that lead to the "studios." Far from having the atmosphere of a commercial space, it looks like an apartment that has been turned into a series of smaller rooms. I smelled burning candles, that aroma of chapels and altars, long before I entered the room. There were thirty or more candles, from tall dripping tapers to vigil lights flickering in cups of liquid wax. They eerily illuminated the room, which would have been eerie even without candle flames. The first object to catch my eye was a steel coffin, standing upright with a cross cut in its lid, and what I took to be a table looked like a steel cage.

"Yes, it is a cage," Nurse Wolf said, "but it doubles as a table. I use it as a cage for overnighters."

Another world, yes, but a recognizable one, for this was clearly a torture chamber. Because of the candle flames the large room was all jumping shadows and wisps of smut and smoke. Black leather predominated. On a suspended steel carousel there was a selection of black leather whips, fifty or more, all types, from horse crops and long whips to the vicious leather whip I recognized as a South African *sjambok,* the very symbol of apartheid. Dangling from other hooks were black leather muzzles, studded black leather masks, bridles and bits, leather gags, and nooses. Nurse Wolf sat on top of the cage in black leather pants and boots and a white T-shirt. Behind her was a large leather seat I took to be a swing.

"What is the purpose of that swing?"

"Sling," she said, correcting me. "Typically, in gay culture you'd say it was a fisting sling. It supports a very vulnerable bondage position where you're completely immobilized. The idea is that you sit on the very edge here. Your legs are shackled and your arms tied. Then you're completely exposed to whatever happens to you."

"And what might that be?"

"Fisting, but I don't do much fisting anymore," Nurse Wolf said. "I loved it. It was like stuffing a turkey. It takes a long time. It can take an hour to open a guy up, but one guy was a lot easier — more open."

And then she mentioned the long autopsy gloves that her doctor friend gave her.

"Or you can do relatively tight bondage in it — which I prefer, honestly. I like it when people don't move at all, or they can move a little bit but they're still not going anywhere."

That tight bondage was more a reflection of her own skill, for it was important to Nurse Wolf that the person to be treated felt completely helpless, unable even to wriggle.

"They get into a state of acceptance much more quickly if they're completely immobilized," she said. "Or they become completely traumatized. It's one or the other."

When I asked "Do they get more excited the tighter it is?" she said that it was impossible to generalize, and she made a larger and more pedantic point. She was insistent that I refrain from generalizing about any part of what she did. "People are all different," she said. I misunderstood if I noticed a classical piece of torture apparatus and saw only a person writhing in pain. "Respecting limits" and "passing to another level" were both repeated mantras in the world of S & M and role-playing. Cross-dressing did not mean that a man wanted actually to change his gender, for this was role-play: "If someone's being forced into cross-dressing, they don't want necessarily to be a woman, but they want to be treated like a slutty woman and kind of forced to do things that are their worst nightmare, that are also very exciting."

"Forced cross-dressing" meant that she dressed them. "I constantly get requests for this kind of thing. Every level of clothing. They say, 'I have to be made to do it.'" If they enjoyed cross-dressing without needing for it to be demanded of them, they often brought their own wardrobe. Sometimes they arrived soberly dressed in a business suit but underneath wore women's underwear. And any sort of dressing might involve a whipping.

I remarked on the whips — their number, their complexity, the quality, too, for they were well made.

"Is that a mace?" It was a heavy spiked ball attached by a thick chain to a club. Traditionally, a mace was a war club used to smash body armor.

"I haven't used it yet," she said. "Let's see, what else? These are nice. I like these padded muzzles."

It was another black leather piece, heavily stitched, with fasteners. The sturdiness of the equipment was impressive, but of course this was not merely costume stuff for a musical of *The Man in the Iron Mask* or *Dracula*, or for dressing up for a costume ball; this muzzle was buckled to a man's face and put to the test.

"This one was made to order, because I wanted to be able to tie it down. I like to do head bondage. I need stuff that you can attach to other things."

She saw me smiling in bewilderment.

"It's a playground," she said.

And there were masks on a shelf above the cage. Silly rubber masks and animal masks and hoods. One that even Nurse Wolf agreed was particularly scary was a hood mask with no eye holes, padded ears to muffle sound, and only a small breathing hole at the mouth.

"It's got headphones in here at the ears, so they're completely disoriented. It's scary. You can try it on if you want. It's really claustrophobic."

I said no and changed the subject, pointing to the huge steel coffin that stood upright and dominated the rear of the dungeon.

"A friend of mine is a sculptor. He made it for me. I watched a lot of

Hammer movies when I was a kid, so this is totally my fetish, you know? I use it very infrequently here, unless I'm playing with someone who's really crazy about it."

"Have you been in it?"

"Yes. I like it. Get into it so that you can hear what it sounds like."

I got into the coffin. Nurse Wolf closed the lid. I felt the sensation of being buried alive: I was squeezed and suffocated and plunged into a soundless blackness. I felt for a way of freeing myself, but I touched only a series of hooks around the edge, which were for restraining the coffin occupant.

"Isn't that coffin totally great?" Nurse Wolf said through the small cutout cross in the lid.

Another day, feeling that I knew only her professional life, I asked her to reconstruct the previous twenty-four hours. I was interested in what a typical day might be, including free time and domestic activity. I was now well aware that she whipped men for a living — and not only whipped them but indulged them in all sorts of ways, from listening to their bizarre fantasies to suspending them from the ceiling in rubber body bags. And there were also the diapers and the sutures.

I had wondered: Does she do it just for the money, or is she compulsive? The answer was, thunderously, that she was compulsive — that thought and fantasy and dedication were all part of her effort; she found what she did exhausting but also vastly enjoyable. She liked her clients — liked them best when they were wordlessly being flogged. The ones she did not like she sent away, and she regarded her refusal to whip them as the worst punishment she could inflict on them.

The previous day had been Sunday. Sundays in the straight world tend to be different from weekdays, but her Sunday — this one at any rate — she said was an average day, except that she had had trouble with her car.

The day had started all right, though. "I woke up at seven or eight and made seared tuna with this wasabi-soy marinade. I have fish every morning for breakfast. Then I left at about twelve and helped my boyfriend with his computer for a while."

So far, apart from the wasabi-soy marinade, this seemed the sort of unexceptional Sunday anyone might have. But it was still only noon.

"I had a session around one," Nurse Wolf said. "I was a little late. He drove in — it's an hour or so — from Queens. When he saw I hadn't arrived, he called me on my cellular phone. I told him to go buy some seltzer water. They're always happier if they have some little tasks. Then he arrives and says, 'Nice pants.' They were new, beautiful tiger-stripe pants. I decided to be nice to him. We talked for a little while. Then I tormented him. I gave him some heavy nipple stuff — really squeezed his nipples. He wasn't tied up. He was still dressed, which is more of a trauma. I tied him up, face-up. Very few are face-down. If they're face-up there's more to play with."

Casting her mind back to her narrative of the previous day, she frowned, and hesitated, and shook her head. I sensed a certain regret in the set of her mouth.

"I decided to try something new," she said. She sighed. That was obviously the regret. "I thought it would be great, but no — it was a mistake. I had to fuck with the perfect mixture. I could have just let him suck my dirty toes. If I had just come from the gym I could have let him lick my armpits. I had forgotten that he didn't like anything anal. But I stuck my finger in him — I was wearing several gloves — and I could tell he was disappointed. He didn't really like it. I love piercing and probing. Here's a body. You can probe it. But he didn't have a great reaction to it. After the session he says, 'It's really uncomfortable. It's really weird. Maybe it's the way I'm built.'"

The man then left, unsatisfied, perhaps disturbed — emotions that Nurse Wolf shared, for she had hoped to bring him to another level, and it had failed. Such men were usually predictable, she said; not like babies in her infantilism role-playing. She should have stuck with the man's own requirements, cliché-ridden as they might have seemed.

As though jinxed, she left her dungeon and had trouble with her car. The key wouldn't turn in the door lock. "I couldn't get my finger into his ass, couldn't get the key into the lock. I didn't push any of the right buttons! It's Sunday — no mechanic. I went to Kmart for some WD-40."

I tried to imagine Nurse Wolf shopping in big biker boots, with her big leather backpack, on aisle 9, "Automotive" — *Attention Kmart shoppers!* — looking for heavy-duty motor lubricants. But there were probably others dressed just like her on this New York Sunday.

The WD-40 didn't work. She fussed with the car lock for a while, then around six went back to the dungeon to change for dinner. She then got a call from a mistress friend, Dale, inviting her over to her place to drop in on a session in progress. "I've got a dinner engagement. I can give you forty minutes," Nurse Wolf said.

The client turned out to be a mystery. Neither Dale nor Nurse Wolf had ever seen his face.

"He always comes in in a business suit, wearing a latex catsuit under it, and that includes a mask," she told me. "It's custom made. He wears dark glasses, too. From the look of his body he's in his mid- to late thirties. He's in good shape. It makes me think that he might be famous or recognizable. You never know. He might just be paranoid."

I said, "If Dale doesn't know his name, what does she call him?"

"Slave, Cocksucker. She calls him a lot of things."

It was early evening, seven o'clock, by the time Nurse Wolf had dressed and put on her makeup. She went in wearing what the man had requested —a catsuit and thigh-high boots. The man's head and feet were tied down, but his hands and arms were free.

Dale was sitting on a throne behind his head, with her feet on his chest. Nurse Wolf said, "Why are this pathetic creature's hands not tied?"

"Oh, because even though he's doing a horrible job, I'm trying to teach him to worship my legs."

"Isn't this a waste of your valuable time?" Nurse Wolf asked.

"I don't know why I bother!" And Dale said to the man, "You don't know how lucky you are. I can't believe she'd be interested in seeing someone like you — she is Mistress Wolf. And you can't even massage my feet well."

"Does he do anything right?" Nurse Wolf asked.

"Hardly," Dale said, stepping on the man's face.

The two women started to laugh. The man made "barnyard sounds" inside his hood. He was tied face-up with chains between two posts on the floor. His hands were free but his penis and testicles were tied with surgical tubing to his toes. Dale got up from her throne and they started to do a dance over him.

The exciting part of a session, Nurse Wolf said, is not quite knowing where it is leading — extemporizing, in the manner of Method actors preparing a scene. So the women danced on the hooded man. Readers of *Vogue, Elle,* and *Harper's Bazaar* will find what followed vividly familiar, for the dominatrices' sharp heels pierced the man's chest as clearly depicted in the Gucci shoe ad for its Stiletto.

Dale said, "I think I have to pee."

Nurse Wolf said, "Well, I really have to go, so I'll do that part if you want — but I don't want him to see."

The man was berated into putting his hands over the holes in his hood while Nurse Wolf squatted and urinated on Dale's toes. "I'd never done that before. It was so great, I loved it. I could care less about men. This is so much not for men." Dale put her feet in his mouth and demanded that he suck her toes. The men hesitated and seemed to panic.

"I'm afraid I'll do it wrong," the hooded man wailed.

"Like everything else you do," Dale said, and the women laughed again. "What a wuss you are!"

The man was confused. Tied up, writhing, he struggled to think of the right answer while the two women stood on his naked body.

I wondered aloud whether he had liked his session.

"They always do when you're enjoying yourself," Nurse Wolf said.

She did not speculate on who the man might be. "I'm not really up on who people are, but someone would probably recognize him." She did not ask: she respected a person's demands, and she wanted hers to be respected. It was important in such a business for people to be comfortable, and — paradoxically, given the fact that they were flogged unmercifully — to feel safe.

The session ended. Nurse Wolf changed her clothes again, met her boyfriend, and they went out to eat at a good restaurant with another couple and enjoyed an excellent meal. All in all, Nurse Wolf thought, not a bad day.

"I didn't start out wanting to be a professional mistress at all," Nurse Wolf said. It had started purely as play, in her prep school. In the seventh grade, at age thirteen, she became a cheerleader. Homecoming was a big Texas thing that lasted a week and involved the whole school. One of the festivities was a slave auction.

"You could buy anyone that day," Nurse Wolf said. "I forget what the other days were. Obviously for me Slave Day was a little more prominent than all the other days. You could buy a slave for the week. Anybody could buy anybody, and there were groups of people that would buy someone."

This voluntary slave auction was for a charity — the Pep Club or whatever the current campaign might be, hunger or homelessness. The stipulation was that within limits it was acknowledged as public humiliation.

"It was flattering to be bought, and it was also a horrible thing," Nurse Wolf said. "Seventh grade was the year I bought Kent Sanford. I'd had a crush on him for years. Finally I bought him, and he was mine. I dressed him in my cheerleading outfit, with full makeup, and that's how it all started."

Kent loved it. Nurse Wolf realized that Kent had perhaps never cross-dressed before that. He was transformed — he fell utterly for Nurse Wolf.

The next year, when she was in the eighth grade, the television series *Roots* came out. The dynamics of the master-slave relationship and the details of domination and submission — the whips, the handcuffs, the shouted orders, the pleading — had a profound effect on her. She saw every episode of *Roots*. She began to think that you could make anyone do anything.

"My mother used to say, 'Men and boys only tease you when they like you.' Basically, I guess I was fascinated by what I could make them do just by telling them. They would do the silliest things. They didn't want to make decisions. They wanted a girl to say, 'Wear my underwear!'"

The notions came through play and experiment. And she admitted that at first she had no clear idea what she was doing, that she was traveling down a road that was first surveyed by the Marquis de Sade. She never read anything about it. Reading did not feature much in shaping or informing her in her tastes. ("You know Krafft-Ebing?" I asked her once, and she said, "Who?") Her tastes were shaped in the time-honored way: learning by doing.

"They said, 'Do I have to?' I said, 'Of course you have to. I won you in an auction.'"

She had a series of "semiplatonic" boyfriends after that. There was no sex, but there was serious play. "In Texas you get all this pool activity. I would draw on them with lipstick and then send them home. They'd worry that their mother or their maid would find out. It was tricky for them."

None of them objected — at least none of the boys she met. She was being playful. The play continued into high school. Her choice of college was fairly easy. She liked art and design. She was a serious student but was also simultaneously broadening her interests in S & M. She had friends at nearby colleges. "I used to play with them and used to photograph their heavy scenes. They were into a lot of blood play."

After graduation in the mideighties, she came to New York. The S & M scene was less open; people met at parties — "play parties." "I dressed. I was a sadist. But you don't learn the skills overnight."

The play at parties seldom goes on in private rooms, and the public nature of these displays of domination and submission means that a practitioner can quickly develop a reputation for being an expert mistress. Nurse Wolf was observed and admired; she was invited to work at various dungeons. The first was the now-defunct West Side Dungeon, which was run by a Hasidic man.

Nurse Wolf says that fifteen years ago there were far fewer establishments in New York than there are now. Even she is astonished by how popular such activity is, how accessible, how much of its imagery is in the mainstream. Still, she is less surprised by the clients than by the mistresses in the houses.

"Some of those people I wouldn't let out on the street. The mistresses were psychotic. And I had more equipment at home than they had in their studios. They'd have a piece of rope and a Ping-Pong paddle. I had beautiful custom-made leather whips."

She had to lay down ground rules: No "toilet service." No foul namecalling. Hasidic men could be trying. "They find women filthy. They want everything to be kosher in a way — 'Is everything safe? Is everything clean?' Then it's, 'Can you beat me on the hands and tell me I'm bad?' They think I'm unclean. They are really into the visual, so it's, 'Take your blouse off.' There's no way I would do that. I am not going to undress for them. This young kid says to me, 'Let's see what you have between your legs,' which I find offensive. I said, 'I have a raw piece of pork between my legs.'"

One day she was asked to do a Hasidic man who smelled terrible. He had not washed. He demanded "a Nazi interrogation" in which she was to be the Bitch of Buchenwald, questioning him, slapping his face, abusing him verbally. He gave her precise instructions: she was to wear shiny black boots, a cap with a shiny black visor, and black leather gloves.

She had been warned about this man, but she knew him by another name. She was too new to the business to know that clients visiting houses had many aliases. This was an unstable man.

He was tied up, but his head was not tied, and at the end of the session, thoroughly interrogated and humiliated, he kissed her when she leaned too close, sticking his tongue in her mouth. That earned him the hardest slap of the session. Nurse Wolf was angry and disgusted — she hurried away and gargled with peroxide. And afterward the man took a shower. "That pissed me off. Not before, but after he had been with me. See?"

In all her stories of whipping and cutting and broken canes and blood, few things offended her more than that unwelcome kiss. Speaking of the risks in her work, she told me about it more than once, always in tones of amazement and disgust.

"So there are some things that repel you?"

"Yes, but mainly I don't want to be told what to do."

The term for this behavior is "SAM" (smart-ass masochist) or "topping from the bottom" (a slave giving orders). Nurse Wolf describes it as backseat driving, and hates it.

"And there are things you like to do?"

"Oh, yes. I love everything I do, or else I wouldn't do it."

There was such intensity in the way she spoke about her fantasies and her own pleasure that the word "work" was inadequate for what she did every day. And as she worked out in a gym most days, she was in superb physical condition: in our usual farewell bear hug, she unfailingly left me winded.

But by almost any reckoning she was involved in the darkest pleasures imaginable. She described many of them to me in detail, down to the exhausted howls of pleasure of a manacled and bent-over man, his skin splitting open and blood bursting from it under the crack of a whip. "The chance to probe someone's body," as she put it, gave her intense pleasure. She was fascinated by Japanese rope bondage and esoteric knots, by any variation that fed her sadism. "Very subtle changes make me very happy." But what was the point of all this pain and darkness? Nurse Wolf said, "Hot things to me are not dark." A look of pleasurable anticipation that brought to mind a sharp appetite lighted her face whenever an image of submission was suggested. "Girls look great when they're tied up," she said. "Some men bring me girlfriends as a sort of offering." But Nurse Wolf was so ambiguous sexually that words such as "gay" or "straight" do not begin to describe the nuances of her polymorphous perversity, nor her quest for erotic variation, which makes *The Story of O* seem like a simple prologue to her pleasures.

One man impressed her by having the highest pain threshold she had ever encountered. "I broke canes on him," she said admiringly. And there was the cross-dressing college friend, whom she described to me as "a rat boy sheltering in the comfort of other men." There are people who would see her for a session every day if she agreed. But shaking her head she admitted the paradox: "These people are junkies."

She told me, "I am looking for a man who can take anything. I have found one, but not a sane one, just the crazies." With one man, a successful businessman and obsessive masochist, it was almost love. He could take anything. He kept asking for more. "I pushed him to another level, and then I couldn't handle it. It was the pain. I don't think he had ever been beaten as hard as I was beating him. And then he was craving it. He was into services — being tied up and played with. I ran him through the wringer. He had to work for everything. And because I was attracted to him, I was beating him harder each time. Usually on the ass. After a caning I don't think he could undress in front of his wife for weeks. I would break canes on him, too."

The man ceased to be a client, left his wife, became Nurse Wolf's lover — well, a sort of lover: her utter slave. But his almost limitless capacity for degradation became such a burden it was as though she was his servant, and at last he exhausted her patience. "I don't think I'd ever do anything like that again. It was awful."

This talk of variety led inevitably to her wondering where my pleasure lay.

"I think I am pretty dull," I said. This talk of pain did nothing but turn my manhood into a peanut.

"No one's dull."

"Maybe," I said. "Funnily enough, the brand name Rubbermaid has always interested me for some reason."

"Yeah." And she smiled wickedly, looking into my heart.

She said, "I like Rubber Queen!"

When she was in a house, she worked in shifts of five to seven hours, getting $70 out of the $200 the client paid. She sometimes did twelve-hour sessions. But she left the house. "I didn't want to be chosen from a book. One time I had a handprint on my face from a slap. I ended a great relationship over that."

Off and on, she had worked in houses for five years. The best place was the Nutcracker Suite, which is still in business. In a house she was on call, and had to see everyone who requested her. She liked the freedom of just coming and going, but there were problems if she broke the rules, and there were penalties, a fine for each infraction. She was fined for being late, fined for running over a timed session. In a dungeon, more than in most businesses, time was money.

Regular work in houses had allowed Nurse Wolf to accumulate some savings. Using that, she set up on her own. To someone unfamiliar with the world of S & M, it may seem unusual that a plumber or an electrician will arrange a sort of barter in return for his work, but this was the case for some subcontractors whose tastes were masochistic. After a day's work putting a ball cock in a toilet or replacing the washers in medical room faucets, the plumber stripped naked, and Nurse Wolf bent him over her flogging stool and thrashed the daylights out of him.

This subject came up when I speculated about the wealth of her clients. Most were powerful men, but some had very little money or had been laid off, and some saved up for a long time to pay for a session. Nurse Wolf said that she often reduced her rates or played with clients in return for work they might do at her studio.

"There's an electrician. He's been laid off his job. He'll come in and do things. And I have people who come in and clean. I do sessions with them if they can't afford it."

"So an electrician or a cleaner will say, 'I'm into forcible cross-dressing.'"

"It will be something that I suggest. And it will only be after I've known them for a while."

"What will you suggest?"

"I needed some errands done. I don't want them to be done by someone who wanted to be a houseboy or a slave. I wanted it to be by someone I trusted, who knew my real name, my bank account, when I sent out chunks of money to pay for things. Someone who could clean a little and that didn't act so slavey that I didn't want him around. So I found someone, and I asked if he wanted to do things every week or couple of weeks in return for a session. He was delighted."

"What did he like?"

"Very heavy corporal things. So I could cane him as hard as I liked. He liked being passed around to friends. He was grateful for every bit of attention."

"Where would he normally be caned? On the ass?"

"Uh-huh. But he could take it anywhere. I just don't want to injure someone. I do it on the back. The soles of the feet are fine. But I've seen people bullwhipped, and it wraps around the calf or their chest, and I think it's dangerous."

Nurse Wolf is not unusual in finding mechanics or housekeepers who will work for a whipping. In the domination newspapers, *S & M News, Dominant View,* and *Dominant Mystique,* there are often classifieds suggesting whippings for work: "Young, attractive & Very Experienced Dominant Female with Complete Dungeon, seeks Dedicated Submissive Male Carpenter . . . to Make Fairly Sophisticated Dungeon Furniture and do alterations to my home in exchange for time spent as your personal temptress, torturer, and object of all your submission."

Nurse Wolf's dungeon was expensive for her to set up, but operating on her own was preferable to being a mistress in a house or large dungeon. For one thing, it was more profitable, but more than anything she began to understand that repeat business was the best, most dependable, and the safest.

Clients from the houses followed her to her studio the way patients follow a dental hygienist who moves to another practice. Some of Nurse Wolf's clients have been seeing her for eight or nine years; others she has known even longer. "I've done people before they've met their wives, before they've had kids. Their kids are now growing up."

A client she has been seeing for seven years recently said that he had something important to tell her. He wanted her to know his real name. It was one of the most dramatic moments in all her dealings with him. Nurse Wolf told him it was not necessary for him to divulge his actual identity, but he insisted.

"For him it was a big thing, that he trusted me enough to tell it to me."

Nurse Wolf likes such people because she enjoys working with clients who have intricate fantasies that become more complex over time and demand intense role-playing, such as the man whose role-playing takes place entirely in an office — and the scene is probably based on his own office.

"The names of the people are very important in this office," Nurse Wolf explained. The cast of characters is large — everyone except this man is female. "He is the only man who's left in this all-woman company. He's wrongfully accused of sneaking a glance at a woman. He's presented with an ultimatum, about losing his job not for making an obscene gesture but for this glance. It's dress-down day. A complaint is filed. It's all women.

They say, 'No man should be allowed to do this.' He has a choice: get fired and lose all his benefits and money and everything, or agree to be a slave."

"And you beat him?"

"No. He's not tied up — we sit here talking. He's forced to make a decision about being completely destitute or to have a contract with the office to live there — to live there naked, to be like a toilet servant. We've now designed a cage for him in one fantasy. It's got a thing that he drinks out of, much like a hamster would — all the toilets feed into that. He licks my toilet. After I've cleaned it. I know he would lick it no matter what, but I don't want him to lick something that's filthy. I don't want people to lick the bottom of my shoes. I know they would. But I don't want them to get some wacky disease."

Among her most devoted clients were the ones she called her babies. Speaking of baby culture, the role-playing called infantilism, Nurse Wolf became almost sentimental. In her smirking sadistic heart there was something strongly maternal. It was her passion for control, her love of detail, and her particular liking for passive clients and unexpected mischief. Babies satisfied her on many levels.

"My fat old babies," Nurse Wolf said, smiling at the thought. "They're so cute. I used to see more than I do now, but I've disassembled my nursery. It's so jammed with stuff. I need more closet space!"

She had a playpen, a big one with steel bars. She even had a baby, Bambi, a grown woman ("She'd scare a real baby terribly") who played at infantilism. "Bambi and I met at the Babyland photo shoot. She wanted a full-time mommy, and I wanted a full-time baby. She was a rotten baby. She got spanked a lot. I didn't have to change her diapers — she wasn't into that. She did things in order to be punished. Which I like. I like that kind of rotten baby. I also like the sweet ones that just lie there."

For babies, she wore a French maid's or a pink satin mommy's outfit. "I'm a cartoon mommy with big high shoes and stockings and lips like this," she said, pursing her lips and making a fish mouth.

Babies are more specific about their wardrobe than any other role-playing client.

"Like three — not two, not four — layers of diapers. They have to be cotton. 'I want those bunnies with the pencils on them.'"

Some babies say, "I want to go on an adventure!" Nurse Wolf, ever obliging, takes them on an adventure. They wear diapers and plastic pants under their clothes, making crinkling sounds as they walk.

"I take this one old baby with one of my girlfriends," Nurse Wolf said. "She comes and visits me. She's a great mistress. She's wicked. We're in a bar with a pool table and I say to the baby, 'You stand over there,' and we make out — this is in a bar around the corner — and she torments him, blows smoke in his face. The baby poops in his pants. We make him play pool, or stand up and sit down really hard."

Of all her clients, the babies are the least predictable. It was possible to make generalizations about leather fetishists, flagellomaniacs, blood players, toilet servants, masochists, slaves, sensory-deprivation junkies, and even bug crunchers, but when it came to infantilism anything was possible. Some are interested only in being dressed. Others have to be changed constantly. Some misbehaved in order to be punished. Others just lay there wanting to be caressed. They loved the smell of talc. Some loved the experience of being diapered, others craved bottle feeding, and you never knew what they wanted in their bottle — beer, chocolate milk, Coke, whatever. Sensual babies wanted to feel safe. Naughty babies tried to get under Nurse Wolf's skirt and had to be restrained. Some babies loved roaming the streets. That baby they took to the bar wanted to be called Stinky Poo-Poo Pants.

In their own worlds, the babies are often power brokers needing to submit, to be caned, to be mommied. These were grown men, big men in every respect — businessmen, heads of companies, stock analysts, real estate speculators, corporate attorneys — who liked nothing better than engaging for an hour or two a week in mommy-baby role-play.

Two generalizations were possible. Baby clients were always shaved. Also, babies loved shoes and often had foot and leg fixations. Nurse Wolf's explanation was that long ago, when these big men were tiny and impressionable, that was the angle they caught, looking up at a real mommy.

I wondered whether babies — or any of these people — had orgasms. After all, wasn't that the point?

"No. I see a lot of people who are denied that. That's part of the treatment. They're sent out without any release. I think there's also a liberating feeling of completely relinquishing your power."

She did not find it odd that most of the people she saw were very successful. "It's a vacation for them to be controlled, to be told what to do — to give pleasure to someone else. I don't engage in any overtly sexual stuff at all, but I can train someone to give the best foot massage."

One of her most powerful clients comes in once a week to submit to Nurse Wolf. His particular fetish is to be a sissy slave and to make her happy. Time is of no importance — five minutes, an hour, five hours; his kink is serving. He is not tied up. He is not restrained, though he does wear a leather collar. He also wears panties. Pleasure for him is nearly always crouching in his collar and pink panties and painting her toenails.

He happens to be a businessman. She sees many such men. She has noticed that the soberest and straightest-looking businessmen have a passion for secret tattoos and hidden piercings. She suspects that the ones from out of town arrange their New York meetings in order to see her. They call and say, "I've got a window between five and seven. I'm definitely coming."

If they say, "Do you have any special instructions for me beforehand?" Nurse Wolf replies, "Go to Victoria's Secret. Get satin panties. Get this color nail polish. Wear the panties. Get your toenails painted by the time you're here." And they obey.

Some of this is so harmless it is almost lovable. The babies, the pedicurist in his panties, the cross-dressers, the obedient attorneys. There is no pain, nothing of what Nurse Wolf would call "heavy corporal," only role-play.

The determiners are cultural as well as in our personal history. In Nurse Wolf's studio there is no censor, no political correctness. No ethnic group is spared and, predictably, the most victimized ethnic groups act out their fantasies in what Nurse Wolf calls "the psychodrama" of role-playing. This is related to the Englishman's "cutely developed sense of kink" and his reliving the exquisite humiliation of a public school caning, but it goes further. In this sense her dungeon is an artifact of the mainstream, something influenced by the ethnicity in child-rearing — the nanny-mommy nexus, the spanking ethic — but darker fantasies are induced by racial history. It is not for Nurse Wolf to condemn; on the contrary, it is one of the paradoxes of her sadism that she is obliged to become a willing partner. Many of the fantasies are imposed on her.

Whenever I mentioned the mothering, the dressing up, the ritual punishments that are common in the most apple pie–eating American households, she talked about how inventive Jews and Catholics could be, because of the repressiveness in their upbringing. They were intensely fetishistic.

I had wondered whether she saw any African Americans. Yes, she said, she did. Like the Nazi interrogation demanded by the Jewish client, the role-playing and submission asked for by African Americans are among the darker desires of her clients.

"I see two black men, both in their late sixties. They're into heavy bondage—abduction scenarios. The scene is in Botswana. They are sneaking around and peeking at me. I've got to capture them and tie them up. He's screaming, 'Don't tie me up!'"

One of them she met at an S & M party some years ago. A friend of hers said, "I want you to meet my slave."

The black man was tied up and being verbally abused ("You little nigger") while having cigarette ashes being flicked at his head.

I said, "Doesn't this go against everything you believe?"

"If you know where something's coming from, and you both enter into a situation where you can explore things that are really dark, it's more pure in a way. I had to ascertain really quickly: Is this guy sound of mind? Is this going to destroy him? Is this going to do something destructive? When I make that determination, it's by mutual agreement."

"How was he dressed?"

The man lay face-down on a table, naked, spread-eagled, with arms and legs tied down.

"I leaned over and whispered, 'I saw you looking at her milky-white breasts. What were you thinking about?'"

The other mistresses came over and took turns beating him.

"We had a great experience," Nurse Wolf said, "but I crossed a real line for myself. I was saying, 'You wanna go here? Then go here—and it might be a lot further than you anticipated.' I couldn't say to this guy, 'Have a positive feeling about yourself.'"

When Nurse Wolf told me she was especially fond of her Japanese clients, I told her about *Pink Samurai,* a detailed book about eroticism in Japanese life, the slave girl fantasies that involve torture, the schoolgirl fantasies in which soiled panties figure—selling panties is a sideline for many entrepreneurial Japanese schoolgirls. As for the defecation fantasies, Nurse Wolf said that her Japanese clients had never expressed any interest, but that she had wanted to see what it was all about.

A few women came in and did sessions. Nurse Wolf understood her own limits then. She was revolted by it. As she told me the story, her face was fixed in a look of utter disgust.

"I have a couple of great Japanese clients. My Japanese are totally into being punished. I know this Japanese guy who is into serious rope bondage. Japanese rope bondage is really beautiful, and each rope has a purpose. It's creative, it's really satisfying. Sometimes, just to learn, I've switched roles — it's great. But I want to be doted on. I want to be dominant."

Not all the clients visit alone. "How do I get my wife interested in this?" is a common question that Nurse Wolf has to answer. She urges them to bring the woman in, wife or girlfriend. Nurse Wolf said that she dominates the man while the woman watches, and often the woman becomes excited while watching the man being forcibly cross-dressed or expertly humili- ated or whipped. Nurse Wolf sometimes makes the man serve the wife or lover; she ties the man up — head bondage, whatever — and forces him to be the woman's sex slave. Some women become obsessed and end up can- ing their men with startling gusto.

A loved one's connivance is an advantage, since most of her clients are forced to be covert. It poses a problem if a man wishes his taste for pain to be hidden from his wife or girlfriend. Are the men going to have to take their clothes off in another room for a month? Nurse Wolf asks rhetorically.

"One man went home with a perfect handprint on his face. He had to come up with a mugging story. Or rope burns on his wrists, or mask lines are another — someone sweating in a black leather mask and they have stains on their face. A whip is likely to wrap around the thigh and cause obvious bruising."

Several couples requested a branding. This is more Blacksmith X than Nurse Wolf, though medicine played a part. She heated a piece of metal, let it cool a little, and branded the man on his buttocks, scarring him for life. But that was the intention. Another man was branded with his wife's name.

Cutting, or blood play, calls for a medical room session and, in addition to satisfying the man's masochism, it calls upon all the resources of Nurse Wolf in her Wicked Nurse role.

"I do a fair amount of cutting and sewing," Nurse Wolf said, describing the actual suturing. "I might sew the penis to the leg, or do cuts around the nipples or the arms."

When I seemed alarmed by her mention of scalpels and suturing, she said she did not cut deep or do anything risky.

Surely sewing a man's penis to his leg did not fall into the category of a mother's sense of fun?

"It's only dangerous if you don't sew it with enough stitches, and they pull out. You sew all the skin. You have to attach it at enough points so the likelihood of it pulling out is not great. There's only a few people I do it with. And the idea is that they go out to dinner with their other mistress, or call girl, or whatever, and they have to stay in that position. I've sutured nipples and wrapped the sutures around their neck so if they didn't stay in a certain position, it was painful, and it was difficult for them to, say, put their coat on. So it's a continual public humiliation."

One novelty was her sewing a man's foreskin together at the tip and then sewing a button to it. The man loved it. She was amazed by the level of pain he endured. He went out to dinner afterward with an Asian woman ("Not a hooker, I can tell"). The woman was part of the treatment. The whole point was that he was not allowed release. The woman brought snippers, and after dinner she snipped off the sutures.

Hearing this painful procedure, I winced and said, "Isn't this dangerous? Any of these things could hurt someone if used to excess. I mean, you can die."

Nurse Wolf became visibly upset and covered her face. "Please don't say that. Touch something! I don't want that negative stuff around here. I've had virtual 911 experiences. Really scary. And I do a lot of really heavy things. I mean, if someone's hooked up to an electrical device and they're hanging on my suspension in the other room — if someone's hanging by their ankles and they pass out, that's a big responsibility. Or there are the ones I electrocute. I use a TENS unit — it's a thing for nerve stimulation — little, like, jolts of electricity. It's been adapted for kinky use."

This was Nurse Wolf at her darkest, wickedest. She described using this nerve stimulator with its accessories, one of which was a catheter. Such equipment is offered for sale in the S & M magazines. A Master High-Frequency model with a selection of electrodes goes for $189, along with "authentic" prison wrist shackles and leg irons, and "enema and colonic supplies."

"An electrified catheter has got to be sanitary," she said. "Got to swab carefully! The catheters come in different thicknesses. I insert it and switch on the electricity."

This was popular with some clients, but now and then a man asks for something he cannot handle.

"One guy is into very heavy bondage. I call it cause-and-effect bondage. If he moves one way, it hurts — for example, a pierced nipple will move on a pierced testicle. He is always affecting his own pain level, too. If he's squirming from being caned on the ass, he's going to feel other stuff. He's also into sensory deprivation, so the combination of all these things that he can't physically handle means that he's going to lose it sometime. If he's not breathing properly in this state, he's not going to be able to say, 'I think I'm going to pass out.'"

"What does he say?"

"I have some safe words. If something isn't working, I have them say, 'This isn't working.' But I don't want them to control the session, like 'Code Red' or 'Mercy,' because that way they're in control."

"But what if they did say that?"

"Then I would back off. Because if they did say that, there's problems. But I'm into heavy chains. I don't want to waste my time. 'A light whipping, please.' Forget it. I'm old and jaded. I think, What's that? You can't take that? I was in one session with a guy and I said, 'Look at you. You said you'd do anything for me. And you can't take it!' Dale was there, sitting in.

"I said to Dale, 'Beat me. Use that on me to show him what an incredible wuss he is. Such a baby.'

"I changed places. I was like, 'I don't like this. I don't even do this and I can take more than you!'"

A serious problem arose with a man who wanted to be wrestled into submission, facing two women wrestlers. Nurse Wolf, who is game for most activities and had trained in boxing, teamed up with another woman in wrestling sessions.

Her name was Daisy. She was on steroids. She was attractive, well built, and covered in tattoos. With a select and devoted clientele, she would fly around the country and do wrestling sessions. It was serious wrestling, in a hotel room, so it was private.

"We'd sometimes do tag team. We'd go to, say, Ohio. I'd wear a long wig. We'd go to these Holiday Inns and do wrestling sessions. Sometimes we'd meet pilots or whoever in the bar, and Daisy would say, 'Hey, want to wrestle for a couple of dead presidents? Got a couple of dead presidents on you?' She was great. The guys would be terrified."

On one occasion at a Holiday Inn in Manhattan they met a teacher who had flown in from Canada for the session. It was almost a disaster.

"He was small — about 160 pounds. Daisy could bench-press him. She could hold him over her head. He was paying three or four hundred, and I was getting a hundred. I was doing head scissors on this guy and I'm squeezing the fuck out of him. I'm squeezing his carotid artery and he passes out and gets a spasm."

Meanwhile, Daisy was saying, "He's fine, keep going!"

"His head is between my thighs and he's spasming. I was torturing him. I let him go and he dropped. I thought he was dead. He spasms, and then he passes out, and I'm thinking, The guy's dead. Then Daisy slaps him really hard and does CPR on him. He comes back."

The man was groggy and disoriented from having fainted, but when he realized where he was, he said, "Okay, let's go." He wanted more.

"I couldn't believe it. I ended up putting my gloves on and beating the fuck out of him. 'I hate you for almost dying!' I don't think he was happy with his black eye. His nose was bleeding. His lip was split. His nose was across his face. I loved it. Afterward I made him take us out for sushi."

There have been other emergencies, many involving friends who know Nurse Wolf's cool head and resourcefulness in a crisis.

"I got this phone call from a guy I know, and he says, 'Something happened to me. I wrecked my ass.' He was using some kind of dildo and ruptured something. He says, 'I'm bleeding — what does it mean? There's a big lump. I think I've broken something.'"

Nurse Wolf, in her role as triage nurse, said, "Call GMHC" — the Gay Men's Health Crisis — an inspired decision. The man called GMHC and was referred to a doctor who diagnosed his condition as serious and performed emergency surgery on him.

Another time she was with a man who was using a vibrator to sodomize himself. And the contraption, about four inches long, torpedo-shaped, simply disappeared. The man howled, but she told him to be calm; she would remove it. But after trying everything — tweezers, forceps, even her barbecue tongs — the thing was somewhere deep inside him and the man was panicky. At this point, Nurse Wolf had one of her flashes of insight.

"I sat him on the toilet and told him to push, and it came out, still buzzing."

One day we were in the restaurant of the Mark Hotel, having lunch, laughing over a menu item described as "weak fish," and Nurse Wolf was saying she certainly didn't want that. She was dressed in her working clothes: short leather skirt, pretty blouse, Doc Marten boots, a heavy chain around her neck. There were young, stylish women in the place who were dressed similarly, for this was the fashion — though probably those other women were not going to spend the rest of the afternoon dressing a banker as a sissy maid or breaking canes on an executive's buttocks, two sessions on Nurse Wolf's agenda. In this giggling about "weak fish," Nurse Wolf used the expression "real sex."

"What did you say?" And I asked her to explain.

"Mutual reciprocity — real fucking. I love that too. I also like playing. I like slaves. I recommend both — real sex and role-play."

It then occurred to me to ask whether these men ever begged to make love to her, just jolly jig-jig cork-in-a-bottle-style sex. She was as shocked by this as she had been by the instance of kissing.

"They wouldn't dare. Are you kidding?" She made a fierce face at me. "They'd be dead. That's a line they'd never cross. Sure, there's some people who want to cross that line, but there's no way."

"Still, your boyfriend knows about this. It must be difficult to go from this — a man being bound up and humiliated — to see your boyfriend, have a drink, and so forth. Then go to bed? Is that transition difficult?"

"It depends on the day. Mostly it's the phone ringing off the hook, people being very needy. I had to take the cell phone to bed because I was expecting a call, and that was a big problem with my boyfriend. I have always done whatever I wanted to do. That's the first time I've ever had to be considerate of someone."

Her boyfriend gets turned off after they have spent a nice day together and she has to go to the studio for a session. He says, "You're going to work." She knows he uses that word because her word for it is "play."

Boyfriends come and go, but the other men have remained loyal through the years. She thought of them less as clients than as men she played with. As for sessions with women, in ten years she had seen only two women on their own, professionally. Her explanation was that women were less inclined to pay for this experience because they could get it in their own lives. It was much more difficult for men to get someone to play with them.

"Do you see yourself doing more of this, or less?"

"I can't do this forever. I get more selective, more specific about what I want to do and what I don't want to do. There are people who call and I say, 'I think you're a great person, but I just can't do this session.' This year I have been cleaning house."

After so much pain, it was, at last, not pain that truly upset Nurse Wolf but the spoken word. Perhaps I should have been warned when she talked of her objection to foul name-calling or her exaggerated response to a dish called "weak fish." Words were much more powerful to her — and to some of her clients — than any whip.

I happened to be reading a new translation (by Husain Haddawy) of *The Arabian Nights* around the time Nurse Wolf told me of her storytelling clients. These tales have been circulating since the ninth century and were written down about six hundred years ago. They have as their point of departure the adulterous debauchery of King Shahrayar's wife with her lover, the black slave Mas'ud, and others. Ten black slaves dressed in women's clothes leap into the palace garden. "Then the ten black slaves mounted the ten slave girls while the lady called 'Mas'ud, Mas'ud!' and a black slave jumped from the tree to the ground, rushed to her, and raising her legs, went between her thighs and made love to her. Mas'ud topped the lady, while the ten slaves topped the ten girls, and they carried on till noon."

King Shahrayar, after witnessing one of these orgies, kills his wife and decides that there is not a chaste woman on earth. As a further act of revenge, he sleeps with a different woman every night and in the morning has her killed. Shahrazad, daughter of his vizier, tries to save herself and the rest of womanhood by spending each night with the king and bewitching him with a new story. The stories in their untidied-up versions involve sex, sadism, kidnapping, and mutilation. In the story of "The Flogged One," a young wife is asked for a kiss by a handsome merchant. The woman turns her face to the merchant. "He put his mouth on my cheek and bit off with his teeth a piece of my flesh." The woman's outraged husband orders the woman to be punished. She is stripped, flogged, and branded.

Nurse Wolf has her Shahrazads. It is role-play so strange that even she is upset. Because she is not passive, she participates in the storytelling — she is sometimes Shahrazad. The most extreme examples of these sessions involve some of her longest-term clients, the ones she calls the Cannibals.

One is a man with a Hansel and Gretel fantasy. With Nurse Wolf's assistance he fantasizes about being a little boy and being cooked alive in a big pot. His fantasy was full of folktale ornamentation: the shadowy cottage, the dark woods, the witch's kitchen. At a certain point the man was eaten, and the prospect of being chewed — his body being the main course — sexually aroused him, especially when Nurse Wolf helped with variations.

Another man, an old man, also sees her to relate stories of cannibalism that would not be out of place in the later, weirder episodes of *The Arabian Nights*. His are similarly serial in nature, and like Shahrazad's, stories within stories. His basic fantasy revolves around the understanding that Nurse Wolf and he are in charge of a tropical island. Young women are abducted and taken to the island, where they are fed and fattened and prepared for a luau. This fantasy includes a French chef, a guest list, and lots of speculation.

This variation on Shahrazad fascinated me, especially the necessity for Nurse Wolf to suggest or elaborate a new plot twist each time the Cannibal showed up for a session. It was certainly literary and seemed to belong to an old tradition of storytelling: the tale intended literally to pass time and to captivate the listener. The way I saw it, the Cannibal, in indulging in these serial fantasies, was perhaps prevented from going out and killing and eating a woman; Nurse Wolf's assistance in his storytelling offered a way of protecting womanhood from anthropophagy. Both Nurse Wolf and the Cannibal talked, but the burden was always on Nurse Wolf to find new aspects of the story to explore. This Cannibal Island story has gone on for eight years. Were it printed, it would fill many volumes.

"It wasn't scary for the first six or seven years," Nurse Wolf said, "but lately it's started scaring me. I don't think about it beforehand, but when he shows up I think: Maybe we'll have a hunt for her this time, or the woman is roasting on the spit, or we'll have an auction and serve up portions that people have bought."

"Is it a particular type of woman he's after?"

"He's very specific. There's a lot of detailed things. They have to be between eighteen and twenty. They have to have a good shape. He's got to measure you. One day he brought a tape measure and he measured my arm, 'Like this.'"

Sometimes the Cannibal brings books to the session, with titles like *Aladdin's Slave Farm,* about girls who are kidnapped by cannibals. The preparation of the meal is more important to the Cannibal than the eating, but it is always understood that a woman is being kept for later.

"We trick them. They think they're going to be sex slaves. They are very carefully groomed, and they are kept in cells together. They are not allowed to speak to each other. They are graded. They are constantly evaluated. They are given daily punishments. They are completely broken down and made to be submissive, and then, when they're prepared, we go into a detailed plan about the arrival of the guests. About how many we're going to have, and what we're going to serve at the luau — the arrival, the roasting of the girls, and then they'll baste them, all our guests will baste the girls. We've had many discussions — I wonder how I can even go here sometimes — like, what is the consistency of their flesh if they die in fear? A logical question. I mean these people at the luau are spending a lot of money, right?"

Now and then, role-playing, Nurse Wolf lets the Cannibal bite her. "He doesn't break the skin. He's got Parkinson's disease and his teeth are shaking. He's got dentures! He bites my arm. He's standing — he bites my biceps, and he's like touching himself, and it's a sick thrill for him. I am in charge. I am, like, 'Bite me. It's tender here.' He takes out his little tape measure. I say, 'You can get the most meat off the upper arm. Or here . . . Or here . . .'"

"Is there anything in it for you?"

"I am bringing something I like to it. You've got to realize my 'freak factor.' The thrill for me is I am exhilarated by Parkinson's disease and dentures, and he's out of this snowy-haired, poly-knit, Poligrip ad, and instead of playing tennis with his wife, he's biting me and having cannibal fantasies. I mean, this is someone's grandfather. Biting me! My arm! It's not about me and it's not about him. I think about it and I snicker. I try to block the ugliness of it."

The man, who is in his late seventies, is so aroused by the sessions that he calls nearly every day and has implored Nurse Wolf to see him three times a week. She can't face it.

"I am up for seeing him every two or three weeks. He totally drains me. It's the reality of it. That I am helping him in his fantasy. But it's so dark. I don't get anything back from him. I get sucked dry. A lot of people feed my imagination. But after a session he changes like Jekyll and Hyde and I just leave the room. It's so embarrassing. I was never into the *words*. I visualized things and I thought, What a great story. But I realized that I could never eat after it. That I dreaded it sometimes."

Yet the man, the Cannibal, was helped. It was possible in this Shahrazad role-playing to see this as the apotheosis of the dominatrix as nurse. There was the fact that by verbalizing his cannibal fantasies he was sublimating them and not acting on them. Horrific as the words sounded, their very utterance perhaps prevented the man from eating women.

And there was the interesting fact of Parkinson's. Oliver Sacks, who has studied Parkinsonian patients, has said that a person who is suffering the mental or physical rigidity associated with the disease often finds release in closely observing another person. The symptoms are alleviated by "borrowing" language and gestures from someone else. Nurse Wolf provided that for the Parkinsonian Cannibal; she loaned him her language and gestures. Though she has no idea that the studies supporting this process are still being researched, she was helping the Parkinsonian Cannibal to function.

Nurse Wolf was not sure about this when I mentioned it, and anyway, the whole subject of cannibalism upset her.

"I always think, One step beyond biting is eating."

"Why do you let him bite you?"

Nurse Wolf said, "I think it's the mommy in me!" And she laughed, but after that outburst she grew gloomy and said, "I am constantly told that I don't see a good representative cross-section of men. 'You are not in the normal world where you can make judgments on things or make generalizations.'"

But it seemed to me that the opposite was true. She understood what most men were really like. True, the covert and the rejected sought her out — no one else would see them. You immediately think of a long line of jostling grotesques and twisted old fruits from George Grosz or Francis Bacon. But no, lined up they were people who were instantly familiar: the electrician, the insurance executive, the construction worker, the stockbroker, the editor, the writer, the white-haired grandpa. The hooded man was hooded precisely because anyone might recognize him.

We did not know everything about them, but Nurse Wolf did. Enigmatic to their wives and girlfriends, hearty and humorous to children and grandchildren, they divulged their secrets exclusively to her.

"One of my slaves was terminally ill," she said to me one day. "He told me almost a year before he told his family. So he and I had this secret. I was the only person who knew."

She went on beating him. He was one of the men who liked "heavy corporal." He kept seeing Nurse Wolf, to be beaten, right up to the month before he died.

This moved me. She told me how much it meant to her to know his secret. She grew fond of seeing him; she looked forward to whipping him. She wept when he died. It was one of the strangest stories I had ever heard; it was as much about strength as it was about human frailty. It was also about that middle ground of connivance where there is hardly a difference between nurse and patient.

I said, "So it's almost like having a relationship."

"Not 'like.' It *is* a relationship," she said.

10
ROBIN WILLIAMS:
"WHO'S HE WHEN HE'S AT HOME?"

One afternoon just before the millennium, on New York City's Central Park West, a few blocks from where a lurking nutter shot and killed John Lennon, Robin Williams, hurrying home to his apartment, was approached by a limping, grizzled man wearing a shoebox-sized radio around his neck. One item of the man's attire was part of a torn plastic trash bag. The man had a grubby package in his fist, and looked like a decaying elf, from the realm of The Fisher King, *as well as, incontestably, a lurking nutter.*

With one shoulder twisted down, the man's movements were almost monkey-like in his sideways approach to the well-known actor-comedian. Robin did not break his stride. Nine years of serious bicycle riding (he had biked in a lengthy workout around Central Park just the day before) have given him the pushing and pigeon-toed gait characteristic of committed cyclists when they are on foot — and there is something simian about that, too.

So the two men converged, the innocent celebrity and the predatory stranger, looking like the victim and the assassin, each about forty-eight years old, each with his peculiar walk, and though the stranger, pawing his pendulant radio, seemed to me to be somewhat menacing in his demeanor, Robin did not look fazed, but instead greeted him with a friendly and disarming shout.

"Radioman! Radioman! What's happening?"

For a moment, as their gaze met, I could see a resemblance, how one man was a version of the other, the stranger like a shadow, and how there was a kind of understanding between them, which amounted almost to warmth.

The man smiled and yanked about twenty large-format publicity photographs of a smiling Robin Williams out of the battered package. His breast pocket, visible just behind the radio, was crammed with ink-smeared pens. He handed over a pen and the pictures and Robin began signing, as Radioman gabbled.

"Whoopi's across town rehearsing a show. I gotta get over there. You know about Bob? He's coming in at eight fifteen. And they're showing your movie tonight, right? I got some of them pictures. So here's what I think I'll do . . ."

The crouching figure named Radioman continued in this vein, sounding a little like Robin himself in a manic mode, with an extraordinary accuracy of names, and precision in terms of places and times.

At last, he said, "You got all the movies and all the money, and what have I got? Nothing."

"You got this, man." Robin handed over the twenty autographed pictures. "Where's your helmet?"

"Lost it. Hey, thanks. See ya?"

After the man had gone, Robin said, "He knows everything that's happening in the city. I can ask him, 'Where's So-and-so?' and he'll tell me exactly where the person is. He rides a bike. He can make it to a location faster than you can in a taxi. He's amazing."

I said, "But do you ever think of giving these autograph hunters the elbow?"

"I couldn't do that to Radioman. I've known him too long."

Radioman's urchin-like appearance and his wealth of information made me think of him as a member of the Baker Street Irregulars — Sherlock Holmes's informative posse — and I said so to Robin.

"Oi, Mister 'Olmes, sir! Oive got a sighting, I do!" Robin said, stepping inside his elevator and instantly becoming a Baker Street Irregular. The elevator operator guffawed, and even continuing into his apartment, Robin kept on with his improvisational role in "Holmes and the Adventures of Radioman."

But later that day, at a bike shop on Columbus Avenue, he bought a Kevlar cycling helmet and assorted gear costing $244.41.

He said, "For Radioman."

• • •

The Cockney accent had just suddenly tumbled out of Robin's strangely pliable and almost pneumatic face, which at times, swelling and distorting, seems to be composed entirely of flubber — perhaps another reason for the success of that movie, since the invention of flubber so exactly matched its creator. Though he has moments of calm, of serious reflection, even of solemnity, "flying rubber" is how Robin seems much of the time.

He had begun the previous day by mimicking Roberto Benigni and leaping into Matt Lauer's lap in the NBC *Today* studio, and before lunch he had been a stern Swiss journalist ("Zees Holocaust movies are passé"), a downtrodden mumbler in shtetl Yiddish ("Bubkiss!"), an equivocating French hotelier, an obscenely drawling Ted Turner, a homeboy, a redneck, a Montana militiaman, a drunken mouth-wiping politician, Goofy, Andy Kaufman, Al Roker, a German (crooning four choruses of "Edelweiss"), an orating and doubletalking George W. Bush, a child frenziedly auctioning Pokémon cards, a shouting urban lout, a prissy interviewer, and, on a cell phone in a car, a Klingon pretending to be engrossed in phone sex.

Then came lunch. At the afternoon taping of *The View*, he created an uproar, mocking Barbara Walters's leather pants ("Those from the Marquis de Suede? The woman's wearing the entire food chain! Get them off and we'll get busy"), jeering at the panel of facetious, overdressed women and mocking the decor ("Hey, did van Gogh have a garage sale?"), putting on a Billie Holiday accent for one of the cohosts, Star Jones, claiming "I just mugged a leprechaun!" (he was wearing a green suit and green shoes), speaking of clubs in San Francisco called the White Swallow and the Cunning Linguist, doing a jig, and finally leading everyone in a Jamaican step dance, calling out improvised reggae lyrics, disrupting the entire show and in doing so giving it life, as he was to do an hour or so later on *The Late Show*, puzzling David Letterman, first doing a dance, then hugging several stagehands, imitating a Mercedes-Benz computer speaking in a German accent, and then imitating a drunk when drinking, an asthmatic when breathing hard, a Scottish accent when describing his trip to Scotland, and "Welcome to Michael Flatline!" as he danced his second furious jig of the day, and a redneck on New Year's Eve ("The lights go out and 'You're mine, pretty boy!'"), and a southern preacher, and Dan Quayle, and Donald Trump, and a riff on New Yorkers wearing headsets and talking to themselves, and finishing grandly with an approximation of echolalia, this explosion of energy and sound lighting up the set.

He said he had been doing this for about the past three weeks, on a tour that had started in Deauville, France, and continued to Toronto and New York, with a guest appearance in Connecticut at Paul Newman's Hole in the Wall Gang children's camp, a charity auction in Las Vegas, and another philanthropic stop in Los Angeles. This, he said, had been an average day.

Five times that day, following him around, I eavesdropped on people asking him, "As a Jew, didn't you have strong emotions in playing the central role in *Jakob the Liar*?" Or, "Have you always expressed yourself in Yiddish?" Or baldly (Mark McEwen, getting acquainted at Robin's CBS interview), "You're Jewish, right?"

The answer to each of these questions was no, always surprising the questioner into a silence that Robin filled with a well-rehearsed quip: "My mother was a Christian Dior Scientist — very stylish!" Or, "There's a tradition of gentiles playing Jews, starting with Charlton Heston — Guns N' Moses!"

The question could have been "Are you Scottish?" or Texan, or Irish, or French, since he is capable of such convincing ethnic immersion. As it happens, he speaks French with such fluency that he can as easily dominate a French TV show, as he proved at Deauville, prompting a French speaker to remark, "Robin doesn't have an American accent in French. It's — I don't know — somehow central European." It is a rum biographical factoid that Robin Williams speaks French with a (perhaps) Romanian accent, but it is fair to ask the question that English people pose of oddballs: "Who's he when he's at home?"

His life so far seems to have three distinct parts. In the first, his boyhood, he changed schools and cities repeatedly. "I was an only child, looking for a connection. Moving from place to place." When I asked him to be more specific, he said, "Moving can fuck you up nicely." His was a middle-class upbringing. He grew up gentile (and genteel), shuttling between Detroit and Chicago, moving to San Francisco at the age of sixteen and, after more moves, eventually settling there. He identifies himself with the spirit of this city of powerful feng-shui, and a number of his films have used San Francisco to good effect.

His father, an executive with an automobile company, was "tough and practical," and a skeptic. His mother was "an optimist." "If my father saw a horse he'd say, 'That thing's going to take a shit any minute now.' My mother saw a room full of shit and said, 'Where's the pony?'" For a while the family lived just across the street from Adlai Stevenson, in Lake Bluff, Illinois. But apart from running track, and in particular the cross-country team, he was little more than a face in a school group photograph. Ultimately, the school was Redwood High, in Marin, California.

The next phase of his life — reckless, exploratory, even dangerous — started with a spell studying political science, which ended when he entered Juilliard in New York City. His acting then ranged from dramatic roles in student productions to extramural improvisation, following strangers on New York streets, imitating them — and, he says, frightening them — as a mime artist. He said to me (it seemed like a modus vivendi), "When you mimic someone, they back away."

He found he expressed himself with the greatest freedom in stand-up comedy, and he became well known as someone who parachuted late at night into comedy clubs, with such a crazed take on the world he seemed like a Martian. Not surprisingly, he was chosen for a cameo role as an alien on *Happy Days*, goggling and gabbling at the uncomprehending Fonz. This singular appearance led to his first success, *Mork & Mindy* (1978–1982), and incidentally, a wild, coked-out life marked by two significant events, the death of his close friend John Belushi from a drug overdose and the birth of his first child, Zachary, to Valerie Velardi. The topic of his drug-taking visibly wearies him, yet the intensity of those years has given him more than a point of view. In many senses, he is a man who returned from the brink — and the brink, a dangerous place that was for years his element, and not very funny, has been a source of his comedy, howlingly funny in retrospect.

Act three, in which he now revels, began with his sobriety and his subsequent marriage to Marsha Garces. "She grew up — I would say — poor," Robin says of Marsha, who was raised in Milwaukee, one of four children. "Her father worked really hard. He was a very proud man." He was a chef, a Filipino, and her mother, of Finnish extraction. "They didn't have a lot. She was working really young and was really independent. That gives you a sense of treating people on all levels with the same respect."

And, as he says, she knows him perfectly. "My strengths and my weaknesses. She isn't there to pander to me. 'You're fabulous!' There's a world out there ready to do that—and to do the opposite, dismember you, and blow smoke up your ass, and so you have to find someone who is truly honest. But you've got to treat someone like an adult and not manipulate them and play off their insecurities. I'm an adult. She can only say so much and then, 'Okay, you're on your own, captain.'"

We talked about a couple we both knew. "If he's electrical, she's the ground," he said, and could have been speaking of himself and Marsha.

To his obvious irritation, Robin is frequently put on the defensive—famously by *People* magazine, but also by others—about his second marriage. In the dithery tone of fake concern that she uses for her most intrusive questions—the manner she adopted to ask the semiparalyzed and wheelchair-bound Christopher Reeve about his sex life—Barbara Walters queried Robin Williams about marrying Marsha, because she had once worked as the children's nanny. Even Lillian Ross—whose romance with William Shawn, one would have thought, would have put her above such speculations—adumbrated a complex sequence of events, with dates, to prove—as though proof were necessary—that at the time Marsha was not the nanny. Does anyone with any sense really care?

On the evidence, Robin Williams is a contented man in a productive marriage, with three children (Zachary sixteen, Zelda ten, Cody seven) and a shrewd and protective wife, who greatly resembles many wives of creative men. Mrs. Kipling (who was American) was like Marsha, and so was Mrs. Robert Louis Stevenson (who was also American), and numerous others. Their husbands' innocence and insecurities and even their querulous, seemingly henpecked quality created the impression that these men were dominated by the women—and these women and others have been deeply criticized. But the women were chosen, and loved, for those very qualities of severity and protection. Marsha Garces Williams fits this mold. And the better I got to know Robin, the more convinced I was that he is a man who, if he were not able to move people to laughter, would be very nearly defenseless.

Though he often lapses into a dreamy admiration of Marsha that makes him look like the Man Who Mistook His Wife for a Hat, Robin Williams has become immensely wealthy through sobriety and steady work and the production company, Blue Wolf, that he formed with his wife in 1993. Their first effort as a team was the irresistible (and profitable) *Mrs. Doubt-*

fire. Next came *Patch Adams,* and then *Jakob the Liar.* Robin appeared in twenty-eight feature films in the 1990s alone, some forgettable, others brilliant, most of them profitable. The couple has substantial residences in New York, San Francisco, and the Napa Valley. They grow grapes. Marsha collects modern art — and that includes Picasso and Mondrian. Robin buys the best bicycles obtainable, but even a great bike doesn't cost much more than ten thousand dollars. The couple travel in their own Gulfstream jet. Robin collects, and wears, extraordinary shoes. "These are Prada," he said of some bottle-green footwear. "And these are custom made in Tokyo," he said of a pair that looked like Eskimo mukluks, a form of hand-sewn clodhopper that guarantees a silly walk.

One is tempted to conclude that while Marsha acquires tasteful trophies — paintings, real estate — Robin, with his twenty bikes, funny shoes, and video games, prefers toys. This is in no sense meant as belittling. I spent a far happier day biking around Marin County with Robin than I would have meditating upon a Mondrian, an experience that seems about as stimulating as staring at a square of superior linoleum.

Robin Williams's resemblance to a self-enlightened patient in an Oliver Sacks case history (not just *The Man Who* but many others) is appropriate enough. Williams was memorable in the role of the Sacks-inspired doctor in the film *Awakenings,* adapted from Dr. Sacks's book. The two men have been friends ever since, and Oliver is one of the shrewdest observers of Robin's behavior. "There is no one like Robin," Oliver says. Coming from a man who has made his entire life a study of human variety, this statement has enormous significance.

When Robin prepared for playing the Dr. Sacks role in *Awakenings,* the effect was unsettling to both men. "Mimicry is an inadequate word," Oliver says. "He didn't imitate me — he *became* me, my fancies, my hopes, my memories. At that point he had to stop. He needed to establish time and distance. He needed autonomy, to find his own voice. He needed to be disenthralled."

And Oliver was struck, as many people have been, by Robin's ability to talk nonstop — seemingly engrossed in performing — while at the same time listening, hearing disembodied mutters or telling noises, and remembering everything on the periphery of his performance. This simultaneity allows him instantly to read an audience — much of his hilarity resides in this skill. It is the skill of the mime artist he was as a student in New York, imitating the gestures and the walk, the hauteur or the fear, of pedestrians for the amusement of passersby; but it is also a reflex of an insecure child who needs to know whether he is being rejected or loved.

"I register everything, positive and negative. I'm like a field sensor." Walking with him in New York, his intense alertness was obvious. He was aware of all sorts of activity and sound to which I was oblivious, and the most unusual aspect was that he was talking to me most of this time. I saw this as a survival skill, the way an animal seeming to browse, deeply preoccupied, is alert to every movement and sound. Robin also has the ability of some animals — I have noticed it mostly among reptiles — of exploding from a state of utter repose to frenzied action. A sleepy, almost catatonic floating crocodile is able to come to murderous life the instant it sees a meal or a threat. Of his sleep habits he says, "I am a marsupial. I can sleep anywhere."

"Robin is hyperspontaneous," Oliver says, and suggests that he verges on the Tourettic, given to alarming impulses and wild associations, those same shouts and barks. "He is never better than doing stand-up comedy in front of a live nightclub audience. It is vivid and transcendent obscenity."

Robin himself sees that stand-up comedy is one of his strengths; it is perhaps where his true gift lies, and he has never really strayed from live audiences. The spontaneous nightclub appearance is a way of testing material, interacting with strangers, and being in touch with the world. But it can be a strange process with unforeseen results. "When you 'go off' in performing," he explained, "you are channeling. It's almost like possession."

Given that in his first years traveling the country with Marsha he often found himself performing in unusual places, and being heckled ("I did stand-up in a hockey arena in Amish country"), he is clearly a man who doesn't mind a challenge.

"In a way he is more naked than anyone else," Oliver says, describing the varieties of Robin's comic performances in stand-up. "Yet you have to interpret it. It is like a dream. I have often felt that the complex forms of Tourette's are like a public dream."

Because he is essentially a satirist, one can easily see his historical antecedents in the nature of the fool, conveying unbearable truth. The classic role is the Fool in *King Lear* — a rich part that awaits him, but it is also a part in *Waiting for Godot,* in which he played Estragon to Steve Martin's Vladimir in 1988 at Lincoln Center (Robin says he loved doing it). Oliver sees this as his strength: "His depth of expression more easily comes out when he is playing the fool. But he is not shallow or dull when he is not playing the fool."

The irony is that he often has a greater intensity when he is not trying to be hilarious — when he is considering a serious question or examining the aspects of a idea. I mentioned to him that one of my favorite short stories is "Ward No. 6" by Anton Chekhov. In this scary masterpiece a doctor who works in a mental hospital in the Russian hinterland finds himself mistaken for a patient, is locked up, and dies miserably, because he is unable to prove his sanity.

"That would be an insane nightmare," Robin said, visibly shocked by the story, which he had never read.

"Let's say you were locked up by accident," I said. "How would you prove your sanity?"

"Oh, God!" he said helplessly, perhaps seeing himself in a straitjacket.

That story is also a favorite of Oliver's, whose personal version of it is a hostile doctor saying, "Ah, delusion of being Oliver Sacks. Lock him up." With his wide experience in neurological wards and medical literature, Oliver Sacks is a wonderfully satisfying and appreciative analyst of Robin Williams's wit and intelligence. Robin was not the so-called holy fool of an extreme condition known as latah, though he is capable of doing a pretty good imitation of frontal lobe syndrome, mimicking "stimulus slavery" and "forced reaction." In spite of the fact that it is almost like possession, Robin is capable of control.

Oliver says, "He can be quiet, and very sensitive, and thoughtful, too, you know." But he added, "Anarchic wit is not possible without experience of a very dark side." When I asked him to expand on this, Oliver said simply, "There must have been grim and difficult passages in his past."

"Grim and difficult" is an understatement. Robin freely admits he is self-destructive, without giving much detail. In press interviews and in his monologues (memorably in the seven Comic Relief performances) he satirizes the wilder indulgences of his earlier life, alluding to excessive cocaine use in his past and to bingeing generally. To paranoia and impotence. To coked-out parenting: "The kid pukes on you and you puke back on him!" To insomnia and hysteria: "You think you've got insomnia and you're doing coke, and then you realize you're dreaming, and you wake up and you find you're doing coke."

At some point, living in Los Angeles, having achieved great success with *Mork & Mindy,* Robin was using cocaine excessively and drinking too much alcohol. (Even telling this story, Robin, with his compulsive verbal marginalia, slips into a Viennese accent and describes Freud's considerable cocaine use.) John Belushi, who was a friend, was a fellow boozer and snorter, but unlike Robin he injected heroin and that deadly combination called speedballs. Being in Los Angeles didn't help, because it was a city where people were constantly asking, "How'm I doing?" with a forced smile and a nervous tapping of the feet.

"Show business, the perception of how well you're doing, all of that," Robin said, speaking of the causes of his former anxieties. "Then you're moving down, and it's 'Are you a commodity that is sellable?' 'Are you worth anything?' 'Who do you know?'"

His voice becomes very quiet, with a growly solemnity that is almost unrecognizable, even to someone who has seen all his movies and watched all his performances. He seems slightly shocked, as though he is reflecting on the life of another man — a crazed, desperate, reckless man, approaching flatline.

"I felt my status slipping and changing. I had gone from being very hot to cold." After a pause he went on, "And then you try to medicate yourself — literally — with cocaine. To keep up your status and do all the things you think you should be doing. And then you think, What have I done?"

Describing the other side of Los Angeles, "the dark-underbelly side," Robin jumped to his feet, twisted himself sideways, and squinted and limped like Igor, and in a low, diabolical, beckoning voice, "Aye, welcome! You're fucked up, are ya? Fallen down through the cracks? Aye, I used to be somebody — did you ever see *Attack of the Cave Bitches*? Here" — gesturing, wild-eyed, lunging for a door in his apartment, and appearing to enter a cave entrance — "I want to introduce you to some people. There's Lon Chaney's stunt double over there. Lon stole everything from him! And over there . . ."

He continued in this vein with such ghastly ferocity that I was laughing, half in horror, half at the weird comedy of it.

"That other side is Chandler Heaven — people just waiting to receive you, saying, 'Come and join us in an angry frenzy of hatred.' It's a whole other culture. It's a netherworld, an alternate universe of trolls and people waiting. Welcome to Hell-Air! It's *Fisher King* territory, even more so than New York."

Drinking heavily, grossly overweight, using cocaine, underexercised, "no kind of discipline, just parties," his self-esteem "pretty low," he fortified his ego by occasionally performing in comedy clubs — the Comedy Store, the Improv.

"Performing was a great outlet at that time, but performing was just kind of getting onstage for some kind of adulation. I remember one night I was onstage and these people kept sending up kamikazis — vodka and lime juice. They wanted me to pass out. I kept drinking and drinking. I stopped, but they wanted me to go on until I dropped."

It was a blank period. "There isn't much to remember of that time. No substantial memories other than going from strange house to strange house. Maybe I blacked it out because it was such a wasted period."

This chronicle of wasted time, which lasted about five years, "from the beginning of *Mork & Mindy* . . . to John [Belushi]'s death . . . was a period of debauched whatever-will-get-me-going, tapping people on the arm and saying, 'You like me?' Very much that seedy kind of thing. Having these conversations until dawn, about nothing."

Eyewitnesses to this downward spiral have provided him with more detailed accounts of the time. In his telling, he is like a homeless man, sleeping anywhere he can, "so loaded and so exhausted, I'd come in and lie on the floor" and go to sleep. The director would come and kick me in the feet and say, 'You have to cross downstage,' and I'd wake up and say, 'Yeah, yeah.'"

John Belushi's life was much the same. And though when he was especially high Belushi sometimes howled "I'm out of control!" he was a living example that it was possible to have a fistful of coke up your nose, a needle of slam in your arm, a cheeseburger in each hand, and to run into a brick wall and remain not just unscathed but cracking jokes. Robin says, "He was a bull."

One night, Robin got a message to go over to the Chateau Marmont. He believes it might have been a setup, "an effort to nail as many celebrities as possible — cocaine busts — to set an example." That same night, after

Robin left the hotel, Belushi died of an overdose. Robin got the shock of his life, seeing the destruction of a man he regarded as indestructible. Soon after, his son Zachary was born. And, as an added incentive to get clean, Robin was summoned to testify at the grand jury convened to investigate Belushi's death.

Death, testifying, and birth equaled trauma, humiliation, and hope: it was all Robin needed. He left Los Angeles. He "decompressed." "Kicking cocaine was easy," and so, he claims, was curbing his drinking. "I didn't go to AA." After such aversion therapy, he hardly needed to. "You can tell people to stop, but [to succeed] there has to be some internal mechanism."

I mentioned that it seemed to me that his experience of the lower depths had been the making of him, not only filling him with resolve but also giving him material. "And I only am escaped alone to tell thee" runs the line from Job at the end of *Moby-Dick,* for Ishmael is the only one left to recount the horrific adventure. Many of us who managed to survive the excesses of the last years of the old century have a similar tale to tell: lucky to have been there, lucky to have made it to the millennium.

He agreed. He said, "You are changed by it, because you've been near the edge and you've come back. I've seen that. It actually dictated the desire to talk about it. Make fun of it. That's why Pryor was funny — freebasing and being burned alive. That's firsthand. People who make the best fun of it are the people who've been through it."

If you can't laugh at yourself, make fun of other people runs the advice on a bumper sticker on Robin's new white Land Rover. Near it, another says, *Madness takes its toll, please have exact change,* and another, *Karma — it's everywhere you're going to be.* These are facetious rather than truly witty, but what struck me was that Robin took the trouble to stick the twenty-five-cent wisecracks on such a serious chassis. The answer is, of course: it's fun. This car is a toy. Driving it is fun. His bike was on the back — a beautiful bike. He owns twenty of them, all different, all bright and high-tech. They are fun, too. He doesn't tell jokes, and he yawns when someone begins one, saying, "So there were these three guys . . ." He much prefers smart remarks; even better, uproarious ones.

The longer I was with him, the better I understood his sense of fun. If the roots of his eagerness to please are tangled up with his childhood dislocations and obscure and unmemorable misery, the effect of his compulsive comedy is pure pleasure. Walking down Columbus Avenue in Manhattan, he was constantly recognized, hailed, greeted with a handshake. An entire junior high of rambunctious girls emptied and accosted him, pleading for autographs. Robin smilingly obliged — posed for pictures, poked fun, greeted them (as the Dalai Lama suggests we should do with all strangers) like old friends. In the same spirit he willingly agrees to two or three fundraisers, even in the middle of a publicity tour.

"It recharges you," he explained, speaking of fundraisers, charity events, celebrity auctions, and appearances for good causes (Comic Relief has raised $40 million so far). "When it bombs it takes something out of you. When it works it rejuvenates you."

Comedians, forever yakking, frequently do not seem to possess a voice of their own. But Robin does, and it is a persuasive and reasonable one. He freely admits to needing the rush of making us laugh, shocking us, demanding to be vitalized by our laughter — astonishing us, jolting us. "I'm a penis!" he cries in one of his turns, standing on tiptoe and shortening his neck and shouldering his way toward the edge of the stage, throbbing in his penile progress, and looking for all the world like a tottering and talkative willy.

In San Francisco, at a photo shoot, the subject of the English two-fingered salute came up. This V sign is to the English what flipping the bird is to an American. Robin began to explain what few Americans (and not even many British people) know — that the "up yours" gesture dates from the Battle of Agincourt, when the English bowmen jerked two fingers at their enemy to show the French (who chopped off the fingers of English captives) that they still possessed the fingers necessary to draw a bowstring.

Being Robin, amid spectators from three European countries, he became a one-man Battle of Agincourt — a hooting French foot soldier, an arrogant English bowman, the lisping dauphin, Joan of Arc, a dazzled peasant; he became a sky full of arrows; he became wind and rain; and he finished in a flourish by toppling backward with a theoretical arrow in his throat. In a frenzied performance, he showed a pretty good grasp of history and a mastery of the theatrical moment. I remembered a line in Wallace Stevens's poem "The Comedian as the Letter C": "this nincompated pedagogue."

It had all happened in a flash, and as soon as he proved himself the life and soul of the studio, he brightened—delighted by the response—and with a gleam in his eye and smiling his crooked, wolfish smile, he became photogenic.

After the heavy schedule in New York, he said he liked being back in San Francisco. He felt much more at home here. People in New York might see him and say, "Hello, how are you?" but they might also scream, "You suck!"

We had just left a bike store where I was picking up a bike for our afternoon spin. He had examined some new technical gear, as he had in New York, and, remaining genial, had continued to ask serious questions about the capabilities of the equipment.

"People know who you are," he said, meaning himself. "But they're like, 'Hey you like bikes!'" Bikes were common ground. "That's what's nice about San Francisco. People say, 'I know who you are! I don't give a shit!'"

On the other hand, from being with this conspicuous comedian in public in two large cities, I could see that strangers, confronted by him, were provoked to compulsive and often incoherent joking. "Just the two of you today!" said the man in the Golden Gate Bridge tollbooth, recognizing Robin and struggling to be funny.

Heading north in his Land Rover to cycle on one of his training circuits around Tiburon, we passed a bus stop poster of him in his latest film. I asked him what kind of response he felt when he saw his face this way.

"I didn't see it," he said with a shrug. "What kind of response is that? But once in a while you see them and people have messed with them. Drawn your eyes out. That's pretty upsetting."

A little later, talking about tabloid journalism, the way a reporter might try to gain access only to cut you down and write a destructive piece, he said, "There's something sociopathic about that."

"Australians are famous for it. I guess it's envy, but it's their way of trying to scare you."

In an instant, gripping the wheel, he was an Australian: "Aw, we got a funnel-whip snake here. That'll kill you. A pit viper, it's so fucking deadly. Sea snakes. And the box jellyfish. They're deadly. Crocodiles—one ate a model last year, not Kate Moss, no meat on her . . ."

We were across the bridge, heading toward Sausalito, and he was still an Australian.

"We grow some great wines here, too." He winced and licked his lips. "A fine Cabernet. Goes great with dingo. Wallaby. Kookaburra. Have you tried the kookaburra wines? Got a great head on them!"

Somehow this led to my mentioning a man Oliver Sacks had met, a man given to compulsive toasting, leaping to his feet with an imaginary glass of champagne.

Bewitched by the idea — and this is a pretty good example of his spontaneity — Robin raised a notional glass, the stammering obsessive-compulsive toaster.

"To my dear friends! To my shit — that I leave behind! To my wife — a good woman — had by all! To you — and you! To my dog — bitch!"

And so on, driving one-handed into Sausalito. Then we got on our bikes. Robin shot down the bike path and was way ahead of me before I got my toes into the pedal clips. "He's competitive," a mutual friend had said, but I have never known a serious bike rider who was not. On the rolling road toward Tiburon he cut corners, hardly hesitating at road junctions, and though I sometimes got glimpses of his yellow jersey, most of the time he was out of sight. He was obviously a strong pedaler, and he knew all the contours of this road, for it was the way home.

At one corner, where I caught up with him — but I think he considerately waited for me — he indicated a driveway and a house set amid the stringy-barked eucalyptus trees. It was an unprepossessing bungalow on a bluff with a fabulous view of the bay, his boyhood home, in a lovely sunlit neighborhood. But he did not pause. The next time he spoke I was gasping and he was saying, "I forgot to warn you about that hill."

He stayed far enough ahead of me to remind me that he was the better biker, but not so far as to rub it in. Under this cloudless sky, in sunshine, racing along the road in the mild air, there was nowhere else I would rather have been. It was a pleasure to see him sprint up the hills, burn around corners, dart through traffic, weaving among cars and changing lanes — alert, swift, spontaneous.

He was not the first person I had seen move from a life of strenuous and destructive self-indulgence to a hell-on-wheels cyclist who competed in triathlons. The true compulsive often makes the greatest athlete. He had a strong moral side, was gentle, kindly — and capable also of screaming obscenities, for laughs. He could carry on a normal conversation, but in seconds he could shout in one of the loudest voices I have ever heard. He was himself, he was his opposite.

Bicentennial Man, based on an Isaac Asimov science-fiction story, shows two distinct sides of his performing gift — and perhaps his underlying personality. Over a period of two hundred years, Robin is transformed from a highly programmed robot named Andrew to a human being. Robin spent a month and a half wearing the robot suit, in order to master it and give it nuance.

The suit itself is an engineering marvel, the brainchild of a hundred sculptors, model makers, engineers, painters, costumers, inventors, stylists. After three prototypes, these people produced a truly inhabitable robot suit — with rigid joints of the sort found on NASA hard suits or deep-diving suits, wrists that swivel, knees and elbows that bend, moving eyes and eyebrows, a usable jaw.

"He's programmed," Robin said, and added that the challenge was that the robot needed to find a way of communicating. It is a useful but rather dumb, predictable contraption until it becomes capable of making a joke. "Humor is the key," he said. "When the robot has made a joke, and knows it is a joke, it is humanized." The thing is liberated, no longer programmed, and happy. It is perhaps the way many of us give order to our own worlds; it is certainly Robin's answer.

Perhaps you would not know if you did not inquire that this hugely talented and friendly man had been through a hell of his own making. But on reflection you have to conclude that it is not possible to enter into his sort of comedy — which is the richest sort — without having been brushed by the bat wings of near madness and experienced one of the worst versions of free-fall drug distortion and public failure, which for Robin occupied much of the eighties. He saved himself, in a more profound way than depicted in any of his mushy medical roles. In this sense he is a wonderful embodiment of Millennium Man: the man who made it through the turmoil of the last three decades, to land on his feet and begin pedaling like crazy on an expensive bike into the new century.

Offered a small fortune to be the opening act for Barbra Streisand in Las Vegas on the millennial New Year's Eve, he said no.

We were driving back from our bike ride.

"Wouldn't that be fun?" I said. "Making jokes in Vegas? A huge appreciative crowd?"

"Vegas is Ground Zero," he said, being funny but also deadly serious. "You don't want to be at Ground Zero if the thing is in any way apocalyptic. The Four Horsemen of the Apocalypse galloping out of Siegfried and Roy's show! No, I don't need a hundred thousand drunk people — I've been there. We've all had our party times, drunk off our ass. 'I love you!' 'Wuss yo name? Eh, let me ask you somethin', sweetheart . . .' I can grab you. You can hit me. It doesn't matter. It's New Year's at Ground Zero. No, no, no, no, no."

"So what's the ideal way to deal with this big night?"

"Be with great friends," he said unhesitatingly. "Wonderful fun people. That's all you need. The simplest things can be the most fun."

11

TEA WITH MURIEL SPARK

Muriel Spark had a bad leg and an amazing reason for it. But her expla-
nation seemed so like a plot twist in one of her own novels, and so stun-
ningly comic, that I found myself listening with mounting hilarity at the
completeness of her apparent invention.

"Well, you see, my hip surgeon in London wrote to me and said, 'I now
wish to be called Sarah, not William.' He said, 'I am a transvestite. I'm going
to have an operation and become a woman.'"

"How awkward," I said insincerely, hoping for more.

"I wouldn't want to be operated on by a transsexual," she went on. "I'd
feel spooky. I don't want to go to sleep on his table and wake up 'Simon' or
somebody. Did you have lunch? We had a terrible lunch. I called down for
some sandwiches. They were just awful. Sloshed with mayonnaise."

I had been longing to meet Dame Muriel Spark, having read and reread her novels for most of my writing life, always stimulated by her peculiar truth, her originality of design, her omniscience, the boldness of
her characterization. Her fiction defies pigeonholing, as she herself does,
joyously.

One day after rereading *Loitering with Intent* on a Hawaiian beach and
greatly admiring it, I wrote her on an impulse to say so. She replied from
her home in Tuscany in a friendly way, with the sort of serenity that de-
scends on some writers after a lengthy period of satisfying literary labor:
you finish a book and are calmed. She confided that she had indeed just
finished a new novel, about Lord Lucan. It seemed to me an inspired choice
of character. In November 1974, Richard John Bingham, the seventh Earl
of Lucan, known to his friends as Lucky—though he was anything but

— bludgeoned his nanny to death in a dark stairwell of his London house, believing she was his estranged wife. He then turned on his wife, who managed to escape and raise the alarm. Lucan vanished the next day, leaving an ambiguous note, saying he would "lie doggo for a bit," and was never found.

Muriel said, *We must meet,* and we did at last when we were both passing through New York City.

Sitting in the half-dark of a hotel room, having tea, seemed a bit like a séance. Muriel is ageless in her talk, bright, funny, forthright — most of all stimulating, because she is interested in everything. The clarity of her pronouncements is like her prose style, crisply sudden and surprising. We talked about *The Driver's Seat,* filmed as *Identikit,* starring Elizabeth Taylor. But she hadn't liked it. "The main character is supposed to be neurotic, and Elizabeth Taylor was much too vulgar to be a neurotic woman." We talked about Africa. She had lived in Rhodesia, now Zimbabwe, where white farmers are being harried by angry Africans, egged on by the president. "[President] Mugabe is mad. He's a power maniac. The press knows it but they pussyfoot around." As for Italy, where she has lived since 1966, "It has a lot of drawbacks. Very inefficient. Not terribly honest. In our sense, you know. Straight dealing is just unknown. Still, they're wonderful. I love their humor." We talked about her ex-husband. "He was bonkers. In and out of loony bins." And her son. "He's a painter, but not a very good one." Then we got to the subject of the transsexual surgeon.

"I had a hip replacement that went wrong. It was done twice. There was a big infection. A surgeon put it right but left me with a half inch less. And then the other hip had to be done. I had that doctor who operated on the queen mother. I can't think of his name. He walked a bit like a ballerina. What was his name?"

"The hip doctor? Like a ballerina?"

"'Please call me Sarah,' he said. It's tragic — the savage desire to mutilate yourself. Dressing up is fine. Dress up! Have some fun! But the actual mutilation — it's really savage."

Anyway, she said, a man could not become a woman but only a transsexual. "That's another category. She's not a woman, she's a concept."

After the surgeon wrote her a letter explaining his decision, Muriel replied, *Thank you for your letter. Interesting. I wish you well in your new life. Yours sincerely.*

"Nothing more I could say. 'Good luck.' I decided against the operation. It's just a bad leg. I can take pain relievers. I wish I could think of his name."

Even so, she was the toast of New York that weekend—invited everywhere, and unfailingly polite and witty. Her manner of speaking is precise, with a disarming brightness and an aunt-like assurance, very little of Edinburgh in it, more the sort of faintly antiquated expatriate English speech that you hear from people who have kept their parents' accent, or that of their headmistress, because they themselves have spent most of their lives outside Britain. Apart from her early youth and some years around the end of the war, Muriel has lived abroad most her life.

There is absolutely no sign that Muriel has had anything but a charmed life, and this is odd, because her earlier life was full of the sort of disruption and struggle that another person would make into suffering and high drama, if not tragedy. For Muriel it has been the source of strength and comedy —and even her darkest novels are full of laughter. "Spark" is perfect. She was born Muriel Camberg, half-Jewish in Edinburgh. But "I don't know much about religion except for the Bible." In her late teens she met Sydney Oswald Spark, and he proposed, then sailed to Rhodesia. Almost immediately after her engagement she followed him to Africa, where they married —she was now nineteen—and soon found herself pregnant. On the birth of her son, Robin, her husband, who "was terribly unbalanced—he could be terribly aggressive," showed signs of mental instability. "It wasn't until I got there [Rhodesia] that I realized it was a mistake."

But she says in her autobiography, "It was in Africa that I learned to cope with life." She left her husband while still in Africa, her son just an infant, but kept the name. "Camberg was a good name, but comparatively flat. Spark seemed to have some ingredient of life and of fun."

Divorced, raising a son, still in Rhodesia, unemployed and with little money, the war at its peak, she applied for a job at an Anglican convent school in Bulawayo. The mother superior, a Nazi sympathizer, said that the war was the fault of the Jews. "Of course, I'm a Jew," Muriel volunteered. When the mother superior said, "It's not so" and became apoplectic, "I took my fair skin and golden locks right out of there." After a single-parent spell in Cape Town, she wangled her way onto a troopship in 1944 and got to

London. "Believe it or not, I chose London rather than peaceful Edinburgh because I wanted to 'experience' the war."

She spent this period of "intense incendiary bombing" at the Helena Club, immortalized as the May of Teck Club in *The Girls of Slender Means*. She got a job with the Foreign Office, "in the dark field of Black Propaganda or Psychological Warfare, and the successful and purposeful deceit of the enemy." After the war she worked on a literary magazine and later at the Poetry Society. She was as her photographs attest, winsome, a beauty. Poems were dedicated to her by hapless admirers. She herself wrote poems and stories and literary criticism. Out of the blue, Graham Greene was so captivated by her writing he gave her £20 a month and occasionally a case of wine ("to take the edge off things") as a sort of literary fellowship, so that she could write a novel. She wrote *The Comforters*. Evelyn Waugh praised it for its deftness in handling the very sort of hallucinations he was trying to depict in his own novel *The Ordeal of Gilbert Pinfold*.

I asked, "How did you feel when you read Waugh's wonderful review?"

"That I could give up my job."

She wrote *Memento Mori* (1957), and by the time *The New Yorker* published *The Prime of Miss Jean Brodie* (1961), devoting an entire issue to it, she was living in New York City and liking it.

"I didn't want to live in England, because I would have had family problems. They would have been on top of me. Especially my mother."

She had placed Robin in the care of her mother, and supported them from a distance. "He doesn't like me at all," she says now. "He liked his father, who was in a loony bin most of his life." While he is not mentally ill, she says she finds her son slow, and "slow people can appear very stupid and resentful. He'd really like me to be a babushka."

"He chose the wrong mother."

"That's what I keep saying. I've done what I can. If you do too much, they turn on you, especially if you're a woman."

After four years in New York she went to Italy, living first in Rome and then in Tuscany with her companion of more than thirty years, the sculptor Penelope Jardine. Muriel has been contented and productive in Italy. I asked her what she liked most about Italian life. She said, "The happy families — Italians accept their families. The parents don't interfere in their children's lives."

Reflecting on this, sipping tea, she added with feeling, "The pull of family is so terrible in some writers' lives."

Her new novel, *Aiding and Abetting*, is her twenty-fifth work of fiction. The main character is Lord Lucan, though the book's subject is duplicity, and that hearty area of masks and shadows where good intentions subvert morality.

"Do you know Lord Lucan? The gambler?" she had asked me over tea, and went on cheerfully, "He was employed by a club, to take on a sucker or two. He bashed his nanny, Sandra Rivett. My book deals with his latter days and with another fugitive from justice, a psychiatrist who had been a fake stigmatist. Lucan ends up in Africa — and he gets eaten. He gets killed by mistake, the same way as he killed the nanny. He has a double with him."

"Who, or what, eats him?" I asked.

"A paramount chief. Trying to make all these little Lucans. You become what you eat."

"You're interested in crime, aren't you?"

"Yes. Very."

What had drawn her to this idea, she said, was that she kept reading about sightings of Lucan. "And then there was the question of whether he could be considered dead from the point of view of the law. And the law said, 'Yes, he is dead — we'll say he is dead so that his son can inherit something.' But the House of Lords said, 'Oh, no, he might walk in at any moment,' and so the son can't inherit the earldom."

Aiding and Abetting is as funny and as dark and allusive as anything she has written. Lucan shows up at the office of Dr. Hildegard Wolf, feeling remorseful, needing treatment. He has chosen this doctor because she, too, has a secret, which he can use to double-cross her should she threaten to betray his identity. Treatment proceeds until another man shows up, also claiming to be Lord Lucan, but who later claims to be a defrocked priest. The two Lucans physically resemble each other. "It's all a very complicated story," Muriel had warned me.

Dr. Wolf employs a perverse psychoanalytic method that involves talking only about herself and her problems for the first three sessions, showing an utter lack of interest in the perplexed patient. This conceit strikes me as an effective mode of inquiry in terms of getting a patient on the boil.

The psychiatrist is as devious as Lucan and her secret much more bizarre than his. As a poor student in Munich, Beate Pappenheim sold handbags. The sight of customers' money made her greedy. Bedridden after a severe "menstrual hemorrhage," she is told by her Catholic landlady of Sister Anastasia of the Five Wounds, a miracle-working stigmatic. Beate hits on the idea of calling herself Blessed Beate Pappenheim, and "every menstrual cycle she covered herself in blood and bandaged her hands so that blood appeared to seep through . . . In between the cycles she wrote out testimonies to her healing power." After soliciting donations "for the aid of Beate Pappenheim's Poor," she becomes wealthy, and in return works some genuine miracles. A cult devoted to her flourishes in Ireland, and she vanishes with her fortune before she is rumbled as a fake.

In Paris, under the name Dr. Hildegard Wolf, she successfully practices her peculiar psychoanalytic method of monologuing. This parallel story to the Lucan story is, according to Muriel, "based on fact."

Much of the novel is concerned with the pursuit of Lucan. Alerted to the possibility that he is in their midst, various people try to hunt him down. It turns out that Lucan has many friends — many aiders and abettors. The phrase is used throughout the novel; indeed, diabolical connivance lies at the heart of the narrative. It is all a wicked conspiracy, a novel about deception and, inevitably, self-deception. As with Muriel's most serious essays into morality and crime — and, in this case, murder one and cannibalism — it is a comedy.

"I've just thought of his name," Muriel said, as teatime ended and she asked for wine to be opened. She had been racking her brain for the name and had come up with some wonderful ones, but they weren't right. She said with certainty, "Muirhead-Allwood — William, but now he's Sarah. What will he do? What man would want a relationship with a cooked-up woman? I think you'd have to buy it. That's my opinion."

12

MRS. ROBINSON REVISITED

My younger self often fantasized about older women, though seldom acted upon it; my younger self seldom acted upon anything. This habit of yearning, these futile fantasies, probably turned me into a writer. People who live rich lives full of opportunity tend not to become writers, while we fantasists do, which oddly makes us seem worldly, when in reality we are anxious geeks, pining after someone confident, glamorous, and truly worldly.

My fantasizing has never been the boring defloration mania that bewitches our Latin friends, nor the connoisseurship of the pedomorphic face and figure, the Hollywood starlet, the pop-music object of desire that looks like a seal pup in a tank top labeled *Boy Candy*. That kittenish teenybopper with soulful eyes and skinny legs is the undoing of many drooling geezers, which is just what they deserve. I don't think I could describe my ideal woman, but my fantasies have often circled around someone resembling Mrs. Robinson. How else to explain myself as a sixteen-year-old boy in a movie theater looking at Ava Gardner in *The Barefoot Contessa* and having trouble breathing?

I have spent much of the past twelve months traveling through Africa, from Cairo to Cape Town, alone, far away from Mrs. Paul. On a Nile cruise near the beginning of my trip I found myself in the company of an exceedingly good-looking woman traveling with a younger man. The woman, who was German, snubbed me, so I talked to her Arab companion —"Oh, not companion, really. I am her physician." He let drop later in an unguarded moment that he was a doctor of reconstructive surgery.

I saw the whole situation at once. Though he looked older, he was actually much younger than the attractive woman, who was his patient, in her late fifties, possibly sixty. I imagined myself a young man of twenty-one and the doctor daring me to take an interest, so that he could prove to the woman that his surgery had been a success. Pure fantasy. All the way through Africa, on buses, on trains, in hotel rooms, I worked on this story, which grew longer and steamier. It was set in a fictional hotel, the Palazzo d'Oro, in Taormina, Sicily, in the early 1960s. I was twenty-one years old then and hopelessly priapic.

Meanwhile, on this Africa trip, I was importuned by women — young women, old women, Congolese, Somali, Ugandan, jumping out of the shadows, buttonholing me in back alleys and on main streets. "Hey, meesta!" "Want a massage?" On the streets, in hotel lobbies, at ten in the morning in Kampala when I was out mailing a letter. "You buy me drink?" You'd think AIDS did not exist, but of course it is through all this activity that it does exist. I resisted and wrote my story, which, like many stories by many men, was essentially autoerotic.

Never mind what authors say about their artistic intentions. Thomas Mann wrote *Death in Venice* after a trip to Venice when, according to his wife, he could not take his eyes off a young boy's bum. We now know that Mann was bisexual. It does not belittle his masterpiece to speculate that its intensity arises from Mann's homoeroticism.

This subject of the younger man having an affair with an older woman still interests me, because time passes and "younger" and "older" mean different things to me. Thirty is old to a young man of twenty. I don't spend much time with thirty-somethings. I am now older than Mrs. Robinson, and yet sex is not theoretical; it is actual, always a possibility. I still stare at women all the time, thinking, Are you beautiful?, and like all men I flunk some, pass others, and give a few of them high marks. This is what most men do all their waking hours.

I have grown older, but this question of age differences and desire is all the more fascinating for its ambiguity. Age is the central point in *The Graduate* — the affair between the young man and his fiancée's mother is what we remember most clearly, and the same drama is central to many masterpieces. The subject is invariably an older man and a young object of desire, usually a girl, sometimes a boy. *Death in Venice* is obsessional on the subject of the desirability, the perfection, of youth, Tadzio's beauty and Aschenbach's helpless adoration of this unattainable boy. *Lolita* is the self-consciously classic study of a middle-aged man infatuated with a teenager.

She is a nightmare, as we know, and hardly virginal, but that does not deter Humbert from his pursuit — it's the source of the novel's comedy, for we see him, as he sees himself, as a much-mocked but willing victim.

Almost twenty-five years ago I wrote an essay, "Homage to Mrs. Robinson," in which I tried to imagine what it might be like to be involved with an older woman. I imagined her as self-possessed, confident, intensely sexual, somewhat domineering, and most of all knowing the score. Her most attractive quality, it seemed to me, was the one we usually assign to the young: the ability to live in the moment. But younger people tend not to do that. They worry about the future, they don't want to waste time, they think: Is this good for my résumé? Is this beneficial to my career? They fear casual sex might erode their self-esteem. They tend to look for Miss Right, not Mrs. Robinson.

I said all those years ago that the older woman is not husband-hunting: she knows what she wants, and if you measure up, you are hers for the taking. She knows the essential things about concealment and has a heightened awareness of time. As a boy sees maturity in a sexual encounter — proof of his manhood, another statistic to relish — the older woman has been granted a reprieve and in that encounter has outwitted her age. For her it is a private, mutual compliment. The classic situation is nothing long term; indeed, she might not particularly want to see you afterward. The preliminaries, the half-truths, the confidences, the wooing — all these are dispensed with. There isn't time. She comes straight to the point and then goes back to her life. She is doing to you what older men do to younger women.

And, unlike many of her younger counterparts, she does not want to be trapped. She doesn't need witnesses. For someone younger, sex is not an end in itself but a means to another end: job, money, marriage, power, family, position. And so, if they never know this older woman and only deal with the twenty-year-old and her tough twinkle, most men grow up believing in sex as a favor they've been granted — sex as strategy or currency or power. Therefore the act itself is full of threat. The older woman typically is indifferent to domination or something given in return — her age has liberated her from those deceptions. She is not interested in power but in pleasure.

At the time I was writing on this subject, I was a theoretician in my presumptuous thirties. I said, "A woman between the ages of thirty and fifty, sexually is alight — her manner might be cool but her body blazes." Now that I am older and know more of hormones, I would raise the bar: women of sixty can be intensely sexual too. And if they have been the least bit active, they know every trick in the book. I am not speaking of love, but of desire. Many are still beautiful.

In general, literature is no help in understanding this mismatch. Robert Louis Stevenson was married to a much older woman, and so was Raymond Chandler. Their wives were extremely attractive if a bit neurotic. Neither of these men wrote fiction on the subject. Turgenev was involved with an older married woman, but his most memorable tale of sexuality is about a man who has an affair with his son's girlfriend. Henry James adored the company of older women but tended to limit his hugs and endearments to younger men. Madame de Vionnet in *The Ambassadors* is his Mrs. Robinson, and Byron offers up one or two in *Don Juan*. Of the other greats, Dickens, Melville, Conrad, Dreiser, Fitzgerald, there are no Robinsonian affairs. The older woman has not been well served by fiction writers.

Movies and plays have succeeded where literature has failed to deliver the goods. The films that come to mind are *Sunset Boulevard*, Bergman's *Frenzy, This Sporting Life, Nothing but the Best, Sweet Bird of Youth, The Roman Spring of Mrs. Stone* (also a novel but better as a film), *A Cold Wind in August, The Last Picture Show, Room at the Top*, and the brilliant Fassbinder film *Ali: Fear Eats the Soul*. Deborah Kerr in *The Gypsy Moths* is the older woman to perfection.

And, of course, Mrs. Robinson — Anne Bancroft seducing Dustin Hoffman in *The Graduate*. The director Mike Nichols was a master of creating a powerful reality in the scenes between the young man and the older woman. The most telling scenes were not in the bedroom but in bars and restaurants, when the young man was out of his depth, leaving Mrs. Robinson to take charge. Taking charge is the essence of sexual vitality. Mrs. Robinson is resourceful, responsive, independent, and a knockout. Was there anyone who saw that movie who did not regret that the hero went off with the daughter and not the mother?

It is nonsense to relate such desire to the Oedipus complex, which is about infants anyway. I think much more often of myself when, at ten or eleven, my mother's old school friend visited and left behind an odor of perfume and cigarette smoke and the aphrodisiacal smudge of lipstick on her gin glass. I think of the first schoolteacher I wanted to possess — Miss

Murphy, at the Washington School, probably no more than twenty-two —
though I did not know how it was done. The first woman who knew more
about sex than I did was older than me, more experienced, and perhaps for
the first time in my life I felt I was in capable hands.

Twenty-five years ago, I wrote, "The older woman gives us something
that is very nearly incomparable, the chance to complete in adulthood what
was impossible to complete as a child, a blameless gift of lechery that combines the best of youth, a maturity, romance and realism in equal parts."

I still think so. Sex is only sometimes procreation, and the rest of the
time it is pure lust, from the imagery imprinted in childhood. The fulfillment in adulthood of childhood fantasies is the very definition of
happiness.

13

TALISMANS FOR OUR DREAMS

About four years ago, I saw what I considered a masterpiece of its kind in the Chor Bazaar, the so-called Thieves Market, in Bombay. It was a reverse glass painting of an Indian nautch girl — dancing girl — caught in a sinuous move, intentionally teasing, probably done in the middle or late nineteenth century, with Chinese characters in black brushstrokes on the wood-slatted back, and set in a decaying frame. I wasn't sizing it up. I was teased, indeed falling in love. It was an old feeling.

The collector's instinct, which is also a powerful appetite, begins with a glimpse of something singular and a smile of recognition, as though the collector has noticed what Auden once called "a soul-bewitching face." The collector has fallen hard, but the feeling cannot be openly expressed or the collector's urgency will be betrayed. Meanwhile, emotion takes hold as the collector lingers, fizzing with curiosity. From fascination to acquisitiveness, the feeling deepens, becomes tinged with a kind of benign lust, next a sense of calculation, and finally a blatant greed for possession. The collector's catchphrase, like the lover's, is *I must have it.* So much ambiguity seems almost dangerous in its seductiveness. Yes, it is a kind of passion.

Money is the least of its motivators. With enough money you can own anything, and you can pay people to find the stuff. Collecting isn't about paying money for something rare. The need to discover is the driving force, making collecting such a complex preoccupation it is almost imponderable. To avoid being self-conscious, I have not deconstructed my own impulse much. I tell myself that I am not "a snapper-up of unconsidered trifles," as Autolycus says in *The Winter's Tale,* and I insist that my travel has been enriched by this enthusiasm.

Another crucial distinction: collecting is not the same as shopping. It has a greater affinity with hunting, or as I suggested above, in the language of desire, with the trawling associated with seduction, resulting in a love affair. Collectors are not merely possessors; they are themselves possessed by the search and at last by the objects of their affection. What lover doesn't know this?

In all collecting, effort matters much more than cash, and uniqueness lends beauty to an object. Intimate knowledge and stealth are part of the quest. Since connoisseurship cannot be taught, collecting involves intense self-education. You must know the history of what you own; *Avoir sans savoir est insupportable,* as the saying has it. In my nearest big library I find books on collecting beer cans of the world, bottles, coins, Chinese porcelain, modern first editions, movie posters, seashells, and much more. But for many of us there are no handy manuals or guides. What has sustained me over the years is the thrill of the chase. Add travel to collecting and you have the sort of passion that can vitalize half a lifetime of pleasurable searching.

That reverse glass painting was probably done by a Chinese painter in Gujarat, I found out later. The process of painting on the back of a pane of glass an image to be viewed from the front was European in origin (a cheaper and quicker version of stained glass), but the style of this piece was Chinese, the subject secular and unusually sensual. Europeans in the eighteenth century introduced this technique of painting to India, where it flourished. The Chinese had learned reverse glass painting from early Jesuits in China at about the same time or earlier, and some itinerant Chinese artists eventually got to India, where they produced many of these secular paintings.

I bought this beautiful thing and I looked for more. It was not easy to find others, but I was delighted by the variety I encountered — religious, mythical, erotic — and the out-of-the-way places where I found them.

With each new painting I was possessed with a greater desire to know more about reverse glass painting in India. Barbara Rossi's *From the Ocean of Painting,* a survey of India's popular paintings; *Glass Paintings: An Ephemeral Art in India* by Samita Gupta; and a piece by Roy C. Craven Jr. in a 1983 *Arts of Asia* magazine were helpful. With the passing years I have found out enough so that I can identify the good ones, the range of subjects, the various styles, the regional differences—places as distant from each other as Tanjore in the south, Bengal in the east, and Gujarat in the west—and the many artistic sensibilities at work, as well as the hands of Chinese and Indians.

As all collectors discover eventually, the objects of their affection become scarcer and more expensive as time passes and their taste develops and their connoisseurship ripens. Whenever I go to India, I look for such paintings. What entrances me is that though reverse glass paintings are superb, they are not treasures in the classic sense, but rather beloved objects from a household, created by an individual hand, someone with enthusiasm and vision.

Not long ago, I was researching another area of my collecting enthusiasm, African artifacts. Verifying a piece, I found quoted in a catalog a wise observation by the French philosopher Gaston Bachelard, who wrote, in *La Flamme d'une chandelle*: "Whenever we live close to familiar, everyday things, we begin once again to live slowly, thanks to their fellowship, and so yield to dreams which have a past, yet in which there is always something fresh and new. The objects we store away in our treasure chest of things, in our small personal museum of beloved things, are all of them talismans for our dreams."

Bachelard, a great explicator of reverie, of the precious space in houses and of old-fashioned handmade objects, like oil lamps and cupboards, is an ideal philosopher for the dreamier collector.

It is hard for me to separate collecting from travel, which seems to me an associated activity. Traveling collectors are people I recognize. One of the greatest pieces of Marquesan art (now in the Peabody Essex Museum in Salem, Massachusetts) is the wooden carving of a graceful human hand collected by Robert Louis Stevenson when he was sailing the Pacific in the 1880s, looking for a place to live. The traveler Sir Richard Burton filled his labyrinthine home in Trieste with his collection of African and Middle Eastern artifacts. On his many visits to Haiti, Graham Greene—one of the least acquisitive of men, but a traveler—became enamored of twentieth-century Haitian paintings and ended up with a superb collection, some of which he mentioned in his novel *The Comedians*.

These travelers were not merely treasure hunting in distant lands, but also giving a point and purpose to their journeys. This is salutary, because travel at its most rewarding is a solitary quest. I also have periods of thinking that travel can seem one of the most annoying, self-indulgent, even futile ways of passing the time. But travel should be about looking deeper into the world at large, into oneself. It is obvious that the study of the material culture of a place reveals subtleties in the history of its people. I don't think it is a rationalization to say that collecting is a creative activity, as well as a spur to wider, more sensitive travel and true discovery.

The collector's passion is something I have felt my whole life, though I did not collect anything for a number of years, not even books. I was nomadic from the time I left college in 1963 until ten years later when I settled down in London. I had lived in Italy, in Malawi, in Uganda, and in Singapore. In this decade of traveling light I had wandered widely: into the Congo, Nigeria, Borneo, India, Burma, all over Malaysia, throughout northern Sumatra, to east Java and Bali. I coveted much of what I saw, but bought nothing. I hardly owned anything, was virtually possessionless, until I was in my thirties. Where would I have put it?

There was another reason. In those days in Africa, most of the desirable artifacts had spiritual power and were in frequent use. Not much was for sale. I recall in the mid-1960s witnessing a frenzied all-night dance of the Angoni people called the Nyau, the image dance, in the Malawi bush, at Mua, a village on Lake Nyasa: drums, masks, bells, rattles, headdresses, and a symbolic image that was paraded in the firelight. Around that time, at the southern shore of Lake Victoria, the Sukuma people held dance competitions where they displayed elaborately carved human-sized figures with movable limbs called *mabinda*. It did not occur to me to buy any of the masks or artifacts that were used in these ceremonies, and probably the dancers would not have parted with them.

After I bought a house, my life changed dramatically. For one thing, with a real home, a place to return to, I became a bolder traveler. And perhaps the collecting passion itself depends on surrounding oneself at home with objects of personal significance. For the first time I was able to collect the things I saw in my traveling.

I set out from this first house in the early autumn of 1973 to take the trip I wrote about in *The Great Railway Bazaar*. On that trip I became an actual collector rather than an ardent fancier, and I began to understand the joy, and the psychopathology, of collecting. I was deeply melancholy on this almost five-month trip alone. I missed my family badly; my spirit needed soothing. I had time on my hands. In Istanbul's Grand Bazaar, the Kapalıçarşı, I spent days comparing jewelry and samovars and carpets. I bought some Seljuk bracelets. I took the train to Iran, and in the bazaar of the holy city of Meshed I found an ancient blue-glazed tile. Going overland, I continued into Afghanistan, where had I wished I could have swapped my gold Omega watch for a crate of tribal rifles with mother-of-pearl inlay in the stocks. In the Lahore Museum I saw a second-century Gandharan statue of the Fasting Buddha, a haunting skeletal image that stayed with me, and forty years later I began to collect Gandharan art. I bought some small Mogul miniatures in Pakistan, some Rajasthani *pichavais* (temple paintings) in India, a dagger in Sri Lanka, a watercolor in Calcutta, a Buddha in Vietnam, and more. The larger items I sent home; the smaller ones I kept with me to Japan and on the homeward leg on the Trans-Siberian Express. In those days, a traveler with a glittering dagger in his bag was not viewed as a threat.

The Rajasthani *pichavai*, I learned, was from the temple at Nathadwara, an image of young Krishna, Shrinathji. I found some of these in London, and the next time I went to India I searched for more of them. Highly colored, beautifully painted, some of them quite large, they seem to me the epitome of the art of veneration — piety and skill given expression on a piece of cotton cloth. Thirty years later I am still fascinated.

In the late 1970s, on the *Old Patagonian Express* trip from Boston to Esquel in Argentina, I discovered Spanish colonial paintings of biblical scenes, of Christ, of patron saints watching over South American cities. I could not afford expensive ones, but I found slightly damaged paintings, beautiful but needing a little restoration. I studied the subjects, the periods, the restoration techniques. When I was traveling in Ecuador, researching my novel *Blinding Light,* I found more of these colonial paintings and by then could distinguish between an original, a good copy, and a brazen fake.

I had first gone to China in 1980, a time when there were impromptu flea markets in many rural towns and villages. I found a large lacquer fish, a teapot, a scroll, a cricket cage, a jade bowl, some gilded lions that had been casualties of the Cultural Revolution. Back home, I researched the objects. The cricket cage, a smooth, pumpkin-colored gourd with a minutely carved ivory top, interested me the most. On subsequent trips to

China and Hong Kong I looked for cricket cages, for cricket paraphernalia — food dishes, ticklers, fighting arenas, containers for catching crickets. I educated myself to the point where, by the time I set off to write *Riding the Iron Rooster,* that trip could have been subtitled *In Search of Cricket Art,* though I did not mention it in the book.

One of the paradoxes of traveling in the Pacific, as I did in the late 1980s and early 1990s, for *The Happy Isles of Oceania,* was the discovery that not much of the traditional material culture still exists. There were exceptions, but on most islands, where there had been wood and clay and thatch, missionaries and traders had introduced plastic bowls and tin pots, aluminum boats and canvas shelters and corrugated iron roofs. If you want an authentic Hawaiian calabash or poi bowl or dog-tooth leg rattle, you will need to go to a dealer or an auction in Europe or New York. (A dog-tooth leg rattle was recently auctioned for about $40,000.) I have never seen any Hawaiian piece I desired for sale in Hawaii, though I have seen many in Paris and Amsterdam.

In quest of *The Happy Isles,* I found that canoe art still existed in some places, notably the wilder shores of New Guinea, the Trobriand Islands and Palau, the outlying islands of the Solomons, and in Vanuatu. There the people still made and decorated canoes in the old way. The epitome of canoe art is found in the splashboard and the prow of a Trobriand voyaging canoe, in the cleverly made and decorated scoops used for bailing the canoe, and in the varieties of paddle. On many islands the people are still firing pots or carving slit drums or making masks and war clubs. I picked up many of these objects, and I saw in some islands the remnants of an older culture, in particular the war clubs.

Collecting and studying Pacific war clubs has occupied me for the past ten years. Every island has created its own form of club, with a specific purpose in battle, out of wood or whalebone. In Hawaii and Kiribati, shark teeth were fixed to clubs, and the Maori fashioned clubs from pounamu, or greenstone. The Fijians created the greatest variety of clubs, and the successful warrior often inserted the teeth of his victim into the club head to give it greater power. Many Pacific clubs are works of art, and not battle-scarred at all, leading me to believe that they served the same purpose as ceremonial swords in Europe — an intimidating object to swagger with. Many old prints engraved by European navigators show Pacific islanders engaged in head-bashing, but quite a few depict men holding a gracefully carved club as a symbol of authority.

With the passing years, the traditional culture of Africa has given way to modernity, to Christian or Islamic conversion, or to the dazzle of electronics. And by degrees, African artifacts of all sorts have become available, even the masks from the Nyau dance and the marionettes from the Sukuma people that I coveted in the 1960s. Of course there are dealers in the great cities of the world, but it is still possible to find pieces in Africa. And some of the simplest are the most evocative. I own a Baga snake sculpture, some Chokwe helmet masks, Yoruba ibejis, and Lunda walking sticks. But I have come to see the beauty in a stool, a bowl, a comb, anything that has been carefully made and used often in a village, the old, worn, everyday things that Bachelard spoke of. Such a masterpiece of simplicity and grace is the African tree trunk, smoothed and shaped by the Dogon people into a ladder, used to gain access to an upper-story granary.

Any scrupulous examination of our pleasures, even our esthetic pleasures, and especially collecting, will probably reveal, deep down, a twisted pathological condition. And it is impossible to be a collector and not to be given pause by such an accumulation of worldly goods. As a collector I am always battling self-consciousness and trying to avoid the bigger questions raised by this happy obsession. I am given heart by Bachelard. In his telling phrase, justifying all the travel and effort, one could not do better than his identifying these collected objects as talismans for our dreams.

14

THE ROCK STAR'S BURDEN

Paul Hewson, who calls himself Bono, can perhaps carry a tune. But what about all the rest of it? While there are probably more annoying things than being hectored about African development by an overpaid and semieducated Irish rock star with a goofy name and a cowboy hat, I can't think of one at the moment. If Christmas, season of sob stories, has turned me into Scrooge, I recognize Bono's Dickensian counterpart as Mrs. Jellyby in Bleak House. Harping incessantly on her adopted village of Borrioboola-Gha, "on the left bank of the river Niger," Mrs. Jellyby tries to save the Africans by financing them "to turn piano-forte legs and establish an export trade," all the while badgering people for money.

It seems to have been Africa's fate to be a theater of empty talk and public gestures. But what is notable about the celebrities involved in African improvement is their need to improve their own image. There are more deficiencies in the people trying to fix Africa than in Africa itself. The notion that Africa is fatally troubled and can be saved only by celebrities and Feed the World concerts is a destructive and misleading conceit.

Those of us who committed ourselves to being Peace Corps teachers in rural Malawi more than forty years ago are dismayed by our return visits and all the stories that have been reported from that unlucky country. But we are more appalled by most of the proposed solutions. I am not speaking of humanitarian aid, disaster relief, AIDS education, or affordable drugs. Nor am I speaking of small-scale, closely watched efforts such as Oprah's school or the Malawi Children's Village. I am speaking of the More Money platform. This once seemed the answer. No longer. I would not send private money to a charity or foreign aid to a government unless every dollar was accounted for — and this never happens. Dumping more money in the same old way is not only wasteful, but stupid and harmful; it also ignores some obvious points.

Malawi is worse educated, more plagued by illness and bad services, and poorer than it was when I lived and worked there in the early sixties, but it is not for lack of outside help or donor money. Malawi has been the beneficiary of many thousands of foreign teachers, doctors and nurses, and large amounts of financial aid, yet it has declined from a country with promise to a failed state.

In the early and mid-1960s, we believed that Malawi would soon be self-sufficient in schoolteachers. And it would have been, except that for decades we kept sending Peace Corps teachers. Malawians welcomed them because it meant that Americans would teach in bush schools, something Malawians hated to do, allowing educated Malawians to emigrate. Malawians avoided teaching because the pay and status was low. When Malawi's university was established, more foreign teachers were welcomed (because they came free), few of them replaced by Malawians, for political reasons. Money was also a problem, though there was never a shortage of ministerial Mercedes-Benzes. Medical educators arrived from elsewhere. Malawi began graduating nurses, but the nurses were lured away to Britain, Australia, and the United States, which meant more foreign nurses were needed in Malawi. Nurses from southern Africa are the backbone of Britain's National Health Service.

When the Malawi minister of education stole the entire education budget of millions of dollars in 2000, and the Zambian president stole even more a year later, and Nigeria squandered its oil wealth, what happened? Bono and other simplifiers of Africa's problems kept calling for debt relief and more aid. I got a dusty reception lecturing at the Gates Foundation when I pointed out the successes of responsible policies in Botswana, compared to the kleptomania of its neighbors, the tens of millions that have been embezzled by politicians in Zambia and Malawi. Donors enable this behavior by turning a blind eye to bad governance and the actual reasons these countries are failing.

Bill Gates has said candidly that he wants to rid himself of his burden of billions. Bono is one of his trusted advisers. Gates wants to send computers to Africa — an unproductive, not to say insane, idea. I would offer pencils and paper, mops and brooms: the schools I have seen in Malawi need them badly. I would not send more teachers. I would expect Malawians themselves to stay and teach. The University of Zambia Medical School has educated thousands of doctors and nurses, few of whom remain in the country. Just ten years ago Zimbabwe was prosperous, with a food surplus. Today it is a ruin because of President Mugabe's destructive policies, resulting in the expulsion of farmers, the flight of skilled workers.

African countries do not lack manpower. They are not the hopeless cases they seem. They have been demoralized by bad governments and subverted by donors, aid agencies, unchecked urbanization, and the crass materialism of the intruding world. The mountains of used clothes that you send there every Christmas have destroyed African textile industries, and the pittance that Africans are paid for their cash crops — coffee, sugar, tobacco, and tea — have been ruinous to agriculture.

Malawi was in my time a lush wooded country of three million people. It is now an eroded and deforested land of twelve million. Its rivers are clogged with sediment, and every year it is subjected to destructive floods. The trees were cut down for fuel and to clear land for subsistence crops. Malawi had two presidents in its first forty years, the first a megalomaniac who called himself the Messiah, the second a swindler whose first official act was to put his chubby face on the money. Two years ago the new man, Bingu wa Mutharika, inaugurated his regime by announcing that he was going to buy a fleet of Maybachs, among the most expensive cars in the world.

Many of the schools where we taught forty years ago are now in ruins — covered with graffiti, with broken windows, standing in tall grass. Money will not fix this. A highly placed Malawi friend of mine once jovially demanded that my children come and teach there. "It would be good for them." Of course it would be good for them. Teaching in Africa was one of the best things I ever did. But our example seems to have counted for very little. My Malawi friend's children are of course working in the United States and Britain. It does not occur to anyone to encourage Africans themselves to become associated with volunteering. There are plenty of educated and capable young adults in Africa who would make a much greater difference than a Peace Corps worker.

Africa is a lovely place — much lovelier, more peaceful, more resilient, and, if not prosperous, innately more self-sufficient than it is usually portrayed. But because Africa seems unfinished and so different from the rest of the world, a landscape on which a person can sketch a new personality, it attracts mythomaniacs, people who wish to convince the world of their worth. Such people come in all forms, and they loom large. White celebrities busybodying in Africa loom especially large. I watched Brad Pitt and Angelina Jolie recently in Sudan, cuddling African children and lecturing the world on charity, and the image that sprang to my mind was of Tarzan and Jane.

Bono, in his role as Mrs. Jellyby in a ten-gallon hat, which he frequently talks through, not only believes that he has the solution to Africa's ills; he also shouts so loudly that other people seem to trust his answers. Absurdly, Bono traveled in 2002 to Africa with former U.S. treasury secretary Paul O'Neil, making a tour of national capitals. His rant was debt forgiveness. He recently had lunch at the White House, where he blathered upon the More Money platform and how African countries are uniquely futile.

But are they? Had Bono looked closely at Malawi, he would have seen an earlier incarnation of his own Ireland. Both countries were characterized for centuries by famine, religious strife, infighting, unruly families, hubristic clan chiefs, malnutrition, failed crops, ancient orthodoxies, tedious sociability, child abuse, dental problems, and crummy weather. Malawi had a similar sense of grievance, was colonized like Ireland, by absentee British landlords, and was priest-ridden, too. Just a few years ago you couldn't buy condoms legally in Ireland, nor could you get a divorce, though (just like Malawi) buckets of beer were easily available and unruly crapulosity a national curse. Ireland, that island of inaction — in Joyce's words, "the sow that eats her farrow" — was the Malawi of Europe, and for many identical reasons, its main export being immigrants, workers, and windbags.

It is a melancholy thought that it is easier for many Africans to travel to New York or London than to their own hinterland. Because your Uncle Manny and Auntie Ruth sent you a postcard with a lion on it from Nairobi, you think they've been all over Kenya. But much of northern Kenya is a no-go area. There is no plane and hardly a road to the border town of Moyale, on the Ethiopian border, where I found only skinny camels and roving bandits. Western Zambia is off the map, southern Malawi is terra incognita, northern Mozambique is still a sea of land mines. But it is pretty easy to leave Africa. A recent World Bank study has confirmed that the emigration to the First World of skilled people from small to medium-sized countries in Africa has been disastrous.

Africa has no real manpower shortage. It lacks belief in itself, and in general it lacks honest leadership. Again, Ireland may be the model for an answer. After centuries of wishing themselves on other countries, the Irish found that instead of begging for alms they themselves could make a difference. Education, rational government, people staying put, and simple diligence have turned Ireland from an economic basket case into a prosperous nation. In a word — are you listening, Mr. Hewson? — the Irish have proved that there is something to be said for staying home.

15

LIVING WITH GEESE

When I first began to raise geese in Hawaii, my more literate friends asked me, "Have you read the E. B. White piece?" This apparently persuasive essay was all they knew about geese, other than the cliché, often repeated to me, "Geese are really aggressive. Worse than dogs!" Received wisdom is not just unwise, it is usually wrong. But I was well disposed toward E. B. White. In his writing he is the kindest and most rational observer of the world. And a man who can write the line "Why is it . . . that an Englishman is unhappy until he has explained America?" is someone to cherish.

Though I had read much of White's work, I had not read his essay "The Geese." I avoided it for several reasons. The first was that I wanted to discover for myself the behavior of these birds, their traits and inclinations, on my own, at least in the beginning. I loved the size of geese, their plumpness, their softness, the thick down, the big feet of fluffy, just-born goslings, the alertness of geese — sounding an alarm as soon as the front gate opened — their appetites, their yawning, the social behavior in their flocking, their homing instinct, the warmth of their bodies, their physical strength, their big blue unblinking eyes.

But it was the second and more important reason that kept my hand from leaping to the shelf and plucking at *The Essays of E. B. White.* It was White's conceits, his irrepressible anthropomorphism, his naming of pets, his dressing them in human clothes and giving them lovable names, his regarding them as partners (and sometime personal antagonists). Talking spiders, rats, mice, lambs, sheep, and pigs are all extensions of White's human world. More than that, they are in many cases more sensitive, more receptive, and truer chums than many of White's human friends. Not just a grumpy partiality toward animals, White's frequent lapses into anthropomorphism produce a deficiency of observation. And this sets my teeth on edge, not for merely being cute, in the tradition of children's books, but (also in the tradition of children's books) for being against nature.

Animal lovers often tend to be misanthropes or loners, so they transfer their affection to the creature in their control. The classics of this type are single-species obsessives. The *Born Free* woman who raised Elsa the lioness as her child was notorious in East Africa as a child hater. Dian Fossey, the gorilla woman, was a drinker and a recluse. Timothy Treadwell, "grizzly man," was regarded as an authority on grizzlies, but Werner Herzog's documentary shows him to have been deeply disturbed, perhaps psychopathic and violent.

Assigning human personalities to animals is the chief trait of the pet owner — the doting dog lover with his baby talk, the smug stay-at-home with a fat lump of fur on her lap who says "Me, I'm a cat person," and the granny who puts her nose against the cage and makes kissing noises at her parakeet. Deer and duck hunters never talk this way about their prey, though big game hunters — Hemingway is the classic example — often sentimentalize the creatures they blow to bits and then lovingly stuff to hang on the wall. The lion in Hemingway's story "The Short Happy Life of Francis Macomber" is sketched as one of the characters, but that is perhaps predictable; so is the canny leopard in Jim Corbett's *The Man-Eating Leopard of Rudraprayag* and numerous other man-eaters in literary history. Moby-Dick is wicked and vengeful, and Jaws was not a hungry shark but a villain, its big teeth the symbol of its evil, just as goodness is embodied in the soulful eyes of a seal pup, so like a six-year-old that at seal-culling season you find celebrities crawling across ice floes to cuddle them.

The literature of pets, or beloved animals, from *My Dog Tulip* to *Tarka the Otter*, is full of gushing anthropomorphists. Does it matter? Probably not. But the writers of nature films and wildlife documentaries are so seriously afflicted in this way that they distort science. How many ant colonies have you seen on a TV screen while hearing, *Just putting that thing on his back and toiling with his little twig and thinking, I've just got to hang on a little while longer,* speaking of the ant as if it's a Nepalese Sherpa.

Possibly the creepiest animals-presented-as-humans film was *March of the Penguins,* a hit movie for the very reason that it presented these birds as tubby Christians marooned on a barren snowfield. "The Emperor . . .

probably the most primitive bird in existence," in the words of Apsley Cherry-Garrard, the first man to visit the rookery of the emperor penguin in Cape Crozier almost a hundred years ago. This story is recounted in his powerful book, *The Worst Journey in the World* (1922). He sledged with two other naturalists from the doomed Scott expedition and endured temperatures of minus-77 degrees Fahrenheit in the pitch-darkness of the Antarctic winter of 1912–13. Cherry-Garrard it was who brought the first eggs to the Natural History Museum in London.

You would not know this from the film. You would hardly know that the entire incubation of an emperor penguin's eggs occurs in total darkness, because of course a documentary can only suggest darkness, not photograph it. Instead, the pairs of penguins are shot as loving, nuzzling couples, with stumbling chicks, mated for life, in little groups, examples to be emulated for their family values. Very little of the cruelty of such an existence is demonstrated. When a bird of prey, probably an eagle, appears in the film and dives to kill a chick, the carnage is not shown, nor is the bird identified. The bird is not another creature struggling to exist in a snowfield but an opportunistic mugger from the polar wastes. We are enjoined to see the penguins as good and the eagle as wicked. With this travesty of science, people try to put a human face on the animal world.

After years of goose-rearing, I finally read the E. B. White essay, and as I feared, I was in the company of a fanciful author, not an observant gozzard, or goose-rearer. Here was "a gander who was full of sorrows and suspicions." A few sentences later the gander was referred to as "a grief-crazed old fool." These are the sentimentalities you find in children's books. A goose in *Charlotte's Web* says to Wilbur the pig, "I'm sitting-sitting on my eggs. Eight of them. Got to keep them toasty-oasty-oasty warm."

Edward Lear was also capable of writing in this whimsical vein, yet his paintings of birds rival Audubon's in dramatic accuracy. Lear could be silly about his cat, but he was clear-sighted. In his writing, White is never happier than when he is able to depict an animal by humanizing it as a friend. Yet what lies behind this expression of animal friendship? It is an eagerness for easy food. Feed birds and they show up. Leave the lids off garbage cans in Maine and you've got bears — "beggar bears," as they're known. Deer love the suburbs — that's where the easiest meals are. The daily imperative of most animals, wild and tame, is the quest for food, which is why, with some in your hand, you seem to have a pet, if not a grateful pal.

But geese live in a goose-centric world, with goose rules and goose urgencies. Unlike ducks, which I find passive and unsociable, geese have a flocking instinct, a tendency to gaggle. This is enjoyable to watch until you realize that if there is more than one gander in the flock, they will fight for dominance, a sort of battle that seems to have upset E. B. White. His essay "The Geese" is one his most tormented pieces, and it is full of howlers.

The essay describes a conventional goose-rearing situation, the successive generations of some geese he owned. He begins by saying that he has a goose and gander who are his friends: "'companions' would be a better word; geese are friends with no one, they bad-mouth everyone and everybody."

"Bad-mouth" is unfortunate. What I found in the first few years of raising geese was the variety of the sounds they made, varying in pitch and urgency according to the occasion, from wheedling murmurs of reedy ingratiation, along with the silent scissoring of the beak, as they step near, knowing you might have food, to the triumphant squawk and wing-flapping of the gander after he has successfully put to flight one of his rivals. (The gander rules by intimidation.) In between are the *ark-ark-ark* of recognition and alarm when the geese see or hear a stranger approach — geese have remarkable powers of perception (famously, geese warned the Romans of the Gallic invasion in 390 BC); the hiss of warning, almost snake-like, the beak wide open; the agitated honk with an outstretched neck; and, among many other goose noises, the great joyous cry of the guarding gander after his mate has laid an egg and gotten off her nest. Ducks quack, loudly or softly, but geese are large eloquent vocalizers, and each distinct breed has its own repertoire of phrases.

As for geese being "friends with no one" — not true. I learned this early. My first geese began as three wobbly goslings, scarcely a day old, two ganders and a goose. The goose became attached to one of the ganders — or perhaps the other way around; the superfluous gander became attached to me. Indeed, he "imprinted" on me so deeply that even years later he will come when called, let his feathers be groomed, scratched, and smoothed, and will sit on my lap without stirring, in an astonishing show of security and affection. Konrad Lorenz describes this behavior as resulting from a gosling's first contact. "Friendship" is of course the wrong word. "Mateship" is more exact: my gander had found a partner in me because his mother was elsewhere and no other goose was available.

The dilemma at the heart of White's essay is that his old goose laid three eggs and then fell dead. White doesn't know what to do with the eggs, which had to be fertile because the goose had a mate. As for the eggs, "they seemed silently to reproach me." The obvious recourse is to put them under a nesting duck or hen, but he cannot find any. A friend offers White an incubator. White studies the directions, and "I realized that if I were to tend eggs in that incubator, I would have to withdraw from the world for thirty days — give up everything, just as a broody goose does."

This statement is made in the same hyperbolic vein as the reproachful eggs. What he means, but isn't saying, is that goose eggs need to be turned once or twice a day in old-style incubators, so they won't cook. Performing this operation hardly means withdrawing from the world; though a sitting goose has a greatly reduced appetite, even the broodiest goose gets up from her nest now and then, covers her warm eggs with feathers and straw, and goes for a meal and a drink.

When Irving, a would-be gozzard, tells White that he has a goose sitting on some eggs, it does not occur to him that he could slip his three eggs under that goose; that she would go on sitting on them until they hatched and she would treat the goslings as her own. Instead, White shelves the three eggs and accepts the offer of three of the man's goslings. The day White sets eyes on the goose and her goslings, the goose is "staked out like a cow. Irving had simply tied a piece of string to one leg and fastened the other end to a peg in the ground."

White, normally the most humane of men, does not evaluate this peculiar torture. But I need to remind myself that White is in Maine. His geese, and Irving's, are in a barn all winter, cruel confinement for big birds that need space for browsing, rummaging, and often flying low. My geese range over six sunny Hawaiian acres every day of the year. Penning or staking them is unthinkable.

White scoops up Irving's goslings, which have "the cheerful, bright, innocent look that all baby geese have." Perhaps to him they have this look, but goslings have always struck me as amazingly precocious, and a few days after hatching they show all the traits of adult behavior, adopting threat postures and hissing when they are fearful.

Introducing the goslings to the old gander ("full of sorrow and suspicion," "grief-crazed"), White is apprehensive. He cannot tell whether the gander's eye gleams with "malice or affection." But malice is found only in humans, and affection is the result of long acquaintance. The gander is merely sizing up three small strangers, which trigger a protective, perhaps paternal, possessive response; but White does not say this. He notes that the gander takes charge, and he says, "His period of mourning was over." White intends a certain charm, but what's the point? It is a bewildered gander being a gander.

The original three eggs are tossed into the town dump. He could have gotten them hatched. Eggs remain hatchable for up to thirty days. He could have eaten them. An enormous thick yolk distinguishes goose eggs, and one egg makes an excellent omelet. Anyway, the three eggs are dumped.

Although he does not know the sex of the goslings, White says, "You tell the sex of a goose by its demeanor and stance — the way it holds itself, its general approach to life."

Not at all, though that may have been White's way of telling the sex of certain humans of his acquaintance. Geese are easily sexed. You tip them upside down and look at the vent in their nether parts: a gander has a penis, a goose doesn't. A little later — weeks rather than months — size and shape are the indicators: the gander is about a third bigger than the goose. White never mentions the breed of his geese, another unhelpful aspect of the essay, but if they were Embdens, the gander would be thirty pounds at maturity, and the goose five to ten pounds lighter; English gray geese bigger, China geese a bit smaller, and so forth, but always the gander is heavier than his mate.

One of White's goslings, the gander, grows into "a real dandy, full of pompous thoughts and surly gestures," and *oh, boy,* I scribble in the margin.

Time passes. "Winter is a time of waiting, for man and goose." Not really — only in frozen places, in barns and pens, and where geese are tethered to a stake in the ground. In warmer climates, the goose's natural habitat, geese develop little routines, favorite places to forage, though they range widely and nibble everything. They get to like certain shady spots, and through tactical fighting, using opportunities, they establish leadership. They stay together, they roam, and even the losers in the leadership battles remain as part of the flock. I can see how this would not happen in a barn or a pen, which are simply prisons, producing perverse—overreactive, defensive, aggressive—behavior, as all prisons do.

Describing the mating of his geese, White seems astonished that they always conduct this ritual in water, as though he is unaware that geese are waterfowl. And, "One got the feeling during the water-pail routine that the gander had been consulting one of the modern sex manuals describing peculiar positions." Which reminds me that facetiousness is another characteristic of the anthropomorphist.

One of the geese lays three eggs and then quits. The other goose is more prolific. White begins to interfere, sorting the eggs by date and by goose. This is unnecessary, though he has so thoroughly taken charge, he has no time perhaps to read a book on the subject, which would tell him that first-season goose eggs tend to produce undersized and weak goslings. In any event, the geese produce five goslings ("My heart leaped up"), and White tosses more unhatched eggs into the dump.

He then remarks that "ganders take an enormous interest in family affairs and are deeply impressed by the miracle of the egg-that-becomes-goose." This has not been my experience. The gander simply takes charge: it is part of his dominance—keeping other ganders away. He is protective, attentive, and aggressive in maintaining his superior position among all the other birds, and will attack any creature in sight, and that includes the FedEx deliveryman way up at the front gate.

White has two ganders, the old one from the beginning of the essay and the younger one that emerged from Irving's clutch of eggs. They fight, naturally. White's description is typically hyperbolic, making the whole business seem gladiatorial. The younger gander wins this fight and takes charge of the new goslings. White separates "victor from vanquished," rusticating and isolating the loser. The goslings have a new protector, the geese a new mate. As for the losing gander, "his head was barely visible above the grasses, but his broken spirit was plain to any eye."

Broken spirit? No, the gander has merely lost that skirmish and has withdrawn, because he is winded and tired and possibly injured. Had White left the ganders together, they would have fought again and the older one might have won, but in any case he would have stayed. Defeated ganders go off for a spell to nurse their wounds, but they always return and remain with the flock. One of the most interesting aspects of a flock is the way it accommodates so many different geese—breeds, sexes, ages, sizes. White does not seem to know that ganders go on contending, and that often an old gander will triumph over the seemingly stronger young one. Only after numerous losing battles do they cease to compete, and then a nice thing happens: the older ganders pair up and ramble around together at the back of the flock, usually one protecting the other.

There is a clue to White's self-deception in this part of the essay. "I felt very deeply his sorrow and his defeat." White projects his own age and insecurity onto the gander. "As things go in the animal kingdom, he is about my age, and when he lowered himself to creep under the bar, I could feel in my own bones his pain at bending down so far." This essay was written in 1971, when White was a mere seventy-two, yet this is the key to the consistent anthropomorphism, his seeing the old gander as an extension of himself. The essay is not strictly about geese; it is about E. B. White. He compares the defeated gander to "spent old males, motionless in the glare of the day" on a park bench in Florida. He had shuttled back and forth from Maine to Florida; his anxiety is real.

At the end, White makes a melancholy business of disposing of more unhatched eggs, though in the course of the essay he has dumped umpteen eggs without a murmur. The last sentence is just strange: "I don't know anything sadder than a summer's day." Does this relate to the eggs? I don't think so. Earlier in the piece, when the two ganders were fighting, he remarks that it was "a beautiful late-June morning, with fair-weather clouds and a light wind going, the grasses long in the orchard — the kind of morning that always carries for me overtones of summer sadness, I don't know why."

These remarks are at odds with the pastoral tone of the piece. The two mentions of summer sadness call attention to what is now called (but probably had no name when White was writing) seasonal affective disorder — not just the gloom that comes over a person on a dark winter day, but also a melancholy that can sadden a person precisely because the day is sunny.

What saddens me about this confident essay is that he misses so much. Because he locks up his geese at night, he never sees the weird sleeping patterns of geese. Perhaps he thinks they are in the barn slumbering, but in fact geese hardly seem to sleep at all. They might crouch and curl their necks and tuck their beaks into their wings, but it is a nap that lasts only minutes. Do geese sleep? is a question that many people have attempted to answer, but always unsatisfactorily. If they are free to ramble at night, geese nap during the day. However domesticated a goose, its wakefulness and its atavistic alertness to danger has not been bred out of it.

Their alliances within a flock, their bouts of aggression and spells of passivity, their concentration, their impulsive, low, skidding flights when they have a whole meadow to use as a runway, the way they stand their ground against dogs or humans — these are all wonders to behold.

I marvel at their varieties of biting and pecking, the way out of sheer impatience a goose wishing to be fed quickly will peck at my toes, just a reminder to hurry up; the affectionate and harmless gesture of pecking if I get too close; the gander's hard nip on the legs, the wicked bite on my thigh that leaves a bruise. I also marvel at their memory, their ingeniousness in finding the safest places to nest, their incredible curiosity — always sampling the greenery, discovering that orchid leaves are tasty and that the spiky stalks of pineapple plants are chewable and sweet.

I had an old, loud China gander that was displaced by a younger gander — his son, as a matter of fact, who ended up with the old goose we named Jocasta. The old gander may have been defeated by the son, but he remained feisty. Then he became ill, got weak, ate very little, couldn't walk, only sat in the shade and moaned. He was immobilized. I penned him in so that the other geese wouldn't take his food. I dissolved in water some erythromycin I got at the feed store and squirted it down his throat with a turkey baster, and added some to his water.

Several weeks went by. He lost weight, but I could see that he was sipping from his dish. From time to time I carried him from the pen and put him into the pond — he paddled and dipped his head and beak, but he was too weak to crawl out. Still, he seemed to respond to this physiotherapy. After a month he began to eat. One morning I was going out to give him more medicine and saw that he was standing and able to walk. I brought him some food and released him from his pen, and as I put the food in his dish, he took a few steps toward me and bit me hard on the thigh. This is not an example of irony or ingratitude. It is gooseyness. He was thankfully himself again.

16

TRESPASSING IN AFRICA

This took place forty years ago in Africa, and still I ponder it — the opportunity, the self-deception, the sex, the power, the fear, the confrontation, the foolishness, all the wrongness. The incident has informed one of my early novels and several short stories. It was something like First Contact, the classic encounter between the wanderer and the hidden indigenous person, the meeting of people who are such utter strangers to each other that one side sees a ghost and the other side suspects an opportunity. It won't leave my mind.

I had gone from America to Africa and had been there for almost a year: Nyasaland. Independence came, and with it a new name, Malawi. I was a teacher in a small school. I spoke the language, Chichewa. I had a house and even a cook, a Yao Muslim named Jika. My cook had a cook of his own, a young boy, Ismail. We were content in the bush, a corner of the southern highlands, red dust, bad roads, ragged people. Apart from the clammy cold season, June to August, none of this seemed strange. I had been expecting this Africa and I liked it. I used to say: I'll get culture shock when I go back home.

With Christmas approaching, I went via a roundabout route to Zambia and on Christmas Eve was sitting in an almost empty and rather dirty bar outside Lusaka, talking to the only other drinkers, a man and a woman.

"This is for you," I said, giving the man a bottle of beer. "And this is for your wife. Happy Christmas."

"Happy Christmas to you," the man said. "But she is not my wife. She is my sister. And she likes you very much."

At closing time they invited me to their house. This involved a long taxi ride into the bush. "Happy Christmas. You give him money." I paid the fare. They led me to a hut. I was shown a small room, and the woman followed me in. I stepped on a sleeping child — there was a squawk — and the woman woke him and shooed him from his blanket into the next room. Then she sat me down, and she undressed me, and we made love on the warm patch on the blanket where the child had been lying.

That was pleasant. I had had a year of women in Malawi, the casual okay, the smiles, the fooling, Jika's bantering, Ismail's leers.

But, in the morning, when I said I had to leave, to go to my hotel in Lusaka, the woman — Nina — said, "No. It is Christmas," and made a fuss.

The brother — George — overhearing, came into the room and said that it was time to go to the bar. It was hardly eight in the morning, yet we went, and drank all day, and whenever beer was ordered, they said, "*Mzungu*" — the white man is paying, and I paid. We were all drunk by midafternoon. The woman was taunted for being with a white man. She answered back, drunkenly. The brother stopped several angry men from hitting her. Loud, drunken fights began in the bar.

We went back to the village hut, and I lay half-sick in the stinking room. Nina undressed me and sat on me, laughed and jeered at me.

I was dressing in the morning when she asked me where I was going. Once again, I said I had to leave.

"No. It is Boxing Day." And she summoned her brother.

"We go," George said, and tapped my shoulder and smiled. His smile meant: You do what I tell you to do. We spent Boxing Day as we had done Christmas: the bar, beer, fights, abuse, and finally that dizzy, nauseating feeling of daytime drunkenness. Another night, Nina's laughter in her orgasm, and in the morning the reminder that I was trapped.

"You stay!"

In her refusal to let me go was not just nastiness but a hint of threat. And her brother backed her up, sometimes accusing me of not respecting them. "You don't like us!"

When I protested that of course I did, they smiled, and we ate boiled eggs or cold peeled cassava roots or a whitish porridge, and then off we went to the bar, to get drunk again in the filthy place. And as she grew drunker, she pawed me and promised me sex — now an almost frightening thought.

Another day passed, and I realized I did not know these people at all.

The food was disgusting. The hut was horrible. The village was unfriendly, the bar outright hostile. The beer drinking was making me ill. I was the only *mzungu* in the place — as far as I knew, the only one for miles around. The language that I knew, Chichewa, was not their language, though they spoke it. Their own language — Bemba, I think — was incomprehensible to me, and I knew they were plotting against me when they spoke it — quickly, muttering, so that I wouldn't know what they were saying.

But I belonged to them. Whenever they wanted money for beer, for snacks, for presents, for whatever reason, they demanded it from me. When I handed it over they were excessively friendly, the woman kissing me, licking my face, pretending to be submissive; her brother and the hangers-on praising me, praising America, saying Britain was bloody shit and asking me to let them wear my sunglasses.

That first night I had been wearing a light-colored suit. The suit was now rumpled and stained; my shirt was a sweaty mess. They were the only clothes I had.

They said what a great friend I was, but I knew better: I was captive. They were out of money. My weakness and arrogance had sent me straying into their world from my own world. And I represented something to them — money, certainly; prestige, perhaps; style, maybe. After the first night we never had a sober conversation. I was a color, a white man, a *mzungu*. I had been captured and they wanted to keep me: I was useful.

When they said, as they often did, "You no go!," I was afraid, because they spoke with such irrational loudness and threat. The boldness in Nina that had attracted me I now feared as wildness. Drinking deafened her and made her a bully as cruel as her brother. George peered at me with odd, brown-spotted eyes, as though at an enemy. Sometimes at night I was wakened by the human stinks in the hut.

I think it was the fourth day. My terror was so great and the days so similar I lost track of time. We went to the bar in the morning, and at noon they were still drinking. I had lost my taste for it, as I had lost my libido; I just stood there and paid with my diminishing wad of kwacha notes.

I said, "I'm going to the *chimbudzi*."

"Go with him," Nina said to one of the tough boys hovering near.

I protested.

"He will not come back," she said, and I realized how shrewd she was. She had read my mind, another suggestion of her malevolence. I took off my suit jacket and folded it on the bar. "Here's my jacket, here's some money. Buy me a beer, get some for yourselves, and hand over the jacket when I get back."

The *chimbudzi* was outside the bar, a roofless shed behind the tin-roofed building, upright bamboos and poles. Maggots squirmed in the shallow bog hole. I stood there and was too disgusted even to unzip, and then I stepped outside, looked around, and seeing no one, I ran — at first cautiously, then really hard, until I got to the road and flagged down a car. Of course the man stopped. He was African, I was white, it was Christmas, he needed money for petrol. He took me to my hotel; I had not slept even one night there. I asked him to wait. I paid my bill and got in again, and when the driver said where, I said, "Just keep going." He drove me twenty miles outside town and dropped me at a roadhouse, where I spent a sleep-less night.

What a fool I had been to trespass. The time I spent had not helped me to understand them. Apart from my initial sexual desire, my curiosity, my recklessness, there was no common ground other than mutual exploita-tion. I was reminded of who I really was, a presumptuous American. In spite of my politics and my teaching in the bush school, I was little more than a tourist, taking advantage. To me they were desperate Africans, seiz-ing their chance to possess me. It was *Tarzan* turned inside out, and rede-fining itself. I saw nothing more. I had simply feared them and I wanted to get out of there. Later the incident kept resonating, telling me who I was.

More dangerous things happened to me in Africa — serious fights, de-portations, gunplay — was there anything more upsetting than being held at gunpoint? But this was my first true experience of captivity and differ-ence, something horribly satirical. It had shocked me and shamed me with the knowledge that I'd been trespassing.

17

THE SEIZURES IN ZIMBABWE

In July 2002, a commercial farmer in Zimbabwe I shall call Jones was phoned late at night and told in a menacing voice, "You have fifteen minutes to leave your farm or you will be killed." This notification was a little unusual for the land reform program. Not the late-night murder threat — that was common — but Jones's farm comprised 110 hectares and only farms larger than 400 hectares qualified for seizure under the government guidelines. The suddenness was also odd. The normal procedure for farm seizures in Zimbabwe is first the serving of an order called a Section Five: notice that your farm has been designated for takeover. This is followed by a Section Eight: notice to vacate the property within ninety days. All of this is arbitrary and politically motivated; it is simple eviction on racial grounds. Even so, Jones was being seriously hounded, with no formalities except a death threat. Jones took the threat seriously, for a few months earlier his closest neighbor had been murdered by a mob for refusing to vacate his farm.

Jones, whose ancestors had come to this part of Africa over a century ago, had bought the land in 1981, a year after Zimbabwe's independence. No one wanted the tract; it was small, and the ground was stony and unpromising. For a decade, Jones and his wife lived in a makeshift hut called a rondavel, borrowed money, dug wells, put in irrigation, used fertilizer, and plowed organic matter into the sandy soil so that it would retain water. Nearly all the commercial farmers in Zimbabwe have done this at one time or another, for the land is not inherently fertile; it is composed of granite sands, with a low water-holding capacity. Farmed incorrectly, the soil turns into desert overnight.

Jones labored for several years to prepare the soil, and then he planted tobacco and roses—the latter he exported to Holland. He also grew seed maize and raised chickens and hogs. He transformed this small farm into a successful operation. He planted shade trees, upgraded his farm equipment, and began to pay off his bank loans. In 1992, in a final flourish of ownership Jones designed and built a lovely farmhouse with stone that he trucked from an abandoned quarry. He made doors and window frames of local teak; the roof was steep and graceful.

The house was his undoing. The elegant roof could be seen from the dirt road that ran past his fields. A prominent Zimbabwean with government connections noticed the house one day and decided he wanted it. It was he who arranged the menacing phone call. Before he could pack, a large mob showed up—men screaming threats. Jones and his wife were forced to run a gauntlet of abusive men, to sing the songs of the ruling party (ZANU-PF), and to praise Robert Mugabe, the president and the man who instigated these illegal farm invasions.

The intruder, an intimate of one of Mugabe's ministers, moved into the house, ate off Jones's crockery, sat in Jones's chairs, slept in Jones's bed, and told Jones to stay away. He fired Jones's forty farm workers and hired ten of his own at lower salaries. He harvested the tobacco and made plans to auction it. Jones, dispossessed of everything he owned, fled to Harare and began filing appeals—for the return of his farm, his crops, his household goods.

The man who told me this story said, "All this happened lately. Since you were last here, more than two thousand farms have been seized. The whole situation is desperate."

I love the African bush, I hate African cities. After my last Africa trip, I swore that I would never go back to the stinking buses, the city streets reeking of piss, the lying politicians, the schemers, the twaddlers, the crooks, the money changers taking advantage of weak currency and gullible people, the American God-botherers and evangelists demanding baptisms and screaming, "Sinners!"—and forty years of virtue-industry CEOs faffing around with other people's money and getting no results, except Africans asking for more.

Then this friend of mine in Zimbabwe told me about the blatant seizure of Jones's farm. And there was apparently more misery than ever: food shortages, no fuel, no hard currency, and the highest rate of inflation in the world, now at 300 percent and rising fast, the economy in such a dire state that the government could not afford to buy the German ink and paper necessary to print bills in Bulawayo. No one could collect a salary because the banks had run out of folding money. As for the farm invasions, they were "much worse. You wouldn't believe them."

And a friend of mine in Malawi, a long-term expatriate my exact age, with my predilection for the bush — the exile I might have been had I stayed forty years in the African hinterland with little else to do except drink beer and chase girls and watch my bananas ripen — this friend complained in a genial scribbled letter that I had not looked him up two years before.

"And you missed the vampires," he said. "There was a hell of a panic about bloodsuckers and some grisly murders a few months ago." He followed this with a story about a monstrous animal that had terrorized Malawi's central region. And more: people were being abducted "for their body parts."

There were other messages, too, from people I had met on my trip, urging me to come back, in the hospitable African way.

No one mentioned acts of God or complained of bad weather. No one asked for donations or even for sympathy. The harvests had been better than expected. No floods, no droughts. The few famines had been regional and political: the governments withholding food aid, a settling of scores with disaffected people, or the opposition, or the more despised tribes. Some rigged elections, some massacres. Like most African events, they went unnoticed or underreported. The outraged headline ISRAELI CHILD KILLED IN BOMBING occurs often in American newspapers, but you never see the headline AFRICAN CHILD KILLED IN BOMBING, for the death of one African child — or even a hundred — is not news.

Joseph Conrad once said, "Before the Congo I was just a mere animal." I could say the same about my own experience of Africa. I became curious again, and thinking about Africa once more, I yearned to go back.

Yes, I had recently published a book about a journey through Africa. The travel narrative implies that it has fixed a place forever. But that is just a conceit, for time passes and the written-about place keeps changing. All you do as a note-taking traveler is nail down your own vagrant mood on a particular trip. The traveling writer can do no more than approximate a country.

So, exactly two years after finishing my long trip in Africa, goaded by friends and provoked by stories from friendly correspondents, I decided to return. I wondered what had happened in my absence. And also, did he say *vampires*?

Two years before in Malawi, an American diplomat had agreed with me that the country was in a dire state economically and riddled with AIDS. "But they're getting cell phones. That's positive." I had jeered at him, saying, "Ha! Cell phones! They'll play with them like toys."

Almost the first thing I saw on my return to Blantyre were three Malawians, two women and a man, in the garden of a hotel giggling at a cell phone on the table that had been switched to Speaker, as a crackling voice chattered like a lost soul in a very badly rigged séance. Everyone had a cell phone. Business was worse than ever.

The Danish government had cut off all aid when it had learned that the Poverty Alleviation Fund had been used to buy Mercedes-Benzes for government ministers. The Dutch had curtailed aid because of the abysmal human rights record. The president, Bakili Muluzi, a Muslim, had hoped to make a friend of Saddam Hussein, and indeed, a few months before the Iraq War he had planned a state visit to Baghdad, bringing bags of rice and schoolbooks. When it was pointed out to President Muluzi that Malawi had no spare rice or schoolbooks, and that donor countries might take a dim view of this self-serving visit, it was canceled. But Muluzi had found an ally in Libya's Muammar Gaddafi, who had sent him helicopters and a fleet of Mitsubishi SUVs for his cronies, as well as money to set up madrassas and Islamic studies centers. As a result, Malawi had become a haven for dissident Muslims. "All Taliban over there," a Malawian said to me, and a month later, on June 26, 2003, four al-Qaeda operatives were picked up and whisked out of the country by the CIA. This caused an outbreak of rioting and looting by angry Muslims in Malawi.

The roads that had been under construction in 2001 were still unfinished. The schools were in worse shape than ever. The highest-paid teachers got the equivalent of $36 a month and complained to me that they could not live on it. There were many more hookers on the streets and in bars, the HIV/AIDS statistics were higher, the coffee and tobacco prices lower. There was no food shortage — in fact, the harvests were better than expected.

"But people here are always hungry. Give them food and they'll vote for you."

President Muluzi was in the process of changing the constitution so that he could run for a third term. Anyone who opposed this third-term bid was kicked out of Muluzi's party. One of these former ministers, Peter Chupa, who was still a member of Parliament, said to me, "Muluzi is a disaster. He has enriched himself and we are still poor. They are all thieves."

Most people I spoke to hankered for the days of the previous dictator, Hastings Banda, who had remained in power for thirty-four years.

"We had no idea that democracy was such a mess," another Malawian who resigned from the government told me. "And no one wants to help us. They don't trust us, because we have wasted donors' money."

Out of this desperate recrimination, self-pity, poverty, and paranoia came phantoms, some real, some imagined.

The monster that appeared one midnight this spring was real enough, but it was not like a beast that anyone had seen. It was a zombie, "a human creation," as though from the island of Dr. Moreau. It was huge and hairy. It became a regular visitor, pouncing on people and "removing legs, noses, arms and private parts." Sixteen people were maimed in one week. Whole villages fled in panic, and soon three thousand people were homeless, cowering from the beast.

The Red Cross and disaster preparedness teams promised help. Rangers tracked the beast and even shot it. Ten bullets found their mark, but the beast survived. "There was no trace of blood." Another thousand villagers joined the cowering refugees.

Two magicians asked to be allowed to kill the beast using juju. The district commissioner said, "The government does not recognize magic."

After months more of beast sightings, and deaths and maimings, the creature was killed by villagers "using traditional methods" — not guns. The beast was stoned, and lamed, and then beaten to death with sticks. Yet "its appearance still baffles people."

"It is a resurrected human being," one villager said.

But the strange beast was a hyena. In Malawi many hyenas had lost their habitat. This one, larger than normal, was starving and desperate — it had not eaten for weeks. And for the months that it lurked in the central region, the months before the harvest, a drama was enacted in which the villagers had found a target for their own anxiety and frustration and hunger.

The vampires were a greater scare. A few months previously the president of Malawi formally denied that his government was "sucking people's blood in exchange for maize donations from some foreign donors." And the mention of bloodsucking was not a euphemism. Vampires had already attacked a woman and her son and tried to extract their blood. There were "bloodsucker scares" in the country's largest town, Blantyre — people blowing whistles and beating drums at night to alert the community that blood hunters were near. A provincial governor was attacked and stoned for being suspected of "harboring bloodsuckers." His house was vandalized. The journalist who reported it in the local newspaper was arrested for writing an untrue story about bloodsuckers and for "causing fear and alarm."

The president, on a private visit to Britain, said the stories embarrassed him and were "destroying the country's image."

Within a day, three Catholic priests were attacked. They were suspected of being involved in bloodsucking.

The government, the police, and the president continued to maintain that there was no evidence of vampires or bloodsuckers. But no one was convinced. Most people believed there were vampires all over Malawi, looking for blood to trade for food.

Like the beast, this bloodsucking episode seemed like another metaphor for African distress. We are being eaten alive, we are losing our lifeblood, and somehow the government is at fault — its denials were proof of it. In Africa, an official denial is like an admission of truth.

The so-called Body Parts Killings were not a figment of the public imagination. Six people were found dead, and the lips, eyes, tongues, breasts, and buttocks had been removed from the corpses. All of the victims were women. Soon there were thirteen more victims, mutilated in the same way. Some were eviscerated: lungs, livers, and intestines removed.

"These body parts are being sold to Mozambique," the president said.

No one asked why. Everyone knew that body parts made the best *mankhwala* — medicine — good for what ails you. Eventually, nineteen men were arrested for these murders, and four men were put on trial. But in the end only one man was convicted of the crime. His name was Thomson Bokhobokho. He was remorseful. He confessed that he ate some of the body parts and sold the others. When asked his reason for the killings, he said, "Poverty."

There were now cell phones in Malawi, but nothing else had changed. I was discussing this with some friends in Blantyre when one of them pointed to some people carrying sacks of flour and jugs of cooking oil.

"They are from Zimbabwe?" one man said. "Ha! We're better off than they are!"

What could be worse than Malawi, I was wondering, and I remembered what I had heard of Jones, the man who had lost his farm to a party man who had taken a liking to it. What did a country like Zimbabwe look like with farms still under siege, limited amounts of folding money, and hyperinflation? How do you run a country with no fuel at all?

In a sort of dystopian tableau, at the perimeter of the new, empty Harare Airport, women and girls were gathering firewood and carrying it on their heads along the highway to their huts. No traffic. Cars and vans were abandoned by the roadside. Desperate doomsday vignettes like this were frequent in Zimbabwe: people scavenging for food and fuel on well-made roads, among modern but empty buildings.

Long lines of people waited at banks. Long lines of cars and minibuses at gas stations, more than three hundred at one station, most of them being minded by urchins because the stations had no fuel. There were no tourists, of course. The hotels were empty. The shops were empty. I bought two crocodile belts for Z$70,000 (the black market equivalent of $40) and had to carry the weighty stack of money in a shopping bag (Harare headline: PICKPOCKETS TURN TO TARGETING PEOPLE WITH BULGING PLASTIC BAGS). I could not carry any amount larger than the equivalent of about ten U.S. dollars in my pocket—the wad was too fat to fold. "The money is like bog roll," the sales clerk said to me, and she pointed out that a $10 bill had the same value and the same surface area as one square of toilet paper. "But is useless, is rougher."

That day, the Zimbabwe president, Robert Mugabe, happened to be in Johannesburg, where he had taken over an entire wing of the posh Westcliff Hotel, with his entourage of thirty—including two butlers, his personal chef, and his bodyguards and flunkies—so as to attend the funeral of the South African hero Walter Sisulu and visit his alma mater, Fort Hare

University. Mrs. Mugabe shopped importantly, and when she applied for a tax refund on her purchases, her extravagant invoices for shoes, jewelry, and dresses were printed in the Joburg papers. At Fort Hare, Mugabe was entertained by a praise singer, Jongela Nojozi, who lauded him in a song for "chasing the whites" out of Zimbabwe, making the president smile.

At independence, roughly 30 percent of Zimbabwe's land was occupied by mainly white-owned large-scale commercial farms. The figure was now 2 percent and falling. In every area, food production in Zimbabwe has seriously declined since the year 2000, when farm invasions began in earnest — tobacco is down to a quarter of what it was, wheat and maize output down 70 percent, dairy production cut in half, and the total head of cattle a third of its 2000 levels. Of the 3,217 large-scale farms operating in the year 2000, only 200 are still fully operational. A serious food shortage was expected.

I started to read the U.S. State Department's "Report on Human Rights Practices" (March 2003). Thirty-nine pages of murder, abduction, beatings, torture, rape, home invasion, "trafficking in people" (slavery, child prostitution, forced labor), and "killing of children for body parts." Selling body parts to South African witch doctors for traditional medicine was Zimbabwe's only verifiable export.

The first week I was in Harare, the *Guardian* correspondent Andrew Meldrum was expelled. Though he had been reporting the truth about Zimbabwe for eighteen years, he was vilified in the *Herald*, a government mouthpiece, as a spy, a meddler, a liar, and "a major disgrace to journalism." Frog-marched to his plane, Meldrum said that the government was trying to intimidate journalists and that no foreign reporters were safe in Zimbabwe.

"Who are you?" a policeman demanded when I turned up at the Norton police station.

The farming town of Norton, sixty miles west of Harare, was the scene some months earlier of the brutal murder of a commercial farmer named Terry Ford. Ford had been beaten, shot six times, and his corpse mutilated by a mob of twenty-seven thugs, acting for a party man who wanted the farm. That was a common occurrence: a crowd of men showed up at a commercial farmer's gate and demanded that he leave at once. These evictions could happen in a matter of days, and the new owner — always a party hack — would be sitting in the evicted farmer's chairs, eating off his plates, harvesting and selling his crops, slaughtering his livestock. One farmer I spoke with (all of them pleaded for anonymity), a man kicked off his land earlier this year, had demanded that his animals be returned to him. The animals were herded by the intruders into a small single pen — cows, steers, pigs, sheep, goats, lambs. Forced into a small space, farm animals panic and fight for dominance. These poor penned-up creatures battled themselves into a bloody mess. More than half of them died. The rest were maimed or useless when they were found the next day by their proper owner.

But Terry Ford, resisting the thugs, had died. Ford's farm was now in the hands of the party man. Soon after the murder, other farms in the district had been *chambanji*'d — mobbed and invaded — and seized by friends of Mugabe. The Norton police were summoned. But they had refused to show up, saying, "This is a political matter."

"I'm just an observer," I said to the Norton police chief. I wanted him to comment on the illegality of the evictions. In the past two years, two hundred policemen had left the Zimbabwe police force because of their disgust with human rights abuses. "I'm a foreign observer."

"Go away." The man was in charge but out of uniform, wearing a dirty jacket. He shuffled toward me in broken-down shoes and faced me, looking fierce, with bloodshot eyes and large, ill-fitting teeth. "We don't want you here."

Harare, with no fuel and no folding money, looked very quiet, though it was full of pedestrians, mainly young people killing time, because the schools were closed, the teachers on strike for higher pay.

HERALD EXTRA! ZIMBABWE STUDENT MURDERED IN LONDON was lettered on a newsstand sign.

"He was my brother," a ragged boy said to me with a teasing look, and pointing at the sign. His mates giggled at his bravado. "So I am going to murder you."

That was the day I noticed that apart from me there were no other white pedestrians in Harare. The next day, a white farmer told me that he had been threatened when he had dropped off one of his workers at the edge of a Harare township. He said, "I don't feel safe here anymore."

Milling crowds, no work, no school, an imploding economy, no rule of law, the leader of the opposition under arrest on a trumped-up charge of treason, the government a defiant kleptocracy with no international friends or local well-wishers. I did not meet a single person who supported the government. The Zimbabwe press, notably the *Daily News* and the *Weekly Independent*, appeared to be unmuzzled, and repeated these accusations and called for change. Yet there was no change, and though there were occasional work stoppages, there was no rebellion.

"It is not in our nature to be rebellious," an African writer told me. Another man said, "We don't have a culture of mass protest." A white woman, a farmer's wife, chain-smoking and furious, was more direct. "It's an arse-creeping culture. A slave mentality."

Her husband's farm had recently been invaded by political thugs, the so-called Green Bombers, and all five thousand acres were now in the hands of a high court judge who owned two other farms. That was not unusual. The government claimed that the goal of land reform was to share wealth with landless peasants and veterans of the political struggle that had led to independence. But this was false. Twelve high court judges had multiple estates and farms, and cronies of Mugabe had simply threatened commercial farmers and taken their land. And the judges helped each other out. When in June of this year a high court judge broke into and seized a commercial farm for himself, the evicted farmer seeking a legal solution was frustrated in his lawsuit by another high court judge, a man who himself owned at least three commercial farms.

A year of fuel shortages had produced several "stay-aways," one-day general strikes in which urban centers had been shut down and no business transacted. But the next day or so commerce resumed, after a fashion. Now there were lines of people — hundreds of them — waiting at banks, in bus queues, at markets. "It takes me two or three hours to get to work, and the same to go home to my township," a clerk in Harare told me, shaking her head.

"Everyone is hungry," a teacher said. There was food, but no one had money to buy it with.

An amazing sight, a whole country running on fumes. Every queue was a mob, but a passive one. I had never seen so many people waiting — every day the lines got longer, the currency weaker, the roads emptier, the food scarcer. I was fascinated by the visible decay, the indifference of the government, the extraordinary decrepitude. I had never in my life seen a place that was so obviously falling apart and yet still limping along. Unable to travel home, many people from the rural areas lived like trolls in the alleys behind the banks and shops and grander buildings in Harare.

Thieves were not apprehended, none of the farm invaders were even cautioned, crime was rife. The police were busy elsewhere. To make money, the police set up speed traps on the perimeter roads of the capital and stopped what few cars passed, demanding that fines be paid on the spot. I was in a car that was stopped. The cop asked for Z$4,000, "but give me two thousand and I'll let you go."

"I gave him four thousand and asked for a receipt," the driver told me as he got into the car. "Just to piss him off."

Two years before, by chance I had met Peter Drummond, a chicken farmer, who also raised cattle and pigs and grew seed maize on seven thousand acres thirty miles from Harare. Back then, Drummond had been threatened with eviction, served a Section Five, and invaded by people demanding land. To intimidate him, the squatters had cut down some shade trees near his house. I had met one of the invaders, a man who called himself Reywa, who had seized fifty acres and complained that his crops had failed because Drummond — the man he had victimized — had not helped him plant them. Two years ago I had jeered at this whining land thief. And he had muttered, "Drummond must plow for me. He must give me seeds and fertilizer."

I asked whether this had happened. And Drummond, who had a sense of humor, said, "Yes, I helped him. I plowed his fields. He's become a sort of friend." Drummond still hung on to his farm, but business was bad. In two years Drummond's chicken production had halved, and the fuel shortage was forcing him to cut back further.

Another commercial farmer I spoke to said that his friend's farm had been seized. The man was driven off his land with only a small suitcase. All his earthly possessions were in his house, and his farm equipment, his trucks, his furniture, and his crops were left behind.

"The man who took up residence trashed the place," the farmer told me. "He fired the farm workers because he didn't want to pay them. He got some of his own people. He tried to plow and broke the tractor. He buggered the tobacco dryers. He pranged my friend's vehicles and most of the animals died. All this in a matter of months. And soon he was on the phone to my friend — the chap who had lost the farm. The farm invader said that everything was broken and that he needed to borrow some money.

"My friend laughed like hell. He said, 'This restores my faith in the native.'"

"Native" was one of the milder words. Mingling with white farmers, I often heard Africans referred to as "munts," "kaffirs," or "houts" — the last from the Afrikaans word *hout-kopf,* wooden head. "Gooks" was common, too, a hangover from the bush war. Now and then "coons." If I winced or took exception, they pointed out that Mugabe was just as bad, referring to whites as snakes, exploiters, vermin, and, often, *mabunu,* a vicious cognate of "Boers."

"This whole business has turned me into a racist," a placid farmer's wife said to me out of the blue one day, frowning and clucking.

Mugabe spent a great deal of time attacking whites and trying to make Zimbabwe's failure into a racial issue, but in fact his human rights abuses have been mainly against black Zimbabweans, and the facts of government-sanctioned torture and murder are horrific, involving electric shock and beatings in police stations.

According to a recent survey by the Zimbabwe watchdog group Justice for Agriculture (JAG), 98 percent of all commercial farms, belonging to approximately four thousand farmers, were scheduled for seizure. Should any of these thousands of people continue farming, they would be committing a crime.

A model of efficiency, with a detailed database of farmers who have been evicted from their land, JAG is run by a group of volunteers and funded by donations. The spokesman and organizer is a bluff, portly, khaki-clad chain smoker named John Worsley-Worswick, who had recently lost his farm. In addition to mounting legal challenges, JAG is helping the sacked farm workers. One of JAG's more ambitious projects is the detailed accounting of the seizure of every farm. This chronicle goes under the rather bland name of a Loss Claim Document. Each bound volume, averaging a hundred pages or more, is a vivid history of a farm, from its inception to its seizure, with photographs of the property, the vehicles, the livestock, and the fields, valuations, flow charts, and a diary of the events leading to the takeover. *A crowd of about sixty chanting men climbed over the fence and began breaking our windows.* Some of the photographs showed dead or badly beaten people — atrocity pictures.

"Obviously we can't go back to what we had, but we need meaningful land reform. Respect for property rights as decided in the courts,"

Worsley-Worswick told me. "The breakdown in the rule of law has been state-inspired and state-sponsored."

In my peregrinations I met farmer Jones, whose eviction story had stimulated my interest in returning to Zimbabwe. Like almost every other farmer I met in Zimbabwe, white or black, he looked much older than his years. He was fifty-one but could have passed for sixty-five. Strangely, he was upbeat. "We're fighting this in court. Everything I have in the world has been taken from me. The thing I most regret is that I can't plant now, so we won't have a summer crop."

We were eating lunch at a chicken restaurant, and this being Harare, only two other tables (of about thirty-five) were occupied by diners.

Jones said, "Have you seen the north — Chinhoyi and Karoi? Virtually all the farms there are gone."

I said I hadn't seen much of the hinterland because of the fuel shortage. There were no vehicles.

Jones said, "You have to see what has happened. We're taking a chap to Zambia — his family was evicted, he's relocating. You can come along."

"When were you planning to leave?"

"In about twenty minutes."

So, less than an hour after I met him, I had agreed to a sudden departure on a two-day trip through farmland and bush, to Kariba and across the Zambezi River into Zambia. He would drop me in Lusaka. We picked up Mrs. Jones, who was good-humored as well as shrewd and capable. Her folks had recently lost their farm. The other passenger, a young man whom I shall call Colin, told me that his parents had recently been evicted. Colin was taking a job in Zambia, in a chicken hatchery that was owned by a Zimbabwean who had been run off his farm, too.

There had been an exodus to Zambia by evicted farmers, who hoped that by staying close to Zimbabwe they would be able to resume farming when Mugabe was out of power and the situation was reversed — either the farms were returned to their rightful owners or compensation was offered. About a fifth of Zimbabwe's commercial farmers had left for Australia or New Zealand, to begin new lives, and even to farm, but this represented to Jones a surrender mentality.

And there was something else, verging on betrayal. Not just running from the injustice, but abandoning a country they loved. All the farmers I met in Zimbabwe loved the land, and though they tended to disparage urban clerks as paper-chewers, and politicians as parasites, they praised their workers and were proud of their labors. They knew the most intimate moods of the climate, the soil, the animals, the birds, the flora, the bush.

"We'll see elephants," Jones said as we headed north. "Look, there's a go-away bird. But I'm not going."

We drove to Chinhoyi, a small farming town of idle people and empty roads, where no one was farming and the lines at gas stations were three abreast and motionless. A week before there had been a rumor that a fuel delivery was imminent. No delivery had been made, but there was nothing to do in Chinhoyi except wait. The bakeries had run out of flour, the shops had run out of cooking oil, there were mealies — sweet corn — in the market for the local starch, sadza, but the price had increased tenfold. Some foreign charities, including the World Food Programme and an Irish NGO called GOAL, were distributing food by giving it to the war veterans, Mugabe's heavies, and asking them to hand it out in the rural areas.

"Food aid is politicized," a white Zimbabwean had told me in Harare. "Our greatest fear is that the NGOs will dig in and undermine agricultural production and make a niche for themselves in perpetuity."

"This was all farms once," Jones said from time to time, as he continued on to Karoi. The gates and fences of large estates were broken, and the fields were weed-choked and unplowed.

"No crops," Jones said. "This should be under winter wheat. There's good irrigation here, but look at the fields — nothing."

All we saw in the next fifty miles was one farm that seemed operational. Jones knew the man.

He said, "They usually leave one farmer in place, but it's hell for him, because he's the man they turn to when they need a tractor or fuel or spare parts or money. And if he doesn't play ball, they'll shut him down."

Not all the rolling hills of this part of Zimbabwe had been farmed. Old Africa still existed in thicknesses of trees and crumbled cliffs, vividly colored in the sunset, the steep outcrops that signaled the beginning of the escarpment that banked down to the Zambezi, Zimbabwe's frontier with Zambia and home to a million animals, large and small.

"Depressing, isn't it?" Mrs. Jones said as we passed a derelict farm. "That place could be producing food. Instead, it's just a ruin."

The dusk was casting a long shadow over these derelict farms and wooded hills, and night came on so quickly that before I knew it we were traveling in darkness. That was when Colin told me that his elderly parents, once prosperous farmers, were working in a hardware store to make ends meet.

At Makuti, just a wide place in the road where there was a turning to Kariba, Jones slowed his vehicle and said, "Look." A slender leopard crept out of the grass onto the shoulder and crossed the road in our headlights, keeping low, its spots bright in the high beams, and penetrated the grass at the far side, its stiff tail bobbing.

"We need fuel," Jones said. "I know a chap in Kariba."

We drove slowly in the darkness for another hour or so.

Jones said, "Look."

An elephant was loping down the road, its bulky hindquarters looming. The animal did not look around at us, did not speed up, did not do anything except continue to tread the white line in the middle of the road with its big flat feet, making us follow at a decent distance. The elephant was absolutely unhurried, hogging the road, plodding at its own speed. Finally, still without glancing back, he turned toward a big, night-black thicket, paused, then crashed through the trees, shouldering the boughs apart.

"How could we leave this?" Jones said.

Twenty miles ahead was the tourist town of Kariba. I had been there four or five times before, because just below the dam was one of the finest stretches of the Zambezi. I had once paddled from here to Kanyemba, at the eastern frontier of Mozambique. In better times Kariba was full of small hotels and bars, houseboats on the lake, good restaurants, suppliers and provisioners. Now, not one hotel was occupied or even open, the bars were closed, and as we arrived at night no one was out. The town was in darkness.

Jones found his friend, the man with the diesel fuel, and filled his tank.

"We'll have to stay here," he said. "The border's closed."

"The hotels are shut," I said.

"I know a chap. He's not here—his house is empty. There's a key in a hiding place."

We went to the house, which was on the side of a hill overlooking the big inky lake, and it seemed that no sooner had I fallen asleep than Jones was clapping his hands in the darkness, saying, "Up, up. Up!" It was four thirty, he said, and he wanted to be first in line at the frontier.

The Zambian side of the border was dense bush and savanna scattered with small villages and mud huts and tiny garden plots, small granaries of woven twigs, women pounding maize in mortars.

"Zim used to look like this," Mrs. Jones said. "Years ago."

Colin looked apprehensive. He was almost thirty and had lived his whole life in Zimbabwe. He had spent some time in England but had never been to Zambia before. And here he was an immigrant, starting a new job as a farm manager, a new life, for his fiancée would be joining him.

Past Kafue, we crossed the railway that continued to Livingstone and Victoria Falls. One station was crowded with people sitting on bundles, sleeping in the shade of the platform, stretched out on the tracks.

"More munts than trains," Colin said, gaping out the window.

We dropped him at the farm, which was owned by a man who had lost his farm in Zimbabwe in June 2002. He had been harassed, threatened, and given a month to leave by a local politician, who now ran it.

Jones said, "We're headed to Lusaka. Just looking around. Anything happening?"

"The big social thing here is polo," the exiled farmer said. "I'm not that keen, but there's nothing else to do. There's a tournament this weekend."

"Notice anything peculiar?" a man said to me at the Lusaka Polo Club, the day of the tournament.

I had fallen into conversation with him and discovered that he was a Zimbabwean who had lost his farm and migrated here to start over. His farm was one of the first in the country to be seized. A *nanga*, a local witch doctor, had demanded a portion of the 1,300 acres the man owned. The farmer refused. "He brought people in. They threatened to kill us. We had to leave." The *nanga* fired all the farm workers — forty of them — and brought in five of his own. "He now controls five farms, all of them useless."

We were sitting near each other watching a match. The polo club, with its small squat clubhouse, restaurant, upstairs bar, and glass cases of dusty trophies, had been in existence since 1946, though I was assured that people had been playing polo here since the 1920s. There were about 150 spectators — the women in wide-brimmed hats, the men in shorts, most people swilling beer, and some children running around — the sputter of sausages on a barbecue, limp pennants on posts, the snort of reined-in horses, the click of the ball against the mallets, the smack of polo sticks, the green field, and high in the sky a single startled fish eagle being harried by a flock of ravens.

"Look, no coons," the farmer said.

White farmers in Zimbabwe talked that way because they had no idea that it was offensive, a journalist in Harare had told me. "They don't know the world disapproves of this language. They are not exposed to anything beyond their own rural horizons."

But that provincialism, revealed in that sort of dismissive language, was one of the biggest differences between these migrants and the white Zambians, who said they were shocked.

"I was at a wedding in Zimbabwe a few weeks ago," another man said to me, shaking his head in disgust, "and I heard little kids using those words."

"These Zimbos used to laugh at us," an elderly businessman told me at the polo match, pointing out the newcomers, the migrants, the exiles, the recent settlers and planters from Zimbabwe. His father had fought in the Boer War and had ended up with a plot of land here, when it was Northern Rhodesia. "They said Zambia was backward, undeveloped, and so forth. Now they're here, and I can tell you we're not that happy about it."

The white Zambians I met at the polo match introduced me to black Zambians. After the circumspection and gloom of Zimbabwe, Zambian frankness was a treat. Rodger Chongwe, who had been appointed minister of justice and legal affairs in the Zambian government in 1991, said that he had resigned in 1995 "because I couldn't sit at the same table with thieves and drug dealers — my fellow ministers, of course." When he began speaking out, he received death threats, and at a political rally in 1997 he had been shot and seriously wounded, the bullet passing through his jaw. He took the hint and escaped to Australia, and had just returned after five years. He said the former president, Frederick Chiluba, had encouraged the assassination attempt.

"What was he afraid of?"

"Of losing power. And he was a thief."

"How much had he stolen?"

"Four hundred million U.S. dollars."

I said that I had read that an elementary school in Hawaii regularly sent money to a school in Zambia so that the Zambian schoolchildren could have hot breakfasts.

"Politicians like Chiluba are laughing at those American kids for sending money."

This brought us to the subject of aid. Chongwe said, "The donors are making us lazy. The Japanese volunteers are doing what the city council used to do—mending potholes. It is better for us to have potholes. We would be forced to do something about them. We'd have to think for ourselves."

Another former member of Parliament was Rolf Shenton. He was forty-one, born in Zambia, and it was hard to tell from his black leather jacket and his earring and wild hair that he was a businessman and a father of four children and had also been the member for Mazabuka. When he wasn't politicking he was a motor mechanic, with a garage in Lusaka. He said, "I get these aid guys at my workshop. I fix their vehicles. Yesterday it was the World Vision Land Rover. I said, 'By giving people food you're destroying their initiative. You're preventing them from farming.' They're entrenched. Charity is a business. They don't even think about leaving. They've created imbalances in food, artificial shortages, sudden surpluses from abroad that undercut the local farmers. They make more problems than they solve."

"What's the answer?"

"We need aid, of course. But much more, we need to be free of aid. We need to break the cycle. They send us doctors. Two thousand doctors have been trained by the University of Zambia Medical School. Fewer than 180 have remained in the country. Does that make sense? We need to get rid of the bilaterals. And the IMF and the World Bank lend money at an extortionate rate."

"What about forgiving the debt?"

"Forgiving the debt is not going to solve the problem. What we need is noncorrupt government. There has not been a free election here since the 1960s."

Donors should be more interested in fair elections, Rodger Chongwe had said to me. Donors lived here, so they knew about the corruption. Donors shielded government thieves because they could tell them what to do. I asked Shenton what he thought of this.

"The donors must fuck off," he said. "Write that down! Use my name!"

Life expectancy was down to thirty-three, and Zimbabwe's statistics for HIV/AIDS infection were similar. Teachers were dying of AIDS faster than new ones were being produced by the teacher training colleges. These were the government's own statistics. A quarter of Zambian women in their thirties were infected. The outlook was bleak for everyone. If you were a fifteen-year-old Zambian, you had a 60 percent chance of death by AIDS before you reached forty-five.

AIDS statistics did not deter the displaced Zimbabwean farmers from relocating. I was told that about fifty farmers were at work, producing maize as well as seeds. The poultry farmers I spoke to were supplying chickens and eggs to the Congo.

"We have the watches, but Africans have the time," one of these farmers said to me. "Remember that. It's the key to living here."

I went back to Zimbabwe. The exchange rate had risen 20 percent in a week. But the opposition party, the Movement for Democratic Change, had become more vocal. The party leader, Morgan Tsvangirai, was a sworn foe of Mugabe. What was needed, Tsvangirai said, was mass action — a nationwide general strike.

There was a great deal of speculation about what would happen. I went to several townships to see what preparations were being made. "What are we doing?" one man said. "We are talking, talking, talking."

One night I was sitting in a Harare hotel bar with a friend.

"We are the only people here," he said.

"True." It was just after eight in the evening, and apart from a waiter there was no one else in the bar or the lobby.

"I am being surveilled." He frowned. "Now, so are you."

The next day another Zimbabwean said, "If you don't leave now, you might not make it," because the mass action would surely happen. There would be roadblocks, police, Green Bombers, and thugs. Mugabe's men would be out, and Mugabe's men would beat anyone who was demonstrating. They also hated whites. I would be beaten if I was outside. All shops would be closed. No planes would fly. The country would shut down.

So I left. People say nothing happens on time in Africa, that nothing will change in Zimbabwe. But right on schedule, from the following Monday, when it was promised, there was a week of protest, of roadblocks, of stoppages, of beatings. Whites were assaulted in Harare, and Morgan Tsvangirai was arrested. Mugabe proved that he had the loyalty of the police, the army, and his thugs.

Ten days later the shops opened, and life, such as it was, resumed in Zimbabwe. But the situation was still so dire that Colin Powell wrote an op-ed piece for the *New York Times*. His message: Mugabe must go. This would be on the agenda when President Bush met in South Africa with President Thabo Mbeki.

There was some good news in late June. Zimbabwe, facing a serious shortfall in food, had found a new food source in Zambia and was planning to import 30,000 tons of maize, as well as soy beans and wheat and 12,000 tons of seed maize. All of this from the bumper crop produced by the Zimbabwe farmers whose land had been taken from them, and who had begun farming over the border in Zambia.

18

STANLEY: THE ULTIMATE AFRICAN EXPLORER

Poor Africa, the happy hunting ground of the mythomaniac, the rock star buffing up his or her image, the missionary with a faith to sell, the child buyer, the retailer of dirty drugs or toxic cigarettes, the editor in search of a scoop, the empire builder, the aid worker, the tycoon wishing to rid himself of his millions, the school builder with a bucket of patronage, the experimenting economist, the diamond merchant, the oil executive, the explorer, the slave trader, the ecotourist, the adventure traveler, the bird watcher, the travel writer, the escapee, the colonial and his crapulosities, the banker, the wanker, the busybody, the Mandela-hugger, the political fantasist, the buccaneer, and your cousin the Peace Corps volunteer. Oh, and the atoner, of whom Thoreau observed in a skeptical essay, "Now, if anything ail a man so that he does not perform his functions . . . if he has committed some heinous sin and partially repents, what does he do? He sets about reforming the world." Thoreau, who had Africa specifically in mind, added, "Do ye hear it, ye Woloffs . . . ?"

These people have been in and out of the continent since the beginning of the nineteenth century, much earlier if we include the Arab slave traders and the tourist Herodotus. A common denominator in this assortment of foreign visitors — high-minded pests and exploiters alike — is their wish to transform themselves while claiming they want to change Africa. Henry Morton Stanley is a classic case.

"We went into the heart of Africa self-invited — therein lies our fault," Stanley confided to his diary. The words are quoted in the magnificent

Stanley: The Impossible Life of Africa's Greatest Explorer, by Tim Jeal, a biography that has many echoes for our own time.

Burton and Speke poked at the edges of Lake Victoria, and Livingstone walked in circles around Lake Bangweulu, speculating on the source of the Nile, pretending to be a missionary. Jeal was the first to reveal, in his 1973 life of Livingstone, that the melancholy Scot had made just one Christian convert (who later lapsed). Even the Arab slave traders stayed away from *l'Afrique profonde.* But a few years after finding Livingstone, on his second African journey, Stanley thrust his way through the midsection of Africa from east to west, and later from west to east. His journeys were valiant, well organized, and the man was a hero. But he was also prone to exaggeration in his reporting the events of his travels, and he had many personal secrets.

"Yet despite the pain and weakness of his physical body," Jeal writes of Stanley's exhaustion after the first traverse of Africa, an almost unthinkable seven-thousand-mile journey to crack the secrets of the central African watershed, "Henry pulsed with almost mystical self-belief: 'For my real self lay darkly encased, & was ever too haughty & soaring for such miserable environments as the body that encumbered it daily.'"

This "real self" is the one that Jeal gets to grips with. Most of what we have been told of Stanley, much of which he wrote himself, is wrong. Jeal nails them as "misguided lies." For one thing, his name was not Henry Morton Stanley. He was not, as he claimed, an American from New Orleans. He had not been adopted. It was not the *New York Herald*'s idea for him to find Livingstone, and the Livingstone he found was not, as he claimed, a saintly figure devoted to the uplift of Africa. He did not utter the words "Dr. Livingstone, I presume." He was not the violent hanger and flogger he was reputed to be, nor was he a willing cat's-paw for King Leopold's infernalities. But, as this book demonstrates in a way that makes it a superb adventure story as well as a feat of advocacy, Stanley was probably the greatest explorer ever to set foot in Africa.

The man we know as Stanley was born John Rowlands in north Wales to a dissolute mother, and at the age of six was confined to the misery of a workhouse. He escaped once but was sent back by ashamed and indifferent relatives. He was discharged from this semiprison at fifteen and got a job on an American ship, which he jumped in New Orleans. He worked awhile there, experimented with a new name and identity, and joined the Confederate army, the Dixie Grays, in 1861. He fought at the Battle of Shiloh, was captured by a Union patrol, clapped into prison at Camp Douglas, and given the choice of fighting for the North or rotting. He changed sides, marched under a Union flag, then deserted and sailed to Wales, where he was again rejected by his hammer-hearted mother: "Never come back to me again unless you are in better circumstances than you seem to be in now."

"Unloved, deeply sensitive, but angry, too," Jeal writes, Stanley searched for a way to prove himself. In being rejected he had also been liberated, and his reading (especially travel books) was another liberation. He made a disastrous journey to Turkey and was for a time a war correspondent, reporting on the massacre of Indians in Iowa and Ethiopians in Magdala. Then, at age thirty-one, he persuaded James Gordon Bennett of the *New York Herald* that he could make headlines finding David Livingstone, who was not exactly lost but who hadn't been heard from for a while and was fading from the public memory.

The success of this African trip from the coast to Livingstone's hut near the shores of Lake Tanganyika was a great coup and a bold headline, and it had the effect of transforming the fortunes of both men. Stanley proved himself a more than able explorer — he was a real leader and had stamina. His account of the trip showed him to be a persuasive writer, though in his wish to justify the effort, he overegged his descriptions of Livingstone and thus canonized him, obscuring the man's oddities and failures. In Livingstone, the fatherless Stanley found a powerful and idealized father figure, whose stated mission to explore and improve Africa could be his own. Importantly (and this is one of the many modern dimensions of Jeal's book), he found a continent where he could transform himself. For a man who had experimented with multiple identities, Africa gave Stanley a name, a face, notoriety, a mission, and problems to solve, and it confirmed his greatness as an explorer.

One of the enduring but creepier features of the emotional life of the British is envy. I see it as arising out of the stifling rigidity of the class system. Jeal anatomizes this corrosive quality in describing how throughout Stanley's life the British press, the big bugs in the Royal Geographical Society, statesmen, and rival adventurers spent much of their time making sport of the shy man, trying to tear him down and belittle his achievements. By inventing and improving his past, Stanley gave them lots of ammo. A self-made man in every sense, he had concealed or prettified so much of his early life that he never seemed anything but dubious — there were always whispers and there were often assaults on his character. Nor did his tendency to exaggerate help him in his quest for respectability. Even in Africa, when he efficiently managed to fight off the spears and arrows of an onslaught of attackers, with a small loss of life, he upped the death tolls, overcolored the encounters, made them emphatically incarnadine, and portrayed himself as a battler. No one quite knew who he was, and he didn't want anyone to know. Jeal movingly describes how even at the end of his life, wishing to write his autobiography, Stanley wandered the streets and cemeteries of New Orleans looking for a plausible family history, "all because he could not endure the thought of admitting that his adoption had never happened."

Yet look what he achieved. The driven workhouse boy dumped by his mother, dreaming of fame, broke free of his class and his country, Americanized himself (he cultivated the accent and the brashness), and became a world-renowned reporter. He single-handedly created the myth of the saintly Livingstone. He then set forth, and in an epic three-year journey he established "the true parent of the Victoria Nile" and followed the Congo River to the Atlantic. Recrossing Africa, he rescued the elusive Emin Pasha (Isaak Eduard Schnitzer, a slippery, fez-wearing German who was ambivalent about being rescued), and — duped by King Leopold, believing that he was civilizing the Congo — he established trading posts as far as Stanley Falls. Five years later, Captain Korzeniowski would steam upriver in the *Roi des Belges* and identify it as the Inner Station, the Heart of Darkness.

The irony was that in spite of his idealism, his boldness in opening the heart of Africa to the world, he was (Jeal writes) "one of the unwitting begetters of the historical process that led to the terrible exploitation and crimes against humanity in the Congo."

But Africa was the backdrop for Stanley's real life. "I was not sent into the world to be happy," Stanley wrote. "I was sent for special work." The epitome of his work, as he saw it, was an ordeal. He was most at ease with Africans, and with Englishmen from humble backgrounds like his own. The wellborn white officers who wished themselves on his expeditions were usually a source of pain and scandal.

Adventure travelers in Africa are nothing new. In the late nineteenth century they took the form of wealthy young men who bought their way onto a journey. They were the feckless and disobedient officers in Stanley's Rear Column who caused the great scandal that dogged his reputation. Take the abominations of James Jameson, the Irish whiskey heir, who stayed behind while Stanley went on searching for the reluctant Schnitzer. "Fascinated by cannibalism" and something of an amateur sketcher, Jameson bought an eleven-year-old girl while bivouacked on the Congo and handed her over to a group of Africans. While they stabbed her, dismembered her, cooked her, and ate her, Jameson did drawings of the whole hideous business.

Bula Matari — "Breaker of Rocks" — Stanley's nickname in Africa, was shy everywhere else, and diffident when pursuing a woman. His love affairs were all failures. He was wooed by a woman who insisted on his marrying her, and she stifled him, refused to allow him to return to Africa, got him to run for Parliament, which he detested, and sent him to exile in an English country house and an early death at the age of sixty-three. Because he had been scapegoated so often, he was refused a burial in Westminster Abbey.

Stanley's life speaks to our time, throwing light on the nannying ambitions that outsiders still wish upon Africa. Among other things it is a chronicle of the last years of the Arab-Swahili slave trade, which was fairly vigorous as little as a hundred years ago, and which Stanley opposed. What would have happened if the Arab-Swahili slavers had remained unopposed throughout Africa?, Jeal muses. "Darfur provides a clue."

There have been many biographies of Stanley, but Jeal's is the most felicitous, the best informed, the most complete and readable, and exhaustive, profiting from his access to an immense new trove of Stanley material. In its progress from workhouse to mud hut to baronial mansion, it is like the most vivid sort of Victorian novel, that of a tough little man battling against the odds and ahead of his time in seeing the Congo clearly, its history (in his words) "two centuries of pitiless persecution of black men by sordid whites."

19

PAUL BOWLES: NOT A TOURIST

The Sheltering Sky was Paul Bowles's first novel, and although he honed his art almost to his dying day—novels, poems, stories, translations, as well as musical scores—it was this strange, uneven, and somewhat hallucinatory novel, and a handful of disturbing short stories written around the same time, that seemed to locate his fictional vision for good in the minds of his readers. So at the age of thirty-eight he was defined, and that definition dogged him for the rest of his life. Even in his eighties he was pestered about details in the novel. I know this to be true because I was one of the people pestering him when he was that great age.

I found him sitting on the floor of a back room in a large chilly apartment in a gray building on a back street in Tangier. It was October and clammy cold. To drive the dampness away Bowles had a sort of superior blowtorch going, a fizzing blue flame heating the curtained-off cubicle, where he was seated like a hawker in a bazaar, on a mat, back straight, legs out, because of a leg infection. Around him was a litter of small objects: notebooks, pens, medicine bottles—everything within reach—a teapot, a cup, spoons, matches, and shelves with books and papers, some of them musical scores. A metronome sat on a low table nearby, among bottles of capsules and tubes of ointment, and cassette tapes and a tin of Nesquik and cough drops and a partly eaten candy bar and a note folded and jammed into an envelope scribbled *Paul Bowles, Tanger, Maroc*, a vague address but it had obviously found him, as I had, with little more information than that.

With a pad in his hand, he was translating a novel from Spanish. His illness and his age gave him a strangely sculpted and skeletal dignity. He seemed sure of himself, and (as a chronic vacillator myself) I admired him for being uncompromising.

Because I did not want to inhibit his talk by taking notes of our conversation, I stopped in a café, the Negresco, on the way back to my hotel and described this meeting in my notebook. I wanted to make it an episode for the end of my Mediterranean journey, the book I was to call *The Pillars of Hercules*. I wrote, *He seems to me a man who masks all feelings; he has a glittering eye but a cold gaze. He seems at once preoccupied, knowledgeable, worldly, remote, detached, vain, skeptical, eccentric, self-sufficient, indestructible, fragile, egomaniacal, frank, and hospitable to praise. He is like almost every other writer I have known in my life.* Seeing me scribbling, a Moroccan sitting nearby asked if I happened to be a writer. His name was Mohamed Choukri. He knew Bowles, because Bowles had translated his first and best-known novel, *For Bread Alone*. He disparaged him in a genial way, then said, "He is a nihilist."

"Everyone is always leaving tomorrow," Bowles had said to me when I told him I was taking the ferry back to Spain the next day.

But Bowles never left. His was the classic case of the person who detaches himself and swims away from the mainstream, to go far away to pursue anonymity — no phone, no name on the house — and discovers that the world beats a path to his door, making him conspicuous. (B. Traven in Mexico and J. D. Salinger in New Hampshire are two other examples of this paradox.) It could be said that Bowles unwittingly popularized Tangier as a louche and literary destination — certainly Jack Kerouac, William Burroughs, Allen Ginsberg, and many others went to Tangier because Bowles had gotten there first. Bowles saw them come and go; he went on living there, with forays to Ceylon and Spain. Bowles had first visited Tangier with Aaron Copeland at the bidding of (so he told me) Gertrude Stein. Copeland went home, Bowles found the place to his liking, and there he thrived, part ascetic, part snob (as he seemed to me), and in his way distinctly rebellious, going against the grain, because the dampness and his rigorous living conditions and the decay of Tangier all seemed to be life-shorteners. But unlike all those others, he was a resident and a traveler, not a tourist.

"I felt strongly then about my not being a tourist as my protagonist Port did in the novel I eventually wrote, *The Sheltering Sky*," he told one of his biographers. He states this explicitly early on in the novel, speaking of Port:

"He did not think of himself as a tourist; he was a traveler. The difference is partly one of time, he would explain. Whereas the tourist generally hurries back home at the end of a few weeks or months, the traveler, belonging no more to one place than to the next, moves slowly, over periods of years, from one part of the earth to another."

Bowles started the novel in Fez, Morocco, late in 1948, and after writing 150 pages went to Oran, in Algeria, and traveled south, manuscript in hand, to Oujda, to Colombe-Béchar, a French garrison, then Taghit, a day's journey by truck, then Béni Abbès and Timimoun, and finally back to Fez. Novelists can be extremely misleading about their methods and motives (Bowles claimed that this book came to him when he was riding a bus up Fifth Avenue), but it seems certain, as he said, that he wrote the book and gathered these details on his trip through Algeria, as he later explained, "a combination of memory writing and minute description of whatever place I was in at that moment."

On his ramble through Algeria, he was writing each morning, elaborating details of places he'd seen. He was also experimenting with drugs, notably hashish and *majoun* ("cannabis jam"); he claimed that some of the novel was written under the influence. In every respect, this was quite the opposite of the romantic idea of emotion recollected in tranquility, much more the insertion of raw experience onto the page, the traveling author creating a picaresque narrative by adding detail to the story line from his peregrinations: the hot nights, the long rides, the wrong turns, the unreliable locals, the hideous tourists — here the Lyles, mother and son.

And the seedy hotels and the bad food. The Grand Hotel in Aïn Krorfa in this novel takes the cake as one of the worst hotels in fiction: the fountain at its entrance contained "a small mountain of reeking garbage" as well as some human infants, naked, their "soft formless bodies troubled with bursting sores . . . pink hairless dogs," and inside, the "predominating odor was the latrine." Here the travelers "engaged three smelly rooms," and one of the rooms has "a jackal skin on the floor . . . the only furnishing."

The meals in this hotel and elsewhere on the trip are so bad as to be almost comical. Weevils in the soup at the Grand, and later Kit "found patches of fur in her rabbit stew" and, in the kitchen, a knife stuck into the table and "under the point was a cockroach, its legs still feebly kicking." In El Ga'a "the meat consisted of various unidentifiable inner organs fried in deep fat," and in Sba the shopkeeper Daoud Zozeph's wife serves up "amorphous lumps of dough fried in deep fat and served cold . . . pieces of cartilaginous meat . . . soggy bread." At Belquassim's, where Kit is captive, "some of the dishes seemed to consist principally of lumps of half-cooked lamb fat." I think we can be assured that Bowles transferred these meals from the table to his work in progress, and that he analyzed it as he ate, or merely gloated over its horror.

The note of fascinated disgust that echoes through the novel is struck at the outset with the three travelers in a seedy café in Oran, studying their maps. The Arabs sit outside, the Americans inside, "cooler but without movement, and it smelled of stale wine and urine."

This motif of grotesquerie occurs so frequently that it becomes a dark version of comic awfulness, causing the reader to think, What next! And this reminds us that the greatest terror in fiction is often achieved by way of black comedy. Bowles was possessed by the notion of extremes, dramatized in the mounting persecution of the professor in "A Distant Episode," surely one of the most terrifying short stories in any language. Bowles claimed *The Sheltering Sky* was "really, a working out of the professor's story in 'A Distant Episode' . . . the same story retold."

The structure of the novel is episodic and seemingly random. Three Americans set off, going south from Oran. They have distinctly different personalities. Port Moresby's name is an intentional joke by Bowles: Port Moresby is of course the capital of Papua New Guinea, named in 1873 by Captain John Moresby after his father, Admiral Sir Fairfax Moresby. The Port of the novel is thin, "with a slightly wry, distraught face" and a sense of nonattachment. His wife, Kit, is a high-strung socialite with a trunk full of evening gowns and makeup — we even see her in a desert outpost wearing a backless number of pale blue satin, for no apparent reason. The third member of this ménage à trois — as it turns out to be — is Tunner, an opportunist, who cuckolds Port and is surprised at one point that it doesn't rain much in the Sahara.

They are wanderers. The Second World War has ended, and they are now free to travel. They know almost nothing about North Africa and are ambivalent about it from the outset, so why have they chosen this destination? "It was one of the few places they could get boat passage" from New York.

The Lyles are Australian, offering farcical comedy of a shrieking racist mother and her creepy son. For long stretches, as much as 170 pages, they drop out of the story. They add very little to the narrative, but they are presented with such gusto they seem to have a point. Tennessee Williams was an early admirer (and reviewer) of the novel, and this mother and son seem like stock figures from his cast of characters.

The Americans move south. Many of the places can be found on a modern map: Messad, Tadjmout, El Ga'a, Sba, Adrar, and distant Tessalit, over the Algerian border in Mali.

It is in Port's nature to nose around, uncomprehending yet undeterred. He is a searcher — but for what? I suppose, the wish to go to extremes. Yet he is chronically restless. When he finds a willing local woman, Marnhia, the whole affair lasts "not more than a quarter of an hour." Later, there are quarrels, misunderstandings; the food gets worse, the weather hotter. "The room was malignant" is one description, and dawn itself is tainted: "the pale infected light of daybreak."

Port's inwardness and sense of self-destruction are intensified. His illness seems to be an illumination, but then — long before the novel ends — he dies. His biographer: Bowles "told Jane [his writer wife] that he meant to kill off his hero halfway through the book. 'He lingers in an agony instead of dying. But I'll get rid of him yet. Once he's gone there'll be only the heroine left to keep things going, and that won't be easy either.'"

In its randomness and especially the exoticism of its setting, the novel was distinctly modern, written for a postwar reading public that was still shockable, and presented by a young man who, though he disdained any idea of a message, could be at times sententious: "The bar was . . . full of the sadness inherent in all deracinated things," and "Humanity is everyone but oneself," and "The soul is the weariest part of the body," and "A walk through the countryside was a sort of epitome of the passage through life itself."

These don't work for me, they hardly even ring true, but there are insights that stay in the mind. After Port's unexpected death, Kit remembers a particular day at home when, seeing an approaching storm, "death had become the topic."

"Death is always on the way," Port had said, "but the fact that you don't know when it will arrive seems to take away from the finiteness of life. It's that terrible precision that we hate so much. But because we don't know, we get to think of life as an inexhaustible well. Yet everything happens only a certain number of times, and a very small number, really. How many more times will you remember a certain afternoon of your childhood, some afternoon that's so deeply a part of your being that you can't even conceive of your life without it? Perhaps four or five times more. Perhaps not even that. How many more times will you watch the full moon rise? Perhaps twenty. And yet it all seems limitless."

The novel moves from observation to observation, rather than from incident to incident. The image of the sheltering sky is enlarged in the unfolding narrative, and of course calls attention to itself. "The sky here's very strange," Port says to Kit. "I often have the sensation when I look up at it that it's a solid thing up there, protecting us from what's behind." And he explains, "Nothing, I suppose. Just darkness. Absolute night."

Ambiguity is menace for him, leading to death, and when Port dies, the darkness behind the sheltering sky is revealed: "A black star appears, a point of darkness in the night sky's clarity. Point of darkness and gateway to repose. Reach out, pierce the fine fabric of the sheltering sky, take repose."

Port's death, "seen from the inside," as Bowles wanted it, is a form of passion. None of the sex or lovemaking in the book — Port and Mahrnia, Tunner and Kit, Kit and her numerous lovers — is described with anything like the power that Bowles gives to this lingering death.

What are we to make of it all? These people are trespassers, not only going too far, but in the wrong place. The desert is described as lifeless, and Bowles writes in one of his grimmer passages, "Now there was a gray, insect-like vegetation everywhere, a tortured scrub of hard shells and stiff hairy spines that covered the earth like an excrescence of hatred." But is it really grim, or is it overegged horror writing, something out of H. P. Lovecraft? I think it is both.

Kit's ordeal, not erotic in any conventional sense, is sexual sadism — written coldly, rather than (as much erotica is written) in a mood of excitement, the writer getting into the spirit of it. For many readers this pitiless and painful woman's journey is the heart of the book, the pretty New York socialite in the desert, rather foolish and ultimately unbalanced, passed from one tribesman to another, subjected to sexual barbarities and ending up in Mali, in far-off Tessalit. It is she, not Port, who is a version of the abused professor in "A Distant Episode."

Bowles was a poet as well as a novelist and short story writer, and this novel especially highlights his poetic gift. Of course it is the story of three naïve Americans lost in the stereotypical alien and forbidding land. And there is a lip-smacking love for harrowing detail — of horrible meals, filthy hotels, foreign habits, and arid landscapes. As for its unspiritual essence, it was written at a time when the word "existentialism" explained a great deal of fiction. It is perhaps one of the important existential texts, many of its effects achieved through ambiguity and vagueness, contrasted with the harsh concreteness of physical description. In this sense it represents a bitter view of life, but it is no more a tragedy than Camus's *Outsider* is a tragedy.

Yet this book matters, particularly for me. It and others helped direct my writing and my traveling life. I was still a student when I read it and Bowles's other novels, *Up Above the World, The Spider's House, Let It Come Down,* and many of the stories. As a traveler, as a writer, I have learned from Bowles's habit of observation, his love of extreme situations, his curiosity about cultures, his love of solitude, and most of all his patience. I am not sure what this novel adds up to — a meditation on death? A warning to the curious? It is a willful adventure story with all the elements of an ordeal. The desert is fatal to strangers. Bowles said he had no message, or rather, "Here's my message. Everything gets worse." But it is obvious that he wanted to give the desert a face and a mood — or moods; he often depicts a landscape in anatomical terms, and he could only do that by describing people somewhat like ourselves crawling around it and becoming its victims.

20

MAUGHAM: UP AND DOWN IN ASIA

In 1922, when William Somerset Maugham was hugely successful as a playwright, short story writer, and novelist, even something of a socialite, he dropped off the map to take the long and occasionally rigorous journey recorded in The Gentleman in the Parlour. *He had gone by ship from Britain to Ceylon, where he met a man who told him of the joys of Keng Tung, in the Shan States of remote northeastern Burma. This provoked him to travel via Rangoon to Mandalay, where he embarked by mule for this supposedly enchanted place. Twenty-six days later, he arrived. He recorded its virtues in his notebook and then plodded on to the Thai frontier, where a Ford car awaited to take him to Bangkok. After that, a ship to Cambodia, a trek to Angkor, another river trip to Saigon, and a coastal jaunt via Hue to Hanoi: up and down in Asia. The book finishes there, though in fact he traveled onward to Hong Kong, crossed the Pacific, crossed the United States, crossed the Atlantic, and, back in London, resumed his writing career and his socializing. But he did not get around to writing* The Gentleman in the Parlour *until seven years later, and I think this needs to be taken into account when evaluating this oblique and selective travel narrative.*

He wrote a great deal in the interval after the trip: *The Painted Veil* (1925), and after another voyage to Singapore and Malaya the powerful stories in *The Casuarina Tree* (1926), *Ashenden* and its stories of espionage (1927), and at least two full-length stage plays. In this time he made at least one more visit to the United States, and in 1927 bought the grand house on the Riviera he named Villa Mauresque. Here, in luxury, he finished his novel *Cakes and Ale* and at last wrote *The Gentleman in the Parlour*. Both of these books were published in the same year, 1930, at what one of his biographers called the peak of his career. *The Gentleman in the Parlour* received the mixed, not to say envious, reviews that Maugham habitually got from critics who, well aware that Maugham was wealthy, successful as a writer, socially connected, something of a snob, and living in style, felt little provocation to praise him.

Maugham was given no credit for enduring difficult travel, yet parts of the trip were arduous. He toured the extensive complex of temples at Pagan in Burma, necessitating a trip down the Irrawaddy, and spent almost a month on the mule on the trip to Keng Tung. In Cambodia he sailed up the Tonle Sap River and crossed the wide lake to view the then remote precincts of Angkor, at the time just a fantastic set of uninhabited ruins in the jungle.

But the delay between the trip and the book interests me. Invariably, a person who wishes to write a travel book goes on a journey and writes the book immediately afterward. The great exception is Patrick Leigh Fermor, who walked across Europe from Holland to Constantinople in 1933–34 but did not write his account of the trip until many decades later — *A Time of Gifts* (1977) and *Between the Woods and the Water* (1986). These books are so fresh and full of detail you'd hardly know that such a long period of time had elapsed.

In Maugham's case, the hiatus made a difference, for both good and ill. I don't think it would have been the same book if he'd written it on his return home. The book's tone and structure are the result of this passage of time. The book is less detailed but more reflective, more deliberate, more artful and even contrived as a result. It summarizes, and avoids divulging much about, the traveler's true personality and predilections. The high points are the mule ride through upper Burma, the period of time in Bangkok, and the description of Angkor.

In the course of the book, Maugham analyzes the wish to travel and the nature of a traveler. These observations are telling for the way they apply to Maugham himself. "When [the traveler] sets out on his travels the one person he must leave behind is himself." The text does not bear this out. And as for the nature of the travel book, "if you like language for its own sake, if it amuses you to string words together in the order that most pleases you, so as to produce an effect of beauty, the essay or the book of travel gives you an opportunity." This assertion also seems to me questionable. A travel book ought to be the opposite of an exercise in style, but rather a personal way of seeing the world as it is.

"Though I have traveled much I am a bad traveler," Maugham says in another place. "The good traveler has the gift of surprise." Maugham adds that he lacks this: he takes customs as he finds them. He views travel as liberating, a refreshment: "I travel because I like to move from place to place, I enjoy the sense of freedom it gives me," and he goes on in this vein, ending, "I am often tired of myself and I have a notion that by travel I can add to my personality and so change myself a little. I do not bring back from a journey quite the same self that I took."

These statements are wonderfully direct, and seem candid, but we know that in this travel book Maugham took extensive liberties, and that in his life and his work he was a master of concealment and indirection.

In great part, *The Gentleman in the Parlour* is a book of stories — travelers' tales, mostly; not Maugham's but those of the people he meets. The book is filled with distinct and well-told stories: the Mandalay tale of the marriage of George and Mabel, in Thazi the irregular alliance between Masterson and his Burmese mistress, in Mong Pying the story of the priest's isolation, in Lop Buri the story of Constantine Faulkon, the Bangkok fable about Princess September, various tales from shipboard, including how the French governor found his wife, and at least two more, one involving the old friend Grosely, the other about the American Elfenbein.

The stories appear to have been related to him by people he met, or in the case of "Princess September," imagined in a sort of delirium during a serious bout of malaria in Bangkok. But some of these stories had been written prior to the trip — in some cases many years before. "Princess September" he wrote for one of the tiny volumes in the library of Queen Mary's Dolls' House in 1922. The tale purportedly told to him on the ship to Hong Kong, the short story "A Marriage of Convenience," had been written in 1906 and was published in the *Illustrated London News* in that year. The Englishman Masterson, who may or may not have related the story of his liaison with a Burmese woman who bore him three children, in the Burmese town of Thazi, appeared as a short story, "On the Road to Mandalay," in the December 1929 issue of the *International Magazine,* and was later published in Maugham's *Collected Stories* under the title "Masterson."

Except for "Princess September," which does go on a bit (and seems anything but a malarial inspiration), the stories are arresting character studies and add the local color (dissipated colonial, lots of drink, love affair without benefit of clergy) that give the Maugham short story, especially the far-flung subject, its tang. They also serve to prove Maugham's assertion in the short story "Masterson": "I was a stray acquaintance whom he had never seen before and would never see again . . . I have in this way learned more about men in a night (sitting over a siphon or two and bottle of whisky, the hostile, inexplicable world outside the radius of an acetylene lamp) than I could have if I had known them for ten years."

But Maugham did not do a lot of sitting alone over whiskey with a stranger. He was by nature reticent — because of his stammer, not much of a raconteur; because of his homosexuality, unforthcoming about his personal life and arrangements. One of the important facts he withholds in *The Gentleman in the Parlour* is that he was not alone on the trip. He traveled with his lover and companion Gerald Haxton, who was eighteen years younger and, although a drunkard and something of a rogue, was helpful in ice-breaking and meeting locals and making arrangements en route — in many respects Maugham's common-law husband.

In *The Summing Up*, Maugham explained. "I am shy of making acquaintance with strangers, but I was fortunate enough to have on my journeys a companion [Haxton] who had an estimable social gift. He had an amiability of disposition that enabled him in a very short time to make friends with people in ships, clubs, barrooms, and hotels, so that through him I was able to get into easy contact with an immense number of persons whom otherwise I should have known only at a distance."

But you get the impression in *The Gentleman in the Parlour* that Maugham was alone, encouraging strangers in their disclosures, battling the uncertainties, struggling against the difficulties, solving the problems of transport and tickets, and all the rest of the hassles that make travel at times such a colorless bore. The first time I read it I admired Maugham's stamina and capacity to deal with solitude. And then I read a few biographies and realized that Maugham was not alone and was often traveling in style.

The revelation that the traveler presented in his or her own book was a solitary wanderer is not that unusual. Bruce Chatwin never said that he invariably traveled with a friend; V. S. Naipaul did not reveal that he was never alone in his travels, but was always (as his biographer showed) with his wife or his longtime mistress, Margaret; Graham Greene was very nearly helpless without a constant companion, since he was unable to drive a car or use a typewriter, and the same can be said for Wilfred Thesiger, who never traveled by himself. There are many other examples of the gregarious traveler presenting himself or herself as a solitary wanderer. There is no shame in this, but it makes the actual solitary wanderers, such as Charles Montagu Doughty on camelback in the Empty Quarter of Arabia Deserta, seem almost heroic.

So Maugham was traveling with his friend and lover. And he said that he dictated the larger part of the book to him en route. He omitted the last part of the trip (Hong Kong to London). He included previously written material. And some of what he wrote appeared as nonfiction in this book and as fiction elsewhere. Despite this manipulation, the book is perhaps his most satisfying narrative of travel.

In the preface to the collected edition of *On a Chinese Screen* Maugham wrote that *The Gentleman in the Parlour* was not, like *On a Chinese Screen*, "the result of an accident . . . I wanted to try my hand again at the same sort of subject, but on a more elaborate scale and in a form on which I could impose a definite pattern. It was an exercise in style." This "style" is not discernible; structurally, it is a conventional travel book, though the itinerary is Maugham's own. And even if they have been manipulated, the stories of the expatriates are wonderful.

Although he seems to be writing about himself the whole time, he discloses little about himself. He loses his temper at one point (his room wasn't ready), but he soon deflates himself. He talks a little about his drinking habits; he reveals that he once took opium. Like many writers who insist that they are not very interesting, he is highly observant. His description of Angkor is one of the best I have ever read, and his account of the Thai court is subtle — an insider's glimpse at Asiatic royalty. And though he claims to be unimpressed, he does justice to the French-looking city of Hanoi. Maugham the narrator has no passion, though passion throbs in the people he encounters and in their tumultuous lives. Maugham's voice is that of the man who narrates his fiction, the watchful writer, humorless but reliable. There is hardly any difference between the man telling this story and the third-person narration of his fiction. Only now and then there is the flicker of a bias, as with the hosiery salesman Elfenbein, about whom he writes, "He was the kind of Jew who made you understand the pogrom," which is vicious. But Elfenbein was the occasion for a Maugham first, perhaps one of the earliest recorded instances of the expression "a chip on his shoulder," as when he says of Elfenbein, "He was a man with a chip on his shoulder. Everyone seemed in a conspiracy to slight or injure him."

Maugham himself had a chip — perhaps more than one. But in general he was stoical, at times intrepid, in his travels. His traveling off the beaten track makes this book not just unusual but (to me the greatest attribute of the travel narrative) a valuable historical document.

In this curious, active, even hearty period of his life, traveling in the Far East and the Pacific, eavesdropping, note-taking, he was at his best, and was perhaps his happiest. A person only sets out on such a trip if he is confident, hopeful that he will discover something new. Maugham, a lonely man, was sensitive to the loneliness of others and keenly aware of his own limitations. Travel was a way of isolating himself, and after traveling became too much trouble, he found relief, if not happiness, in his own splendid isolation at Villa Mauresque, where he wrote *The Gentleman in the Parlour,* recalling his happier moments on the road.

21

ENGLISH HOURS: NOTHING PERSONAL

I see that the Yorkshire Ripper is seeking a release date, and might get it, having served thirty years for killing thirteen women by crushing their skulls in the late 1970s. He is ready to be your neighbor again, perhaps resume his nickname of Metal Mickey and pick up his profession of truck driver or, possibly, gravedigger — he was digging graves when (so he testified in court) he heard the ghostly voices commanding him to kill women. Yorkie Pete Sutcliffe back on the roads and in the lanes again! That memory stirs so many others.

It is the delusion of the alien that he or she is a witness to an era of significant change. I understand this as a necessary conceit, a self-important survival skill that helps to make the stranger watchful. I lived in England for eighteen years, as a pure spectator, from the end of 1971 until the beginning of 1990. I was just an onlooker, gaping at public events that did not involve me. I was a taxpayer, but couldn't vote; a house owner, but still needed an entry visa at the airport; and for quite a while I had to carry an Alien Identity Card.

Having lived for six years in Africa and three in Singapore, I knew how to be an alien. The alien method is to keep your head down and stay current, to save all documents and receipts, and to take nothing for granted. You are not owed anything. Detachment is imposed on the alien, and "nothing personal" is the alien's motto, because the alien has no security and no discernible future. I had a family, a wife and small children, to protect. I was anxious. "You Yanks," people sometimes said to me when they heard my accent, as though I needed to be reminded I was an alien. But an alien is reminding himself of that every moment in the foreign country. The alien has to practice cunning to disguise this twitchy state of mind; but insecurity stretches the nerves, heightens the attention, and makes the alien remember. Mine wasn't an era, it was simply eighteen years of events. For an alien, life in the foreign country, never completely comprehensible, is always eventful.

Early on, it was a period dominated by smoking: the top deck of the bus was a designated smoking area, people chain-smoked in doctors' waiting rooms, British Airways allowed pipe smoking at the back of the plane, and some movie theaters had smoking sections—an era of blue smoke and fruity coughing. The craze for bar billiards and snooker crested in the 1970s, with a surge of interest in the snooker on TV, a show called *Pot Black*. The single-screen cinemas began to be transformed into bingo halls. Later, when cinemas became scarcer, churches were deconsecrated and gutted so that they could serve secular purposes, bingo among them. This surprised me, and I was shocked when Christian churches were turned into mosques. The year I arrived in England, my little family prepared for some feast days by polishing the brasses in the local church. Not many years later it was "Bingo!" or "*Allahu akhbar!*" and the brasses were left to blacken.

Public events dominated my attention, as they do all aliens looking for ways to fathom the foreign country and their own slender connection. The stories unfolded: The Ripper, the miners' strike, and the three-day week, when a shoe mender in Sydenham refused to serve me and pushed me out the door (it was his day to close early, to save coal, to subdue the miners). A plane crash in the spring of 1972, the aircraft dropping like a stone into Surrey, and the emergency vehicles unable to get to the scene, because so many people on this sunny Sunday drove to see the carnage (118 people killed), blocking the narrow roads with their cars.

The deaths in Northern Ireland were always in the news, the bombings all over. Bloody Sunday occurred about two months after I arrived: fourteen Irish protesters gunned down by British soldiers, and many wounded. "The paras know what they're doing" was the line up at the pub, where I listened, "and one of those dead blokes had a nail bomb in his pocket."

Bombs, bombs! So many of them on lovely days, in parks and public houses, on Christmas, in hotels, nearly all of them the work of the IRA, whom I saw as aliens, like me. Even the House of Commons car park was a bomb site: the MP Airey Neave, about to be named Northern Ireland secretary, blown up in his car. The Guildford pub bombing of '74, four people killed, many injured, and the same year, in two pubs in Birmingham, twenty-one people murdered. Lord Mountbatten and three others, including two children, blown up on his yacht, *Shadow V,* while on an August holiday in Ireland. To the mournful echo of the bomb came the vindictive crowing, the toothy triumph of Gerry Adams, cock-a-hoop with the deaths on the yacht.

The official IRA line was always "Look what you made us do. It's your own fault!" A large nail bomb in '82 in Hyde Park killed four soldiers and seven horses. Another the same day, a large bomb under the bandstand at Regent's Park, instantly killed seven of the band members and seriously injured all the rest, including many people in the audience — a sunny day, the band playing selections from the musical *Oliver!* Six people killed at Harrods in '83, at Christmastime. The bomb at three in the morning at the Grand Hotel in Brighton that was intended to kill Prime Minister Thatcher and her whole cabinet — five people killed, many injured, and Thatcher, working on her speech at the time, survived.

There were much worse bombings in Ulster, just as cowardly, just as vicious, just as pointless. And IRA member Bobby Sands went on a hunger strike, demanding prisoners' rights in Long Kesh, where he was serving fourteen years. Refusing to be force-fed, he intended to call attention to his list of demands, "the right not to wear a prison uniform" and others. He wished, punishing himself, to arouse pity. But the IRA bombs were on everyone's mind. Not understanding that most people didn't care, and certainly not the prison staff, who were probably glad to see him suffer, Sands died of self-imposed starvation.

The clearest memory I have of the whole nasty Ulster mess, of cruelty and bloody-mindedness, is a newspaper picture of a skinny teenage Irish girl whose boyfriend was a British soldier: tarred and feathered, gleaming black, with white tufts stuck to her body, her head shaven, terrified, pushed along a street by a howling mob of Catholics. She looked like an alien to me, suffering the alien's fate of rejection — in her case, extreme and humiliating.

· · ·

It was years before anyone dared openly to mock the royal family.

The queen, with her hint of spiritual authority—Defender of the Faith—was spoken about in whispers. "She works jolly hard" was the mantra. Princess Anne was named Sportswoman of the Year in 1971. I wondered: was the princess in her show jumping such an inspiration to the footballers in the council estates that they saw this award and cried, "Wicked, guy!"

One night a man named Fagan climbed the wall of Buckingham Palace and broke into the queen's bedroom. Unable to summon help, Her Majesty sat with Fagan in her dressing gown until they were finally spotted and Fagan taken into custody. But he couldn't be charged with breaking and entering—it wasn't a criminal offense. How was an alien like me to know that? Fagan was found guilty of stealing a bottle of the royal wine, and at his trial when the subject of the queen came up, he grew indignant and said, "I won't have that woman's name dragged through the mud!" or words to that effect.

Prince Charles got publicly married and appeared in an iconic pose with Diana on a postage stamp. Prince Andrew's marriage to Sarah Ferguson was memorialized with a special label on bottles of cheap champagne, about the same time it was revealed that Sarah's father frequented a massage parlor, the Wigmore Club, for a weekly wank.

Wank was a new word for me. I learned others in those years that I had never heard before or didn't know: pantechnicon, pastilles, salopettes, anorak, ginger wine, trifle, syllabub, riddling (the coal grate), gaiters, trug, secateurs, borstal, Boche, Gorbals, yobbos, scotia (a sort of household trim), valence, shandy, chicane (as of a set of racing cars), gauntlets, whitebait, infra dig, subfusc, knackers, Christmas crackers, Dutch courage, Dutch cap, double Dutch, Screaming Lord Sutch.

I watched the conductor on the 29 bus on Lavender Hill making change, working his ticket machine with two hands and holding the money in his mouth, biting on the pound note, and when I stumbled, he quipped, "Have a good trip!" and the other passengers hooted. The estate agent in Clapham explained that the five-bedroom house on the market for £10,000 had no central heating: "Just arm-swinging." The Labour politician Denis Healey said in a speech, "You're out of your tiny Chinese mind." George Brown demanded to be in the House of Lords, because he had just turned fifty-three, had worked hard enough in his political life, and needed a sinecure. He didn't seem very old to me, but he got his sinecure and became drunken, idle Baron George-Brown.

Another Labour lord, George Wigg, Baron Wigg — he had enormous ears — was arrested for "kerb-crawling," another new expression to me. He denied it, and was acquitted of the charge, but it was apparently true. It was known that he stalked strolling prostitutes in his car. He was a mate of the prime minister, Harold Wilson, who had ennobled one crook after another, Lord Kagan, Lord Miller, and others. Those were Labour men. The Conservative Party's deputy leader, Jeffrey Archer, a similar piece of work, became Baron Archer of Weston-super-Mare: another crook, a proven liar, slimy, with a history of fiddling funny-money schemes, and now a lord. News to the alien: so this was how the system worked!

A news item that struck me — this was in the 1970s — described a woman who was charged with trying to encourage her mother to commit suicide so that she could inherit the house. "Mummy, take the pills," and the mother sweetly replying, "I'm not sure I want to, love." The daughter persisted, "Go on, Mummy," and almost succeeded, until the mother's nerve failed her, and the plot fell apart.

Sir Anthony Blunt, the queen's adviser on paintings, expert on Poussin, turned out to be a Soviet spy and a traitor. This fascinated me: here was an intelligent and well-connected Englishman, authentically horse-faced, who (so it seemed to me) had set out to make himself an alien. But Blunt was living proof that such a man could not succeed in becoming an alien, even in his treachery. He held a grand position; he was exposed; he did not fall far. He had betrayed many people, but still had many friends, and his connoisseurship was widely respected. He was asked how he felt about being a traitor. "Dreadful," he said languidly, in the tone of an afterthought, as though he was talking about having a bad cold. He summed up for me another way British society worked. He hardly suffered, was never put on trial, still had his gay chums and defenders. It was a victory for suavity, and after he was unmasked he wrote his *Guide to Baroque Rome*.

No one knew much about the SAS — even the initials themselves were obscure — until 1980, when the Iranian embassy in London was taken over by Iranian separatists, a whole pack of aliens. Hostage negotiations continued; London was watching. Then black-suited soldiers abseiled into the building from helicopters, killing all the hostage takers except one. "You let one of the bastards live," Denis Thatcher said, smiling, to one of the SAS men at the award ceremony afterward.

The killing of a police officer, Yvonne Fletcher, never left my mind. It was in the spring of 1984; she was patrolling a crowd of protesters outside the Libyan embassy in St. James's Square. And then she fell, killed by a bullet from a gun aimed by someone inside the embassy. When the embassy was closed not long afterward, and the scowling diplomats swaggered out to the square — to fly home to Libya — the TV announcer said, "One of these men killed Yvonne Fletcher."

Of the many scandals, each contained a memorable line.

"Bunnies can and will go to France," Jeremy Thorpe, leader of the Liberal Party, had written to a man who was said to be his former lover. He was entangled with this male prostitute, yet denied everything and got off. The man in question, Norman Scott, had been targeted by one Gino Newton, who shot his dog Rinka but failed to kill Scott. Scott revealed love letters from Thorpe with the "Bunnies" quote. It turned out that Thorpe might have been involved in the plot to murder Scott. But Newton was no genius, confusing Dunstable with Barnstaple. The magistrate lowered his head and said to him, "Even a moron in a hurry would know the difference."

"Lie doggo." The Lord Lucan scandal: In an attempt to kill his wife, Lucan bashes in the head of his nanny, Sandra Rivett. The name Rivett was always repeated with a smile (like the name Olive Smelt, whom the Yorkshire Ripper had attacked). Lucan tries and fails to kill his wife, who runs from the house covered in blood, to the Plumbers Arms in Belgravia, screaming, "Help me!" Later Lucan wrote in a letter to his friend Bill Shand Kydd, "I will lie doggo for a while."

"If you stay here much longer you will go home with slitty eyes," Prince Philip said to some British students in China in 1986.

"Gotcha!" was the *Sun* headline when 323 Argentine sailors died on their ship, the *Belgrano,* sunk by a British nuclear sub days after the beginning of the Falklands War. The Argentines struck back with missiles. "It's like two bald men fighting over a comb," the poet Borges said in Buenos Aires. And when this unnecessary war was over, Margaret Thatcher hooted in triumph, exhorting the country with the single word "Rejoice."

After Idi Amin expelled the Indians from Uganda in the early 1970s, they began to run the corner shops, newsagents, and off-licenses in London. The shops were kept open later and later — unprecedented hours. I identified with the Indians as fellow aliens and sometimes spoke Swahili to the newsagent on St. John's Hill, from Tanzania, who missed the place terribly. We drank in the Fishmonger's Arms, an Irish pub, and he would frown into his beer and say, "It's mango season," meaning in his town, Mwanza, on Lake Victoria.

These Indians knew everything about being aliens. They had lived as outsiders in East Africa and had great survival skills and a kind of accommodating and contemptuous deference. In Britain they began to take over failing local post offices — the bill paying, the parcel weighing, the banking, the albums of postage stamps. None had run post offices in Uganda, but some had been duka-wallahs, shopkeepers, and could handle complex paperwork, the smudgy pads of carbon paper. As aliens, Indians were willing to work on weekends, or on early-closing days. But the post office was shrinking — it had begun to shrink in the first decade of my residence.

No one seemed to notice or care, though it was an inconvenience to me when the Sunday evening pickup at the mailboxes ended. I worked during the week on my own books, but on weekends I usually did a book review. I would read the book on Saturday, write the review on Sunday, and post it that evening so it would be on the editor's desk the next day. The Royal Mail was a good name for this efficient system. As the years passed the post offices contracted, and then they became like toy shops, selling sweets and knickknacks. Often a television blared at the waiting customers, as a diversion, and no one got their mail on time.

My alien assessment was that England did not have a climate; it had weather, seldom dramatic. So I was astonished when the worst windstorm since 1703 hit the south of England one dark early morning in October 1987, killing eighteen people. I was woken by my own burglar alarm and the racket of many nearby alarms. I had no lights; big branches had fallen from the sycamore tree in my back garden. I called the Battersea police station, and though the phone was promptly answered the policewoman could not help me. She said that everyone had the same problem: "It's the wind." When I asked for more information she said, "I am sitting in darkness." In the gray light of dawn I went out and saw the downed plane trees on Wandsworth Common and across side roads. A man walked toward me, animated by the chaos, smiling, excited, an uncharacteristic Englishman blurting out to me, a complete stranger, "I've just come from Clapham Common. It's worse there. Trees all over!"

Of the many riots, in Belfast, Derry, and Liverpool, in Notting Hill, Brixton, Clapham Junction, and elsewhere, the riot that scared me most was not any of the ones that erupted near my home. Many times I had seen vandalism and riot damage, broken and boarded-up windows, just down the road in Clapham Junction. I was becoming used to observing sudden mayhem, football hooligans, racial incidents, windows casually smashed, and cars broken into in south London, where I had learned how to be an alien — and I learned to smile the ambiguous alien smile when English people said, "America's so violent."

But the riot in October 1985 in Tottenham, north London, on Broadwater Farm Estate, made me wonder. A howling mob, intent on destruction, chased and hacked to death an isolated policeman, Constable Keith Blakelock. He was overwhelmed by screaming masked rioters wielding knives, and when they got him down, they used the knives to try to behead him. They found that a human neck with all its bones and tight muscles and tendons is a hard thing to sever, and these maddened murderers failed, though they sawed at the flesh and bone for a long time, hoping for a trophy. Were they ever caught? Had they been aliens, they would have been, but they were English yobbos, of the sort who persecuted aliens.

What I remember best was Bernie Grant, the unapologetic local councilman, weighing in. He was about my age, black, born in Guyana. He had been an alien once, but was now an accepted political hack, with a following. I was fascinated by his confident smile, by his saying that the police had asked for trouble, and, "What the police got was a bloody good hiding." He did not mention that the fallen policeman, covered in blood, his face smashed, killed by the crowd, had been partly decapitated. I understand that a municipal building in Tottenham has been named in his honor — not Keith Blakelock, but Bernie Grant. An arts center.

These violent public events gave me a greater detachment, a growing sense of not belonging. I always listened for clues. The alien has an ear cocked to the radio. The lineup of panelists on *Any Questions?* sometimes indicated what the prevailing opinions on the issues were, for or against. They talked about the shows — one was *The Family,* a BBC series that was broadcast in 1974. Terry and Margaret Wilkins and their family, a big vulgar shouting bunch, had allowed cameras to film all their comings and goings, one of the earliest of what now would be called a reality show.

"I tell my children that they are lucky that we live in a happy home," one of the *Any Questions?* panelists, journalist Jacky Gillott, said when asked about the propriety of the show. She described how dysfunctional this TV family was. "Not all families are like the Wilkinses." She seemed sure of herself, but one night about five years later, Jacky Gillott went upstairs and, with her children in the house, killed herself.

I wondered if the news of these crimes and misdemeanors made other people feel like aliens — onlookers, disconnected. It seemed that disconnection was a natural feeling in such a divided country. And then there were the silly movies, the awful music, the bad art, the sports failures, all the defeats, the public cheats, the liars, the nine-day wonders, the stars — Simon Dee, Dusty Springfield, Erica Roe, Russell Harty, the talked-about actors of *Coronation Street, Crossroads,* and *The Archers* — all of them described in Dr. Johnson's trajectory: "They mount, they shine, evaporate, and fall."

The bombs were the worst, for the awful deaths and for the way they changed the texture of life. It is so easy to be a bomber or a sniper in a civilized country. And the dreary result was metal detectors in unlikely places — museums, for example — and bag searches, and the Left Luggage facility was declared too dangerous to continue. It got so bad that any briefcase in a pub looked like a potential bomb.

The sleazy aristocrats and the crooked politicians, the spies and the trimmers, seemed to taint the whole society. Jeffrey Archer's books were stacked and sold everywhere, and they always seemed to me a visible sign of corruption. This horrible man wouldn't shut up, wouldn't go away. And though an apology from any of these creepy people might not have undone any of their crimes, it would have been something, a gesture. But in a society where "Sorry!" was almost a catchphrase, on most people's lips, no one who should have ever said sorry — not Wilson, not Archer, not Blunt, not Major Ferguson, not Bernie Grant, not Gerry Adams, none of them. "Sorry" was never uttered by one of the biggest crooks of the lot, Robert Maxwell, a certified alien, born Jan Ludvik Hoch in Carpathian Ruthenia. But he had changed his name, gotten a British passport, and become a member of Parliament, a schemer in publishing, an insider in the Labour Party, and a greedy embezzler. Cornered in his crookery, he jumped from his luxury yacht off the Canary Islands, drowning himself. No suicide note, no regret. Regret was perhaps implied in the last act of Harold Wilson's crooked friend Sir Eric Miller, a Jew, when he killed himself on Yom Kippur, the Day of Atonement. But it wasn't an English thing; it was the gesture of an alien, on the high holy day when guilt must be acknowledged.

For me, the daily life of an alien is less like living in a country and having attachments than like sitting at the back of a darkened theater watching actors on a stage — sometimes tragic, often melodramatic or comic, invariably ending as farce. Because I followed these rogues in the press, and never knew any of them, their faces were always enlarged, grotesque, brightened and flattened by flashbulbs — no one was smugger than Blunt or piggier than Maxwell, more freckled and fatter than Sarah Ferguson. Archer's simpering con-man smile, Ian Paisley's huge jaw, or Gerry Adams's fangs: it was as though you had to be hideous-looking to be in the news. I had never seen uglier people.

I endured the horrible unapologetic faces in this national farce until the action became repetitive, or incomprehensible, or frightening, or frustrating. Some of the people I knew were transformed, their lives changed radically. A few got knighthoods or into the Royal Academy or the House of Lords; half a dozen killed themselves or got rich or vanished. Many of my English writer friends ended up in the United States, participants in my culture as I never was in theirs. Always I was in the stalls, watching from the shadows. "Nothing personal," I said to myself. As an alien, I was living in a house that just happened to be in England. I never stopped writing; it was my mode of being. And then one day, knowing there was no place for me here, I slipped out, as some aliens do, and never went back.

22

TRAVELING BEYOND GOOGLE

In the bungling and bellicosity that constitute the back and forth of history, worsened by natural disasters and unprovoked cruelty, it is not just the humble citizen who is punished. The traveler, too, usually a stranger to such ructions, is inconvenienced, pushed aside, or trampled to death. But if the traveler manages to breeze past such unpleasantness on tiny feet, he or she is able to return home to report, "I was there. I saw it all." The traveler's boast, sometimes couched as a complaint, is that of having been an eyewitness, and invariably this experience — shocking though it may seem at the time — is an enrichment, even a blessing, one of the trophies of travel, the life-altering journey.

"Don't go there," the know-it-all, stay-at-home finger-wagger says of many a distant place — I have heard that my whole traveling life, and in almost every case it was bad advice. Yet a familiar paradox of my experience is that these maligned countries are often the most fulfilling. I am not saying they are fun. For undiluted jollification, you can bake in the sun at Waikiki with a mai tai in your fist or eat lotuses on the Côte d'Azur. As for the recognition of hard travel as rewarding, the feeling is mainly retrospective, since it is only in looking back that we see how we have been enriched. At the time, the experience of being a bystander to sudden political or social change can be alarming.

Throughout history the traveler has been forced to recognize the fact that leaving home means a loss of innocence, encountering uncertainty. The wider world has typically been regarded as haunted, a place of darkness: *There Be Dragons*, or as Othello reported, "Cannibals that each other eat, / The Anthropophagi and men whose heads / Do grow beneath their shoulders."

But it is the well-known world that seems particularly dire at this moment. Egypt has been upended, and I smile at the phrase "peaceful mob" as an oxymoron; all mobs contain an element of spitefulness and personal score-settlers. Tunisia before the mass demonstrations and the coup was a sunny shoreline, popular with European vacationers, where the chief annoyance to the traveler was the overzealous rug dealer. Libya is a war zone, but only the other day the Libyan tourist board was encouraging visitors with promises of Roman ruins and *cuscus bil-hoot* (the Berber version of couscous with fish). Baghdad may have been the Paris of the ninth century, as Richard Burton described it, but James Simmons points out in *Passionate Pilgrims* that it has disappointed most travelers since then as "a city of wicked dust," "odorous, unattractive, and hot," with an "atmosphere of squalor and poverty" — and these descriptions are from the 1930s, long before invasion, war, and suicide bombers.

Yet Afghanistan in the 1960s and '70s, for all its hassles (gunslingers, scolding mullahs, ancient buses, bowel-shattering cuisine), was astonishingly rich in tradition, ancient pieties, and dramatic landscape, shimmering with the still-intact Buddha sculptures in Bamiyan, and penetrated with a sense of the medieval, robes, ragged turbans, daggers, and a certain dusty romance, dark eyes peeking Shmoo-like from a burqa. Kiss that goodbye. I well remember the jolting bus ride from the border city of Meshed in Iran, the walk across the stony frontier to Islam Qala, and the small-scale magnificence of the ancient city of Herat. But it will be a long time before any *farang* with a backpack, or a Gucci bag, takes that bus ride again.

The recent disaster-in-installments in Japan of earthquake, tsunami, damaged nuclear reactor, and near meltdown is an unexpected shock, since Japan has always been regarded as one of the safest countries in the world. Now it seems a perilous place of inundated cities, contaminated air, and undrinkable water. But the earthquake itself was enough to inspire a sense of deep insecurity. The idea that Christchurch, New Zealand, would be flattened and felt as dangerous — that polite, orderly, beautiful, underpopulated, provincial, hymn-singing place — is yet another surprise.

Few natural disasters are more upsetting, more apparently unnatural, than an earthquake. Charles Darwin, in his account in *The Voyage of the*

Beagle of an earthquake he witnessed in Valdivia, Chile, in February 1835, described that strangest of events when the trusted firm earth begins to give way and slide in a brisk liquefaction under us. "A bad earthquake at once destroys our oldest associations: the earth, the very emblem of solidity, has moved beneath our feet like a thin crust over a fluid; — one second of time has created in the mind a strange idea of insecurity, which hours of reflection would not have produced."

This seismic alteration can also be compared with the sudden mob in Egypt, the overthrow of a long-standing government, the eruption of a volcano, and the release of radioactivity into a blue sky and cows' milk. What then is the traveler to do except huddle and observe?

Tourists have always taken vacations in tyrannies — Tunisia and Egypt are pretty good examples. The absurdist dictatorship gives such an illusion of stability, it is often a holiday destination. Burma is a classic case of a police state that is also a seemingly well-regulated country for sightseers, providing they don't look too closely — Burmese guides are much too terrified to confide their fears to their clients. Kenya's twenty-four years of kleptocracy under President Moi, which ended in 2002, never discouraged safari-goers — might indeed have encouraged them to believe they were safe with so many conspicuous cops (though one of my Kenyan friends was held and tortured in Nairobi's main police station for being an outspoken journalist in this flush safari-going period). It is only relatively recently that tourists and hunters have begun to stay away from Zimbabwe. At a time when President Mugabe was starving and jailing his opponents in the 1990s, visitors to the country were applying for licenses to shoot elephants and having a swell time in the upscale game lodges.

By contrast, the free market–inspired, somewhat democratic, unregulated country can make for a bumpy trip and a preponderance of rapacious locals. The Soviet Union, with nannying guides, controlled and protected its tourists, while the new Russia torments visitors with every scam available to rampant capitalism. But unless you are in delicate health, and desire a serious rest, none of this is a reason to stay home.

"You'd be a fool to take that ferry," people — both Scottish and English — said to me in the spring of 1982 when I set off at Stranraer in Scotland for Larne in Northern Ireland. I was making my way clockwise around the British coast for the trip I later recounted in *The Kingdom by the Sea*. At the time and for more than ten years, a particularly vicious sort of sectarian terror was general all over Ulster. It seemed from the outside to be Catholic versus Protestant, centuries old in its origins, harking back to King Billy — William of Orange — and the Battle of the Boyne in 1690, the decisive event still celebrated by marchers in silly hats every year on July 12. Ulster violence in the 1970s was pacified and then stirred by British troops, and the terror given material support by misguided enthusiasts such as U.S. Representative Peter King and Libya's Colonel Gaddafi, bedfellows in this self-destructive nastiness.

How do I know this? I was there, keeping my head down, eating fish and chips, drinking beer, and observing the effects of this confederacy of murderous dunces, the splinter groups, grudge bearers, and criminal hell-raisers of the purest ignorance. "I'm a Muslim!" a man cries out in a Belfast street, in a dark joke that was going around at the time. And his attackers demand to know, "Are you a Catholic Muslim or a Protestant Muslim?"

The narcissism of minor differences was never more starkly illustrated after that rainy night when I boarded the ferry from Scotland and made the short voyage into the seventeenth century, setting off to look at the rest of Northern Ireland. What I found — what I have usually found after hearing all those warnings — was that it was much more complicated and factional than it had been described to me. And there were unexpected pleasures. For one thing, the Irish of all sorts were grateful to have a listener. This is a trait of the aggrieved, and to be in the presence of talkers is a gift to a writer. Yes, there were checkpoints, roadblocks, bomb scares, metal detectors, pat-downs, but these have become a fact of American life today. There was the occasional outrage. Ambushes by and against British soldiers were fairly common, as well as other features of uprisings from Israel to Sri Lanka — the kicked-down door, the humiliated civilian, the stone-throwing children. But the prevailing quality of war is not noises or gunfire. It is suspense, something like boredom: nothing happening for long periods and then everything happening at once, in indescribable confusion.

What I saw in Ulster on that trip was unforgettable. It was first of all the recognition of the utter uselessness of the conflict and its self-destructive element. But it was also the way in which, in the worst situations, life goes on. Market day was observed, even though a bomb was now and then detonated in a market square. Rituals were observed: at one such, in Enniskillen in 1987, eleven people were killed when the IRA detonated a bomb at a Remembrance Day ceremony — murdered as they were mourning their dead.

Still, life continued: a cake sale, a bike race, farmers mowing their fields, the sound of a choir from a church, "Have a cup of tea?," birds singing on country roads where I waited for a bus, the blackening rain coming down, and the exasperated good humor of humane people who were sick of it all.

It was all a revelation that has become a rich and enlightening memory. And it had been far from the only time I was warned against a place. "Don't, whatever you do, go to the Congo," I was told when I was a teacher in Uganda in the mid- and late 1960s. But the Congo was immense, and the parts I visited, Kivu in the east and Katanga in the south, were full of life, in the way of beleaguered places. In the mid-1970s, when I was setting off from my hotel in West Berlin for a train to East Berlin, the writer Jerzy Kosinski begged me not to go beyond the Brandenburg Gate. I might be arrested, tortured, held in solitary confinement. "What did they do to you?" he asked when he saw me reappear that evening. I told him I had had a bad meal, taken a walk, seen a museum, and generally gotten an unedited glimpse of the grim and threadbare life of East Germany.

Not all warnings are frivolous or self-serving. Passing through Singapore in 1973, I was warned not to go to Khmer Rouge–controlled Cambodia, and that was advice I heeded. There is a difference between traveling in a country where the rule of law prevails and one in a state of anarchy. Pol Pot had made Cambodia uninhabitable. I traveled to Vietnam instead, aware of the risks: this was just after the majority of American troops had withdrawn, about eighteen months before the fall of Saigon. I had flown from Singapore, where I was warned not to go. Vietnam then was defenselessly adrift in a fatalistic limbo of whispers and guerrilla attacks. It was less a war zone than a slowly imploding region on the verge of surrender. My clearest memories were of the shattered Citadel and muddy streets of Saigon and the stinking foreshore of the Perfume River in Hue, up the coast, the terminus of the railway line. Now and then tracer fire, terror-struck people, a collapsed economy, rundown hotels, and low spirits.

Thirty-three years later, I returned to Vietnam on my *Ghost Train to the Eastern Star* journey, which was a revisiting of my *Great Railway Bazaar.* I went back to the royal city of Hue and saw that there can be life, even happiness, after war, and, almost unimaginably, there can be forgiveness. Had I not seen the hellhole of Hue in wartime, I would never have understood its achievement in a time of peace. Seven million tons of bombs had not destroyed Vietnam; if anything they had unified it. And Hanoi, which had suffered severe aerial bombardment over the many years of the war, looked to me wondrous in its postwar prosperity, with boulevards and villas, ponds and pagodas, as glorious as it had been when it was the capital of Indochina, certainly one of the most successful and loveliest architectural restorations of any city in the world.

Just a few years ago Sri Lanka emerged from a civil war, but even as the Tamil north was embattled and fighting a rearguard action, there were tourists sunning themselves on the southern coast and touring the Buddhist stupas in Kandy. Now the war is over, and Sri Lanka can claim to be peaceful, except for the crowing of its government over the vanquishing of the Tamils. Tourists have returned in even greater numbers, for the serenity and the small population. There are more people in greater Mumbai than in the whole of the Democratic Socialist Republic of Sri Lanka.

Sri Lanka was on the might-be-your-last-trip list of the traveler Robert Young Pelton. He has made a career of clucking about hazards, descriptions of which fill his books, notably *The World's Most Dangerous Places*. But on the one occasion when we met — on a TV show that was taped in New Jersey — he came across as a genial if torpid Canadian, except when he was talking about the horrors of Sri Lanka, the Philippines, and Colombia. I had made pleasurable trips to all three, I said. And I was compelled to point out to him that we were just a few miles from what a local newspaper called "America's homicide capital" — Camden, New Jersey.

Many people think of global travel as though presented on a menu, one of those dense, slightly sticky volumes that resemble the Book of Kells. It is a changing menu, the places of shifting importance, often a Place of the Day, and some deleted. Iran was on the menu once; Albania was not. I found it impossible to get a simple tourist visa to Iran a few years ago, but had no trouble going to Albania in 1995. After decades of being closed to the world, Albania opened up and was a mere overnight ferry ride from Bari, Italy (*"Si prega di non andare!"* my friends had said, begging me not to go); it was and remains one the weirdest places I have ever been, as I tried to show in my *Pillars of Hercules*. Not risky, but a tumble through the looking-glass.

The earth is often perceived as a foolproof Google map, not very large, easily accessible, and knowable by any geek drumming his fingers on a computer. In some respects this is true. Distance is no longer a problem. You can nip over to Hong Kong, or spend a weekend in Dubai or Rio. But as some countries open up, others shut down. Some have yet to earn their place on the traveler's map, such as Turkmenistan and Sudan, but I've been to both not long ago, and although I was the only sightseer, I found hospitality, marvels, and a sense of discovery. The stupendous Greco-Buddhist ruins of Gandharan monasteries in and around Taxila, not far from Peshawar, in Pakistan, are unvisited except by jihadis, and even then, their only mission is to deface them.

The Kingdom of Sikkim, in northeastern India, is open for business, but when I was there late last year the hotels were empty, and they were not much fuller in Darjeeling, where I'd driven from. For that matter, the coast of Maine is pretty much unvisited in the winter months, but it is just as friendly, and as lovely, as in other seasons. In my own *Tao of Travel*, the fact that a place is out of season doesn't make it less interesting, just more itself, and a visit perhaps more of a challenge. In the same way, while weighing the risks and being judicious, travel in an uncertain world, in a time of change, has never seemed to me more essential, of greater importance, or more enlightening.

23

HAWAII: ISLANDS UPON ISLANDS

Hawaii seems a robust archipelago, a paradise pinned like a bouquet to the middle of the Pacific, fragrant and fluttery and freely accessible. But in fifty years of traveling the world, I have found the inner life of these islands to be difficult to penetrate, partly because it is not one place but many, but most of all because of its fragility and the almost floral way in which it is structured. But it is my home, and home is always the impossible subject, multilayered and maddening.

Two thousand miles from any great landmass, Hawaii was once utterly unpeopled. Its insularity was its salvation. And then, in installments, the world washed ashore and its Edenic uniqueness was lost. There was first the discovery of Hawaii by Polynesian voyagers, who brought with them their dogs, their plants, their fables, their cosmology, their hierarchies, their rivalries, and their predilection for plucking the feathers of birds; the much later barging-in of Europeans and their rats, diseases, and junk food; the introduction of the mosquito, which brought avian flu and devastated the native birds; the paving over of Honolulu; the bombing of Pearl Harbor; and many hurricanes and tsunamis. Anything but robust, Hawaii is a stark illustration of Proust's melancholy observation: "The true paradises are the paradises we have lost."

I think of a simple native plant, the *alula*, or cabbage plant, which is found only in Hawaii. At maturity, as an eight-foot specimen, you might mistake it for a tall pale skinny creature with a cabbage for a head ("cabbage on a stick" is its common description, *Brighamia insignis* its proper name). In the 1990s an outcrop of it was found growing on a high cliff on the Na-pali Coast in Kauai by some intrepid botanists. A long-tongued moth, a species of hawk moth, its natural pollinator, had gone extinct, and because of this the plant itself was facing extinction. But the botanists, abseiling and dangling from ropes, pollinated it with their dabbling fingers. In time, they collected the seeds and germinated them.

Like most of Hawaii's plants, an early form of the *alula* was probably carried to the volcanic rock in the ocean during the Paleozoic era as a seed in the feathers of a migratory bird. But the eons altered the *alula,* made it milder, more precious, dependent on a single pollinator. That's the way with flora on remote islands. Plants lose their sense of danger (so to speak), their survival skills — their thorns and poisons. Isolated, without competition and natural enemies, they become sportive and odder and special — and far more vulnerable to anything new or introduced. Now there are many *alula* plants, but each one is the result of having been propagated by hand.

This is the precarious fate of much of Hawaii's flora and its birds. Its native mammals are just two: the Hawaiian hoary bat (*Lasiurus cinereus semotus*), Hawaii's only native land mammal, and the Hawaiian monk seal (*Monachus schauinslandi*), both severely endangered, and needlessly so. I have seen the slumber of a monk seal on a Hawaii beach interrupted by a dithering dog walker with an unleashed pet, and by onlookers in bathing suits hooting gleefully. There are fewer than 1,100 monk seals in the islands, and the numbers are decreasing. The poor creature is undoubtedly doomed.

Hawaii offers peculiar challenges to anyone wishing to write about the place or its people. Of course, many writers do, arriving for a week or so and gushing about the marvelous beaches, excellent food, and splendid weather, filling the travel pages of newspapers with holiday hyperbole. Hawaii has a well-deserved reputation as a special set of islands, a place apart, fragrant with blossoms, caressed by trade winds, vibrant with the plucking of ukuleles, effulgent with sunshine spanking the water — see how easy it is? None of this is wrong, but there is more, and it is difficult to find or describe.

I have spent my life on the road waking in a pleasant, or not so pleasant, hotel, and setting off every morning after breakfast hoping to discover something new and repeatable, something worth writing about. I think other serious travelers do the same, looking for a story, facing the world, tramping out a book with their feet — a far cry from sitting at a desk and staring mutely at a glowing screen or a blank page. The traveler physically enacts the narrative, chases the story, often becomes part of the story. This is the way most travel narratives happen.

Because of my capacity for listening to strangers' tales or the details of their lives, my patience with their food and their crotchets, my curiosity that borders on nosiness, I am told that anyone traveling with me experiences an unbelievable tedium, and this is why I choose to travel alone.

Where I have found a place or its people to be unyielding, I have moved on. But this is a rare happenstance. The wider world in my experience is anything but unyielding. I seldom meet uncooperative people. In traditional societies especially I've found folks to be hospitable, helpful, talkative, grateful for my interest, and curious about me, too — who I am, where I'm from, and by the way, where's my wife? I have sometimes encountered hostility, but in each case I have found that conflict dramatic enough to write about — a rifle muzzle in my face in Malawi, a predatory shifta bandit in the northern Kenya desert, a pickpocket in Florence, a drunken policeman at a roadblock in rural Angola, a mob in India, teenage boys jabbing spears at me in a shallow lagoon where I was paddling in Papua New Guinea. Such confrontations go with the territory.

My love for traveling to islands amounts almost to a pathological condition known as nesomania, an obsession with islands. This craze seems reasonable to me, because islands are small, self-contained worlds that can help us understand larger ones. For example, in *Easter Island, Earth Island,* the authors Paul Bahn and John Flenley convincingly argue that the fate of the world has been prefigured by the eco-disaster of Easter Island, the history of this small rock standing as a parable of the earth. Literature is full of island parables too, from *The Tempest* to *Robinson Crusoe* to *Lord of the Flies,* and notably in each case the drama arises from people who have arrived on the island from the outside world.

One of the traits that I've found in many island cultures is a deep suspicion of the outsider — a *palangi,* as such people are called in Samoa, suggesting they've dropped from the sky; a *haole* in Hawaii, meaning "of another breath"; a "wash-ashore," as non-islanders are dismissively termed on Martha's Vineyard and other islands. Of course it's understandable that an islander would regard a visitor with a degree of suspicion. An island is a fixed and finite piece of geography, and usually the whole place has been carved up and claimed. It is inconceivable that a newcomer, invariably superfluous, could bring a benefit to such a place; suspicion seems justified. The very presence of the visitor, the new arrival, the settler, suggests self-interest and scheming.

"They will break your boat!" an islander howled at me in Samoa when I met him on a path near the beach and told him I had paddled there. "Or the boys will steal it!"

"Why would they do that?"

"Because you're a *palangi* and you're alone. You have no family here. Let's go — I'll help you."

It was true: a gang of boys were lurking near my kayak drawn up on the beach, looking eager — and the man confirmed this — to kick it to pieces. Because I didn't belong there, because I had no connection, no friend, except this man who took pity on me and volunteered to warn me.

At the time, I assumed I was one against the many, and that the islanders were unified, with a common consciousness that caused them to oppose the arrival of a *palangi*. Perhaps this was so. I was well aware when writing a travel book about Pacific islands that, because I had no friends or relations onshore, I was never truly welcomed in any set of islands. At best, the islanders simply put up with me, waiting for me to paddle away.

Most of these islands had a single culture and language. They were not xenophobic but rather suspicious or lacked interest in outsiders. Hawaii is another story, a set of islands with a highly diverse ethnicity, ranging from Hawaiians, who refer to themselves as *kanaka maoli*, "original people," whose ancestry goes back 1,500 (some say 2,000) years, to people who arrived just the other day. But the mainland United States can be described that way, too — many Native Americans can claim a pedigree of 10,000 years.

I have lived in Hawaii for more than twenty years. Though I have written a number of fictional pieces, including a novel set in Hawaii (*Hotel Honolulu*), I have not considered myself successful in writing any nonfiction about the islands, nor have I ever read anything that accurately portrayed in an analytical way the place in which I have chosen to live my life. I have been in Hawaii longer than anywhere else. I'd hate to die here, I murmured to myself in Africa, Asia, and Britain. But I wouldn't mind dying in Hawaii, which means I like living here.

Some years ago, I spent six months attempting to write an in-depth piece for a magazine describing how Hawaiian culture is passed from one generation to the next. I wrote the article, after a fashion, but the real story was how difficult it was to get anyone to talk to me. On the Big Island, I went to a charter school in which the Hawaiian language was used exclusively, though everyone at the place was bilingual. Aware of the protocol, I gained an introduction from the headmaster of the adjoining school. After witnessing the morning assembly, where a chant was offered, and a prayer, and a stirring song, I approached a teacher and asked if she would share with me a translation of the Hawaiian words I had just heard. She said she'd have to ask a higher authority. Never mind the translation, I said; could she just write down the Hawaiian version?

"We have to go through the proper channels," she said.

That was fine with me, but in the end permission to know the words was refused. I appealed to a Hawaiian language specialist, Hawaiian himself, who had been instrumental in establishing such language immersion schools. He did not answer my calls or messages, and in the end, when I pressed him, he left me with a testy reply.

I attended a hula performance. Allusive and sinuous, it cast a spell on me and on all the people watching, who were misty-eyed with admiration. When it was over I asked the *kumu hula,* the elder woman who had taught the dancers, if she would answer some questions.

She said no. When I explained that I was writing about the ways in which Hawaiian tradition was passed on, she merely shrugged. I persisted mildly, and her last and scornful words to me were "I don't talk to writers."

"You need an introduction," I was told.

I secured an introduction from an important island figure and managed a few interviews. One person sneeringly reminded me that she would not have bestirred herself to see me had it not been for the intervention of this prominent man. Another gave me truculent answers. Several expressed the wish to be paid for talking to me, and when I said it was out of the question, they became notably monosyllabic.

Observing protocol, I had turned up at each interview carrying a present, a large jar of honey from my own beehives on the North Shore of Oahu. No one expressed interest in the origin of the honey (locally produced honey is efficacious as a homeopathic remedy). No one asked where

I was from or anything about me. It so happened that I had arrived from my house in Hawaii, but I might have come from Montana — nobody asked or cared. They did not so much answer as endure my questions.

Much later, hearing that I had beehives, some Hawaiians about to set off on a canoe voyage asked if I would give them sixty pounds of my honey to use as presents on distant Pacific islands they planned to visit. I supplied the honey, expressing a wish to board the canoe and perhaps accompany them on a day run. Silence was their stern reply, and I took this to mean that though my honey was local, I was not.

I was not dismayed. I was fascinated. I had never in my traveling or writing life come across people so unwilling to share their experiences. Here I was, living in a place most people thought of as Happyland, when in fact it was an archipelago with a social structure more complex than any I had ever encountered — beyond Asiatic. One conclusion I reached was that in Hawaii people believed that their personal stories were their own, not to be shared, certainly not to be retold by someone else. Virtually everywhere else, people were eager to share their stories, and their candor and hospitality had made it possible for me to live my life as a travel writer.

Obviously, the most circumscribed islanders are the Hawaiians, numerous because of the so-called one-drop rule. Some people who regarded themselves, before statehood in 1959, as of Portuguese, Chinese, or Filipino descent identified themselves as Hawaiian when sovereignty became an issue in the late 1960s and 1970s and their drop of blood gave them access. But there are forty or more contending Hawaiian sovereignty groups, from the most traditional, who worship deities such as Pele, the goddess of fire (and volcanoes), to the Hawaiian hymn singers in the multitude of Christian churches, to the Hawaiian Mormons, who believe, contrary to all serious Pacific scholarship and the evidence of DNA testing, that mainlanders (proto-Polynesians) got to Hawaii from the coast of the Land of Joshua (now California), when Hagoth, the Mormon voyager (Book of Mormon, Alma 63:5–8), sailed into the Western Ocean and peopled it.

But it wasn't just native Hawaiians who denied me access or rebuffed me. I began to see that the whole of Hawaii is secretive and separated socially, spatially, ethnically, philosophically, academically. Even the University of Hawaii is insular and uninviting, a place unto itself, with little influence in the wider community and no public voice — no commentator or explainer, nothing in the way of intellectual intervention or mediation. It is like a silent and rather forbidding island, and though it regularly puts on plays and occasionally a public lecture, it is in general an inward-looking institution, esteemed locally not for its scholarship but for its sports teams.

As a regular user of the UH library, researching my *Tao of Travel*, I requested some essential books from the library system that happened to be located on a neighbor island.

"You are not on the faculty," I was told by one of the desk functionaries in a who-might-you-be-little-man? tone. "You are not a student. You are not allowed to borrow these books."

It made no difference that I am a writer, because apart from my library card — a community card that costs $60 a year — I had no credibility at the university, even though my own forty-odd books occupy its library shelves. Books may matter, but a writer in Hawaii is little more than a screwball or an irritant, with no status.

Pondering this odd separation, I thought how the transformative effects of island existence are illustrated in plants, like the *alula* that had become cut off and vulnerable. Island life is a continuous process of isolation and endangerment. Native plants become hypersensitive and fragile, and alien species have a tendency to assault and overwhelm this fragility. The transformation was perhaps true of people, too: the very fact that a person was resident on an island, with no wish to leave, meant he or she was isolated, in the precise meaning of the word: "made into an island," alone, separated, set apart.

This perception of mine is not fanciful. It is, in Hawaiian culture, an established way for people to define where they live. Every island in Hawaii is divided like a pie, into wedge-shaped areas, narrowest at the center of the island, widest at the coast, each called *ahupuaʻa*, a term suggesting a sacrificial altar — *ahu* is sacrifice, *puaʻa* is pig. The subdivision of each *ahupuaʻa* is a collection of *moku puni* — literally "islands." So "islands upon islands" accurately describes the manner in which Hawaiians live.

This has become more complex over time, as non-Hawaiians arrived and settled. In an archipelago of multiethnicity the trend to apartness is not a simple maneuver. To emphasize separation, the islander created his own metaphorical island, based on race, ethnicity, social class, religion, neighborhood, net worth, and many other factors — islands upon islands. In my years of living in Hawaii, I have begun to notice how little these separate entities interact, how closed they are, how little they overlap, how naturally suspicious and incurious of others the groups are, how each one seems to talk only to itself.

"I haven't been there for thirty years," people say about a part of the island ten miles away. I have met born-and-bred residents of Oahu who have been to perhaps one neighbor island, and many who have never been to any—though they may have been to Las Vegas.

"We sent a large group of musicians and dancers from Waianae to the Edinburgh Festival," a civic-minded and philanthropic woman told me recently. "They were a huge hit."

We were speaking in the upscale enclave of Kahala. The obvious irony was that it was possible, as I suggested to the woman, that the Waianae musicians who had gone across the world to sing had never sung in Kahala, or perhaps even been there. Nor do the well-heeled Kahala residents travel to hard-up Waianae.

It is as if living on the limited terra firma of an island inspires groups to re-create their own island-like space, as the Elks and other clubs were exclusive islands in the segregated past. Each church, each valley, each ethnic group, and each neighborhood is insular—not only Kahala, or the equally salubrious Koko Head, but the more modest localities, too. Leeward Oahu, the community of Waianae, is like a remote and somewhat menacing island.

Each of these notional islands has a stereotypical identity, and so do the actual islands. A person from Kauai would insist that he or she is quite unlike someone from Maui, and could recite a lengthy genealogy to prove it. The military camps at Schofield, Kaneohe, Hickham, and elsewhere exist as islands, and no one looks lonelier on a Hawaii beach than a jarhead, pale, reflective, perhaps contemplating yet another deployment to Afghanistan. When the George Clooney film *The Descendants* was shown on the mainland, it baffled some moviegoers because it did not depict the holiday Hawaii that most people recognize—and where were Waikiki and the surfers and the mai tais at sunset? But this film was easily understood by people in Hawaii as the story of old-timers here, so-called *kama'aina,* children of the islands, and all of them *haole,* white. They have their metaphorical island —indeed, one *kama'aina* family, the Robinsons, owns its own substantial island, Niihau, off the coast of Kauai, with a small resident population of Hawaiians, where off-islanders are forbidden to go.

Even the water is circumscribed. Surfers are among the most territorial of Hawaii residents. Some of them deny this, and say that if certain deferential rules of politeness are observed ("You take dis wave, brah," a recently arrived surfer calls out to humble himself in the lineup), it is possible to find a measure of mutual respect and coexistence. But much of this is basic primate behavior, and most of the surfers I have met roll their eyes and tell me that the usual response to a newcomer is "Get off my wave!"

All this was a novelty to me, and a lesson in that nebulous genre known as travel writing. As a traveler, I had become used to strolling confidently into the oddest places — approaching a village, a district, a slum, a shantytown, a neighborhood — and observing the dress code, the niceties, the protocol, asking frank questions. I might be inquiring about someone's job or lack of employment, their children, their family, their income; I nearly always got a polite answer. Recently in Africa I made a tour of the townships of Cape Town, not just the bungalows, the dusty dwellings, the temporary shelters and hostels, but the shacks and squatter camps, too. My questions were answered: it is how the traveler acquires information for the narrative.

In the worst slum in India, the meanest street in Thailand or Cambodia, chances are that a smile will make you welcome. And if you have a smattering of Portuguese or Spanish, you will probably have your questions answered in a Brazilian *favela,* an Angolan *musseque,* or a Ecuadorian *barrio,* in each case a shantytown.

So why are islands so different, and why is Hawaii — one of the fifty United States — so uncooperative, so complex in its divisions? This, after all, was a place in which, after the attack on Pearl Harbor, more than three thousand men from Hawaii, nearly all of Japanese ancestry, volunteered to fight, and their unit, the 442nd Infantry, became the most decorated regiment in U.S. history. But that was the army, and they fought in Europe.

First of all, what looks in Hawaii like hostility is justifiable wariness, with an underlying intention to keep the peace. Confrontation is traumatic in any island society, because, while there is enough room for peaceful coexistence, there is not enough space for all-out war. Just such a disruptive conflict got out of hand and destroyed the serenity of Easter Island, reducing its population, upending its brooding statues, and leaving a legacy of blood feud among the clans. Fiji went to war with itself; so did Cyprus, with disastrous results. Hawaii, to its credit, and its survival, tends to value the obliqueness, nonconfrontation, and suspension of disbelief that is embodied in the simple word "mellow." (What I am doing now, taking an unmellow look at Hawaii, is regarded locally as heresy.)

So there is obviously a reason for Hawaii's separation. Perhaps this tendency to live in specific zones is a conscious survival strategy and a mode of pacification. Fearing disharmony, knowing how conflict would sink the islands, Hawaiians cling to the mollifying concept of aloha, a Hawaiian word that suggests the breath of love and peace.

In spite of its divisions, Hawaii is united, and perhaps more like-minded than any islander would admit. Each self-regarding metaphorical island has an unselfish love for the larger island, as well as a pride in its brilliant weather, its sports, its local heroes (musicians, athletes, actors). Another unifier is the transcendent style of hula, danced by *kanaka maoli* and *haole* alike. Hula is aloha in action. Just about everyone in Hawaii agrees that if the spirit of aloha remains the prevailing philosophy in Hawaii, it will bring harmony. "Aloha" is not a hug; it is meant to disarm; it is a verbal formula for gently keeping people happy. More and more I have come to see this subtle greeting, a word uttered with a floating ambiguous smile, as less a word of welcome than a means of propitiating a stranger. But perhaps all words of welcome perform that propitiatory function.

As for the fanciful assertion of largeness, it is reassuring for an islander to know that the island is big as well as multidimensional, and to maintain the belief that much of Hawaii is hidden and undiscovered. It helps, if you want to cherish the idea of distance and mystery, that you do not stray far from home, your very own metaphorical island.

Further defining the zones of separation is the bumpy and jagged topography of a volcanic island, its steep valleys, its bays and cliffs and plains, its many elevations. In Hawaii there's also a palpable difference in weather from one place to another, the existence of microclimates that underline the character of a place. I can drive twenty miles in one direction to a much drier part of the island, twenty miles in another to a place where it is probably raining, and in between it might be ten degrees cooler. The people in those spots seem different, too, taking on the mood of their microclimate.

Never mind that Hawaii is seven inhabited islands; even on smallish Oahu — about fifty miles across — there are many places that are considered remote. This whimsy of distance enlarges the island, which inspires the illusion of a vast hinterland and the promise of later discovery. I am bemused by the writer from the mainland who, after five days of gallivanting and gourmandizing, is able to sum up Hawaii in a sentence or two. I was that person once. These days, I am still trying to make sense of it all, but the longer I live here, the more the mystery deepens.

24

MOCKINGBIRD IN MONROEVILLE

The twiggy branches of the redbuds were in bloom, the shell-like magnolia petals had begun to twist open, the numerous flowering Bradford pear trees — more blossomy than cherries — were a fragrant froth of white, and yet this Sunday morning in March was gray and unseasonably chilly in Monroeville, Alabama. A week before, I had arrived there on a country road. In the Deep South, and Alabama especially, all the back roads seem to lead to the bittersweet of the distant past.

Over on Golf Drive, once a white part of town, Nannie Ruth Williams had risen at six in the dim light of a late-winter dawn to prepare lunch — to simmer the turnip greens, cook the yams and sweet potatoes, mix the mac and cheese, bake a dozen biscuits, braise the chicken parts and set them with vegetables in the slow cooker. Lunch was seven hours off, but Nannie Ruth's rule was "No cooking after church." The food had to be ready when she got home from the Sunday service with her husband, Homer Beecher Williams — H.B. to his friends — and anyone else they invited. I hadn't met her, nor did she yet know that one of the diners that day would be me.

The sixth of sixteen children, born on the W. J. Anderson plantation long ago, the daughter of sharecropper Charlie Madison (cotton, peanuts, sugarcane, hogs), she had a big-family work ethic. Nannie Ruth had heard that I was meeting H.B. that morning, but had no idea who I was or why I was in Monroeville, yet in the southern way, she was prepared to be welcoming to a stranger, with plenty of food, hosting a meal that was a form of peacemaking and fellowship.

Monroeville styles itself "the Literary Capital of Alabama." Though the town had once been segregated, with the usual suspicions and misunderstandings that arise from such forced separation, I found it to be a place of sunny streets and friendly people, and also — helpful to a visiting writer — a repository of long memories. The town boasts that it has produced two celebrated writers, who grew up as neighbors and friends, Truman Capote and Harper Lee. Their homes no longer stand, but other landmarks persist, those of Maycomb, the fictional setting of *To Kill a Mockingbird*.

Among the pamphlets and souvenirs sold at the grandly domed Old Courthouse is "Monroeville: The Search for Harper Lee's Maycomb," an illustrated booklet that includes local history and images of the topography and architecture of the town that correspond to certain details in the novel. Harper Lee's work is a mélange of personal reminiscence, fictional flourishes, and verifiable events. The book contains two contrasting plots: one a children's story, about the tomboy Scout, her older brother Jem, and their friend Dill, disturbed in their larks and pranks by an obscure housebound neighbor, Boo Radley; and in the more portentous story line, Scout's father's combative involvement in the defense of Tom Robinson, the decent black man who has been accused of rape.

What I remembered of my long-ago reading of the novel was the gusto of the children and their outdoor world, and the indoor narrative, the courtroom drama of a trumped-up charge of rape, a hideous miscarriage of justice and a racial murder. Rereading the novel recently, I realized I had forgotten how odd the book is, the wobbly construction, the arch language, and the shifting point of view, how atonal and forced it is at times, a youthful directness and clarity in some of the writing mingled with adult perceptions and arcane language. For example, Scout is in a classroom with a new teacher from northern Alabama. "The class murmured apprehensively," Scout tells us, "should she prove to harbor her share of the peculiarities indigenous to her region." This is a tangled way for a six-year-old to perceive a stranger, and this verbosity pervades the book.

I am now inclined to Flannery O'Connor's view of it as "a child's book," but she meant it dismissively, while I tend to think that its appeal to youngsters (like that of *Treasure Island* and *Tom Sawyer*) may be its strength. A young reader easily identifies with the boisterous Scout and sees Atticus as the embodiment of paternal virtue. In spite of the lapses in narration, the book's basic simplicity and moral certainties are perhaps the reason it has endured for more than fifty years as the tale of injustice in a small southern town. That it appeared, like a revelation, at the very moment the civil rights movement was becoming news for a nation wishing to understand was also part of its success.

Monroeville had known a similar event, the 1934 trial of a black man, Walter Lett, accused of raping a white woman. The case was shaky, the woman unreliable, no hard evidence, yet Walter Lett was convicted and sentenced to death. Before he was electrocuted, calls for clemency proved successful, but by then Walter Lett had been languishing on death row too long, within earshot of the screams of doomed men down the hall, and he was driven mad. He died in an Alabama hospital in 1937, when Harper Lee was old enough to be aware of it. Atticus Finch, an idealized version of A. C. Lee, Harper's attorney father, defends the wrongly accused Tom Robinson, who is a tidier version of Walter Lett.

Never mind the contradictions and inconsistencies: novels can hallow a place, cast a glow upon it, and inspire bookish pilgrims — and there are always visitors, who'd read the book or seen the movie. They stroll in the town, using the free guidebook *Walk Monroeville* in the downtown historic district, admiring the Old Courthouse, the Old Jail, searching for Maycomb, the locations associated with the novel's mythology, though they search in vain for locations of the movie, which was made on a Hollywood backlot. It is a testament to the spell cast by the novel, and perhaps to the popular movie, that the monument at the center of town is not to a Monroeville citizen of great heart and noble achievement, not to a local hero or an iconic Confederate soldier, but to a fictional character, Atticus Finch.

These days the talk in town is of Harper Lee, known locally by her first name, Nelle (her grandmother's name, Ellen, spelled backward). Avoiding publicity from the earliest years of her success, she has remained reclusive. She is back in the news because of the discovery and disinterment of a novel-length fragment she'd written and put aside almost six decades ago, an early version of the Atticus Finch–Tom Robinson story, told by Scout grown older and looking down the years. Suggesting the crisis of a vulnerable and convicted man in the Old Jail on Mount Pleasant Street, the novel is titled *Go Set a Watchman*.

"It's an old book," Harper Lee told a mutual friend of mine who'd seen her while I was in Monroeville. "But if someone wants to read it, fine."

Speculation is that the resurrected novel will be used as the basis of a new movie. The 1962 film of *To Kill a Mockingbird*, with Gregory Peck's Oscar-winning performance, sent many readers to the novel. The American Film Institute has ranked Atticus Finch as the greatest movie hero of the twentieth century (Indiana Jones is number two). Robert Duvall, who at age thirty played the mysterious neighbor Boo Radley in the film, recently said: "I am looking forward to reading the [new] book. The film was a pivotal point in my career and we all have been waiting for the second book."

According to her biographer, Charles Shields, in *Mockingbird*, Harper Lee started several books after her success in 1960, including a new novel and a nonfiction account of a serial murderer. But she'd abandoned them, and apart from a sprinkling of scribbles, she apparently abandoned writing anything else — no stories, no substantial articles, no memoir of her years of serious collaboration with Truman Capote on *In Cold Blood*. Out of the limelight, she had lived well, mainly in New York City, with annual visits home, liberated by the financial windfall but burdened — maddened, some people said — by the pressure to produce another book.

It seems, especially to a graphomaniac like myself, that she was perhaps an accidental novelist — one book and done. Instead of a career of creation, a further apprenticeship and refinement of this profession of letters, an author's satisfying dialogue with the world, she shut up shop entirely in a retreat from the writing life, like a lottery winner in seclusion. Now eighty-eight, living quietly in a nursing home at the edge of town, she is in delicate health, with macular degeneration and such a degree of deafness that she can communicate only by reading questions written in large print on note cards.

What have you been doing? my friend wrote on a card and held it up.

"What sort of fool question is that?" Nelle shouted from her chair. "I just sit here. I don't do anything!"

She may have been reclusive all her life, but she is anything but a shrinking violet, and she has plenty of friends. Using a magnifying glass, she is a reader, mainly of history, but also of crime novels. Like many people who vanish, wishing for privacy — J. D. Salinger is the best example — she has been stalked, intruded upon, pestered, and sought after. I vowed not to disturb her, though while I was in Monroeville, as a gesture from one writer to another, I signed my book *The Tao of Travel* for her and left it at her place of residence.

. . .

Nannie Ruth Williams knew the famous book, and she was well aware of Monroeville's other celebrated author. Her grandfather had sharecropped on the Faulk family land, and it so happened that Lillie Mae Faulk had married Archulus Julius Persons in 1923 and given birth to Truman Streckfus Persons a little over a year later. After she married a man named Capote, her son changed his name to Truman Capote. Capote had been known in town for his big-city airs. "A smartass," a man who'd grown up with him told me. "No one liked him." Truman was bullied for being small and peevish, but his defender was Nelle Lee, his next-door neighbor. "Nelle protected him," that man said. "When kids would hop on Capote, Nelle would get 'em off. She popped out a lot of boys' teeth."

Capote, as a child, lives on as the character Dill in the novel. His portrayal is a sort of homage to his oddness and intelligence, as well as their youthful friendship. "Dill was a curiosity. He wore blue linen shorts that buttoned to his shirt, his hair was snow-white and stuck to his head like duck-fluff; he was a year my senior but I towered over him." And it is Dill who animates the subplot, which is the mystery of Boo Radley.

Every year, a highly praised and lively dramatization of the novel is put on by the town's Mockingbird Players, with dramatic courtroom action in the Old Courthouse. But Nannie Ruth smiled when she was asked whether she'd ever seen it. "You won't find more than four or five black people in the audience," a local man told me later. "They've lived it. They've been there. They don't want to be taken there again. They want to deal with the real thing that's going on now."

H. B. Williams sighed when any mention of the book came up. He had been born in a tenant-farming family on the Blanchard Slaughter plantation, where "Blanchie," a wealthy but childless white landowner, would babysit the infant H.B. while his parents worked in the fields, picking and chopping cotton. This would have been at about the time of the Walter Lett trial, and the fictional crime of *Mockingbird* — the midthirties, when the Great Depression gripped "the tired old town" of the novel, and the Klan was active, and the red clay of the main streets had yet to be paved over.

After the book was published and became a bestseller, H.B., then a school principal, was offered the job of assistant principal, and when he refused, pointing out that it was a demotion, he was fired. He spent the next ten years fighting for his reinstatement. His grievance was not a sequence of dramatic events like the novel; it was just the unfairness of the southern grind. The pettifogging dragged on for ten years, but H.B. was eventually triumphant. Yet it was an injustice that no one wanted to hear about — unsensational, unrecorded, not at all cinematic.

In its way, H.B.'s exhausting search for justice resembles that of Bryan Stevenson in his quest to exonerate Walter McMillian, another citizen of Monroeville. This was also a local story, but a recent one. One Saturday morning in 1986, Ronda Morrison, a white, eighteen-year-old clerk at Jackson Cleaners, was found shot to death at the back of the store. This was in the center of town, near the Old Courthouse made famous twenty-six years earlier in the novel about racial injustice. In this real case, McMillian, a black landscaper, was arrested, though he'd been able to prove he was nowhere near Jackson Cleaners that day. The trial, moved to mostly white Baldwin County, lasted a day and a half. McMillian was found guilty and sentenced to death.

It emerged that McMillian had been set up, testified against by men who had been pressured by the police, and who later recanted. Bryan Stevenson, a civil rights attorney, took an interest and appealed the conviction, as he relates in his prize-winning account, *Just Mercy* (2014). After five years on death row, Walter McMillian's conviction was overturned, and he was finally released in 1993. The wheels of justice grind slowly, with paper-shuffling and appeals; little drama, much persistence. In the town with a memorial to Atticus Finch, not Bryan Stevenson, another, much later miscarriage of justice, but this one with a happy ending.

And that's the odd thing about a great deal of a certain sort of Deep South fiction — its grotesquerie and gothic, its high color and fantastication. It's almost as if the emphasis is on freakishness. Look no further than Faulkner or Erskine Caldwell, but there's plenty in Harper Lee too, in *Mockingbird,* the Boo Radley factor, the Misses Tutti and Frutti, and the racist Mrs. Dubose, who is a morphine addict: "Her face was the color of a pillowcase, and the corners of her mouth glistened with wet, which inched like a glacier down the deep grooves enclosing her chin." This sort of prose acts as a kind of indirection, dramatizing weirdness as a way of distracting the reader from day-to-day indignities.

Backward-looking, few southern writers concern themselves with the new realities: the decayed downtown, the Piggly Wiggly and the pawnshops, the elephantine Walmart on the bypass road, where the fast-food joints have put most of the local eateries out of business (though AJ's Family Restaurant and the Court House Café remain lively). Monroeville people I met were proud of having overcome hard times. Men of a certain age recalled World War II: Charles Salter, who was ninety, served in the 78th Infantry, fighting in Germany, and just as his division reached the west bank of the Rhine, he was hit by shrapnel in the leg and foot. Seventy years later he still needed regular operations. "The Depression was hard," he said. "It lasted here till long after the war." H. B. Williams was drafted to fight in Korea. "And when I returned to town, having fought for my country, I found I couldn't vote."

Some reminiscences were of a lost world, like those of the local columnist George Thomas Jones, who, at age ninety-two, remembered when all the roads in town were red clay, and how as a drugstore soda jerk he was sassed by Truman Capote, who said, "I sure would like to have something good, but you ain't got it . . . a Broadway Flip." Young George faced him down, saying, "Boy, I'll flip you off that stool!" Charles Johnson, a popular barber in town, worked his scissors on my head and told me, "I'm from the child abuse era — hah! If I was bad, my daddy would tell me to go out and cut a switch from a bridal wreath bush and he'd whip my legs with it. Or a keen switch, more narrah. It done me good."

Mr. Johnson told me about the settlement up at Franklin and Wainright, called the Scratch Ankle community, famous for inbreeding. The poor blacks lived in Clausell and Marengo, the rich whites in Canterbury, and the squatters up at Limestone were to be avoided. But I visited Limestone just the same; the place was thick with idlers and drunks and barefoot children, and a big toothless man named LaVert stuck his finger in my face and said, "You best go away, mister — this is a bad neighborhood."

There is a haunted substratum of darkness in southern life, and though it pulses through many interactions, it takes a long while to perceive it, and even longer to understand. The other ignored aspect of life: the Deep South still goes to church, and dresses up to do so. There are twenty-four good-sized churches in Monroeville, most of them full on Sundays, and they are sources of inspiration, goodwill, guidance, friendship, comfort, outreach, welfare, and snacks.

Nannie Ruth and H.B. were Mt. Nebo Baptists, but today they'd be attending the Hopewell C.M.E. Church in the northwest corner of Monroeville because the usual pianist had to be elsewhere, and Nannie Ruth played the piano well. The pastor, Reverend Eddie Marzett, had indicated what hymns to plan for and had furnished the sheet music. That Sunday was Women's Day. The theme of the service was "Women of God in These Changing Times," with appropriate Bible readings and two women preachers, Reverend Marzett taking a back pew in his stylish white suit and sunglasses, Daddy Faith to his fingertips.

Monroeville is like many towns of its size in Alabama — indeed in the Deep South: a town square of decaying elegance, most of the downtown shops and businesses closed or faltering, the main industries shut down. I was to discover that *To Kill a Mockingbird* is a minor aspect of Monroeville, a place of hospitable and hard-working people, but a dying town, with a population of 6,500 (and declining), undercut by NAFTA, overlooked by Washington, dumped by manufacturers like Vanity Fair textiles (employing at its peak 2,500 people, many of them women) and Georgia-Pacific, which used it as a source of cheap labor until they could find cheaper labor elsewhere. The town had the usual Deep South challenges in education and housing, with almost a third of Monroe County living in poverty.

"I was a traveling bra and panty salesman," Sam Williams told me. "You don't see many of those nowadays." He had worked for Vanity Fair for twenty-eight years and was now a potter, hand-firing cups and saucers of his own design. But he had lucked out in another way: oil had been found on his land — one of Alabama's surprises — and his family got a regular check from the oil wells there. His parting shot to me was an earnest plea: "This is a wonderful town. Talk nice about Monroeville."

Willie Hill had worked for Vanity Fair for thirty-four years and was now unemployed. "They shut down here, looking for cheap labor in Mexico." He laughed at the notion that the economy would improve because of the *Mockingbird* pilgrims. "No money in that, no sir. We need industry. We need real jobs."

"I've lived here all my life, eighty-one years," a man pumping gas next to me said out of the blue, "and I've never known it so bad. If the paper mill closes, we'll be in real trouble." But the paper mill, Georgia-Pacific, had already shut down several of its local plants, and Willie Hill's nephew Derek had been laid off in 2008, after ten years fabricating Georgia-Pacific plywood. He made regular visits to Monroeville's picturesque and well-stocked library (once the LaSalle Hotel, where Gregory Peck had slept in

1962) to look for jobs on the library's computers and update his résumé. He was helped by the able librarian Bunny Hines Nobles, whose family had once owned the hotel.

Nannie Ruth was most of the way through her cooking before I left Selma, two hours on the country road to Monroeville, returning on a back road, marveling at living history.

Selma was a surprise to me — not a pleasant one, more of a shock, and a sadness. The town was an easy drive from Monroeville; I had longed to see it because I wanted to put a face to the name of a town that had become a battle cry. The Edmund Pettus Bridge I recognized from newspaper photos and the footage of Bloody Sunday — protesters being beaten, mounted policemen trampling marchers. That was the headline and the history. What I was not prepared for was the sorry condition of Selma, the shut-down businesses and empty, once-elegant apartment houses near the bridge, the whole place visibly on the wane and, apart from its mall, in desperate shape, seemingly out of work. This decrepitude was not a headline.

Just a week before, on the fiftieth anniversary of the march, President Obama, the first lady, a number of celebrities, civil rights leaders, unsung heroes of Selma, and crowders of the limelight — Jesse Jackson, Al Sharpton, and politicians — had made speeches and looked suitably solemn. They invoked the events of Bloody Sunday, the rigors of the march to Montgomery, and the victory, the passage of the Voting Rights Act of 1965.

But all that was mostly anniversary gush, political theater, and sentimental rage. The reality, which was also an insult, was that these days in this city that had been on the front line of the voting rights movement, a mere 24 percent of the 18-to-25 age group bothered to vote, and the figures were smaller in local elections. I learned this at the interpretive center outside town, where the docents who told me this shook their heads at the sorry fact. After all the bloodshed and sacrifice, voter turnout was low, and Selma was enduring an economy in crisis. This went unremarked upon by the president and civil rights stalwarts and celebrities, most of whom took the next plane out of this sad and supine city.

Driving out of Selma on narrow Highway 41, which was lined by tall trees and deep woods, I got a taste of the visitable past. You don't need to be a literary pilgrim; this illuminating experience of country roads is reason enough to drive through the Deep South, especially here, where the red clay lanes, brightened and brick-hued from the morning rain, branch from the highway into the pines. Crossing Mush Creek and Cedar Creek, I saw flyspeck settlements of wooden shotgun shacks, old house trailers, and white-planked churches. I went past roadside clusters of foot-high anthills, gray witch-hair moss trailing from the bony limbs of dead trees, on a mostly straight-ahead road of flat fields, boggy pinewoods, and flowering shrubs, and just ahead a pair of crows hopping over a lump of crimson roadkill hash.

I passed through Camden, a ruinous town of empty shops and obvious poverty, just a flicker of beauty in some of the abandoned houses, a closed-up filling station, the whitewashed clapboards and tiny cupola of old Antioch Baptist Church (Martin Luther King had spoken here in April 1965, inspiring a protest march the next day), the imposing Camden public library, its façade of fat white columns, and then the villages of Beatrice — *Bee-ay-triss* — and Tunnel Springs. After all this time-warp decay, Monroeville looked smart and promising, with its many churches and picturesque courthouse and downtown mansions. Its certain distinction and self-awareness and pride were the result of its isolation. One hundred miles from any city, Monroeville had always been in the middle of nowhere — no one arrived by accident. As southerners said, you had to be going there to get there.

Hopewell C.M.E. Church, in a festive Women's Day mood, was adjacent to the traditionally black part of town, Clausell. The church's sanctuary had served as a secret meeting place in the 1950s for the local civil rights movement, many of the meetings presided over by the pastor, R. V. McIntosh, and a firebrand named Ezra Cunningham, who had taken part in the Selma march. All this came from H. B. Williams, who had brought me to a Hopewell pew.

After the hymns (Nannie Ruth Williams on the piano, a young man on the drums), the announcements, the two offerings, the reading from Proverbs 31 ("Who can find a virtuous woman, for her price is far above rubies"), and murmured prayers, the minister, Mary Johnson, gripped the lectern and shouted, "'Women of God in These Changing Times' is our theme today, praise the Lord," and the congregation called out, "Tell it, sister!" and "Praise His name!"

Minister Mary was voluble and funny and teasing in her sermon, and her message was simple: be hopeful in hard times.

"Don't look in the mirror and think, 'Lord Jesus, what they gonna think 'bout my wig?' Say 'I'm coming as I am!' Don't matter 'bout your dress — magnify the Lord!" She raised her arms and in her final peroration said, "Hopelessness is a bad place to be. The Lord gonna fee-all you with hope. You might not have money — never mind. You need the Holy Spirit!"

Afterward, the hospitable gesture, my invitation to lunch at the Williams house, a comfortable bungalow on a road off Golf Drive, middle class by Monroeville standards, near the gates to Vanity Fair Park, which was off-limits to blacks until the eighties, and the once-segregated golf course. We were joined at the table by Arthur Penn, an insurance man and president of the local NAACP branch, and his son, Arthur Penn Jr.

I raised the subject of *Mockingbird,* which made Nannie Ruth shrug. Arthur Sr. said, "It's a distraction. It's like saying, 'This is all we have. Forget the rest.' It's like a four-hundred-pound comedian onstage telling fat jokes. The audience is paying more attention to the jokes than to what they see. Look what happened to Walter McMillian."

In Monroeville, not noted for any great courtroom trials, the dramas were intense, but small scale and persistent. The year the book came out all the schools were segregated, and they remained so for the next ten years. When the schools were integrated in 1970, the white private school Monroe Academy was founded. Race relations had been generally good, because people kept in their place, and apart from the Freedom Riders from the North (which Nelle Harper disparaged at the time as agitators), there were no major racial incidents, only the threat of them.

"Most whites thought, 'You're good in your place. Stay there and you're a good nigger,'" H.B. said. "Of course it was an inferior situation, a double standard all over."

And eating slowly, he was provoked to a reminiscence, recalling how in December 1959 the Monroeville Christmas parade was canceled because the Ku Klux Klan had warned that if the band from the black high school marched with whites, there would be blood. To be fair, all the whites I spoke to in Monroeville condemned this lamentable episode. Later, in 1965, the Klan congregated on Drewery Road wearing sheets and hoods, forty or fifty of them, and they marched from there to the Old Courthouse. "Right past my house," H.B. said. "My children stood on the porch and called out to them." This painful memory was another reason he had no interest in the novel, then in its fifth year of bestsellerdom.

"This was a white area. Maids could walk the streets, but if the residents saw a black man, they'd call the sheriff," Arthur Penn said.

And what a sheriff. Up to the late 1950s, it was Sheriff Charlie Sizemore, noted for his bad temper. How bad? "He'd slap you upside the head, cuss you out, beat you."

One example: A prominent black pastor, N. H. Smith, was talking to another black man, Scott Nettles, on the corner of Claiborne and Mount Pleasant, the center of Monroeville and steps from the stately courthouse, just chatting. "Sizemore comes up and slaps the cigarette out of Nettles's mouth and cusses him out. And why? To please the white folks, to build a reputation."

That happened in 1948, in this town of long memories.

H.B. and Arthur gave me other examples, all of these exercises in degradation, but there was a harmonious postscript to it all. In the early sixties, Sizemore — a Creek Indian, great-grandson to William Weatherfield, Chief Red Eagle — became crippled and had a conversion. As an act of atonement Sizemore went down to black Clausell, to the main house of worship, Bethel Baptist Church, and begged the black congregation for forgiveness.

Out of curiosity, and against the advice of several whites I met in town, I visited Clausell. When Nelle Harper was a child, the woman who bathed and fed her was Hattie Belle Clausell, the so-called mammy in the Lee household, who walked from this settlement several miles every day to the house on Alabama Avenue in the white part of town. (The Lee house is now gone, replaced by Mel's Dairy Dream and a defunct gas station.) Clausell was named for that black family.

I stopped at Franky D's Barber and Style Shop, on Clausell Road, because barbers know everything. There I was told that I could find Irma, Nelle's former housekeeper, up the road, "in the projects."

The projects was a cul-de-sac of brick bungalows, low-cost housing, but Irma was not in any of them.

"They call this the hood," Brittany Bonner told me — she was on her porch, watching the rain come down. "People warn you about this place, but it's not so bad. Sometimes we hear guns — people shooting in the woods. You see that cross down the road? That's for the man they call James T — Jimmy Tunstall. He was shot and killed a few years ago right there, maybe drug-related."

A white man in Monroeville told me that Clausell was so dangerous that the police never went there alone, but always in twos. Yet Brittany, twenty-two, mother of two small girls, said that violence was not the problem. She repeated the town's lament: "We have no work. There are no jobs."

Brittany's great-aunt Jacqueline Packer thought I might find Irma out at Pine View Heights, down Clausell Road, but all I found were a scattering of houses, some bungalows, many dogtrot houses, rotting cars, and a sign on a closed roadside café: *Southern Favorites — Neckbones and Rice, Turkey Necks and Rice.* Then the pavement ended and the road was red clay, velvety in the rain, leading into the pinewoods.

Back in town I saw a prominent billboard with a stern message: *Nothing in this country is free. If you're getting something without paying for it, Thank a Taxpayer.*

Toward the end of my stay in Monroeville, I met Reverend Thomas Lane Butts, the former pastor of the First United Methodist Church, where Nelle Harper Lee and her sister Alice had been members of his congregation, and his dear friends.

"This town is no different from any other," Reverend Butts told me. He was eighty-five, had traveled throughout the South, and knew what he was talking about. He was born ten miles east, in what he called the "little two-mule community" of Bermuda (*Ber-moo-dah* in the local pronunciation). His father had been a tenant farmer — corn, cotton, vegetables. "We had no land, we had nothing. We didn't have electricity until I was in the twelfth grade, in the fall of 1947. I studied by oil lamp."

The studying paid off. After theology studies at Emory and Northwestern universities, and leading parishes in Mobile and Fort Walton, and taking part in civil rights struggles, he became pastor of this Methodist church.

"We took our racism from our mother's milk," he said. But he'd been a civil rights campaigner from early on, even before 1960, when in Talladega he met Martin Luther King. "He was the first black person I'd met who was not a field hand," he said. "The embodiment of erudition, authority, and humility."

Reverend Butts had a volume of Freud in his lap the day I met him, searching for a quotation in *Civilization and Its Discontents.*

I told him the book was one of my own favorites, for Freud's expression about human pettiness and discrimination, "the narcissism of minor differences" — the subtext of the old segregated South, and of human life in general.

His finger on the page, Reverend Butts murmured some sentences: "'The bit of truth behind all this . . . Men are not gentle creatures who want to be loved . . . can defend themselves . . . a powerful share of aggressiveness . . .' Ah, here it is. '*Homo homini lupus* . . . Man is a wolf to man.'"

That was the reality of history, as true in a proud town like Monroeville as in the wider world. And that led us to talk about the town, the book, the way things are. He valued his friendship with H. B. Williams: the black teacher, the white clergyman, both of them in their eighties, both of them civil rights stalwarts. He had been close to the Lee family, had spent vacations in New York City with Nelle, and still saw her. An affectionately signed copy of her novel rested on the side table, not far from his volume of Freud.

"Here we are," he intoned, raising his hands, "tugged between two cultures, one gone, never to return, and the other being born. Many things here have been lost. *To Kill a Mockingbird* keeps us from complete oblivion."

25

BENTON'S AMERICA

On a low bluff of salt-crusted and tussocky grass in a corner of Menemsha Pond on Martha's Vineyard, a neatly set flight of stone steps is flanked by a retaining wall of fitted boulders, leading to a gracefully paved landing that shows as a tessellated slab beneath a foot-deep pool of wind-nudged bubbles. Who shaped this marvelous stairway to the water? Anyone can see that a dedicated and skilled mason with an eye for sculptural symmetry must have made it with his hands, to protect the natural contours of this part of the lovely pond. All the chosen stones had been sucked smooth by the sea.

"Daddy did that," Jessie Benton told me as I stood admiring its simple beauty and function. Jessie, Thomas Hart Benton's daughter and eldest child, now a dark-eyed and energetic woman of seventy-five, is the embodiment of her parents' mingled temperaments — the bold midwestern father, the resourceful Italian mother. "He built the wall and all that stonework himself, so that we could walk down to our boat or go swimming," she went on. And then she looked around the pond and glanced up-island, smiling with satisfaction. "This was our world."

It was Thomas Hart Benton's world, too. This restless man first visited the island in 1919 with his wife, Rita, and they spent every summer there until his death in 1974, easily earning themselves the hard-won designation as islanders. Given the length of time he spent there, and his paintings of the place that are the sinuous obliquities of a master, he could be ranked next to Edward Hopper and Andrew Wyeth as a coastal New England painter. The oversimple label of Benton as a regionalist, one he once embraced himself, misses the point. The ten panels of *America Today*, his most important mural, show Benton as a painter celebrating (and some-times critiquing) the whole of American life.

The word "mural" means "related to a wall" and calls up the vision of a single painted wall. This is misleading in the case of *America Today,* which is a whole painted room, four walls, ten panels, floor to ceiling. Like all great art, the mural does not reproduce well; illustrated, it is dim and simplified, its colors untrue, much detail lost. All masterpieces must be seen at first hand. This was the reason for the Grand Tour. It is the reason that people still visit the great museums of the world, and they discover, as I did with *America Today,* that being in that room, enclosed by those glorious walls, is the way Benton conceived his project: not as a set of pictures but as an enlivened space. It must be seen that way for its subtlety to be appreciated and the full force of its color and vibrancy to be experienced.

In 1930, Benton was asked by Alvin Johnson, director of New York's New School for Social Research, to do a large-scale mural, ten panels altogether, for the boardroom of the school's new Joseph Urban–designed building. The school's academic program was a departure in higher education, and Benton's commission was something of a novelty, too. Not only was he to create an ambitious mural that would encompass a room, he also had to agree to do so without compensation — no money, but the materials he needed would be provided. "I'll paint you a picture in tempera if you finance the eggs," Benton said when he was told he wouldn't be paid. One inducement was that the work, once completed, would enhance his reputation (he was thirty-nine and still struggling) and win him other commissions.

In terms of detail, he was well equipped. He had been traveling throughout America since 1926. "Benton had accumulated all the necessary raw material for a monumental painting of American life in the modern era of rapid change," Emily Braun writes in *Thomas Hart Benton: The America Today Murals.* "All he needed was a patron and a wall."

The room in which the mural is displayed, in the American Wing of the Metropolitan Museum of Art, is identical in size to the New School's boardroom. The sketches and paintings in the adjacent rooms are proof of what Benton said of the veracity of his mural: "Every detail of every picture is a thing I myself have seen and known. Every head is a real person drawn from life." None of it was fanciful or exaggerated; it is a true portrait of the Jazz Age, which was also an age of intense industrialization in the United States, when cotton was king and oil was beginning to gush; a time of clearing the land for the planting of wheat and corn, the making of steel, and the mining of coal; when New York, its skyscrapers rising, was bursting with life — burlesque shows, movie houses, dance halls, saloons, and in its crowded subways, straphanging coquettes stood before seated intellectuals and bankers under signs advertising toothpaste and tobacco.

All this Benton shows in his pictorial chamber. But what of those misshapen torsos and long-reaching arms and — a distinct feature of the panels — the incredible variety of human hands: grasping, pleading, holding tools, beckoning, praying, hundreds of hand gestures, scores of bodies depicted with unusual plasticity. Speaking of the Mannerist style of the sixteenth-century Dutch painter Abraham Bloemaert, the Met catalog helpfully explains how "both artists filled their compositions with undulating, unnaturally elongated figures and diffused the viewer's attention across the picture plane."

I moved counterclockwise around the room, beginning with "Deep South," which is entirely devoted to cotton, but with contrasting figures, the standing black cotton picker looming over the seated white man on his harrow, the steamboat *Tennessee Belle* in the center loading cotton, and the obscure detail, a chain gang being watched by a mean-faced guard cradling a rifle. As in all the panels, the workers are heroic and powerful.

Next to it, "Mid-West" shows an altered Eden, lumberjacks clear-cutting a forest for timber and for land to grow corn, the grain elevator in the background mirroring the skyscraper depicted across the room in "City Building." A book illustration might not catch the swollen menace of the rattlesnake in the lower left, nor would it show well the boxy Model-T Ford Benton used in his travels. "Changing West," the next panel, is an unromantic study of the oil boom in Texas, dominated by thick smoke and a derrick; yet portions of it show the vanishing professions of herdsmen and cowboys, the confrontation (lower center) of a Native American facing a painted floozy.

No humans appear in the central and largest panel, "Instruments of Power," which is more proof that Benton did not abandon abstraction and that his deftness in rendering movement by controlling color must have impressed his student Jackson Pollock, whose early paintings show Benton's influence. I don't think any reproduction would do justice to the blur of the whirring propeller, nor is it possible in leafing through a book of pictures to see how the red of the plane is repeated in a man's red shirt in one panel, a red blouse in another, the red dress of a dancer, or the crimson leotard of the trapeze artist flinging herself across the top of the opposite panel. The whole mural, among many other things, is a study in attention-seeking roseate colors.

The red shirt of the work-weary miner in "Coal" seizes the eye, as do the smokestacks, the fires, and the power plant. But you need to stand on tiptoe to see, on the upper right, the rough shacks of the mining town, a reminder of the humble home where that muscular miner lives. The furnace flames and fire-lit bodies in "Steel" seem to heat the whole painting, and illuminate the strong bodies and gripping hands, but the tiniest grace notes are those of sparks flying.

"City Building," directly across from "Deep South," shows a similar dynamic pattern of workers, black men and white men working together — in both panels the black workers loom larger. An almost imperceptible detail is the sight of two dark-suited figures — gangsters — one handing over money, at the center of the picture.

Seated for a while at the center of the room, before the two New York panels, "City Activities with Dance Hall" and "City Activities with Subway," I watched people entering *America Today*. None of them strode to the facing wall to see "Instruments of Power" with its planes, trains, and power plants. All the viewers turned to the city panels, where spirit and flesh vied for dominance. They leaned to the right to see the burlesque show (50 GIRLS) and the preachers (GOD IS LOVE), or to the left to see the frenzy of the dance hall, the drinkers, the circus performers. These city panels are the most satisfying of all, the most crowded, the most vital and paradoxical.

Benton appears life-size in that last panel, clinking glasses with his patron, Alvin Johnson, his wife Rita seated nearby, like a Madonna, with her son T.P. In this panel the only contraption is a ticker-tape machine, a stockbroker brooding over it, a clue to the Depression that was about to hit hard, as Benton showed in the rectangle over the boardroom door, of human hands — reaching for food, grasping for money. Benton did not know how bad the Depression would be, but throughout this room he was painting the truth, and the truth is timeless and prophetic.

· · ·

"The Vineyard was his awakening," Jessie Benton told me.

The Vineyard when he first knew it was still an island of fishermen and dirt roads and ox carts, a remnant of the nineteenth century, where the Bentons eked out a summer existence gathering mussels and clams, Thomas working in his self-built studio, Rita Benton bartering the fluffy rolls she baked for the local farmers' vegetables. "We weren't poor," Jessie said, in an echo of her father's observation. "We just didn't have any money."

The Vineyard was not Benton's entire world, and neither was his portion of the Midwest. His view took in the whole country. Benton was one of the gamest and greatest wanderers in this land, as he shows in his forthright and superbly observed book of travels, *An Artist in America* (1939). In 1924, after the death of his father, with whom he had a prickly relationship, he decided to travel around the country, "to pick up the threads of my childhood." He went down rivers, up mountains, along country roads; camped and hiked and bunked in farmhouses; and went into the heartland and confronted the cities of roisterers and skyscrapers in the making, obsessively sketching.

Born in 1889, in Neosho, in the lower left-hand corner of Missouri, near the Arkansas uplands that beckoned to him, he knew the mule-drawn plow and the sharecropper's shack, and he traveled by the clumsiest conveyances — some of the oldest riverboats, by wagon and horseback and old jalopies, and by the steam locomotives he loved and which he hallowed in his work.

He was that ideal creator, in the words of Henry James: someone upon whom nothing is lost. He made piles of sketches. He had seen the West, the Deep South, the Midwest, the cities. He had lived in New York; he had recorded the making of buildings, the smelting of iron, the harvesting of cotton. He knew from close observation the work of a field hand, the performance of a violinist, the movements of a dancer in a burlesque show, the tedium of a straphanger in the subway, the fatigue of a steeplejack. I can't think of another American painter who knew so well the faces of the American landscape and the figures in it, and the many forms of the American worker — industrial, agricultural, office clerk, musician, dancer, trapeze artist.

"He is an anthropologist of American life," his biographer Henry Adams said to me as we lingered over an ink-and-wash picture of three black farm workers in a wagon near a cotton shed. Adams has written in detail of Benton's mission to record types of work in the United States. (Adams has also detailed, in *Tom and Jack*, the complex relationship between Benton and Jackson Pollock, who was twenty-three years his junior, his student, and for a while an informal member of his household, living in a chicken coop behind the Vineyard house, painting sunsets and seascapes.) "Benton was a child growing up on the American frontier," Adams told me. "There was a way of life that was disappearing, and he wanted to record that."

"I'm afraid I can't title it 'America Today' anymore," he said to *Newsweek* in 1957, which Emily Braun uses as an epigraph. "I'd have to call it 'What Life was like in America in the Twenties.'" Later he said, "If it's not art, it's at least history."

It is indisputably art, of a vital kind ("the energy and rush and confusion of American life"), yet not all critics were convinced of that, and some still resist acknowledging Benton's achievement. He has been faulted for being too narrative or too illustrative, and yet it seems to me, like the great traveler-artists (of which George Catlin and Edward Lear are good examples), Benton's work arises from a tradition of storytelling, and reporting from the road. The mural is news, and it is also a mirror of life observed firsthand. As Sinclair Lewis did around the same time in fiction (*Main Street, Babbitt, Elmer Gantry*), Benton showed us who we were as Americans.

Still, the innovations of Benton's art, and even his subtle abstractions, are lost on some. In his time, he had Marxist detractors; in our time, Robert Hughes has been the loudest denouncer, accusing Benton of gratuitous dazzle, in effect of being too brilliant.

"Benton was recoiling against the anti-narrative impulse of his time," the art historian Leo Mazow told me over a Mexican lunch in Fayetteville, Arkansas. As for Hughes's bluster, Mazow said, "Hughes saw criticism in literal terms, as criticizing — rather than describing, interpreting, or analyzing."

You want to say to Benton's detractors (and carpers or philistines generally): These paintings are not on trial — you are. And the technique, the arrangement of elements in the mural, lead the viewer through the work. In his way of connecting the parts to the whole ("a rotogravure style," Mazow suggested), Benton uses diagonals to direct the eye, X patterns for focusing activity, and subtle balance in the placement of figures. So the eye is guided through the narrative, not from left to right but in a circular way, from figure to figure, deeper into each panel.

The greatest painters and writers teach us how to see. With this in mind, I had decided to visit some sights in the South related to Benton, and happened to be passing through Fayetteville on my way from Neosho, Missouri, Benton's birthplace. He was born in a grand house that burned down in 1917. It is easy to see how a boy from a small orderly town, with its grid of streets surrounded by creeks and gentle hills, was energized by the steeper hills and isolated villages farther south in the Ozarks.

Among the vintage memorabilia and ephemera displayed by the Neosho Historical Society, near the center of town, is a small news item from the *Neosho Times* of August 15, 1907, about a fistfight Benton was involved in outside the town's bank, when he was fifteen. "Tom Benton and Harry Hargrove had a very interesting 'scrap' Sunday evening," the front-page piece begins. "Both boys were arrested and in police court Monday. The Benton boy admitted he was the aggressor and pleaded guilty to assault."

"He loved to fight," one of his school friends recalled, when Benton returned for a celebratory homecoming with Harry Truman in 1962. His uncle was a famous senator with the same name; his father, Maecenas, was a lawyer and congressman, but Tommy (to the despair of his father, whose sternness he resented) grew up a poor student but a free spirit. "The Neosho Creeks . . . where we went to swim," Benton recalled, "and learned the arts of chewing and smoking tobacco."

Into Arkansas, over War Eagle Creek and Onion Creek, past Dry Fork and the tiny hamlet of Old Alabam, the Ozarks rise, not mountains but a succession of low ridges, a series of elevations, a sea of long lumpy hills. No single feature is apparent, there are no peaks, but the whole panorama of it — the broad shifting vista of elongated hills, like thickly forested mesas — is dramatic. And it is especially moving because it still seems unpeopled, the isolated communities hidden in hollows and behind the slopes, some of which are bunchy with old-growth trees.

In Benton's time, as a traveling artist, this was the forest primeval, but even today the Ozarks are remote and beautiful. "And thinly visited," as I mentioned to an old-timer in a junk shop in the hard-up town of Leslie, which was once prosperous making oak barrels. He replied, "I hope it stays that way."

This man, in his overalls and boots and faded hat, had the beaky country profile that occurs frequently in Benton's sketches of the Ozarks, some of them transferred to the "Deep South" and "Mid-West" panels of *America Today*. On any given morning in the small-town diners in the Ozarks — Harrison, Marshall, St. Joe, Bellefonte, and Yellville come to mind — the older men are Bentonesque. In this place of enduring backwoods, the forms of work, which Benton recorded, are unchanged: family farms, hog-raising, turkey-rearing, cabbage patches.

"Welcome to Hillbillyville," a man said to me on a side street in Alpena, with the self-deprecation that is common in Arkansas. "People are poor here, but that's a good thing for them. The economy don't affect them. Up or down, they live just the same."

This man also mentioned that when he first moved to the town from not far away, he had a visit from the Grand Wizard of the Ku Klux Klan, who had driven over from Harrison, encouraging him to join.

I asked him what his reply to this was.

"I said, 'You and me don't have enough in common for that to happen.' He took it pretty good and went away."

Old times there are not forgotten, but not all oldfangledness is salutary. It is worth noting that in significant places in his panels Benton painted black men working harmoniously among white ones, and his sketches are full of the details of black life — the sharecropper, the preacher, the cotton grower. In this unusual landscape, peculiar to Arkansas, among these small farms and their antique plows and harrows, and its isolated people, Benton felt like a discoverer. Such is the hardly altered and traditional way of life, and the unspoiled forest, that it is still possible to feel that way, and even to sense the same conflicts.

The Buffalo River is the central artery in the heat of the Ozarks. Benton went down the river in the 1920s and again later in his life, when he was in his seventies. He followed it on its eastward course to the confluence of the White River, then continued south.

With Benton in mind, one early September morning I rented a boat and paddled for a whole day, from Baker Ford to Gilbert, stopping at intervals to inhale the fragrant air, to watch the sun flashing on the rapids and the insects stirring on the surface of the shallows. The river was greeny gold in the stiller pools as two deer, a doe and her fawn, picked their way across the river ahead of me, occasionally pausing to nibble or sip. I saw herons and a cormorant. The drumming of a woodpecker echoed from the cliffs and sheer rock faces, which made it seem that some parts of the river were coursing through a canyon. In this silence and solitude, I had the reassuring sense — because of the visible slope of the river — that I was sliding downhill.

It is easy to understand why Benton loved his time on the Buffalo River, and why his experience of traveling in the heart of America rekindled his love of the land that he elaborated in his paintings and murals. It is one of the achievements of Arkansas environmentalists that the Buffalo River remains untampered-with and undammed.

"Interested at the time in my projected history of the United States," Benton says in *An Artist in America,* "I was looking for some of the old river towns where I might get next to authentic first-hand material." Soon after, traveling near Natchez, he hears of a location, a levee near the Red River, where he might observe an old steamboat — one of the last — being loaded with cotton bales. In Benton's telling, it is an adventure, finding his way with his friend Bill across the Mississippi to Louisiana, and through the bayous and back roads to the narrower tributary and Red River Landing.

"I was determined to make drawings of a riverbank loading," he writes, "a rare event in these days." It is a whole week in the heat, under the thorn trees by the river, his food and water running low, before the *Tennessee Belle* appears at the landing for its cargo. But this is the boat that is depicted in the center of the panel "Deep South."

"Ya'll came too far," an older man told me in the tiny Louisiana farming community (soybeans and sugarcane) of Lettsworth, where he'd been born and never left. "Every time there's a flood here we get a new channel or two."

He sent me back upriver, along the levee, past the new canal with its complex of locks, and some cotton fields looking wintry, thick with blown-open tufts, to low-lying woods where I inserted myself down a side road. After a few miles on this broken road, I took a gravel road to the Red River, where I found a landing — perhaps not Benton's landing, but the shacks, the beached boats, the thorn trees hung with Spanish moss, and the air of abandonment combined to make it appear Bentonesque. I had not found the location I'd been looking for, but in the search I'd found remoteness and beauty.

Benton was seldom on a hunt for something particular. Like all great travelers he launched himself into the unknown, content that he was in the United States — preferring the countryside to the cities — eager to record the life of the land. The fruit of that search can be found in the ten panels of *America Today,* now restored and rehung, one of our national treasures.

"He has some magic by which he gets to the soul of things," Henry Adams said to me. We were looking at an oil painting of Jessie, done by her father as a present for her eighteenth birthday, a lustrous portrait of a young woman holding a guitar that she is about to strum. I was thinking how Benton's genius enabled him to make family affairs and discovered pieces of social history into works of art.

"It took him all that summer," Jessie said. And giving a practical meaning to the rosy adjectives "genius" and "magic," she added, "All his life, Daddy got up early, with the light. He worked all day, until the light went."

26

MY LIFE AS A READER

It seems quaint today — and hard to imagine, unless you live in a dictator-ship, where the truth is dangerous — but not long ago in the United States many books were illegal, regarded as subversive, or provocative, or so lewd they were likely to corrupt a reader. Book banning (often accompanied by book burning) has been common throughout history — as long as books have existed, which is thousands of years if you count papyrus and scrolls. And the fact that it touched my town was a direct link between my little library in Medford and the barbarities of the big world: the destruction of books by the Chinese emperor Qin Shi Huang in 213 BC, the burning of the library at Alexandria by Julius Caesar 48 BC, the Nazi book burnings, and other such violent and idiotic suppressions.

So, coming of age at a time of forbidden books, when some writers were regarded as outlaws, I was fascinated, my attention seized by this apparent wickedness. With banned books and notorious writers in mind, I sought out those objects of malevolent power and was profoundly influenced in becoming a reader. From the beginning, reading for me was an act of trans-gression and rebellion.

Some rare, tattered, much-thumbed paperbacks were passed from hand to hand, though to own one of these titles was like possessing a drug or a bomb. I had a friend whose father kept a copy of D. H. Lawrence's *Lady Chatterley's Lover* in a bottom drawer, and my friend flourished it and showed me the dog-eared pages. In my youth, several of Henry Miller's titles, notably *Tropic of Cancer* and *Tropic of Capricorn,* were banned; the Lawrence, William Burroughs's *Naked Lunch,* and Edmund Wilson's *Mem-oirs of Hecate County* were not available until they were subjected to a judicial evaluation. *Huckleberry Finn* has been a problem from the time of its publication in 1885. And because some books were vicious or vulgar, writers, too, were suspect, as corrupters, and consequently they were power figures. The idea of the writer as someone dangerous was greatly appealing to me. What fourteen-year-old boy does not wish in his idle moments to be associated with someone notorious?

I also remember when books were unbanned and became freely available in the mid-1960s, but by then I was in Africa, reading and writing. Nowadays, except for occasional eruptions over words regarded as offensive (*Huckleberry Finn* once again), or a literary depiction seen to be subversive, books are taken for granted and writers are seen as ordinary people — nerds, drudges, bearded, boring, the talkers on TV, the signers at the bookstore.

Never mind. Reading has been my refuge, my pleasure, my enlightenment, my inspiration, my word-hunger often verging on gluttony. In idle moments without a book, I read the labels on my clothes or the ingredients panel on cereal boxes. My version of hell is an existence without a thing to read, but I would hope to correct it by writing something.

Literacy is widespread in the world, yet in my early life, as a teacher in central Africa, I lived among many people who were unable to read. This was not a hardship for them — as toilers in the bush, they had other compensating skills, and they viewed me as someone with a peculiar habit of idleness, holding a book before my face and staring at it for hours. I admired their self-sufficiency as subsistence farmers spending long hours in the fields, as they observed the cycle, and sometimes the cruelty, of the seasons. There were others in the village who had learned to read but who never picked up a book. As the saying (erroneously attributed to Mark Twain) goes, those who didn't read had no advantage over the ones who couldn't read. Indeed, in their arrogance and their presumptions, the literate nonreaders were at a considerable disadvantage.

The great distinction in the world I know is not that there are old people and young people, black and white, Third Worlders and First Worlders, rich and poor, educated and uneducated, employed or out of work, but that there are people who read and those who don't. Most don't.

Out of pride, people claim they read, because reading is praised as a wise and wonderful activity, and they don't wish to be thought of as foolish or lazy. But reading requires mental effort, an ability to concentrate, a lively curiosity and intelligence, as well as a mastery of solitude. "Curiously enough, one cannot read a book: one can only reread it," Nabokov writes in *Lectures on Literature*. "A good reader, a major reader, an active and creative reader is a rereader. And I shall tell you why. When we read a book for the first time the very process of laboriously moving our eyes from left to right, line after line, page after page, this complicated physical work upon the book, the very process of learning in terms of space and time what the book is about, this stands between us and artistic appreciation," and he later concludes, "A book, no matter what it is — a work of fiction or a work of science (the boundary line between the two is not as clear as is generally believed) — a book of fiction appeals first of all to the mind. The mind, the brain, the top of the tingling spine, is, or should be, the only instrument used upon a book."

Reading is a serious matter, but readers are seldom lonely or bored, because reading is a refuge and an enlightenment. This wisdom is sometimes visible. It seems to me that there is always something luminous in the face of a person in the act of reading.

A great part of the appeal of reading fiction is the discovery that the reader knows much more of the inner life of the characters in the book than of his or her own family members or friends. This intensity of the reading experience cannot be communicated to a nonreader, which is why fictional characters seem real, exemplary, tragic, comic, and accessible. I am thinking of passionate readers, who read everything, people for whom Hamlet is a believable figure in the middle distance, paradoxical, witty, and burdened by a mission to avenge his father's death; for whom Madame Bovary is a sneaky, self-deceiving romantic, and Huck Finn one of life's buoyant survivors; for whom Jane Austen's Emma, Dickens's Pip, Melville's Ishmael, Joseph Conrad's Marlow, Graham Greene's "whisky priest," Kafka's Gregor Samsa, Nabokov's Lolita, and other characters are deathless, persuasive, and ready to be summoned, along with Lady Chatterley, Henry of the *Tropics*, and Flem Snopes, the ultimate imaginary friends.

These are from the great books, but even the wayward masterpieces can seize our interest. Flann O'Brien's *At Swim-Two-Birds* is an oddly written novel but an engrossing narrative, and the same can be said for *The Sound and the Fury, His Monkey Wife,* and many other works of fiction—children's books, romances, scientific narratives both speculative and fantastic, detective stories, and Westerns. Most of our reading has an effect, though with time, as with other aesthetic concerns, the reader practices discrimination and learns connoisseurship. From this a reader develops a common language, the language of books.

Most readers can trace their love of books to their listening to stories. My father read *Treasure Island* to my brothers and me at bedtime; my mother read us *The Five Chinese Brothers,* the *Snipp, Snapp, Snurr* series, *Sonny Elephant,* and the many Dr. Seuss books. At school, as second- and third-graders we were read *Epaminondas and His Auntie* and *Little Black Sambo,* two books with racial overtones that would make them unsuitable for an eight-year-old today but seemed jolly at the time, especially as they were written to be read aloud. When I reflect on all these titles, I am struck by their exoticism—pirates, China, Swedish boys, the Deep South, and Sambo (not an African American but a Hindu Tamil boy in south India). My interest in the wider world was stimulated early.

A few years later in school, as a Friday-afternoon treat, Miss Sullivan read the class Frances Hodgson Burnett's *The Secret Garden,* a chapter at a time. The novel was originally written as a serial for a magazine, so the chapters are shaped for effect, short and vivid, and the thrust of the book is conflict, illness, neglect, and loss, as well as healing and growth. That novel left a deep impression on me as an example of the drama of fiction, with structure and plot building, showing how circumstances can be altered: a blighted garden made whole and healthy, a sick child made well, a mood improved. That it was set in Yorkshire, England, with allusions to colonial India, with oddly named characters (Dickon, Weatherstaff, Mrs. Medlock) and unfamiliar dialect ("Tha munnot waste no time"), made it exotic to me and memorable.

I emphasize this book because, utterly foreign and yet understandable, it opened a door for me, like the door to the secret garden itself. I began to understand how a book that had no relation to my own life could possess my imagination. That, of course, is one of the pleasures of reading. The great books cast a spell, admitting the reader to another world, sometimes exemplary, like the Polynesian Eden of Melville's *Typee* or the English dystopia of Orwell's *Nineteen Eighty-Four.*

I should say that all my reading, with a few exceptions (swapping with friends, lurid paperbacks, or the violent horror comics of the early fifties), was of library books. We had the Bible and Shakespeare and Grimm in the house, but not many others. I did not buy a book until I was a college student, but I remained — and am still — a library-goer.

At some point, quite early — I was perhaps thirteen or fourteen — my reading diverged and I began to live a parallel life as a reader, supplementing school books with library books I chose for myself. The required reading at school I often found dismaying, insufficient, or overanalyzed. Seventh grade, we were assigned Saroyan's *The Human Comedy*. We studied it for a month. It seemed thin to me, and I hated its coyness and its simplicities. Later on, Hemingway's *The Old Man and the Sea* — portentous, self-consciously sagacious, and the old man lost the fish, so what was the point?

On my own, not telling my teachers, reading for pleasure, I used the town library and ranged more widely: *The White Tower* (mountain climbing), *Kon-Tiki* (sea voyage on a waterlogged raft), and books of humor, especially the collected pieces of S. J. Perelman, whom I found hilarious for his verbal magic and his love of both slang and the oddest words. I realized, with a bit of self-congratulation, that Perelman was speaking to me and enlarging my sense of the absurd. And from his allusions it was clear that Perelman was also a traveler to far-off countries. Now and then I recognized my own world in a book and discovered a counterpart: Holden Caulfield, a boy wealthier than I was (New York, private school, fencing classes) but just as innocent and disillusioned; and the wry outsider in Max Shulman's *The Many Lives of Dobie Gillis*. What a pleasant surprise to find worldly priests with human weaknesses in the stories of J. F. Powers, especially those in his collection *The Prince of Darkness*. They behaved and sounded just like the priests I knew, bossy, red-faced Irishmen who cracked jokes, played golf, and had submissive housekeepers.

Haunting the library, stalking the open shelves, I developed a taste for books of adventure. The origin of this was probably *Kon-Tiki* and Richard Henry Dana's *Two Years Before the Mast*, augmented by Kenneth Roberts's *Boon Island*. Roberts's subject was a true story of mutiny, shipwreck, and cannibalism, and the fact that these events occurred on an island off the coast of Maine made the harrowing narrative all the more appealing. I began to seek out books about survival in the wilderness, of dramatic mishaps at sea, or in jungles or deserts — in a word, ordeals. They were never political, nor had they anything to do with warfare. These books were concerned with overcoming adversity and hostility in the natural world, the worst that can happen to a wanderer. I was not on any sports team. My private pleasure was hiking. I'd become a Boy Scout at eleven, I owned a rifle (Mossberg .22), and wished to know more of the dangers in the world, especially in the woods and at sea, and the ways to brave them. I was fascinated by the strategies of survival, the limits of human endurance, and — though I knew the concepts but not the words for them then — by transformation and redemption.

It was School Books versus All Others, the books I was told to study and anatomize set against the books I delighted in. It seemed odd to me that Hemingway was taught so thoroughly and his contemporary F. Scott Fitzgerald, whose writing I loved, was ignored. Dickens was hailed, his contemporary Anthony Trollope not considered; Dostoyevsky and Tolstoy, but not Turgenev or Gogol. And in college we were saturated with Shakespeare, but were told very little of his fellow dramatists — Thomas Kyd, Marlowe, Cyril Tourneur, Middleton, and Rowley. This is still the case in high schools and colleges — the notable names chosen over the others. Probably this is so because, unfortunately, time is limited. That is a shame, because reading cannot be compartmentalized; it is a skill and a pleasure that needs to be inspired, so that it becomes a lifelong passion.

People sometimes tell me they have read one of my books and liked it. I say, "Have you read any of my others?" Often the answer is no, for which I blame English teachers, who make a virtue of skimming from one author to another, believing this to be the best initiation in the humanities. It is actually an error in judgment and a sad sort of dilettantism. My method of reading is the opposite. When I find a writer I enjoy, I make his or her writing a personal project. I began this while living in Africa, the earliest of my intense reading years. I read Albert Camus's *The Stranger.* Then I read *The Fall* and *The Plague,* and along with these a biography of the man and his essays, including *The Rebel,* and finally his two volumes of *Notebooks.* Then I knew Camus.

Rather than read a book, I read a writer. I have done this with most of the writers I have enjoyed, not merely the obvious ones — Henry James, Conrad, Fitzgerald, Faulkner, Trollope, and Turgenev — but writers outside the canon, Ford Madox Ford, Nathanael West, Anthony Burgess, Djuna Barnes, Nadine Gordimer, Elias Canetti, Borges, Jean Rhys, and many others, devouring all the novels and stories, and then whatever biography I could find. I mentioned this once to the head of a university English department in a seminar I was conducting with his students, and he said, "That's all right for you, but we don't have as much free time as you civilians." Tact prevented me from telling him he had a salary, which I lacked, and that he was a lazy and philistine fathead.

The 1950s, when I was in junior high and high school, was a time of racial turbulence. My first awareness was the lynching, in 1955 in Mississippi, of Emmett Till, who was exactly my age. Some of my fellow students were black, but they were reticent, and anyway this was the North. No KKK threat or voter registration hassles here. It was only in books that I was to encounter the black experience. One of the books read to us at school very early (I guess after 1951, when it won a literary prize) was Elizabeth Yates's *Amos Fortune, Free Man*, about a slave who, after many tribulations, buys his freedom and prospers as a tanner in Jaffrey, New Hampshire, a novel based on historical fact. Later I read Ralph Ellison's *Invisible Man*, the works of Richard Wright, James Baldwin, Langston Hughes, and Zora Neale Hurston. And that intimacy I mentioned earlier, the way a reader is admitted to the inner life of a fictional character, meant everything to me, and shaped my sensibility, and gave me some understanding of racial conflict in American life.

It is a common misconception that an experience of books turns a reader into a writer. Reading does not make you a writer any more than a love and understanding of pictures makes you an artist. The reading experience can be so intimidating it would discourage many who think they might like to make a stab at it. I think of the readers of Nabokov or Joyce or Samuel Beckett, the dazzlers, the virtuosos, the self-conscious stylists. Perhaps that is the key to the canon — the simplicities of Hemingway or Dreiser give people the hopeful delusion that they might aspire to do the same.

I did not set out to be a writer. My desire was to be a medical doctor, but this was thwarted by ten years of travel, during which I fell into writing, served an apprenticeship, and fifty years went by, and I am still at it. To me, what writers read is as interesting as what they write. Which writers do great writers admire? We know that Dostoyevsky read Dickens, that Tolstoy read Thoreau, that Thoreau read Melville. Henry James read Flaubert,

George Eliot, and all his contemporaries. Joseph Conrad read widely, but said his favorite book was one of scientific exploration, Alfred Russel Wallace's *The Malay Archipelago*. Jack London read Conrad, to whom he sent fan letters. Mark Twain sent friendly letters to Kipling, whom he admired. Faulkner read Georges Simenon, and so did André Gide and Henry Miller. In Miller's long and detailed book on the subject of his reading, *The Books in My Life*, one of his chapters is "Reading in the Toilet" ("a habit which is widespread"). Simenon, who published hundreds of novels, a dozen of them brilliant, claimed he only read books about forensics, medicine, and psychology. I cannot think of any writer of stature in English who has not shown a knowledge of the Bible.

Though I hate being read to now — I am too impatient, I need to create my own rhythm and intonation, I like to see the pattern of words on the page — I have never ceased to read. I am not a speed reader except when absolutely necessary (for a book review). The better the book, the slower I read. I sometimes ponder a single page for a long time, often scribble in pencil in the margin. Reading a book quickly is no virtue.

It would take a *Books in My Life* tome to describe the books I've read, and I haven't the heart for that, but one hint to some of its contents would be all the books and authors I've mentioned here. Each travel book I've written has necessitated the reading of scores and sometimes hundreds of books. For my *Tao of Travel* I read about 350 books and quoted from many of them. The pages of my work are filled with references to books I've loved.

I seldom read the newest, most widely hyped books and tend to avoid my illustrious contemporaries — their voices in my head would be a distraction. I seem always to be delving into the past. Recently I decided to reread B. Traven, a mystery man who tried as an exile in Mexico to hide his German identity. Most people know *The Treasure of the Sierra Madre*, but Traven wrote much more. I bought and read all his books, including the little-known ones — *The White Rose, The Kidnapped Saint*, and the six jungle novels — as well as Will Wyatt's biographical search, *The Man Who Was B. Traven*. With the help of a dictionary I am reading *Land des Frühlings*, Traven's account (with his photographs) of the Mexican state of Chiapas, which, though published in 1928, has never been translated into English.

I have also been searching for the overlooked and scarce books by and about Conrad, and have bought and read *Notes on My Books*, his theatrical adaptation of *The Secret Agent; Letters to My Wife*; and his wife Jessie's

Joseph Conrad as I Knew Him. I read a new book of Hawaiian history by a friend, and reread *Moby-Dick* after I found a copy of the edition illustrated by Rockwell Kent. On my bedside table, to ease myself into sleep, I have a new translation of *Death in Venice,* a book I have read countless times.

You'd think from all this that I have a well-stocked library, but I don't. I am not a serious book collector or even a book saver. I don't have the space or the inclination, and books can be a burden. They're heavy, they gather dust, they eventually become malodorous. If I don't intend to reread a book, why would I keep it? I give books away — to libraries, to schools, to prisons. What books I own are ones I intend to read again or are treasures: beautiful editions of *Ulysses, Seven Pillars of Wisdom,* an early Samuel Johnson *Dictionary,* and *The Voyage of the Beagle.* I also own the New York Edition of Henry James (twenty-four volumes), the signed twenty-two-volume edition of the works of Joseph Conrad, all of Graham Greene and Kipling and Nabokov, and first editions of Henry Morton Stanley's Africa travels (with maps), three different editions of *The Worst Journey in the World* (Apsley Cherry-Gerrard was a constant reviser), and the three hard-to-find travel books of Edward Lear, about Albania, Calabria, and Corsica. But most of the books in my library are editions of books I have written.

I have kept some signed books. The first one I acquired in Amherst, Massachusetts, in 1962. I was walking down the road and saw Robert Frost walking toward me. He agreed (after complaining a bit, he was a cranky eighty-eight) to sign a copy of his new book of poems, *In the Clearing.* Since then I have added to my shelves of signed books, mostly by friends: Bruce Chatwin, Jonathan Raban, V. S. Naipaul, William Styron, Philip Roth, Hunter Thompson, Haruki Murakami, and many others. A signed book is something of value — sentimental value in the eyes of a reader, hard market value in the estimation of a book dealer.

Though it has never been my intention, my reading has been a way of remembering where I've been, since I associate the reading of particular books with specific locations. Madame Blavatsky's *Isis Unveiled* I read as a student in Amherst, curious about the doctrines of Theosophy, but I also read Ralph Ellison and Jack Kerouac then. I read, for obvious reasons, Chekhov's stories on the Trans-Siberian Express, Carlo Levi's *Christ Stopped at Eboli* in southern Italy, and Thomas Hardy in Dorset. Less obviously, on a sea voyage from Singapore to North Borneo, on the MV *Keningau,* I read Naipaul's *A House for Mr. Biswas.* "Why do you laugh?" a Malay rubber planter asked me again and again. I have described in my *Old Patagonian Express* reading Poe's *The Narrative of Arthur Gordon Pym* in Costa Rica and the spell it cast on me. Stuck for a month in writing my *Mosquito Coast*, I read John Cheever's prison novel, *Falconer;* its energy reminded me of what writing must do and lifted my spirits to the point where I was able to go back to my book. I wrote Cheever a note thanking him.

In Africa, where I was a teacher more than fifty years ago, it was a two-hour round trip by bicycle from my little house through the Kanjedza Forest to the small town of Limbe. Once a month, the latest cargo from the coast included the new Penguin paperbacks that were displayed on the revolving wire book rack at the Nyasaland Trading Company. I felt the books were being sent to me, two oceans away, because no one else in Limbe seemed interested. These inexpensive Penguins were my further education —the obvious Orwells and the lesser-known novels, *Coming Up for Air* and *Burmese Days;* the earliest Anthony Burgess novels, including *Enderby* and *Nothing Like the Sun;* the Penguin Classics such as *The Iliad* and Dante; the Simenons and other crime paperbacks in green bindings; and writers unknown to me: Henry de Montherlant and Laurie Lee. Reading took the curse off the long dark African nights and gave me relief and hope, for no matter how badly the day went, a book was waiting for me at home, and this has continued to be the case.

27

THE REAL ME: A MEMORY

Standing by the side of the road with a fixed, propitiating smile and my
thumb out, I felt puny braced against the beat of oncoming traffic. I was
hitchhiking under the pigeon-haunted girders of a huge high bridge span
that was like an iron sky. The sound of speeding cars was a howl and then
a fading-away whine of farewell as they whipped by, throwing up grit and
exhaust fumes in sudden gusts, and scattering the dirty birds. The buffet-
ing wind from the slipstream pushed me back, my heels chewing gravel.
All northbound hitchhikers from New York City at that time knew that the
best place to thumb a ride was on the stretch of Henry Hudson Parkway
beneath the George Washington Bridge.

Although it was not raining, a fine mist softened and simplified the world
to a bearable unreality. But I knew better. It was a dim, clammy-cold day
in April 1962, a year of uncertainty and bad news: spies, Cuba, atom bomb
tests, a recent plane crash in New York, and I had no money. In the shadow
of the bridge, under the spell of Kerouac, or so I liked to think, I was eager
to get to Amherst and see my friend Jonquil J. Christ. She was an undergraduate at Smith — witty, confident, a worldly New Yorker, who praised
my writing and said that she had plans to write, too, "but under a nom
de plume." From what Jonquil told me, she was from a classy family, the
Christs so upright — so Christlike — she intended to protect their respectability with a pen name.

"You need a good one," I had said. "Like Céline. Or Saki. Or George
Sand."

"Mine's better than those. I am going to be Betsy Brenhouse."

I envied her for that, the future memoirist, Betsy Brenhouse, and her revelations of high society. I had met her that winter. She and her bright friends, disheveled nymphs of Smith, Julie and Sydney, drove up from Northampton to tease me with their wit and beauty in my cluttered room on South Main Street. "See the house across the street, behind that hedge? Emily Dickinson's." With Jonquil it was not a question of romance, but of the assured hilarity and comradeship I needed, a sense that with her and her friends I was connected to the real world of class and influence.

After twenty minutes or so, a car slowed down and pulled partway onto the shoulder. I ran to it and the driver called out, "Hop in."

He was probably forty, though he could have been less. As a twenty-one-year-old I had no sense of people's ages. Thirty was middle-aged to me. Kerouac was forty and old, though youthful in his energy and rebelliousness. The driver was casually friendly, which was a relief. Often a driver seemed somewhat suspicious of a hitchhiker, and cranky until he was reassured you were harmless.

"Where you headed?" Saying so, he gnawed his fingernail, twisting it in concentration in his teeth like someone biting open a pistachio.

"Springfield," I said, because the way to Amherst was on a side road.

"College kid?"

"Yes. I'm premed," I said. "But I do a lot of writing."

"Me too," he said.

"Really?"

"Sure. I'm a writer."

This statement was magic to me then, and he smiled at my sudden attention. He was a big, loose-bodied man, with a paunch showing in his gray sweatshirt. His smile enlarged his jaw in his wide sloping face, and when his attention tightened, two deep vertical creases appeared in his forehead, like the number 11. He was sitting, so I could not tell how tall he was, but he was bigger than me, and fleshier, and he seemed to become self-conscious because of my stare. His fingertips were licked clean from his nail-biting.

"I'm out of shape," he said. "All the sitting. Hey, writing's not much exercise. I used to be a bodybuilder."

"What sort of things do you write?"

"You really interested?"

"Yes," I said, because the only writers I knew were English professors in Amherst, some local poets, and Jonquil, or rather, Betsy.

"Pulps, mysteries," he said. "Paperbacks."

Paperbacks in those years suggested sleaze, lurid covers, yellowish pages, crime, violence, sex, and always something of the forbidden, for thirty-five cents.

"Have you written many?"

"Oh yeah, maybe a dozen."

I was distracted, so it did not occur to me to question his vagueness, that he would not know exactly how many books he had written. What distracted me were the car's red leather seats, which should have added elegance but were worn and scuffed and cracked — and smelled, not of leather but something sharper and sourer, the sweaty odor of an unwashed human body. And it struck me that perhaps it was not the odor of the leather at all, but of the fattish smiling driver, who was still talking.

"It's money," he was saying. "You could do it. You seem like a bright kid."

And I thought: Write one of those paperbacks, yes, it would be wild, wicked, sexy. The writers lacked all pretension and were like outlaws. Some were arrested on charges of obscenity and went to court and were branded criminals. The idea of a writer being someone criminal and dangerous was attractive to me, and my book would impress Jonquil, who knew nothing of lawlessness. And there was the money.

"How long does it take to write one of those, um, paperbacks?"

"Oh, I don't know — depends," he said, and it seemed he had stopped listening to me and was looking in the rearview mirror, slowing down and letting cars pass, and in this thoughtful pause nibbling a fingernail. The set of his teeth was fangy and ugly and briefly evil.

"Where are we?" I asked, because he had begun to make a turn.

"I just gotta get something. I live here." He wiped his wet finger on his sweatshirt. "You mind?"

"Not really."

He had turned into a side street off the parkway somewhere in Yonkers, and continued a short distance up a tree-lined road toward an apartment house, a façade of sharp jutting balconies. The trees had just come into bud, and on this misty day the damp air had soaked the road, and the large parking lot in front of the apartment house gleamed black.

"Come on in, I won't be long," he said, gently insisting, and when I got out of the car the dampness in the air smelled sharply of dead leaves and muddy earth, one of those days so stifling and gray you feel you're partly underground.

He had made me curious, so I followed him into the stairwell and up two flights to an apartment facing the parking lot, somewhat reassured that it was high enough and facing the road to be well lighted. It was an open-plan kitchen, dining area, and living room, but messy. I looked for a typewriter and books or any sign of its being a writer's apartment, but all I saw were dishes in the sink, magazines on the table, a coffee cup on a windowsill.

"Did I mention I was a bodybuilder?" he said.

"I think so." Now I noticed, shivering slightly, that the apartment was clammier than outside, and some degrees cooler.

He held out his arms as though presenting himself. "See, this is what happens when you stop exercising. I was all muscle, but if you let yourself go it turns into flab." He snatched at the magazines on the table as if to straighten them, and pushed them away from me into a pile, but they remained ill assorted. "You spend any time in a gym?"

"No — just —" *A gym?* I could not think of a reply.

"Know who spends a lot of time in gyms?"

"Bodybuilders, I guess."

He laughed. "Homos," he said, and paused on the word, fixing his gaze on me. "They love hanging around gyms, where guys are lifting weights." He went to the sideboard near the sink. "Want a cup of coffee?"

"No, thanks. Don't bother."

"It's instant. No trouble."

And now I knew that coming into the apartment had been a mistake. He had said there was something he wanted to do, but he showed no sign of doing it. He looked relaxed, as though he had no intention of leaving, and he was taking his time filling a kettle with water and putting it on the stove. I had now been in the apartment long enough to see that it was so untidy and cold it seemed no one really lived there.

"By the way, what's your name?" I asked.

"Who wants to know?"

"I might want to read one of your books."

Saying that seemed absurd, because of "bodybuilder" and the chill and bareness of the apartment. I saw no books anyway, only the clutter of tattered magazines, thickened from reading or the dampness of the room, pushed into a pile and impossible to identify.

"Gary," he said, and smiled in hesitation, as though he'd forgotten he'd told me he was a writer. "But I write under the name Rod"—another gulp of hesitation—"Rod Fisher. You can't write that stuff under your own name. You'd have to think of an alibi."

"Maybe I will," I said, wondering why he hadn't said "pseudonym," but "Fisher" resonated—fissure, like the upright, number 11 creases in his forehead. I was now trying to think of an excuse to leave, and started to say, "I should probably—"

"Coffee," he said in the same remembering voice. He turned his back on me and went to the counter, spooned coffee powder from a jar into two cups. This he did with deliberation, taking his time, as if he was thinking of something else.

In the silence, the odor in the apartment became stronger, the sweat smell of the car that was like a wet animal, intensified by the dampness of the day. And then I knew: it was the man's smell, body odor, a hum of unwashed clothes that was like decay, and flesh that was sharp now, and as he came closer with the coffee, a stink. Some smells suggest danger; his did.

"Want to look around?"

"It's okay." I sensed myself becoming more compact, holding my elbows against my sides and my hands over my chest, as women sometimes did with me when I got too close.

"Because I see you're kind of curious, looking at my stuff." He slapped the magazines and disturbed a page, and I saw flesh, a bare torso, a muscular man. "I've got lots of room in the back, a lot of great stuff. I'm a photographer, too. I've got a darkroom. I develop all my own pictures." He drew a lump of wallet out of his back pocket and flipped it open to a snapshot of a muscleman, a large gleaming body with a narrow, turtle-like head. "See? That's the real me."

I said, "Look, I really have to go."

"Plenty of time," he said. "What made you want to be a writer?"

"I don't know." He was leaning toward me. That smell like a foul cloud around him. "What made *you* want to be a writer?"

He nodded and chewed his lips with satisfaction, as if tasting something familiar, and wagged a bitten fingernail at me.

"I get it. You're one of them smart guys. I ask a question, and instead of answering you ask me the same question back."

He said this in a new tone, with a sharpness that matched the smell of his sweatshirt. Closer, I could see that the collar of the sweatshirt was chewed.

"I'm planning to be a doctor," I said.

"Got a girlfriend?" He lifted a finger and gnawed, turning it in his teeth.

"I thought you were going to give me a lift. If not, I can just—"

"I'm taking you to the Merritt Parkway," he said, sounding indignant, and shoved at his sweatshirt sleeve and looked at his watch. I noticed the leather wristband was cracked and rotted. "Lots of time. Enjoy your coffee." He sipped and peered over the rim of his cup. "So you don't have a girlfriend?"

"I actually do."

"What's her name?"

"Jonquil."

"She pretty?"

"She's really nice. Goes to Smith." And I thought, Save me, Jonquil. She was funny and friendly and would forgive me for my saying she was my girlfriend. Something—she might say—for Betsy Brenhouse to write about. And I had the sense that if I needed help, she'd provide it; she had status and connections, and with Smith College poise she always had an answer.

"The real thing, eh?" he said without any interest.

"I guess so."

Instead of replying, he half raised himself from the chair and dragged it, making the metal legs stutter on the hard floor as he came closer to me.

Just then the phone rang, deeper in the apartment, indicating to me how big a place it might be, the echo of the ring making it emptier and darker. He did nothing, looked stubborn, his lips pressed together, until after many rings, it ceased, and then he relaxed again.

"Let me see your hand."

I thought he was going to snatch it and use it to subdue me, so I kept my hands in my lap. That made him smile and go silent and stare at me. Then he held up one hand, his palm out, vertical, at the level of my face.

"Go on, let's see what you got."

I raised my hand and placed it against his, but gingerly, because his palm was damp and his fingertips were sucked clean where he'd bitten his nails. He pushed against my fingers and adjusted his hand so that the meat at the base of his thumb met mine. I looked away and saw a page in one of the tumbled magazines, a naked kneeling man in a black dog collar.

"I have to go," I said, and tried to move my chair back.

But he held me with his upraised hand tightening against mine. "Now I know," he said.

"Know what?"

"What you really got."

The phone ringing again from the far-off room made him twitch with anger, the creases in his forehead deepening.

"Goddamn it." He skidded his chair away and hurried across the room and through the door, saying, "Hold on a minute."

But as soon as he was out of the room, I got up and walked quickly to the front door. I pulled but could not open it, and saw it was locked with a deadbolt, which I twisted and slid back with fumbling fingers. Then I was out the door and hurrying toward the stairs.

A smallish balding man with a monkey's squashed face and big ears, in a blue tracksuit, was just mounting the landing at the entrance to the stairwell. He had to have seen me leaving the apartment, because he said, "Where's George?"

"I don't know," I said without pausing.

"But you'll do," he said in an actressy voice, skipping next to me and reaching to pat me.

I stepped past him and ran down the stairwell, two flights to the parking lot, where there were only a few cars. I knew I was exposed in the gleam of the great wet expanse of the lot, aware that from above I could easily be seen, like a hurrying insect, a small figure scrambling toward the main road. I had the idea that I was climbing into daylight from underground.

Instead of hitchhiking from there, I walked back in the direction of the George Washington Bridge, knowing that if the man tried to follow me in his car, he would not be able to make a left turn on this lane of the parkway. I walked to where a young hitchhiker was standing with a hand-lettered sign, HARTFORD.

"I'm going there, too," I said. "Mind if I go with you?"

"Okay by me, but it's up to the driver."

We got a ride. I sat in back. The driver was a salesman, who asked each of us for a dollar for gas: "Hey, gas isn't a quarter anymore!"

In Hartford, I hitched to Springfield and then to Northampton, where I called Jonquil at her dorm. No answer, so I went to Amherst by bus, in the dark. I tried her again but she didn't pick up, so I called her friend Julie, to tell her what had happened with the man who'd picked me up: the detour to his apartment, and how Jonquil had given me heart by giving me a destination, and I wanted badly to see her. "In a way, Jonquil saved me."

"Who?" Julie asked, and then quickly, in a hushed voice, "Oh, her father just died."

"That's terrible."

I heard a murmur of hesitation, then, "He was killed."

"Killed? How?"

"It's a really complicated story, and I only know a little bit of it," she said. "She's probably taking the rest of the year off. She's really upset."

I sent a letter of condolence to Jonquil at Smith, but it bounced back to me, the envelope stamped *Addressee Unknown — Return to Sender,* and I assumed she had gone home for the semester. After failing to find her, and distracted with work, I slipped into the routine of classes and studying, and drinking, and casual romance. I had never known Jonquil well except as an occasional visitor, descending from Smith with the other disheveled nymphs from the heights of their respectability, to tease me and be witty. Now and then, hearing myself say, "Want to come home with me?" reminded me of the man who had picked me up, what I now regarded as a close call, and I winced, remembering details of it.

I did not see Jonquil again. I lived my unexpected life, and occasionally thought of that day hitchhiking, the man in the sweatshirt with the bitten fingers and the creased forehead and the snapshot: "This is the real me." As the years passed I became more frightened for my younger self, that reckless fool pretending to be poor, dreaming of Kerouac, thumbing under the George Washington Bridge with enough money in his pocket for bus fare, believing he was real.

At last, much older, with the retrospective horror one feels in maturity for a long-ago close call, I was provoked to look for Gary, or George, or Rod Fisher. I had survived into the Internet age of revelation, the randomly sorted archive of ancient trivia and accumulated names and places; the repository of the past in a virtual vault where anything can be known; an answering service that had never existed before, to tell us of our dead ends and what happened to our former friends. Though I found some instances of hitchhikers on the Henry Hudson Parkway being raped and murdered in unsolved cases, I got no hits on names, and no mentions of Rod Fisher, the writer of pulp fiction.

The ease of the search made me curious about Jonquil J. Christ. I tapped her into my computer. Her name did not occur anywhere in the twinkling galaxies of cyberspace. She was returned to me, like the letter I had sent long ago to Smith College. So much for Jonquil. As for her father, the words "Christ" and "killed" produced far too many Internet stories for me to sift through, most of them biblical.

I wondered whether Jonquil, as Betsy Brenhouse, had written about this, or about anything else, so I tried the pen name and discovered that Betsy Brenhouse had been a student at Smith in the year in question, and I felt thoroughly teased. I looked for more — easy enough, Googling the name — and swimming onto the screen a number of story titles surfaced, among them MAITLAND BRENHOUSE MURDERED. SLAIN MILLIONAIRE was a headline in the *Yonkers Herald Statesman* in April 1962, when I had been hitchhiking, sustained by thoughts of Jonquil.

"Maitland Brenhouse . . . 50-year-old financial wizard . . . Police theorized he had been shot through the head while watching TV in his house in Hastings-on-Hudson . . . He had a habit of leaving the rear door to his home unlocked. He was in lounging clothes." The murder weapon was a .32 caliber pistol. In subsequent news items there were mentions of loan-sharking, buying debts and collecting on them, "Brenhouse pressing for loan payments at a high rate of interest . . ."

"At least ten persons had a good motive for shooting Brenhouse," the Yonkers newspaper wrote when reporting the arrest of a "material witness, William Degna, 34, the Bad Check King of Westchester." But Degna was released for lack of evidence. Then this: "Brenhouse won a $20,000 judgment against Frank Sacco" over a "bitterly contested promissory note." Sacco was described as "a wise guy" and a member of the Genovese crime family, and he lived near Brenhouse (his "business associate") in Yonkers, where he "had been arrested numerous times on loan-sharking charges." The boxer Jake LaMotta, in a two-hour interrogation in the Hastings-on-Hudson police station, provided Sacco with an alibi for the night of the murder and caused a stir, his startled, ruined, palooka face in a front-page photo with his tubby lawyer on the station house steps. LaMotta mentioned the Brenhouse murder in his 1970 memoir *Raging Bull,* because by then the case had become notorious, and a mystery.

N.Y. MURDER PROBE GROWS MORE BAFFLING was a headline in the *Chicago Tribune,* which described the murder as "a perplexing whodunit." Contradicting the wealth of the victim was this fact: "Brenhouse was contesting federal income tax claims exceeding $1,800,000." In other stories, denials, accusations, and names such as Jimmy "Dimps" DeMasi, "Nutch" Birretela, and other toughs appeared, and in 1988 the arrest for murder of Frank Sacco, who had served time "for shylocking and other fraudulent financial practices." Though he had been acquitted of murder in other trials, he was ratted out by his nephew, and was convicted of the murder of a drug dealer and wise guy, Robert Meloni, whom he shot and dumped in a landfill.

A later *Herald Statesman* story, under the headline FAMILY FIGHTS TO CLEAR NAME OF FATHER, published a statement by the Brenhouse family, among them a daughter, Elizabeth — Betsy. "He was a good man rather than a ruthless businessman. And we are willing to spend our last cent to clear his name."

I searched for a postscript but found nothing, except in a story on the anniversary of the crime: "The shroud is as opaque as on the first day of the murder."

The killing of Maitland Brenhouse remained unsolved. Nothing was ever published by Betsy Brenhouse, and Jonquil J. Christ did not exist.

28

LIFE AND THE MAGAZINE

Life *magazine was like life itself for about fifteen years of my youth, until my parents stopped renewing our subscription. I remember the images of the Korean War, the movie* Cleopatra, *the funeral of William Faulkner (reported by William Styron), the space program, and the Vietnam War. One issue in 1953 contained the entire text of James Michener's novel* The Bridges at Toko-Ri, *and in 1960 the whole of Hemingway's* The Dangerous Summer, *in three issues, the man himself smiling serenely on the cover.*

Reading *Life* in a bungalow in Medford, Massachusetts, I beheld a world that was remote and alluring, places I would never see, parties I would never attend, politicians, celebrities, actors, millionaires, and up-and-comers whom I would never know — examples of the great and unattainable. It is how the mass of people lived, vicariously, following the fortunes of famous names in magazines and newspapers; and how they live now, overlooked, unregarded, grinding away, not celebrated, not up-and-coming.

I left Medford and kept going. I went to central Africa as a Peace Corps volunteer and, provoked by the wonders there, had something to write about. I remained in Africa, as a schoolteacher, then as a university lecturer in Uganda, and moonlighted as a stringer for Time-Life, helping with stories about mercenaries in the Congo, witch doctor excesses, and military coups. After that I was an English prof in Singapore. Many of the places were familiar to me from photographs I'd seen in *Life*: klongs in Bangkok, rickshaws in Malaysia, Burmese temples, and many people, too — the races of Asia.

When my contract was not renewed in Singapore in 1971, I abandoned salaried employment and moved to England. By then I had a wife and two children, and five books published. I never again entered a classroom or had a boss (no order of "Meeting on Thursday. Be there"). Seventeen years passed, years of travel in which I had flashbacks of *Life* — in South America and China and India, and in Britain, too: I had seen my first Beefeaters in *Life,* my first Scottish kilts and bagpipes. I got to know Bill Styron, and told him how I'd read his evocative Faulkner piece in *Life* in 1962.

At the end of 1989, I left my wife and traveled throughout the Pacific. I ended up in Hawaii, a place I had first seen in *Life* — hula girls, luaus, volcanoes, big surf. I married again, a woman from Hawaii. I continued to write — it was my living. I had paddled a kayak for years, and the folding kayak I owned was one I had first seen in a cover story in *Life* magazine in 1957, the Klepper kayak paddled by Hannes Lindemann in his epic ocean voyage: "Across Atlantic by Canoe — Dr. Lindemann in Canvas Craft." (That issue also contained a story about the American South, "Embattled White South Digs In: Legislative and Judicial Fronts for Civil Rights." All I knew about segregation then I learned in *Life.*)

I did not know any other writers in Hawaii in those early days. But I was happy writing in the morning and paddling in the afternoon, beyond the surf zone in Waikiki to the buoy off Diamond Head (first seen in *Life*), or on the North Shore, out of Haleiwa, where I eventually bought a house. Some fellow paddlers said that I should meet Gardner McKay, a paddler and also a writer. I knew his name from his local radio program, *Stories on the Wind,* and his sonorous voice — maybe a little too sonorous?

The word got to Gardner. He invited me for a drink. He lived in Portlock near Maunalua Bay; I lived fifty miles away near Waimea Bay. It took several months for us to arrange to meet, in Honolulu, at a bar on Makaloa Street. He greeted me with a bear hug, which winded me.

He was way over six feet tall, handsome, deeply tanned, ten years older than me, with a paddler's broad shoulders. Like me he wore an aloha shirt, a pair of shorts, and the flip-flops known in Hawaii as slippers. We talked in general — I had just published my *Happy Isles of Oceania,* which he said he'd read and liked. He was working on a novel, and though he was far from finishing it, and said nothing about its subject, he surprised me by telling me its name, *Toyer.*

When I said I heard him on the radio, he took this to mean I listened to his programs. His calm, easy voice in conversation was not the overdramatic radio voice, and I wondered to myself why he did not talk this way on his broadcasts. He said he normally paddled out of Maunalua Harbor. We discussed conditions there, and elsewhere. We groused a little about Hawaii—the traffic, the crowds—as local *haoles* do.

Then I said, "Makaloa Street. Have you read Jack London's story 'On the Makaloa Mat'?"

"Yes. I love Jack London."

That I took to be perhaps the beginning of a friendship. A mutual liking for an author of many books is often a great bond.

He said in a teasing way, "When I read *The Happy Isles* I figured you were really cranky."

"Ha! But you can see I'm not. Cranky people don't travel well. You need to negotiate and make friends."

"I agree." He drank the last of his beer and said, "So how about dinner? Come home with me. My wife's a gourmet chef."

"I figured we were just having a drink."

He laughed—he had a great booming actor's laugh—and said, "Yeah. I thought, if you turned out to be a pain in the ass, it would be just a drink. But you seem okay. Hey, come on. Dinner."

So this was a sort of interview, and he was gauche enough to crow about it. But I found this annoying: being tested, then told I was being tested, finally told I had passed the test.

I said, "I've got other plans."

"Maybe we could go paddling together sometime."

He then grabbed me, another bear hug, but more energetic than the greeting had been, leaving me gasping and giggling a little.

But I did not go paddling with him. He lived far away, in an enclave of wealthy people and gated mansions. I lived in the country among my beehives. And he showed no interest in paddling on the North Shore. He was probably as reluctant to put his boat on his roof rack as I was.

Eventually, he sent me his novel, *Toyer,* with a note. His handwriting was impressive, an artist's bold cursive—"a good fist," as graphologists say: fountain pen, wide nib, black ink. He wrote, *Let me know what you think, even if you hate it.* I didn't hate it, but I found it humorless, with many first-novel faults, slow going and sententious. It was about a psycho who toys sadistically with his women victims. Instead of telling him that I was not entertained by sadism against women, I encouraged him to write another book. This book helps me with dates, because *Toyer* came out in 1998, about six years after the beer on Makaloa Street.

I did not see Gardner again, but I heard from him, always a note in his bold penmanship. He invited my wife and me to a dinner party. A dinner party is an odd and rare thing in Hawaii, where people entertain informally in restaurants or clubs or on the beach, and this dinner party meant a one-hundred-mile round trip. So I declined. He suggested another drink. But we were never able to find a mutually suitable time. I felt he was struggling to write, and I wished to maintain a distance from his struggle. *Toyer* had seemed to me unpromising, yet clearly he had a gift.

"He's a famous actor," my wife said. "You never saw *Adventures in Paradise*?"

"I must have been in Africa." (I had lived without a television and a telephone for nine years.)

In a later message, Gardner said he was ill, and he added that he was reading my *Sir Vidia's Shadow*. My paddler friends elaborated: Gardner had prostate cancer. His wife, Madeleine, the gourmet chef, had devised special meals for him — these friends said — to restore his energy, to help him continue to write his memoir, which was going to be called *Journey Without a Map*.

In 2001, Gardner McKay died. His wife asked me to speak at his memorial service. I said of course. Though I had hardly known him, I felt I should make an effort, because I had not offered him the hand of friendship when he was alive, and perhaps struggling.

The service, in a large auditorium in Honolulu, was well attended, hundreds gathered, the stage filled with flowers. In the Hawaii tradition, everyone wore an aloha shirt, and some were garlanded with leis.

The grieving eulogists filled in Gardner's biography, and it was there at his memorial service that I got to know him. He was praised as a certified yacht skipper, a drama critic, a sculptor, a professional photographer. And one speaker described how in his Los Angeles compound Gardner had raised fierce African lions. There were many testimonies to his days in Hollywood, the greatness of his TV shows that I had never seen, and the word "heartthrob" was used. I had remembered him as the man in the bar on Makaloa Street, patronizing me, but now I saw he'd been a golden boy.

When my turn came I extolled him as a writer and paddler, and mentioned how I'd gathered from the previous speakers that he had seemed a golden boy. I summoned the Robert Frost poem "Nothing Gold Can Stay" from memory, and recited it.

Leaving the hall, I passed through the foyer where an easel was propped with many photographs of Gardner pinned to it, and on a table, surrounded by orchid blossoms, a copy of *Life* magazine, Gardner McKay on the cover, handsome in a white knit sweater. Above his portrait: *How About Him, Girls? The New Challenger for American Good Looks.* And under it: *Gardner McKay — Actor, Athlete, Artist.*

I did not need to open the magazine to know what was in it, the story of a young actor who (it was written) was destined to be a Hollywood star. He was a yachtsman, a traveler, and a great actor with a brilliant career ahead of him. And the photographs showed his career — the movies, the TV show.

Seeing that copy of *Life,* I vividly recalled reading that story in the summer of 1959, about to graduate from Medford High School, with no idea of what would happen to me and only the gloomiest prospects. The next issue, which I had pored over, miserably, contained a modest letter to the editor from Gardner McKay, claiming he had been overpraised. I remembered it all, because "The New Challenger" was one of the stories in *Life* that made me feel overlooked and small and unregarded, with an uncertain future, holding a magazine, looking at the big world from a bungalow in Medford.

And though I knew nothing of Gardner's subsequent career, his fame as an actor, his leaving Hollywood to travel, and coming to rest in Hawaii, I often thought of this handsome man on the *Life* cover, whose name I had forgotten, and wondered what had happened to someone of such promise, someone I had envied.

29

DEAR OLD DAD:
MEMORIES OF MY FATHER

My father — whom I loved, and who loved me — never read a word I wrote, or if he did, never mentioned the fact. It was like an embarrassing secret we shared, of a creepy proclivity I had, something that we couldn't discuss without awkwardness. And what was odd was that from 1967 until his death in 1995, I published more than thirty books and hundreds of essays and magazine pieces. He would have had to go out of his way to avoid reading them, actually to step over them, since many were in his house.

It was not that he didn't read. He enjoyed history, especially local history — of Boston, New England, his ancestral province of Quebec. The Lewis and Clark Expedition fascinated him to the point where he would declaim the hardships the team faced, with the stouthearted Sacagawea, the bad weather, the plagues of wasps. ("They were taw-mented!" my brother Alex would cry, wagging his finger, imitating Dad's characteristic way of speaking.) He read everything he could find on the assassination of Lincoln and had a detailed knowledge of the conspirators. He read the newspaper every day, and he read his Holy Missal the way a Muslim reads the Koran — and his missal had the thickened and thumbed look of a Wahhabi's Koran. He read James Madison Usher's dense and very dry *History of the Town of Medford*. He read about whaling and could tell you what flensing was, and about the composition of baleen, the Gloucester fishermen, the Civil War, the Battle of Lexington, the works of Edward Rowe Snow, all of that, but no works of mine.

At first I was bewildered, then relieved, and finally I was indifferent.

My father did not read novels — anyone's novels, at least not modern ones. And I had not become a writer to please my parents, only myself. A writer is rarely able to do both, and I know that, far from wishing to please them, I wrote as an act of rebellion.

Edmund Wilson's mother said she'd never read a word of his. D. H. Lawrence's father mocked his son's writing and called it a kind of slacking. Joyce's wife famously jeered at his verbal ingenuity. The Japanese writer Haruki Murakami told me that he did not know if his parents had read any of his books. "They never said anything." At the end of his memoir *Family History*, John Lanchester comments, "Once my mother wasn't able to read my books, I finally began writing them."

Edith Wharton wrote in a letter, "My literary success puzzled and embarrassed my old friends far more than it impressed them, and in my family it created a kind of constraint which increased with the years. None of my relations ever spoke to me of my books."

These reactions do not shock me.

My father satirized himself as "dear old Dad" when he felt especially put-upon. "And who'll end up doing it?" — cleaning the garage, shoveling the walk, washing the car — "Dear old Dad." That's how I thought of him — beloved. But when I look at his sketchy history, I'm not sure I understand him or know what his life was like. His was a life with no documents: no long letters, hardly any letters at all, no serious diaries, no affidavits, not even a will, nothing written down. A birth certificate, a death certificate, nothing in between. This is a crucial lack — dealing in suppositions is like dealing with a mythical character, mostly guesswork. He was a writer of postcards — but postcard writers are great obscurers and evaders and mythmakers. *Just a line to say we're having a fantastic time.* My father was not a joiner. He did not have many friends, and no close friends, so there are no witnesses outside the family. Except for the last years of his life when he was ailing, he didn't drink. Even then, in pain, it was merely a measure of Wild Turkey. He didn't smoke. He seldom went out at night, except to church or choir practice or the Holy Name Society, always, in his term, "the Holy Name." He was quietly amiable, with no strong opinions, and generally uncritical. His genial nature made him, I now see, impenetrable, almost impossible to know. Assemble all the evidence, scraps of paper, snapshots, scribbled postcards, and what do I have? Just bones, or less, bone fragments. "Mr. Bones," he called himself, at the minstrel show in which he appeared.

He was born a hundred years ago. I clearly remember when he was sixty-five — the age I am now — when I set out to write *The Great Railway Bazaar*. My children are now in their midthirties; at my age, Dad still had a seventeen-year-old in school — my youngest brother — who, inevitably, has different memories of him: a gray-haired man at his high school graduation, an elderly man at his Harvard commencement. Dad might have enjoyed my travel book, since it was a journey, and factual, but I know that he would not have liked my novels. Without saying so he believed that most fiction was frivolous, absurd posturing that made the author look ridiculous; immoral, too, unless it was a historical romance or a certain category of classic.

He loved *Treasure Island* and read it to my brothers and me in our attic bedroom, which we named (in homage) the Benbow Inn. He read us *Kidnapped* and most of *The Deerslayer* and *The Last of the Mohicans*. These novels had real heroes, and adventure, and a point; he believed them; they lived for him. *Ask No Quarter* (1946) by George Marsh was a novel he'd read as a young man and praised because it was based on verifiable fact. Another book he recommended to me was *The Americanization of Edward Bok* — an editor's and writer's autobiography. Neither of these books interested me, convincing me that our tastes were irreconcilable.

He was often too busy or, being fully employed and hard-pressed his whole life, too tired to read anything but the newspaper, sitting in his bathrobe under a lamp, usually the *Boston Globe*, now and then the *Medford Mercury*, sometimes the Catholic paper the *Pilot*. He wrote notes, sent postcards, and for the early years of his marriage — during World War II — kept a laconic, one-line diary. The entry for April 10, 1941, was *Anne had another boy at 7:25*. That was me.

My mother claimed that I was his favorite. This can't have been true. He was impartial. It was my mother's way of saying that I was not her favorite — and that was true. She was a mercurial, insecure woman — domineering people often are — and she feared me for my defiant aloofness. I knew this and made myself more noncommittal and cooler. It antagonized her that she didn't know what was in my head. Eventually, she did read my work — some of it. On the publication of my first novel she wrote me a letter complaining that she had been overcharged for the book and that the book was (her word) "trash." I kept the letter — indeed, still have it after all these years and have often reread it as a goad. She felt that my work did not reflect well on her as a mother, and that was all that mattered to her. She often exclaimed in a shrill warning voice, "The written word is forever!"

So there it was — my father, who was proud of me, never read a word; my mother, who read half a dozen of my books, didn't like them much, and either told me to my face or whispered about them to my siblings. "Paul's writing filth [or "porno"] again" — and of course they jeered at me. Of the two, my father's nonreading was the more helpful and humane, as though he was forgiving me for indulging myself.

I thought of my parents as totally separate beings: my sympathetic but rather formal father, my emotional and talkative mother. Alone with my father I was nearly always happy, but facing them together could be difficult, because my father deferred to her, saw her weaknesses, supported her even in her irrationality. The two sent out contradictory signals. I didn't know what to say. If my mother became sufficiently wound up about something, my father would hit us to placate her, though I knew it hurt him to raise a hand to any of us. We were, however, threatened constantly — the chief transgression was insubordination. If he hit us especially hard, he'd say, "That was a love tap. Next time I'll really haul off and tan your hide."

It is probable — certain, I think — that my six siblings would disagree with much of what I say here. But it is my contention that each of us had a separate upbringing, that my mother and father behaved differently toward each of us, their sympathies and personalities revealed uniquely to each child, and that we as children were different, too. Their child-rearing was spread over many years and their circumstances kept improving, from the dire postwar period, to the turbulent sixties, to the seventies, when things looked up, to the eighties, when they began to live in comfortable retirement.

I asked one of my brothers to verify a simple incident in my father's life. He disagreed strenuously with something I regarded as an established fact. I began to think that each of us believes he owns the family story, owns our memories of Dad, our tales, the history of Dad, and regards this version as beyond dispute. I have often wondered aloud about Mother's oddities and received angry glares from some of them. How dare I? So the Dad

I knew might be unrecognizable to the rest of the family, though he was real enough to me. His death was such a blow that for ten years I could not think of writing about him. But now I can describe him and his peculiarities without becoming upset. I had tried in the past a number of times, but got so sad I could not continue.

Because of his natural reticence, perhaps shyness, and his unease in unfamiliar social settings — well, how can a more or less indigent father of seven children be gregarious? — no one knew him well. He had a deflecting and concealing manner, in which he became so supremely accommodating, he made himself almost invisible, a challenge to my trying to re-create what I know of him.

He was proud of his family, tended somewhat to idealize this big happy family notion, could be deeply contented, was of a reflective, even meditative cast of mind, and was capable of enormous and infectious happiness. It is possible that he lacked self-esteem — an outsider might suggest this. But I don't think it was the case. He was the least egotistical person I have ever known, with an almost Buddhist sense of vacancy, detachment, and generosity. He was a natural giver, and rather awkward when he received anything of value or substance, which was in any case seldom.

He was a man of limited, or at least not active, ambition, but with a strong capacity for work, great loyalty, honesty, and politeness, yet what seemed his sense of unworthiness was actually piety. He was personally modest, to a degree I have never found in anyone except the most devout lama or holy man, always demurring when he was praised. Yet he was quick to praise other people; he was punctual, deferential, appreciative, sober, and correct.

In traveling, especially in Asia, I meet men like my father all the time: shy, conscientious, reliable, uncomplaining, law-abiding, and a bit unworldly and innocent: rickshaw drivers, menials, clerks, shopkeepers — humble men, curious and eager to assist, men who get to a point where they want to help more but can go no further. These are the older men of provincial towns who know the times of the trains but have seldom been on one, who look a bit fearful and smile nervously when in the lobby of a fancy hotel, who are often on their way to or from the temple, who want to please, who talk lavishly about their children, who are not cynical at all but seemingly always in awe of someone bigger, different, wealthy. My father didn't scorn powerful people; he was respectful of them until he had clear proof that they were cruel or rude or — one of his favorite words of disparagement — fakers. My father was someone who hardly exists in America anymore, but a person of old-fashioned modesty I meet often in foreign parts. It is no accident that I began to write these memories in Burma, where I met many men like my father, indestructible and incorruptible men of the underclass.

He was the eldest of six children, adored by his mother, respected by his father (for whom he was named), admired by his five siblings — he seemed the most civilized, restrained, and decent of them, also the most intelligent. His mother's maiden name was Eva Brousseau. His grandmother Brousseau was born Picard, or Pecor, and was part Menominee — a Native American nation that once occupied the whole of Wisconsin, eventually subverted by colonists and intermarrying with French soldiers and settlers in the seventeenth and eighteenth centuries. Eva was born in Belleville, Ontario, but the family circulated back and forth, to Flint, Michigan, and Detroit, speaking French, hardly recognizing that an international border existed.

"Grandma played with Indians when she was a small girl," my father said. He did not mention she was part Indian, but this was an indication he knew of it. "She saw Buffalo Bill," he also said. Bill Cody's Wild West Show went everywhere, even to Belleville and Flint and Detroit.

My grandfather Eugene Theroux was descended from a man who lived in Detroit at its founding, when it was a garrison and a trading post for fur trappers. This man, our original ancestor in North America, was Antoine Theroux, or Terroux, born in Verdun-sur-Garonne, near Toulouse, France, in 1675. It is not a common name in France, though Alexander Dumas was born in a street in Paris named Rue Thiroux. Antoine was not a native French speaker but a Gascon who spoke Occitan. During his first winter in Canada, instead of moaning "*Le temps est très froid*" or "*Il fait froid*," this much more effusive son of Gascony would have uttered something like "*Dieu vivent! Fa pla fred a pr'aici.*" And feeling far from home, he would have muttered, "*Soi pla lan d'enta ieu,*" rather than "*Je suis bien loin de chez moi.*" Most of his fellow soldiers would have been from Normandy, native French speakers, so Antoine would have been babbling to himself, on his own, establishing a family tradition, the first in a long line of odd men out. He sailed from Rochelle with a brigade of musketeers to New France in 1693, and his last bivouac was as a soldier in the army of Antoine de la Mothe Cadillac, the man who founded Detroit.

Antoine Theroux's nickname was La Ferté, "the Fiery One," probably because of his quick temper or because he was passionate in other ways. He had a liaison with a woman outside his marriage, so there is a parallel branch of the family. He was granted a plot of farmland after completing his army service; this was in a Quebec village called Yamaska ("Place of the Reeds"), near Sorel, where most of the headstones in the churchyard of St. Michel are chiseled THEROUX. He died there in 1759.

Ten generations later, my grandfather was born, one of eleven children — nine boys, two girls. When my grandfather was three, the family farmhouse caught fire — it was in the winter of 1882. His mother snatched him from his bed and brought him to the upstairs window, where she lobbed him into a snowdrift below. He was saved by the deep Yamaska snow; his mother died in the flames.

My grandfather remained on the family farm until his midteens, old enough to travel and work, when he joined his older brothers in Nashua, New Hampshire, to work in the mills. For a time they lived in Lawrence, Massachusetts. I have a studio photograph of the nine brothers in black suits, some of them heavily mustached, looking like a baseball team posed at a funeral. Eugene met Eva Brousseau, who had come all the way from Belleville to work at an adjacent mill in Nashua — the French Canadians were the first real workforce in New England — and he married her.

Around 1905 my grandparents bought — or perhaps built — a small house in the woods outside Stoneham, Massachusetts. In this house my father was born. My grandfather was a night watchman and a worker in a shoe factory. As a child (so my father told me) my father accompanied his father at night, keeping him company "on his winds": a watchman patrolled the premises of the empty factory carrying an L-shaped handle, winding the various clocks. Although my father was a good student, an able athlete — a starter on the high school football team — and a fluent French speaker, on graduation from Stoneham High in 1926, there was no question of his going to college. His father brought him to the shoe factory and (so my father related) introduced him to the foreman, saying, "He's all yours."

He lived at home and worked in Wakefield in the factory, and a few years later commuted to Boston — a long way — to work at the American Oak Leather Company. My father said he was glad for the work, for any job, and often spoke of all the unemployed people ("college graduates!") selling apples out of crates on the sidewalks of Boston during these years of the Great Depression. Perhaps this gave him a lifelong craving for steady work, a safe job, no matter the salary, and a skepticism of college degrees.

He was selective in talking about his early life. Obviously he was a conscientious high school student. He would have been a reliable worker at American Oak. Once, talking to a friend, he referred to his father as "my old man" — his father beat him for it. My father said he deserved the beating: he was ashamed. He called his father Pa. His father raised chickens, and my father would have helped. One summer, he visited his aunt in Montreal — his mother's sister. He ran out of money. His uncle, a contractor, put him on the payroll of a job, though he was not required to do any work. It was just a scam. He bought a pair of overalls and collected his pay every Friday.

"Imagine. I showed up in clean overalls and all these men who'd worked all week, in their dirty clothes, lined up with me. I felt awful."

He had a memory for these hurts and transgressions, slight as they were. He had a serious respect for hard work — that is, manual labor, getting your hands dirty. He did not regard anything else as work — writing, banking, preaching, fiddling with figures, or investing didn't really count as labor, but a more refined sort of scheming.

There is no suggestion of carnality in his early life. He had a few male friends. He would have needed their encouragement in order to range more widely. He drove with them one day to drop off one of their number at Amherst — Mass. Aggie, as it was then known — and sixty years later still remembered where he'd had lunch that day, in a diner on Main Street. In his rather uneventful life, this simple outing counted as an event.

His years of bachelorhood he spent living at home in Stoneham, commuting on the train and what he called "the electric car" to Boston. "I handed over my pay packet to my parents every week without fail." In the winter it was all work. In the summer there was an occasional outing, to

Salem Willows amusement park, Nantasket Beach, or the honky-tonk at Revere Beach.

"Your father was a reader!" my grandmother told me in a praising way when I was a child. "Albert used to sit there with a book in his hand and a few apples. He would read the book and eat an apple" — and she dramatized that. The book in one hand, the apple in the other. Another unhelpful, much-too-neat family story. How old was he? When was this? What was the book?

Reading impressed her because she could barely read, and her husband, my grandfather, could not read at all, had never been to school, though once, mentioned by name in the Stoneham paper, probably a church-related item (St. Patrick's Church), he looked at the mass of newsprint and found his name, put his finger on it, as if to defy the belittlers. Like many illiterate people I have known, he was very shrewd, a reader of faces and gestures, prescient, patient, rather silent, and watchful.

On one of the summer outings, my father was introduced by his friend and neighbor Charlie Farrow to a single woman from Medford. She was a college graduate and a teacher, though she gave up teaching eventually. They courted for four years, saving their money, and married in 1937, when my father was almost thirty. They had enough money to buy a house outright. I had thought that because of his work in the leather company, footwear a crucial industry in wartime, my father was exempted from the draft. But it was his asthma and his three children that prevented him from being drafted.

He had few regrets in his life. Not going to college was one. Not having a marketable skill was another. But his keenest regret was not serving in the military; it was mingled shame and sorrow made more vivid because, even though asthmatic, he was able-bodied. Both his brothers served in the army, three brothers-in-law too, as well as one of his sisters, all of them seeing action, and one — Richard Long, "Uncle Dick," a full-blooded Native American, married to his sister Florence — was captured and kept in a German prison camp for almost three years.

One of the more melancholy aspects of my father's one-line wartime diary is the way the mention of the fall of an Italian city or the bombing of a German one is accompanied by *Rain all day* or *Went to the movies*.

In the early part of his married life, until he was crowded by children and had no spare time and not much money, my father was a moviegoer. He had definite opinions about actors — disliked the cowboy actor Ward Bond, liked Charles Laughton in *The Hunchback of Notre Dame* — preferred musicals to thrillers, and disliked violence of any kind.

His vocabulary was widened if not enriched by the movies of the thirties and forties: "kiddo," "toots," "skeezicks," "I'll tan your hide." Liked the radio, too, of which he was a nightly listener: "Parkyakarkus," "Tain't funny, McGee," and all the catchphrases of W. C. Fields, from "my little chickadee" to "Who stole the cork out of my lunch?"

"Give us here," he said when he wanted something handed to him. "Give it a rest" when you talked a lot. "Stop gasbagging" when you talked far too much. "Shift" when he wanted you to move. "He took and folded it," a New England locution. "He's a faker" described an unreliable person, and "He's a good scout" was the opposite. "He's a piker" indicated penny-pinching. "He lit into the woods just as tight as he could jump," a self-conscious Maine expression he liked. "A lazy man's load" indicated you were carrying too much and would drop some of it. Amazed at anything he said: "For Christmas sakes!"

"Do it *comme il faut*" was my father's frequent demand. "*Mo' psi' bonhomme*" (*mon petit bonhomme*) was his expression of praise, with the Quebecois pronunciation "*petsee*" for *petit,* as with "*clem*" in "*crème à la glace.*" A frequent Quebecois exclamation, "*Plaquoteur!*," meaning "fusser," is such an antique word it is not found in most French dictionaries, but I heard it regularly.

He was not a coward, but he was restrained, overly modest, somewhat shy, deferential, even submissive, especially among strangers. I cannot imagine my father giving anyone a direct order, but I can easily see him taking orders — and going beyond the call of duty: working late for nothing, working weekends, ignoring rudeness or a blunt tone from a superior to keep the peace, or pretending (for his own self-respect) that he had not heard it. He could be intimidated by big confident men, whom he half admired and half despised. He would have made a good soldier.

He hated disorder, disobedience, chatter, backtalk, bad posture, idleness, long hair, loud noises, any sort of indecency, foul language, slang, pretense, frivolity, showy wealth, nudity, coquettishness, falsity, silliness, superior airs, and overbearing intellectualism as opposed to subtle wit. He deplored ostentation of any kind. He loathed lengthy explanations and longwindedness.

He liked silence and space, and had a boyish admiration of heroism, especially heroism accompanied by modesty. ("Anyone would have done what I did.") He was fascinated by new scenes — a place he'd never been, a new road, a new bridge. New buildings did not interest him.

He was easy to please. He liked his mother's Quebecois food: thick kidney stew, mashed potatoes, pot roast, asparagus on toast, pea soup, strong tea.

Pea soup and johnnycake
Make the Frenchman's belly ache.

He was addicted to jingles like that.

We're the boys from Nova Scotia,
We're the ones who choke the fish.
We hate the goddamned Irish,
We're the boys from Antigonish.

I slept in the long attic room we called the Benbow Inn with my two older brothers when we were very young. After lights out we listened to the radio: *The Green Hornet, Mr. and Mrs. North, The Shadow,* and *The Great Gildersleeve.*

"Turn that thing off!" Dad would call out from the bottom of the stairs, which were steep, like a ship's ladder.

One night the radio wouldn't turn on. It was an antique, with big bulbous vacuum tubes that glowed in its innards. One of them was missing, and because of this the radio was unworkable. A note had been tucked in its place, my father's scribble:

Lives there a man with soul so base
Put him last in the human race.
He'd stoop to steal a radio tube,
And treats his kids like little boobs.

Mildly anticlerical, he found most priests unbearable in their piety, obtuse, and out of touch. "What do they know about raising a family?" He smiled in reproach at the notion of priests having maids and housekeepers to cook and clean for them. I think in a compliant way he resented authority, though he never defied it. He avoided conflict all his life.

He was somewhat despised by my mother's ambitious, competitive, sententious, and parvenu family, but he quietly endured their boasts. He didn't respect them enough to stand up to them. Anyway, he was a passionate FDR Democrat and they were Republicans with a sentimental love of Italy, even during the war. He was a classic underachiever in a world that didn't know the word. He was intelligent, fluent in French, always up on the news, totally dependable, a fast learner, with a phenomenal memory.

Yet he began his working life in a shoe factory, among cutters and stitchers, and on his marriage had only risen to the rank of shipper, the mysterious word I wrote on the specified line "Father's occupation."

"Shipper" meant the stock room, the mail room, the level of Doraisamy ("Sammy"), my Tamil peon in Singapore — writing labels, sorting mail, tying parcels, and in my father's case, wrapping up crates of new shoes. But so what? He seemed to find it companionable, and often mentioned his workmates, Chester Pyne among them, and another man, a Syrian immigrant who taught him some Arabic greetings. You might guess at his training when you saw my father take a ball of twine and quickly tie a parcel, making the knot, slipping the loop, and snapping off the extra twine in one motion.

For a period in the late 1940s he was a traveling salesman, selling cowhides — sole leather — to the faltering shoe factories in northeastern Massachusetts and southern New Hampshire. Most were Jewish-owned — my father did business with Jews all the time (I knew it from their names), but I never once heard him make an anti-Semitic remark. Later, he would begin sentences with "When I was on the road . . ."

He had almost no interest in making big sales, but he was attracted to the serene monotony of the long drives, the freedom of the open road, meeting familiar contacts at warehouses and factories, eating at roadside diners, making side trips to historic and scenic sites — the House of the Seven Gables was one, old sailing ships moored at Gloucester and Portsmouth, the Rebecca Nurse house, the Old Man of the Mountain, Mounts

Chocorua and Monadnock, battlefields of the Revolutionary War, equestrian statues on the village greens of small towns.

My brothers and I sometimes went with him. I don't remember any sales, but I do recall an all-afternoon tour of a cigar factory in Manchester, New Hampshire (the 7-20-4 brand). He might have resembled Willy Loman in this phase of his life, yet he was happy and, unlike Willy, sometimes took his boys along with him for company.

He liked showing us around such sights. "A good take-in" was his expression. He might have been a generally patient and lovable high school teacher but would have found student insolence and laziness unendurable.

One day my father went to work and found the door locked; the company had folded. Without any notice, obviously to avoid creditors, American Oak Leather Company went into liquidation. This was in 1949. He had the idea of opening his own shoe store — he even leased an empty shop — but was saved from this certain failure by the chance to run a shoe department in a just-opened men's clothing store, O'Brien's, in Medford Square. He worked there for thirty years, earning such a small salary that eventually, when there were only a few children at home, my mother went back to teaching.

My father's goodness was sometimes exploited. He was innocent, but he did not make a fuss and never bore a grudge. With only a high school education, he was uncompetitive in a world of fierce competition. He was grateful for a safe job.

A natural father figure, he was forgiving, loving, soulful, generous. But his innocence made him rather fragile in some ways, bewildered by the cruel world, which threw up unexpected problems.

I had a serious problem early in 1961. I was nineteen. My girlfriend was pregnant. I went to my oldest brother — the eldest in such a family occupying the role of a wise counselor, except in my case. He was frightened rigid by the news. "Tell Uncle Jim . . . Maybe Father Foley will help." My drunken uncle, our unforgiving pastor.

I fled with the girl to Puerto Rico. I have written elsewhere of this amazing year. When we returned, she went to a home near Boston, then delivered the baby at the Mass. General, and I visited her there. A very cute baby boy. "He looks like you," my girlfriend said. She gave the baby up for adoption. We found out almost forty years later that he had gone to a childless couple — a wealthy, grateful family who became his benefactors. This boy, educated at an Ivy League college, became an innovative businessman and ended up a multimillionaire.

At the time of the birth, my parents were informed, and they were stunned. They realized I'd endured almost a year of exile, a kind of poverty, miserable fear, and desperation. But only I had seen the baby.

"What have you got to say for yourself?" my mother said afterward. I had nothing to say. She said, "You should be ashamed."

Later, trying to shame me further, she said, "I told Dad. He went to bed. I found him lying there, crying his eyes out."

My father's sorrow was something I had never witnessed. I had hurt him deeply. He never said a word of this to me, never alluded to it. It was a foretaste of his way of dealing with my writing — not something to mention or discuss.

I was relieved. What was there to discuss? But when I had needed them, they did not help, could not help, simply were not there, except — in my mother's case — to blame. It was a great lesson to me, a motto for my escutcheon: I am alone in this world.

My father had a wide knowledge of the process of tanning leather, of shoemaking, of shoe styles, all the elaborate names (cordovan bluchers, brogues, wingtips, pebble grain, the shank). But this was really a sort of dilettantism; there was no profit in it. And having gained this knowledge over the years, it was mainly anecdotal, the fruit of talk with old-timers and work in factories.

His real life was lived between his long spells of work. First was his family. Yet having fathered seven children, it was as though he didn't know what to do with us. Such a sprawling family meant great activity and confusion and responsibility, but he seems to have been mellow enough, optimistic enough, not to worry too much about how he would support all these children and a temperamental wife. He was gentle and protective, with occasional episodes of anger, usually provoked by Mother: instead of defying her, he turned his wrath on us. We were a jostling, rivalrous, teasing, and talkative bunch, but we were not rebellious. I was always somewhat shocked to be disciplined, because I studied, read for pleasure, kept to myself, didn't smoke or drink, didn't have a car or even a bike. My only indulgences were my secret fantasies of life as a backwoodsman, tracker, skier, marksman, scout; my tendency to escapism in reading.

The church was important to my father's life. His faith, his sort of devotion, I have seen among pious Muslims, among Buddhists in Burma and Vietnam — humble and hard-pressed men with an unswerving belief in the uselessness of vengeance, the importance of forgiveness, and that goodness is inherent in humans. He would have subscribed to the you-too-can-be-a-Buddha notion of enlightenment as possible through prayer and meditation, kneeling and prostrating yourself in places of worship. He lived Buddhism's Five Precepts without realizing it.

One of my father's church-related activities was the choir, of which he was a member until a few years before his death, which would have been sixty or more years of hymn singing. He had a strong, confident, rather tuneless voice, with a gravelly character, and even if there were thirty other people singing, I could always discern my father's baritone.

Singing was for him a joy, a pleasure, a relief. He loved Benediction for the hymns alone, his favorites being "Pange Lingua" and "O Salutaris." His friend Charlie Farrow once said that as a young, unmarried man my father entertained people by singing "with a lot of feeling" the song "Plaisir d'Amour."

The choir became the cause of one of the strangest episodes in my father's life. For two years in the early 1950s he performed in the church minstrel show. This antiquated and quaintly objectionable entertainment involved a number of white middle-aged men in blackface, wearing fuzzy and ill-fitting wigs and outlandish vests and frock coats in a variety show that was both slapstick and songs. He was "Mr. Bones," an "end man," and the others were "Tambo" or "Lightning." Because he practiced so often and so loudly, I knew all the words to the songs he sang in the successive years: "Mandy (Is There a Minister Handy)," "Rosie, You Are My Posie," and "Rock-a-Bye Your Baby with a Dixie Melody," all done in a general imitation of Al Jolson, who had also performed in blackface and was a musical icon when my father came of age in the 1920s. "Nobody" was another favorite, which had been written and made famous by Bert Williams, who, unlike the other minstrels of his time (around 1910), was a real black man. The song was broad and bitter.

The stereotyping, the lame jokes, the mockery, the heavy satire of Dad's minstrel show — the embarrassing wrongness of it — were obvious to me, and probably to many people at the time. My father had black acquaintances and shoe customers, yet this was just fun, a parallel activity that was not regarded by him as offensive. He was tolerant and humane and would have been indignant and hurt if anyone had characterized the show as racist. The first minstrel shows had begun in the 1830s and continued through the nineteenth century, many of them satirizing slave owning and the supposed nostalgia of the slaves for plantation life, as well as commenting on the events of the day. Such shows, regarded as subversive in the South, were an entertainment fixture in the North, where they flourished until the 1930s. After that, they evolved into vaudeville and burlesque revues, and only amateur players — like my father and his fellow churchgoers and choristers — put on the blackface shows. They were finished by the late 1950s, but they had been dated and doomed long before then.

I had found it excruciating to watch my shy father doing a soft-shoe shuffle, or rattling a tambourine and singing "Mandy," wagging his white-gloved hands. His jokes were not funny. "You're stupid." "You should see my brother — he walks like this." He loved performing. Playing a part gave him latitude and allowed him to overcome his reticence. In blackface, as Mr. Bones, he was a man in a mask, liberated in this role.

That was the happiest and most assertive I had ever seen my father, followed by times, in the late fifties or early sixties, with his friends on summer evenings at cookouts in the backyard, eating hamburgers and singing along with a Mitch Miller LP. Then, I remember being upstairs in my room, reading a book, probably a bootleg Henry Miller novel, and listening to the music and loud voices, belting out those songs.

While a student at UMass, in '62 and '63, I went home on some weekends but we never talked about the past, about the child I had fathered. We did not talk about my studies or my grades or about money, nothing about the future. These were my problems. My father never gave me money — he had little to give. He did not offer any career chat, no suggestions or advice. I worked full time in the summer to save, and did odd jobs in Amherst during the semesters.

Now and then he would drive me up to Route 2 where it crosses Route 128. He would wish me luck ("Be good" was his usual salutation), and out I'd get to hitchhike to Amherst. He might park nearby and watch me standing with my thumb out until a car stopped. Then he'd beep his horn and head home. Why did he not give me the dollar or two to take the bus? you ask. The answer was, As long as there are people to give you a ride, why pay for a bus? It was about seventy miles from that junction to Amherst, hours of hitching. But he had hitchhiked himself as a young man, and as a traveling salesman had often picked up hitchhikers.

"Close the door tighter, Jack," he said to one hitchhiker. He called all male strangers Jack.

"How did you know my name?" the man said, suddenly spooked, believing perhaps that he was being abducted.

My mother lamented the fact that her father was a frustrated intellectual, condemned to a boring job. I see him now as a neurotic and manipulative man who had endured an orphaned childhood, shunted among foster homes near Ferrara in Italy. But he was now a prosperous tailor and property owner with a big, successful family, well respected in West Medford.

"Why?" I asked. The man, Alexander Dittami, had money, an adoring family, social position, and seemingly great satisfactions.

My father said (to my mother's approval), "He was cut out for better things."

But never once did I hear my father, grateful for whatever came his way, express the thought that he had been cut out for better things.

He was not an effusive letter writer, but he was a regular sender of notes. When I was in college, and afterward when I was in Africa, he would jot me a note, like a memo, nearly always from his little workstation at the store. He was excited by my having joined the Peace Corps, and when I had first said I was going to Africa — Nyasaland — he said, "Wonderful. Imagine that!"

No intimation that I was abandoning him or that I would be in danger. Probably it was something he wished he had done himself, a fantasy of departure — just push off and hit the road. Though he had no interest in Africa.

While he wrote me notes, my mother wrote newsy or sanctimonious letters about her doings. I published my first novel in 1967. When my mother wrote to say it was "trash," my father said nothing.

I also got married in 1967. He was pleased to meet my English wife. Later, when we had a child and were home for a visit, I could see how uncertain he was with babies. My father held my son awkwardly as he screamed, no idea how to pacify him or what to do. When in relief he handed the kid back to me, I understood something of his reticence as a parent of small infants, though he was wonderful as we grew older and became his companions.

In the 1970s he visited London. He was lost in the huge city. He could barely understand Londoners' English, and leaving the shop of a Cockney butcher, he marveled that I was able to hold a conversation. "I couldn't understand a word he said!"

Most London restaurants were cramped, the tables close together. In Wheeler's, in Victoria, with other diners a few feet away, my father, against all the rules of English restaurant etiquette, tried to strike up a conversation with the man at the next table — much to the man's consternation and annoyance. My father did this later at the café at the Royal Festival Hall, and again in a restaurant in Old Compton Street. And when he was rebuffed, he just laughed. He believed that ignoring someone who was right next to you was ruder than attempting to banter with them.

In Egypt the following year, visiting his youngest son, my brother Peter, in Cairo, my father discovered that he loved the utter foreignness of that big chaotic city. Londoners had intimidated him, but Egyptians were humorous and talkative, more responsive and welcoming. This human warmth probably reminded him of Boston in the 1930s. He was an adaptable man and easily fitted in, buying a red fez and wearing it for two weeks, striding up and down the bazaars, more like a pasha than a Shriner, in his element as a stranger.

He had a smile for everyone, never looked for trouble, and was genuinely interested in the details of other people's lives. Uncomplaining, he asked for very little, was so unimpressed by luxury he ridiculed it — "Waste of money!" — and hardly cared about comfort. Discomfort was something true to him. If he'd had the money, he would have made a great traveler in the old style, as a wanderer, not as a scholar. He always encouraged me in my travels, and unlike most people was a patient listener to travelers' tales.

• • •

His chief burden was ill health, and his adult life was dominated by asthma — audible breathing difficulties and sometimes choking fits so severe he seemed on the point of gagging to death. His asthma was the formal reason we could not have a cat or dog, but in fact my mother hated pets. "What's the point of them?" was one sally, and "Do you want to kill your father?" was another.

For relief my father used a nebulizer, an old-fashioned glass retort worked with a rubber bulb, producing a dense medicinal vapor that he inhaled deeply. The brand name was DeVilbiss. This seemed to ease his breathing, but all that inhalation of mist and medicine may have soaked and shredded his lung tissue. Certainly he had little lung capacity, and in his seventies was plagued by emphysema, though he had never smoked; it was this that eventually killed him. He simply suffocated. I know, because I was with him when he breathed his last, with great effort — "agonic breathing," the nurse called it — just before he expired, like a man trapped beneath a heavy stone.

Because of his asthma he could not walk fast, exert himself in games, or bend deeply. Dusty places were unendurable to him, and so were humid days. We climbed Mount Washington in 1956, but he didn't make it to the top. His lungs were clogged, clotted, and my recurring memory is of him squeezing the nebulizer and panting. Much later he used a small aerosol inhaler. I am convinced these clumsy remedies destroyed his lungs. He lived his whole life in a harsh climate — damp winters and humid summers. "I should go to Arizona," he would say, with the same mild chuckle as when he said, "I'd buy a new car this year but I don't like the *lines*."

"Lines" was a word that fakers used, and it was laughable to Dad that anyone would be fool enough to buy a car for the look of it. Cheapness and dependability were all that mattered to him. He never bought a new car. He never bought a new suit, for that matter. He wore the cast-off suits of Harry O'Brien, his boss — good suits that he got altered to fit him. Buying anything brand new was to him a waste of money, something foolish, pure vanity. He sometimes even refused hand-me-down suits as "too dressy."

It alarmed me to hear him choke, to see him redden, at times unable to draw a breath. And so I would watch helplessly until he somehow cleared his throat and wheezed and poked the nebulizer into his mouth. He had the loud, gargling, phlegm-gathering hoick that I have heard delivered into a spittoon or onto a pavement, with the same slushy gusto as a Chinese peasant.

One of the theories of asthma is that it is sometimes self-induced, psychosomatic, the result of low spirits or repression, the heavy breathing a kind of grieving. I can believe that repression contributed to my father's asthma. He could not express himself fully because of his wife's weak ego and need for attention, and her own complaints. But though my father clearly suffered, he did not use his asthma as an excuse, and often made himself ill in his exertions. But if any of us children needed a favor, a ride somewhere, a sympathetic ear (provided the problem was not too great), my father was willing. "Where are you?" he'd say to the stranded midnight caller and would immediately set off on a rescue mission. He never had any money, but if he had been wealthy, he would have eagerly shared it, saying, "How much do you need?"

We did not own a TV set until the mid-1950s or perhaps later. Dad hated it for its noise, its intrusion, its obvious falsity, its hype. Just hearing advertising pitches or promises could make him angry. "Someday, I'm going to put an ax through that thing!" Interesting: he had grown up in the Stoneham woods, where axes solved problems. But he watched *The Ed Sullivan Show* and *The Honeymooners* — he laughed at Jackie Gleason, who ranted but was at bottom a sentimental slob, and he had a love for the odd humor of Jimmy Durante. Early television was full of vaudevillians; it was live and could be unpredictable, and that alone added to the interest. He did not watch much else until the 1970s, when he followed episodes of *Bonanza,* a hokey Western. After that, all he watched were baseball games, the only sport he cared about, but even so, he was hardly a fan, merely an occasional spectator. He was engrossed in a Red Sox game the night he was taken to the hospital, a few days before he died.

Memories, fragments, generalizations — what do they add up to? This recollection of mine seems insubstantial, yet that itself is a revelation. I thought I knew him well. On reflection, I see he was strange, and he seems to recede as I write, as sometimes when I asked him a question about himself, he backed away. In writing about him like this, I realize I do not know what was in his heart. He is just like those skinny old men in Burma and Thailand and Vietnam who inspired me to think of him.

What were my father's passions? I don't know. Did he have any fantasies of success? I draw a blank. Ambitions? I have no idea. He enjoyed fishing, beachcombing, tinkering in his shed or in the basement. These are trivial things. What were his dreams? I don't have a clue. Did he ever cheat on my mother? I doubt it, but how would I know? He had stereotypes of some ethnic groups, Italians and Irish, the loud, pushy Boston tribes, but nothing serious. He was tolerant in matters of race, an intuitive humanitarian, and was proud of the fact that Boston sent black regiments to fight in the Civil War: one of his personal landmarks was the Saint-Gaudens memorial to Robert Gould Shaw and the Massachusetts 54th Regiment on Beacon Street. There is no better example of how vivid a Yankee he was in his beliefs and how little sympathy he had for the South in that war, nor did he have any romantic notions about the South generally. But if he had secrets or personal hurts, he did not share them. His most remarkable outward eccentricity was his habit of talking to himself. He murmured constantly, in a private and unbroken narrative.

One memory we shared — a family story — was of my father looking out the window on a winter afternoon, staring hard, and after a long pause uttering, in an almost theatrical manner, one word: "Never!" Then nodding in satisfaction.

What had he been thinking of? What question, what issue? Perhaps he saw a face, or heard or remembered something. The word was said with King Lear–like decisiveness, in his characteristic accent. *Nevah!*

He did not hover over me or anyone. True, he did not guide me either, but neither did he impede me. Now and then he would give me a word of warning, but it was general, just a well-meant platitude. He was not sagacious, but he was gentle and knew his limitations. He was greatly in awe of my eldest brother — his trips to China, his hobnobbing with politicians, his audience with the pope.

My father never spoke a word to me about sex. He never taught me to throw a ball. He did show me how to skip a small flat rock on the sea, how to bait a hook with a worm, how to play a stone-throwing game called

Duck on a Rock. My homework was a mystery to him. I wanted a bike and a dog. I did not get them. I wanted a gun — I got a Mossberg .22, in a swap with my friend Eddie Flaherty. My mother said, "I hate guns." Dad said, "Watch where you point that thing." He never took me to a baseball game, or a ball game of any kind. Or a movie. It is possible that he took me to a restaurant, but if so, I have no memory of it — nor do my older brothers remember any restaurant or dining out.

Even on the days I drove him from Cape Cod to Boston for radiation treatments, when he was diagnosed with prostate cancer, he brought his lunch in a brown bag, a sandwich and an apple, which he ate in the car in the hospital parking lot. On those drives I tried to get him to talk about his early life, his childhood, his parents, his ancestors, but he would not be drawn; he was brooding about death. He hated hospitals and feared doctors. He found them cold and impersonal; his treatment, he said, was "humiliating." Yet he overcame the cancer. He had his privacies and allowed me mine. He never asked me an intrusive question, never welcomed one from me. We never discussed a book, a movie, or a song. Now and then he might drive to the other end of Medford to attend a play at the Tufts University theater. He loved the tragedies of Shakespeare — *King Lear* and *Othello* in particular, also *Macbeth* and *Hamlet*. He especially relished the self-conscious soliloquies and flourishes of the hammiest productions. "I am not what I seem!" He was in his heart a groundling — the action of the plays did not interest him, but the rhetorical denunciations held him, and afterward at home he might declaim them. "Sharper than a serpent's tooth . . ."

There was a certain amount of ham in his own life. One of my brothers got a speeding ticket, and my father accompanied him to traffic court. When the trivial case came up, the judge asked a blunt question, and my father said, clutching his hat in his hands, "Your honor, we throw ourselves on the mercy of the court."

I never introduced my father to any of my girlfriends, nor any woman I knew, until I was married and brought my wife home. Twenty-odd years later, on my divorce, he said nothing. But what was there to say? Only, "Everything works out for the best," his stoical motto. He never gossiped, never used profanity, never told an off-color joke. Scantily dressed women on TV embarrassed him; he'd leave the room.

He was a gardener — not a fancier of flowers but a grower of vegetables. He cultivated beans when I was young — Kentucky Wonders, pole beans — and grew tomatoes and squash. He was methodical. He knew how to space the plants, how to fertilize them, was a diligent waterer and weeder. He nearly always succeeded in producing a good crop. He must have learned these skills from his father, who was also a vegetable gardener.

A shy man himself, he would dare his children to take risks, as if on his behalf — trespass at the Boston Navy Yard, where we were shouted at by an armed sentry, or crouch on a rock and let the tide come in and isolate us. "I'll give you a quarter!" Some of his challenges and temperament I gave to Allie Fox in *The Mosquito Coast*. He would dare us to jump into the very cold water of Cape Cod Bay in late spring. Like Allie, he was a contriver of splintery inventions, hinged contraptions, shoe scrapers, window boxes and wind chimes, labor-saving devices with wobbly wheels. None of them were made well — he lacked the tools and used found or scavenged materials — and some were outright dangerous.

He saved string, scrap wood, old screws, nuts and bolts, jam jars, coffee cans, cigar boxes, orange crates. He threw nothing away. Garbage he buried in his garden, which the raccoons would dig up. He never passed a trash barrel or a wastebasket without looking in and seeing if there was something usable to salvage. He believed that people were foolish in most of the things they discarded. The day I received my honorary doctorate from the University of Massachusetts, I was walking on the campus in my ceremonial robe with my parents and noticed that my father had dropped behind. I spun around but he was nowhere to be seen. Then I spotted a pair of kicking legs: he had tried to retrieve something from a big steel barrel and tipped himself into it. He was upended and stuck. When I helped him out he was red-faced from being upside down but was clutching a fistful of yellow pencils, which someone had thrown away. "Pencils!" he gasped. A find. *Those'll come in handy someday.*

He banged the nails out of old boards, then flattened them and saved them. Nails are cheap. Why would a carpenter make anything with old rusty nails? He used a straight razor his whole life, a cutthroat blade, which he sharpened with a leather strop, and lathered himself with a brush and a puck of soap. Mornings he always shaved in the kitchen, leaning into a little mirror hanging at the end of a cupboard, so as to leave the one bathroom available for his large family. Concentrating, he held the tip of his nose to the side with one hand and scraped with the other.

My mother was a worrier. He was not. His serenity irked her and made her even more fretful. He had no solutions, therefore (he seemed to think) it was pointless for him to contemplate any problems. His fatalism was rosily tinged with optimism. He believed there was justice in all things and that there was always a price to pay: if you had a swimming pool, you or a neighbor would probably drown in it; if you had an expensive car, you'd probably crash it; if you had a lot of money, you'd lose it or be robbed; an expensive tie would only have soup slopped on it. To all such happenstances he'd say, "Serves them right."

He also believed that goodness was rewarded. My brother Alex sees this as Micawberish. I agree. Mr. Micawber's farewell to Copperfield is a florid echo of many of my father's own farewells to me: "If, in the progress of revolving years, I could persuade myself that my blighted destiny had been a warning to you, I should feel that I had not occupied another man's existence altogether in vain. In case of anything turning up (of which I am rather confident), I shall be extremely happy if it should be in my power to improve your prospects."

He prayed. He was devout, even pious. He felt that God would provide answers — surprises, happy endings. Faith was a shield. God protected the devout.

"Everything's going to be all right" was his general and often irrational view, his response to querulousness. The odd thing is that not much in his life was all right: he never had money, we had no space, we had no idea where we were going or what we were doing, pure chance sent us to college, and we had to grub for our tuition. Just about all the useful advice I got in my life was from strangers.

Dad was nearly always out of his depth. He seemed to know this, so he hated scrutiny or searching questions or anything personal. The truth would have been devastating. This made him a natural listener and appreciator of other people's lives and problems.

He was calm, humorous, undemanding, and, because of his gratitude and lack of complaints or snobbery or ego, easy to be with. Yet he had no idea how I was living my life, and he would have been bewildered if I had told him I wanted to be a writer. He would have said, Why? Or, How? Or, What will you write about? And, Where's the money going to come from?

A job was not something you created or carved out for yourself. A job was something that someone gave you and allowed you to keep. In his feudalistic mind, work was handed out, something to be grateful for. Work was done in silence, humbly, under the eye of a boss or a foreman or a manager, a sort of lord whom you had to please. It was all drudgery, but at least you had Sundays off.

Writing was not work — certainly not a job or a profession. The very fact that writing was published made it a cause for alarm, something that would call attention to you and the family, something disreputable for being a public act, an arrogant display of vanity. An egotistical gesture like publication was not praiseworthy, but probably, like all impulsiveness, something you'd have to live down.

I am exaggerating, but only slightly. The more I reflect on my father's self-consciousness, the better I am able to understand his lack of interest in my work, perhaps his fear of it.

All art was to my parents an indulgence, superfluous, something that other people did, necessitating a private income. "But how will you make a living? What will you fall back on?" It did not strike me as odd that they felt this way. I felt this way myself, and it worried me.

Behind her back, we satirized Mother, mocked her parsimony, her catchphrases ("You'll be in a peck of trouble," "I'll bet you dollars to donuts"), her explosive temper, her little-girl sniveling, her vanity, her repetitions, her studied piety. To some of us children she was a bore and a burden, fussing about nothing, but to the others she was a reliable ally — a source of money, adept at the sort of bribery and backhanded gifts that are common among weak people. It was a divided family. Satirizing Mother was an act of defiance. It meant you were a rebel — strong, or else pretending to be strong.

Yet we never satirized Dad. It wasn't that we didn't dare to; we were habitually disloyal to each other, as Mother was, mocking us secretly to one another: "He's put on weight in all the wrong places." We could easily have jeered at Dad. But we spared him. And it was odd, because he had his obvious faults. He too was repetitive and predictable, his catchphrases were no less hackneyed than Mother's, he could get flustered, especially in a car — he was a terrible driver, he learned late, and always made beginner's mistakes, letting the clutch out too fast, braking too hard, not using the rearview mirror.

Did we spare him because he was so kind to us, unselfish and loving? That would have been an admirable reason, but even sweet, kindly people were mocked by us; almost no one got off the hook. Yet Dad did. Perhaps we saw his innocence and goodness, but I don't think it was that. At bottom we pitied him, felt genuinely sorry for him, because he was not the wise and revered patriarch he wanted or sometimes pretended to be. He was henpecked. He was ill at ease. He was too preoccupied to worry, and in alarming ways he had accomplished very little as a workingman. He was a clerk — barely a clerk. Our mockery would have done more than hurt him; it might have destroyed him. And he wanted us as friends. He had no idea how to help us, and yet, as I said, if he'd had money or influence or power he would have shared it. He gave us his love, which is a great deal; he had nothing else to give. And he gave his love unselfishly, in the best way, without burdening us with it or expecting anything in return, a rare thing, a gift not many people know.

Normally you understand an enigmatic person by his or her close friends or recreations. Hunting, darts, the Elks club, piano playing. Dad had no close friends, no recreations except beachcombing. We were his whole world, his society, his companions. There was no one I knew who, as Dad's friend, illuminated any aspect of his personality or revealed a secret — no drinking buddy, no golf partner, no fellow gambler or girlfriend or sidekick — no one, as Dad would have put it, he chewed the fat with.

Some communicants from St. Francis Church attached themselves to him, the odd customer might linger, an O'Brien's employee might chat, but no one was close, no one Dad would have confided in. Some people in the choir were acquaintances, but the pleasure of the choir was that it was all about singing together, not swapping stories.

Certain men, French Canadians with a similar background he could relate to — Louis LeComte, who was an accountant, and Camille Caron, who had known him as a young man — tough, rather laconic men my father liked, obviously because they were aloof like him and spared him the details and spoke the same patois. But French Canadians are not clannish and defensive immigrants. They are not immigrants at all, but settled and placidly at home, with no memory of a foreign land — more like Native Americans, which indeed they often are.

My father's world was his family, but even so, he didn't know us very well, certainly did not know me, and wordlessly gave me to understand that it would be futile for me to unburden myself to him. He would not be able to help. Don't worry, he would have said — uselessly. Things will get better, everything works out for the best, just don't call attention to yourself. Don't be a *plaquoteur*, you'll only make it worse. And if it gets worse, just soldier on with it, as I did.

He also inclined toward Mother's belief that a noisy complaint meant you were exaggerating, and if you howled you were not suffering that much. "People in real pain don't make any sound at all. Doctors will tell you that." I heard this a thousand times. People who cried were fakers.

Dad was an example of self-control and stoicism, so I could never tell what was on his mind or in his heart. I do not know even now. I set down all my memories of him and he remains an enigma — perhaps there is no more to know? He was raised in a large poor family. He went to work. The Great Depression lay like a black frost all over the country. He raised a big family while America was at war. He didn't prosper, yet he didn't go under. He survived and ended up counting his blessings. His spiritual life, his churchgoing, accounted for much of his spare time and his most serene moods. Other kids' fathers had cronies, drinking companions, confidants, belonged to social circles, or were members (like Harry O'Brien) of country clubs; they hunted or tinkered with cars or collected stamps. None of these activities interested my father. His life was either his family or the church. Work was too tedious to talk about. He attended the Holy Name, Novenas, the First Friday, High Masses, and Benediction. He usually sat toward the back of the church with his head down, the embodiment of the humble Publican in the parable of the Publican and the Pharisee, praying with his eyes cast down, twisting rosary beads in his fingers, or in the choir, singing his heart out.

In the course of writing this I reread Edmund Gosse's *Father and Son*, J. R. Ackerley's *My Father and Myself*, and Henry James's *Notes of a Son and Brother*. A number of biographies, too, in my search for answers to the question, What are other writers' fathers like? For one thing, other writers' fathers were often themselves writers. Two books that astonished me were *The Life of Kingsley Amis,* by Zachary Leader, and *Experience,* by Martin Amis. I say astonished because if there was a man who was the opposite of my father in every way, it was not nutty Philip Gosse or jolly Roger Ackerley or grandiose Henry James Sr.; it was outrageous Kingsley Amis.

Amis led a messy but highly productive life. He had great and lasting friendships with other writers. He was in part a public man: his life is there in his books, and he seems to have been an amiable drinking companion, not an angry drunk but a witty one for whom alcohol was creative fuel. For many years he drank heavily, often as much as a bottle of whiskey a day. His hangovers were a daily event. He was phobic and a philanderer — he had sex partners and casual women friends. Panic attacks plagued him. Air travel was one of his phobias; he never boarded a plane in his life. He could not bear to be alone in a room. He raged, screaming "Fuck!" at his wives and children. He made a lot of money but saved little, ran up debts, was burdened by overdrafts, went through two traumatic divorces, over-indulged in food, made racist remarks to amuse his pals, was amusingly foulmouthed. He was old at sixty, ill later on, and dead at seventy-three. He received a knighthood. He left behind him a mountain of paper, a long shelf of books, a whole archive of documents.

That man was more foreign to my father than almost anyone I can imagine. My father would more easily have got on with a Bedouin or a Zulu or a hawker in a Cairo bazaar. But he would have been baffled to the point of incomprehension by Amis.

If I had said to him, "Kingsley Amis worked every morning, wrote sixty books, wrote poems, reviewed books, wrote essays, appeared on television, won the Booker Prize, published novels . . ." my father would have said, with economical sarcasm, "Really?" And he would have underlined it with "Ha!"

In my father's eyes, no book, no poem, no prize, no gong or title, could justify a life like that. Just the drinking would have roused my father's scorn, just the women, just the swearing. Amis did not believe in God: "It's more that I hate him." My father believed in a loving God who, propitiated with prayer and good works, might bail him out. But my father wasn't judgmental; he did not offer gratuitous opinions about people who were debauched or dissipated. Pressed for an opinion about Amis, he would have frowned and thought, "For what does it profit a man if he gains the whole world and loses his soul." Words he lived by, but would have said only, "A wasted life," and then perhaps try to temper it, as he often did, in a familiar phrase: "He's more to be pitied."

The conversation would have had to end there. I would not be able to convince him of the hard work, imagination, seriousness, and value of Amis's writing — the gusto, the humor, his ability to catch a tone of voice or draw an English — or Welsh, or American — type. (However, there is no character in Amis's many books who resembles my father.) Amis's poems I now see as the equivalent of his close friend Philip Larkin's, and I had always assumed Larkin the master.

Reflecting on Amis (who fathered a respected writer) just confuses me more when I think about my own father. How did he influence me? Not in any bookish way, certainly, though he was not a philistine. Not intellectually, since my father was superstitious as well as devout. He taught me not to be selfish, showed me how to listen, and left me alone to grope toward the profession of letters. His memory — perhaps I inherited that, a great gift. Maybe, too, his love of narrative in the children's classics.

In the Amis household conflict was in the open — shouts and accusations — and it was in the books. The Amis life can be unpacked and put on view like one of those mammoth yard sales spread out on a lawn, where you see empty gin bottles, old books, dated clothes, letters, dandified canes or shoes, funny hats, photographs, theater programs, cracked plates: not pretty, but everything can be explained in nine hundred pages. In many ways Amis's life resembles the lives of other writers. Ford Madox Ford's was just as tumultuous and productive. Norman Mailer's more so for being longer — more books, more wives and children. Simenon's was just as boozy but sadder. Robert Lowell's much crazier and shorter.

My father bears no resemblance to these men. Yet there was disorder and tension and conflict in our household: in the angular splinters in the woodwork, pulsing in the air, a disturbance that was deep, subtle, and without any voice, a noiseless bewilderment and uncertainty, the vibrant presence of low-pitched rivalries, and paradoxically, it was all masked by politeness, or was affectionate, or sometimes hostile teasing. This sets it apart and makes it harder for me to understand. It seems, if one were comparing, that not Amis but my father was the more complex, more enigmatic man, his buried or hidden life more of a mystery.

In some ways I know I resemble my father. I yawn like him, growling. I scowl like him at small print. I talk to myself all the time. When I am bored, I feign interest in just the way he did: "Is that so?" I snort and clear my throat like him. His gargle is now mine, and so is the reflex to say, "Serves him right," because my father, without knowing the concept, believed in karma, just as he understood the subtleties of the atman concept in Hinduism, though he would have said "soul."

My father hated gabbers, gasbaggers, and ear benders, and so do I. My father had a way of inhaling deeply through his nose when he was impatient, and I do it, too. Sometimes I feel I am my father — never mind the writing. I have a similar temperament. I am generally humane, relatively serene, and like to be left alone, as he did. I will sometimes agree to anything to keep the peace, because he felt (as I do) that you can't really change the narrow stubborn mind of a person who is set in his belief, and anyway, why bother?

If something is seriously wrong, my father believed, there's not much you can do to fix it. The world is large, you are small, nothing matters enough for you to get steamed up about it, and in a profound sense nothing matters except your immortal soul.

My mother was demanding, thin-skinned, and impatient. She was all right with babies but hopeless with children who had a will of their own. She struggled with us, replying with her own presumptions, and when I pointed out they were illogical, she accused me of defiance.

She criticized my father, made him submit by nagging him, and after having weakened him she faulted him for being weak. Dad was unselfish and strong, though lacking in ambition. She made him submit to her will, and in time she destroyed his will, holding him responsible for wrong decisions and their slender and uncertain finances. He tried to please her, but of course there was no pleasing her. She could only control him (and us) by being dissatisfied. Naturally, we always came up short. And how could anyone know what she wanted when she herself didn't know what she wanted?

She was the sort of nag who would repeat, "Be careful, you're going to drop that!" so many times that at last you bobbled the thing and dropped it.

She so completely dominated him that even at his most submissive he was uncomplaining, always at her beck and call. She became more of a pest as they grew older, rejoicing in the charade of theirs as a marriage of equals, when anyone who knew him well could see that it was a pure tyranny. She did the talking, he did the listening, he took the blame, and when Dad became mortally ill she blamed him for that, too — rolled her eyes at his pain as though he was faking, or at least exaggerating. What a trial it was for her to have this sick, coughing, and spewing man in the house.

"I could kill him," she said once, out of his hearing, when he was acutely ill and suffocating with emphysema. An interesting remark, because of course she was killing him.

If there was a lesson for me, these family experiences resolved themselves in my horror of weak and vain, nagging and castrating women. As soon as I sense an echo of my mother in a woman's voice, I recognize the snarl of a she-wolf and flee. Needless fuss, denial, an utter absence of logic, no memory of the hundred things I've done well but only the one thing I've failed to do, ultimately a cynicism and a merciless refusal to see my pain — when in my life I've heard those things, or heard something as subtle as a sniff, a snort, a harrumph, a certain tilt of the head, I have mentally shut myself down and vowed to end the relationship, because I do not want to become the person that my father became in his old age, reduced to dependence on an unhappy woman who not only didn't know what she wanted, but needed most of all someone to blame.

That was my father's example to me. In a way, I think he was hinting at it all along: Don't do what I've done, don't live my life, don't make the mistakes I've made. He cheered me in my going to Africa, in taking months off to hike around Britain's coast, in paddling my kayak, especially in the winter. "Here, let me feel your hands!" He loved the calluses on my paddler's hands — they represented work, effort, freedom, and happiness, doing what I wanted. Never mind the books that came of those experiences; it was the effort of traveling that counted.

Walking through a house I was building on Cape Cod, a lovely place sitting on four acres, he said, "I wish my mother were alive to see this." A meaningful remark, because he had been loved by her and he wanted his mother to be proud of him, wanted to give something back to her. By then she had been dead for thirty years.

He welcomed my wives and children, but he would have been just as happy — happier maybe — if I'd never married. Then I would have been completely free. He was a kindhearted man, but not a particularly doting grandfather. He had had his fill of small children, and so had my mother.

Go your own way, he'd say, and he often quoted Kipling without knowing the lines were Kipling's: "You can travel faster and farther alone."

Now I see that I was constantly trying to protect him, rather than the other way around. I spared him the details of my life. He would have been wounded by any revelation of immorality, offended — more than offended — by an coarse joke. He once stopped and shamed a priest (of all people) who was telling one. "Is that a blue joke, Father? I don't want to hear it. The boys here" — because we were listening. "It breaks down discipline."

He would have been appalled if he ever got wind of instances of my wayward behavior. I had a mediocre school record. I was arrested by the police at a campus demonstration in 1962 in Amherst. I had fathered an illegitimate child. I was kicked out of the Peace Corps ("terminated early") in 1965 for a number of transgressions, my first wife and I split up in 1990, I wrote umpteen books — and these events or topics were never mentioned at all, and perhaps in my father's mind they never happened. Or was it because they were *faits accomplis* that there was nothing to say?

In some ways he was more like an uncle than a father to me. He did not want to know too much of me. He craved companionship without intimacy. He did not want to reveal too much of himself. He wanted us to think well of him. And I did, respecting his wish for restraint and remoteness, admiring his faith and his good heart.

Apart from his episodes of being Mr. Bones, he did not burden me with his personality or his hopes for me. He never pushed me or gave me advice. He left me alone, and by implication I understood that he just wanted to be left alone.

30

THE TROUBLE WITH AUTOBIOGRAPHY

I was born, the third of seven children, in Medford, Massachusetts, so near to Boston that even when I was a small boy kicking along side streets to the Washington School, I could see the pencil stub of the Custom House Tower from the banks of the Mystic River. The river meant everything to me: it flowed past our town, in reed-fringed oxbows and muddy marshes that no longer exist, to Boston Harbor and the dark Atlantic. It was the reason for Medford rum and Medford shipbuilding. In the triangular trade the river linked Medford to Africa and the Caribbean — Medford circulating mystically in the world.

My father noted in his diary, *Anne had another boy at 7:25.* He was a shipping clerk in a Boston leather firm, my mother a college-trained teacher, though it would be twenty years before she returned to teaching. The Theroux ancestors had lived in rural Quebec from about 1690, ten generations, the eleventh having migrated to Stoneham, up the road from Medford, where my father was born. My father's mother, Eva Brousseau, was part Menominee, a woodland people who had been settled in what is now Wisconsin for thousands of years. Many French soldiers in the New World took Menominee women as their wives or lovers. In the early nineteenth century, the U.S. government intimidated their descendants and swindled them out of their land. Today, with only about thirty-five fluent speakers of the language, the culture of these Native Americans, aristocrats of this continent, faces extinction.

My maternal grandparents, Alessandro and Angelina Dittami, were relative newcomers to America, having emigrated separately from Italy around 1900. Many Italians would recognize Dittami ("speak to me") as an orphan's name. Ecco, Esposito, Trovato, and the obvious Orfanelli and Del Orfano are others. Though he abominated any mention of it, my grandfather was a foundling in Ferrara. As a young man, he got to know who his parents were, a well-known senator and his housemaid. After a turbulent upbringing in foster homes and an operatic incident (discharged from the army, he threatened to kill the senator), Alessandro fled to America, and met and married my grandmother in New York City. They moved to Medford with the immigrant urgency and competitiveness to make a life at any cost. They succeeded, becoming prosperous, and mingled piety and smugness made the whole family insufferably sententious.

My father's family, country folk, had no memory of any other ancestral place but America, seeing Quebec and the United States as equally American, indistinguishable, the border a mere conceit. They had no feeling for France, though most of them spoke French easily, in the Quebec way. Heroic in World War II (even my father's sisters served in the U.S. military), at home they were easygoing and self-sufficient, taking pleasure in hunting, vegetable gardening, and raising chickens. They had no use for books.

I knew all four of my grandparents and my ten uncles and aunts pretty well. I much preferred the company of my father's kindly, laconic, unpretentious, and uneducated family, who called me Paulie.

And these five-hundred-odd words are all I will ever write of my autobiography.

At a certain point — about the age I am now, which is sixty-seven — the writer asks, "Do I write my life or leave it to others to deal with?" I have no intention of writing an autobiography, and as for allowing others to practice what Kipling called "the higher cannibalism" on me (Henry James called biographers "post-mortem exploiters"), I plan to frustrate them by putting obstacles in their way. "Biography lends to death a new terror."

The mysterious B. Traven (born Otto Feige in Germany), author of *The Treasure of the Sierra Madre* and ten other novels, succeeded in frustrating any biographers by assuming multiple identities, changing his name three or four times, and living as a recluse in Mexico. He wrote, "The creative person should have no other biography than his books." Kipling paraphrased this in a terse poem:

And for the little, little span
The dead are borne in mind,
Seek not to question other than
The books I leave behind.

But, laying false trails, Kipling also wrote a memoir, *Something of Myself,* posthumously published, which was so oblique and economical with the truth as to be misleading — just jottings. In its tactical offhandedness and calculated distortion it greatly resembles many other writers' autobiographies. Eventually, biographies of Kipling appeared, questioning the books he left behind, anatomizing his somewhat sequestered life, and speculating (in some cases wildly) about his personality and predilections.

Dickens began his autobiography in 1848, when he was only thirty-six, but abandoned it and, overcome with memories of his deprivations, a year later was inspired to write the autobiographical *David Copperfield,* fictionalizing his early miseries and, among other transformations, modeling Mr. Micawber on his father. His contemporary Anthony Trollope wrote a short account of his life when he was about sixty. Published after his death in 1875, it sank his reputation.

Straightforward in talking about his method in fiction, Trollope wrote, "There are those who . . . think that the man who works with his imagination should allow himself to wait till inspiration moves him. When I have heard such doctrine preached, I have hardly been able to repress my scorn. To me it would not be more absurd if the shoemaker were to wait for inspiration, or the tallow-chandler for the divine moment of melting. If the man whose business it is to write has eaten too many good things, or has drunk too much, or smoked too many cigars — as men who write sometimes will do — then his condition may be unfavorable for work; but so will be the condition of a shoemaker who has been similarly imprudent . . . I was once told that the surest aid to the writing of a book was a piece of cobbler's wax on my chair. I certainly believe in the cobbler's wax much more than the inspiration."

This bluff paragraph anticipated the modern painter Chuck Close's saying, "Inspiration is for amateurs. I just get to work." But Trollope's *Autobiography* was his undoing. This bum-on-seat assertion especially was held against him and seemed to cast his work in so pedestrian a way that Trollope went into eclipse for many years. If writing his novels was like cobbling (the reasoning went), his books could be no better than old shoes. But Trollope was being his crusty self, and his defiant book represents a particular sort of no-nonsense memoir in the English tradition.

All such self-portraiture dates from ancient times, of course. One of the greatest examples of autobiography is Benvenuto Cellini's *Life,* a Renaissance masterpiece full of quarrels, passions, disasters, friendships, and self-praise. (Cellini also says that a person should be over forty before writing such a book. He was fifty-eight.) Montaigne's *Essays* are discreetly autobiographical, revealing an immense amount about the man and his time — his food, his clothes, his habits, his travel — and Rousseau's *Confessions* is a model of headlong candor. But English writers shaped and perfected the self-told life by contriving to make it an art form, an extension of the life's work, and even coined the word "autobiography": William Taylor first used it in 1797.

Given that the tradition of autobiography in English literature is rich and varied, how to account for the scarcity or insufficiency of autobiographies among the important American writers? Mark Twain's two-volume excursion is long, strange, rambling, and in places explosive and improvisational. Most of it was dictated, determined (as he tells us) by his mood on any particular day. Henry James's *A Small Boy and Others* and *Notes of a Son and Brother* tell us very little of the man and, couched in his late and most elliptical style, are among his least readable works. Thoreau's *Journals* are obsessive, but so studied and polished (he constantly rewrote them, trying to improve them) they are offered by Thoreau in his unappealing role of village explainer, written for publication.

In the same self-conscious vein, as a letter writer E. B. White seems to have had his eye on a wider public than the recipient, even when he was doing something as ingenuous as replying to a grade school class about *Charlotte's Web.* White idealized Thoreau and left New York, aspiring to live a Thoreauvian life in Maine. Two editions of *Letters of E. B. White* were published in his lifetime. Is this self-promotion, or candor, or his gratifying a readership eager for his epistolary briskness? He was a modest and kindly man, without much vanity; still, personal letters published by a living writer are rare. In most cases, the life-in-letters collection appears after death — the letters of James, Stevenson, Steinbeck, Faulkner, and many others are examples. But such a collection usually illustrates that the selected letter is a charming but not always telling form, especially when the author is writing for posterity.

Hemingway's *A Moveable Feast*, which is glittering miniaturism but largely self-serving portraiture, was posthumous, as were Edmund Wilson's voluminous diaries. Thurber's *My Life and Hard Times* is simply jokey. S. J. Perelman came up with a superb title for his autobiography, *The Hindsight Saga*, but only got around to writing three chapters. Wright Morris's three memoirs are precious and unrevealing. No autobiographies from Faulkner, Baldwin, Steinbeck, Bellow, Mailer, James Jones, Philip Roth, or William Styron, to name some obvious American masters. They lived in an age when American writers were shamanistic figures who nurtured personal mythologies ("We were like rock stars," Styron said to me once, reminiscing). You get the impression that such a venture might be regarded as beneath them or perhaps would have diminished the aura of shamanism. Some of these men encouraged tame biographers and found any number of Boswells-on-Guggenheims to do the job. Faulkner's biographer neglected to mention an important love affair that Faulkner conducted, yet found space to name every member of a Little League team that Faulkner chanced to meet one day.

The examples of American effort at autobiography tend to be rare and unrevealing, though Kay Boyle, Eudora Welty, and Mary McCarthy all wrote exceptional memoirs. Edward Dahlberg's *Bottom Dogs* is a bitter evocation of a bumpy childhood. Gore Vidal wrote an account of his own life in *Palimpsest*, and John Updike had an early stab at his in *Self-Consciousness*. Both men were distinguished essayists, which the non-autobiographers Faulkner, Hemingway, Steinbeck, and some of the others never were — perhaps a crucial distinction. Lillian Hellman and Arthur Miller, both playwrights, wrote lengthy autobiographies, but Hellman, in her self-pitying *Pentimento*, neglects to say that her longtime lover, Dashiell Hammett, was married to someone else, and in *Timebends* Miller reduces his first wife, Mary Slattery, to a wraith-like figure who flickers through the early pages of his life.

"Everyone realizes that one can believe little of what people say about each other," Rebecca West once wrote. "But it is not so widely realized that even less can one trust what people say about themselves."

In America there are far more show-business autobiographies, self-portraits of sports figures, and political memoirs than writers' accounts of their own lives. In most cases, these celebrity lives are known to be ghostwritten, but some are promoted as solely the work of the subject, even when this is demonstrably not the case. The questionable authorship of such books compels me to stick to literary autobiographies, because one can be fairly certain they were written by the subjects.

English autobiography generally follows a tradition of dignified reticence and raconteurism that perhaps reflects the restrained manner in which the English distance themselves in their fiction. The American tendency, especially in the twentieth century, was to intrude and obviously draw on the life, at times blurring the line between autobiography and fiction (Saul Bellow anatomized his five marriages in five novels). A notable English exception, D. H. Lawrence, poured his life into his novels, a way of writing that recommended him to an American audience. The work of Henry Miller, himself a great champion of Lawrence, is a long shelf of boisterous reminiscences, which stimulated and liberated me with their horseplay when I was young. Oh, for that rollicking sexual freedom in bohemian Paris, I thought, innocent of the fact that by then Miller was living as a henpecked husband in Los Angeles.

It is almost expected that the English writer, glimpsing the bottom of the barrel — cracker barrel, perhaps — will in the later years of his or her life turn aside and write an autobiography. I have mentioned how Trollope's was as forthright as his attitude toward the process of writing itself, but there are many examples of the subtle, the oblique, and the exhaustive in English autobiography. Some of these books are extensions of the subjects' imaginative work, or even surpass it.

The types of literary self-portraiture are so wide-ranging that it might help to sort out the varieties of this form, which is nearly always egomaniacal and never exhaustive. Excluding the publication of diaries (the favorite diversion of politicians), and the prehumous (in the case of E. B. White), as opposed to the posthumous, collected letters, there are many ways of framing a life.

The earliest form may have been the spiritual confession, originating in a religious passion to account for a life and to find redemption. Saint Augustine's *Confessions* is a pretty good example. But confession eventually took many secular forms — not disclosure in search of atonement but the confession subverted as personal history. The appeal of Casanova's *History of My Life* is as much its romantic conquests as its picaresque structure of narrow escapes. The more modern confessional form is something like the relentless boasting of *The Confessions of Aleister Crowley,* in which his comparing himself favorably to Shakespeare is only one of many preposterous sallies. Crowley, a diabolist, poet, and playwright, fancied himself the incarnation of the Beast from the Book of Revelation, proclaimed, "Do what thou wilt shall be the whole of the Law," and promoted himself as a womanizer (one of his women he designated the Ape of Thoth), but failed to mention in the seven hundred pages of this confession that he was a homosexual. (The subtitle of his book, by the way, is *An Autohagiography.* He had promoted himself to sainthood.)

Neither would you know from Somerset Maugham's *The Summing Up,* written in his midsixties (he died at the age of ninety-one), that, though briefly married, he was a lifelong homosexual. He says at the outset, "This is not an autobiography nor is it a book of recollections," yet it dabbles in both, in the guarded way that Maugham lived his life. "I have been attached, deeply attached, to a few people," he writes, but goes no further. Later he confides, "I have no desire to lay bare my heart, and I put limits to the intimacy that I wish the reader to enter upon with me." We end up knowing nothing about the physical Maugham in this rambling account of his life and opinions. His sexual reticence is understandable, given that such an inclination was unlawful when his book was published, but there isn't so much as a hint, and at its best the autobiography is a hinting form.

The memoir is typically thinner, provisional, more selective, undemanding, even casual, and suggests that it is something less than the whole truth. Joseph Conrad's *A Personal Record* falls into this category, relating the outward facts of his life, and some opinions and remembrances of friendships, but no intimacies. Conrad's acolyte Ford Madox Ford wrote any number of memoirs, subtitling them "reminiscences," among them *Return to Yesterday, Thus to Revisit, It Was the Nightingale,* and a reminiscence of Conrad. But even after reading all of these memoirs you have almost no idea of the vicissitudes (adulteries, bankruptcies, scandals) of Ford's life, recounted by a plodding biographer in *The Saddest Story.* Ford rarely came clean and had a genius for mendacity, as well as the vigorous rehashing of well-polished anecdotes and improvisations. He called his writing "impressionistic," but it is apparent that the truth bored him, as it bores many writers of fiction.

Among the highly specialized, even inimitable, forms of small-scale autobiography I would place Jan Morris's *Conundrum* (1974), which is an account of her unsatisfactory life as a man, her profound feeling that her sympathies were feminine, and that she was in essence a woman. The solution to her conundrum was surgery, in Casablanca in 1972, so that she could live the remainder of her life as a woman — "gender reassignment," as the operation is called these days. Her life partner remained Elizabeth, whom she had, as James Morris, married many years before. Other outstanding memoirs-with-a-theme are Fitzgerald's self-analysis in *The Crack-Up*, Jack London's *John Barleycorn*, a history of his alcoholism, and William Styron's *Darkness Visible*, an account of his suicidal depression. But since the emphasis in these books is pathological, they are singular for being case histories.

In contrast to the slight but powerful memoir is the multivolume autobiography. The prize goes to Augustus Hare, who wrote virtually his entire life in his six-volume (three in 1896 and three in 1900) *Story of My Life*, an extraordinarily full (three thousand pages) and candid account of this obscure Victorian, filled with travel (Hare was a writer of guidebooks), tales of the uncanny for which Hare was well known, and odd sidelights: "It used to be said that the reason why Mrs. Barbara had only one arm and part of another was that Aunt Caroline had eaten the rest." Hare was making notes for a seventh volume up to a few days before he died. Osbert Sitwell required five volumes to relate his life, Leonard Woolf five as well, adding disarmingly, in the volume *Sowing*, "I feel profoundly in the depths of my being that in the last resort *nothing matters*." The title of his last volume, *The Journey Not the Arrival Matters*, suggests that he might have changed his mind. Anthony Powell's *To Keep the Ball Rolling* is the overall title of four volumes of autobiography — and he also published his extensive journals in three volumes. Doris Lessing, Graham Greene, V. S. Pritchett, and Anthony Burgess have given us their lives in two volumes apiece.

This exemplary quartet is fascinating for what they disclose: Greene's manic depression in *Ways of Escape*, Pritchett's suburban upbringing (*A Cab at the Door*) and his literary life (*Midnight Oil*), Burgess's Manchester childhood in *Little Wilson and Big God*, and Lessing's disillusionment with communism in *Walking in the Shade.* Lessing is frank about her love affairs in that book and also its predecessor, *Under My Skin,* but omitting their passions, the male writers in this group exclude the emotional experiences of their lives. I think of a line in Anthony Powell's novel *Books Do Furnish a Room* where the narrator, Nicholas Jenkins, reflecting on a slew of memoirs he is reviewing, writes, "Every individual's story has its enthralling aspect, though the essential pivot was usually omitted or obscured by most autobiographers."

The essential pivot for Greene was his succession of romantic liaisons. Though he did not live with her, he remained married to the same woman until his death. He continued to pursue other love affairs and enjoyed a number of long-term relationships, virtual marriages, with other women.

Anthony Burgess's two volumes of autobiography are among the most detailed and fully realized — seemingly best recalled — I have ever read. I knew Burgess, and these books rang true. But it seems that much was made up or skewed. One entire biography by a very angry biographer (Roger Lewis) details the numerous falsifications in Burgess's book.

V. S. Pritchett's two superb volumes are models of the autobiographical form. They were worthy winners of literary prizes and were bestsellers. But they were also canny in their way. Deliberately selective, being prudent, Pritchett didn't want to upset his rather fierce second wife by writing anything about his first wife, and so it is as if wife number one never existed. Nor did Pritchett write anything about his romancing other women, something his biographer took pains to analyze.

I never regarded Pritchett, whom I saw socially in London, as a womanizer, but in his midfifties he revealed his passionate side in a letter to a close friend (printed in *V. S. Pritchett: A Working Life,* by Jeremy Treglown), saying, "Sexual Puritanism is unknown to me; the only check upon my sexual adventures is my sense of responsibility which I think had always been a nuisance to me . . . I am peaceable, a non-quarreller, amiable — really a hedonist you know. But I notice people prefer jealousy to love, unhappiness to happiness, power over others to pleasure for themselves, unkindness to kindness . . . Of course I'm romantic. I like to be in love — the arts of love then become more ingenious and exciting."

It is a remarkable statement, even pivotal, which would have given a needed physicality to his autobiography had he enlarged on this theme. At the time of his writing the letter, Pritchett was conducting an affair with an

American woman. But there is no sentiment of this kind in either of his two volumes, where he presents himself as diligent and uxorious.

Some writers not only improve on an earlier biography but find oblique ways to praise themselves. Vladimir Nabokov wrote *Conclusive Evidence* when he was fifty, then rewrote it and expanded it fifteen years later, publishing it as *Speak, Memory*, a more playful, pedantic, and bejeweled version of the first. Or is it fiction? At least one chapter of this improved version he had published as a short story ("Mademoiselle O") thirty years earlier. And there is a colorful character whom Nabokov mentions in both versions, one V. Sirin. "The author that interested me most was naturally Sirin," Nabokov writes, and after gushing over the sublime magic of the man's prose, "Across the dark sky of exile, Sirin passed . . . like a meteor, and disappeared, leaving nothing much else behind him than a vague sense of uneasiness."

Who was this Russian émigré, this literary paragon of wayward brilliance? It was Nabokov himself. V. Sirin was Nabokov's pen name when, living in Paris and Berlin, he still wrote novels in Russian, and — ever the tease — he used his autobiography to extol his early self as a romantic enigma.

Like Nabokov, Robert Graves wrote his memoir *Goodbye to All That* as a youngish man, and rewrote it almost thirty years later. Many English writers have polished off an autobiography while they were still relatively youthful. The extreme example is Henry Green, who, believing he might be killed in the war, wrote *Pack My Bag* when he was thirty-five. Evelyn Waugh embarked on his autobiography in his late fifties, though (as he died at the age of sixty-two) he managed to complete only the first volume, *A Little Learning*, describing his life up to the age of twenty-five.

One day in the Staff Club at the University of Singapore, the head of the English department, my boss, D. J. Enright, announced that he had started his autobiography. A distinguished poet and critic, he was then in his late forties, and would live another thirty-odd years. His book, *Memoirs of a Mendicant Professor*, appeared in his fiftieth year, as a sort of farewell to Singapore and to the teaching profession. He neither revisited this narrative nor wrote a further installment of his life. The book baffled me; it was so discreet, so impersonal, such a tiptoeing account of a life I knew to be much richer. It was obvious to me that Enright was darker than the lovable Mr. Chips of this memoir, that there was more to say. I was so keenly aware of what he had left out that ever after I became suspicious of all forms of autobiography.

Although I regard the autobiography as an unreliable little creature, or even a loose and baggy monster, this form of personal narrative exerts a horrible fascination on me. When a writer's autobiography is published, I pounce on it. I want to know what this lonely business was like for him or her. And though I favor the gut-spilling mode, I understand why writers skimp on disclosing their adulteries. But while it's wise to be selective, what's the point in presenting such a life as complete, leaving it to a cannibalistic biographer to sort out the unseemliness?

"No one can tell the whole truth about himself," Maugham wrote in *The Summing Up.* Rousseau disagreed, and so did Simenon in his vast *Intimate Memoirs,* though his biographer called the book "a self-justifying fable." Simenon's own appearance in his crime novel *Maigret's Memoirs* — a young, ambitious, intrusive, impatient novelist, seen through the eyes of the old shrewd detective — is a believable self-portrait. I'd like to think that a confession in the old style is attainable, but when I reflect on this enterprise, I think — as many of the autobiographers I've mentioned must have thought — how important keeping secrets is to a writer. Secrets are a source of strength and certainly a powerful and sustaining element in the imagination.

Kingsley Amis, who wrote a very funny but highly selective set of memoirs, prefaced it by saying that he left out a great deal because he did not wish to hurt people he loved. This is a salutary reason to be reticent, but the whole truth of Amis was revealed to the world by his assiduous biographer in almost nine hundred pages of close scrutiny, authorized by the novelist's son: the work, the drinking, the womanizing, the sadness, the pain. I would have liked to read Amis's own version.

It must occur as a grim foreboding to many writers that when the autobiography is written, it is handed to a reviewer for examination, to be graded on readability as well as veracity and fundamental worth. This notion makes my skin crawl. The very thought of offering one's life for a hack to evaluate has to be discouraging to many writers. It certainly discourages me. Fiction — a thing I make — is something that is inevitably handled by the reviewer's inky fingers. I can't help that. But I am more protective of my personal flaws and passions and don't wish them to be graded. I begin to understand the omissions in autobiography and the writers who don't bother to write one.

Besides, I have at times bared my soul. What is more autobiographical than the sort of travel book I have been writing for the past forty years? In every sense it goes with the territory. All you would ever want to know about Rebecca West is contained in the half-million words of *Black Lamb and Gray Falcon,* her book about Yugoslavia. But the travel book, like the autobiography, is the maddening and insufficient form that I have described here. And the setting down of personal detail can be a devastating emotional experience. In the one memoir-on-a-theme that I risked, *Sir Vidia's Shadow,* I wrote some pages with tears streaming down my face.

The assumption that the autobiography signals the end of a writing career also makes me pause. Here it is, with a drum roll, the final volume before the writer is overshadowed by silence and death, a sort of farewell, and an unmistakable signal that one is "written out." My mother is ninety-eight. Perhaps, if I am spared, as she has been (she still reads and writes and manages on her own on Cape Cod), and I live into my nineties, I might do it. But don't bank on it.

And what is there to write? In the second volume of his autobiography, V. S. Pritchett speaks of how "the professional writer who spends his time becoming other people and places, real or imaginary, finds he has written his life away and has become almost nothing." Pritchett goes on, "The true autobiography of this egotist is exposed in all its intimate foliage in his work."

The Graham Greene expedient tempts me. He wrote a highly personal preface to each of his books, describing the circumstances of their composition, his mood, his travel, and then published these collected prefaces, stories behind stories, as *Ways of Escape.* It is a wonderful book, even if he did omit his relentless womanizing. Henry James wrote prefaces for the New York Edition of his work, and while he revealed very little of himself, he provided a detailed account of how he approached each book. Tellingly, these theoretical prefaces were published after his death as *The Art of the Novel.*

The more I reflect on my life, the greater the appeal of the autobiographical novel. The immediate family is typically the first subject an American writer contemplates. Get the family saga out of the way — "misery lit" in today's parlance — and then move farther afield. But I began my writing career by describing the lives of others. I never felt that my life was substantial enough to qualify for the anecdotal narrative that enriches autobiography. I had never thought of writing about the sort of big, talkative family I grew up in, and very early on I developed the fiction writer's useful habit of taking liberties. I knew I would find it impossible to write an autobiography without invoking the traits I seem to deplore in the ones I've described — exaggeration, embroidery, reticence, invention, heroics, mythomania, compulsive revisionism, and all the rest that are so valuable to fiction. Therefore, when my *Copperfield* beckoned, I wrote *Mother Land.*

ACKNOWLEDGMENTS

The following essays previously appeared elsewhere:

"Introduction: Study for Figures in a Landscape" (as "Writing and Traveling"), *Washington Post.* "My Drug Tour: Searching for Ayahuasca" (as "Honey, the Shaman Shrunk My Head"), *Men's Journal.* "Thoreau in the Wilderness," introduction to *The Maine Woods* (Princeton University Press). "Liz in Neverland," "Robin Williams: Who's He When He's at Home?" and "Tea with Muriel Spark," *Talk.* "Greeneland," *New York Times* and introductions to the Penguin editions of *Journey Without Maps* and *The Comedians.* "Hunter in the Kingdom of Fear," *Guardian.* "Conrad at Sea," introduction to *Typhoon and Other Tales* (Folio Society). "Simenon's World," introduction to Simenon's *The Widow* (New York Review Books). "Dr. Sacks, the Healer" (as "My Friend the Doctor"), *Prospect.* "Nurse Wolf, the Hurter," *The New Yorker.* "Mrs. Robinson Revisited" (as "Here's to You, Mrs. Robinson"), *Harper's Bazaar.* "Talismans for Our Dreams" (as "Private Obsessions of a Collector"), *Departures.* "The Rock Star's Burden," "Stanley: The Ultimate African Explorer," and "Traveling Beyond Google (as "Why We Travel"), *New York Times.* "Living with Geese," "Hawaii: Islands upon Islands" (as "One Man's Islands"), "Mockingbird in Monroeville" (as "Return of the Mockingbird"), "Benton's America," and "The Trouble with Autobiography," *Smithsonian.* "The Seizures in Zimbabwe," epilogue to the paperback edition of *Dark Star Safari* (Mariner). "Trespassing in Africa," "English Hours: Nothing Personal," and "Dear Old Dad," *Granta.* "Paul Bowles: Not a Tourist," introduction to *The Sheltering Sky* (Penguin). "Maugham: Up and Down in Asia," introduction to *The Gentleman in the Parlour* (Vintage Classics). "My Life as a Reader," introduction to *Reading,* photographs by Steve McCurry (Phaidon). "Life and the Magazine," *New York Times Magazine.*